MW01174321

RICHARD IV

THE LAST WHITE ROSE

ERIC OWEN BURKE

Note for Librarians: A cataloguing record for this book is available from Library and Archives Canada at www.collectionscanada.ca/amicus/index-e.html
ISBN 978-1-4251-6726-4

Printed on paper with minimum 30% recycled fibre. Trafford's print shop runs on "green energy" from solar, wind and other environmentally-friendly power sources.

Offices in Canada, USA, Ireland and UK

Book sales for North America and international:
Trafford Publishing, 6E–2333 Government St.,
Victoria, BC V8T 4P4 CANADA
phone 250 383 6864 (toll-free 1 888 232 4444)
fax 250 383 6804; email to orders@trafford.com
Book sales in Europe:
Trafford Publishing (UK) Limited, 9 Park End Street, 2nd Floor
Oxford, UK OX1 1HH UNITED KINGDOM
phone +44 (0)1865 722 113 (local rate 0845 230 9601)
facsimile +44 (0)1865 722 868; info.uk@trafford.com
Order online at:
trafford.com/06-2222

10 9 8 7 6 5 4 3 2 1

This novel is based upon the times, and the true history and circumstances, of Prince Richard, Duke of York, imprisoned and thought-to-be murdered in the Tower of London by his uncle, King Richard the Third, only to re-emerge, years later, under the names of Piers Osbeck, or Perkin Warbeck, used to conceal his true identity until the time was ripe to claim, by all rights, his crown and title: King Richard the Fourth.

I wish to thank my wife, June, for her design of the book cover, and for her thoughts and caring during the process.
To my son, Greg, and my daughter, Jackie, for their media input.
To Sylvia Pollard for her understanding and commitment.
And to that unknown that always guided my hand.

Edited by Pollard Editing
www.pollardediting.com

PART ONE: KING EDWARD IV

April 1483 …

Chapter One.

The King is Dead.

'Twas the year of our Lord fourteen hundred and eighty-three. The month of April lingered with its cold of winter still about o'er this Isle of England. Damp did it lay with chilling winds to bite all that would venture forth. The sky to tell naught 'twas mid-morn's hour, for London Town was dark and grue.*

The horse and rider clattered out from the yard, which lay within the palace of Westminster. The black-edged document he carried tucked in his pouch was most secret. Sealed with the royal seal upon red wax, destined only for the eyes of a prince, the messenger sped his way, his big horse of shiny black snorting and panting in time to its gait; in great haste were they upon this fateful day. The rider's dark coat fluttered and flapped, his hood pulled tight about his neck, the mist beaded his cloth. The bridge was soon to gaze, and in little time was to rattle o'er its oaken boards. Pikes stood aside the way showing their grisly prize atop. The severed heads looked down upon him as he clattered by, as if disturbed by the din. With their smirked mouths and popped eyes they swayed in the mist-laden light, some at rot, some still bloody, and watched as he crossed o'er the fogged Thames.

Below, in the dark arches where the black water slapped its gringed** slime, the river dwellers lurch in their rotting craft. They live in a vile state; nameless, ragged, and lost were they; the dank and dripped wet they lived in made short their lives. All had the bloodied cough; forever spat into the river as from boat to boat it could be heard. Rat-bitten and infested with lice as animals themselves they lived. The victuals they ate were that which was thrown into the river as waste, or washed down the sewer channels from the town of London. Or such they could steal. No grave would mark their pass; a gentle, rippled slide into that black gloom to float seawards on the river's flow, and become fodder for such creatures that awaited them.

Now upon firmer ground, the horse and rider picked up their pace, and soon, with pant and sweat, were away along the road to the castle at Ludlow.

---

* *grue* gruesome, foreboding
** *gringed* [coined] grimy, black

The message there to be delivered? "The king is dead!" … Lechery and debauchery had rotted him away, he was alas done. The messenger rode on; quickly he raced through the villages and hamlets, bent was he upon his task. No markings or insignia showed upon him as black upon black went he, for many enemies and spies lurked about who would give much to know the message that was secreted within his pouch.

The peasants in the fields saw him fleeting by. As they toiled their day with ached back and thirsted throat, they had seen the blessed fellow whose only labour was to ride a horse. They would not ride a horse; their master's watchdog gazed o'er them from the dawn's light to the sun's sleep.

Through the thickest forests and upon narrow paths he rode, the branches and bushes taunting his ride, tugging his coat and lashing his horse. A clearing at times would show, cleared there the trees as the woodsmen cut and hacked at the great logs. Sawn into lengths of two paces for the great fireplaces needing to be fed at the castles and manors. His horse was changed for a fresh steed, as he took victuals and supped a little ale at the changing stations along the way. He was now hardly able to mount his ride from the aches laid upon his frail shape, but then he was upped and upon his shaking way once more.

Edward IV, the king of this Isle, dead. The fact was not known to many, for such news took many days to spread about. The king's oldest son, Edward, the Prince of Wales, was now heir to the throne of England; his younger brother, Richard, the next descendant. Both brothers were feared of what may be placed upon their young heads, for strife and bloodshed oft came to such as they. Edward was lodged at Ludlow Castle, far from his home at the palace of Westminster. He but twelve years of age, his younger brother almost of ten years. Edward, though, was almost of age to ride before the king's army, to seek honour and bravery against those who desired to take this dearest of lands. The Scots, the French, the Spanish. All with devious intentions to cage this place and to bend it to their evil ways.

Such thoughts, though, are not to their minds at this time, more so to the hunting and fishing that they are engaged in. The royalty and the upper class were oft to travel their many estates, to partake in the towns' feasts and festive occasions. Vintery was mostly the cause of their visit this day. The wine cellars, after the winter feasts that took place in the manors and castles, were almost empty. Barrels of wine were now being eagerly sought. These gifts would be most gratefully accepted by the lordly lot, though naught to the vintner's pocket would come.

The journeys of the lords and landowners were also obliged to collect any taxes that were owed from the overburdened peasants, to also act as a travelling court, metering out punishment and fines regardless of any hearing. Justice was hard to find for they without the chink of coin.

Ludlow Castle was set high in the hills of Shropshire and close to the border of Wales. It lay overlooking vast rolling fields of grazing and sown land, bound by thick woods and low brush spreading as far as the eyes could see into the misty far, all alive with fowl and game, a royal arena where only the finest gentlemen were to roam.

The castle at Ludlow stood as it did in the thirteenth century; a pace thick were those stone walls; cold and foreboding they stood as high as oak trees, melting to the clouds' fold. Built from the local stone 'twas chiselled and shaped by craftsmen all in trade. Carpenters had worked the huge beams aloft, high above the masons who crafted below laying the floor of sandstone and slate, they who seemed but little people from their view on high. The tradesmen were all brought from London to work their craft, for the ties of the guild were strong, placing those who were its members into good state. They were waged far above the other menial workers, for only the guilded were allowed to work with such skills that had been apprenticed, to the exclusion of all others. The only menial labour hired came from the local farms, for trivial tasks and for strong backs.

This day the rafters overhead are blackened by the fires that burned below them in the huge fireplaces, and no more to be seen was that rich white oak. The glow of torches flickered kindly upon the walls to bless this dark place with some glimmer of light. The black oily smoke was painting all as it wended its journey to the roof's far reaches, laying now the timbers with the tarred residue of many years. And mingled there, in that warmly place, were the pigeons that did flutter, laying their droppings upon all below with light feather and heavy crod.* The words unspoken: Do not upwards gaze.

Smells from the kitchen did waft about, both good and bad did stray; forever it seemed the cooks did labour therein both day and night, always mouths seeking to be fed. Oxen, chicken, venison, eel, lamb, and rabbit, all at boil or roast. Bread baked, wine made, and ale brewed. The black-charred fireplaces burned continuously with their incessant desire for attention, like the newborn babe they had no desire to be left without fuss. Ashes were removed and panned into the tin boxes, hot and of spit, and glowing with the grey soot. As each tin was filled a bar was struck between the two handles and was lifted by two underlings, who carried the hot mass with its spraying and rocking through the many passageways, to be at last outside in that cool air of the day. The ash blustered about liken

---

* *crod* [coined] a combination of slop and crud

to the clouds above, as they dumped the burning lot into the waste pit, and like ghosts of grey went back to seek more.

The great logs were carried in with grunt and groan, and then laid gently upon the ash to keep the warmth flowing through the cold ways that whistled the castle. A team of servants was kept in attendance of the hungry places where the flames did glow. The logs were piled at the courtyard entrance, making long the trek with the heavy load for those servants and skivvies. The fuel was covered in thatch; dry they must be, for the fires must not spit too freely. 'Twould the pile be closer to the need, but those who worked such tasks were kept far from the nobles. They were not to mingle, and was best they were unsighted. This system was the way for all, as was decreed.

The woodsmen who toiled at the great trees, the peasants who toiled the fields, the maids and house servants were all lowly upon the ladder of life, and the struggle to survive each day took its toll, for oft stricken by some malady, or some injury, death would come soon and take its victim. The taxes they were assessed placed them with little monies left, and oft 'twas that violence was brought against the tax collectors, hated for the monies they took, which went straight into the king's coffers, and was wasted upon the royalty who lived in luxury and in excess. The laws though were of change for the peasants and all the lowly creatures; the working class was needed to build roads and cottages, as this land of England was at last dragging itself from the sticky mire of wars, and of turmoil, to see now the ground laid to the future. Appeased they had to be, and the Parliament were passing bills to protect such as they, but minutes were hours, and days were years.

Ludlow Castle was somewhat quiet this eve; the crack of the fire, the whisper of servants were all that laid ear. Half sitting, half lying upon the settle—which was usually the place where the king would sit—Edward, heir to the throne of England, reclines. Upon the demise of his father he would be king, but as yet 'twould be in name only, for he would require more years to mature. One score and four he would have to reach before he could rule alone, which left many years that he may be bent and squeezed to others' desires and to others' intrigues. For good or for evil, he stood to be moulded.

His mother, the Queen Elizabeth, was to be the prince's Protector until he became of age; her desires though were self-serving and of much evildoings. She had waited this day when her husband would succumb to those long indulgences in every excess that he had engaged in. The queen had been sowing the seeds for her own harvest, planting them in Edward's mind to succour and grow. His mother's relatives and other devious persons, all of ill intent for their own reward and gratification, surrounded the prince. Elizabeth would hold the power to remove anyone who stood in the way of her desires and aspirations of unlimited wealth. She, so blinded upon the path taken, was rank.

The Earl Rivers was not of this ilk, and was one of the Prince Edward's constant companions, appointed by the King Edward to school and guide the prince upon the way of right until he did become of age; to lean him away from any who may try to show him the easy path. Rivers was a scholarly person and a fearsome knight who had stood beside his king in many a fray, and had earned all the respect bestowed upon him, not in the Parliament or within the Church, but upon the field of battle where men did bleed and heroes walked. Now he was in the position he held as designated by the king, and had the closest and most continuous access to the prince, and as such was able to influence the young Edward and to send him upon the desired path. True he was to his king and gave only the best council to the prince. The earl knew too well that if that bitch, Elizabeth — such did he call her, for he knew her ways — if she had the chance she would get her craggy hands upon this prince's flesh, and dig in her bloody fingers till naught is left. Rivers knew the danger in which he was placed, and with little doubt that one day he would be brought to answer for his ways, for one such as he could break the wheel and tip the cart. But shouldered with the king, he feared not such reprise.

"This day was a good day was it not, my lord?" the earl spake, breaking the silence.

"'Twas so, my Lord Rivers; some good fish and venison we did gather this day," the prince answered. A slight boy was he, with light hair and eyes of grey, more his mother's demeanour than of his father's. Dressed in the fashion of the times, with green shirt and stockings, a black doublet, and black leather high-laced shoes, he sat relaxing by the fire's crackle, and watched the shooting arrows of light that showed upon the castle's grey walls. Others in the party, eight in all, were in other areas of the hall. Some half slept from the wine and ale they had supped. Others in the dark reaches of the room, dimly about where the torch did not show its light, whispered into close ears, and bringing stifled laughter to some lewd remark, played upon the ears of those ladies, who were always available in these places of intrigue and cuckoldry. Ready were they to please their lords. Some had, with pleasures touch, wayed to their bedchambers where privacy had little hand in such meets, for when bedded, the waiting ladies were always in attendance to their mistress, bending to her needs at all times, and did remain so during all the amorous excursions that were flaunted.

"What say you, sire, that we retire for the night?" the earl posed to the prince, who he saw was having some difficulty in remaining awake; but the prince was taking upon himself a manly tack, and wished not to be seen as a child who sought slumber's pose. "This day has been too long. Come, more sport awaits us upon the morrow, and an early start would be most apt." Before any answer could pass the lips of Edward, the light tap of the head butler upon the door that stood partly open did draw both from their chat, as most silently the butler entered, bowing reverently as he did so. Came he attired in his long black coat, with his white stockings showing as he grovelled along. Black shoes did he wear, with large silver buckles, that seemed to give a most odd appearance to his feet. His collar of white protruded from his coat; thick dark hair laid upon his head cropped neatly above the ears and about the neck. He stood, a man in his fortieth year, or thereabouts. It seemed he was always bowing and grovelling to his masters to some excess. To see him one would imagine that he had been in service from early childhood, and over many years had attained the position he now held through much labour and demeaning activities. But 'twas not so, for once he too was a lord, and once time ago had held this land and properties, and indeed did have riches abound. He had an army, he owned peasants and farm workers, and he lived in high style. But a king dies and in his place comes some tyrant who cares not for that which went before and does bring forward his own leeches to usurp the properties and to steal the lands from those who were loyal to the king demised, then to cast them out upon the road, penniless and destitute. The law was writ that such people, as these who walked with the dead king, must not receive any help or succour in any way from any person, in as much as they would be deemed traitorous, and death would be the punishment. The butler had children, but they were dispersed and he knew not of their whereabouts. His lady-wife worked in the kitchen, and they had a small room for accommodation. The new lords of the land took in such outcasts as they, for they knew not what the morrow may bring. Fate may have it that one day they too may have to buttle. The law did speak one thing, but survival did speak another. For the humble butler may one day strut again. *The night be long, but the dawn cometh.*

"My lord," addressed he with his educated voice. He spake clear but his tone was quiet. "A messenger has arrived at the inner gate, sire; he seems to be agitated and in some hurried state."

"From where does he come, my man?" Edward asked. The earl, with the same question upon his lips, looked on.

"He travels from Westminster, my lord."

"Send him in at once; we will receive him." The butler in silence did leave, gliding away as if upon some ghostly legs. Edward, after sending the butler upon his way, turned with worried brow toward the earl.

Also, of some concern himself, was Rivers, but he concealed the fact in his reassuring tone. "May that your father is sending to you some kind of tribute for your labours in replenishing the crown's coffers."

"Methinks that is not the case, my friend." The prince was wary of the kind words laid upon him by Rivers.

"If the news is not to our liking, be of strength, sire, and remember you are of royal blood and do not shake as others."

The butler came slowly into the chamber of the prince; the messenger, close at his heels, did follow with two soldiers of Edward's guard in close attendance. At the entrance the messenger had slowed a little, as he clasped his dispatch case tightly in his hand and glanced quickly about the chamber, as if to guard it still from any unwanted gesture, even in this most secure place.

"Bring to me the dispatch, Marshall." The rider stood now from the reverent state he had taken, unbuckled the message pouch, and passed the red-waxed message to the butler, Marshall.

"Begone, rider," spake the prince once more. "Wash, and take some victuals, for you may ride again before this day is done." The fellow was dismissed curtly, for they wanted not the uncouth person to remain near. The rider bowed his respects and slithered away, as glad to go as they were to rid of him. Marshall brought the document to Edward, and then made to depart.

"Stay," Edward gestured to the butler, sensing the calmness about this man, which in these unknown circumstances felt reassuring. The prince's hands became unsteady, for he feared what may be writ within that sealed fold. He fumbled with the half-open document; it slipped from his hands like a worm in oil, and fell as a fluttering bird upon the floor. The floor seemed as cold as a grave's slab, bringing a bad omen to any who wished to seek the letter upon it. Rivers stepped forward to assist his young ward, but Edward gestured him to stay and picked up the butterfly letter from where it lay, reading the little he could see as he rose … "My royal Highness, we regret—" It slipped once more from his useless fingers. He now in some distress did slump back upon the settle, where but minutes before he had been of a more jovial nature. Marshall came then close and placed a comforting hand upon Edward's shoulder, for he knew well the pains that followed the nobility. 'Twas not all the loss of someone beloved that brought such ache, but also the burden that would be placed upon shoulders of one so young. Rivers stepped forward and retrieved the message that lay upon that cold slab once more, as with some dire thoughts himself of its contents.

"May I, my lord?" he queried. The prince could only wave a consenting hand in response to the request. Rivers read on. "My royal Highness, we regret your father, our most beloved and holy king, passed in peace from this cherished land to the heavenly place of our fathers, upon this eighteenth day of April, in the year of our Lord fourteen hundred and eighty-three. With all our sympathy, we await your most regal self at Westminster. You will be king. Long live the king! Your devoted mother, Elizabeth."

Both Rivers and the butler kneeled before the one who would be king, and did pledge to him their oath of loyalty.

"Arise," Edward spake, recovered a little now from the anguish he felt. "Marshall, make immediate haste and prepare for my departure; with all speed we will make to the palace. Also inform the captain of my guard to make ready our soldiers."

"We ride tonight, my lord?" Rivers spake now, concerned was he of the rash move taken by Edward. For he knew well the perils of the night ride with that black moonless night that did cling close about, and, if most fortunate, only the tracks of carts to guide the path. Peril could show its shape most foul.

"Yes, Rivers, we go with haste. I am well aware of your concerns, but I fear such plotted mischief at Westminster with no king about, and I am feared for my brother, who in all his innocence sits alone in that place. I wish no longer to tarry here, as you well know too many games can be played 'twixt and waye.* Rivers knew the prince was adamant in his decision, and did not try to press the matter further.

Edward was much in thought as he readied for the journey that was to be taken. Most concerned was he of all that had been thrust upon him, upon this boy of few years, he feared he could not survive such that may come his way. He prayed that Rivers would always speak to him in the voice of truth.

Marshall methodically saw to his orders, first informing the duty officer of the demise of the king, then conveying the orders of the prince soon-to-be enthroned. The officer quickly went his way to inform his commander of the latest orders, and then to proceed in rousing the guard. They, broken from their slumbers, cursed and moaned at all who were the wearers of the officer's garb, but were soon assembled with little more ado. Marshall then made his way to the servants' quarters, where he awakened his own underlings and the lord's manservants, who were to dress their masters in attire suitable for their journey. Soon the whole castle was apprised of the king's death, and of the ride to be taken into the night's dark fold. There

---

* *'twixt and waye* [coined] to convey there is no master with a stick

was a constant chatter and speculation all about as unlikely stories were spread to intrigue the mind. The manservants finished their dressing as they hurried their way to the lords, pulling on their boots and stockings as they ran, stumbling and twisting about as they did so, struggling with shirt and coat liken to the court jester with the act of a clown. Eventually they became of presentable dress to enter their lords' quarters, and to clothe them.

The time came in that black of nights for them to depart, for Westminster was at need for its king. A short stay they knew would have to be made upon the travelled way, horses to change, victuals taken, and, may, a little rest, for the miles were many and they were far from Westminster's gate. They left with their small army, the cold black at cling to their bodies, the chill did creep the bones and slow their ride.

Marshall looked upon them as they made their way. Stood he in the open doorway as the wind-blown torches within waved their smoky heads about, blustering in that blowed cold that came upon them, making to dance the silhouette of the butler, to jiggle his grey shadow about as a graveyard ghost. What may come now? thought he; what will the next twist be in this rope of life? Would he once again strut as master of this place, or still skivvy about in some degraded fashion? He watched on as the night quickly drank them in, the hooves' clatter, the bridles' clink and rattle. "Forward" he heard as the party moved away. There was no torch at show, for discreet were they as the blackness welcomed them into its cloak. Soon only sounds stayed the air to let know aught was about. The butler closed the door, and his dancing figure was gone.

Chapter Two.

Richard Cometh.

There came then this day with their rattling armies, two dukes of proud heritage, returning from the northern borders where they had been at fight with the Scots. They filled with ambitious desires tread the road; they were aware of the King Edward's impending death, but knew not of his demise. Though upon such a fate had devised some plan to bring about their aims. As yet they were only scraggled lines upon a canvas, awaiting the time when they would know of which colour to use, and of the place where it would be dabbed.

They came, those dukes, one ahead of the other by twenty miles. Their destination was Northampton, where they would rest overnight and then proceed upon the morrow to London—there they were to report to the King Edward of their activities. The Duke of Buckingham did trail aback, as the Duke of Gloucester closed his army to the castle that stood within the walls overlooking the town. The late afternoon lay dark with mist and rain; a putrid smell was rising from the bogs and swamps that lay each side of the cart tracks; this was the road that did choke the throat, and wetted the eyes of such travellers. Gloucester sent forth his outriders with their torches to guide the army along this path that was not familiar. The duke did not wish to be pulling horses and their riders from the muddy clutches that lay close. Every move he would make was of cautious tact, his mind and eyes on all things of danger. 'Twas the reason he did survive when others had fallen to their lax ways.

Richard, Duke of Gloucester, rode before his army; he wore his riding harness with his long-sheathed sword swinging by his side, clattering against his black riding boots. He was slouched in his saddle now, for many miles they had plod and weary was the gait. The duke's white charger, with head drooped, lopped on. This horse he cared for more than aught else, for many a skirmish had they survived together, and oft without guidance had brought his duke to safe ground. It stood out as a pearl placed upon a cloth of black velvet as it trod its muddied way. The duke gave out the look of fatigue, but sly as a fox was he, for 'twas told that with both eyes closed tightly he could still see the enemy a mile afar. And 'twas many who thought they had the advantage, lay now with heads severed and armies destroyed to their own folly.

Clattering along behind their leader with good horse and well armoured, came the dukes, followers of noble blood, a warring lot and the last of the true knights; though muddied and worn, still proudly they came. Then came the soldiers of the foot; old campaigners and young sprouts, they trudged along. Soldiering for Richard they had seen many a fierce battle and bloody massacre. Bitter times when their comrades were cut down before them, but they still survived, and through all the hardships they would all in a whispered moment lay down their lives for Richard. The archers next trod the way, each with their longbow clutched and the hemp hanging slack as they marched. Their quivers, full of feathered flights, await to fly from the strong arms that now swing limp. These the heart of the English military, dreaded for the firepower they did bring, for, in less than one minute, each man could unleash six arrows; twelve could be shot if a loader were to hand. They, able to rain down death and havoc from the sky, to bring down all who stood beneath this shower of doom. One thousand strong were they, all proud of their skills, all invincible, as were their leaders, always ready to fight. They were fed well, clothed well, and goodly booted. Their helmets glinted from the torches flickering light, as they trod that set gait with ne'er a step faulted.

The swordsmen in close dress followed with the White Rose of York showed upon their tunics. The sheathed English steel clattered against each, were they so close. That steel that wrought such bloodshed upon those who dared to stand before it. Superior to any yet forged, with its honed edge so sharp, 'twas easy with one blow to sever a head in 'twixt. The rest of the army did follow; as always the cooks with their pans and irons, and their stores of food and their livestock, tied to the carts. The bowmakers, the blacksmiths, all trudged the way, for all manner of folk did come with the army; they wore no uniform, but not one soldier could march far without their presence. They all jogged along behind in this late afternoon of fourteen hundred and eighty-three.

Through the dark of the long hours in that late afternoon, glimmering torches showed coming a horseman dark. He approached from ahead escorted by Richard's outriders; they came through the mist and dark as ghostly figures. The horse's breath was seen covering them with great bellows of steaming fog. A messenger they bring, one of Richard's devious fellows, planted he like a weed in the court at Westminster. The duke stayed now his horse and waited for the cloaked rider to near.

"Forgive me, my lord; I bring most important news from London." The rider apologized to the duke for not showing full reverence to his lord, but knew he well the message brought would bring the duke's forgiveness.

Nothing was writ; only quiet words were spoken upon such matters.

"Come closer." The duke beckoned the rider to come ear-close; their horses, restless and fidgety from the stop, pawed at the muddy track, snorting their steam and tossing their heads. "What news do you bring, fellow?—though I feel within me the gist of the message you are about to speak."

"The king is dead, my lord," was the message whispered into the lordly ear. A twitch cricked the corner of the duke's mouth, then a misted eye was seen. Outside some remorse did show upon the lordly face. Inside, though, 'twas all thoughts in turmoil, as many things ran through his mind that his time could be close. He saw the spotty prince all of a gangle hanging from some royal thread. Then the queen of evil, about with her slimed followers, she with snip shears to hand, ready to cut the thread and take that prince into her keep. She may snip, but, by God's good grace, she will net but a thread at dangle, for it will be I who will hold the thread with the jiggling Edward upon it.

"And, pray, what of the Prince Edward? Where does he lay in this?"

"My lord, the last report we have is that he was lodged at Ludlow Castle, but on hearing of the demise of his father he did, in the dark, leave that place, and he is believed to be on his way to London. We have riders out seeking his whereabouts, and it will soon be known to us of his circumstances."

"You have served us well, my good fellow. But I must have Edward's journeyed place with haste, for things must quickly come if we are to have our day. We will tarry at this place to await your dispatch; so let your horses fly, and bring to us the place without delay, for a soon word will bring to you and your riders a goodly reward."

"Thankee, my lord; with all speed I will have the dispatch soon in your grasp." Then, with a bowed head and a pull upon the reins, he was away, with mud flying about and with the horse's steamy breath ghosting, he was gone into the eve's dim.

The Duke of Gloucester, silhouetted by the light of the torch-runners about him, was seen coming over the hill, approaching slowly to the place that would be their stay. He stopped close to the entrance, proceeding no further whilst his guards searched about the dark places for any lurking misdoers. He looked at the castle as he waited. 'Twas an imposing place, built of the grey stone that had been cut from the quarry that lay close. Those thick walls did stave the place from any onslaught. A moat, deep and black, surrounded the walls with only one bridge there to enter the gate. Oak were the doors that filled the gate, as hard as the stone they did swing upon.

The sun then shows itself, shining through the mist and the fog that rose from the moat's waters. A muted, eerie wash of pink that layered itself upon the grey stone, engulfing those walls and towers as yet not seen. The proud duke stood before this drape; his horse was restless and ready to feed after the long journey taken this day. And then, like the closing of the eyes, the sun was gone, and gloom played about once more as the bright from this day was done.

A lone torch waved to give Richard the sign that all was safe within the grounds, and a voice then did call from the dark there. "All is well, my lord."

"Care for your horses, and feed your soldiers, then bed for the night. We move again at the dawn's break."

"Yes, my lord," the officer of the guard answered; but before he could move away, Richard gave due state to further the order, as close came his words.

"Be in all readiness to move quickly, for this night may not be liken to others that have passed."

The officer saluted his leader and bowed in respect as he left to carry forth his duties. The others of the entourage were now dispersing and going about their tasks of making camp. The cooking of victuals would soon be started; some wagons had to be repaired, bedding and feed provided for the horses, and much ado before any rest could be taken, and then to be at the ready for Richard's call that could tumble them out to ready again and be away.

After a pat upon the neck from his master, Richard's horse is taken away to the stables, and the duke to the castle door strides, followed he by his lords and earls. The great door starts to open as he nears, then wider does it creak to drape the comers in the light from within. The torches and the fireplaces show their flickering glow all about. The fresh logs placed to greet their new guests did crackle and spit their welcome.

"Humble tidings, my lord master." The keeper of the castle, with head bowing and with humble manner, backs from the door he had discreetly opened, to cringly* let the new guests enter his domain.

"Where is Buckingham?" The duke chides the question to the humbling servant. The words spoken in such commanding tone, to seem more of an order than a question.

"Not arrived yet, my lord, but 'twas related that he is but one hour away, and making of good haste." The reply came with more grovelled beggings. The keeper of the castle was a tired old man with limp and stoop, and had been in service there since the time he was but a small

---

* *cringly* [coined] based on cringe

boy running barefoot in the kitchen, emptying slop, and burdened with all other tasks to degrade, deemed to run from dawn's break to moon's rise. Through the years, under strict and difficult masters, he had risen to his position of power. His face was craggy and aloof, and seemed always to bear a cynical smirk, giving the impression that he had seen and heard of all things many times before, and was so deemed the ruler of this small kingdom. But within this castle, upon this day, 'twas Richard who did dwell, and all who would trifle with such as he may not the morrow see.

Richard, Duke of Gloucester, brother of King Edward IV. And, in lineage to the throne, after Edward and Richard—the sons of his dear brother, king—he was indeed the next rightful heir. His ambitions, though, were to seek such things by other means, for he would be king even though princes stood in his way. Built of fearful size he was not, but he did possess an overpowering presence that made other men creak. Not for him stature tall and wide, but he with crooked back, and with one shoulder much higher than the other. Under his cloak hid within the folds, his withered arm did dangle gruesome. But a more feared warrior there was not; his high ambitions added to the fire that was at burn within; for him, there was only the path to the crown, and all else was the dung of cows.

"I will take victuals now," he stated. "Apprise me at once when Buckingham arrives, and do not delay, for there is no time that I dally this day."

"Yes, my lord," the castle keeper did reply with lowered head, as he beckoned his master forward to the dining table. The duke began removing his cloak and his harness as he strode as if there was no time to waste upon standing still. Manservants appeared out of the gloomy niches to help him and to remove the discarded attire, then to disperse with the dripping robes into the dark ways from whence they did come.

The rough-hewn table stood immovable before the great fireplace, still spitting its shards afar, as the flames wrapped all lovingly about the new logs placed. The shadows danced about those stone dank walls as the duke seated himself at the table. Richard's commanders, the earls and the lords, had followed his steps to the victuals spread, shedding their garb as they came along, and once more to be retrieved by the scurrying servants. Those coats, wet and heavy, those capes that dripped about, to be once more floated away into the lost passages of the castle.

They were all seated now, around that table that did offer to them all manner of victuals, with breads and wines to bring their stomachs to full. Then, to enter from the dark passages of the castle, came forth slowly one by one the courtesans, their heady perfume drifted in before their sight, as they brought their games of the night to play, to play upon these virile members of the aristocracy, and with flaunt they did their wares display, to snare whoever desired to spend time and trinkets in their warm folds …

That royal party, who were coming south from the castle at Ludlow in that darkest of nights, were approaching the abbey at Oxford. The Prince Edward with Earl Rivers by his side, and their noble entourage at their backs: Sir Richard Grey, Sir Thomas Vaughan, Sir William Stanley, Sir Richard Croft, and Sir Richard Hawte. These all members of the council of Protectors, all supposed of one mind: the care and protection of their royal charge. But there was not one who did not have his own agenda, for regardless of the queen, they too had great sway over that Edward, who believed that one day he may rule this land. For they, as well as many others, had such thoughts that were not so, and had in their own mind another to rule as king, one in their own clique, one who would serve well as a ruler and would need no bending, and naught to be spent, for would he not already be so bent?

'Twas in the late hour of that eve when Edward's party arrived at the abbey. Within the courtyard there the monks awaited their coming. Forewarned of their arrival, they stood there in the darkness; only the light that did creep from the open doorway showed where they waited, for in drab robes did they stand, against drab walls hidden, for their calling was of a discreet nature, and they wished not any pomp that would stray them from their most devout of ways. The entourage dismounted, the wind billowing their capes as the sails of ships to float them away upon the rolling sea. But then came forth the monks to guide them into the harbour of the abbey, warm and safe from that cold lash that blew, and to make their way into the Great Hall there. The small guard that escorted them was but three score; too small an army for any enemies that may play a hand against them. The way then so deemed was by travel quick, to be in the safer walls of Westminster afore any action could be fashioned against their persons. *Like pimples upon the buttocks of a queen, they would be hidden in the dark and unseen, known to no one.*

The hall greeted them with blazed fire and tabled victuals. They quickly made goodly comfort around the inviting spread. And then, with some short hours of rest, they would ride again to be in London upon the morrow with God's caring grace. They began to make loose their harnesses and their coats as they ate and supped their ale, for time had been long since food did fill their bellies, and they had little time to remove such as clung to them whilst their stomachs churned. The manservants in numbers moved about them, helping to remove the reluctant garb. They tugged with grunt and swear to pull off the riding boots, so wetted as to be shrunk upon the leg. Others did bring bowls of water hot, and began to wash the hands and the feet of the grubbed riders, who still scoffed down the victuals through the inconvenience.

All were now engaged in such activities except the Lord Rivers, who during the arrival had been engaged in the deepest conversation with a messenger, who had stood patiently awaiting the prince's coming for some while. The Prince Edward whilst being groomed had spied across the hall, and had seen in the dark there that Rivers was in some deep council, and it seemed that something of importance was pending. He saw then the Lord Rivers pressing some coinage into the man's hand, as he made away behind some discreet coverings. The Lord Rivers then came to where Edward did sit, and then in some discreet tones imparted the message that had been received.

"Sire, it is reported that Richard of Gloucester and Henry of Buckingham are but a thirty-mile distance away, and I feel that upon hearing of your father's demise, they may have intentions dishonourable to their prince."

"I pray 'tis not so, my lord, for Richard is my uncle, and to me has shown naught but kindness, and to my father his utmost loyalty. I do not believe he would ever bring harm upon me, and for him to bring such against his beloved England … No, sir, it is folly, and I will have none of it."

"I too pray it is not so, my lord, but if you will take my council in this matter, and, with me, proceed with caution. Ride to London as quickly as you may, then, if I am wrong, little harm will be done, but, if I am right, you will be safe in the protection of Westminster." *The ship does not sail into the squall, but does wait another day for skies that are clear.*

"You, my lord, are wiser than I, and so shall do your bidding. But do you not think, sire, that if Richard is bent upon some plot that he has the hand, for our horses are not yet rested, and at this place there are no fresh horses about. If it is true that he is within thirty miles, if not even closer by this hour, he can surely overtake us with ease."

"That is so, sire, but I do think there are some ploys that we can consider to slow their coming. With your permission, I will go forth and seek out Richard and Buckingham at the castle where they are abode. Or to any place upon the way where they may be, in pretext of your prince's desires to greet them, and to bestow upon them your continued trust and honour pledged as so aptly applied by your father. With such words I can delay them with your most honourable thoughts. For they will see then that any fears they may have had, due to your father's demise, were unfounded, and they will trot, in all good faith upon the morrow, to greet you at the abbey at Oxford, where, sire, you will be long parted."

"I fear for you in such intrigue, my friend, but it would indeed solve our dilemma. Blessing I do give upon this enterprise, but, my lord, be thee of much vigilance, for I need you by my side, and not with shoes cocked. You may be like a dove entering a cote, with a falcon at flutter within."

Rivers, with a hasty farewell, was soon at stride down the long hall to delay Richard as best he might …

The meal was half finished at the castle that lay at Northampton; the usual scene was now being acted out. The lords slumped, mostly drunk from the wine and ale so liberally proffered. The ladies of the night tripped about, they also with their fill of ale. Stumbled they from one lord to another fulfilling each favour desired, and gleaning from those nobles such trinkets and such privileges for their husbands that could be called upon. Many of them were in a wedded state, but only so for such lands and possessions that one family could reap from another, and to have a lord who owed a favour would be of much advantage to climb that ever-higher ladder.

Richard was not inclined to taking part in such activities this night, and the deemed conversation at the table was of such pleasures of the night, which had left Richard with no interest but for the pleasure of wiping away, from his fingers and face, the fat of the chicken and pork he had feasted upon. The manservants slowly moved forward with their bowls of water and cloths, and with permission did wash the rest of the grease from his person, to then pick out his teeth of any remaining strands of meat that may be secreted in there. After their menial duty was done, they gently dispersed themselves to the areas of the room to await the next activity that may show itself.

The fire grows dim as the housekeepers enter carrying the heavy logs to liven it once more. They begged forgiveness for the intrusion as they laid them with care upon the hot ashes, and quickly, almost as they were placed, did the fire cycle begin with the spitting and crackling and of smoke and sparks, till all is at flame again. To the torches set upon the walls now went they, filling the copper funnels with black oil as brighter they did glow, and would last until the morrow's morn. They looked at the thick candles that burned in their crude holders, seeing that they lit the table still and glowed steadily, and knew that they would burn for many hours yet. Their tasks were soon done, and with a "Thankee, my lord" they drift into the dark passageway, leaving behind the odour of their bodies and their clothes that soon mingled with the smoke from the fire and the black drift from the torches, but 'twere all unnoticed by Richard, who had seemingly dozed through all of the activity.

"My lord!" Richard is stirred from his restful state by the castle keeper.

"Buckingham has arrived, sire." As he alerted the duke, Buckingham came by him, half knocking him over as he curbed his way. In his harness and with his riding coat fanning behind him like some banner, he strode like the wind across the moors. Richard's brother in intrigue has at last arrived; stirring now, Richard jumps to his feet and greets his comrade, calling to him as he comes closer.

"How fare ye, my friend?" Richard asks as he embraces Buckingham, a soldier's embrace … to a comrade.

"I am well, my lord." Comes now the strong voice from the warrior whilst returning his affection to Richard. He, strong of arm and of feeling, and with Richard's burning desire for the crown, they did strengthen each other. Greetings followed from the other lords who were at wait and adding to the changing atmosphere, as each therein greet Buckingham with their respects. Although only a few months older than Richard, he is younger looking, fair of hair still, as 'twas when he was a boy, stood he now though over six feet tall, he showed then with an imposing air. Straight of back, with handsome features, he was the very opposite of Richard in appearance, but both minds were quick and both as eager. They were well educated and very intelligent in the matters of state and the laws that did bind it. Buckingham was Richard's closest friend and his most-sought adviser.

They had suffered many battles together, where one was totally relied upon by the other, where one would lay down his life to spare his comrade. They were as one, and double the threat to any enemy that may chance their hand. They had matured as two young oaks growing side by side to become one tree.

The ritual of disrobing, of removing boots, continues again. Buckingham brushes the servants aside with their water and cloth—he needs victuals now! Soon his features are painted, shiny with the grease from his food and with ale that did drip off his short beard; he feels again more content. "What of —Edward—my friend?" he utters from his meat-filled mouth.

"I await my rider … We pray he may return soon so that we may plan our course of action," Richard replies, trying hard to understand his friend, whose mouth is so full he oft wondered if he were able to draw breath.

"I hear he is local," then comes the voice, a swath of ale clearing out the mouth and throat, making the conversation easier.

"We believe him to be so, but we must hope he has not moved too quickly on us, for I fear if Edward reaches Westminster, and that sorceress Elizabeth and her lecherous advisers continue to manipulate him, it could be hard times for such as we. For surely now our king has gone we are without any power, and our followers will find it hard to come to such as we. Without doubt, we will lose all to her crew, and even if our lives are spared, we would become but humble persons."

Buckingham stirred to the words spoken by his comrade. "Like you, my friend, I will never become such a man. I would die upon the axeman's block before I would yield to such."

"Aye, my good lord, and I will be stood aside of you proudly awaiting my turn, and when you are cut, I would take up your severed head at drip from the basket, and kiss those blood-drained lips, then upon high would I hold it and declare to all: This man hath more love to his kin, and is of such noble visage, that even as he does dangle, he stands tall above all of you who still breathe. God bless you, my dear Buckingham," spake Richard.

"Aye!" came the rousing reply as all in the chamber gathered together and embraced. Richard and Buckingham knew well the ways to rouse their followers, and oft with timely words would instill into them their own passions and desires. The time that was coming upon them was meaningful to the White Rose of York, for they knew if they would fail in their act it would be the end of them. They did fear their rose may perish, as the winter of their hated queen would flow over their garden, and render all with its death.

The long-awaited messenger arrives as Buckingham is in the midst of being washed and dried. The keeper, as fast as he was able, brought him in to the chamber where all did wait about.

"Come here straight … here to the table," gestured Richard. "What dispatch do you tender?" The rider attempts to kneel and to bow his head, but he is soon grasped under the armpit by Richard who roughly pulls him up. "We have not time for that, fellow." But before he could continue, Buckingham was slopping some ale into the rider's mouth to refresh his rusty throat, and spilling it all about as the fellow tried to drink and to speak at the same time. As he waited for the rider to recover, Richard then turned to the ladies who were in the vicinity, and to the servants and keepers. "Get thee away now! … We will have no spies here to stumble our way." They scurried away with little ado, and in quick time made to the farthest reaches of the chamber where no shot could be gathered.

The messenger, trembling and ale-soaked, came under the gaze of the lords, and stated in some quivering tones his much awaited words. "Sire, the prince at this moment is resting at the abbey at Oxford, and is slated to move toward Westminster at dawn's early light."

Richard was listening close, with the others there leaning o'er to grasp more of the situation. They listened intently to the whereabouts of Edward, and Buckingham, still drying his face from the ale that was splashed upon him, did listen in with ears perked.

"We move!" Richard stated, he then stirred quickly as if his legs were already striding toward his horse. But before aught else came about, the messenger speaks once more.

"Forgive me, my lord, but there is more."

"More! Then for God's sake, let's hear it, fellow; I wish not to stand here like some cloth upon the line."

"There is a rider heading to you from the abbey. We are not yet sure if it is the Lord Rivers, or may the Lord Sir William Stanley."

Richard was stayed in his tracks, and for a few seconds did stand in contemplation.

"They are playing a card in the game, are they not? This is the first card they show; it will bear little in winning. We, my friends, hold the last card, the one that will bring the fortune, the one that will triumph. It seems they plan to delay us in our endeavours, so we must appear humble and subject to their ways … Go nourish yourself, fellow, then get yourself a fresh mare from the stables, and await there in discretion, for soon you will be of need to guide us to Edward's location. Now be away and make ready."

"Aye, sire," came the reply from the weary agent, and with a bow he exited to the kitchen, and to the aroma of satisfaction.

"I feel, upon your council, my Lord Buckingham, that we must make our new guest most welcome and less suspect to our moves. Our fellow commanders must engage him in some council, whilst we send a small band of our best soldiery to bring out our Edward, and return him to our midst, for do you not think, my friend, that he needs muchly to be in some safe keep?"

"I agree, sire, but I pray we have no blood upon our hands in this endeavour; we must indeed be gentle in our labour and must refrain from any attack upon Edward's guard, for 'twill bode well for our cause if it is known that we were not hostile towards the future king. Once hands are placed in a bowl of cherries crushed, it takes long for the stain to be washed away. And, my lord, as you did so speak, we must secure our prince and bring him into the safety of our fold, and so to secure our own freedom."

All then was agreed, and 'twas planned that Richard and Buckingham would excuse themselves whilst the earls and the barons would hold the lord in some deep council. The troop commander was now called. He came standing straight, clean, and mannered—though he was not fully attired in his uniform, for he had been supping and preparing his equipment for the morrow when the message came. But he knew when Richard called, you came with haste and naught else. For 'twas better for the soldier to be standing there naked in two minutes, than fully clothed in five.

Both Richard and Buckingham were close to their commander now. They spake in lowered tones away from everyone, huddled in a darkened corner far from the firelight and the torches, as if all about them were spies and agents of disrepute.

"Send to the village; we shall need outriders with torches … One of our light wagons with speedy horses, and bring also spare torches and pitch, and be sure we have enough runners to make it to Oxford, for we must make most hastily; there will be no time to dally—" Richard then was slightly interrupted by Buckingham.

"And make thee sure that the runners are familiar with the tracks; we would not be lost this night."

"Aye, sire," the commander replied.

"Twenty good men, upon well-rested horses," Richard continued, with nodding approval from his comrade. "Bring also a farrier suitably mounted. Be on standby in the stables close to the hour of one of the clock, and in all silence remain there, for in stealth we must depart. Bring along the usual needs, and plenty of ale for the runners."

"Regarding guards upon the route?" Buckingham half asked and half reminded Richard, as was their way, one to the other.

Listening to the words of his comrade, then repeating them, Richard took his heed. "Place guards upon the way, from here at the castle to one mile out; let all pass who are journeying to this place, and be not seen in such endeavours. Anyone that you see travelling south from the castle, detain them and hold them until we pass, then bring them in close guard to the stables in shadow, and keep them locked until our return … Let us see what fish we may catch … You are dismissed, commander."

"Aye, sire," he answered, and with suitable reverence he was quickly about.

Returned they to the table, which still dripped with its victuals and ales, and 'twas that the wood beneath barely showed was it so laden. Fresh logs were ordered for the fire, though still abright with flame; the less activity occurring when the guest arrived the better 'twould be for their intrigue. They all laid and lolled about as before. The ladies were brought back in; their bodices seemed even lower now as they displayed their soft-powdered bosoms, showing an enticing glow as they moved by the firelight, pleasing to all those who did gaze. The scene was set for things to come. The waiting ladies and the servants returned to their stations. The normality of the evening returned and all upon the surface showed without intrigue. The sticky web hangs unseen. As all then waited, some knew for what, others did not.

"My lord, the Earl Rivers has arrived, and wishes that he may have audience with you?" the keeper spake as he entered to bring the message so awaited.

"He may, with all pleasure, join us." Whilst still speaking, Richard gave a slight look at the Lord Buckingham. Richard stood then in slowly fashion, as Rivers was now entered into the chamber by the keeper.

"My dear lords, I pray you are well in spirit?" Rivers spake as he came forward and grasped Richard's hand and arm, and then gave the same greeting to Buckingham.

"We indeed are well, my lord, except of course for the grievous news of Edward's demise, which has surely brought much pain and anguish to our hearts. It has so played upon our stomachs that we are only able to partake of a few morsels from our table, so we may have at least a little nourishment. Our dear friend, Buckingham here, has been sorely tried to take any victuals at all." They looked over as Buckingham nodded his sad head in agreement.

"'Tis good that you are afflicted this way, for it does show your love and loyalty to our departed king, whose sweet manner and piety, and the deep love he carried for his kin, and for his most honourable lords, tears fearfully at all our emotions. Edward, our prince, and soon-to-be king, is so deeply gutted he can hardly mount his horse, and finds it most difficult to proceed upon his journey to Westminster, for he is struck with such grief over the death of his father. He indeed wishes not to travel without you, my lords, his most cherished of all the nobility. The message I have been so entrusted to bring to you, his most beloved uncle, is that he will tarry for you in the abbey at Oxford, so you may proceed with him to London to give him strength upon his track, and thereby showing his followers of how highly he bears his Lord Gloucester and his Lord Buckingham." *If lies were yarn, then this weaver could make cloth enough for an army.*

Richard then did take his own wheel and brought to the spin his own yarn, and did wrap it to the bobbin and thread it with most care, and began his foot upon the pedal, and did fashion his own tangle. "'Tis so honoured we are, all who are gathered here, to be thought upon with such reverence by our dearest of princes, and, in such, look forward with joy to the morrow when we may bestow such thanks to him in person, and to most humbly march in his presence to Westminster under his royal cape trust. We pray the morn will not be late in its coming, for do not our feet itch to be sided with our soon-to-be king?"

The preliminaries were now over, as they gathered with the earls and barons who were readily sat about the table. Richard and Buckingham did but peck at their food in some sad fashion like two caged birds. The Lord Rivers ate and drank most heartily, for it had been many hours since he had last supped. The ladies were still flaunting about and Rivers demised that they were there so that all so grieved could have some distraction to forget their anguish even if only for a short time. But to himself he did not in truth speak, but believed only that which he did wish to be so. All now were engaged in council with the Lord Rivers, and feeling he well puffed as the most likeable person in that chamber. "What are the latest happenings at court?" ... "The hunting at Ludlow, how did it fare?" ... "What of the French?" All asked between the plied malmsey. 'Twas then tried to obtain more information from the now relaxed Lord Rivers regarding more secretive matters, but he, just a little drunk, spake of only mundane things. He knew he had set his mark upon the outcome of the morrow and was cat-pleased with his effort. He had made the journey alone, except for his two manservants; a journey well worth the taking, for he had no doubt that the two dukes would proceed with him to the abbey on the morrow, where he would be as surprised and dismayed as they to find the prince had already left, and indeed was now approaching London. He thought, what a day of sadness for the two lords as they saw their prize gone, and tears almost filled his eyes. Poor dim fellows; all war and little brain.

"The Lord Buckingham and I must ready our troops for the morrow and prepare our most colourful banners and buntings," Richard spake as he and Buckingham pulled from their chairs, and gave polite bows to be excused by Rivers.

"Of course, my dear lords, you have much to do. Begone, and upon the morrow we will ride in such pomp and glory to our Edward who awaits eagerly your coming, and to be such a sight entering London as never before seen." Rivers stood as he spake, waving his arms about in some pompous display, with slurred words and drunken manner. Which convinced not the lords, for a wily one like Rivers would not leave himself in a vulnerable state. Richard and Buckingham left the chamber, as one of the evening ladies began helping Rivers forget the anguish he was feeling from his king's demise, as came she with warm cheek and soft touch to send such misery away.

The lords, with just a nervous glance back into the chamber, made straight to the stables, crossing the wet courtyard and keeping they close to the walls of the castle, blending in the darkness with the dank stone that towered about them. Unsighted and with much stealth they slipped through the old oak door of the stable ... The lock clicked silently behind them as they slithered in. Then, in the darkness, a light was struck and a small torch was lit from its flame, though at first refusing to offer its glow, but then gradually it flickered to show a small smoky light in the darkness of their meet. Seen first was the grubby-haired faces of the outriders who had been gathered from the village; their aroma reeked the crowded space. Richard though cared not to such things, for he would delve in the pigsty and roll about in the mire if it meant obtaining his ends. No word was yet spake, and horses became restless upon the lighting of the torch and the sighting of the others who invaded their place. Some began to kick their hooves and to snort with displeasure, but were soon quieted by their riders who calmed them with gentle tone and soothing hands.

"All is ready, my lord," the commander in his husky voice whispered close.

"Move gently out with the utmost care; go in any order until we are without from the castle. Proceed." The stable doors were eased open, but still chose they to squeak their song across the yard, as then 'twere held back by two lightly-armed soldiers, as Richard spake to the party and then made toward the open door. As the small light was snuffed, the loyal group slowly, one by one, left the stable; their black shapes showed barely visible in the dinginess, for the night was clouded and the black dampness clung about them; but it seemed not cold, for they were filled with the dangers of the coming ride and their hearts beat fast upon the thought. They continued on in single file: a peasant, a soldier, an officer, a horse — led by its rider, a lord, a cart. And so they did tread in the early hours of the morn, no sight could be seen. But heard … The gentle clink of harness brass, a slight squelch of boots in mud, the neigh of a horse, the rattle of the light wagons. To look … Naught could be seen of the dark parade; only ears in shot would know of any undertaking about, as the line continued until all were from the stable. The two soldiers last gently closed the stable doors then turned the key in the heavy cast-iron lock. As they turned to be upon their way, a torch passed one of the windows of the castle's upper chambers that lit upon the courtyard to stay their way. They leaned back against the wall there, but then in an instant the light was gone and in its place darkness loomed once more. They followed the way of those before and soon came up to the back of the party.

They all had gathered in a small clearing surrounded by trees, huddled aside the track that would take them to Oxford. They were now out of sight and shot of the castle as they readied in this goodly place. The pitch torches were lit, and the peasant voices could be heard clear as they gathered for the task placed upon them. A small light at first glowed in that dark arena like a firefly in the forest's black deep. A rough-bearded face did it show with long hair, but no eyes yet were seen; a brighter torch was then lit, and a small man whose hair was cropped did show, then from one to the other the ratty lot became seen. Light was all about now, and the party was able to organize into the force desired. The torch-carriers walked to the head of the group; their lights showed their heads wrapped in the roughly-woven cloth of the peasant and covering the bottom half of their faces so only the dark holes of their eye sockets could be seen. Their hands and arms were bound in the same way. Legs were covered and tied with rope so only the foot of their boot did show. They had undertaken these journeys before, and knew they well the perils of running with the pitch torches. They knew of the molten tar that ran down upon their hands and arms, of it splashing onto their faces and not cooling until it had burnt a pit hole into the flesh, and then as it cooled to become solid again, staying upon the flesh like black leeches to fall off in their own time. They made their way, being fifty paces ahead of the main party, along the track that was to Oxford. Six of them waited there with torches that burned bright; like ghostly mummies they stood, wrapped in their cloth of the dead.

Other runners did wait in one of the carts, torches at the ready but not yet lit; some sat all bandaged, others were still tying on their crude protection—all readying themselves for the time when they would relieve their fellow runners. A barrel of water slopped in the cart at the ready for anyone who may catch fire, so they may be plunged into the cold relief, to bathe off the pitch sticking to their skin as best they were able, all whilst rocking and splashing down the rough track.

Spare torches lay in the cart, the pitch and straw kept dry with sheets of canvas, that cloth treated with the oil of the whale. There they did sit in the still cart waiting to be dragged along the track; six were they, mummified like the others, six mummies rocking in a land boat. They sat silhouetted in the light from the torches that waved about, waiting for their turn to run their mile in the blackness, and hope they would not come tumbling down, for if down they went, they prayed they would be able to rise again as from the tomb. For at day's end only those who stood would receive their wage. If you did not show, pride in your pocket would be all you would reap.

The rest of the military were soon in order, as the group of horsed soldiers settled behind the runners who jigged about in their wait. The military giving some protection to the two lords from the smoke and the grease that would come from the spitting torches. After the lords came the rest of the soldiery assembled, followed by the mummy cart, the wagon of supplies, then the farrier and his boy with the spare horses.

"Come, Buckingham," Richard spake to his comrade. "'Tis time for us to writ upon this page, and pray when the page is turned we are still scripted in history's book."

"Aye, my lord, so be it," came Buckingham's reply, with clasped hand to Richard's.

"May God be with us upon this night of our royal endeavours!" Richard called about as he waved all forward, and at last they were away into the gloom. A strange party to be spied indeed. All darkly clothed, they picked up their gait set by the torch-carriers. The carts rocked and swayed in the tracks of the wagons gone before. The horses at trot, trying to maintain the strange gait that had been set by the runners; riders bobbed and rocked about as they tried to control their steeds. The lords with their billowing cloaks that almost hid their horses, like a skirt upon a maid.

The runners afront were now only seen as torches, as they jigged up and then down, and then to one side, then to the other, some seeming to disappear then appearing again, as if their was a stumble and then a recovery as the torch showed bright once more. The noise of the party though was of lowly intent. But clear in the windless night came the cries of the runners as they called to each other, and sounding clear to all.

"To the left up there, John!"

"No, this be Comrey's Corner … To the right, then left!"

"My torch be going!"

"Run on … Run on, 'tis good yet!"

"Coming to Black's Hill now! Push on lads—it's a climb! … Push! … Push!"

On went they with their chat, as the black smoke was seen above the light from the torches, it drifting into the night of black.

"Tom's down! … He's down!" The cry came about as one lost his footing to be tumbled in the dark. The party passes by the runner who is seen picking himself up and looking for the torch cart; he spies it coming through the black trees and hobbles along with twisted knee, to be grabbed then by his brothers as he leaps on, breathless and blackened. Another torch is lit, and a fresh runner leaps out with torch above his head into the dark way, then lengthening his stride he gradually overtakes the soldiers and fills the empty place left by his comrade.

"Did see—Tom?" came the breathless question from ahead.

"Aye, he lays in the cart; he will be well."

On they ran, the horses snorting, their shoes now quiet, then rattling at times as they came upon the stony parts of the track, clatter-click-clatter, one after the other their brasses chiming against each, bringing new sounds to the music of the ride that played with the creak of the carts, and to the talk of the torch-runners as they bounced around in the night.

They had been upon the road to Oxford for over two hours now, the runners changing at every mile. So far no stop had been made, but the time was coming to change horses and to partake of some victuals. They had covered seventeen miles with close to another ten miles to go. 'Twas now three-thirty o'clock, on the morning of April the fourteenth, fourteen hundred and eighty-three.

One of the soldiers begins to move ahead after receiving orders from Richard to slow the troop down, and to make ready for a stop. They gradually slowed and were shown into a sheltered area by the carriers of the torch. As they pulled into the area, the runners had already lit the tall torches and staked them into the ground, guiding all to the place of rest. Came then Richard to quickly post the guards about the area. Though this place lay far from any habited places, much was at stake this night and lax actions could end their game. They took no chances, for stumpy trees and ill-shaped bushes were not always as they seemed. This was one of the many things that made Richard, and Buckingham, such wily foes, and why his troops were so loyal to him, knowing that they would be protected as much as the lords were able. The carts and the horses, with much clatter and rattle, were the last to pull into the safe lot. The victual cart had hot water at the ready, to begin the washing of the grime and the grease from the faces of the lords and of the troops, though at this time 'twas waived, for the hour would not spare such luxury.

All began to crowd about the victual wagon, but then stood back a pace to enter the lords through that they may pick whatever they needed from the chicken and pork, and to take a tankard of ale to sup. After the lords had taken their fare, the others in the party moved back to the tuck, all shoulder to shoulder—the officers, the soldiers, and the peasants—all rubbed together as one group showing no distinction in their class. The situation though was not appealing to those of high rank, but the orders from Richard deemed it so, for he knew that this kind of camaraderie would bind his soldiers together, and bring reliance from one to the other. The usually uncaring peasants even felt some allegiance to those about as they elbowed for their victuals with grinned faces.

The farrier and his boy were most busy now, and had no time to sup. They changed the saddles to the fresh horses, then looked over the used horses to replace missing or damaged shoes. The blacksmith's fire burned bright, the bellows lay limp, but soon the smell of smoking hooves wafted through the sparking air, as the farrier pulled the glowing iron from the now raging fire, and the boy pumped the leather with frantic suck and blow to make the iron glow red. That colour that had to be most perfect. A few dull taps with the heavy hammer soon drove the nails into the hard hoof; they were then fed and watered, washed and rubbed down with fond care. 'Twas that in some short time all the horses were ready to run the track again when their hour did come. Then at last the farrier and his son, with their labour done, went with hunger to their sup. Smells drifted heavily about this once sweet smelling place. The smell of the oil from the torches, the droppings and urine from the animals as 'twere trodden by the men who busied about, the sweat from the horses, the wet saddle leather—all lingered with other smaller aromas, the ale, the sweat of the bodies, the burn of food—all mingled about to create the smell of soldiery.

The torch-carriers were the most in need of a stop from their black run. Burnt wrappings had to be replaced, and the cuts and scrapes they had suffered from the trees and rocks that cluttered their way needed some lard and a bandage. Some were dipping their heads into the water barrel to cool their smoking hair; head bandages had become loosened and hot tar had run through their scalps.

"Mount up!" came the cry from somewhere afar; a last gasp rush was about before they moved again, a quick gulp of ale, a quickly tied rope upon some burned wrappings, a mouth-filling bite into the chicken leg, stuffing a pocket with some buttered bread, the tying of boots. Some though were surprised more than others, as they roughly wiped their rears with cloths and dock leaves, after relieving themselves at the outer reaches of the area. They were still pulling up their breeches as they half ran and half stumbled to their stations, with the sound of a wild boar grunting and foraging about, spurring them on.

The guards were called in from their stations and climbed into the victuals cart to replenish themselves as they started to trundle from the clearing. The tall torches had been pulled, and the runners gathered about them lighting their small torches from the still burning flame. Quickly they had their fuel bursting to life and did light the eerie group—those raggedy men who jogged to their place upon the track. God was surely smiling upon them, for they had not lost any of their brothers to the night. They had all at the beginning of the run voted to share their wage amongst all, so any who did fall would still receive their share. For who could say in that black of nights who may fall and who may stand?

"God guide us all!" came the word, and they were away once again into that curtain of blackness, to move on for another hour or more. They had been running for only, may, fifteen minutes when two of the runners were already missing over this treacherous stretch. One of them was seen from the runners' cart; he did lie at the side of the track, but could not run to leap upon the wagon. They could not stop to help him, but they saw him wave a hand as they rattled by, showed from the lone torch that flickered in the cart. A smouldering wrapped hand, underneath the blackened fingers showed.

"Thomas! ... Thomas! ... We will return!" one of the men called as he peered back into the dark where lay his friend.

"He has his dagger ... He will be safe," spake another.

Time had gone painfully by and the party was slowing once again, looking for some stopping place, then soon to trundle into a wooded clearing that was a goodly hide, and to be but two miles from the abbey of their seek. The time was now half past the hour of three of the clock, and the hours were closing. The party had to reach the abbey before the sun did rise, for this would be the time Edward's horses would be rested and he would be able to continue his ride. They wished to abduct him at the abbey and not upon the open road where all could not be properly contained. The outer farms and hamlets of Oxford were close as they prepared for their only chance to snare the princely one.

All was as ever in the secluded stop, all to their different tasks. They were very close to their objective and other ploys were being tabled. They had to get to the prince before anyone knew of the danger about, for once the prince was theirs, then blood would not be spilled in his name.

Richard and Buckingham had planned their tactics earlier in the castle at Northampton. They had obtained the cape of the Earl Rivers with its royal motifs, bright and regal, and had brought with them his horse from the stables, the distinctive piebald mare he always rode when possible, and was well known to all.

The carriers were again assembled at the cart knowing that only two of them would be required to finish the journey. Too many lights burning in the still dark morn would certainly arouse some activity at the abbey, for 'twas surprise that was the key to Richard's endeavour. The two runners made themselves ready, they being chosen because they had not suffered any injuries upon the way and were in good stead. They wetted their bandaged arms in the barrel of brown grubby water, retied their head and face coverings, and made sure their leg ties were still tight upon the wrappings that covered them.

The other runners, who had finished their task, were removing their head coverings to feel the cool morning air breezing past their hot skin. Some had lost part of their hair where the boiling tar had broken through areas of the wrappings. The scalp showed red and blistered, with black leeches still sticking to them; it would be some days before they dropped off, and would leave a legacy of their timely mission implanted upon them for all time. Faces were marred. And eyes were swollen. The mouths though were strangely unmarked, as if each burning drip had been eaten up before any damage could it do. The black teeth showed some rise to this, as they showed glinting like tombstones in the night's graveyard.

The runners were all smiling in the childish smile that their labours were done, and thoughts ran of their jaunty ride back to their homes, to show there with pride their scars of battle and to jingle their coin upon the table. They sliced away the bandages from arms and legs, and cut around the places where 'twas stuck to their skin, leaving there the leeches with tufts of cloth sticking out from around them. Six of them did sit there with the smile of the fool upon their burnt-red faces. Black teeth, tufty hair, black leech-like blobs wearing cloth caps—all rested upon the skin of this group of peasantry. They had their own level of proudness, and this day they were full.

The farrier was turning his hand at repairing one of the carts. A deer, startled by the lights that jigged along the track, had run into the side of it, cutting a deathly gash upon its head as it ran into the hub of the wheel; so severe was the hit that a new wheel had to be fitted. The king's deer was now draped over the victuals wagon ready for a feast, and was looked upon as some good omen. For may not the prince too succumb to this party's agenda?

The soldiers were changing horses once again, pulling the saddle off one and throwing it over another. The fresh horses, at first, pulled and twisted away from the unwanted chattel upon their backs, but once secured there they settled into calmness, as if giving up the struggle was based only upon principle. After readying their mounts with bridles and bits, the soldiers cleaned off themselves the greasy paint that had layered upon them. With hot wet cloths, they tried to find the faces that lay beneath that macabre mask that had been applied. Wiping and rubbing they did try to see themselves once more, but seemingly the best that could be done was to thin the black to a brown, and to spread it more evenly upon the skin … Making them look more like the soldiers returning from the crusades, than from the midst of the cold hills of England.

The two lords were also engaged in cleaning themselves, also trying to remove the blackened lot that had been painted upon them. With no manservants there to help, they helped each other, with each wiping the other's eyes and mouth and scrubbing at the beard. Closely they talked to each other during this activity.

"Time is pressing, my dear Richard." Buckingham talks through a mouth that is twisted out of shape by the pushing and pulling of Richard's efforts to bring his friend to some state of respect.

"'Tis so, my dear Buckingham." The reply came clear, though somewhat subdued. "But with some good fortune over these last miles we may be timely in our arrival. The tracks leading to Oxford are more in keeping with a faster ride than was the case earlier. Our messenger knows the path well, and knows the most direct way to the abbey, and surely he will guide us with much haste." Richard then began to help Buckingham with the cape he is to don; the royal insignia was brightly shown by the torches' light; the gold and blue patterning did shimmer most regal. A glimpse of the White Rose seen as 'twas draped around Buckingham, as then a hat was placed upon his head; 'twas his own hat but in the style that the Earl Rivers did wear, and in the half light would be judged the same. Richard helped his comrade to mount the piebald, while one of the officers steadied the shaking head of the animal as the lord was lifted aboard. He sat there high upon the steed, and, in a show of bravado, spread his cloak about in flurry, as one earl was oft seen to do. Richard stepped back a pace to see the result.

"I am deceived!" cried he as he saw the recreation of Rivers before him.

"Then, my friend, shall all others be so deceived," answered Buckingham from his high perch.

Richard mounted his horse, as the messenger was sent to the lead with the two runners by his side; then all was ready.

"May God guide us upon our most royal enterprise!" shouted Richard.

"Aye!" came the reply, again and again. "Aye! Aye!"

They trundled off to quickly set their gait to the runners' trot. And to be seen ahead only a dim flicker of flame showed, as they jingled in the subdued light toward the abbey at Oxford. Good time was afforded them and, a little after the hour of four of the clock upon this long and eventful day, were sighted the cottages and then the spire that was near to their destiny. The torches were now snuffed, with the tar starting to quickly cool, and return to its solid state as it trickled down the wooden shaft. Both runners left the party to return to the cart and to clean away the grime that was layered upon them … To see once again that hidden smile, the fool's smile.

Richard's entire group had stopped; they peered into the half-light trying to make out the landmarks that lay ahead, but quickly the messenger had seen his bearings and knew of the place he was at.

"'Tis but a little way now, my lord," the voice whispered quietly in the darkness of the trees. "Just to the left of the spire stands the gates to the abbey. We will know when we are but minutes away, for soft is the track until we are near. And then, just before the gates, cobblestones are laid for may thirty paces; the sign will come when our footing changes from soft to hard. We will then be but strides away."

The carts were left in the wooded area to wait unsighted until the return journey. Two guards were left to care for that which they left behind. One watched their comrades depart, as the other searched for some ale in one of the jumbled wagons.

With the messenger a little in front, the lords and the soldiery moved in all discreetness toward the abbey. As the cat to the mouse, to pounce in silence …

"What say you?" 'Twas the Earl Rivers who shouted in some agitation.

"My lord, I could not gain any presence with you; guards are stood outside your room and below stairs, and would not allow my passage." 'Twas one of River's manservants who tried to explain the dilemma that was forced upon him. He had been in the kitchen with the second manservant earlier that night and had heard rumours of Richard's departure. "Being unable to see you, my lord, we decided that John, the other manservant, would take a horse from the stable and proceed with haste to our Prince Edward to where he is abode, and to hasten him to flee the abbey and in all haste to depart from the place, for fear of Richard's intent."

"So they have let you in to see me now?" The earl searched the manservant with his words and his eyes.

"Aye, my lord, to bring you victuals," the manservant answered his master with bowed head.

"Victuals!" the raged earl cried out now in anger. "Victuals! … 'Tis not such I need. For my need is to depart this evil place most urgently. Come and dress me with haste." Quickly the manservant clothed his blustering lord, until he stood a more imposing figure in his breeches and tailored doublet. Far more striking than the long nightgown and the red headwear at flop he had worn, for he would strike no fear in such garb. The only pain he would cause would be from laughter's aches. "Now, where are those guards?—I will have their heads!" The manservant scurried to open the heavy oak door for his master, and as he opened it he stood back out of harm to release the raging lord with sword to hand. Rivers stepped out into the passageway, puffed he to his full height, but was stopped by such words that met his coming, which he did not believe would be spoken to a nobleman.

"Hold, sire!" The voice rasped as two pikes barred his path, held they by soldiers of Richard's personal guard, and the voice shouted from the commander in charge.

"*Hold, sire? …* You say to me?—an earl? 'Hold, sire!' I will surely have you severed today with your *Hold, sire!*" He ranted, but they would not yield. It mattered not one boot to the guards; their knees did not tremble from the threats being made, and they stayed their ground, with the white-faced manservant peering from around the door, seemingly to be only as tall as the latch. The earl then altered his tactics, for he saw bravado would not let him pass. "On what grounds do you deny me passage from this place?" Again he spoke in a sterner, but much calmer tone to the guard commander.

"My Lord Gloucester orders such through this humble being who does grovel before you. I am to impart to you—your most royal earl—that you are detained here until my Lord Gloucester dost return. And—"

"Get to it, man—The reason I am detained here? And cut the fiddle-faddle."

"You are, sire, detained here for treasonable acts, perpetrated against our beloved Prince Edward, soon-to-be king."

"Treasonable acts!" The earl raged loud again, forgot was his more calm demeanour. "I have no explaining to proffer to peasantry who bar my free passage. Now—Step thee aside!" The earl moved as if no one of any value stood before him, but, as he did so move, the pikes were pushed close to him and the officer drew his sword.

"Sire, you cannot leave; we would die by our master's sword if we did not die by yours. We, in all respect, implore you to wait a while upon our master's return, for we wish not to shed blood; but be sure, my lord, we will not allow you passage." The guard spake with more firmness now, and the earl seemed he was climbing the greased wall at the fair, and he knew he would keep sliding down all to no avail, for these peasants would not be dealt with. He would wait and use his guile upon someone who had some chivalry. The earl, still red of face and mumbling beneath his breath, took his sword and returned to his sleeping chambers, and, with the help of his servant, slammed the big door thudding shut, closing off the guards who blocked his freedom, feeling with the action that they who stood without had been taught a lesson. The earl prayed his other manservant had made the journey in time for the prince to flee, as the two guards who stood the door glanced at each other as calmness came about, and with a crooked smile lilt to their mouths, they stood easy once again …

Clip-clop—the sound of the horses changed from the soft to the sound that came upon the cobbled way, echoing their arrival to the open gate of the courtyard. The light was breaking at this morning's hour as the Lord Buckingham, in his guise, clopped into the lighted yard. The Lord Gloucester was still a shadowy figure and stilled near to the gateway, but then came slowly on as he watched Buckingham getting closer to the prince. 'Twas a timely arrival indeed, with the Prince Edward standing upon his brightly-coloured mounting stool ready to board his pawing mount. His servants were all about him, helping the young boy in every way to safely stride the tall animal. The nobles of the prince's entourage were over to one side of the yard, also being helped to mount their steeds, but they all in different states, some half mounted, some still having their boots tied, others pulling at their capes. The prince's guards were in the same fashion, all at total disarray, with no one at alert. A feast of disorganized victuals for the hungry Lord Gloucester.

The Lord Buckingham rode calmly on. Some doffed their hats at him as he came by. Others gave a bow to the man. Some who knew him well gave a wave of the hand. The lord rode without challenge to within one yard's distance of the Prince Edward.

"My lord—" The young prince was startled at first as he saw the shape before him, and at first was ready to welcome the Earl Rivers, but then did see 'twas the Lord Buckingham who stood before him.

"Richard cometh!" was the cry before aught else could be spake. The shout came from one of the monks who was atop the tall ladder that stood against the tower. He had spied him coming for he knew his colours, but alas too late was the call, as all stood in stunned state, and could only look from one to the other to cast blame about where it may lay. The prince tried then to downplay the situation with talk of some mundane nature.

"It is with great joy I see you here my Lord Buckingham, and also my dear uncle, Richard." Who had now joined his comrade. "What of my Lord Rivers? Is he not with you?" The prince glanced with some puzzled look at the cape worn by Buckingham, to await some answer to the reason of this strange occurrence. All eyes in the courtyard were looking at the story that was unfolding before them. As they looked on so enthralled, Richard's soldiers were silently entering the outer areas of the yard, though they still hid by the close darkness of the walls.

"My dearest, and most beloved, Edward," Richard spake in the most sympathetic manner that was available to him. "We do, sir, have disturbing news of your Protector, in that he has acted in a most traitorous manner, and with the other nobles of your party are planning less than noble doings against your royal self."

Those in the courtyard, whose names had been slighted, stiffened as if to come to the aid of their prince, and to deny such traitorous charges that were levied against them. They were all dismounted now, some with hands readied upon the sword, and stood with defiant gait but yet took no step. The troops of Edward stood still and did not move, for as yet they did not see any danger to their prince, for only his dearest uncle stood by him close.

Richard then dismounts and strides across the dusty courtyard to where the nobles are standing. The Prince Edward's Protectors, all in name, stood: Sir Richard Grey, Sir Thomas Vaughan, Sir William Stanley,

Sir Richard Croft, and Sir Richard Hawte. Came Richard at stand before them with legs apart and finger pointed, his voice half to a shout.

"We accuse you of conspiracy against our beloved Edward, and would give to you fair trial to belay these charges. But if you feel you are without guilt, then come, draw your swords to me, I who will smite you down in the name of right. Do it now if you are of innocent mind." He stood, but not one would move against the challenge of Gloucester, for they were all of courtly ways, and were not the warriors of Richard's ilk. "Then let the chicken hearts beat under your noble garb, and let us not see your legs that shake within your breeches." Richard moved closer to one of the lords, glaring close into his face and just a breath away from his whiskers. Buckingham thought it possible that Richard may make a rash move and spill some blood, for he was oft to become angry. But he did not; he ranted only to carry his play to the full, as if writ upon the stage. "Come, my lord, draw now if indeed you are in the right." Richard forced his presence even closer by pressing his uniform against the lords. The noble who stood lowered his eyes upon the challenge, and stepped back a little away from the menace that was before him. He would have none of it, and reasoned to himself that he would have more of a fair accounting in any trial than he would within the courtyard of this abbey.

Richard, in his last show of contempt towards the nobles, turned his back to them and walked toward Edward. He knew if no one tried to attack him from the rear then the day was his. No one did. He walked then back across the yard to where Edward watched and, upon reaching his prince, lowly bowed to him in deep respect. "It doth grieve me most painfully, sire, that my lips must be those that bring unto you such bad tidings."

"But I need Rivers by my side," the prince in his boyish voice pleaded with his uncle.

"You will see, my prince, from all that I relate, that he has such treacherous leanings towards you, and in no manner is he faithful to your cause … My Lord Buckingham, who stands by your side, had to wear such guise upon our journey to you, so as to appear as the Lord Rivers, for 'twas the only way to obtain such safe passage to our prince. For as surely as we stand before you, we would have not survived the journey to apprise you of the situation. If we had travelled as Richard and Buckingham, we would be muddied in some ditch awaiting the rot of death … If it pleases you, my most loving prince, I place myself before you, in all my humbleness, to offer you protection from all of this wickedness that is about, and to keep all conspiracies gone."

The prince could contain himself no longer, and cared not that royal blood ran in his veins, as then, with welling eyes, did burst into the tears of the young, and he was not content, but accepted all he had been told, for he had no advice to do other.

The prince after a little while, and with a caring arm about him, began to recover, and was seen then to whisper quietly into the ear of his uncle; and Richard, as if repeating the prince's words, spake out to all. "My prince orders his guard to take all orders and directions from his Protectors—the Lord Buckingham, and myself, the Lord Gloucester—and to move under our orders, and to place under arrest the lords so charged with treason: Grey, Vaughan, Stanley, Croft, and Hawte."

Upon this order, the guard under the command of the new Protectors stepped forward and there disarmed the traitorous lords, and did secure them in their keep.

"We will at this time avail ourselves of the abbey church," Richard spake solemnly to his nobles. "We will pray for the heavenly entering of our late king into the glory that is Heaven. And to pledge our fealty to our blessed Edward, soon-to-be king. From whence at nine of the clock upon this morn, we will all be readied and will depart for the castle at Northampton, where our Lord Rivers will join with us upon our journey to our most beloved prince's Westminster, to visit with his dear mother—the late king's Elizabeth."

The prince did chirp when he knew his friend Rivers would be by his side, for such treason unfolded to him had not reached any belief within the mind of the Prince Edward. And Richard knew a happy prince was a gullible prince.

The party entered into the monastery and the doors behind them were closed, as all the dignitaries entered within. It slammed shut, as if one epoch was ended, and it would seem that when the doors again opened another would begin. 'Twas not bright within the cold walls; a dimmed torch and a dimmed prince were about. They sat all upon the hard benches as the prince's servants came to them, carrying some of the monks' red wine to be used in the service pending, but drank not as such, but to liberate tongues and to quench the thirst. They were soon being washed and cleaned from the grime and sweat of their endeavours. Boots were wiped and coats were brushed as the two lords continued to pacify the young king-to-be. They appeased him with their complete loyalty to him, and to his royal kin, and, with a little time in persuasion, the Prince Edward was in higher spirits, and was grateful to the lords for their vigilance and loyalty in bringing such traitorous actions to a close.

The prayers in the abbey began, as mixed with the spoken words of the abbot came the uncontrollable sobs of the lords, as their past king was praised, and were pledged all sincere and loyal actions towards the new king of this England. Edward was of no doubt of how highly he was held by his new companions, for they were struck with trying grief as the words from the abbot rang about the abbey. Edward was doubting the loyalty of his old Protectors, and was minded to place all his trust in Richard and in Buckingham. For had they not saved his life by a hair, and suffered much in protecting this young prince?

In the darkened yard of this abbey, upon this day, upon this morning, intrigue and murder were starting to be painted upon the picture of this blessed Isle.

Chapter Three.

The Royal Prince.

The time was closing towards the hour of nine of the clock, as the high oak and iron doors of the abbey creaked open once more. The monks, three to a door, pulled them open, grunting as they pushed them fully wide. From within, all dark and of shadow, they looked back and saw coming to the dark doors of the abbey the Prince Edward. He appearing slowly into the morn's sunlight, a dull figure shown in the abbey's dim, firstly; but, as the brightness of without came o'er him, was seen a colourful tunic and feathered hat, brightened by the boyish face that peered from beneath. The dukes followed in their black and dull attire; soldiers pledged, more than courtly lords were they. The servants and guards followed into the courtyard with the sight of the proud troops mounted upon fresh steeds. Richard's guard and Edward's guard were in separate files; they stood three abreast, but now were one unit under Richard. The wagons were ready and laden, full of victuals and trap, and of worldly things befitting a prince. Manservants climbed onto the carts fixed with benches upon each side, and made for the transport of such persons. Those once Protectors of the prince were mounted, but chained together like scoundrels, as if their fate was already addressed in the book of death. They were closely guarded by Richard's own troop, upright and loyal.

"Forward to the castle at Northampton!" came the duke's cry. Then, loud and clear, "God bless our royal prince! God bless our royal prince!" came back the cry. They were away with their royal banners flying as they left the abbey at Oxford. The royal standard fluttered at the head, to let all about know that this was a royal parade. The last hooves clattered out of the abbey, as the monks slowly closed the outer gates, stopping only to peer down the cobbled way through the gap that remained, to see the party go further and further from their sanctuary. As they were all but a cloud of dust in the distance, but seen still above the lay the royal standard on high, a mast of a royal ship as it dipped and rose northward. The monks then closed fully the gates, and all was tranquil once again.

As the gates were closed, from the stables there came some murmurings … 'Twas not yet all quietude in the abbey.

"God's grace, are they at last gone? … Bring the steed, bring the steed;

at last, can I ride?"

"Yes, sire," some awaited reply came. But only from within the stable was such heard with yet no sign of any movement. As the monks stood about, all looked toward the paddock from where the voices had come, awaiting some action from the words heard. Then the rattle of harness sounded, the kiss of brasses, the grunt of someone mounting. The monks ran quickly back to the courtyard gates, and pulled open once more the great doors. They feared a great rush of horse and man was soon upon them. Now the restless snort and the kicking of a caged mare were heard, as then the horse and rider burst out, the doors rattling open as they are forced by the animal. The need to escape that black restraining hole and to run free into the sunlight was its want. Its front legs lifted from the sacred ground as it came, whinnying through, its strong teeth and the uncontrollable lips distorted to release its joy. It seemingly thought it would never run again, but now 'twill. The rider was small of stature, but with the look of a skilled horseman dressed for the fast ride. The smooth boots. The tight breeches, dark blue in colour. The fitted coat of black from the skin of the deer. A hat that fitted close and tied about the neck. The royal crest did show upon it, for this was the queen's spy, who had been secreted within the abbey to supply his mistress with all that was about during Edward's journeys. For when the monkey is away from the cage, who will know what mischief may come.

But the spy of Elizabeth had more black doings to relate than she could ever have imagined. A wayward monkey would have naught on this tale. He rode out from the abbey like fury unleashed, remembering to duck his head under the stone portal that lay o'er the gate. As he blustered out, the gates were already being closed by the abbey monks—were they so glad to be rid of the troublesome lot that had rent their tranquility. Their rough brown cloth of the cottage dragged in the dust; though tied with a good rope at the waist, it made little difference to the grime that blew about their knees. Their hoods hung backwards from their shaved necks, and shaved still more above the ears where their hair stuck out from the cropped heads, like turtles of the swamp were they.

The rider galloped southward; the day was now bright, the weather warmed. 'Twas half past the hour of ten of the clock upon this day of foulish play, as sped he toward the capital of this land—London, which did lie but sixty miles hence. He made quick time now as the tracks turned into better surfaces, and then into good roads. His sword clapped at one side, his sheathed knife swung at the other. The riding gloves of goatskin were tight upon his strong hands and wet with sweat as he struggled with the reins. The energy of his mission spread from rider to horse, and now it seemed as if they were one. An hour later, with his horse steaming and excreting white saliva from mouth and nostril, they pulled into The Coach Inn at High Wicombe—'twas time to change mounts. The stable boys quickly removed the saddle from the tiring animal and placed it, still sweated, upon the fresh steed, fastening up straps and bridle with haste as was ordered by the queen's confidant. Whilst the horse was made ready, the rider was washed by one of the servants at the inn; he drank some ale and took some cheese and bread. He strode away to his new companion, as he pushed two apples into his pocket. Then, chinking some coin into the innkeeper's palm, he mounted once again and carried forth upon his journey. He repeated the change at Uxbridge, and then again as he entered London Town. Close now was he to his destination … the palace of Westminster, which was the queen's abode.

He rode at last into the courtyard there, where he dismounted and his horse was taken away by the lad. And, though he was weary, he still bustled about in his duties of the queen. He was duly recognized by guards and courtiers alike, and was swiftly passed through all the security, for the queen's confidant was not subject to the rules of others. In little time he was striding toward the door of his queen's chambers, as along the stone passageway he came, with the tapestries that hung the walls glancing at him as he strode by. A knock was rattled upon that crested door, placed by the lone guard who did lead him in, and then, with little ado, he was before his queen, kneeling in all reverence, his hat—crumpled in his hand—lay across his body to assist in his lowliness. His other hand rested upon the hilt of his sword, pushing it forward to give movement to his homage.

"Stand and report yourself," the queen Majesty ordered. The confidant rose slowly, only slightly lifting his head as he did so. He, in reverence, had not yet gazed upon his queen, and when he did 'twas with head still bowed and with eyes not lifted, as was required in his lower state. For would not it be a slight against her Majesty if their eyes did meet? She stood before him as he began to see more of his most royal of queens. First, the small shoes he saw with their French embroidery, then was seen the folds of her silk skirt of rich dark blue, her white bodice of Egyptian cotton with pearls stitched upon it showed high upon her neck. He saw sleeves puffed to the shoulders; he dared not to gaze any higher, but could picture mistily the pearl ear ornaments that did dangle and glitter, the auburn hair, clean and shiny, the lightly painted lips, and the creamy colour of her skin that was without pox. Her brown eyes and painted brows. A pearl cap atop her regal being, as then he dared no more. In private there was no mourning for her king-husband, of whom she was glad to be rid. She demanded the utmost fealty and respect from all in her presence. A bitter woman she, not to be crossed.

The messenger was now shaking nervously. He was a brave soul who had dealt with many situations in his profession wherein valour and the strength of his character were much to be held; but, when he had to face his queen, all his strength seemed to wash away like the running stream. For he feared muchly the queen Majesty's reaction to the message he was to utter from his quivering lips. Then it spilled out, though his chin did tremble.

"Madam ... The Prince Edward has been abducted by the Lords Gloucester and Buckingham. The Protectors are all under arrest for high treason ... The prince, with the two lords now proclaimed Edward's Protectors, are expected in London within a few days. They have pledged, madam, their total allegiance to the prince ... My queen, Richard doth come."

"How dare you, sir! ... How dare you bring to me such tidings. You are but a traitor yourself to bring to me such discourse." The confidant, numbed, spake naught and could only drop to the floor and grovel before the raging queen. "Take him from me!" she shrieked at the guard who had stood by. They came quickly to the messenger and attempted to stand him and to walk him from the chamber, but his legs were not able to move, and so they lifted him, arms pitted, and took him away, he trying to move his legs to walk but no movement came as they dragged him like a frog.

"God's Death," cried the queen as she crumpled upon the rushes that covered the floor, sobbing now. "I am done ... My day is done." Her rich clothes shook from her demeanour as she slumped upon the grassed covering. She lay in all sadness, desolate and dismayed. The waiting ladies were all about now, but could not assist their queen without her permission. The queen's first lady gazed upon the dilemma, and then ran from the chamber to the quarters of the queen's adviser. Silken hands, small and delicate, pulled her skirts above the ankles to hasten her step; she was soon whispering to the guards that stood at the adviser's chambers. They knocked for her, with one of the guards entering with the lady in some distress following. He informed therein the chancellor's clerk that the queen's lady most urgently required council with the chancellor. In little time she was curtsying in the presence of the Lord Rotherham. The Lady Blanche, with tear-laden eyes and unstill lips, related her queen's demeanour and its cause. The chancellor consoled the lady with a sympathetic hand upon her shoulder, which still shook in despair. And then, with much calmness, as was his wont, he escorted the Lady Blanche back to the chamber of the queen. They entered to see that the waiting ladies were much closer now to their mistress. They all though sobbing with reddened eyes and consoling each other, as they looked upon their queen's distress.

"Allow me, your Majesty, to give you some consolation, and to reassure you that our Duke of Gloucester will offer no harm to our beloved prince. He is, madam, a man of honour and has much reverence both to you and to your kin." Though the words from the chancellor were kindly spoken, the queen would not be consoled and did remain in her state of distress, crying and sobbing.

Then at last she stood shakily. "Do not touch me … I need no help. We will take my younger son, Richard, and my waiting ladies, and my servants, and any chattels that may make our stay bearable, and make sanctuary in our blessed abbey of Westminster, to await what will alight from these acts of treachery. I am in a fearful state as to the outcome of these changing ways ... not wanted, but thrust upon me and my royal person. Done such by those who wish to bring about their evil upon us." The ladies were allowed to help her now as the sighing and the sobbing gradually faded away, and to begin the move to the abbey, which lay but a short walking distance away. As the chancellor left the chamber to pursue the matters that had opened before him, Blanche gave a perceived glance over to him, and saw that he glanced back upon his leaving, and their eyes for a moment did meet …

Richard was now approaching the clearing where awaited his wagons and horse, and the peasantry of the torch. They stood awaiting his return, but saw firstly the banners rising from the dust of the track that was now dry and crumbling. As they came closer to their sight, they spied the royal banner and the decked horses, the wagons brightly decorated, and now the nearing sounds of such a ride. The horses' plod, the rattling carts, the far talk of the soldiers from one to the other. As they came into the clearing the noises though became dulled, muffled by the cheers of the waiting party. And, as the Lord Gloucester approached, a sudden quieting came about, for then, seen close to their duke, did ride the Prince Edward, as all bowed with solemn reverence towards the prince. But within a short spate of his passing, jeers did rent the air as the shackled lords were paraded by. 'Twas the time to vent feelings of disgust at the traitors who came their way. They sloped by in a sullen and dismayed fashion as the abuse rang about them.

The end of the parade came along, with the victuals wagon passing out bread and cheese to the men who were now waiting in the carts to follow behind. A cask of malmsey from the winery at the abbey of Oxford was passed into the cart where sat the runners of the torch, and was seen their eyes to widen at the sight. The waiting party turned slowly their carts and their horses behind the train, and added to the entourage. They were soon upon the road but many stops were taken, for leisurely was this ride. Came then to view the castle at Northampton, seen but two miles hence. Now the carriers were most boisterous and loud as they, helpless, rolled in the last cart, with appetites fulfilled, and the malmsey swilling about, as the happiness of returning home lifted even higher their spirits. Lying in the cart was Thomas, he who had waved his bandaged hand to them as they passed him by upon that black night, a broken leg the medal of his escapade. Edward's surgeon had taken care of the injury; no breaking of the skin showed so healing would take place. Splinted he then did lay in the cart with the smile of wine upon his face. The other runner lost upon that night had been making his way back along the track when he came upon his friend and comforted him until the party came upon them and their plight was eased. The ballads of the time laid their blanket of humour and raunch wafting about. Sometimes clear, other times muffled, as the breeze played with their harmony over the troop.

"Molly, the landlord's daughter—" was heard as it drifted about. "With open heart would greet all guests—" To fade again, then soon was heard "The Sailors' Return" that came with more raunchy verse with the words again fading to nothing, then rising to be heard clear again, then to fade. "The Ballade of Tilly Tucker" came clear: "Tilly Tucker, soft in the night …" And then to fade once more, but the soldiers of the party still mouthed along, for knew they well the rhyme that drifted. And so it went with one song after another, with wicked comments and wine-washed laughter, to come they now close to their village. The cart stopped as the paymaster gaited up to them, and as each one did place his feet upon the ground, he was given his set rate. Thomas struggled from the cart helped by his friends.

"Can he stand alone?" asked the paymaster, as he looked at the hobbling Thomas, held up by his comrades.

"He doth stand with us, sire, his brothers."

"Then he will receive full pay, for 'tis with more honour to stand hobbled with your brothers than to speak with a tongue untruthful." They each pushed the coin into their pouches, and then formed themselves into some sort of a mummery group, as they swayed with arms about each as the malmsey splashed about in the near-empty cask. From their bags, bread and cheese protruded, a chicken leg, some turnip, and a pork pie grasped in grubby hands. They waved and shouted and laughed their toothy grins as they went in the direction of their village. They were going back to their oppressive existence, but a more contented lot would be hard to find. Thomas, supported by his brothers, struggled upon his good leg, swinging his medal of the day all wrapped. Staggering and swaying they went on, still laughing, still singing, still swearing, as they slowly left the party of abductors behind and staggered toward their homes. A jingle in their pockets, and the story forever told of the day when Thomas broke his leg, and they stole a prince from the evil queen.

Richard spake to Buckingham as they rode along. "That we will be of such cheerfulness, my friend, upon one of these soon days."

"Aye, my lord," Buckingham half replied, half at thought elsewhere. "Yet the affairs of state are of not such a joyous nature, and I fear 'twill be many a moon to see us of a different frame."

The party, with its royal guest and its royal trappings, clattered then into the walled courtyard of the castle at Northampton. Rivers heard the coming as he did lay upon his cot, and quickly upped and peered from high o'er the sill of the window of his confinement, for even standing full and of stature tall, *and* at stand upon his stooled servant, 'twas as much as he could do to see into the yard below. He saw his dear prince, Edward, being assisted from his mount, and then to step upon the cobbles that lay far below his window's look.

"Come fellow, time to meet with our prince." Rivers turned from his stretched stance and addressed his now upped servant. "'Tis time to put these villains in their proper place." The servant helped ready his lord, to bring forth his innocence against the charges of treason that had been placed against him. With the love and devotion he had shown to the prince in his late father's name, he knew that Edward would be by his side in this fateful matter. He knew also that the two lords, Gloucester and Buckingham, would be cast away, and all their possessions stripped. Death would be their coming. How could those so clever appear now so foolish? Dressed he soon in his most fine attire; washed and shaven, he waited, as sat he near the door to be dutifully called in some short time, with no doubt … He waited.

All were dismounting now. The Prince Edward and his servants passing into the castle. The lords there bowing graciously as the prince, with slim smile acknowledged them as he entered, and then was past them and into the main hall where thought he some meet with Rivers may take place.

The soldiers busied themselves, some leading horses to the stables, some helping the lords in keep to dismount, and handling them not in any chivalrous fashion. They were guided to an unused cellar still in their shackles. A guard was stood inside with them, for there would be no chatter and no scheming. All was of silence in there except for the splashing and spraying, as some relieved themselves against the dark walls of the old wine cellar. Outside, another guard stood the door; no one would enter without his know. Carts were rolled away, now empty of their load, some to be repaired, and some to await the next journey ... The journey to London.

Against one of the side doors some close conferencing was taking place; one of the senior guards, who had been placed along the route, was giving the lords details of an event that had taken place. Buckingham and Gloucester drank in the mundane report from the guard like bitter ale, but 'twas soon to turn into the sweetest of wines. The guard had stopped a rider coming fast and heading south upon the Oxford road. The horse was stayed and upon seeing closely now, the rider seemed to be dressed most poorly, though his horse and saddle were of expensive taste. On removal of his tattered coat, 'twas found beneath that he was more elegantly attired than one would have thought, looking to be more of a manservant than a pauper. The two lords seemingly had heard enough for their appetite, and gestured to the soldier to take them to where he was in keep. They followed him into a small room at the side of the stable where the rider was secured. The door was opened and the lords stepped inside. All about harnesses and bridles hung from the walls in large numbers, and the smell of leather filled the air. Then the room brightened as the afternoon sun shined through the opened doorway. The shadows of the lords intentionally fell upon the frightened servant. Like vultures over their prey did they stand, speaking yet naught.

"You now have to come forth with the truth, for of the truth we do know of it. If you tell all, no harm will befall you, but, if one untruth is spoken, you will be pained with much anguish, for we know what you are about. So choose thee with care that which you are about to speak, for a mouth without a tongue will utter naught ever again." The menacing Richard spake harshly to the servant who did shiver.

"My lord," he bleated, "I am in truth all that you say, in that I am indeed the manservant of the Earl Rivers, and, upon hearing of your lordships' journey to Oxford, and being unable to make words with my master, I rode out to seek the prince and to bestow upon him the need to leave this abbey as would be wished by my master. But I was unable to do so, for I was detained by the guards upon the way and then held here in captive."

"So that is your truth?" Richard asked, and toned to disbelieving in one sentence.

"I humbly beg, it is so, my lord."

"Is it life that you wish, or is it the axe that you seek?"

"'Tis life I wish, my most noble of lords."

"It is seemingly to me that you did confer with the Earl Rivers, your master, and from him did receive some direction. Not to bring any message to our prince, but to bring a traitorous dispatch to our lords — Grey, Thomas, and Vaughan, those leading members of the Protectors of our prince — and in so doing to bring about murder. The message you did bring was one to bring harm to the next king of this land, and to warn of our mission of mercy to protect our beloved Edward. And further to harm us upon our quest by lying in trap for us, and the doing of harm to our persons. Does this not seem more of the truth than the lies you try to fool us with? Those lies that can only bring upon you anguish."

"Yes, sire," the servant replied trying to find the way that would spare his life. "You are correct in the happenings upon that day and I beg your forgiveness for my childlike memory."

"We are well aware of such stresses, but are most pleased that the truth has now surfaced." Buckingham spake then with calm tones to the servant. "And you will relate this true event at conference with our prince and the Lord Rivers?"

"I will indeed do so, my lord," he replied, as the lords slowly left the bridle room, leaving the servant still in some fear, for he was so close to the sword that he did grasp at the only rope left dangling, even if it dangled o'er a cliff.

"Feed him" was all he did hear as the door was closed once more upon him.

Rivers waited, dangling upon another rope o'er another cliff, becoming more agitated as time crept by. The dukes, though, knew that the meat hanging for the longer time was more to the liking, and would be more the sweeter when the meal did come.

The lords entered the castle and went straight to their chambers, to bathe and to be shaven. With hair clipped and washed, and in more lordly cloth, they readied for the dinner at eve. The time now upon this historic day was at the five of the clock, upon the thirteenth of April, a long, decisive day for our two lords.

All were dressed and refined and about to sup. Buckingham entered the chambers of Gloucester.

"My lord is looking of extreme nobility ... A new doublet I see, and most refined."

"Yes, 'tis so, my lord, from our French tailors ... Wouldst ours could work so fine, but their fingers seem as thumbs and cannot make such fine ware ... What of our prize in the bridle room?"

Richard continued after such pleasantries had been lavished. "A gift from heaven, my friend; we could not have wished for a more fortunate happening, and for his eventful story to be so close to our own, one would think 'twas planned."

They smiled that deceitful smile to each other, and then came down the stairs of the castle to the dining hall, where stood the laden table before the logs that burned upon the firegrate. Dressed in finery and being content in their labours, they were now ready to lay more direction toward the Prince Edward. They sat close awaiting their princely boy.

He came all shiny of face, the washed and combed locks about his forehead and ears hung in royal curl, a princely person indeed was he, as all the lords did rise and bowed in lowly unison, greeting him with such sincere devotion.

"You are looking in such good spirits, my lord," spake our Richard. "And decked in such fine cloth you indeed put ours shamely."

"You flatter me, my Lord Gloucester, with your charming manner."

"Nay, my dearest Edward, you are in all a most handsome and royal prince," Buckingham spake, laying on his own praises.

They ate, they drank, and warmed by the fire. A content trio of different destinies.

And still did Rivers wait for his call, but as yet 'twas not heard, and left he alone to know naught of what 'twas that may come.

"'Tis time now, my prince, to speak of worldly things," Richard spake over his goblet of wine, as the Lord Buckingham and the Prince Edward sat contentedly and listened to what the wise uncle may say. "It is our traitorous Rivers, sire, that gives us such pain to speak of. We regrettably have news of a plot against your most royal person. A servant of the earl has come forth and related to us a devious act played out by our most trusted Lord Rivers and others of the Royal Protectors, and also relating to the murder of your most loyal of servants—Lord Buckingham and I, Richard of Gloucester—your most devoted kin. And they bring upon you, my prince, such grave intentions. We would bring this servant to you if you wished, but have not yet done so for the grief it may cause you in hearing such damning issues."

"I will hear him, for I am want to end this matter," Edward spake from the deep chair that scorched by the fire.

"Then it will be so, my prince," Buckingham spake as he beckoned one of the guards and ordered the bringing of the servant before the prince.

Soon the shackled servant was at kneel before his future king. The prince gazed the trembling hands as the wretch bowed before him.

"Tell me of this deed, fellow, and do not be feared, for I will let no harm befall you as long as you speak to me, your prince, the truth of this matter." And the prince did place upon these words the sternest voice available to him. The servant went through his story with ne'er a change as that he was advised. The prince was taken aback by the final realization that the pointing of fingers was indeed true, causing him to slip into some tearful repose. The lords, with a nod, ordered in the guard to remove the bowed confessor, and he was removed and taken back to the bridle room. He too waited.

"It grieves us deeply, my prince, to see you in such distress," spake Richard as he laid a caring hand upon the boy's shoulder seeking to console him. The prince then rises to his uncle and wraps his arms about him and sobs as if in the arms of his mother, looking he for love and affection. For yet in his heart he is still a child and only painted as a prince. After the tears had abated somewhat, Richard pulled him away and, facing the prince, held his upper arms in a fatherly grip; the prince's head hung low as if in dismay.

"If it pleases you, my prince, the Lord Buckingham and I will apprise the Lord Rivers of our knowledge in this matter, and will take care of all the unsavoury things that have to occur, and in doing so would take all manner of hurt away from you and burden it upon ourselves in your name. But only if it may please you, my prince."

Edward did not gaze up from his dismal state, only to nod his head but once in approval. Thankful was he that he had such loyal subjects to relieve him of life's terrible burdens. Then slowly he turned to his servants as to retire, a very sad boy.

"Be of some cheer, my prince," Buckingham spake as the prince readied to depart. "For upon the morrow in pomp we ride to London, and you will again be close to your mother, the Queen Elizabeth, and to your brother, Richard, and they will be joyed, and she will hold you close to her bosom in deep affection."

"Aye, my lord." In lowly voice answered Edward as in courteous manner he made to his chambers.

The Lord Gloucester and the Lord Buckingham then made their way to the chamber of the Earl Rivers to rid themselves of this thorn. They asked not for entry, only to bade the guard who stood to enter them. They walked in to the now unshaven earl, slumped he in a hard chair.

He stirred himself and stood as the hundred questions that he had all tried to come together as he spake, but came out they only bumbled in some foreign tongue. He swallowed now and spake again. "Why am I confined in such a dire state when I am innocent of any wrongdoing?"

"My dear earl, the heartbreaking confessions of your manservant has rent us quite sickly, and so 'twas a while before we were able to address the matter with you," answered Richard.

"I demand an audience with the Prince Edward!" the earl shouted amongst his spray of saliva.

"*Demand?* My dear Rivers. Our royal prince is so fraught with the schemes he has heard to injure his royal person that no demand can bring him to your sight, for is he not in great dismay with all of his Protectors?—which, sire, is a mockery of the very word. And, as such, the Lord Buckingham and I have regrettably had to take up the task of interviewing you, to belay any more hurt upon his young state. Regarding these acts that have been perpetrated, it pains us most deeply to have to broach them, they bringing such anguish to our stomachs, so much so that, since taking upon ourselves this burden, victuals may not pass our lips for many days."

"It seems to me, sirs, you should soon waste away to naught with the grieving of our king, and the distasteful task you have now taken on to deprive you further of your appetite."

"We, sir, speak sincere, and expect only to hear such derisive remarks from the mouth of a peasant and not from some lordly person!" Gloucester continued as the earl seemed without words. "We must now keep you in all security until your treasonable actions have been reconciled. Tomorrow you will be in the ride to London; so ready yourself for six of the clock."

They bowed a courteous bow, and left a frightened and dejected earl standing alone with no friends stood by his side.

The lords smiled slyly at each other as they went to their guarded chambers.

The light tap came upon the bedchamber's door, and then the low creak to open and then to close. The dainty slippered feet dimly shone by the lone candle. The swish of satin. The waft of French perfume. The flickering light bouncing off soft breasts. The creak of the bed upon the mattress of horsehair. The slim body of a young court lady slid into the arms of Gloucester; long, unpinned hair brushed his face. He felt the now shoeless toes against his legs. The jingle and rattle of bangles were heard. The ear hangings then tapped against his face. "Yes, this has been a goodly day indeed."

The queen, and those directed by her, had set the coronation of Edward for the fourth day of the month of May. But now, with the change of the Protectors, that date would not be met, and all would have to await the arrival of Edward and his new lords to settle the matter.

Yet the sun had not risen o'er those lowly hills of Northamptonshire as began the early stirrings at the castle. The break of day meal was being prepared in the kitchen, with its smells of bread and the pork at fry. The eggs brought but this morn from the cackling hens were being cooked over the open fire, with its hooked irons and hanging pots swinging in and out of the wrapping flames. A cast oven, upon each side, baked and cooked out of sight.

The kitchen for this meal was also used as the dining room, with its warmth and smells making good the start to the day rather than the cold and formal hall. Benches were placed about the long preparing table, which was all cleaned now from the morning's activity and replaced with the basic fare and appetizing aromas of the meal. Flagons of ale full for the quaffing and steaming dishes did lay upon the scrubbed boards. From lords to manservants would tread about this kitchen's place at this morning's time. A few soldiers here sat talking through their food, some entering, some leaving; manservants there—those who were not engaged in the cleaning and the dressing of their lords and making them ready for the journey to London. Stable lads were tucked away in the farthest corner at a small table readied for them. The smell of the stable and their unwashed state deemed they be hid away as far from all others as they were able. More soldiers came, boisterous and loud of mouth, laughing and pushing, struggling two upon one. The fake swordplay to escape. The graphic stumbling from the knife wound received. The staggering with eyes half closed and the hand clutched to the chest. Falling now upon one of his comrades engaged in his victuals. The stabbed soldier though quickly recovered from his plight as he slyly lifts a sausage from the platter of his unsuspecting friend, and then bites through it with eyes that did twinkle. A better fare; the finest sausage cooked this day; far better than a chosen one; ah, so sweet the stolen. And with that bite came the smile of the young boy in the uniform of a soldier. Trickery had been fulfilled with more laughter ringing from his comrades. The time ticked the comings and goings. The tables cleared of dirty platters and empty tankards and then piled again with food and tankards full.

Kitchen maids were all about, toing and froing; young maids and old maids alike drifted. Delayed by bawdy remarks and with grabbing and pinching hands as they flitted the tables, returning to the fireplace and ovens sometimes blushed of face. They stood in their kitchen garb—the dress of black worsted cloth, the white collar, the white bonnet tied about the neck and the stiff linen apron hung. The young ones a-giggling and a-nudging as they talked of the things that had been said and done upon their innocent persons. As they prepared another dish they straightened their clothes, and fixed their twisted bonnets to make another foray with platters full into the seated fray. The older maids, who had spent much time in these dealings, were giving back with boisterous remarks of their own amongst the laughter from the soldiers, and did engage in some grabbing of their own with even more comic pain, and more laughter, as they did so.

My lords did enter, and calmness and respect took over from the gaiety as the officer of the day shouted the order. "Stand for my lords!" All stood, some though still trying to curb their jolly time. A nod from Richard brought the officer's voice again. "Continue in respect." And they were all at their meal once more with much chatter but little foolery.

The prince, eating in his chambers, nibbled at his food with little zest, and cared not when he had to leave it to be readied. They were now pulling on his stockings after they had bathed him, then fastening his fine doublet and applying a little courtly powder to dull the childish glow of his cheeks. Cotton gloves were then pulled over his dainty labourless hands. The collar of Belgian lace was then fixed about his neck. A hat of fine felt with a peacock feather protruding, purchased from the French milliners in Paris. Shoes he wore of fine Italian leather imported from Verona. He was surely a most handsome prince.

He tried to dull the events that had turned his world, and thought of the maid instead who had brought the victuals to his room. The bowing of the narrow waist as she curtsied in respect to him. A girl of fifteen years, he thought; he had watched her as she had struggled in with the tray. He remembered her leaning over the table in front of him as she laid down the platters and tankards, revealing a discreet glimpse of her bosom as she did so. Then a quick look she gave into his face, with a demure smile, a sincere smile for this prince. She had curtsied once again before him upon finishing her task and had flashed once more her eyes to his. And then, with a swish of her skirts, she was gone. She was not like any of the courtly ladies he had seen, all breasty and pouty, all maked with powders, all promiscuous. But a sweet country girl of devotion. Ah, he thought, to wish that it could be such, but for princes such as I they have naught to say of such matters, but all left in the hands of others to be then betrothed to some infanta who is the princess of some place not even known to the wisdom of London.

Six of the clock neared upon this May morning. The sun was not yet risen as all was made ready in the dim courtyard. The prince's troop, now readied at the head, showed in its most regal finery, they mounted on bedecked horses as all did show of princely splendour. The fife and drum a-ready. Another troop of soldiers, Richard's men they. Not so bedecked as the others, but clothed in a more warlike dress; a heavily armed, protective group. They were without the pomp and regal soldiery that stood afront.

The prince, though, was about Richard's group, for they wished a safe journey this day, and Richard would not have his prize guarded by maidens. He had seen the bone in their back and 'twas indeed wanting. The Lords

Buckingham and Gloucester were flanked each side of the prince, though a little to heel at a reverent place. More guards came to the rear of them, followed by the wagons full with food and clothes and all the trappings of a royal march. The spare horses and the servants did jiggle at the back.

The whereabouts of the prince's Protectors was upon Edward's mind, but fearing more tearful happenings he thought of it no more. He had decided to let his new Protectors proceed with their plans to care for all strifely business, and to protect and honour him as their soon king.

Very early upon that same morning, before many were about, the Lords Gloucester and Buckingham, having no conference with the Earl Rivers, sent him under guard to the castle of Pomfret and not upon the ride to London. Sent he there to be in keep during our lord's pleasure. The other Protectors were sent under the same veil to other castles, so there was no audience from one to the other and bereft of all news from without, upon death.

"Let us to London now with all speed and pomp to deliver our most beloved Edward safely to his coronation, and to place him in the bosom of his loving mother, our dearest Queen Elizabeth. And also to his most loving brother, Richard, and to his people of this land, who await with all loving greetings to praise the royalty of our princely Edward … On!" shouted Richard as his speech concluded. They all moved out from the castle leaving the darkened courtyard behind them. Then, outside upon the cobbled way, they unfurled their banners and high they were in the breaking dawn. The fife and drum started setting the gait at a slow trot, and to soon be seen the last of the troop leaving the castle—the sun like some child awakening raised its round head from its cloudy pillow to see what this new day was about. It lifted slowly from the brightening hills of Northamptonshire, then laid its bright pleasure upon this day that was clear, this morn of spring, with the warmth leaking into the uniforms and clothes of all who were in its sight.

Stopping for short rests and a change of horse, they continued on into the far of the days. Their last stop would be overnight at Watford upon the eve of May the third. They were now within twenty miles of London and the palace at Westminster. The prince's soldiers rode some distance ahead of the main party; they were to arrange overnight lodging for the entourage. If there were no manors or a large estate house, as was the case upon this journey, then lodgings would have to be sought at the coach house, at the tavern, and the stables—at any place that could be found, for there were many persons to be bedded and fed.

The inhabitants of these small towns, where such stops were made, were not pleased to have such thrust upon them. Beds and food had to be provided — with no gifts or funds given in exchange. 'Twas deemed an honour to offer the nobles such hospitality, but not looked upon as such by the providers. For to provide bed and victuals for the royalty and for their army of soldiers and servants left the townsfolk mightily poorer. Patrons were removed from the inn. The maids and servants, the cooks and butlers all moved in and made ready for the royal prince and his lords who were soon to arrive. The stables were cleared of horses and stable workers, and in moved the prince's men with fresh straw and water for the coming horses, and cleared they areas so the soldiery would have some place to rest with the animals.

Cooks did come setting their fires in the side streets and squares, bringing in their pots and cauldrons, with barrels of ale taken from the inn brought and set upon trestles. Pigs and fowl were soon cooking, brought as gifts from the village folk to feed the small but hungry army. Tables were set up with breads from the cottages, with pies and tarts also placed.

The cottage dwellers had all left their homes; some crouched outside upon the walk, others sat upon benches, whilst their abodes were being prepared for the quarters of the maids and the servants and whoever else could be squeezed into the small places. 'Twas good the night was warm and dry, for the sleep of the dwellers would be under God's stars this night. All within the town will be glad to see the back of the last cart as it trundles away upon the morrow.

The royal party was getting close to the overnight stop. News was spreading about quickly to all the people about of their coming, and small groups from local places were now appearing at the side of the track that the prince would travel. They would wish a glance at their monarch-to-be as he travelled to his coronation. Stood they aside the way, tattered and dirty, bowing and curtsying at the parade as it passed, and gazed open-mouthed and in awe of such a worldly sight. But not a slight acknowledgement came from the royal party; they passed as if no one stood the way, as they who watched were deemed mere nothings — chattels.

Pulling into the small town, the crowd was thickening at the sides of the cobbled road as Edward's party, with much pomp, did ride past. A braver lot stood as their numbers grew. They stood more boisterous in their acts and talk, some cheering, many booing with sarcastic words pressed. Others called: "God bless the prince!" Shouting and waving, jeering and praising were they, but the haughty still saw and heard naught.

The morn of the fourth of May, which was meant to have been Edward's coronation day, was now not to be. The day came with red and purple skies; the dark oaks silhouetted against the bright backdrop. Stout and full-leaved they stood casting their shadows over the mounting parade before it. The prince's troop had increased during the night with royal guards that had been sent from Westminster. More musicians, more unfurling banners waving atop the pikestaffs, wearing the strawberry glow of this morn's light. The pageantry and pomp of the ride into London grew in splendour as would befit the most royal of kings.

Once more the cry of "God bless our Prince Edward!" as the more regal parade moved away. The sun was rising higher o'er their left shoulders; half were in the light, half were in the dark from the broad oaks that covered their way as they left that small town. If the parade had looked to the rear, they would have seen many folk, waving and cheering them upon their way, in the great relief that they could return to their lives and recover from the loss of such worldly things they did possess, to work once again to recover from this royal usurp.

London was in great anticipation of the arrival of the royal party. Boats rocked upon the river Thames, full they of different supporters and of different factions. The servants and followers of Gloucester floated about in many numbers, sidled with the boats of the followers of Buckingham. Boats with Edward's supporters and his royal companions. Boats that held many of the old Protectors loyal to the prince. The Earl Rivers' followers. The queen's supporters all bobbed about in their brightly-coloured craft. Each with their own banners flying, with some dressed in most frivolous attire, all shouting their support for their cause, one across the other. Sang they songs of loyalty to their chosen one, bumping boats and sweared words, more shouting, then pushing at each other with their oars, prodding and poking as the boats closed, then a slimy splash as one party was tipped into the grimy waters, with many cheers ringing about from those with a dislike to the flailing crew. And so 'twas with each trying to win support for their candidate.

The master knights and royal lords were donning their harnesses and making ready their troops, for they did not yet know whither the axe of Richard, the axe of Edward, or the axe of Rivers would fall, or upon whose head. For who would come to this town as the strongest would be determined the outcome. All was of turmoil in the streets, the crowd rowdy in its wait of the royal party. Would the prince be a prisoner? Would Richard be as king? What would be?

They came then this regal group slowly into the city, and made heading for the palace of Westminster, where Edward had dwelled with his mother since he was born. The crowds cheering louder as they saw the banners all unfurled and heard the music coming of the fife and drum with such proud notes drifting o'er the throng. The royal guard brightly bedecked came next, followed by the boy-prince. Proudly he sat upon a white charger with its brasses at shine. The saddle cloth with the royal crest all blue and gold, was draped o'er the whiteness of the animal, with Edward all pompous and glorious in his regal attire floating above all. And there, a most reverent distance aback, showing great respect with their bowed heads and submissive bearing, came our Lords Gloucester and Buckingham. Showing to all about that all was indeed well within the royal house. And no discourse would come about from this new alliance.

The royal palace was becalmed after the turmoil of the day. 'Twas noontime as the prince went forth to seek his mother secluded in the abbey. He came to bring her forth and to give her the good council she must be awaiting. He would bring to her the good message that the new Protectors were all faithful and in much devotion to the crown, and that she must fear naught and so take her rightful place amongst the royalty. The prince strode toward the main entrance with his now manly gait, followed by his close guards and his servants ...

The Dukes of Gloucester and Buckingham went they straight into the council chamber, to relate all of the details regarding the abduction of the prince, and of the imprisonment of the Earl Rivers. Awaiting them there did sit the Parliament.

"My lords of this privy chamber, it is humbly that I have to pass such bad tidings through these lips to your most loyal ears. I can only be thankful, no matter what the outcome of this meet, that I, and my Lord Buckingham, with the grace of God, were able to save our dear prince from the dire circumstances that were to be thrust upon him." Richard began to relate the reason for his actions. "We have a true confession given without the use of torture from the servant of the Earl Rivers. We have it in written fact all others so involved in this act of treachery. This statement was also heard with great sorrow by our beloved prince, who, as you will see, has marked the document with his royal seal as having heard this confession. We have the fellow in our keep if our lords wish to hear his sad story. We, my lords, are filled with such deep sorrow to have to place before the king's council such woeful admissions. The confinement of the Earl Rivers and the others so imagined as Protectors of our prince were all involved in the murderous acts being planned. And, in the bringing to light of this disgrace, my Lord Buckingham and I took the great responsibility upon ourselves to become the Protectors in a most humble fashion to our future king."

"We wish to question this manservant." 'Twas the Chancellor Rotherham who stood, being urged to do so by the Lord Hastings, two of the queen's lackeys.

"With the greatest of pleasure, my lord." Richard then ordered his guard commander to come about and bring forth the manservant that was detained in their keep. They waited upon him, and during the wait the council was in conference amongst themselves, perusing the statement and the seal upon it which had been passed to them by the two lords. They too were in conference with close words at the bench where they sat, and not being in shot of the council's bench. They leaned in lordly manner and lowly did speak one to the other.

"Do they have some doubts about the seal and the writings that we have placed before them? It seems they look for some slight against our actions, do you not think?" Buckingham queried to Richard.

"Do not fret, my dear friend, they but snatch at flies in the dark, and try to stay themselves upon anything they can. They can find no recourse without offending the prince, and that they would be feared to do. But the Lord Hastings seems somewhat more mistrustful than the others, do you not think? Soon his ways may have to be curbed."

Rivers servant was then brought in and was stood to face the council as he worded with the clerk the sworn oath of truth. Gloucester and Buckingham stood a little behind and to one side of him. He stood still now, shaven and freshly clothed, awaiting the first question.

"This statement so given by you ... Was there torture involved to obtain such?"

"Nay, lord. All respect I did receive," he answered clearly to Rotherham.

"Off with your shirt," next was gestured. The servant untied the shirt and slipped out of it, undoing the wrist ties lastly to release it to the floor.

"Raise your arms and turn around," he was then commanded, and, as he did so, 'twas Hastings that stepped forward and looked upon the servant's skin, who stood with his arms high and his back to the council; his eyes were gazing at the two lords, but no glimmer was passed to any eye in that brief time. The inquisitor stepped back to his place as no abuse upon the flesh of the servant could be seen. The torture did not lay upon the outside but upon the inside; unseen was the screw. "Put your cloth back on." He bent and picked from the floor his linen shirt, so recently provided, and proceeded to pull it on again, but he was unable to tie it properly as the council continued to question him. He stood the puppet of Gloucester to be jigged when needed.

"You say the Earl Rivers told you to only inform the Protectors and did not name the prince?" The question came from somewhere in the midst of the council, and no one knew for sure who had spake the words.

"That is so, sire, to only relay the message to the lord Protectors."

"Whence did you obtain this message, being that our Earl Rivers was under close arrest and could receive no visitors, and he was not allowed contact with anyone?" A murmuring drifted through the council at the pertinent question. First looking from where the question had come, and then to the servant to hear what reply he may bring forth.

"My lord had beckoned me from his high window o'er the courtyard, and I, from his signs and what I could hear of his orders, gathered what he wished, being that I should make to his chambers upon some pretext. He then threw down coins to me for which to buy the guards at the entrance to his chamber. I went then to my lord's chamber with a platter of victuals and some ale, for all knew he had not yet eaten. The guard at the door firstly refused me entrance. So I offered the coin and he did take it, in exchange for a short time alone with my lord where he apprised me of his wishes. 'Tis the truth I speak, for I am a devoted servant to my lord R—"

"Yes, yes, no need to bumble on. Remove him; we have heard all we wish." Hastings beckoned the guard who had brought him in to now return him in keep, and he was most humbly gone.

Gloucester and Buckingham stood side by side as the council were once again talking and gesturing amongst themselves, some with heads shaking as in disbelief, a whisper here, a sigh there, as Gloucester then spake.

"My dear lords, please forgive my most irreverent interruption, but I deem to say our most cherished Edward, soon-to-be king, has put his utmost faith in the guidance of your most humble servants, the Lords Gloucester and Buckingham, that it seems want and shameful that having been pained by the traitorous acts of his Protectors, that to offer at this time others to guide him would be most harmful and of much hurt to his young self. We, with all devotion to our most beloved Edward, believe that he would be most pleased of the continued love and guidance we bring to him."

The council was now almost compelled to let the new Protectors continue, for not to do so it seemed would go against their prince's will. This would then place the council in a position of mistrust and loss of stature in the eyes of the prince. And may to lose their seats upon it, which were lucrative positions indeed. After more intimate discussion was taken, the chairman, the Lord Hastings, did agree.

"After having given much thought to the situation, we find it would be in our dearest Edward's best interest to let him continue with the guidance so lovingly shown to him by our dear Lords, Gloucester and Buckingham. We will take into consideration all that has been approved here this day and all such laws will come under review at the next Parliament that which is set for this year of our Lord, fourteen hundred and eighty-three, on the twenty-fifth day of the month of June. All those in favour of this bill shout aye!" ... "Aye!" was the shout and the chamber came into disperse. Richard had what he wanted ... Time.

Chapter Four.

The Bloodied Tower.

"Mother! Mother!" shouted the prince as he ran into the chambers where she dwelled in sanctuary.

"Edward, my son, come, let me embrace you, come." The queen held out her arms to welcome her prince and to embrace him with much devotion.

"Edward! Edward! You have returned!" 'Twas Edward's younger brother, Richard, who now joined in the closeness and affection towards Edward.

"I pray you are both well, but wonder why you conceal yourselves such for we see no troubles about."

The queen then gave her reason to the young prince. "My dearest Edward, I fear the sword of Gloucester and his ally Buckingham, for naught but the crown will settle their fever."

"Mother, you are mistaken, for all I have received from them is a loyalty beyond all bounds and such devotion to us, the royal family, to deem others who have given their pledge to us as mere seekers of fortune and despots."

"Do you not see, my dear son, that they have covered themselves with silk, and the snake that lies beneath is hidden from your young eyes? No, we will not come from this place whilst Richard holds you as he does. Your brother and I will wait until the Parliament has met. When upon that day Richard will be stripped of his powers, for the majority will be at seat that day to vote against him. He has not enough lords to stand with him to win a parliamentary vote. That is the day I will step from sanctuary; I will not step out before that day."

"So be it, Mother, if that is your wish, but I believe, before the date of the sitting, Richard will prove to you that which lies under his silk is no snake, but a heart that beats warm towards his royal family, and he will show to you his colours true." He bade farewell to his mother and to his brother. He was saddened, but knew in his heart that his dear uncle would bring forth his mother and place her in her most royal place upon the stage of kings, of this he had no doubt.

After leaving the council chambers, Richard and Buckingham called close to them their officer of the guard, and with some discreet talking and furtive glances they placed some coinage into his hand, and with courteous bow he left to carry forth his masters' orders.

"The servant's confession stood us in good stead, Buckingham, but it must stay that way for our comfort, my friend."

"Yes, sire, little choice do we have, for he could become a cackling hen and leave troubled eggs all about." They left then for their horses with one more thorn ready to be cut.

The officer of the guard paced toward the wooden door of the cellar whereat stayed a guard. With loyal bow he clicked open the door, and the light did shed upon the devoted servant of the Earl Rivers. 'Twas time for him to be rewarded for the royal service he had given to our lordly pair.

"Come forth!" called the officer into the dim corner wherefrom some movement was heard.

"Where are you bringing me?" came the reply.

"We are taking you to the open fields, away from the city, where you will be freed." The servant moved to the officer, wary of his fate, but praying the lords would be true and fair to him as given by the pledged oath of knights. He was taken outside where the officer mounted his horse, then reached down and pulled the servant up behind him. They clattered from the quarters behind the palace and rode some miles from the town of London, to a large building of murky bodings that lay close to the river Thames. No signs did hang from this place, but it had the bearing of a workhouse where death was part of the stone 'twas built from. Through the open gate they went as the stench from within worsened the more they entered. The rain was drizzling all about and dark were the skies. The smell rose about as from a slaughterhouse as they circled to the back of the building. Sackcloth was seen lying upon the muddied ground, some with still rotting heaps beneath, from the days when death came upon those who toiled there and they were dumped for the crows. 'Twas neither a pleasant place for the living, nor for the dead. The servant dared not speak as he was then ridden through the evil place hoping they would pass it by. But the officer dismounted, and pulled the reluctant servant from the horse to which he did cling fearfully; his knees did begin shaking for he saw no meadow there for his freedom.

"Down on the ground!" ordered the officer, pushing the servant into the mud. "Stay your head." A rough hand pulled his hair to set him in a good position. 'Twas then heard the sound of the sword, left its sheaf to glint high in the air. The servant was numb as fear ran his body. The blade when next gazed upon was covered in blood as red as one could ever see.

With a head one way still blinking its eyes, still the brain trying to move some part, the body upon the other side twitched about still wanting to continue. But the gushing blood drained all and now 'twas still. The officer wiped his sword upon the part of the servant's cloth that was bloodless, and returned the cleaned blade to its lay. A wave of the officer's hand then brought the dead cart to view from out of the shadows. A black cart, a black horse, the rider all of black. It paced over to them slowly, the driver then stepping down lifted the body into the cart, turning he picked up the head and, holding it with the hair, tossed it to the back where it rolled into the corner, its eyes gazing at the other corpses that were placed there. A sackcloth was thrown o'er the cart, and a chink of coins was rattled into grubby hands. The officer mounted his horse, gave one quick look at the head that grinned there, then rode upon his way, for all this day was done. 'Twas not yet done though for the driver of the dead cart, who began to rifle the pouch and clothes of the bloody servant for any monies that may still be there. A grunt though was all that was heard for the pockets were empty. He threw back the sackcloth onto the stinking cart, and then he too was aboard, and clopping soon on his way to the mass grave of the paupers.

The date of the coronation had been set for the twenty-second day of June. The date of the bill for the new Protectors of Edward was passed upon the fifth day of May. Many intrigues were to be played before the Parliament would meet, which was after the coronation and set for the twenty-fifth day of June.

Our two lords went to Crosby Place instead of the palace at the Tower where the General Council of the Realm resided. Richard and Buckingham wanted separate discreet doings, away from eyes seeing and ears hearing. They held all their meetings within these walls, where they had set up their own parliament to control without sworn council.

Crosby Place was not a large residence but close to the size of a manor house, far less than a palace. This was a place that was owned by Richard and was his residence whilst in London. 'Twas a quite regal place, close to the palace at Westminster and near to the palace at the Tower. There in the bookroom they continued their schemes, as their goals became lofty as time waived.

"I believe, my dear Buckingham, that we can make events flow into our river, and it appears without much hardship." 'Twas early evening when Richard spake these words, for the time had come to sit by the fire and to relax some from the day's chores. They sat drinking wine from the dull pewter goblets, in close to the pitch torch that did flicker with the firelight. Richard continued slowly, choosing with care his words, for he was about to broach his friend of the certain feelings he had, and to lay these feelings upon his ally in a way that would not incur any ill will. "I will ask you, Buckingham, about the thoughts I have to attain the state of king of this Realm, which may ask for some dire actions." Quietness then hovered but for a moment. "What say you, my friend, upon the matter?"

"My dear Gloucester, I have never believed our journey would end at being the Protectors of the prince. For regardless of our goals we would have to endure much from the changing councils and parliaments, and always someone would want us stripped of such power. Then, one day, without doubt we would surely lose all and would be in some dire state. So, my lord, I am with you, for we cannot aim for anything less than to rule this land. And whatsoever flows o'er you flows o'er me, whether good or bad."

"Good, good, my lord, in my heart I knew of no other answer you would give."

They shook hands and arms heartily and lifted their goblets, and clinked them together in their friendship, and did quaff the contents with ne'er a breath.

"We have many allies and followers, my lord, but at the moment the council has far more voices against us. We must with haste gain some significant souls in their stead, many voices that will shout your name— Richard."

"I know of this dilemma, my friend, but believe me we will be louder upon the opening of the Parliament."

On the days following they drew upon their supporters, the lords and earls, the barons and landowners; any who would increase their vote were courted. In many meetings at Crosby Place things were shaped the way of Richard. He had the full confidence and the love of Edward, and the signet of the prince was placed upon many a document mostly upon the guidance of the Protectors. Buckingham was granted most powerful positions. Constable of Royal Castles and Forests. The government of Wales was his, with many more desired posts to his name. With such acts they were able to bring more of their own supporters into the government. Many changed their allegiance to support Richard rather than contest their lands, which were threatened, for they knew it would be wanton indeed to even try, had he so much sway. The Prince Edward signetted the documents implementing these acts, with the words always to follow: By our Lord Protector of England, the Duke of Gloucester. Protector and Defender of our Realm of England during our young age.

During this time, many documents about the Queen Elizabeth were being sifted. She was the sister of the Lord Rivers, and was formally the Lady Woodville, once married to Sir John Grey, and by him had two children. The late King Edward IV, the father of the Prince Edward, on visiting Sir John was besmitten by the beauty of Elizabeth, and soon, through contrivance, did marry her. This act was later to be the downfall of the queen, of her kin, and of her friends, whom she had elevated in her protectoral position over the Prince Edward.

In short time our two lords had changed many positions within the Realm. From landowners, to dukes and earls, and all manner of nobility. Changed even were the keepers of jails, the harbourmasters, the royal guard, and in many other positions that one day may benefit Richard, for these positions brought with them allegiance and more strength to his cause. Although he had gained many votes in the Parliament, which was soon to sit, the incumbents had not been idle, and had recruited many of their own to vote against this Richard who does presume too much.

The lord then did not have enough on his side of the house and was still short of winning the day. But in his mind he knew that when the time did arrive, either through contrived events or by natural occurrences, he would one day soon be king.

The meetings at Crosby Place continued well into the month of June, and upon the twentieth day, five days before the coronation, came they to place various tasks upon themselves. For still behind with a few ayes the two lords played their hand of slight.

Upon the twenty-first of June fifty persons of noble bearing were, by royal request, ordered to attend at the Tower for the purpose of receiving knighthoods at the coronation. The purpose was that they may be in practice for their positions on the parade, and to be familiar with the words of acceptance upon this most regal day. They stood about in groups talking in one of the Tower's rooms of the palace. The walls of stone, cold and uninviting, received some light from the two high windows that made the only bright in the chamber. The room, though not large, was well suited for the assembly; seats and benches were about, dark and blackened from the oily pitch lamps' smoke. A large table, painted with the same brush, stood in the chamber's middle. The temporary residents were mostly standing as they talked. They were dressed most finely, and in a joyful mood of anticipation for the coming coronation and for their knighthoods. Though the positions would be more upstanding to them, 'twas the remuneration from the Parliament that lit their eyes.

A little impatience showed in their mood as they waited; Richard was yet to appear, and 'twas well past the time of the meet. Gloucester at this time was still engaged in converse with Buckingham and his officers. They were stood inside the writing room where the queen and her councillors engaged in their underhanded business. Many of this nobility were amongst the group that waited upon Richard's presence, others had been requested away upon other business, and the queen was at asylum in the abbey. This placed Richard in the position to view any documents he could find to assist in his cause towards the throne, for all eyes were gone from this place.

The duke at last strode away and headed toward the party who awaited him, leaving his associates to carry on with the search. Upon entering he carried a most pleasant look.

"I greet you, my lords, upon these most joyful of days. I must apologize firstly though for my unforgivable lateness, but the affairs of state hang long upon us all." He stood about before their coming was discussed, and spake to many with the most cordial of words as they stood at wait, and all were in the most pleasant of frame. Then, after a short spate, the door to the chamber was opened slightly by one of Richard's officers, and through that small opening he caught the eye of Richard with his polite bow, and to request our lord to spare time for a moment to receive some information upon a small matter of importance. Richard prepared to depart the room, and with much apology conveyed to all that he would be but a short while. He then left the meeting leaving inside the continuing conversations, not impatient any more for they had been reassured with Richard's charm, and were anticipating their good fortune.

He came, walking the short distance down the dim-lit passageway, knowing that something of importance must have been found. He entered into the writing room and heard the door latched behind him by one of his officers—locked so all within was of secret doings. He saw his men still searching through papers and scrolls that had been kept in secret, but now laid open to our lords. Buckingham's hand was under his cheek as he rested his elbow upon the table as in some scholarly mode. He nodded upon seeing Richard and waved some papers at him as closer he came. They held the documents flat down upon the table for 'twas wont to spring back to a scroll again.

"This, sire, was the first document of interest." Richard listened as Buckingham read aloud that which was written and our duke mouthed along silently to every word that was spake. "The document is making a referral from the Queen Elizabeth to diverse persons of her court, and refers to the distribution of certain lands and properties which, sir, are in our names, and the names of our loyal colleagues. Then it does state to take all necessary actions to diminish our authority over the prince and over all other states we have gained. To make us powerless in the Realm, all this to occur when our prince has been crowned."

Richard did not yet speak, and he seemed surprisingly calm upon hearing the revelation. But upon the next document Buckingham knew that such a state would quickly end, and he blessed the day he laid upon Richard's side of the bed.

"Read on, my lord, upon this second instrument."

Buckingham rolled it atop the first as he spake as then they continued in the same manner of reading. "This was found, my lord, behind some secretive panel that became known to us. They are documents written by her royal Majesty the Queen and is the list of guests that will attend the prince's coronation. The heading states that this is the final list of dignitaries, as assigned by the queen and her advisers, that will be in attendance of our dear Prince Edward upon his coronation. The said to take place upon the twenty-fifth day of the month of June, this year of our Lord fourteen hundred and eighty-three. This document, my lord, was of the English royalty and nobles—there being a separate list for the European royalty and nobles who are to attend. Read on, my lord, of this document of our countrymen." Buckingham passed over the parchment to Richard for he desired that he read it for himself; he wished not for such words to pass through his own lips for what may come. Richard slipped the sheet from the fingers of his friend and slowly began looking at the list of names that showed before him. Our Lord Rotherham. Our Lord Hastings. The Lady Shore. Our Lord Rivers. Sir Richard Grey. Sir Richard Hawte. Sir William Stanley. On went the list as he continued to look down the names, speaking not one word as he did so. The look upon his face began to change, twisting more with each name read. Faster he glanced now. At the end of the page he came to the last of the listed names, and then, as if not able to understand, he turned over the document in one last attempt, but knowing there would be no writings upon the back that would ease his mind. Richard was in some contained rage, but it would be a short time contained. He was severely displeased, not with the names he saw but more so with the names that were absent.

"We are abandoned as a child in a forest. God's Death upon that wanton bitch, Elizabeth! She has not brought upon us to hold any position in the prince's future. She plans to eliminate all of us who are in opposition to her desires. We would, it seems, have been most fortunate to come away from this with our heads … Reasons are, Buckingham, for us to hasten our plans and to claim our right to the council of this land, and I swear that mangy jackal, Elizabeth—she who ran with the lion and became a lion because of our King Edward—well, the lion has gone and she is but a jackal once more; once more she is but Elizabeth Woodville. I will sort things this day, my friend, and it is to Elizabeth's good that she cringes in sanctuary at the abbey, for she would lay with her husband before this day would be done. Now I go, and I will spill some blood."

Richard strode out with an "Aye, sire" from Buckingham. The door was pulled closed behind him as he strode away in his slanted gait. With head lowered and in much thought he was upon that short journey through the arched passages, dark and not inviting. He then stayed his step near to an alcove where lurked the captain of his personal guard. He ordered him forth.

"Sire," he whispered as he came close to Richard. His leader talked to him closely, giving to him the precise orders he wished carried out. To wait as positioned by the duke with swords and daggers drawn, and upon the command of my fist's clap upon the table board, to cry from without most loudly: "Treason!" And to rush the chamber to contain all within. Be readily alert of any resistance from those so held. And if any act, no matter how slight, in some untoward movement, to bloodily quell it.

The officer bowed to Richard and turned toward his shadowed soldiers. Richard watched, with the a scowl of anger maintaining his face, and listened as his orders were passed. Then, upon command, the guards drew their swords and daggers and marched most quietly to the chamber door. Twenty in all were they, dispersing each side against the walls as ordered and out of sight when the door was opened. Richard stepped to the door, which was opened by his standing guard. The Lord Gloucester entered then into the den that would soon be filled with mischief. Chatter and laughter were his greeting for they had not yet noticed his entrance. The feathers of the bright hats bobbed above groomed hair and trimmed boards, breastplates glinted but worn by few; most wore doublets and breeches, silver-buckled shoes and boots stood. All armed with sword and dagger, slim white hands dripped many rings. The nails cleaned and shaped waving about in many gestures. Richard's glance was of warriors not, but idlers and vain. He was not feared of these lords.

He was seen, and the room quieted as he was greeted with bows and loyal voice, and every respect was paid unto him. But 'twas seen by all, that in the short time he was gone, that those most amiable of features that were last seen had now left his face. In its place came a scowl and lip at quiver; something was afoot and seemed it would not be to their liking.

"My lords, here gathered," Richard spake as the murmur and chatter died away. "I ask you, what would any person who planned my destruction expect from me if such a circumstance did prevail?"

"That they would be tried as heinous traitors and be subject to the laws so written for such an offence," Hastings replied to Richard's question amongst the urgings of his noble friends.

"And tell me, what of those such people who knew of such a course and yet said naught?"

"They would truly be as guilty as the one so charged." Another lord spake his piece with a knowledgeable smirk to his friends, as Richard spake once more.

"Then if I did say to you that the Queen Elizabeth has devised these acts against my person, what say you now?" No answer this time was coming from any corner, for fear was replacing joy therein and no one knew the move of the other, or to what answer would be the best forthcoming. "You will see what that sorceress the queen and that other witch on her council—Shore's wife—have done to me with their unholy craft … They have wasted my body and twisted it to their will to make me into a poor deformed wretch." And upon speaking such he was pulling up the sleeve of his shirt, up to his left shoulder he tugged it. Whereupon he showed them all a withered arm, thin and much shorten than his right with rippled skin and showing bones. A most disturbing sight as all who did gaze upon it gasped and tried to recoil from the grisly scene. But all knew this sad affliction of Richard's was as such from his birth, though they bested to remain silent upon the matter. They knew also that Shore's wife was of no council to the queen, she being the mistress of the late king and that the queen was in favour of the liaison, did have regard for her, and that was all to the matter. All who stood within the Star Chamber knew that things were becoming dangerous for them, and their minds began to linger upon some thought of escape from this lord who had seemingly gone mad.

"Well certainly, my lord, if they have so heinously done so then indeed they are worthy of heinous punishment." Hastings at last answered the question that had been proffered. Trying he to find the words to bring some sanity to the situation so at least they may find enough respite to escape.

"*What?* … What!" Richard cried with gnawing lips frowning and fretting. "You speak to me with ifs and with ands and with buts, when I tell you they have done this with no ifs. They are witches! And I, sir, will make good on your body … *Traitor!*" And, with great rage flowing through him and with all his might, he clapped his fist upon the table with a great rap that echoed about the numbed chamber. And, at this token, someone without the door was heard to cry: "Treason!"

No sooner was the word sounded than the door was flung open wide, forcing those who had slyly crowded there—making ready for a timely escape—to be the first pushed back by Richard's soldiers; causing the nobles to be falling over each other as they were manhandled, and fetched back against the far wall with grazed faces and scraped elbows all tumbling about. The guards had rushed forth at the signalled cry, with knives and swords to the ready, and soon filled the chamber, which being small made it nigh impossible for any of the nobles, if they dared, to draw their weapons. Richard's voice rose above the tumult.

"I arrest thee, traitor!" Richard had the cloak of Hastings within his grasp as he bleated, bewildered and shaking. And with the great strength he possessed in his good arm, Gloucester continued to shake him about, to extract from him every small piece of revenge from the one he had selected to be the goat.

"What, me, my lord?" Hastings foolishly asked through his rattling teeth.

"Yes, thee, traitor—Thee!" was the only answer to be spake.

One of the guards, upon seeing the Lord Stanley making some movement toward Richard, brought down his sword from where it waved above his head, cutting through the hat and the grey hair and through the skull, which was cleft in two to the teeth that had been chattering joyfully but minutes ago. To the floor, amongst the scattering of legs, twitching and heaving, he dropped. Blood spurted like a fountain from his gaping skull, splashing and spraying upon those who were close and wincing at the sight of the blood upon them. They attempted to brush it away with their bejewelled fingers. Fine nails were embraced in lordly blood. Richard too was bespattered, his cloth now more red than blue and gold, but it mattered not for he had been bloodied many times before. The red stream spread upon the stone floor soaking into the boots and shoes of those who stood. The guard had done his work well, for Richard's orders had stated that any untoward action must be met by severe and deadly action, and so 'twas. Never mind, truth be told, the Lord Stanley had merely fainted and had been in the process of falling forward. One less vote for the queen was a very good death, and would not disturb Richard's thoughts more upon the matter; indeed, would it not be advantageous to seek out more who may wish to give their life for another seat taken from the bitch?"All will end as this!" Richard raised his anger once more toward the nobles who stood with the fearful words ringing in their ears. "Guards, take these traitors to separate chambers, and do not be feared of your swords if any make any gesture that you think is not apt." That was all he need say of those nobles for he knew they would now bend easily to his breeze. "All except the Lord Hastings … For, by Saint Paul, I shall not dinner until I see thy head off. And I, sir, will not be late for my dinner."

After being waved forward by Richard, his guards took Hastings in their keep as was ordered, sparing upon him few niceties. He cried out, pleading desperately, but knowing his fate was written.

"My Lord Gloucester, in your most benevolent heart, please do not avenge this upon me for I am innocent of any treasons towards you. I am sworn to an oath as a knight of this Realm and I have always stood by that vow I did enter into, which swore me to the right of all good people. I plead with you for my life. I beg of you, do not do this thing; do not take my life."

"Sire, you gave up your oath of a knight when you deemed me and mine to be stripped of our heritage by placing your signet upon the bitch's document. If, sir, you cannot act as a knight you must not expect another knight to do so … My dinner cools." Hastings was silenced, having no more hand in his fate, and so gave into what would be his end. Richard turned and with his bloody steps dripping upon the stone, made with steady pace to his dinner table, where Buckingham and his loyal followers awaited him well apprised of the situation.

Hastings was pushed and abused as he was ushered from the chamber, watched with little envy by the nobles who still shivered. His bloody footmarks traced the others down the spiral stairs, dim and damp. He trod the worn steps of the many who had gone this way before him, jostled by the guards at his sides and followed by the officer of the guard, whose hand dwelt gently upon the hilt of the sword that would soon breach the air. They stopped against a narrow door arched above with black stone. Ushered into the brighter side of the gateway, then pushed again, the lord stumbled to a small green at the side of the chapel there. He was brought then through the dandelions now brightly flowered to a log that lay stained and dark. Around him the grim-faced guards with no words spoken forced his head over the block.

"May God have mercy on your evildoings." He half heard it spake. And there, with sword flying, Hastings' head was severed from his body. The deed had been done and Richard was not late for his dinner.

Our Lord Gloucester was in mind of the feeling that may prevail over the land and about London upon the hearing of the demise of Hastings, and he knew many would be in some unrest and in some quandary over their allegiance to Richard. For he knew well of the stories that became exaggerated, for it seemed the further the distance the more bizarre became the tale and did puzzle the minds of men. And they would search for the right path to take, and Richard would have to devise that path. Some means had to be contrived to belay all thoughts that the two lords had done aught wrong in their actions. For the allegiance of his lords and their votes had to be guarded whilst the episode was still at the moment contained.

'Twas the day after Hastings' death when the lords went to the Tower.

The execution was still only known to a few who were sworn to secrecy. They readied themselves, as firstly a message was sent to all diverse persons of lordly state to come in haste to the Tower, where Richard and Buckingham were under duress. The message 'twould be delivered by one of Richard's officers and would show himself in some agitated state. Whilst the officer went upon his way, the two donned some harness that was ill fitting for both of them, with rusty and broken straps squeaking and rattling and muchly dented. Buckingham's was too small: the legs only covered to above the boot, part of his arms showed past the arm metal, the helmet protruding upon the top of his head like a turnip in the field. Richard showed as no less a sight: his harness was big, and showed all loose and rattling, together with broken straps dangling and helmet too big, he having to tilt his head backwards so he may see. Old swords they carried, not sharp but rusty and broken.

Soon the summoned lords came with much bustle and purpose to the Tower; armed as asked and grouped together with swords drawn, they followed Richard's officer up the spiralled case and along the arched stone passageway with little light to show. In haste they had come to the call of their lords, and to the chamber where sounds from desperation did come. The doors were open wide as they came inside, and saw there the Lords Buckingham and Gloucester both breathless and red of face. Buckingham leant upon his sword with his head lowered upon the hilt; Richard half slumped upon the bench there, both looking fatigued and embattled. Richard then looked up and breathlessly did speak as Buckingham wearily raised his head from his sword.

"My lords," he panted. "Your coming here with much haste warms us most heartily."

"What has happened here? Who has attacked you? … Why, my lords, are you dressed in such lowly armour?" One of the lords started to ask the questions all wanted to know.

"We were called here, my lords, to converse with the nobles, so we may bring final arrangements to the matter of their knighthoods that are to be bestowed upon them at the coronation. We came, the Lord Buckingham and I, with much joyful pleasure and light of heart, for to see such nobles enter knighthood is dear to our Edward's heart and to ours. We came here to this chamber, which did stand empty, and waited quite long for the lords to arrive. Our thoughts were that, may, we had in our enthusiasm arrived a tad early. Then, after a short while, one of the guards brought to us a folded message. We know not from whom it came, but one day when such is revealed I will endow him most generously, for it warned us of an impending plot upon our lives. We came not prepared for such a foul deed and we had but one officer with us and he the only one who was armed. We then dispatched him to bring your good lords here to save our humble persons. We deemed the uniformed guard on his own could exit the Tower. As we were unarmed we felt we could easily be set upon, whereupon we went to the guards storeroom and were able to arm ourselves, but having to don the only harness that was there. We thought it best then to hide within the chamber at the far to where the place was dark, and there to await our enemies or that you, my lords, may arrive in time to delay their actions. But, alas, they came and charged with swords drawn into the place where we crouched. And surely 'twas a devious plot against us to bring murder upon us and they to become Edward's sly Protectors. They came in the chamber, and not at first seeing us they relaxed their weapons. That is when Buckingham and I struck from the darkness and did severe aggravation upon them, and with bloody swords flailing we were able to overpower them as you see from this gory mess." Richard pointed down with his broken sword as the lords looked down upon the sticky blood-soaked stones. "Then, by God's grace, our officers appeared with many of our guard and did take those villains in secure keep, where they are now detained."

The lords who had been summoned were agape at the story, which seemed not unlike a child's fantasy. But, as no other story as yet was unfolded, so they did question the story that had been told.

"Sirs, whose blood is this in which we stand?"

"At first we knew not, for in the dim light all was of flailing swords and black shadows, and 'twas not until our guards came and all was subdued that bringing closer a lantern we were able to see those who swam in blood, and they were perceived as the Lord Hastings and the Lord Stanley. We were indeed shocked to see who lay at our feet but both were under the queen's spell, and seems that they were her cohorts in this miserable deed."

"My Lord Gloucester, you say you hold others of this act and that they are imprisoned?" one of the lords probed further.

"Yes, that is so, my lord, but at the present time they have pledged themselves to silence and will speak naught to any person. Soon though they will speak of their evil plot, and will name the lady behind such doings."

The summoned lords looked about at the floor and the splattered footsteps that trod all about the chamber, and down the passageways to thin their track to naught. Then it did seem that they were satisfied with the story, and to await the talk of the prisoners to see who indeed was behind this terrible occurrence.

"'Tis indeed a bloodied tower, my lords."

"Yes, indeed a bloodied tower," Richard and Buckingham replied.

Richard then ended the meet with the drift of his objective, that the gathered lords and diverse persons would go out to their different parts, and relate the terrible act that had been directed at the prince's most loyal Protectors. And that they would speak of the brave action that ensued to continue their protection of the soon-to-be king, their Realm, and all citizens therein.

They all with tumbled minds had left the Tower and did relate the story that was unfolded to them, of the brave action of our Lord Gloucester and of our Lord Buckingham.

Notices were posted all about London, placed there by Richard, relating to this event, that the queen and her bloody adherents, they who intended, and still do intend to murder and utterly destroy us and all those who are our beloved, and to end the old blood of this Realm.

The queen was most disliked long before this happening, and so the populace regarded that all that was relayed to them did speak of the truth. The queen's advisers, who had been thought of as speaking for the nation, were now also in marked danger.

Chapter Five.

Treason's Price.

The clearing of the old guard from the Parliament continued. The Lord Cardinal Archbishop of Canterbury, Thomas Bourchier, was sent to the Tower and imprisoned there, with the Archbishop of York, Thomas Rotherham, and the Bishop of Ely, John Morton, amongst many others of such prominence; their townhouses and country manors all placed in the hands of the new Protectors and their party. The Mistress Shore was imprisoned; Richard did not attempt to maintain his charge of sorcery against her, but seized instead her goods and her lands. Later she would be taken from the Tower to be placed in a nunnery where she did remain.

Richard was becoming more powerful and, through devious means and subtle persuasion, the coronation date had been postponed. Thoughts then were turned to Richard, the queen's younger son, who was at sanctuary with his mother at Westminster. The Prince Edward was well wrapped in the lordly covers of our two lords, but the Prince Richard was not, and was still a threat.

"We must separate the Prince Richard from his mother before she corrupts him to her ways." The Lord Gloucester was speaking to his council, called towards the end of June at Crosby Place. "I am feared she may flee with him, and secure him in safety for some future plot to gain for him the throne of this Realm."

All at the council were loyal to Richard, for he was most generous with his gifts, and they would pleasure in any mission he deemed them, for a happy Richard they all wished to see. They had at times seen him angered and did not revel at the sight.

"I put it to you, gentlemen, that we need to enact a legal document to remove the prince from his mother's keep. She is of a devious nature, and we fear for the good of our young Richard and the danger that hangs about him. He must be placed in a safe haven with his brother who pines most heartily for him."

A bill was draughted to this effect by the royal council, and because the queen was in asylum and guarded by the Church, excommunication would be the penalty if she were harmed. The imprisoned Lord Cardinal duly signed it upon draught, and, though bound to the Tower, he was given certain privileges for his signet. Thus 'twas approved by the Church to be placed before the queen without penalty.

Buckingham came with writ in hand to the stables with long, determined strides to carry him along, and a small group of guards trying to keep pace with the carrier of the task. All mounted in the small yard and soon had left the chambers at Crosby Place behind them, to clatter over the cobbled roads of London Town and struck toward Westminster Abbey. Through the narrow roadways they went with capes fluttering at their backs and the horses splashing through the open sewers that lay; the people about all cringing closely to the walls so as not to be trodden under by the wayward hoof.

They trundled along, a spare horse in their midst saddled but riderless, a mount worthy of a prince no less. Soon the short ride brought them to the sight of the refuge, and they rode into the massive court in front of the abbey. The building with its towering steeples seemed to cast its dark shadow over half of London Town. This was a place of religious fortitude where they had to break the sanctuary of the Church. Not only was this task before them, but also they had to approach the wrathful queen, which was fearsome in itself, for she still carried the bearing of a ruler. They dismounted and left their horses in the care of two of the guard that were with them. They came, then, with their dire task to the great oak doors that stood before them, and entered into the Great Hall through a smaller door that was placed within the larger doors. Bare-headed now were they, with hats underarm clutched as they came toward the religious keeper of the abbey, who stood await.

"What is your business in this place, my lord?" he asked.

"We have legal documents from the Prince Edward's council to remove the Prince Richard from this place." Buckingham then handed the document to the keeper. He read the message, as the red, blue, and green light from the windows high fluttered their hue upon his black robe. He read on with moving lips as if the paper before him was a prayer. To the signatures then did he gaze, to raise his brows upon the sight of the name so signed that sat most regally: the Lord Cardinal. If the cardinal had placed his signet upon such a document then, in all lordly reason, Richard must be in some mortal danger. He then bowed in his solemn state and returned the document in silence to the lord. The keeper then beckoned the party to follow him as they echoed their steps in the cavernous building, until they came soon to the great door of the inner chamber. Black and foreboding it stood like some giant guard to deter all who may wish to enter. A broadsword with all its might could not gain access. A battering ram with twenty men to charge could not. But upon this day a wafting flimsy paper could, to wherein was secluded the queen and hers.

Firstly a rap upon the door, and then, not immediately, but in a short time, a stern voice rattled: "Enter"—sounding through the thick oak that barred. Buckingham and his party entered with little reverence as they closed towards the queen, who quickly upped from her settle and showed upon her face the rage at the disrespect being shown to her. For in her courtly days when she was most powerful she would demand the utmost obedience from all who were in her presence. When she dined all except her closest guests would have to remain bowed throughout the meal, which at the evening dinner could last from two to three hours; even her mother was obliged to adopt this position, and much pain and degradation was brought upon all so encumbered. Servants were only to move when dishes were brought in or removed, or upon the signal when the queen's mouth needed to be wiped with the fine lavender-dampened cloths by her ladies. Or, at her command, when she wanted to spit, they would be allowed to move to place a cloth in front of her mouth, so she may expel that from within. This was then her demeanour: cruel and pompous to the extreme.

The imposition imposed upon her was unbearable and she took to raging and screaming at the insolence, but it meant naught this day for those heady days would be no more, and all the threats she uttered were to no avail for she had naught to carry them out. She knew 'twas so, which made her more angered, as she saw all her past glory tipped from its bucket into the sewer. Buckingham then bowed, a sarcastic attempt at reverence as he completely ignored all that the queen did rant.

"I have a writ, my lady, to take within our keep the Prince Richard, to safeguard him from all intrigue that may befall his regal self within these false walls." The queen stood ready to denounce all with their foolish utterings. But before such did happen, the prince in fair pace entered the chamber to attend his mother's distress. Then misfortune came about, for he had entered the chamber where stood the guards and they resisted his passing to reach his mother. 'Twas the beginning of the separation. Richard was only ten years and six months old but he knew well what was afoot, for he had been warned of such things in his schooling. Warned of kings and queens and devious persons making to do foul things.

"Do not take my child!" she shouted, now showing her anguish at the situation. "He is in less danger in my arms than in your keep!" The queen then attempted to move toward her son, her youngest babe, but barred from doing so by the guards who stood her way. The prince was stilled also knowing to resist would be of no avail.

"You are to come with us, my prince, to join your brother under the cloak of your most loyal Protectors." With a slight bow Buckingham spake reverently to Richard.

"May I say goodbye to my mother, sire?"

"Of course you may, my prince." Buckingham bowed once more and then beckoned him over toward his mother as the guards eased their stance for his passage.

Tears flowed upon their fine garments; if they did flow upon sackcloth the pain would be no less. In little time and with sobbing clutch, they were eased gently apart, and the small prince was taken from her as he looked up at the soldiers who seemed mountainous at his side; he then was ushered away to join his brother who dwelled in the palace at the Tower. They left the chamber and, with a glance back, the queen was seen in deep distress. She had been desolate and friendless before, now she was childless.

The guard marched on through the clattering abbey with their prince amidst them; eyes peered from many a corner upon this day, to see the young Richard and to pray indeed they may see him yet another day. Soon outside were they amongst the restless horses, frolicking and dancing about in some disturbed state, as if all was revealed to them and they liked it not; but soon, with gentle words and coaxing hands, all was again of calmness. They mounted outside the abbey's peering watch with the prince already astride the spare horse, and quickly all went upon their way. Buckingham would meet with the Lord Gloucester, and the young prince would be united with his older brother.

On through the narrow streets of London went they, clopping past the houses whose upper stories overhung the road beneath, leaving little light to see the people who waved from the windows or from those who waved below. In the open places crowds had gathered, cheering as they saw their young prince safe in the keep of the Protectors and away from the evil queen, she so set to do him harm. Underfoot was wet and soft, and still the stench of the sewage rose. Left contained, though, within the narrow almost covered ways, there 'twas left to linger that gaseous fume. They rode on and soon the entrance to the Tower showed, as the smell was more behind them except that which did cling to their clothes and lingered about their persons.

They came with dulled hooves over the wooden bridge that led to the entrance of the courtyard. The young prince had resided here many times before with his close family and enjoyed all that royalty commanded. He looked up at the dark grey granite as they came nearer to the entrance. It seemed darker now and higher and did not show any comfort. It seemed more of a confining place than the joyful one he had known. He more than ever longed to see his brother, for all about him were strangers and he but an orphan in their midst. *To see his brother, oh, please, may it come soon for this lost soul.*

They had stopped, and an officer was quickly about to help the prince down from his mount; then he, with caring, held his hand as they made their way to the entrance bringing to Richard some comfort. As they walked, he gazed at the strong hand, brown from the sun it showed with many light marks upon it, scars that showed the shape of healed wounds, the nails cut square and not all clean, his shirt showed below his sleeve, grubby and soiled from the days doings. He saw then his own hand clutched within it, the slender hand of a child with a regal ring upon the finger. A lace cuff showed below the blue velvet of his doublet. He looked up, his face still looking clean as if freshly washed, a dishevelled golden curl hung upon his royal forehead. He held onto the hand that tugged him along the dimly-lit passages, running three paces to every stride his guide did take, the officer not being familiar with the step of a child. Then, as he was swung around a corner, Richard saw ahead a door open wide, and standing before it in great joy was Edward.

"Edward! … Edward!" shouted the young soul as he slipped his soft hand from the heavy grip that held it and left his guide, who slowed and watched as Richard placed his arms about his elder brother. A little sob was heard as he did so for the nearness of his kin had brought much relief to him. The emotion he had contained, so taught to a prince, now welled out with tears of joy. But as quickly as the tears had come he again became composed and returned to his princely ways; he stood back to look once more at his brother, seeing that he was cared for.

"Do not distress yourself, my dear Richard," Edward spake with his arm strung about his brother's shoulders bringing to him comfort. "We are with our friends here and they are sworn to protect us. We will be safe with our dear uncle, the Lord Gloucester, who is close and caring for us. And while he stands as our most loyal Protector, harm will not show about us in any shape."

Gloucester was standing behind Edward, but so enamoured to see his brother was the prince that he had only seen that which he desired above all things. But now he was able to spread his sight to other further places, and leaving Edward he came to his uncle who crouched down to give a comforting hug to the young prince, and showing to him such deep affection.

"You are safe, my dear Richard; do not fret, for we are here to defend you with our lives. And to foresee that the royalty of this Realm will flourish under our care."

"Thank you, my dear uncle. My heart is lighter now that I am in your keep, and all fear has now indeed left me. But, sire, I do fear for my mother for she is alone and appears most distraught." The young prince aired the concerns that he still held within him.

"Do not be feared, my prince," Gloucester spake softly to the young boy. "These things of concern will soon be settled, and your state will be of complete happiness."

"Thank you, my uncle," he replied. "I am in complete trust of your words so spoken."

The two princes then started to move toward their chamber with the duke in between them; on one side he held the hand of Richard, and upon the other he held the hand of Edward. He to comforting the warm hands within his own. Gloucester reassured the princes once more, as he then excused himself for the business of state did press upon his time. He left the two princes chattering together, and they seemed in a more playful spirit now they were reunited. He closed gently the door, and left after a quick glance at the two guards who stood discreetly within the dark covering of the walls, silent and unseen.

Gloucester went with pondering steps to the conference chamber, and there, with Buckingham and the others of Richard's council, sat around the planked table, discussion was of the traitorous Protectors they held in those various places north of London. It had been agreed that the time was apt to bring them to trial and so to end any scheming they may have with the queen. The Lord Northumberland was given the task of bringing this part of the drama to a close. *There were many cottons that dangled below the skirt, and they had to be clipped off before someone was tripped.*

The next morning at nine of the clock, Northumberland left with his troop to carry forth the task that had been placed upon him. With them this day rode the Bishop of Bath who had been a close adviser to Edward IV, and after Richard's purge was imprisoned in the Tower as a follower of the queen. But he had since paid a ransom to Richard and had been released, and held now a position within the council of Gloucester. Their journey was to the castle at Pomfret where Rivers was being held. Northumberland had sent soldiers from his troop to the other castles where the other Protectors were imprisoned, they with orders to bring all to the castle of Pomfret. A trial would be held there, encompassing them under one incriminating document.

Northumberland approached the castle late upon the following day, as the blustering winds blew about the grime upon the track and dusted the travellers, as if in a lowland fog and not upon that hill's crest. They all made for the comfort that lay within the shelter of Pomfret's walls, seeking some respite from that wind that billowed their flapping capes; they, soon to sup and warm by the raising fire, would be of all content. Others not so; those all so charged with treason sat not by some warm fire or supped mulled ale. They were in their cold keep and would await the hour that would bring them to face justice. That hour would be upon the morrow, and sleep would be hard to find this night within those walls of trial.

The morning came dull and stormy, filled with the wind still adding to the drab state, blowing the rain through the ill-fitting windows of the assembly hall where the trial was to be held. In it blew, splashing down the walls and wetting all who dwelled below. The chamber was so crowded that no one could move about, they but to soak up the wet where they did sit. There were shutters upon the east side of the castle where the weather did come most hard, and at last they were closed by the servants, darkening the gloomy hall even more as they were rattled shut. The shutters, though, were of rot and in need of some repair, with gaps all about them that still let in the lashing rain.

The court was seated upon the wooden benches that were close around the oak table; its boards were hid by the papers and books that lay upon it. Nobles and others who had gathered to see the trial sat jostled closely together, all wishing to be in some advantageous position when the inquisition came about.

"Bring in the prisoners!" sounded about, as Northumberland beckoned to the guard with his shouted order. The guard pushed the door open until it would open no more, and there it stayed jammed against the uneven flag. He then leaned his head through the opening and cast his rattling voice down the empty passageways.

"Bring in the prisoners!" was his shout, and sounding all about as if ten voices had called such as it echoed far. Then from outside the hall could be heard the sound of feet; softly at first was the step then gradually louder with each closing stride, until the accused entered the chamber and were within sight of all who had awaited their coming. Many were the guards about them as they came, the Earl Rivers, with the Lords Grey, Vaughan, Croft, Hawte, and Stanley, whose brother, unbeknown to him, had been struck down at the Tower. They were stood before the table, dishevelled and needing to be bathed, though they were still dressed most finely, still bearing the aloofness that stated that all who stood or sat about them were most inferior to themselves. Their impression given was that they were untouchable, and they were confident to the extreme that the trial would bring to them total vindication of the conjured charges. Seated at the centre of the table before them were Northumberland and the Bishop of Ely. He sat with a sour face, stern and unforgiving, scripture strict … except when the coin was proffered. Two of Richard's most loyal officers sat each side to confirm that all their lords' wishes had been carried out. Guards were posted about the dark walls as well as the close guard that were stitched to the accused. A flagon of malmsey and some goblets of silver were placed upon the table; they danced by the lone candle placed there. Notes of the trial were being writ by a clerk who sat apart at a small desk. Already the sound of his quill squeaked and scratched upon the parchment.

Remaining seated, Northumberland was the first to speak.

"You are charged, this thirtieth day of June in the year of our Lord fourteen hundred and eighty-three, that you, the said Protectors, under vows given to our royal monarch Edward IV, did not carry out your duties so pledged to the Parliament to protect and to guide the Prince Edward whilst in his young years, but indeed did deceive him and bore to yourselves and yours gifts and properties, by misusing the signet of the king, the monarch of our Realm. And further, to conspiring with the Queen Elizabeth to do damage and harm to our beloved Gloucester and Buckingham, now our prince's Protectors. How do you plead to the charges laid against you?"

To answer stood the Earl Rivers. "We have the greatest..." Rivers started to place his words in wrappings of silk, but did not many of them speak.

"How do you plead of these charges against you, sir? Is it that you do not understand the question?" Northumberland shouted as he stood and banged the flat of his hand upon the table, interrupting the long recourse that was intended to follow from the mouth of the Earl Rivers.

"We are not guilty, and we demand—" Again his words were cut.

"Sir, we are not here to listen to your demands. You are not some royalty who stands upon the hill with two thousand soldiers at its back. A traitor charged is why you stand here and all we wish to hear from you is your plea. We will hear nothing more from you; no talk will be allowed in defence of your actions. The jury here will decide if you are guilty or not guilty. Your words will not be considered as deemed by the laws that cover the acts of treason."

They were sickened, as a doomed air hung about them and all of their haughtiness left, numbed by the dreadful words upon their ears.

"I protest that we are unable to defend ourselves of these vile charges!" shouted the Earl Rivers once more. Northumberland sighed heavily at this latest outburst. He did not answer Rivers but turned to the close officer of the guard.

"Draw your sword!" Which the officer did. The sound of the metal leaving the sheath had sparrows twittering in the far of the rafters. And, with the scratching of the quill upon the parchment, were the only sounds within the chamber. "If any one of the accused speaks again, run him through and be not subtle in doing so for I am truly peeved with such whimperings." Now even the quill's scratch did stop at the words from Northumberland.

The assembled jury spake quietly and briefly amongst themselves, and in little time 'twas Northumberland who came to his feet. And in such brief and short words did speak that which all knew would be told. *As if the rabbit had to be snared before the sun set upon the moor.*

"The jury before you, as designated by our Lord Gloucester, find you all guilty of treason, and that you are to be beheaded by the axe and then quartered, as is the punishment for treasonable nobles. This act will be carried out before the sun sets upon this day." *So indeed the rabbit did have to be snared with haste*. Knees gave way within the lordly group as some retched upon the stone floor; they stood and clung to each other for comfort so sickened were they at their fate. For death would quickly come and there would be no time for bargaining. The trial had taken less than one half of the hour, from promise to despair.

The guards marched the stumbling lot into an enclosed area within the courtyard of the castle, where before them the block of death sat grimly. The executioner stood discreetly against the shadows of the wall, his presence though was shown with the small glint that caught upon his shiny axe, gripped there most firmly with the strong hands of his trade. Some of the castle's servants were peering through the windows at the scene below, others crowded the doors that opened onto the yard. Many stood within the arena, as children gleefully ran about, unaware of the gruesome act about to take place. Their voices shouted about, mingling with the desperate whines from the prisoners. All kinds of folks were being ushered in who had come from the close villages and towns, to stand about in their groups and to watch the event of an execution unfolding before them. They were pressed by the soldiers to attend the act so they could see what fate would bring upon them, if they involved themselves in such intrigues against their nobles and kings. They needed not to be cajoled but did come gladly. Not to be awed by such happenings, but to see close the nobles whimpering and grovelling as they were brought to the block. Soon they to be twitching their lordly shapes … This was the sport that they had come for, and not for any lessons to be learned from the noble lot.

Rivers was the first to be brought to the stage, refusing to have his eyes covered as he was knelt down and his head placed upon the block. His lips still moving from the chant as he mouthed his last prayers to his God. No words were spoken over him as he breathed his last air … The noise of the axe came like a hawk in its killing dive. The lords awaiting their fate closed their eyes and cringed away from the noise of death—the noise of a dull thud as axe met flesh and bone. The axeman though was off his target, and the blade had sunk itself into the left shoulder below the neck, flooding the courtyard with such a cry of pain, that it echoed about the stone walls.

"Damnation," the executioner mumbled as he with haste pulled out his axe, and with another strike, this time with more resolve, struck the death blow clean. The head rolled away, bumping upon the cobbled yard, with blood spurting from head and from body, as both came then to still. The remains of Rivers were dragged away to be quartered by the guard who stood by the carts at wait. The executioner beckoned for the next victim upon the court's list. Others who came his way were not so proud and brave as was Rivers. Some had to be carried to the block, for as fish upon the riverbank they flopped about not knowing up from down. Others tried to flee but were quickly caught by the villagers who revelled in the chase; the soldiers then took them still struggling to be forced upon the wooden cradle. Others came in shock with minds gone to an idiot and not knowing as to what journey they were on. And soon the lives of all the Protectors were ended with cheering and much gaiety from the crowd about; 'twas a day well spent as the children still danced and played their happy games.

Richard, in some regard for the noble being of the Protectors, brought upon them death in a less cruel fashion than those of commoners, for they were neither gutted nor subject to castration as was the law, but death was brought upon them with some leniency, though death did still come.

The quartering was being carried out in some brutish fashion. The guards with readied swords hacked and chopped at the bodies to sever them into quarters. Each quarter was labelled as to whom it did belong, written upon parchment and tied to a body part, either to an arm or to a leg. All the left-leg quarters were thrown into one cart; all the right-leg quarters thrown into another. All the left-arm quarters and the right-arm quarters thrown into two more carts. Four carts then trotting from the castle of Pomfret upon this evening of late June. Their grisly meat was covered with sackcloth as they rolled upon the way from the executions. The road divided after a short distance and each cart took a separate path to the four corners of the land. And upon each reaching its destination the parts of the lords were hung within the town square of these far places. Hung there so all could see that the justice of the land had been carried out to the people's will, and all rumours put to bed. And to let it be known that this was the fate of all those who did seek to usurp the Realm. 'Twas indeed that treason's price had been paid this day.

The following morning in the castle of Pomfret, Northumberland and the Bishop of Bath, with the others of the court, eat their daybreak meal seated in the castle's warm kitchen. Hungrily they pulled at the fresh loaf with their hands, to tear large pieces with their brown teeth that hid behind their rough beards—swathed in grease and fat from the eggs, pork, and chicken. The breakfast table was filled with the usual morning victuals, with frothing tankards of ale being swallowed, it seemed that one gulp did suffice to empty the vessel, and 'twas taxed muchly to fill again and again.

"My lord," the bishop broached Northumberland in some quiet manner, "on our return to Crosby Place, I would be most grateful to you, sir, if you could arrange some council with the Lord Gloucester for my humble self."

"And what, my dear bishop, is the purpose of this council? I can relay any message you may have to our Lord Gloucester with the utmost confidence."

"Yes, sire, I know of the utmost trust in your council, and I do not wish you to think that your trust is my motive, for it is not. This, my lord, is the most delicate of matters and when it does come to light, you will understand my motives. I must relay my words into Richard's ear only. But to show you that I am all sincere in this matter, and that there is no intention of any slight upon you, I would wish, with Richard's consent, that you are by my side when such an audience can be made." The bishop spake as tactfully as he was able, with Northumberland drawing no hurt from the words spoken.

"Then it will be so, my bishop, I will by your side dwell when this meet is proffered." An almost unseen nod came from the bishop who, with his usual quietness, thanked the lord for the consideration given in the matter. He though was somewhat subdued in such a situation as this, but made up for all his meekness as soon as he embraced the pulpit, where all his corked fervour did burst from his bottle of oration.

Later upon this same morn, with weather undecided as to its act this day, with first bright sun then to cloud, then back to sun again, not knowing which it wished to play upon those below its twirling sky, they began their journey, leaving behind them the bloody Pomfret Castle to await its next intrigue.

One of the clock in the afternoon saw them close to the town of London, and to the bridge that came to sight that crossed over the twinkling Thames. They drew closer, as poles then could be seen standing there, eight-foot in height were they and swaying like small dead trees. At least thirty of them stood in the light breeze; all seemed top heavy with a black fruit as big as a turnip atop the branchless sticks. Strange plants these that grew upon this bridge of London Town. Nearer they came and all knew of this scene; there were no strange trees upon this bridge, and 'twas not some fruit that was atop, but the heads of murderers and thieves, of traitors and treasoners. The very tops of the poles were hid as they entered the skulls; they stood not straight but all at grotesque angles. Some heads leaned forward upon their stick bodies; some did slant backwards. Poles gone awry with the point sticking through the eye socket, with decaying eyeballs upon the tip. Crows and ravens were all about; some circled above whilst others stood atop, pecking and tearing at the feast that was provided for them. All manner of faces swayed there. Half faces, eaten or rotted away, some smirking faces, some sad, all swaying as in some dance upon the bridge.

Northumberland's party came amongst the small crowd that was gathered there, they who came to see who were upon the poles, and to see if they could recognize the disfigured remains that bobbed there, and who was the latest addition to this rotting army. As the soldiers dismounted and made toward the cart, the throng went with them to the sackcloth that covered the cargo, showing shapes beneath like muslin over a basket of eggs. They knew what lay beneath, as some tried to lift the cover to be the first to see the dismal sight, but they were soon pushed aside by the guards and were unable to glimpse aught. They remained close to the cart though, no matter how hard they were shoved.

The soldiers who carried out the dismembering then came forward peering at the heads that sat upon the poles that swayed above them, and shading their eyes in the bright light to see which were the most rotted. Spaces were needed for six more new partners to join the waltz. They chose their poles, lifting them out of the blocks in which they stood, and then knocked the sucking heads from the sticks upon the planks at the bridge's edge. The heads fell into the murky waters below, with bystanders leaning over the wooden rail to see them tumble and splash into the river. Not until they had bobbed from sight did they return to the cart where the crowd was growing into a sizable gathering. Word had spread about that some new victims were being added to the wretches who nodded there.

The scene was becoming rowdy as impatience took over. Northumberland, still mounted, stood tall above those about him, and with a few cracks about some ears with his horsewhip soon had things under control again. More people came, still noisy and jostling; all were anxious to see the heads that were in the wagon. A soldier coming pushed through the crowd that parted to let him pass, for he carried one of the bloody poles that were stood upon the bridge. He leant it upon the side of the cart with the point showing upwards and black with congealed blood. Other soldiers were moving poles about so that there were six empty spaces at the front that faced the town, a place where they could be more easily seen and more easily reminded of the fate of wrongdoers. Another soldier jumped into the cart with sarcastic cheers from the crowd. "Hooray," they called half-heartedly as if at last something was going to happen. He pulled the cover back and kicked it out of the way, clear of the cargo that lay there. Some of the crowd were clutching at the side of the cart and managing to peer over the boards at the bloodstained sacks that leaked its blood to thicken at the bottom of the cart. The soldier, bending over, pulled off the twine that secured the first bag, and, pushing his hand inside, felt a tangled mass of hair and dragged out the first trophy. Then, standing, he held it up so all may see, but the bag still stuck to the head and had not dropped. The crowd at the cart chanted: "Take it off! Take it off!" The soldier tugged at the bag and it fell away from the head that gazed its lordly ogle to all who were close, and then a cry went up as the head was lifted arm's-length high. "Yea!" they shouted.

"'Tis Vaughan!" a one-eyed man called about him

"Yes, 'tis," shouted another; "I'd know that sour face anywhere!" The laughter took over from the curiosity that was before. "He looks better now than when last I saw him!" And on with much sport were the jibes. Mothers who pushed at the back of the crowd lifted up their children so they could see the grisly sight. "Mam, I cannot see!" they cried with blubbering eyes. The guard threw the sack into the crowd where they tugged and fought over it, until one stood victorious holding his trophy high for all to see; a beaming smile upon his red cheeks for the grand prize was indeed his. He held the very sack that once wrapped the head of the Lord Vaughan.

The guard held the head by its ears as he forced it onto the pole, with a squish and a squirt of thick blood trickling slowly down the shaft; a soldier below held the pole tightly so it would slide on easier. 'Twas on, but the guard in the cart did not care for the way it sat, being 'twas too much upon one side and did lean too much. He pulled it off with the sucking sound of wood from raw meat, then did reposition the head, and plunged it down again so the point pushed into a fresh part of the brain. He then stepped back a pace and looked at his work with his head slightly tilted like an artisan, and to smile at the result, receiving then from the crowd many a "Bravo," which he acknowledged with a deft bow. The soldier below then helped his comrade bring the prize to its hole upon the bridge, and both slid it in until it would slide no more; then, looking up, they turned it to be sure the head faced the town. The crowd began cheering at every little move that was made. The next head left the sack and was held high.

"Rivers!" was the cry from the one-eyed man again, seemingly an expert on dead faces.

"Yea, Rivers!" went the cry. "The traitor, Rivers; he's one of them!" ... "Good, good. Death to the traitors!"—all such was shouted about with jovial remarks quickly to follow. "No bed games for you tonight, my lord; you have lost more than your head!" The crowd was having now a most pleasing time, laughing and jollying about. Then at last 'twas six heads that were gazing toward inner London, but saw they little. Their white, drawn features of death but food for the crows. Some of the crowd still lingered, taking a last look at their sport as many now dwindled homeward to tell of their day, and six amongst them with bloodstained sacks to show.

The soldiers and the lords gathered together and made upon their way to Crosby Place. A few latecomers came looking up at the new display, as the crows gathered about not fearful of the citizens below as they screeched their circles and others landed awkwardly upon the swaying heads, their wings aflutter trying to peck the eyes that stared glassily.[*] A meal of a lord as the party of Northumberland entered the city.

---

* *glassily* dull and lifeless

Chapter Six.

Murder Now Comes.

Upon his arrival, Northumberland made to report to Richard and went immediately to his chamber where the guard who stood the door entered him upon sight.

"Was your journey successful, my lord?" Richard was alone in his quarters to receive Northumberland for he wished no ears about at this meet, though he was well aware of the outcome of the enterprise for his spies were not all for the enemy.

"Aye, my lord, all was done as you asked with little trial. If you will pardon my words, sire, the heads of the traitors are all displayed upon London Bridge and the other remains have been dispatched for display, and should all be at view upon the morrow."

"I am well pleased, my lord, for now we are beginning to see some sight of victory in our endeavours. You will be well rewarded, my Lord Northumberland, for your loyalty in this sordid affair." Richard as always spake with much generosity.

"I do all to serve you, my lord; my intent is not for rewards for proud I am to be able to stand by your side." He bowed politely to Richard who acknowledged the lord for his sincere words. "If I may further impose upon your time, sire, the Bishop of Bath has requested an audience with you, and it seems as if it is a matter of some importance. I think, sire, 'tis to our cause to confer with him, though he would not state to me of what tack 'twas. He also requested, sire, as a gesture for obtaining such a meeting, that I, with your permission, be allowed to privy such a meet."

"Very well; we will receive the bishop and yourself upon the morrow at ten of the clock within this chamber, and let us hope the bishop offers us more than a sermon. By such a time our Lord Buckingham will be with us from his duties and may join us."

"Aye, my lord, I bid you a good day till the morrow." With this Northumberland left to be washed and to partake of some victuals, and to relate to the other lords the outcome of his journey to the castle of Pomfret, and all the doings that did occur.

The morning of the meeting with Richard quickly came. With the lord and the bishop making their way along the echoing passages to their place of council. 'Twas a little before ten of the clock as they were admitted into the chamber. They entered with all respect to Richard and to the returned Buckingham, who was reporting the events of his journey to his castle at Brecknock where he had taken the Bishop of Ely to secure him and to keep him in his house. It seemed all was going well for Gloucester for he was in good spirits upon this bright morn. Northumberland, though, prayed that whatever the bishop had to say would not put a stop to Richard's happy demeanour.

They gathered about the table—all polished, with the hardwood chairs set about it for their council. The room filled with light that beamed in through the windows this bright day. After Richard sat at his desired place, all seated themselves with no word yet uttered, as all eyes turned to the bishop and did wonder of what tale would be told. Sat he in his dark robe of rough cloth as determined by the Church, tied at the waist with silver chain and dangling cross—a thing for fondling when he was in some nervous state. To be now fondling that cold metal, for the secret he held could change all as never before and turmoil could ensue. He had to choose with care the words he was to speak, not only for England but for the rewards to be gained from that which he held in sacred trust. That trust that he was about to sacrifice so given under the vows of the Church. A small man was he with balding head, elderly, and bent with cricked back, his face filled with stern religious features that looked as if it had never borne a smile. And 'twas certain he had never laughed and the only thing that did please him was to count his coin, which twinkled his eyes. He at last stood as all still gazed upon him, and he was beckoned by Richard to speak his piece.

"My Lord Gloucester and all the nobility at this table, as you know I have been a most loyal and faithful servant to our late King Edward, and have done all that was ever asked of me in my capacity as Bishop. I have done all that was asked, and that my place was to remain silent, as I had sworn in the house of God to do so. Now that Edward is no more, I deem my sole intent is to serve my new masters in the same devoted manner. I then have to relate to you that which I was compelled to keep secret, for I cannot serve you with full devotion unless it is revealed." Richard did not usher the bishop along but was desirous that he would get to the tip of the sword, for had he not polished the handle too long; he, though, fought his impulses, and his face retained the features of one that was really interested in all of this. "I pray I do the right thing by this, but I know through our Lord's divine messages that you will soon be the ruler of this Realm, and I deem it my right as a servant to you to speak of the truth … The fact being that during the time before the King Edward married the

Lady Elizabeth Woodville, who was to be our queen …" As the queen's name came to light, all were of cocked ears and backs straightened from their bored slouch. "In a discreet ceremony I did marry the King Edward to a young lady of noble blood and many properties. The marriage was so secret that I was sworn upon the Bible and upon the pain of death, to never reveal such as was placed upon me. And, sirs, I do hold the certificate of marriage that holds my story to be of the truth."

"What is it you say, sir?" Richard was standing, unable he to sit longer, as he sought more incriminating words. Buckingham and Northumberland remained seated, but stared in some disbelief at the bishop, stunned at what they had heard.

"I say, my lord, that Edward did not receive any papal dispensation from the Church regarding this first marriage. He had then a legal wife and, therefore, was bigamously married to our Lady Elizabeth, and in doing so made the children of this marriage, Edward and Richard, illegitimate and not rightful heirs to the crown."

"The name of the lady who is our late king's wife?" Richard asked.

"Dame Eleanor Butler, my lord, is the name so written in the marriage document, and the name proffered at the ceremony."

"This is too much to believe; all is about now; up is down; the rabbit flies. Soon the rooster will chase the fox." These were the only words that Richard could find to speak.

"You have upon your person this document of marriage?" Buckingham now asked.

"I do, my lord." The bishop, guiding his hand beneath his robe, produced a rolled parchment sealed with the royal signet; he passed it to Northumberland, who then passed it to Buckingham.

"Read it, my friend," Richard bade Buckingham as he slowly seated himself. He was in a calmer state now, though his eyes showed all that was being conjured within his mind. The document was broken open with the brittle wax flaking onto the table. Buckingham read aloud from the statement he clutched as all within this chamber listened to every word that was spake.

"This, my lords, is a legally binding certificate of marriage, signed by both Edward and the Dame Eleanor Butler and duly witnessed by the Bishop of Bath. I see the date stated here relating to this marriage, and indeed it did take place a full six months before Edward's marriage to Elizabeth." He held the document out, and passed it then to Richard who took it but still could not believe that which had been related to him, and the good fortune this document would bring to his house. He stood this day as the clear heir to the throne. The two princes were bastards, the queen was not a queen, and he was, with little trouble, to become ruler of this land. And, with just a few trifling things to overcome, he would make that rocky path smooth and level once more.

"Your disclosure of this document, my dear bishop, has shown to us that you are as loyal and devoted as you were to our beloved King Edward, and you will be brought into our fold as one of our most trusted advisers. Your lands and incomes that were forfeited during our turbulent times will all be returned to you, for you have shown the faith that we dearly search for."

"I humbly thank you, my Lord Gloucester, and will, in all my doings, be, at all times, your most faithful servant and will preach such in your name."

"We shall call a Parliament of all the lords and nobles and bring to them details of this document. Go forth, my dear friends, and arrange such with some haste. Buckingham and I will remain here in some further discussion of that which remains to be unfolded." And, with bows of gratitude, both left to their duties; the chamber door was quietly closed, leaving the two lords once more to their schemes.

"This day has indeed turned in our favour, Buckingham," Richard spake, as he still tried to place his mind fully upon all that this event would bring.

"It is so, my dear Richard, for at this day's dawn who could have foretold of such happenings. What say you, my lord, of Elizabeth and her illegitimate offspring?"

"Elizabeth is of no threat, for she is bereft of all: no husband, no friends, and royal princes, she has none … Though they have to be dealt with, for there are many still loyal to them in this land who will take little heed of their state, and will still try to bring them to the throne. They have much to lose in this game and will not fold lightly. Without doubt they will try to view the marriage document as a forgery, and we can do without such a dilemma. We must deal with the situation quickly before devious plots can be formed to harm us."

"And what do you want for the children, my lord?" Buckingham asked but knew he without doubt the outcome of his question.

"Buckingham it grieves me most sadly that they will have to be silenced. We will have to murder those bastards for to let them live will bring much harm to our ambitions. If they do not bring trouble now, they will bring it later."

"I must agree with you, sire, that it is the only way we can secure ourselves, but I am truly grieved of it for they are but innocent children."

"Fear not, my friend, I will arrange all so the pain within your heart is lessened."

"Aye," said Buckingham with sad resolve, for he was deeply grieved by the action that had to be taken. He knew it would be a bloody path that they would tread but he did not like this bloodshed.

"Be of strength, my friend, for well it will be. 'Tis best I away to Baynard's Castle, and await there in all humbleness whilst you address the Parliament to place me as the only true king of this land, and with your persuasion you will obtain all the needed votes for your Gloucester, for we are indeed in full majority and now have the right. I wish you to relay to all the nobles there gathered that I am so overcome by the feelings shown towards me that I deem it improper to impose myself on the Parliament upon this day. I will await your coming Buckingham, and let the feelings of all who are so dear to me be as a surprise to my humble self. And of all the other matters so discussed I will undertake all that is required concerning such."

Buckingham started his duties organizing the sitting of the Parliament, and to sending out his riders to diverse lords of the council. In all directions did they cantor, requesting all to attend the Parliament upon the sixth day of July in the morn at ten of the clock promptly.

At this time Richard stayed secluded in his chambers at Crosby Place to show himself humbly when came the time. But at this hour he was not on call to anyone, and he was able to spend his time arranging the devious task that squirmed Buckingham: the murder of the two princes. He called first one of his most trusted lords. Sir James Tyrell, who, as with all the other nobles in his position, had been apprised of the bishop's document. Sir James was ushered into the chamber of Richard and was taken straight to where Richard did sit. In that room where many devious schemes had been hatched and many debates mulled ... the privy. He entered to the row of benches fixed to the wall with holes atop in a suitable size, all with rough wooden lids covering the buckets showing dark beneath. Two windows let in the light and aired the chamber, as this was not an odourless place of council. Richard sat with his lumped back against the wall, his breeches flopped about his ankles. He was leaning from one side to the other as his easement dictated. His wooden cover leaned against the wall close to some rough cloths that hung upon pegs there, placed to clean away as much as they needed, before a servant arrived with warm water and towelling to wash them thoroughly.

"Take a seat, my lord," Richard beckoned. Tyrell accepted, lifting off the cover next to Richard where he had been asked to sit, and did lean against the wall noting the contents of the bucket below as he did so; 'twas over half full but enough room was left. They seemed a little lax in their privy duties he thought as he pulled down his breeches to his ankles, then the rest of his underclothing. He sat and in doing so let good wind, which was a friendly sign and did please Richard.

"Are you well, my lord?" Tyrell inquired.

"Indeed, I am, sire, much with the news that will soon be heard by all in this land, and may I say, bring much fortune to those who are in my close council as you are so to me, dear Tyrell, my trusted one."

"Thank you, my lord, for your trust. I am as always at your complete and loyal command and it pleases me well that you are in such good spirits." Tyrell's face had become distorted into some kind of strain as he winced a little, forcing his function loudly into the bucket below with the pungent smell rising from it ... As if not to be outdone from this action—indeed, was he not soon-to-be king?—Richard let forth the same, but a more loose effort did show, which splattered about the top board and the bucket, spraying all about, and then 'twas accompanied by a loud passing of wind. Richard had been saving this for some time and was often fighting off the discomfort to do so. Tyrell had given his best but 'twas not good enough to compete. Richard smiled at the lord sat aside him knowing once more he had triumphed. Tyrell lolled with only the light breeze scenting the chamber; first one and then the other, their amusement finished. He would come better prepared upon his next visit, his mind floated ... The game was over, and more serious things were mulled.

"I have a most difficult task for you, my lord," Gloucester began his request to his trusted colleague as they sat still upon their reddening rears. "And of all the decisions I have had to make over the years, even such as upon the field of battle, I have never been so pained by the deed to be done. Such a task has been forced upon me against all that I hold dear. 'Tis the only path I can take; so regrettably, though I do not totally agree with my advisers, I see it must be done ... Sire, we must erase the princes from the picture and not dally about it; let us get it done and finished with."

Tyrell listened to the words again and was not in shock, for he knew when Richard had the princes together under his hand there would be only one exit for them. "Whatever your command, my lord, it will be done."

Richard then continued. "They have to be murdered and their remains buried so no trace of them can injure us. First, I wish you to go to the Tower and arrange that the princes sleep in separate chambers. We want not the cries of one to awaken the other and cause more hardship to our act. Then, approach the lieutenant of the Tower, Brackenbury, and order him to carry out the murders in our name. All this to be done most hastily. Then I ask you to remain steady whilst the act is committed. Afterwards you are to review the bodies and undertake that they are indeed the princes, and, after their most discreet burial, report back to me, for I wish to know of all the details."

"I will do so immediately, my lord." Tyrell stood as Richard also rose from his seat, roughly wiping themselves so they were in more comfort.

"Come!" Richard shouted to bring in the servants who came with their warm water and linen cloths. The two lords leaned over resting their hands upon the bench with legs parted and their backs to the skivvies, as they came and wiped the lords clean with their wetted cloths. Then they were sprinkled lightly with perfumed water and then dried with the warm towelling that had hung by the kitchen's fire. The servants helped with the dressing of their masters. And after they were readied, the lords made their way toward the doorway with Richard almost entering his chambers, but turning before he did so to chasten the servants who were still busied in the privy. "By my God, clean up this place instead of wasting half your day warming in the kitchen. Do you delight in that we have to piss in a sty? Get to it now or you will be made to drink the slop." He slammed the door shut upon them, to leave them well fretted.

Richard signed some documents in his chamber to finish his pressing business. He then mounted his most favourite charger and left Crosby Place with his retinue. Their journey was to Baynard's Castle there to await the outcome of the called Parliament. The outcome would not be in doubt, as sure the sun will rise in the morn …

Tyrell went alone to the Tower, his steps to tread the way of discretion, for the order he had received had to be passed in the most secretive of fashion, to the one who knew not yet of its coming. Soon he passed the guards who stood the main gate, and then was dismounting in the Tower's yard. The fog drifting about dampened the clothes and made all about glum and foreboding. The tall stone walls hid the devious schemes that oft played within, and it seemed to the lord that dark tasks always came with dark days. The stable lad came running through the dim yard; raggedy he came toward Tyrell, shoeless and unkempt with the dirty face of a boy peering through the roughly-cut fringe of his hair. Then, bowing lowly, "Sire," was all he spake in respect as he took the horse to be wiped down and fed, and for the farrier to see that the shoes were of good stead, and that the animal had no injuries and was not suffering from any cough. The horse was cared for more than the young boy. For which indeed was of the greater value. They could always, with little ado, get another boy, but horses were costly.

Inside went Tyrell; a small side entrance was his way, being less seen than other doors and was closer to the means of the evil act he was wrapped in. The low arch lit by the smoking torch above was burning gloomily in the fog, showing little his way into the narrow passageway, seeing only glimpses of the dripping walls with the worn flagstones beneath. He came to the chamber of the Officer of the Tower, and was shown by a guard through the thick blackened doors to an inner closet. Windowless, with a lone pitch torch lighting the miserable hole, the black smoke peeled about the place as it floated up to the high roof and then out through an opening at the rafters' loft.

Brackenbury was seated at a table, which had many documents thereon. Some for the release of prisoners who had served their time, or had paid a ransom agreed upon. Others there for pardons granted. Documents for the jailing of accused persons and to what treatment they would be subject to. Their food, their visitors, their cell. And of death warrants to be carried out. There laid a never-ending stream of pain, brutality, and false justice. All did lie upon this wooden table under moving shadows and flickering torches.

Two prison guards stood close by the table, they awaiting their orders from the Officer of the Tower. As yet, none had seen Tyrell entering the chamber as most quiet of foot did he tread.

"And, for the sake of God, this time be sure you torture the right prisoner. If you cannot read the order then speak of it." The officer, almost despairingly, passed over the documents to the guards who seemed to care little about their mistake. Upon receiving their orders they at last turned from the table; being the first to see the Lord Tyrell, they bowed most loyally with a "Sire" and then backed from the table so that Brackenbury could see his visitor. He, upon seeing Tyrell, stood as quickly as he was able, causing two or three of the documents he was reading to be dropped to the floor; but for the moment he had to ignore them, for to greet the lord in a proper manner was most important.

"A good day, my lord. I pray you are well?" The words coming with the most polite bow offered to his visitor, whom he now recognized.

"Good day to you, keeper. I have need to speak with you hastily and in all privacy."

"Go to your duties; we will continue with the rest of your orders at a later time," the Lieutenant Brackenbury dismissed his guards.

"Yes, sire," the guards spake together, saluting their officer and bowing to the lord, as the keeper picked up the fallen documents and placed them back upon the table, as if he knew exactly where they belonged. The door was clicked shut by the soldiers to hold only two within the cold smoky chamber. Brackenbury was a goodly officer and served with all his will to whomever was king and to be always loyal. He was a tall man with the carriage of a leader and being most thorough in all he did. He had held the position of Officer of the Tower during the reign of Edward, and after his death was retained by Richard because of the deep devotion he had shown to his position and to his masters. His face bore a look of calmness; he was now forty years old and slight of hair. Always it seemed he was involved in many intrigues that were thrust his way from the royalty and their advisers. But in all he tried to be a fair man when 'twas possible, and carried principles when others had none. He had always laboured in the Tower, placed in one capacity or another, and for many hard years had lived among the death and pain that slinked about this dark foreboding place. In this, the most evil of hides, he, through all trials, remained committed, even though at times he was pained by the Tower's torments.

"I bring a most difficult task to you, Brackenbury," Tyrell spake, trying to choose his words with care upon this most delicate of matters. I bring this task to you as directed by the Lord Gloucester, who, I must tell you, will be our king ere two days pass. He wishes you in all discretion, but with the utmost expedience, to end the lives of the two princes that are in your keep."

"The royal children!" Shocked was the response from the officer as he listened to the task placed upon him. "Sire, I cannot … I cannot. For to do harm to those innocent royals is something I will not carry with me. I know I would die of grief if I were to bring about such a task. I would be ravaged with night dreams and fearful visions of devils and ogres, and damnation would be my end."

"*Murder,* my dear lieutenant, would be all that would come upon you if Richard did hear such drift. You have been chosen for your loyalty, yet you flap and cackle like some mother hen."

"Sire, if it is death I have to bear then so be it, for the request bodes all of evil, and I say I will not do such a task."

"I tell you now, my man, I will not be the one to lay such news upon Richard for I fear his wroth would come down upon me in your name."

"With your permission I will ride with you to Richard and I will tell him of my will, and naught then will fall upon your head."

"You speak brave talk, sir, but you are asking for death if you do not obey this order. You do know this, do you not?"

"I know, sire, but it is God's will and I can do no other."

"We will ride then to Richard at Baynard's Castle where he awaits more pleasing tidings to be sure. We must go with haste for he expects this matter to be unfolding to his desire at this very time, not to be dragged out upon the backs of horses."

Leaving the second lieutenant in care of the Tower during his absence, the two rode quickly out from the still dismal yard and made way to Richard's retreat. They had ridden for little more than an hour when they entered the yard of Baynard's Castle, and made their way to the chamber where Richard did wait.

"He is somewhat engaged at the moment, my lord, and I do not know if I may disturb him." Richard's personal guard answered Tyrell's request for entry.

"I think he may, my man. Come, let me try." The lord pulled out his dagger and rapped loudly upon the door with the butt, the sound echoing about the stone walls.

"Who knocks?" came the annoyed voice from within.

"'Tis I, sir, your servant, Tyrell; forgive me, sire, for disturbing you."

"Come in," the more cheered voice called. But how long would it be of cheer, worried Tyrell.

They came into the chamber and saw why Richard had desired not to be disturbed. He was in the process of entertaining three or four courtesans brought with him from the nearby palace. The Lord Tyrell, and the Officer Brackenbury stood in the middle of the chamber, not yet knowing their next movement, for Richard was lying aback upon the settle, barely clothed was he. Those garments he did not wear were strewn about the chamber as in some frenzied fashion. There he sat caring not as they stood their place.

"Come, come, my fellows." A wine-soaked slur painted his words, and they deemed he was in some high spirits, but he was a wily fox, and what you saw was not always what you reaped. They greeted him with due respect, but he cared not for such things at this time. They glanced at the ladies who waltzed about, which caught the eye of Richard, who deemed more should share his pleasures, or to be toyed with as such. He introduced one of the ladies sitting next to him to Tyrell, who was not so inclined to such activities. She beckoned him closer with her mouth speaking as foul as a fisherwoman, and tempted him with her bared enticement; but he cared little and stood his place to decline most gracefully the offer from Richard. But the lady still jabbered.

"Sires," she slurred, "come closer and show me your documents." The giggling words slid through the over-painted lips, as other lips about rang with muffled laughter.

Tyrell stood somewhat fazed by the situation, for the happier Richard became, the further would be the fall to reality and the worse would be his demeanour. He did fear most earnestly that more than the head of Brackenbury may roll from this untidy affair, and he wished not his own head to be tossed into the same cart.

The lady upped and made toward the stood lord. The steps she trod upon her heeled boots were not of the steadiest, though she did manage to bow before him in an enticing manner, with apples bobbing in some hidden water. As she rose she had to steady herself upon Tyrell's leg, clutching it in an unmistakable manner, which he allowed, for upon her drunken journey she was most happy to cling to anything that would steady her lilt.

"I would be most happy to see you at any time, my lord," she spake as she was able to release her grip, and then turning she swayed back to her place. She showed her back to the lord and to the officer. The gown she wore was seen to be open from the shoulder and continued down in a wide vee, not to her waist, but far below to reveal as much cleavage as the front did show. She glanced back at them as she walked away, and her thoughts were that she was desired, for the French gowns they wore were to this end.

The ladies went about in some giddy state beginning to dress Richard so he would appear more lordly to his guests. Upon finishing their task they were dismissed and did sway with their heeled lilt from the chamber to leave only their perfume to linger behind them. The room was emptied of any distraction, and Richard was of a more noble appearance. And so posed the question to Sir James."So, all is done, Tyrell. Is my path clipped of those bothersome thorns?"

"May I speak, sire, in my Lord Tyrell's place?" posed Brackenbury.

"What is this? No, you may not! I have given my orders to Tyrell and I need the answer from Tyrell … *So?*" The irritated Gloucester riled as Tyrell reluctantly spake.

"It is with much regret, my lord, that I have been unable to urge the lieutenant to do your bidding, for even under the threat of death he would not."

"*Would not? …* Would not! Tell me of this 'would not' Brackenbury," Richard ranted with glaring eyes.

"It is with heavy heart that I cannot obey your orders, my lord. I cannot kill two innocent princes who are of England's royal blood, for I am oath-bound to defend all royalty no matter who or of which is their rose. I am, my lord, a loyal servant and I have never before disobeyed an order, but this order I must, or I lie in hell's basket. If it is death that you place upon me, I would need no guard, I would need no shackles or blindfold. Tell me of what time and of what place you wish to execute me, and in all humbleness I will come. I will come alone to look a traitor amongst all good men. I have failed you, but I would give my life proudly for I did not break my oath and no man can do more. This order, sire, I cannot fulfill."

Richard and Tyrell looked at Brackenbury, for his words spake only of truth. Richard mulled that had he a son who was threatened, would he not pray that one such as this man would stand upon the same ground, and would not undertake such a foul deed.

"Fear not," Richard spake. "One with such devotion and loyalty I cannot lose." The duke could be most brutal but also most benevolent. He was a knight, and he knew that before him stood a brave and chivalrous man. Brackenbury had risked his life in defence of the crown. He could ask no more of any man.

"Guard!" called Richard, and quickly did enter the officer. "Take our good keeper to sup and make ready for him to stay the night, for such devotion shall have its reward." Our lieutenant left with a most grateful bow to the one who had shown him such benevolence. "Before you go, Brackenbury," Richard called, "leave with me the keys to the Tower, for I have need to keep them secure; place them upon the table before you depart."

"Yes, my lord," he replied and clinked the twine-tied lot upon the table, and, with more respect, he left the chamber with the guard.

Brackenbury supped most royally at the table feast set out in the warm kitchen, then when he was filled he was taken to a small antechamber where he was washed and shaved, and pampered as he had never been before, for lived he at this moment the life of a lord. He was then entered into a most regal bedchamber as fine as in his dreams and told of in tales he thought could not be true. Clean covers were his. A flagon of wine sat upon the table, as then to drink from the full goblet as he lay abed. The room was dimly lit with but a single tallow, not showing the dark corners that were as black as night there in those deep recesses. But felt he well content as the wine lessened in the flagon, and peaceful feelings lulled him. He heard the creak of the door from within the dark place where no light shone, and fear spread that wrath was upon him, for he knew that what men spake oft came from two mouths. He lay awaiting what may befall him. A last gulp of wine was swallowed, and he was resigned to the fate that was about to render him. He was not afraid for he knew his soul would be in heaven and not in damnation. Two shadows he saw close to his bed, shapes that held to him as yet no form. But before he could determine, came the heavy perfume wafting over his face and drawn into his nostrils. Two maidens he then saw, not bent upon murder, but bent on giving just and loyal rewards for such devotion to the monarchy. They slid into his covers sidling one each side of him. He became drunk with the heady perfume rendering him helpless. The warmth of the maidens' skin seemed to cover him from head to toe as he drifted. "If this be murder then carry forth your devious plot."

"So, Tyrell, what say you?" Richard posed the question, but heeded no answer. "Here are the Tower keys." He dangled them from his ringed first finger, showing them with some menace to the lord. "'Tis your task now; do not fail this time." They swung jingling close to Tyrell's face, who took them calmly off the finger offered, bowing as he did so.

"Aye, my lord," was the answer he gave with much disquiet in his voice, and sadness showing in his gait as he made toward the door.

"And Tyrell—" Richard spake once again.

"Aye, my lord?" Might Gloucester have noticed I still have my head? Tyrell pondered.

"Do it with haste, for too many hours have been wasted this day. And do not seek some other loyalist to stay you from your task, for 'tis your neck that lays bare now."

He left behind him the chamber so full of murderous words, and closed the black door to hide the evil, but it still did not sit well within him. He leaned upon the door's frame outside the room as if fatigued; he felt he had not the courage to commit the outrage placed upon him. With head low he thought for a moment more, then with a sigh he with troubled step made his way to the stables, and there mounted his horse and clopped away from the evil that was within the castle of Baynard.

The horse and rider made their way toward London, but shortly Tyrell diverted himself to a track that lay upon the way, covered with high overhanging trees and close bush. One cart's width was all that could pass this lane, which led to his manor, darkly hid along the twisting way. He entered the small courtyard, the house lay dim amongst the knit leaves that scraped and rattled against the dark stone. As he dismounted, the stable boy came running upon hearing the horse arrive; he took the bridle with a polite "Sire" in acknowledgement of his master; he then walked the horse gently away, talking to the animal in his child's voice as he did so, promising all good fare to the steed. Tyrell, only two paces into his walk to the manor's entrance, stopped and, turning slowly, looked back at the stable lad leading his horse away.

"Boy!" he shouted; as he did so call, his mind was amok with tumbling thoughts of whether he would be able to do that which jumbled his head, and to which would be the best tack to do such, and what fearful act would be bestowed upon him if the deed was uncovered. All these things milling at once in his mind as he became dazed with his thoughts; words then left his mouth, seemingly spoken by another being. "Come here, close." The lad turned the horse and came with hurried step and meek bearing, fearing for trouble coming his way.

"Sire?" he spake, not knowing yet the reason he had been fetched.

"Of what age are you?" Tyrell queried the lad.

"I am of eleven years, my lord."

"How do you speak with such educated tongue?" Once again Tyrell searched.

"I have been taught to read, sire, and have also schooled myself."

"You have no lilt of the London tongue. Where are you from?" The boy was getting concerned as the questions became more searching; he nervously brushed the hair back from his forehead. Tyrell's face then came close to the lad, and grasped his wrist as 'twas leaving his locks and looked at the hand he had clutched. Pale and soft it showed, though 'twas covered in grime; he turned it over, and holding the fingers in his hand looked at the boy's nails; though some dirt lay under them he could see they had been cut, and some were still very clean and cared for, as if in his waiting time he had been trying to keep himself in some respectable state. These were not the hands of a stable lad. Raggedy was his cloth but he was of straight back with some bearing to his frame. Tyrell stood back a pace and looked the boy over, pushing him around by his shoulder until he was facing him again. He saw his footwear, as stood he in sturdy leather shoes too rich for this boy. Others who worked the stables were bare of foot; or, if they were fortunate to own boots, they were of poor description and ill fitting. "Boy!" Tyrell held the lad by the collar of his ripped shirt and shook him as he tightened his grip, nearly lifting him from the ground. He spake not loudly but menacingly, pushing his bearded face onto the soft skin of his dangling prize. "You, sir, had better bring forth to me the truth of your situation for I know you not to be the lad you show me ... Choose well your words, for one more untruth and you will see not the morrow."

The boy swallowed, a lump in his throat as a chestnut, his knees as jellyfish, but he stood still as he was let to the ground, and though not in tears he was most fretful and feared for his life. "My lord, I beg you to forgive my childish ways of deceiving you; I am in fear, sire, and was trying to be truthful unto you, but the need was to protect myself. At this time I am a stable boy, my lord, but I am also the son of the Lord Ludlow who did lose all his lands and holdings and was cast out. When our beloved King Edward came to the throne we were left with naught but the tattered cloth we wear, and so our family made apart to diverse places so that we may survive, and may, with God's good grace, pray we become a family once again. My brother and I came to many places but there was no help for us in any part of the land."

"You have a brother with you? How old is this brother?"

"He is all but ten years of age, my lord."

Tyrell looked as if he had found two pearls instead of one in the latest twist that had befell him. "And of what demeanour is this brother? Is he a shadow of your kin?"

"Yes, my sire, he is very much so, and cannot be mistaken for my brother."

"Go on then, boy, get on with your tale," urged the royal officer once more.

"We came then, my lord, as stable boys to your manor and have been so here this past while—I cannot remember for how long but a winter did pass. Please, my lord, do not take revenge upon us for we meant no disrespect to your house."

"Take my horse and stable it, then come with your brother to my chamber, and be short time in your task."

"Yes, my lord." And with the polite bow of the gentry, the boy turned with Tyrell's horse and made his way across the courtyard to the stables. The lord then went to his chamber through the main door and along the passageway. So deep in thought and intrigue was he that he did not notice the flagged floor that was beneath his tread, or the bright tapestries that hung the walls, or even the maids who dipped in respect. Soon he found himself in his outer closet; his mind was so full he remembered neither the door that closed behind him nor the servant that stood.

The boy entered the stable and beckoned his brother. "John!" he called toward the dark corner that was their place, a half whisper, a half shout, and again he called, "John!" Then, with a rustle of straw, out from the shadows came his younger brother, whom he had been fathering until one day they could return to their family and all would be as before. He told John the conversation that had taken place with the Lord Tyrell, talking as he hurriedly took care of the horse in his charge; John then began to help in the fetching of water, and filling the feed box with oats as he listened to what his brother spake. They struggled with the heavy saddle but soon had it hanging in its place upon the iron pegs. The horse was soon content as it munched into its oats. They both quickly wiped it down so it would not shiver and catch a chill, placing a saddle cloth over it and tying it secure, their task now finished.

"What will he do, Paul? What will the lord do to us?" John asked.

"I know not, dear brother, but do not fret for our lord seems of a noble sire and I believe he means not to harm us; but we must go and do his bidding." They came together with hands clutched, as they crossed the yard with the wind-blown trees rustling about them to the entrance of the manor. The lord's first butler brought them in and took them to the door of the chamber wherein was their meet. He raised his hand to rattle upon the door but stopped before he did so, turning to look at his charges shaking there; he looked them over in despair, tut-tutting at the boys who stood dishevelled before him; he ran his fingers through their hair like a human comb, but to no avail, and then began pulling at the ragged clothes they wore, but no more could be done for them so tattered were they; he stepped back a little to look at them again, and shaking his head knocked upon the door; and, with the "Enter" only he heard, opened the door to the chamber.

"The boys, my lord," he spake as he pushed them in with the small of their backs, closing the door with a click of the latch behind them …

The Parliament were now arriving for their summoned council; there was no true feeling amongst most to the reason of their meet. Soon, after standing in the outer chamber, the numbers increased and many were gathered in groups mulling the reason for their call. Rumours came about of all different discourse but one was repeated more than the others, that was the bringing of the Lord Gloucester to the throne of England, which was met in quiet tone with tittering laughter and derisive jokes, for 'twas a fact that they had no cause to agree, for the Prince Edward was the only rightful successor to the throne that waited and no other had the right.

The great doors creaked open, and the musty smell from within stayed their chat as they shuffled in through the doors' gate; but, inside the Parliament, they began again murmuring the questions that lay upon their minds. The dark-panelled walls and oak benches a familiar sight to all as each made toward the place that over time was to their suiting. The light was shafting in from the windows that were placed on one side of the chamber. The other walls bore no openings and showed only the damp patches upon the stone where the rain would creep. Some soon were seated at their places, whilst others stood about, still talking of such acts they could not place.

In short time Buckingham entered with the Bishop of Bath at his side; they came to their place and the assembly all stood in respect of the king's Parliament. As they did so they saw not Richard's face and were surprised by such, for he had always been at his seat to see his desires flower. But he was absent, and though puzzling it eased the tensioned air of the chamber, for the anger that befell them often from the Lord Gloucester would not rage this day.

"Please be seated, my lords," Buckingham spake and waited whilst everyone settled into their places. "Thank you for your presence at this Parliament, my dear bishop, and I have a most painful task to bring to you this day, but pray at the outcome all will be appeased and in good frame within my lords. We come assembled here this day to put our dear Lord Gloucester forward as the only true leader and monarch of this Realm." All gathered listened intently to the opening speech, and did remain hushed as they awaited the reason for such a claim. "We hold a most disturbing document, that after this Parliament has heard all that is writ, you will be as one in our dear Richard's will to take upon himself this heavy burden of state." Rumblings of something foul floated about the chamber that tingled of another attempt by Richard for something unsavoury, for there was no reason upon God's earth that could bring such a deed about. "Gentlemen, I give the floor now to our revered Bishop of Bath."

"My lords, it is with heavy heart I bring forth to you this document." He showed it to all as he raised it above his head, waving it tantalizingly back and forth as an army's banner before the trooping soldiers. "This, my lords, is a wedding contract; it is a contract tying our late King Edward to the Dame Eleanor Butler. It is dated, my lords, as you will see, a full six months before the wedding of our said king to our Lady Elizabeth Woodville. Thus making the union with Elizabeth bigamous, for the king had not been granted any dispensation from Rome." The meeting then turned its face to shouts and discord and turmoil.

"No! No!" came the dissent from the floor. "Shame on you, Bishop!" came about the chamber. "Forgery!" was heard with many harsh words that did bandy about. The bishop waited for the air to calm and in little time did continue in the now quieted place, for the lords wished also to hear the other words that were writ upon the document.

"Also, gentlemen, this act so done places the royal children of Elizabeth's marriage into the state of illegitimacy, and as such renders them not of royal title." Once more the Parliament was in uproar at the latest revelation. Amongst the unrest, the bishop passed to the bailiff the marriage certificate with its broken seal of Edward's, but still seen as such with the royal crest showing clearly in the red wax that clung; he then took a pace and placed it into the reaching hands of the lord that was close. The lord brought it to his gaze as he read aloud from the paper he clutched. Others rubbed his shoulders as they craned for a closer look at the contract to determine its value. The paper was passed one to the other, and as they did so the bishop continued and began answering the many questions needed to be asked.

"I see, my lord bishop, that your name is struck upon the certificate of marriage, as having conducted the ceremony that joined Edward to the Lady Butler." The words came from within the throng that stood the floor of the chamber.

"That is so, my lord," did answer the bishop.

"In knowing such a marriage was still of legal binding, why did you not then bring to your archbishop the fact that the marriage to the Lady Elizabeth would be illegal?"

"Yes, sire, as you see 'twas I who conducted the ceremony of our Edward to the Lady Butler; by my signet upon the document I swore to such. I was indeed shook to illness on hearing that Edward was to marry Elizabeth without dispensation from the first marriage. But with haste I was called to the palace before I could submit any views of such to any person. To the palace, ordered by the king, I did go as the humble servant that I am, and under death's shadow I was reminded to remain silent on such matters, and, in the words of the king, 'I can soon get another Rome lackey to take your place.' I was then sworn once more upon the Bible to remain in dumb state, and so would my oath have stayed had it not been for the king's demise, and for the most loyal and honourable presence of Richard, who prayed with me to God to be relieved of this heavy burden, and in these circumstances I revealed to him the marriage document, and he was saddened by the devious act and was brought to tears in his dilemma."

"We believe all you have spake, for it comes from your lips, our dear bishop. If such is sought for Richard, and he indeed is deemed monarch of this land, to what would be the fate of the Queen Elizabeth and the two princes whose states are dire?" Another question floated to the table above the murmuring of the nobles, still unbelieving of such things that had passed before them. Buckingham stood, beckoning to the bishop that he would bear the questions.

"I put it to you, my lords, now that you know the true facts that have been placed before you, that the only choice for king is Richard, who has been a loyal and devoted servant to you all, for has he not increased your lands and properties manyfold since he took upon himself this heavy task of the Lord Protector? There will come forth, as you know too well, many pretenders to the throne of this land with their many intrigues, bringing this Isle into turmoil and rampage. And when these rebels finally bring forth a king, in what state will you, my nobles, lie? For if these pretenders are not of your ilk, then what say you, my friends, when your families, your lands, and your fortunes are all washed away, as the tidal sea washes all away in its relentless pursuit of the sand? And even if fortune smiles its happy face upon you, your reward would be that through all this mischief you may come from such with your life but with naught else. It is known to all that which has been writ in the past script of this land's bitter history; let us not writ another page such but say this day 'tis enough, and no more shall turmoil come upon us. Now, my lords, I speak of Richard, for if you place him upon the throne of this land your fortunes will not be forfeited, your riches will remain with you, and the bosom is where your families will lie. You will continue in the same manner as before and your state will be swelled, for Gloucester is of a most generous personage and doth give many rewards to his most loyal nobles."

The council was quieted even in the high, echoing chambers of the ceiling. The creaking of the rafters was all to hear as the regal chat floated about from the lips of Buckingham. "And, my lords, we assure you that our beloved princes will have not one hair upon their heads touched in this endeavour, and further that our dear bishop, who sits here in all his humble bearing, has given his personal oath that he will care and protect both innocents from all harm and to keep them in most royal comforts." The bishop nodded approval of this statement, clutching the cross that hung about him as he did so, bringing sanctity to the pledge he had given. "And of the Queen Elizabeth, whom Richard bears no malice or ill, and has always spoken of her with the most pleasant of tone, shall be given titled lands and properties befitting her state with a yearly income so approved by this Parliament. I rest, my lords, in my duties to this Parliament, and state to you that our lord, the Duke of Gloucester, at this time resides at Baynard's Castle, and is waiting, in all reverence and humility to you, our Realm's nobles, praying at the altar there that whatever decision you carry forward, he will, in all his humbleness and servitude, carry forth to your lords' desires. He prays there at Baynard's, for he wishes not his presence to affect your decision, and does await your pleasure."

The murmuring now was the murmur of agreement, not for their own avarice but for England. "Richard!" came the cry filling the air, seemingly from far aback where Richard's guards stood. "Aye, Richard!" was another cry, and then another and another. "King Richard!" was the next shout. "King Richard!" they all cried like rain filling a barrel until it all became one and overflowed. 'Twas done; the royal parchment was produced as if waiting for the word to leap upon the table. Buckingham read aloud the words writ, and then 'twas given the "Aye"—one lord at a time, until all present there had shouted for its passage and all were of much joy.

They made ready then for a most regal procession to go forth to Baynard's Castle, and to declare indeed that Richard was to be their king. All a-bustle 'twas in the courtyard of the Tower palace as they prepared for their journey. On entering the Parliament earlier in the day this outcome seemed an impossible quest and detached from all thought, but changed were they and joyful, for their lives would become abundant in all the things they treasured, without the troubles that an unknown monarch would bring, for naught could be gained to play Richard down; yes, indeed they had climbed the mountain and were now heading into the valley of abundance, and would forever roll in the clover of the gentry ...

The boys had entered into the Lord Tyrell's chamber. He stood with his servants about him, all looking at the boys and each with a task it seemed. Two of the servants, John Dighton and Miles Forest, beckoned the boys forward and took them both to the open window that they may see them more clearly; they both stood as the inspection carried on about them, still feared yet for what may come upon them.

"Clothes off, boys!" called the Lord Tyrell. They started to unfasten their ties as some of the servants began helping them to discard their rags. Soon they were naked and standing uneasy as they faced the group before them, stood they with clutched hands to comfort each other as they stood a-shiver. Maids bustled forward, and as they did so could be seen the large wooden barrels filled with hot water that had been hidden behind them; then gently they pulled the boys apart, and, lifting them, lowered each into the clean water of the barrels. The discarded clothes were quickly removed as one of the servants took charge of them, hurrying them away at arm's length to burn them in the pit that always smouldered, scurrying hastily before the fleas invaded his person.

"Hold your nose and duck under the water," came the instructions from around the barrels. The boys understood what was happening; they were being deloused and knew well the drill. They both dipped under the water with a deep gulp of air; no boys could be seen upon the surface water of the barrels; all was still; not even a bubble did show. Then something came to the top and floated upon the water, then again and again, the fleas and lice were coming to the surface to breathe; skimmers were at the ready, wooden rings covered in a rough cloth with a shaky handle bound to it; they skimmed it through the water's surface collecting all the vermin as it went back and forth, then banged them into another tub to drown. The boys came up for air, sucked in as much as they could, then disappeared again, repeated often until nothing came to the surface to be scooped. The brothers then were washed and scrubbed clean by the maids under the watchful eye of the lord. Two cherubs appeared from the grime that had painted them, as a slight smile came to ease the royal officer's troubled face. The lye that they were scrubbed with had given to them the glow of cleanliness. They were pulled from the tubs, then rubbed dry with the heavy course towels that were used also to dry off the horses. Soon the two stood. That skin that was once as white as snow was now red where they had been scrubbed and rubbed; shiny hair, dishevelled and looking like the rooster's comb, clean though for the first time in many months. They were sat side by side upon a bench with all manner of folk about them. Their hair was being worked as they sat with only the rough towel about them for warmth; their hands showed blue with cold, and shivering were they once again, not only with cold but also with fear, for they knew not yet what the game was to be played. For some reason the lord wanted the hair upon their heads to be of a light colour and not the mousy brown that grew; 'twas wetted with some cloth dye and soon came to the lightness that was required; and the shears clipped their song as the locks were cut to a more suitable length. They came next with the hot irons, those that were used by the ladies of the household, to bring out the curls and ringlets that were the fashion. They clamped and turned the boys' hair; the sound of sizzling and the smell of burning hair invaded the chamber, but in short spate the boys were the wearers of blond locks that curled about their heads with some hanging lightly above their eyes.

"Good," said Tyrell as he saw his tree coming to fruit. "Clothe them and let us see what we have." Clothing was brought forth, that which was used by the young servants in training, and most suitable for Paul and John, showing young lords and not stable lads. Soon they were dressed in blue doublet and short black breeches, with black stockings and shoes. Surely a royal couple of boys.

"Why are we treated so?" At last Paul could stay his mind no longer.

"Fear not, my child, we have some lordly children who are in need of some new friends to play with; they are tired of their play together and look for new companions. You will have much joy and good victuals and be well cared for; far better than the life of stable boys."

"Oh," was the only sound they uttered as Tyrell spake of his reasons for their change. They were then ushered out to a covered cart, leaving the servants and maids behind to clear the water-sodden cloths and to dry up the soaked floor, to empty the barrels, and to hastily bring the place to that which 'twas before as if naught had taken place. Left alone the servants started their play, and were soon laughing and giggling and running about, with false screams from the terrible men who were after their virtue, but somehow being caught and kissed, showing the resistance of a mouse, no master or head servant were about to contain them; they were free for a little while.

The boys were placed in the cart and covered with a canvas. Told to remain still and quiet, they huddled in their finery under the dark mantle, hearing only, seeing naught. "Mount up," they heard in the oily smell of their cover. They felt the cart move and the wheels roll and bump over the cobbled courtyard, shaking them like the sea rocking their little ship. On they went for may it have been but half of an hour, when they swayed a little and came to a stop, and heard then from a little distance the sound of many a fife and drum beating a steady march, the pipes filling the air with their lilt and of a crowd cheering and shouting. They could not contain themselves, and managed to pull up the corner of the canvas that tented them; the bright light squinted their eyes as they peeked at the parade that was coming close by. The cart had been pulled to one side of the road to let the procession pass. The bright, colourful sight came upon them and in all regality and pomp marched by, the swinging of the drumsticks, the sashes swaying with the walk all astep, the banners waving on high with the White Rose aloft all. Soldiers did march, striding proudly, fully armed with bright armour plates on show. Lords and bishops came horsed on their chargers, the saddlecloths fluttering with their coats of arms fresh in reds and blues and golds. The horses' fittings all at shine and glint clinking as they rattled by, more soldiers came, then came decorated wagons draped in bright silks, then more banners were marched by, until the music began to drift away as the parliamentary procession made its way to Bayard's Castle, and dust and banners were all that were left to see. Someone pulled down the canvas and all was dark again. Rattle, bump, they were on there way once more. Two ships passing both to different ends. On they trundled through uncobbled track and muddied way, then once again the cart was clacking over the cobbles until the wheels rolled quietly except for the click, click repeating itself, rolling noisily over the flagstones of the Tower courtyard. They stopped and the two boys could hear orders being given as the horses were dismounted, and the drivers of the cart quickly leapt to the ground and were heard removing the animals from the shafts, and then taken to the stables with the clatter of hooves lost; all seemed quiet.

The light filled their faces making them again peer through slitted eyes as the canvas was pulled from them. "Out you get me beauties." 'Twas the servant, Miles Forest, who called them out, with the other servant, John Dighton, standing close by; both were dressed in the garb of servants, but they were big rough fellows who it seemed were ready to do more dirty work than serving and fetching. Dighton carried a somewhat large box strapped to his back; it looked not too heavy but 'twas of some bulk, as he watched the boys clamber from the cart and onto the yard's stone. Tyrell held them back for a moment, his arm hung to block their path as he glanced about the courtyard looking for curious eyes that may be about; all seemed clear as he beckoned them on with a hasty wave. They made to a small portal covered in ivy, and with thick brush that hid the way to the black door unseen amongst the hanging cover. Tyrell jingled his key bunch and selected one that looked a fit; he rattled it in the lock but it would not open; he tried another and still it did not open. The two servants looked nervously about but all was still and they remained unseen; the two boys shadowed in by the two rough fellows hidden and unsighted to all who may pry. They could see naught, only the belts and buckles about them, belts that held sharp knives and daggers, which did not fray, for all folks who could afford such weapons did carry them. Another try with a rusty black key sprung the lock that held the oaken door. Tyrell clicked the latch; the wood creaked as it reluctantly let in the light and gave way to the beings that entered. They stood in a small closet as the door was closed, with the latch's click creaking loud in the dank place. 'Twas locked behind them as Tyrell withdrew the key from the rusty-edged keyhole; he looked at it closely in the dim light looking for some mark to remember which key he had used; he saw then V stamped upon the face; "Five"— he would not forget. The others waited whilst the lord was engaged in his musings, then he came pushing by them, to squeeze belts and knives against heads and ears with muffled ows as he did so, and pressing the smell of leather into their faces. They stepped to the bottom of some spiral stairs and looked up to where they disappeared into the darkness above their heads. The blackness under the stairs hid a place of secrecy with soft sand underfoot, a good hiding place that had been observed by Tyrell. They went up the stone steps of the little-used entrance single file; the lord leading, followed by a servant, the two boys holding hands for safety on the slimy steps, then, at the rear, the other servant, glancing behind him as he steadied himself, his hand upon the wet wall to help in his task. The steps were steep and there were many of them, the stairway becoming narrower as they climbed, made so that whoever had to defend the steps would only have to face one man at a time. A little stumbling came from the boys, as they struggled to lift their feet and legs over the high steps that were all uneven, built they of soft sandstone that had worn deeply in the middle from years of use, and a level footing was not always had. The boys wondered, as boys do, of how many feet had gone before them to have worn the steps so deeply, and who had trod this way, and for what purpose, and why, and when, and …

At last the door at the top came to view and once more the correct key was being sought; the jingle broke the trance of the boys. The keys were being tried more quietly at this door for it did lead into the passage where the princes' chambers lay. Quickly the key was found and the lock gently sprung, held back by the key in Tyrell's hand so the spring therein would be silent. He removed the key but kept it in hand. Gently he lifted up the latch pulling upon the door as he did so to ease the iron from the lock's gate, so that metal did not rub upon metal, which may disclose their presence. As he opened the door, he lifted it as best he could so the hinge would be less made to squeak. It seemed that the lord had been through these events many times before in his dark doings. He pushed his hatless head through the opening cautiously, though he did not expect to see any guards, for they were mostly placed at the main entrance and at the doors outside the passageway; but he still played his game warily for much was staked for him this day. All the other doors to the princes' chambers were locked and no entrance could be gotten there, and the only keys were held by the Officer of the Tower, who was now far from caring of this state, and such were clutched in the warm grasp of the lord.

They came out quietly into the torch-lit corridor; the boys did wonder of the strange entrance that had been chosen, but had no answer to such a scheme and just followed the black coats about them. No windows broke the walls, the torches burned their light continuously, and the air not so damp and musty as they reached the upper level of the Tower. Tyrell checked his key; he knew now they were all numbered, and saw this lock had been key eight as he clipped the bunch to his belt and pulled his coat over them. They took a few steps along the passage and came to the two doors that was the entrance to the princes' chambers. A fine doorway, heavily gilded, with the royal coat of arms carved deep into the frame above the door, covered in gold leaf and trimmed with royal blue and silver. Tyrell knocked quite loudly upon the imposing door; a small voice from within shouted, "Enter." Such a small voice for such a big door, thought John, his eyes levelled at the ornate door handle that soon became covered with the hand of Tyrell as he pushed it open and entered, followed by his servants and the two boys.

"My prince," said he, bowing lowly in deep reverence, and in so doing all followed his manner; the boys now realized that they were to be the playmates of princes. They had done such before when their father was the lord of many castles and manors and when they had much wealth. Oft times they were visited by the nobility, and did spend many hours at play whilst their parents attended courtly functions. The room, surprisingly, was not well lit and made some difficulty to determine what was about.

"What do you seek, my Lord Tyrell?" 'Twas Edward who, on recognizing his guest, queried his intention.

"My most royal prince, I come from your most loving uncle, Richard, whose heart is saddened that you are so kept here, and deems it will be soon that you can safely take up your rightful place in our Realm, for the heinous and crafty who are out to do you ill will soon reap their dire end. To bring some gaiety into your wait he has sent unto you two boys of lordly manner, who are pleasantly gifted to ease the burden of your keep." Edward peered around Tyrell to glimpse the boys, and in doing so, saw that they were of similar state to the boys of the nobles he had oft played games with; they stood attired mostly as the prince was, with light hair and dressed in likewise manner as berries upon a bush.

"Good, well done, my uncle. My dear sir, may I ask further of you this day, it seems the door between this chamber and my brother's is locked, and we have seen naught of each other for these past seven days."

"Say naught further, my prince, for the Lord Gloucester has instructed me to open the adjoining door so you may reunite with your brother Richard, and, with the two friends we have brought for your pleasure, we hope soon your heart will be uplifted." Tyrell went to the adjoining door with the prince's permission, murmuring a little as he searched for the right key. "Forgive me, sire, for taking so long; I am not familiar with the key." Edward said nothing but waited patiently during the lord's endeavours. Soon the lock dropped and Tyrell removed the key, but, before he could move the latch, it began to move on its own as he stared at the door, then to step back as the door opened with a quiet motion; then, half in one chamber and half in the other, stood the younger prince, Richard. "My prince," spake Tyrell, but he did not register one bit as Richard passed him by, and went to his brother's welcome with hugged embrace and tearful sob; he had been apart from Edward for some time and feared that they would not again be so close. The princes then broke apart as tears turned to sniffling for the younger boy, but still hands were joined for his comfort.

"My dear brother, it seems that our loving uncle has been in some distress at having to protect us in this way, and has sent the Lord Tyrell here with two lordly boys." The prince looked to them. "By what name are you?" he queried.

"I am Paul, my prince," he answered with refined voice, "and this is my younger brother John; we are most pleased to be acquainted with you once more."

"As you know, we are Edward and Richard, and wish you to call us such without pomp." The prince's eyes brightened, as thoughts of fun and play came bouncing forth from the mind that had struggled through much boredom. "We have swords and shields that the carpenters have made for us; now we can have some royal battles for I am well tired of winning over my brother." He said such with a wicked smile. The four left with much joy, from the chamber where stood Tyrell and his servants, to search out their warlike weapons in the second chamber.

The servants moved forward to the middle of the room as shouts rang from boyish mouths—they had found their weapons and turmoil would ensue. One servant helped the other to remove the box that he had carried. They placed it upon the floor and untied the rope that held it tight and removed the lid; they all peered inside. A feast there lay in the box, a feast for boys, of strawberries, of cream, of buns jam-filled, of small meat pies, of pork thinly sliced and fried, of Banbury tarts and Eccles cakes, and, ominously, wine for the quenching of the thirst of young boys who had little practice to taste the liquid of the grape, but no guardians this day watched over them. *The field had been ploughed and raked, and ready was the seed to be sown.*

Tyrell and his servants dismissed themselves from the melee that was about to start. The boys had entered the fray of battle upon this desolate moor that was their battleground. The swords clashed on shields and helmets, with cries of anguish that flew about as first one fell to the mighty sword then another, only to rise up again and continue to fight once more.

"My lords, there are victuals at your ready; we will leave you to your victories."

"Aye!" was the faraway answer, for who could talk of aught when battle raged?

They left them to their foray and awaited outside in the passageway, knowing that soon thirst and hunger would claim them, and that the victory feast unattended by adult persons would be as a feast of soldiers victorious, and naught would be the boundaries of sup and bite; they would gorge and drink as warriors until they fell.

The battle late was done after many escapes and bloodied sword; they came to the chamber where lay all the victuals; they came still with swords in hand, belts slimly at the waist, buckled with the close combat daggers sheathed there, helmets askew, all red-faced with beaded droplets running down, for if one fought such battles then this was the feel, to be master of the sword and slayer of all that is evil. They sat wearily, cross-legged on the rush-covered floor, still in their battle harness with the swords laid down beside them at the ready, for they would not be surprised by any that may skulk about. They picked from the wares big red strawberries and dipped them in the clotted cream from Devonshire, and slowly placed them into the soft tastebuds of their mouths, sucking the sweetness off the green stalk and flicking it at their comrades. The fruit filled their mouths and melted there with the flavour of nectar slipping down their parched throats. "Drink we need," said one of our soldiers as they pulled out the keg of wine, then came a glint of mischief passing from one to the other as their eyes met in the dim room. They pried out the bung of the keg with a knife that lay upon the table, a cheese knife but well suited for the task, and, found in the box, silver goblets to hold their prize. 'Twas poured as each one gazed at the ruby liquid filling their vessel. They sniffed it before drinking to have upon them some idea of what would be the taste; a musky smell, sweet and beckoning, drifted to them, sparkling their eyes with devilment, and was most appealing to their dry throats. "To battle!" was the cry as they clinked their goblets and drank into the quenching liquid. It slipped like honey down their rasping throats, the taste better by far than anything they had ever supped before. At their castles and manors they had drank the drink of the young, the fruits of blackberry, of raspberry, cherry, and loganberry, which were all crushed together then strained through muslin cloths into the kitchen jugs, and brought to them to sup at their pleasure; the drink so sweet and rich, gallons they could easily sup, but they were never allowed to drink too much for their parents were concerned of the soft stool it produced, and were feared it could be the start of dysentery, which most times brought death upon those who were inflicted. But this drink was different, not as fruity but sweet liken to honey; they drank it down with much vigour, for this warlike activity brought upon them great thirst. They ate more, the pies and buns quickly eaten up; they drank more as the cask was passed around and each one filled up his goblet. Strange laughter came to be bantered about, laughter that for some reason rang in their ears as if they were in some cave deep in the ground; the wine was being slopped as hands and heads became unsteady, but they noticed not such things. Still they shouted with slurred words about the great victory they had won this day, and started into some bawdy songs as soldiers do at their victory feasts, for come the next battle they may not be the ones who rejoice such, so all good had to be made of this moment for like times may be few. The cask was passed about once more to fill the swaying vessels, but only two goblets came to fill; the other warriors lay slumped upon the rushes, no longer thirsty, their battle was done, as goblets lay, tipped, flowing the wine upon the stone floor.

Outside the doorway the trio of doers listened and waited; they heard the battle's lull and all was then as still as the midnight's hour. The three cronies of Richard waited a little longer, and when some time had passed they gently opened the door to the chamber and saw the four innocents all asleep, dreaming the dreams of boys. They entered in there; Tyrell clinking his keys and springing the lock to close behind them, now in all privacy were they. Moving slowly into the room, they picked up Edward and placed him upon the bed within the chamber where they had eaten; then they did place his brother by his side, carrying them like puppets at the fair, lifeless things with arms dangling and heads aside. They gently lifted the covers over them so only their sleeping heads showed.

"The wine in these brats make them more to my liking," spake the servant Forest as they each took one of the flopping boys to the next chamber to be apart from the princes; for murder soon will come and two bodies not of royal stock were to be done.

"Aye, and a few jiggers of gin in the barrel makes it the more potent," Dighton conceded as they laughed the laugh of villains. They laid down the brothers, Paul and John, who stirred a little as they were placed upon the cot in the far chamber; the covers were placed over them as they lay upon the straw-filled mattress there. Gently, with quiet tread, they left the chambers and met once more with Rivers who stood in the passageway.

"We will let them settle for a little before our action is carried forward. Do not forget this day, my friends, for murder now comes most evil. The princes must not be harmed and will be taken to sanctuary; the two other boys will be sacrificed, for two bodies are needed of princely gaze for our dear Richard to note of their demise. And further, in the name of God, if any whisper of this day escapes your lips, the lamp of incense will be swinging for you and you will be of clay!" They nodded to the statement made to them and agreed to all that was spoken, as they had done many times before.

They talked outside the chamber in whispers, letting time slip away and slumber deep to come. Inside the room, though, Edward had awakened somewhat and began to shake his brother's slumped body, and began speaking to him in slurred tone. "Brother, we have not danced with the maidens upon our victory feast as true warriors do on such occasions."

"What say you, brother? You want dancing?"

"Aye, I want dancing as the warrior wants dancing. Come."

He dragged the limp Richard from his slumber, and across to the other sleepers who lay with heavy heads. "Wake! Wake!" shouted Edward as he shook the boys from their slumber.

"What is it?" John asked fearful of what may be afoot.

"We did not dance the victors' dance with the maidens." Edward nearly fell over backwards as he breathed his sickly breath over the two boys. He dragged them from their sleep and pulled them roughly from the bed, all swaying as if stood upon a rocking boat. "The victors' jig!" shouted Edward as he began to dance about the chamber, twirling and falling and rising to dance again as if all were part of the steps that went with the jig. The others joined him, if only to be rid of the dance so peace may come to their heads so sick. Soon all were stepping out with spinning and stomping to the sound of the lute that rang in their heads. They fell and jumped quickly up to fulfill their act of triumph—one more goblet of wine they took as they staggered about, falling then to sleep where they stood. But cold and hard was the floor and even in their stupor they upped and went to find some soft bed to lay upon. Richard crawled on hands and knees, for to walk on sea legs he could not. He made soon to his bed and did climb in, but it seemed there was little room, and through beady eyes saw there were two already abed; so on his knees, once again, he made his way to the next chamber and found there the bed with but one that lay in sleep's folds; he climbed up from the floor to the mattress, and soon lay in slumber, though the bed swayed and rocked to spin him into some unknown state he had not known before.

The waiting party amid their own yawns, opened the door gently to see the princes' pillowed curls, both in deep respite were they as they lay in their rolling bed. Tyrell waited without the chamber, as his two servants entered to do their grisly work. Past the sleeping princes they slithered with their evil intent and into the chamber where lay the two boys; heard were the sounds of heavy breathing, the sound of the deep induced sleep, the last breathing sleep. The servants slinked into the gloom. One each side of the bed, and with gentle act did take the pillows from beneath the golden locks. They looked at each other in the dim, as only white of eye did show. They dropped the pillows onto the faces of the numbed sleepers, and held them tightly there for they expected a struggle for air for which their lungs would crave, but so drugged were they from the wine they had taken, little was felt from either, and their dreams flowed into blackness, and death was upon them in the cold room of the Tower. All was done as they took away the pillows and looked down with little feeling upon the still shapes beneath them; they came close to the boys' faces and could hear no breathing, and deemed that death was here. Dighton and Forest were of a most devious personage and wished to end the deed with the blade, but bloodless was the order, for if something went awry the bodies would not be bloody, and the death that overtook the princes could be deemed a natural demise. They lifted the limp bodies and in silence carried them through the chamber where the princes lay, and out into the passageway where awaited the master of the deed.

He gazed at them as he gently closed the door to the chamber. "Are they finished?" he asked as he moved toward the one held by Dighton; the boy's arms and legs dangling without life as he looked the boy over, pulling the head to one side and feeling the neck below the ear as the boy was held towards him. He felt for the beat in the vein there, of which his barber-surgeon had related to him 'twas the way to see if life remained in the body. Tyrell had practiced the act upon the surgeon, and felt life being pumped through such a place. He searched the neck of the boy and found no life; he tried again fearing he was not on the right vein, but all was still beneath his fingers and he could feel the skin cooling. He went to the next boy and felt the area where the spot lay. His stomach turned and came up to his throat; he could find life still beating in the small frame. "This one is alive, you fool. Do you not know death when seen?" Forest lay the boy down on the stone of the passage and in that dim light moved his hand toward his dagger, to finish the job as he felt should have been done from the start, for when blood did spurt from the neck's slash 'twas over. He had never seen anyone rise from such a wound, but he was stayed by the hand of Tyrell. "Get once more the pillow and finish it bloodless; you know well it has to be so." Forest moved once more into the room, cursing the lord with his uppity ways; once more past the princes he went, glaring at their royal pose laying there. A quick slash, thought he, and there would be two less to order me about; but he went into the far chamber and retrieved the pillow that would end it. He came out with it and began to hand it to Tyrell. "Finish it. Your task awaits not mine." Tyrell pushed it back toward his servant. Forest pushed the pillow once again onto the young face, holding it tightly there as they watched in the chilled night to another life gone. The servant lifted off the pillow so that Tyrell could try his skill once more and see if life was still within the boy; he felt for a moment and determined that indeed the boy had succumbed and was dead.

The servants followed Tyrell once more down the stone stairway, young bodies slung over their shoulders to clear the narrowness of the walls. As they reached the bottom, Tyrell pointed to the dark place under the stairway, the place where he wanted to hide them in that black corner. The servants placed the bodies down, and with bare hands moved away the soft sand therein to make a shallow hiding place. They lifted the boys into the hole and arranged the arms and legs to fit more discreet, then covered them over with the sand, which they levelled so it looked as it did before, left in this place until Richard had been told of the deed done, and to what end he wanted next with Edward and Richard.

"Wait in all discretion by the cart and I will bring down the princes," Tyrell spake as he unlocked the door to the yard that they may wait there for his return. He upped once more the dingy wet steps of the staircase; to the top he went and peered again into the empty passage, then went quietly to the princes' chamber and inside did slip, his dark figure came to the bed of the siblings.

"My princes," he spake in hoarse tone so as not to startle them. "My princes," he said once more as he gently shook their shoulders. Again he shook, and again; they were so drugged he had to shake them with more vigour, and his words came forth with loud call as he shook them awake. "My princes! Wake! Wake!" And at last they began to stir from their respite.

"What is it?" a disturbed voice from the covers spake.

"My lord, it is your most loyal servant, Tyrell."

"What do you want, Tyrell?" came the voice that wished to be left alone.

"My princes, you are in much danger here; there is a threat to your lives. I have come at others' bidding, as well as for my own loyalty, who deem it their duty to bring you forth from this act. Please come with me from this place so plagued with evil, so I may place you in a more secure state."

"Does my uncle Richard know of this?"

"Yes, sire, he sends me to rescue you from this ungodly scene." The two innocents managed to arise with much swaying and unsteady bearing. "We must move you in much secrecy. Please do not be feared, for we are most loyal and care only for your well-being." Tyrell held the hand of one, who held the hand of the other, and led them from the room, only releasing the hand to lock the chamber's door; he moved to the hand again and led them across the lit passage to the door at the top of the stairs. Inside now he pushed past them and found the key to the door from his bunch and sprung the crusty lock. He slid back once more to clutch the small hand that was offered, the hand that sought safety in this black hole. They started down the steps. "Be wary of your tread, my princes, for these steps are most difficult." They could not move; the dark was overwhelming; the steps slippery and worn. They sat upon the top cold stone, both with heads resting in their hands, trying to stop the dizzy games that fluttered within, and the sickness that lurched in their stomachs; they could not, would not be moved. Tyrell came and picked up one of the royals, breaking the clutch that held tight to the other's hand. "Sit still, sire, I will fetch you in one moment; hold to the stone's edge and do not let it go." He carried the first one down and leaned him against the bottom step. "Hold there, my lord," said he as he went to get the other swaying boy. "Come, sire," he grunted from his stair climbing, and, breathing heavily, lifted him upon his shoulder and carried the second one down to the bottom. When he placed the boy down he saw that that the first prince had slid down and was slumped sideways; his head lay in the soft sand near the underside of the stairway. He pulled him up and placed the prince's hand back into the hand of his brother.

Tyrell slowly pushed open the door to the courtyard to spy his two servants waiting there crouched by the wagon; they saw their lord at the open door and came over to him, then each took one of the princes and lifted them into the wagon, covered them with a blanket, and pulled over the canvas cover to conceal the royal cargo. Tyrell jingled his keys once again as he locked the door behind them and came to the cart. "Take the royals to the manor and mind you treat them with respect. If they awake, be secretive in all you say and do, for the little they know will suit. I must seek Richard at Baynard's Castle to see of what he may desire of us next. I will return to the manor with haste for we still have much to do." The servants mounted the cart and struck their way to the manor house, whilst Tyrell took the other tack and headed to the one who will be king.

Chapter Seven.

Devious Games.

Richard's informant from the Parliament had ridden forth with haste far ahead of the official party who slowly made their regal way. He came as directed to bring to his master the outcome of their meet that day, for though Richard wished to be surprised, he had no doubt of the outcome that the dusty traveller would bring. The rider arrived at Baynard's Castle and dismounted in the courtyard. He entered the great door where stood the guards, tall and shiny; they knew of this man and he was quickly beckoned forward to set his step to the chamber of his dear Lord Gloucester.

Our soon king waited, not so much in holy prayer, but with his young niece, Elizabeth Plantagenet, the two enraptured by each other's company and tasting the joys that came from such a liaison, both filled with playfulness as they awaited the message from the Parliament. The Lady Elizabeth, daughter of the King Edward and Queen Elizabeth, pranced about, her dress below her bosom in reckless mood, arms about Richard's neck with the most tender caresses when the knock awaited came upon the door. She slipped off her lover in no haste to cover herself, but stood provocatively leaning upon the settle as was her way, always filled with mischief and dare. The servant was bade to enter by Richard, and came he more into the room than was usual so he could speak to the lord more discreetly in his musings; he whispered softly of the arrival of the lord's informant, glancing as he spake with much discretion at the soft plumpness that showed of Richard's companion, which brought a favourable smile from Elizabeth, as she flaunted herself in her usual girlish way.

"Why you whisper, I know not. Bring him forth. Let us hear what he has to say."

Richard spake as the lady pulled up her lowered dress to appear more demure in her manner. The servant left the room but with not the gait he had entered; his voice was heard calling the informer forward to have audience with the Lord Gloucester. He came in, bowing lowly at Richard who stood before him.

"My lord—" he started to speak, but was interrupted by Gloucester, the one who did stand in some mood of impatience; first a dribbling servant now someone who wants to bow and grovel.

"Rise and come here, man, and stay this time wasting hogwash; tell me of the news you bring."

He came forward as beckoned, a strong man, set thick and shaved clean, his hat clutched under one arm, his other hand lay upon the hilt of his sword, his belt and harness were wet with sweat and mist as the leathery smell drifted about him. Elizabeth perked up noticeably at the sight of the rider and his stirring aroma that came about; the sweat from his horse that still clung to his breeches added to the earthy smells that he brought. She looked at him through lowered eyes as innocently as she could with all kinds of desires running through her young body. A look from Richard, which would wither many a man, only made her giggle in her childish way, and he could do naught about this woman–child who could render him as helpless as any who saw her joyous pleasure.

"The Parliament are on their way as I speak, my lord, to offer you the crown of England, which was granted as your right this day. May I, in all my humbleness, congratulate you, sire, and add that I will always be at your command and your most loyal servant."

"Yes, yes—how far are they aback of you?"

"They are but a half of the hour away, my lord"

"Good, good, good." Richard was pleased by the message. "Your service will be well rewarded. Depart, my man, for I must prepare myself for their coming." And with a pleasing "My lord," and "My lady," he bowed his departure, as he took a quick glance at the demure and innocent-looking lady that delighted his eye, and who stood at Richard's elbow and gave the rider her wicked smile as he departed the chamber, and knew when it came to loyalty Richard indeed did keep his promises of reward.

"Begone, my hussy," Richard whacked at Elizabeth's rear as he spake, "I have to become surprised and humble." The crooked smile he gave suiting his stature.

"No, my king, I will not!" Elizabeth defying and teasing, leaning over so her bosom showed almost fully. "I will not!" Standing up she with legs apart and with hands upon her hips stood daring her lover.

"You vixen, go now. Time runs short."

"If you can catch me, then I will go." She, lifting her skirts above her knees, showing her white stockings, ran from Richard to safety behind the broad oak table, mocking him to catch her. "Come then, my big brute king, come on, catch me."

Richard leapt at her, sliding across the polished table taking Elizabeth so much by surprise, her knees trembled though she knew 'twas only a game, and her game to boot. She ran, skirts hitched once more squealing as she went to the adjoining door, which stood half open; she managed to gain the room but before she could fully close the door, Richard was upon her, snarling and growling liken to some evil animal; she tried to escape but he had caught hold of the back of her dress, pulling her to the floor with squirming giggles, kicking and screeching; she tried with timid strength to push him off, but all was lost for he was too powerful for her willowy frame; up came her dress above her waist, her underclothes gone in earlier games, she was a lady defenceless. "No, no, sire, please do not sully me, for am I not a pure maiden?" Her pleas mattered not as Richard took her as she lay in tousled array.

Soon all was calm again as Richard rolled off his Elizabeth; she still of mirth as she saw his rumpled sight. He with fatigue trying to lift himself but finding much difficulty in doing so.

"I must ready myself," he said. "Time is becoming short." His face still red from his exertions he started up at last, but was pulled back to the floor again as Elizabeth tried to pull down his breeches, while Richard tried to pull them up.

"My lord!" A voice shouting called to Richard.

"Yes?" replied the lord, still trying to break free from the clutches of his mistress who seemed to have a dozen hands.

"Pardon me, master." 'Twas one of Richard's servants who called, for when not receiving any answer to his repeated knock, had entered slightly into the outer chamber to see if all was well, to peer in, and to call to his master. "Sire, there is a delegation of lords entering the castle wishing audience with you."

"Bid them up to my chamber, and make known my surprise that these honourable guests should be calling upon me this day. Relay to them that I am just leaving from my prayers and will be with them most hurriedly."

"Very well, my lord, I will relay your message to them." The servant waited outside the door of Richard's chamber as the party arrived and did relay the message so given to him. They stood there await, for they knew that the time of prayer was most sacred and understood their arrival to be of some surprise, and giving them some time to dust off their clothes and to stand supping a goblet of wine, which was offered to them.

"Get off me, woman; I am in much haste, can you not see?" Richard was showing some anger as he was not able to make himself ready.

"Ooh," Elizabeth cooed with hurt tone in her voice. "You are frightening me, master." And then in her baby voice teased, "Please do not punish your humble niece; please do not tell papa." Richard was able to straighten his clothes as he shook his troubled head at Elizabeth's games. He brushed his dress with the palm of his hand trying to make the rumpled clothes smooth again but they seemed as if they would sooner stay rumpled. He found upon the floor his prayer hat that had been strewn about during the rumpus, and put it on his ruffled mop, then touched the hair that showed into a more fashionable state.

"My lord," he heard from the outer chamber. "Your guests have arrived." The servant unable to delay the party any longer had to admit them into the room to await the Lord Gloucester.

"Coming!" he called to his servant as he heard the voices of the delegation making their way into the chamber. Picking up his Bible and at the same time blowing the dust off it, he began to open the door to greet his guests, but difficulty had come upon him for he seemed to be held back in his progress. Elizabeth had placed her hand into the top of his breeches and was pulling them back and down. Quickly with his free hand he roughly pulled her hand away to free himself. "Ooh," again he heard from behind him as he was then able to go forward.

"My lords, I am deemed most pleased that you are visiting me upon this day. To what do I owe such pleasure?"

"My dear Lord Gloucester." 'Twas Buckingham who spake; he had been the one selected as spokesman for all gathered there. "We come all in deep homage, sire, to you upon this joyous occasion, and wish to state that after council at this day's Parliament we have all agreed to solicit you to become king of this Realm. We would deem it most pleasurable if you would give us your aye to this request, albeit the shadow of the terrible illegitimacy of the two royal princes still saddens us so."

"My dear lords, I am taken aback with surprise that you would, in all this land, have chosen such a humble person as myself before all others who are far more worthy than I. But, my lords, if it is your wish then I humbly fall upon my knees before you, and will, in all goodness and loyalty, take to me this heavy task." And he fell to his knees before them in such humble state; the lords somewhat puzzled by the red perspiring face that gazed at them from beneath the prayer hat, with thoughts, though, of a very robust service indeed.

"Nay, my lord," the lords urged Richard to rise from his pose. "We humble ourselves before you, our King Richard. Aye, King Richard!" they chimed and all knelt before the chosen one. Richard was then helped to his feet and made most reluctantly to stand before his honouring subjects. The dark eyes of the mistress Elizabeth peered through the narrow slit of the door with a little smile upon her painted lips. She knew that never could she be queen, even if Richard's wife were dead, for to marry her would not strengthen the crown nor bring fortune to it. But Richard's wife, Anne, was in ill health, and, if she was no longer a door between them, she would be more to Richard than a mistress; a queen without title would suit finely.

Estates and riches would abound, as delight fluttered within her.

Richard went hand to hand now, thanking each of the lords gathered and to speak of rewards for such loyalty they had shown. With Buckingham knowing of all so gathered he would reap the most, for the hand of Richard was in comrade with his. Though for the first time he was feeling a disturbing ache within his body, for he knew that this act of making Richard king would end the lives of two innocent princes, and he was mired in the same mud that clung to Gloucester. Now that Richard was to be king, it may pass that his act toward the princes may mellow, and Buckingham would use all the power he had to persuade his comrade to be more lenient, and to stay any violence. He had decided, with God's help, that he would do such and try to stave off the dreadful act; he felt easier that he had some hope within himself. He continued again with his lordly duties as chief adviser to Richard; the ache that dwelled was no longer within him.

All were engaged in setting the date for Richard's coronation; 'twas suggested to him that the sixth day of July would be most apt, which was well agreed to. They all were stood, talking amongst themselves, sipping the wine so well provided and standing about in merry groups; the end to their meeting was nigh.

Came riding into the courtyard at Baynard's Castle, as all the lords were so gathered there, Lord Tyrell, showing all discreet as he kept close and secret to the walls, and did not dismount until he was within the darkness of the stables; the stable boy took the horse from him with a "My lord" as it clopped into the black of its stall. Tyrell entered through the kitchen as he had done times before, for such dealings were to him ordinary in nature. All were at work therein, cooks and helpers, servants and maids, all about the steamy place; some sat at the table having their meal whilst things for them were at a lull. Not all saw Tyrell enter but those who did acknowledged him with due respect. He caught hold of one of the servants by his arm, who had been a contact for him on previous occasions, and talked closely into his ear, informing him to make it known to Richard's head servant of his arrival and that he would await the Lord Gloucester's pleasure. The servant took the lord to a closet so he could bathe and refresh himself. First he had to make use of the privy, and on entering was pleased that 'twas empty, for he wished to be in secret and not to converse with anyone. Quickly he was in there and quickly he was out, taking care of his own bathing, and back within the closet in good haste. Victuals had been placed there in his absence, with a large pitcher of inviting ale. He poured the brown liquid into the tankard until it frothed over, and whilst it still ran down the sides of the vessel he drank it down without a breath drawn between. He sat and troughed into the meat and bread and cheese, and pouring once more another tankard he drank but half this time, as the hunger and thirst that he had entered with was with him no longer, and he was now satisfied, filled and clean once more, the mud and dust gone.

Almost as he wiped his whiskers, a knock did sound upon the door. A quiet questioning "My lord?" he heard.

"Yes," he answered, wiping the grease and ale from his mouth with the linen cloth there placed, picking his teeth as he stood, twisting the wooden needle through the gaps around them and flicking bits of grease and gristle all about the table and onto the floor as he did so; no matter, the mice would soon clean it up, except they would replace it with their own droppings.

"Lord Gloucester sends for you, sire."

Tyrell came to the door opened for him, to thrust the soiled cloth and toothpick into the hand of the servant; he brushed past him as he went down the passage to the closet where he was to meet with Richard. A guard stood close at the entrance; he on orders clicked the latch open then pushed the door wide, and with a bow stepped aside so that Tyrell could enter freely. He entered the closet as the door once more closed behind him; he stood alone in the small room maybe of ten paces each way. The light came from a high westerly window, and at this time was still bringing its light upon the dull stones of the place. Two rough benches and a planked table the only furniture therein; no tapestries or paintings hung the walls to bring some cheer to this drab corner. He sat at the end of the bench and looked straight before him at the blackened door, the door from which Richard would enter. No more the thought as quickly did swing the door open and Richard was standing there before him, showing upon his face some princely troubles.

"My dearest Richard, I hope that now I may call you your Majesty?"

"You may call me so, my dear Tyrell, as in all reverence I have indeed been given the honour of ruling our great land. To more disturbing things though I must turn, my lord, to hear from you the outcome of your task that bedevils my soul with such anguish."

"I bring such facts, my king, of heartache, in that our two royal princes have suffered to have their lives ended this day so bright, when it should be dark with gloom."

"Oh, no, do not tell me such, for were not those royals the joy of my life?" Richard spake in riddles, as a piece of string with one end, so difficult to fathom was he. "I am so deeply saddened by such tidings. We must seek out those who have done such a villainous act, and all revenge must be brought down upon them. Do you know Tyrell who is responsible for so terrible a deed?"

"I do so, my lord, and would deem it my honour to see these evil persons murdered, and with pleasure will carry out such entitlement."

"Be it so, my dear Tyrell, for I wish not to know who they are, for I am grue with such doings. I wish no more blood upon my hands as I am come of kingly stature. Where are the princes at?"

"They are kept in secret, my lord, at the Tower, far from persons and not seen. I beg your forgiveness, my king, in such that I broach, but is it your wish to see the children so that with your own eyes you may see them lifeless?"

"You tell me they are so, Tyrell; that is all I need, for I have all trust in your allegiance to me. And so foul would be my vengeance upon any mistruths that I know, for fear of such, no lies would come for 'twould be folly. They though are of royal blood and must be given prayer and proper rites as befits their standing, for cursed would we be to shy from such. Get the priest from the Tower to remove them from their place, and to take them afar, unknown to all, and to bury them with all reverence."

"I will in all haste do as you bid, my king."

"The valuable service you have given us has placed you in such high esteem that any favour we may grant will be laid before you, and the reward for your actions will be large. I tell you though you must make concealment of yourself for many a while, until all manner of this deed so wickedly done has been dulled, for there are many spies about who may try to use such things against us, and no doubt would seek you out and through devious means bring forth some ill-gotten lies to bring down our royal self. But, when all is forgot, you may return from such concealment; your lands and estates will await you and will be duly increased in soil and in gold. This must be done for our greater safety. You will be allotted such benefits to keep you and your loved ones in a goodly state of luxury for a full five years to keep you within our gratitude."

"I am honoured to be held in such high esteem, for I feel that I am but a lowly servant to you, my lord; I am indeed blessed to be able to serve you, my king."

"We have prepared a writ for you to be taken to the treasury where you may obtain the monies I have pledged. The writ comes with the royal seal of the king and is fact. Tyrell, finish up your business and be as the doe in the morn's mist."

"Aye, my lord king." He knelt and took the rolled document; 'twas wrapped with blue ribbon with the royal signet waxed upon it. He accepted it from his king and kissed the ringed finger that was offered and departed his audience.

He left the castle of Baynard's in the dimming light and slowly was swallowed in the cool mist; soon being no longer seen, as a dream forgotten, Tyrell rode to the treasury that was at the Tower to obtain his pledge. He arrived in short time and tethered his horse to the wall ring; he did not stable it for short would be his time here. With a few strides he was at the portalled gateway to the treasury, which was heavily guarded; two soldiers stood close to the gateway and two more lingered about under the dark walls almost unseen. Tyrell waved his writ in front of the guard there who was barring his entrance with a mean gaze upon him. The royal seal thereon was floating at the guard's eyes and changed the features to a more willing state.

"This way, my lord," he said, and with the guard ahead of him, he was walked to the treasury along some dimly-lit passageways, up worn steps of stone and low archways, and thought it may be difficult to steal from this place for the way to freedom would be hard to recall. They came then into a small guarded area, with the keeper of the king's treasure looking a scholarly scribe from the little that could be seen of him. He was seated there at the lonely table hiding behind neat stacks of scrolls and documents, to show only the bald head in the candles' light, but the scratching of the quill made it known that someone was awake behind the sheets. The scratching stopped and Tyrell was able to see more of the head and was taken back a little by the sight of the keeper. How could someone so old and withered still be alive? he thought after seeing more of him; a bony hand stretched up from out of the grave. He placed the scroll in the bones and watched as it floated from his sight to be hidden behind the papers high. A strange squeak came from the mouth of the clerk, which appeared to be his voice, quite worn out it seemed from more than a hundred years of chat.

"My lord," he said in a somewhat uncaring fashion, for living past his supposed lifespan he had naught to fear of death, and so treated all his fellow men with disrespect, whether lord or peasant, and cared he not for any banter. Tyrell heard the seal being broken and the scroll unrolled as then silence came about. Two aged eyes looked over the pile upon the table and peered at the Lord Tyrell.

"Guards!" the voice came all nurdled* and stiggy.** Two guards immediately came forth and stood behind the treasurer; the scroll rose higher, floating upon dead fingers so the guards could see that which was written thereon; they looked at the document held there and then both raised their gaze to Tyrell. A sickness came over him. Had he been plotted to his

---

* *nurdled* [coined] croaky
** *stiggy* [coined] squeaky

death by Richard? For he knew not what was contained in the scroll.

"Guards!" again was called; one of the soldiers, an officer that stood aback of the treasurer, shouted his order, a more commanding voice was this one. Tyrell felt them stand each side of him as if detained. The treasurer stood but seemed no taller standing or sitting; he floated along as if by a breeze, for a wind would have been too fast. He went to the iron gates that stood in the darkness behind him, his keys rattling as the gate was opened, like the sound of a prison door it swung. Tyrell was wary of what may come, but no movement was made toward him. It came upon him that all was for the security of the treasure so held here, and not to detain him. The guards followed the jingle of the keys into the dark; the flicker of the candle carried played the shadows upon the grim walls; mumbles and cursing came from within as they dragged about the moneybags. Then, out of the black grave, came the ghost of white gliding toward his table. The two guards followed him out, carrying the coin in brown bags of canvas, all dusty and bundled tightly, they stood behind the seated keeper holding securely onto the heavy bags. Scratch, scratch. Tyrell heard the familiar sound again as the quill made its mark.

"Sign here," the squeaky voice ordered, as a paper receipt came over the piled table, then appeared a quill held in stained fingers. "Sign the document … You can sign your name, can't you?" Tyrell noticed the remark little as he signed with shaking hand the receipt note for five thousand pounds, a royal amount indeed. The keeper took the signed paper and the quill back, with no word spake, for to him 'twas monies from his own purse and 'twas begrudged. The guards carrying the bags came forward and headed Tyrell out from the treasury, and, with the lord's guidance, came to his horse tied against the shadowed wall, and helped to pack the fortune into his saddlebags and secured them with the leather straps.

"Thank you, my lord," the guards spake as they departed, calling back as they went their way. "Be alert, sire, for the light is dimming and there are evildoers about."

"Yes, there are," he replied. "Indeed, there are." He mounted his steed and with slow gait rode from the treasury. On entering he was as a dull signet with feathers dirty brown, but upon leaving he was like a swan, all white and full of plumage. Off he went into the night to make toward his manor where lay his intrigue. Within the half of the hour he was at his destination and clattering up to his stables, past the cart, now horseless and empty in the shadows, with the canvas pulled back and to bare the boards. He dismounted as one of the stable boys came to take his horse. "My lord," he said as he held tightly the reins whilst Tyrell removed the saddlebags and threw them upon his shoulder, waving the boy away with his free hand, the other holding onto the heavy bags. He walked the short distance to the manor door, and in that short time in his mind thought of the devious ills that had been enacted since last he had slept. He now had the two princes safe in his keep, unknown to Richard, and, except for his manservants, not known to any other person. Richard had been appeased and was in grateful mood. He had a cache to take care of his family and the princes. And, most important, one day, on reaching age, they may regain the throne that had been pried from them, the throne that was rightly theirs. But more acts had yet to be carried forth, for no person must hold the information that the princes were still alive, and such must not reach the ears of Richard.

He entered into the manor as the door was opened by his manservant. "Sire," said he, greeting his master; forward he came to relieve the burden from Tyrell's shoulder.

"I will manage these," Tyrell said. "Where is your mistress?"

"She awaits in the master's chambers, my lord."

"You may return to your duties; I need you not at this time." The servant bowed and went his way as Tyrell moved his steps to the direction of his chambers; he entered them without formality. His wife heard the door being opened and turned to look who had entered, and seeing 'twas her husband, stood, as her waiting lady took from her lap the stitching she was engaged in; both lightly curtsied to Tyrell.

"My lord," said his wife.

"My dear," answered Tyrell. "Are you well?"

"I am, my lord, and pray you are likewise well."

"I am so … Please dismiss your lady for I must have most important converse with you."

The lady, upon hearing such, did curtsy and left the room, glancing at the fire as she did so to be sure 'twas still burning well. She closed the door behind her and left the Lord and Lady Tyrell in the glow of the fire. The Lady Tyrell looked at her lord with kindly face, for he treated her with much respect, and, though 'twas an arranged marriage, they had a deep caring bond with each other.

"My dear, I have been given a most important commission from our King Richard, which must take me away from you. Until the task so pledged upon me is completed, I cannot return, and it is not yet known how long the commission may take. The monies from the lands and estates will keep you amply, and, from the funds received to complete the task, will leave you with two thousand pounds to supplement you. I know you are of a shrewd nature and will do all good until I return." He placed the saddlebags upon the table lit by the candles that burned bright upon it;

he untied one side and, lifting the leather strap from its clasp, pulled out two of the moneybags, and did rattle them down upon the old oak table, shaking the candles so they flickered and dimmed for a moment before burning bright once more. He looked tenderly at his wife but dared not tell her of the devious games he was playing, and wished to leave her with no such burden upon her sweet self. "After I have eaten, I must away most hastily. I leave you with much affection and wish that I may return soon." He gave a low bow of respect to his wife who returned the gesture with a low curtsy and bowed head.

"My lord, I will await in deep devotion for your return."

Naught else was spake for service to the king came with such duties, and service to the king was above all else. He tied up the open sack and placed it back in the saddlebag lifting them to his shoulder as he left the chamber. Then, with no backwards look, he was gone, making his way toward the kitchen for victuals and to see that his two servants were well with their charges.

He entered the hot kitchen, the fire crackling there with blackened pots a-bubble with their aromas of meats cooking and breads baking, filling the space with its tantalizing lure. Placed upon the long table there, many kinds of dishes were spread to meet any fancy that may come to those with hunger and thirst. Flagons of ale in excess were placed, with the grinning faces of Tyrell's servants well supped into the table's offering. They stood unsteady, with discreet hands holding onto the table so they could appear more to the lord's liking.

"Sire," they both in respect spake, with a nod of the head and a loud burp, which Tyrell ignored without a flicker.

"All is well?" Tyrell asked as he looked toward the princes seated at the far end of the table, and only noticed by their light hair that showed above the pile of victuals that lay.

"All is well, my lord," came the answer from the unsteady. Tyrell went down to the end of the table, still clutching his bags as they sat upon his shoulder, but at last placed them close beside him as he sat with the two princes, whose heads hung quite lowly over the table. He held the hair of one and pulled up the head so he may see in what state they were. A white and sickly face showed, lit by the fire's glow; the eyes showed of little brightness, all rolling and seeing naught, with low moans coming forth as if in some malady. He lifted the other boy's head in the same manner and it showed in the same lost state; both still suffered much from the wine.

"Can you hear me, my prince?" he shouted as he tried to shake some response from the limp boy. "Can you hear me?" he called again as then he shook the other boy.

"Yes," came the whimpering voice, softly spake so as not to injure his head any more than was necessary. "Yes," spake the other, equally as soft.

"Listen to my words most carefully for your lives depend on such that I speak. From this day forth, for your well-being, you will no longer be princes." He spake closely and whispered to them in all secrecy, for there were in the kitchen many ears seeking all kinds of gossip—pantry maids and biddies, cooks and servants—all seemingly with the ears of bats, able to hear a whisper from ten paces. "You will just be boys who are within my guardianship and will be deemed to obey all the commands I give unto you, for dire peril could overcome us all if you fail in doing such. Do you hear me?" His voice raised now, bringing startled glances from about the kitchen, but they knew not of his council.

"Yes, my lord," came the sickly whisper once again.

"Cook!" Tyrell shouted loudly to the far of the scullery. A large shape loomed from the fireplace, casting an enveloping shadow it seemed over all who were stayed at the table.

"My lord," she said as she curtsied to the lord.

"You have boys, do you not?"

"I do, my lord. Six of them, my lord."

"I wish you to bring some of their clothing that will suit these two here. Breeches, shirts, and such."

"But, my lord, the clothes of my boys are old worn, and are not of such grandness, surely not befitting of your charges."

"Woman! Just bring forth two coats and two hats that will fit. I wish not for silk and lace, but rough tweed or worsted cloth. I will give you sixpence for such wear, so you may purchase more clothing for your children. Go and fetch to me these articles and be of haste."

"Yes sire, surely with haste," she answered as Tyrell pushed a whole sixpence into her chubby hand. It closed around the coin as a serpent, and he was just able to retrieve his hand from the closing vice. And as she turned to be upon her way the voice of Tyrell she heard.

"And make you sure they are not flea-ridden, and remove all lice from them or they will be of no use to me."

"Sir," she called without looking back as quickly she went her way.

He looked at his two servants, they slumped at the table with heads at rest within their folded arms almost asleep from the ale they had supped. Tyrell drew with much discretion a small corked gallipot from the inner reaches of his coat, a brew from his barber-surgeon, a brew to bring tranquility to those in need. He slid down the bench leaving his bags close to the two boys, then, selecting two of the goblets, poured half the liquid into each vessel from the pitcher of malmsey that sat upon the table. He filled both to the brim, then poured himself a small amount of wine into another vessel. He placed the two drinks in front of the servants, and then standing behind them shook both vigorously at the shoulder.

"Come on, my faithful ones, drink up your wine, for soon we must make away from this place." In a daze, they both looked up, and all they could see in their heady state were the goblets of wine, for a full goblet of wine left upon the table was a sin to behold and an insult to the host, and with such thoughts drank it down with the thirst of a crusader. But as soon as the vessels were emptied they slumped again in deep set.

He left them and sat at the bench to sup, drinking his wine and filling his belly with the good victuals from the table. Soon the cook arrived returning with clothes for the two boys; she placed the bundle upon the bench by the side of Tyrell.

"My lord," was all she spake and with a curtsy went back to her bubbling pots. Tyrell unrolled the bundle, and, holding the garments up one at a time, looked them over as an expert in boys' attire would do. They seemed to be of good thread and suitable for his want; the drab colour would hide all that was within. He pulled up one of the boys and saw he was the taller one, still sickly and swaying about. He took one of the long coats and pushed the boy's arms into the sleeves, then tied it at the front covering the bright cloth of his doublet; he then pulled one of the hats over the golden curls that hung his head, and all was now hidden beneath and did nicely hide the face with its heavy brim. He carried on with the smaller boy, who was soon bedecked with similar garb. No more princes showed as they sat in their meagre cloth; mere travellers they upon the weary road.

"I need to take these drunken servants back to their places, for they will never make home this eve if left to their own devices." Tyrell spake loudly to the manservants who awaited in the far of the room, at the same time looking over to the two lads who sat lonesome at the table. The servants quickly came upon the order and began to drag the two sleepers to the cart outside. The canvas was pulled back as one at a time the drunken bodies were dumped onto the wooden boards, and the canvas pulled back over them to hide the miserable wretches that were tangled in there. The horse was being hitched to the cart as Tyrell climbed up onto the wooden seat; one of the servant's coats wrapped about him and a full-brimmed hat upon his head, a lord unseen, and but a servant alone at the reins of a cart, he trotted his cargo slowly from the manor. The skivvies watched as he became lost behind the thick of the trees, and mulled that most strange was the act, that the lord would take it upon himself to return two humble servants to their dwellings when such as they were at his bid; but he was of noble stock and they assumed his small brain worked in ways not of the normal person.

A short distance from the manor lay the marshes near Battersea, to where the lord was went. Soon in the blackness, with only the horse to guide him to his destination, he slacked off the reins and let the animal freely trot, the track seemingly known to the horse as it picked its way through the thick brush. The way was invaded by the moon and could be seen the glimmer upon the water that was there as he slowed the cart to the edge of the swamp. The lord stepped from his seat and placed his feet upon the wet ground; the mud squelched under his boots as he went to the back of the cart and pulled back the canvas cover; and there lay again two more helpless children, asleep and in dreams like babes in the gloom that was about them.

He dragged one of the heaps off and rolled it almost to the swamp's bank where he loosened the ties that were about the sleeper's neck, and as he held the servant still he drew the dagger from its keep, and in the moon's bright he looked for a moment at the weapon, and, selecting the most trusted edge, slashed it across the dirty neck. The blood gushed, pumping away the life; a gurgle was all to hear in the still air, as with his boot he pushed the draining body into the stinking swamp. He dragged from the cart the next faithful one and placed it upon the swamp's edge where the other had laid; he pulled back the shirt from about the neck to reveal the beating vein, then went straight to the spot with his dagger, the eyes opened for a moment but then closed with a gurgling throat and a squirt of life, as the second body was pushed into the marshes. That most tedious task was finished. He wiped his dripping dagger to shine again, free of all trace of murder, sheathed it, and boarded the cart again, turning it back to the manor and to the princes. All evil was done.

The Lord Tyrell was well worn as this long day drew to its close; the horse again brought him to his place as he dozed at the reins; the stable boy's voice brought him to life as they stopped in the manor yard. Wearily he lopped to the kitchen's warm entrance. There, lying upon the rushes, were the two princes, dark at the fireside except for the red glow that played upon their curled bodies fast into the land of peace were they. Tyrell lay down close to the fire and soon joined the somnolent detachment; the steam rising from his wet clothes and muddied boots; as he slept, tales of a dark night drifting his slumber. Only for a short time did he rest for he wished to be away in the dark of the early hours. The fire cracked and brought him from his rest with a startle, crossing his mind came thoughts of the devious acts that were placed upon him. The fact was that the soon-to-be King Richard was paying monies to have the princes in safe keep, and that he had already paid monies to have them murdered. "Am I not stuck in this spider's web? Will I not free myself from such turmoil? Pray I may, and pray I avoid the king's wrath that he never finds my hand in this deception, for I could not endure the pains of the Tower and the pain of my dear wife's destitution." He stood and shook from himself the malaise that pained him. But this be the path chosen, through the brambles and briars to the meadow of flowers. He washed his face with the hot water from one of the washing cauldrons, and stood by the fire drying himself with one of the warmed cloths that were hanging from the mantle. He drank a flagon of ale, for thirst was upon him this early morn. He strode over to where the children lay still in their sleeping stupor. He shook them both most abruptly with some sort of mischief within him, as he had often been so awakened by his elder brother, who had many times frightened him from his restful sleep, and he could still hear the guffing laughter that came from him as he gazed down upon his younger kin. The princes looked up in bewildered fashion not knowing yet their circumstances; but Tyrell came with more of a fatherly tone and did not wish to frighten them as his brother may have chosen to do.

"Wash yourselves, boys; 'tis soon time we must away and make you safe." They both arose and washed in the water placed there and dried themselves in childish fashion. Their features were still white and sickly. They noticed the clothes that in some strange way bedecked their bodies, for they knew nothing of the happening, they being too full of crapulence to ask any questions. Tyrell bundled some of the food off the table into one of the large cloths, and tied the corners together to make a food bag for their journey; he slung the moneybags over his shoulder and picked up the food.

"Come, my children, away we must before this morn breaks of light." They followed behind him as he went to the door as ducklings behind the drake. Tyrell opened the door and was shown the cold black morn. The boys, with the cold at their faces and the warmth at their backs, hid behind their mentor as he stepped toward the readied wagon.

"Where are we bound?" the elder boy asked, feeling most sick as he summoned up the question, and could speak no more because of the vomit he could feel rising from his stomach and into his mouth; he tried to contain it but could not as out it came. Yesterday's victory feast left his mouth to end up steaming at his feet, the craddy* smell rising with the steam that reached the other boy's nose, causing him the same distress, as forth it came like porridge tipped out of a pan, hot and vile. When all

craddy [coined] vile

had calmed and they had wiped their faces upon the cloths they carried for this occasion, they looked with sad face at the Lord Tyrell, as a sick dog would gaze.

"You will feel more yourselves, now that you are relieved of your stomachs' ills. How about a goblet of wine to purge out your mouths?" The mischief was within him once more, but this time he could not resist. "Ugh," they uttered and turned even paler at the thought of ever again drinking such an evil brew.

"We, my boys, are away to Folkestone, there we will gain passage to Portugal, which seems the most favoured of the lands that lay across our Channel, the place where we will be safe until you are older, and you can return to this England and regain the throne that is your right. It will take us three days to reach the coast, and you must be of all vigilance upon this journey and do all that I tell you for your safekeeping."

They looked at Tyrell and nodded that they would indeed follow his bidding, and, without hesitation, jumped into the cart as Tyrell covered them with the canvas. The moneybags were their headrests; the bag of food there was pushed as far away as they could, wishing not to smell its aromas. They lay close to the seat board where their guardian was sat, and heard clearly the "Walk" as the horse took the command and moved out from the manor, black as the night it lay, and soon onto the roadway that was signed to Folkestone. They were rumbled and rocked as the cart moved along the cobbled streets in the morn's sky that still showed its blackness. Then the rattling gave way to the soft tracks of the lanes that took them away from London Town. They passed the marshes at Battersea, with no glance from Tyrell at the still waters that winked at him as they went by; he guided the horse along the muddy way to leave far behind the evil that lay there. The cart rattled and bumped, and the boys could hear from beneath their covers that the sounds came from the timbered bridges they were crossing, the planks banging loosely against the wooden wheels as they did so, and the morn's light began taking a peek at them through the holes and edges of their cover.

The cart came to a stop and the canvas was pulled back to uncover the children. The light squinting their eyes as they tried to see about them, but quickly lids were opened and the forest around them came to view.

"You can sit back there now without the cover, for we are clear of the city, and you are just my children taken to visit afar." Tyrell climbed back into his seat and slapped the reins onto the horses back; they were journeying again. The boys were able to breathe more easily without the canvas, damp and heavy, over them; the sickness they had felt had eased a little, though the rocking of the cart still caused them some discomfort.

The trio carried on through the morn, with a change of horse near Bromley at about ten of the clock in the morn, and on to the evening where they stopped their journey this day at Wrotham, and made to obtain rooms at the inn there; they turned into the yard with the stable boy running out to take the horse's reins as it tossed its head and snorted as the smell of its feed drifted from the barn. The travellers stepped down from the cart and made their way to the entrance. Tyrell called across as the boy guided the horse to its stable. "Six of the clock, lad! We leave at six in the morn. Be all ready."

"Yes, sire," came the answer from the grubby face.

With Tyrell clutching his bags and one boy carrying the food bundle, they went in and made straight to the landlord's table; a narrow passage led to it, seen dim even in the still bright eve and full of strange smells to the boys, of ale and meat pies, and urine; they liked it not as it did remind them of the folly they had taken upon themselves. 'Twas brighter in the small room where the man stood counting his monies; as they came to him he looked up.

"Yes, sire," said he in an accent the boys had not heard and deemed it hard to understand; but Tyrell heard naught strange in the tongue, but then our master seemed to know all manner of things, but then he was very, very old.

"We need rooms for the night and victuals."

"Three of you, are there?" questioning as he looked them over. A man of portly stature was he, overfed on the inn's cooking and large amounts of ale; his head was almost bald; his face was very red as if he had bathed in the juice of strawberries; he had two front teeth amiss. A green shirt with long sleeves covered his thick arms, a brown waistcoat of worsted over top, his legs were hidden beneath the table but glimpses of more brown worsted was seen there. The inn showed of a very low ceiling with blackened beams; the dust and cobwebs hung up there like a lace cover, looking ready to fall upon any who may linger too long under its net. The doorways were wide but so low that a person of average height would have to lower his head to pass. Thick wooden doors gated with iron hinges and latch were black, rusty, and old. Walls were of a rough plaster-like covering, made from crushed limestone and sand laid on with a wooden float and brushed over with a dye wash from the weaver's house. The floor was of black flagstones quarried nearby, and all covered in sawdust to make sweet the smell, also to soak up the spilled ale and the slimed spit. Tables and benches were placed around the small room with the torches burning in their holders, their black smoke and odour marring the walls and ceiling. The small windows, with their shutters wide to rid the room of the smells there, rattled in the cool blow that came about the inn, laying open to the fields beyond.

The talking and laughter rang about even at this early hour, as many were already swaying about and slopping their ale. The landlord's daughter moved about the tables with her jug of brew, filling the tankards and dropping the pennies clink into her pocketed frock, made from some stiff cloth that made it rustle as it swung about her ankles. The neck cut low, a bonnet atop her head, a young lass of comely bearing watched closely by her landlord father, for many crude folk frequented such rowdy places. At this early hour all was of jollity and laughter, a friendly place of meeting, but as the night went on and bellies were filled with ale, as the cards were dealt and the coin lost, fighting would almost certainly break the occasion.

"Three pennies for your bed, one for your horse, and two for your victuals at supper and breakfast." Slowly the landlord added the amount up from his ledger. He looked up, "Sixpence, my lord." Tyrell withdrew a handful of coin from his money pocket, and poking at it with his free hand, took six pennies from the mound and laid them upon the table before the innkeeper, returning the rest to his pocket secure. The keeper scooped up the coins. With his beaming smile he seemed a most jolly fellow, as he undid the ties on his heavy moneybag and clinked the coins to settle with the others that bunched there. "Mag!" he shouted as another daughter came from the shadowy room, she most similar to her sister, as she curtsied to the new guests. "Take 'em to the backroom, my dearie, and make sure the pot's empty," his cheeks almost bursting with his big toothy grin.

"Yes, Father," she answered, and beckoned the trio to follow her to the passage which led them to the narrowest and the lowest stair anyone could ever encounter.

The boys followed the swishing skirts and trim stockinged ankles up the stairway; her leather shoes treaded softly as they reached the landing, waiting at the top for the others to catch up to her. The boys were quickly there, but Tyrell was slow to come, as a loud bump and "Ouch!" was heard to crack his head upon the ceiling overhang, still mumbling some curses at the innocent beam. Mag swished them to the door of the backroom, pushed it open, and entered with the party close behind her. The room was small of size, beamed as downstairs, with rushes upon the floor; two wooden-planked beds covered in straw, and a rough-hewn table with a small bench was all that it held. Mag brought in a lit taper from the torch burning in the passageway and lit the torch that was affixed to the wall in the guests' room. She then busied to the corner of the room to inspect the chamber pot that was set there; she peered into it, and 'twas not so delightful. The boys sat upon the edge of the bed; not such a royal chamber they thought, as they watched whilst Meg picked up the pot and held it as far from her nose as she could, the contents slopping about as she left the room, and made toward the window in the passageway that overlooked the road. She peeked out of the open shutter to see that all was well below, a lesson she had learned with some abuse, and wished not to hear such blasphemy again; all was clear so she threw the contents out through the window onto the sewery road below, pulling the pot back inside and gazing into it to see if all had been thrown out; well enough, she thought, and went back to the room and replaced the pot in its discreet setting. Then with a curtsy, Mag's duties were finished.

"Is there anything else you require, sire?"

"No, Mag," answered Tyrell.

"No, Mag," mimed the boys. Finding at last some mischief in their bleak situation.

"Will you be eating here or downstairs, sir?"

"We will eat here this eve, and take breakfast downstairs at five of the clock."

"I will see to your request, my lord." Then with her eyes twinkling, "Will there be anything else I may do for you?"

"No, Mag."

"No, Mag," the boys chimed. She turned and drifted from the room.

"I will bring your supper shortly," she called over her shoulder as she left.

The boys flopped back onto the bed as Tyrell took off his heavy garb and dropped it upon the rushed floor, his heavy moneybag, the saddlebags, his bulky overcoat, his sword, his belt, all at lay. He sat upon the creaking bed and pulled off his wet cavalry boots and placed them in regimental order upon the floor, then laid back with a relaxing gasp, his stockinged feet with steam rising hung over the end of his bed.

Morning came, and the supper was still untouched as they arose, for fatigue had overcome them and they knew naught of the maid's visit and had slept till the cock's crow. They had taken breakfast in the tavern room below and now were on their journey once again. The boys were feeling much better now as the sickness they had was past and they were able to eat food once again, but swore they that never again would they sup aught but boiled water. Tyrell guided the cart along the wet lanes as they passed through country towns and small hamlets. They went many miles this day, and as dusk was closing about them they approached the outskirts of Maidstone where stood the King's Head Inn to be their night's stop.

They were but two miles from the town as they moved along a narrow lane; the bushes and trees hugged close to their sides; underfoot was wet and muddy as the horses searched for footing in the squelching mire; they came to a bend in the narrow track with the dark bushes hiding the road that was ahead. At first it seemed as if the wind had stirred the leaves and branches, making them shake in a strange fashion, but then the cover split apart as two ruffians stepped out in front of the horse.

"'Old there, sire!" came the rasping voice in the dusky light; they barred his path and Tyrell had to stop the cart.

"Get down and stay below the canvas," he whispered to the boys, half turning so they could hear his low speech; but the two robbers had heard his talk and knew his game, and let know such to Tyrell.

"Get down me lads, eh!" they laughing and mocking the voice heard. Came forward from the dim light the bigger of the two men, the breeze blowing the odour of him over the cart; an overpowering brute was he, fearful in looks without the knife that glistened at his belt; his hair long and unkempt, he showed a full beard; his thick bruising arms bulging from his tight shirt, which was thick with dirt with a week or more of slop spilled upon it; his dirty leggings disappearing into the dark of the ground on which he stood. He moved his hand toward the horse's bridle to contain the animal.

"I tell you, sir, do not touch that horse! And, for your well-being, stand aside and let us freely pass." Tyrell was standing as he bent over and tied the reins in anticipation that his warning would not be heeded. The boys huddled lower under the canvas as their guardian defied the ruffians who barred their way, and closed their eyes in some fear of the outcome.

"Stand aside? You are not in your master's house now; you are in my house; these trees, these bushes, this track—all mine, and you trespass upon it. I will take you and your siblings to task and rake you into collops." The fellow's voice was raised to bring fear and dread into the lonely party, but Tyrell would have none of it, as the boys cringed once more at his defiant words.

"I tell you only one more time, for no more will I utter these words: Stand aside and let us pass, for my wroth will fall upon you if you do not."

"Ha, ha, hear that, Mar?" turning to his partner and repeating Tyrell's words again as seemed his way. "His wroth is going to fall upon us; we shake with fear, do we not?"

"We do indeed; indeed, I shake with fear as when my lady-wife doth scold me for not feeding the hens; all of a shake I am, yes, indeed," spake the man, Mar.

"Throw down your moneybag, then we will, in all honesty, let you pass; if you do not, you will not see the morrow's light and we will still have your monies and your boys—no doubt a tidy sum they will fetch." The ruffian pulled his dagger as he spake and made toward the cart. Tyrell jumped down to the muddy ground; no more his patience left within him as he threw off his heavy coat and stood with hand on sword ready to do battle. The ruffian stepped past the horse and, with dagger raised, made quickly toward Tyrell, as the other robber also started to become more brave and followed his accomplice a few paces back. The sword slid silently from its rest and, with one lungeing slash, was brought down upon the arm of his assailant, and seemingly with little effort did cut off the arm and it fell into the mud. The robber at first had felt nothing and was still pacing toward his victim, raising his severed arm higher, when upon him came the terror of the night's doings as he gazed at the half arm with his blood spurting all about. In anguish he cried of his misfortune. His accomplice was already on the run into the bushes as he saw the tirade that had been leashed and wanted none of it. Just to sit by the fire with his family in one piece was all he prayed for upon this dismal night. Tyrell moved forward again, his anger crazing his mind as he went after his foe; his sword slashing and swishing in the cool air. The robber squealing like a pig fled as the sword came by his ear, to cut through the long hair that flowed behind him as he ran into the woods.

"Come and fight like a man, you blaggart!" Tyrell shouted as the dark took the assailant from his sight; he slowed now and let the ruffian escape into the night; the smell of urine and excretion filled the air and he was gone.

Tyrell returned to the cart as the boys came out from underneath the canvas hide. They had seen some of the struggle as they bravely peeked from their hiding place, and had some deep respect for their new guardian, for they knew of his bravery, and that he did indeed speak truthfully when he swore that he would uphold their safety in all manner of things. They had seen that his words were not short of action when the time showed. And, if nothing else, he was prepared to defend them and to maintain their well-being.

The arm caught the gaze of Tyrell as it lay there in the red mud at his feet; it lay still clutching the dagger that was to be their harm; he liked not the sight and kicked it to the edge of the track so that 'twas clear of the cart. One of the boys reached toward him from the cart and handed him a cloth with which to clean his blade, for the blade had to be cared for as a prized possession, shiny and clean at all times. With care he wiped it clean and handed back the cloth to the boy, then he ran his finger along the edge, and looked closely at it for any nicks it may have suffered. All appeared well as he placed it back in its scabbard to keep safe and at the ready for the next time it may be needed.

"Remember, my princes, always keep your sword sharper than the next man's, for one blow with such will bring you victory over the dull blade." They knew of that which he did speak, for they had seen the sharp blade and would bear his council, for 'twas good council.

Tyrell climbed back once more onto the cart and sat again on the wooden seat, steady of breath and not agitated, as if he had just been to relieve himself and not to have chased off some would-be robbers. They carried on to Maidstone, and in blackness came upon the inn they were seeking. The jovial sounds rang from the open windows, making it easy to be guided there. They stabled the horse and made their way inside to the noise of laughter and of shout; a tumult of people were before them as they pushed inside. There all kinds of people—tall, short, stout, thin, men, women, children, mostly dirty and raggedy—tattled their story. But some there were clean and better attired as merchants and shopkeepers would be. A mix of all kinds and all manner of odours, some vile some pleasant. The smell of the oil burning in the torches, of the food that was cooking, of ale, of dampness, of the wood blazing from the open fire, all wafted through the small inn overfull with mankind.

The boys followed Tyrell to the counter table where he had spied the innkeeper; they made their way through the bodies and legs that barred their passage. As they came closer to the keeper, the boy who trailed the group a little stumbled to the sawdust floor, tripping over a leg that was not there before, as quickly 'twas pulled out of sight as the boy fell, with much laughter about as he took his fall. The red-faced fellow smelling of much supped ale and fish pie took the boy by the arm and helped him to his feet.

"Oh, my poor fellow," he spake in another strange tongue, "did you trip? I do hope you suffered no discomfort."

"Yes, sire, I did stumble but to no harm, thank you." He took two more steps and was tripped again, sliding into the spit and sawdust that lay wet and grimy upon the floor. Louder was the laughter as he rose covered in sawdust and slime. Tyrell came back to where his slippery boy stood.

"Come, my son, and do not delay us with your silly games." Tyrell went along with the pranks that were being played with a smile upon his face that had not shown for many a day, as he ushered the boy to the counter. This was the jest one did meet at the inn, for no malice was intended; this action only to break the toils of the day, for pleasure was hard to find at this dismal time for many folk.

"Landlord," Tyrell called to the innkeeper, who was at this time talking to one of his patrons and had his back to the them as they stood at his table.

"Aye, sir," he spake as he turned toward the voice that beckoned him, and as he turned the same features appeared before them, as if all keepers of inns were bred from the same parents. Here he was: rotund, red of face, and most jovial. A grin that showed the missing tooth, but where there was baldness before this keeper had hair that was bright red, but of the same ilk as all the others they had seen.

"We need a room for the night. There are three of us."

"You will have to see my wife, sire; she does all the stopovers. She is at the back in the kitchen." And he waved Tyrell the way to take.

"I will be but a short while," he spake to his boys. "Sit here at the end of the table. Do not speak to anyone and all will be well." They sat meekly there as Tyrell glanced back at them in a fatherly way as he went toward the kitchen; he knew if any trouble came their way it would be of a jovial nature, and it would be good for them to deal with such people, for as princes they would never know of this life that jollied all about them.

They sat at the table with all about them rough-looking and smelly peasants; all seemed drunk, for they knew something of the state as the sickness rose from their stomachs at just the thought of it. There was laughing and shouting and none seemed interested in their new company. Some were standing as loud voices came over some argument. Their table was covered in empty ale tankards, with pieces of bread and cheese lying there; they gazed at the messy lot.

"'Ow 'e doin', lads?" the rusty voice spake in twisted words, the face but three inches away from one of the boys; hairy and unshaven it swayed there, yellow and black teeth, eyes crossed as bewitched, pushing these strange words before them; the smell of ale and raw onion drowned the boys in its spit as the words were spoken, and with the smell of dried sweat made them retch as if the sickness was upon them again. "Looking fur a drop o' ale, are we lads?"

"No, sire, but we would like a drink of milk that has been boiled, if we may." The boy trying some means to be rid of the odorous peasant that clung about them.

"If we may? Blimey, 'ear that Jim? If we may."

"Aye, I 'eard," said Jim. "Maybe that Nell will get them some milk," he said to Tom, both showing a mischievous grin upon their faces.

"Aye, Nell!" shouted Tom. "Nell, Nell!" he shouted across the room, loudly above the din that was about. "Nell, Big Nell!" he called again, and then from far across the room a shadow rose from the corner and made its way toward the voice. Shouting and talking to the pub dwellers as she came, she being ragged as she passed them by, calling obscene words to her as she bundled along, and giving back equally vile comments, some made to grab her, and Nell with fists swinging stopped their game with loud smacks as her thumping hands met soft flesh with the laughter ringing loud. The shadow loomed over the boys, a big obese hulk with golden hair splayed as wide as her shoulders it lay, the lips painted giving the face of the court clown, big chubby shoulders fought from her dress, which was so low at the front that when she leaned toward them, they felt they may be crushed by the two huge breasts that were ready to fall out upon their hapless bodies. The dress she wore was larger at the waist than the shoulders, and down to the floor it went, sticky and slimy at the bottom; where the floor had been cleaned with the heavy cloth, two dirty boots stood before them, half hidden by the thick sawdust. Her face looked at them closely; two teeth were missing at the front, one each side of her discoloured front teeth, showing even more their grime by the overly painted lips, painted on without the aid of a reflecting glass it seemed, all smeared and uneven, yet meant to be enticing. The smell of some sickly flowery scent mixed with the sweat of her hulk came over them, drifting about the boys' heads like gas from the swamp.

"What do you wish, my dearies?" she said, the voice so deep and booming, sounding more akin to the sergeant of the guard they had heard from the army barracks, than from some folly maiden.

"They ask for some milk, Nell. What say you to this?" the peasant nearest to the boys asked whilst staring at them through his crossed eyes.

"Some milk, my dears. Would you like it warm or cold?" asked she with her red smile.

"Warm, Nell, we would both like it to be warm, thank you."

"Just one moment, my dears, and I will get it for you." Everyone in the room knew what was about to happen, everyone except the two boys, all innocent, who sat most politely awaiting their request.

While they sat, Nell pulled down the front of her dress so that her released bosoms fell out all plump and overwhelming, and, before any action could be taken to avoid them, she planted one then the other over the boys' faces, covering them completely with her abundant flesh. Darkness fell over them and the heaviness made it impossible to breathe as she pressed herself against them even harder. They struggled to be free as the bar revelled in laughter at their plight; asking for milk when Nell was about was a femme fatal—not fatale! At last they struggled clear from under the weight of the bosoms; red-faced and sweaty, they gasped for air.

"So, what think you of Big Nell's milk?" she asked. No answer could yet come as the two boys were still trying to recover their breath from the ordeal. "Need more, my dears?" She made a mischievous move toward them as she spake. They beckoned as best they could that they wished no more, and, as the laughter rose again from their pleadings, Nell inquired further in her most soft and motherly tone, "Would you like to wipe your faces dry?"

"Yes, Nell, that would be most welcome," they replied. The bar seemingly hushed now, closer came the patrons to the table where Nell floated. Still innocent were the boys, bewitched by the kind tones now coming from the painted mouth, and spoken with such sincerity. Easy pickings for Nell these two; cherries from the lower branch laden with fruit. She bent down as if to retrieve some cloths from her pocket, as the boys sat close together hoping that Tyrell would soon return, for only upon his showing would they feel completely secure. Nell, speaking though with much kindness now and with soft tone, felt no more a threat to them.

"Here we are then, my beauties, try ye this," still in her comforting tone did she speak. Then in one move she lifted up the hem of her skirt and raised it above her head, revealing her stockinged legs with folds of flesh overflowing from atop; her dirty knickers showed full of holes and seen never washed with her fat beneath pushing through the holes and edges, liken to the bread dough rising through old muslin cloth, oozing out of any opening. Then, with little warning, she dropped the dress tent over the top of the boys, and as they disappeared beneath the folds she hugged the two squirming bodies close to her legs and rotting wear, her thick strong arms clamped about them. Then, in this state, with the boys helpless, she let forth a mighty wind that she had been keeping warm for some while, and now did rent it out like the cow in the field. The tent filled with the odorous smell of cabbage at rot; the boys beneath struggled even more but was to no avail, as to move from the lock they were gripped in was impossible. The fumes rising about was making it difficult to draw breath; the smell of the urine from the rotting knickers made their eyes flow with tears, but breathe they must and so sucked in the rancid air that was with them in this dark cave, coughing and choking as they did so. At last the grip was loosened and the tent lifted as they came out from their prison of smell and silence, to drink in the clean air of the tavern, no longer was it so vile. The laughter rang all about them as they were able to look about, and among the raucous remarks that flew about they had burst from their confinement, and ran with outstretched legs leaping over the limbs that lay before them to hinder their way, slipping upon the slimy sawdust as they skidded toward the kitchen and to safety from Nell, whose bellowing laughter rang about the tavern room far louder than any other there.

"Come back, me beauties, I've more for you to savour." But the boys wished to hear naught as they made their exit into the tranquil kitchen; they came to Tyrell as he was about to return to the tavern bar, rushing in they held onto his thick legs in stark fear of what may be lurking them.

"Easy, my boys. What troubles you?" He spake in a concerned manner, ready if need be to avenge any misdeeds done to his wards.

"Nell—" was all they could utter through their air-seeking gasps as they pointed to the laughter-filled room.

"Nell?" said Tyrell; "you're feared of a woman? Come, come," said he with a smile upon his face, he well aware of the antics of Nell, for this had been his stop on previous occasions and Nell was no stranger to him. "Two big fellows like you scared of a little lady in the taproom? Fine warriors you will make, my lads." His teasing over, he guided his wards back to the table where they had sat before; food and drink was brought as one biddy roughly cleaned it with the table brush, so all that lay there was now mingled with the floor's sawdust. The other laid down the fare before Tyrell and his wards.

The laughter had died now, and things calmed to the normal rowdiness. They ate and they drank and were most content. Readying themselves to make way to their room, for fatigue was draping their tired bones, they stood to leave and, as they did so, the last boy felt his sleeve tugged strongly. He was pulled toward the cross-eyed peasant; 'twas he who brought the boy's arm toward him so he may speak closely in his ear with just a little thought to help the poor fellow sleep.

"Nell says she will visit with you this night to lay all her charms upon you, my dear, near the midnight hour she will come," he whispered most secretly into the small ear draped in golden curl. "Do not let your master hear of this, for he may wish to have her for himself; 'tis our secret." The boy pulled away from the grinning toothy face, smelling no better than it did before. The ward, though, was white of face and fearful, for he could not bear the visit of Nell to his bed, and he wished not to put such childish fears upon Tyrell.

They all left and went up the narrow way to their room. Soon, all were asleep, but one who lay with his back upon the straw bed, his eyes open wide, with the rough cover pulled to his neck, clutched by a pair of white hands, listening for any telltale noise, he watched the door as the fear of Nell squirmed through his body; he lay in the black room helpless; there would be no sleep this night, for vigilant he would have to be till dawn's relief. Then a noise he heard; Nell was coming; he struggled as a hand came upon him.

"Get away!" he cried. "Get away from me!" He tried to push away the hand that was upon him.

"Come on, boy, time for us to ride again." 'Twas the voice of Tyrell; the morn had come and he was safe; the room brightening, as the dawn came splashing through the open window. This was the boy's most thankful morn, for soon they would move away from Maidstone, and the inn where dwelt Big Nell.

They rode through that bright day of early July, of the year fourteen hundred and eighty-three, making fair way to Folkestone. They came over the limestone hills there, and saw below the harbour with the fishing boats bobbing about, toing and froing they went there ways. The dockside they saw was of a busy seaport with many merchant vessels there, some loading some unloading upon the dock. Labourers they saw carrying overweight sacks to the waiting carts, barrels and boxes being moved about, looking like ants with their eggs, forever moving to some objective, as they, from afar, gazed at the sight below them.

Soon they clattered into the town filled with noise and busy folk, all manner of them about their business; the warm sunny day did bring much brightness to the old town, giving such gaiety to the scene that met our travellers. The smell from the open sewers, though, took the joy from their eyes, and in its stead brought the vile stench to their noses, even more rancid in the warm summer air. Coming along the harbour's way they rattled along the cobbled road. The docks stood on one side with the vessels tied up at the thick splitting posts. The gulls flew above, swooping and diving; with squawk and screech, they dipped about helping to fill the din at the harbour side. The vessels loomed large above the boys as they passed; in wonder they gazed at the rolling ships that hugged close the harbour's wall, creaking and scraping their hulls upon the stone, crying to be freed, to be released from their captivity so they may billow their sails in the windswept sea that called for them. Thick ropes hung down from the unseen decks; other ropes, with fifteen or more men, lowered down the wooden platforms filled with all kinds merchandise, as then with gentle care they did bring them to land softly upon the wharf's side; as then quickly the cargo was covered by another group of workers who pulled and tugged at the boxes and bags as soon as it came to sight; as if no time could be spared to breathe, they picked out something to carry and in doing so were off with their find to the waiting carts. The scene looked of complete mayhem, but then some order came as the overseers took over, checking the writings upon the cargo and matching them with their papers, then pointing and shouting to which cart they were to go. As the ships were emptied, 'twas soon they were being filled once more from the other platforms that sat awaiting at the side of the dock, as wearily the labourers pulled again upon the hanging ropes, heavy the load, for up it must go to the high part of the deck, where shouted the captain in stern voice to move on with haste. Thus was the wharf on one side of the way; on the other side lay the inns and taverns, the bakers and the butchers; all manner of business was there, richly done with the heavy trade that came off the ships.

They moved on in their cart to come to the place where they would bed. The inn stood on the corner of a small wynd* leading to the stables; they trundled down the bumpy way as Tyrell stopped at a side door short of the horse's shelter, and climbed down from the cart, stiff and aching from the journey, as the two wards stood in the back of the cart and stretched their bodies, wondering as to the next move to be made.

"Stay at the cart, and do not leave it for any reason; I will be but a short time to arrange a bed for the night." They did not speak but sat once more lowly in the cart and waited for their guardian's return. Tyrell went back to the road from which they had come, and turning the corner came to the doorway of the Sailors' Rest. He entered up the high step, such that during a storm the sea would not flood the inn, but deemed a curse by all of the drunkards who came out of the taproom. In he went to the aroma of stale ale and wet sawdust. Many people were about with their usual joviality, but here was a more affluent group and seen well attired were they; shopkeepers and merchants made up most of the body that supped there, a more refined lot than the last place they had visited.

"Good day, Bogle," spake Tyrell as he caught the landlord's eye.

"Good day, my Lord Tyrell. How be you this summer's day?"

"I am indeed well, Bogle, and I see you are of the same spirit." Having rested at the inn many times before, Tyrell knew well the landlord.

"'Ave your usual room, sire, if you be staying."

"I am so, and will take the room; there will be three of us on this journey." The landlord reached for his jingling keys that were upon the wall behind him, hanging in rows were they like bats waiting for dusk.

"There yar, my lord," he said as he handed over the keys.

"I take it, Bogle, the key to the side door is amongst these?"

"Yes, my lord, 'tis this one with the twine attached," pointing and fingering the key to use. Tyrell dug into his pouch and paid the landlord with the chink of coin into the outstretched palm. "My lord," he said in thanks.

"Bogle, I have not been here; you have not had eye of me." Tyrell spake as he thrust another coin into the hand.

"Yes, my lord, 'tis so."

"We will eat in our room, if you will send victuals for three at six of

---

* *wynd* narrow passageway usually between buildings

the clock. Thank you, Bogle."

"Thank you kindly, my lord, I will see to it."

Tyrell left the taproom, carefully striding the deep step, and taking little time to turn into the wynd and make his way to the wards at wait. He saw them sitting upon the cart seat talking closely to each other; and they did not notice Tyrell until he was almost upon them, whence they stopped their jargon abruptly at his presence, and sheepishly did not look at the lord directly after seeing him.

"What are you talking of?" Tyrell asked, concerned at the secretive conference.

"Nothing, my lord, just the chatter of boys." The Lord Tyrell looked at them, and it seemed to him that the Prince Richard was the one who seemed to answer all the questions, and not the elder brother, Edward, but he thought no more of it; he cared not for the sulking of children and their strange ways.

"Come, we have rooms for the night."

"We will not be visiting the bar room, will we, my lord?" With a most pleading voice came the question from one of the boys as they climbed down from the cart.

"No, not this time; we will eat in our room." No words replied but an air of relief seemed to dwell. Leaving the cart where it stood, they entered through the side door and went up the private stairway to their room. They came to the doorway directly at the top of the landing and entered to a more accommodating dwelling; the rushes upon the floor were fresh and smelled clean; two beds of comforting dimensions, a table and benches of good stead were in the middle of the room; a stand in the corner and placed upon it a wash bowl, with a pail of clean water beside it with drying cloths hanging over the rail. A small section was boarded at the side of the room, where hidden behind lay the privy; the bench and the wooden lid were scrubbed clean, and clean sawdust covered the floor. The ceiling beams hung low against the washed walls as candles glowed upon them. The candles showed that this was a place that catered to the more distinguished client, for in most inns the smelling torches were the source of light and chosen for their frugal glow. The candle being too costly for such places and only burned in the more expensive places.

"Stay here, boys, I will return shortly." Tyrell had settled the boys into their lodging, and now had business to do.

"Where are you to, my lord?"

"I have to obtain some vessel for our journey to Portugal."

"Why do we go to Portugal, sire? I believe you told us before but seems our heads were somewhat befuddled at the time."

"'Tis known that France and Spain are in so much conflict with our Realm that it would be unwise at this time for us to seek refuge in these countries. As Portugal is the closest and the least hostile to us, this would be our best choice, and, to add, there are fewer spies about in that place than Spain or France. That, sirs, is the reason for such a choice."

"Oh, thank you, my lord," was all they spake. Tyrell left the room and the two wards now sat at the table looking at each other with unmoved looks upon their faces; but no one could judge the thoughts within their young heads.

Tyrell was once more upon the cart and making his way but a short distance this time; went he no further than the far reach of the docks where the smaller craft were tied, bobbing their watery waltz as they awaited their dance upon the sea. The cart was tied to the hitching post and he entered the tavern that stood close there, and amidst the usual ruckus he quickly caught sight of the landlord.

"My good man," Tyrell spake.

"Yes, sire," came the reply with the thick accent poured over it. A thin man this time, not of the usual type encountered before. Rather small he with meekly nature.

"Can I help you, sir?" came a more commanding voice from close by. The landlord's wife with haughty bearing stood up from her stool, showing much larger proportions than her husband and obviously the real master of the house.

"Yes, madam." Tyrell turned away from the landlord and addressing his wife came closer to her, close enough that he could smell the aroma of her ale-stained apron, and to quietly talk into her close ear, being careful not to make his request heard, other than to the ear in which he did speak, for many spies of many different masters were about. "I am seeking a boat for my two companions and myself to convey us to Portugal in a discreet fashion. Do you know of such a person who may help us in this endeavour?" She looked about the taproom for a boatman who would be suitable, then her searching stopped as she eyed a rough-looking fellow, as he supped his ale in the company of a group of boatmen, they all at wait for their next orders but for them the pickings were few, so they drank their ale as they listened for the call of the wharf bell, when a few boats would be chosen for some task but not all would have luck shine upon them.

"Josh!" she called over to the place where they were sat, and beckoned the boatman to her who had already caught her eye, as 'twas searching the room. He stood and bottomed his tankard at the same time, belching as he left his fellows at the table and letting stinking wind, as he spit a pile of ale-soaked saliva onto the sawdust—the sawdust lying there to suck up all manner of liquids, as it turned the wet gob into the slimy soup of the floor. He rolled his sailor's roll over to the table where Tyrell stood with the landlady. A short swarthy man was he and appeared to be of Spanish or Portuguese stock; his clothes, though appearing well made, were very dirty and in much need of washing; big high boots he wore, they matching his clothes in refinement and dirt. Roughly shaven with his thick black hair hiding his ears, he came slowing from his sailor's gait as he neared Tyrell. The landlady sat then a few paces away having no interest in the conversation that was about to take place; the less she knew of such things the safer she felt.

"Sire," he spake with his broken English, and with two grubby fingers he saluted from his unseen hat, a seaman's salute as a tar to his captain, and always the way he seemed to greet folk.

"Yes, my man. Josh, is it not?"

"'Tis so, sire."

"Where are you from, Josh?"

"I from Portugal," said he in his troubled English. Tyrell came close to the fellow to speak in low tones.

"I seek transport to Portugal for three passengers," quietly spake Tyrell, but Josh could hear the words that were said most clearly.

"I do that, sire, for you, but you know many risks about; the king's coastal ships always seeking close to shore; seek tyrants escaping to lands." He tried to convey his concerns with arms waving about and with hands gesturing, of the king's vessels stopping many craft that left Folkestone, for there were many fleeing the land, taking their rich possessions with them before they could be taken by the new king that reigned, and others fled for different ills—murderers, rapists, thieves, and traitors—all fleeing justice. Tyrell knew the risk he took; he had safe passage as writ by the soon-to-be King Richard, but he had no passage for his cargo; little choice he had if he wished to take the princes to some safe keep. "I understand your concern, Josh, and as such deem that we must travel in the dark hours, and the less time I spend here the safer I shall feel, and wish to go this night at the hour of midnight. What say you? Are you game? And of what is your price for this journey?"

"I sail at midnight; I ask ten shillings."

"Done," said Tyrell. "I will see you outside the tavern at twelve of the clock, and will pay you your dues then, agreed?" Tyrell stuck out his hand, which was clasped in the binding agreement of the shake.

"Agreed," said Josh as he swayed back to the table of his fellow mates.

Tyrell was speaking to the landlady who had been beckoned to come to his side, now that his council was over.

"Madam, for your service to me, I have tethered outside a horse and cart, both in good stead, of which I am no longer in need, and would give to you for the most likeable service you have shown me. If you would like to see it before you accept, please do so."

"Tom!" she shouted, as if her husband was suffering some kind of deafness. "Go out and look at the horse and cart that is tethered outside and see its worth."

"I'm getting these fellows their ale, my dear, I will be but a short while," the landlord pleaded.

"Come here with that," she spake as she made toward him and bounced him out of the way with her hip as she took over the chore. "Go look at the horse, Tom. Why do I have to do everything about here?"

"Yes, my dear," he said as he moused his way to the door.

"Hullo, dearie," Tyrell turned to the voice that spake as one of the tavern hussies sidled her comely body close to his, pushing her knee up into his groin. "Want to come in the alley with me?" she asked brazenly. Her bosom pushed almost to his face as she pressed even harder to him. All this did happen in the shortest time as he looked into the face of a thousand stories, each one written there with its own line. Before time did her features show the weariness of her life and the hardness of her existence. Her face made to look more appealing with the heavy cream and powder layered upon her poxed skin. He gently pushed her away a little so that there was some space between them.

"No, madam." And then spake in some kindness, "My time is pressing," and in speaking gave her three pence so she may eat tonight.

"Thankee kindly, sir, if you call this way again, you can do it for naught." Swaying her hips as she left him, she went to the end of the crowded bar. "Gin," she called as she put her penny down.

"'Tis in good order, my dear." The mouseman on his return relayed what he had seen to his wife. "Both horse and cart are in fine order and worth well over fifteen shillings."

"Does he think now that he's some kind of expert on horseflesh?" the landlady quipped to Tyrell, who wished not to make any comment on the matter. "Thank you, sire," she continued after her little asperity upon her husband. "Your gift is far more than my service to you and I feel in debt."

"Do not fret, madam, for I have no further use for either."

"Please call anytime you are passing, for the ale and victuals will be of no cost to you or your friends."

"You are most kind, my lady. I bid you good day." Tyrell touched his hat and once more stepped upon the road outside, and went toward the inn where his wards did wait. He slowed down at a small opening amongst the tight buildings, for if you were a horseman you would not be able to pass by this yard, for the smells and sounds tantalized your mind and held you. The hostler was at work there, his fire burning of wood and peat; the young lad pumping away at the bellows, his face red with sweat, but still he pumped, the smell of the wrought iron, and the sound as 'twas worked with much skill upon the old anvil. The horses saw Tyrell as he stood and gazed the scene, tied at the back in the cool shadow of the stable, snorting their song and pawing the ground. The hissing sound as the red iron was plunged into the water with its steam and shower bursted about. As always the smell of the horse manure filled the air, coming out of one end as quickly as the hay was fed into the other. When the pumping was done, the boy began to move the manure that was piled near the horses, and brought it to the pile that was outside upon the street, passing by Tyrell with its sweet smell as he went. Later the pile would be picked up and taken away to the place of smell along with many other heaps that were about. The lord moved slowly on, realizing it would be many years before he would see such English places as these, and cared not for time as he savoured the life about him. The smell from the bakery reminded him that he had not yet eaten, and thought of the enjoyment of relieving such with good victuals. Then came to his ear the loud buzz of bluebottles as they flew about the hanging meats outside the butcher's shop, entertaining themselves upon the fresh meal. The tailor's shop, and the bootmaker he passed. Gentlemen stood at the street corner talking with much zeal about their businesses and how they fared. Children ran about. Horses and carts rattled past. The smell of sewage on its way toward the sea. Other smells—sickly, vile, sweet, tempting—all separate, blended; this was Tyrell's England, and soon it would be gone as he made down the way that did lead to the old inn of the Sailors' Rest, that secure place of their keep where his wards awaited his return. He unlocked the side entrance door, and locking it behind him stepped up the narrow stairway to the room of his two princes. He entered with no need to knock, surprising the boys as they quickly separated on seeing the lord enter; they had been once more in deep conference. Tyrell saw their commotion but heeded not there action.

A knock came lightly upon the door that led to the inner stairs of the inn; as it broke the silence, Tyrell pointed to the boarded area of the privy.

"Get in there, boys, until we see who our visitor is, and stay in stillness." They did so at once and were soon unsighted. Tyrell discreetly opened the door to see standing there the kitchen maid, a young girl of no more than thirteen years dressed neatly and holding a large platter full of food and drink, ordered for six of the clock.

"Come in," he said as he held the door open, wondering how such a frail thing could carry such an unwieldy item up a flight of stairs, along a passageway, and, to place this juggling mix onto the table without a spill, deemed him most pleasant towards her. After she had placed down the platter and upped from the table, she gave a childly curtsy to the guest and turned to leave.

"Here, my dear," Tyrell spake as he placed a penny into the small hand that met his outstretched offering.

"Why thankee kindly, sir," she said in her tiny voice, and with another curtsy she left, closing the door quietly behind her.

"Come, my boys, time to eat then abed for a short while; we have a meet at twelve of the clock to take our boat to Portugal."

They came slowly from their hide.

"Tonight, my lord?" asked one of the boys.

"Yes, tonight we must go, for to tarry may bring us closer to exposure, and it is long into the day for such to come upon us now."

"Yes, sir," came the reply. Tyrell looked at the hatless boys in the light that was growing dimmer; he seemed to think that one of his charges, Edward, the older prince, that the hair upon his head appeared to be somewhat darker and less curled than he recalled.

"Your hair, Edward, what has happened to it? Does seem to me of a duller colour—how is this?"

"'Tis but my time of changing, my lord, and seems I am losing my childlike locks and becoming more of a manly shade; my curls coming less, and more of a soldiery nature."

"Yes, Edward, that seems to be so. Do not forget on leaving this place to keep your heads covered and your features scarved as much as you may, to keep you unknown to those eyes that pry."

They sat and supped around the table in their small room, talking of the journey ahead, the boys asking who would be taking them, the length of time at sea, would sickness come upon them, and all manner of things, to which Tyrell gave answers and was able to dispel all that troubled them. Finished then their late meal, they washed themselves and picked their teeth clean, and went to rest for the journey ahead.

Little sleep befell Tyrell as he watched over his princes, and looked moonward to place the time of the meet. Shaken at the shoulder, first one prince was awakened and then the other, they stirred themselves in the dark nightly hour. Tyrell took the striker and taper from its holder and lit a candle, and from the flickering light bringing only its shadowy glow to see by, the boys washed their sleepy faces, to bring back some life into their still awakening bodies. They had all slept in their travelling clothes to speed their departure from the inn, each boy helping the other to don their heavy coats and to tie them closed to keep out the chilled night, for they knew that this night they would be tossed about in the cold Channel for many hours. They pulled their hats down, and secured them tightly about their necks, then brought up the stiff collars high about their faces and hooked closed, hiding all but just a little flesh and four black eyes to be shown of their faces. Tyrell donned his coat and hat and he too was soon ready, and in short time were all at the narrow stairway, the boys tripping carefully down the dark passage with Tyrell throwing the keys upon the table, and making sure no chattels had been forgotten. He then hugged his saddlebags with one arm as they lay over his shoulder, closed the door, and followed the boys to the bottom of the stairs where the noise of the night could be faintly heard. They came from the alleyway to the road that went alongside the harbour, turned the corner, and made way to their place of meet. There were still many folk about, with the torch-lit shops still selling their wares hoping for one more buyer. The smoking torches lit the path to take, glowing upon the heads of the people roaming there. Drunks fell all about as the taverns still sold their brew to the soggy lot; late into the night 'twas offered until there was no one standing to buy. Shouting and laughing were those who had not yet succumbed; rowdy and troublesome were they. Tyrell took the boys over to the dockside, away from the tavern's spill, but still they were all about; two or three trying to hold each other up, passing them by as they made to their dismal homes, others fighting and falling, another group swaying as they looked at some poor soul lying bleeding on the mud and slime of the road, the sewage oozing around his legs and boots, the brown turning red with his blood. Too many boisterous sailors were approaching them with their drunken games played upon the harbour's edge, to fall with the cold splash of the sea below as all gathered about to rescue their friend, swaying and shouting as the dripping tar was pulled from the sea with shiver and shake. Tyrell moved back over to the other side once more where the lit torches gave them some protection, for he sought no trouble.

They came to the street in which women were standing around each tavern along their way. Each waiting to catch some drunken fellow who still had a coin in his pouch to make their night to profit, for most this night, all their endeavours had brought little reward. And not until some naval vessel berthed letting forth its randy crew, would their fortune change for a short while. The women waited all dressed for the teasing game that would engage those whose brain was not in his hat but in his breeches. As they passed, the overpowering, sweet, flowery scent mingled over them, with bosoms fighting to be released from their bindings and red-lipped faces painted bright. Pastilled eyelids fluttered over watery, twinkling eyes trying all to entice a penny.

Tyrell dragged his wards through the crude callings falling about the boy's ears, as they came at last to the inn of their meet. Naught could be seen of Josh as Tyrell looked about the crowd that lingered outside; but, as they moved further into the throng, the glimpse of the small swarthy man came into view, hidden it seemed by the giants about him as he stood leaning against the wall, a tankard in his hand.

"Josh!" Tyrell called as they closed toward him.

"Aye, sire, you are ready?" came the reply in Josh's best English. "And these your crew?"

"Yes, this is my crew, and here is your fee." Tyrell discreetly placed the monies into the rough seafarer's hand. 'Twas gazed upon for a short while as Josh studied the amount, then, leaning off the wall, he bottomed his tankard and placed the empty vessel upon the sill. He then deposited the coins with a clatter into his money pouch and tied the string, pulling it tight to his belt in all security.

"We go—please to follow." Josh stepped through the crowd as the trio tagged on behind the seafarer's gait; his legs it seemed would never adjust to any land that did not sway or rock. A short distance they went, then across the road to the harbour steps that would take them to their means. A crowd of rowdy sailors there from a small vessel of his Majesty's fleet slightly blocked their passage.

"Scuse," said Josh as he gently tried for a way through, but they just looked down at him and closed their ranks, making it most impossible to pass; the drunken group full of the courage of numbers and of ale. Tyrell stepped back with his wards to keep them from any troubles, watching closely the scene opening. "Scuse." Once more came the plea from the small man. No move was made to let them pass. Tyrell's hand was upon his sword with the boys behind him in safety, but the need for him to show his metal was not needed, for, with the quickness that blesses the small and agile, Josh's dagger came from under his cloth. He slashed at one arm barring the way, and on the return, slit the cheek of another who stood close, then pushed them using his stocky legs into the rest of the tars, then again with speed he had his dagger at the throat of another. "Scuse!" he shouted, and the passage was opened with sprawling bodies and bloody splash. Josh pushed the drunken sailor who he held into the others as they made to care for their shipmates. "Come!" said Josh; quickly he ushered his cargo down the steps to the dark waters below, as the sailors above were still trying to understand what had happened, so quickly had it come; they picked themselves up and peered over the harbour wall into the dark below where went their assailant, a little fellow, who by morning's light would be spoken of as well over six feet tall and very broad of shoulder. "Quickly—We go please," said Josh, wanting to put to sea before any more ruffians could be brought to the aid of the sailors. Tyrell and the princes—the would-be seamen—followed Josh onto the rocking vessel, which they could hardly see in the darkness. The shadowed moon offered no help to their eyes as they stepped from the solid ground to the lilting, unsteady craft. Soon they were all on the vessel and hugging the mast to keep themselves steady. Josh untied the line and wound it into a neat pile upon the deck board, then went to the back of the boat and began steering and pushing with his oar away from the harbour of Folkestone.

The moon began breaking out from the curtain that hid its brightness and making all about clearer to their eyes. The sailboat was a sturdy oak vessel of thirty feet, with a strong, straight mast poking into the stars above their heads, and a box-like area at the stern covered in canvas to afford some shelter from the lashing waters. They moved further away from the dockside as the lights and sounds and the moving shadows were gradually faded; they floated calmly seaward. Josh busied himself going through his routine of tying off the rudder and securing any ropes or spigots that were about, for a trip over such could be fatal on the small craft. He pulled hard upon the long wooden arm of the keel lock and lowered it down into the becalmed water. His crew watched all this time, as he worked his seafaring skills upon the boat, still in the calm of the harbour's arms. He went to the canvas sail that was rolled in orderly fashion at the bottom of the mast. Untying the ropes that held it secure, he started to pull upon the winch block, and took the heavy sail in quick time railed to the top of the mast, his sinewy arms bulging and straining as he did so, glistening in the light spray. He looked up as he tied it off; the light breeze flapped the sail, and then billowed softly to give the vessel a steady push as it quietly crept from the harbour.

Tyrell and the princes made some comfort for themselves in the canvas shelter, sitting and gazing through the open back at the place where Folkestone did lay, but all now was of mist and black sky. They looked on hoping that another sighting would come, but it did not. Sadness filled them upon the waltzing water, as they made their wake from the only home they had ever known and headed for the darkness that was the English Channel. The silhouette of Josh steering his boat seated at the rudder was all they could see; the craft started to lurch and sway as they headed into the open waters, almost clear were they of any coastal vessels of his Majesty that could reach them.

Tyrell's thoughts were mingled with all manner of things. The ability of Josh with the knife troubled him a little, for it seemed he was rather more adept at such actions than the poor sailor he was should be. He hoped the crossing would not be stormy, for he wished his charges not to be sickly, and for the small craft they held tightly onto not to flounder and to lose all he had gambled for. Would this be the last fence they would have to climb before a more peaceful time would come upon them in the land of Portugal, away from the dangers that threatened them at this time?

As the cold and lashing waters pushed their vessel about, the princes looked for the dawn at its bow with thoughts of the warm, caressing sun they hoped would soon come.

PART TWO: KING RICHARD III

July 1483 …

Chapter Eight.

Buckingham Turns.

Richard was preparing, with his wife, Anne, for his coronation at Westminster. He stood alone in his private closet, longing, in the dusky light, for the gentle tap that would come upon the door. Tap, tap, it came; the rap he knew, so slim and delicate did it sound. His shadow darkened the door as he opened the latch. And his eyes melted upon his niece, Elizabeth, who had been summoned to him.

"Come in, my dear," spake he in his most soft voice. She entered with the sparkle she had flowing from her all; the perfume she wore captivating her soon king as she knew it would. With her back to Richard she slipped off the hooded cape she wore and let it fall to the floor. She turned to her partially-clothed love, who was smiling at the sight that was being uncovered before him. Quickly they closed to each other and with gentle fondling, and girlish giggles about his ears, he lifted the short, comely frock she wore so that she was bared before her king.

"My lord, my body grows weak and trembles with your advances." He now had forced her to the cot and was upon her in much frenzy, and in the darkness ravished her childlike body until both were exhausted, but soon she was all a-giggle again, as Richard stood and began to put on his underclothes and his breeches. She lay upon the down bed and watched as Richard made himself more presentable, a smile upon her red lips, her face as an angel. Even though she was young in years, her mind was not, and behind all the laughter and pranks lay an astute woman, who would, in all of her being, live a life of joy and to want of naught. Not through devious acts, for she was not such a person, but through patience and with a caring heart and pleasant demeanour and other attributes.

"Elizabeth, my dear," Richard spake caringly, but with a more serious tone to his voice as he pulled up his mistress from the bed; her slim bangled arms encircled his neck as he did so, and her soft bosom pressed gently upon his bare chest, his withered arm discreet in the darkened room. "We must talk of our relations after I am king—" Before he could continue she interrupted him, for she knew all he was to say and did not wish him to be troubled in having to say it.

"My lord, I understand the conditions of a king and know that I can never be your queen, for such would bring troublesome times to yourself. I am your mistress and content to be, until you tire of me."

"Elizabeth—" Richard tried to intervene in her converse, but was quietened by the two tender fingers that were placed upon his lips, the musky perfume from them drifting to his nostrils and bringing calmness to him.

"All I need, my lord, is to please you whenever you may call upon me, for I will come to you at any hour and to any place, for you, my lord, are my life, and I am not saddened at all at this state as long as I can be with you whenever you desire."

"I thank you, my dear, for your understanding; my heart was knotted for the thought of you being no longer in my life, but now it is joyed at your loving talk." He embraced her with deep affection as his eyes teared. In battle torn and through all strife only strength would he show, but with this little dimple he could be turned into a child. "I will see that you are kept in a most royal fashion, and you will never need for aught." He spake into her sweet smelling hair, as with eyes closed and her head to one side she rested her cheek upon his chest, a pleasant smile upon her young face, all fears of the future, whether of love or of fortune, were sealed in this liaison.

They gathered up their strewn clothes and dressed quietly. Elizabeth was hooded once again and at the door being opened by Richard.

"Until the coronation, my dearest one, when I will place my gaze upon you once again, and in the ceremony amongst all its regal trap and pomp 'twill be you that will tumble my head at all times. She smiled from beneath her hood as a child would gaze of all trust, and kissed her king upon his cheek as a niece to her uncle may.

"Goodbye, my king," she smiled, and her small shape waltzed away from the closet of Richard.

'Twas the sixth day of July, the day of Richard's coronation. A good clear day rose from the black night before it. The king-to-be and his wife, Anne, made ready at Crosby Place; the waiting ladies at last finished with their fussing and fetching to adorn her in the rich garments befitting such a splendid occasion; the manservants making their master most regal and primping him to everyone's delight, from a man's soldier to a prince of royal bearing in short spate.

Away most timely, they were at the noon hour to the abbey at Westminster, their golden coach pulled by six white horses bedecked in fine bridles and saddle cloths. Ushered closely by horsed soldiers at the front and at the rear, they passed by large groups of people waving and cheering as they clattered their way. Houses were bedecked in royal banners, some hung across the roadway, from one upper window to another, to flap in the warm midday breeze. The fifes and drums beat out their royal medley as the bells from the steeples peeled their chorus most pleasant; the air seemed to be filled with the joyous sounds.

The parade came to the abbey, and they took their way from the coach and went up the stone steps to the great doors there that opened wide upon their arrival, and greeting them with the choir that rang its heavenly blessings about the sacred building. They seated themselves upon the old thrones that had been used in such ceremonies for three hundred years. And there they were given their crowns of the royal guardians of this land, and were deemed king and queen as writ in the laws of the land and of the Church. Within one hour the solemn act was over, and they left the darkened abbey, with its old musky smell, to breathe then the air fresh of the mid-morn's hours. Their crowns glistened in the bright sun that beckoned them forth; they came all regal with cloaks of blue of purple and of gold, with the White Rose of York shining from the banners held above them. The servants, with ponce, came forward, and with much honour showing from them, removed the royal shoes. As then the new king and queen, in royal homage, came barefoot down the red cloth that had been laid before them upon the steps of the abbey, and most humbly with heads bowed they made their walk along the cloth that stretched upon the road before them, as they slowly took their way past the cheering throngs to the royal feast that was to be held in the great hall of Saint Edward's shrine. "God save our king, Richard!" was called all about as banners were waved, and small babes held high so they might see the royal pair in all their glory. All manner of lords and ladies following the path of the new king. Abbots and bishops, with mitres and croziers, came in their most solemn bearing. Northumberland, with the pointless sword unsheathed held high to his lips as to be kissing the hilt, walked alone. Suffolk with the sceptre, Lincoln with the cross and ball, Norfolk came carrying the royal crowns on the silver platter, covered with blue cloth of the royal house, and Buckingham bearing the king's train, with lowly reverence did he walk behind his king and friend. The Lady of Richmond carried the train of the Queen Anne, followed by the Lady of Suffolk, the Duchess of Norfolk, and by twenty other ladies who followed the most regal procession.

As the last person treaded the last step upon the first length of the red cloth, the royal pages came from within the watchers and carefully rolled up the long stretch, and, with much haste and many harsh words from their masters, who shouted about them, picked up the roll; six boys did run through the thinning crowds, stumbling and tripping as they went their way, under much duress as the cane held by the overseers whacked across their thin legs and welted their tender skin, whelping as they ran from the stinging, as they hasted as quick as they could, but 'twas never fast enough. They moved better now as they left the crowds and cut through the side alleys and roadways, they dry of mouth, red of face and of leg, to pant for breath, and then to emerge at the last cloth laid, with not yet the royal party upon it, and with much direction and harsh words from the parade officer laid down the cloth they had carried, to join with the other that was already laid and made another twenty feet of royal humbleness possible. The pages raced to the back of the parade once more as another group repeated the act, the cloth then retrieved at one end then placed at the other, to be seen as one continuous piece to those who upon it did tread.

In short time the royal party had reached the steps of Saint Edward's Great Hall, and upon climbing the many steps there, turned and waved to their subjects from their high place above the road, which brought even more cheers to ring about, and then the royal couple faded from sight as they entered into the hall. As they did so victuals and ale were brought out to the throng that filled the roadway. 'Twas deemed they would not want upon this festive day, and they would be of good cheer with their families and able to rejoice of their new king and queen, and upon the happier times he had pledged to bring forth to them.

In the Great Hall 'twas filled with joy, banners on high like angels floating above all who revelled below. Wall tapestries hung in many splendid colours, and the dress of all who thronged there, brought such brightness to the solemn building as they cavorted amongst each other. The noise of laughter and music rang all about the chamber. The music still played as they were seated, and ate and drank their fill; then, near to the end of their sup, the great doors of the hall swung open wide, creaking their displeasure as they did so, and all inside were subdued from the banging and creaking and rose to see what the intrusion meant. And then came riding into the hall Sir Robert Dymoke, the king's champion, his horse all trapped in silk of red and white, the rider dressed in the best white harness. The heralds blowing upon their bannered horns as he clattered amongst the banqueting throng, he came close to middle of the hall and with his steed rearing up, he then declared in deep ringing voice: "Be their any man here who will say against King Richard the Third, why he should not be king, speak thee loud now?" And for a while the hall was of complete quiet. Then said he, "No one sayeth so—" and drawing his sword and wielding it above his head cried with much fervour, "God bless our king, Richard!" And all the people so gathered cried forth: "King

Richard!" and on "King Richard! King Richard!" as with one voice did it ring. And the king stood with his wife in hand and they most humbly bowed before their most loyal subjects, and slowly, as the praises slowed, the king and his wife sat and all was of a most pleasing lot.

Richard turned then to his adviser Buckingham; he had noticed that he bore not such a joyous face as was his custom.

"Come, Buckingham, fill yourself with much joy, my dear friend, for you seem a tidy dull."

"Nay, my king, I am full of much pleasure for you, but my heart though is a little sad for our dear princes at this time, for they are so alone in their young state."

"Trouble ye not, Buckingham, for no harm will touch their princely persons; 'tis my word I give."

"I know of this, my lord; please forgive my concern," and he raised his goblet with his king as they clinked their vessels together and drank the rich red wine. But still the anguish was within Buckingham, as he had already heard whispers of the supposed death by murder of the two princes, and was feeling the need to depart from Richard's side if this were true, for he could not serve a child-killer. But the truth he did not know and had to dismiss such from his mind, for the wrath of this king he did not want to suffer. It seemed to him that one day he would walk upon the mountaintop teetering upon its edge, to be pushed one side he would still feel the love of Richard, to be pushed the other he would feel the treachery and hate of his friend. Fate and truth would say which side he would be pushed.

The days passed, and the King Richard engaged in many parliamentary acts and writings, to repay his many adherents and high nobles who had favoured his cause, to bring knighthoods and monetary awards to them.

'Twas now put about that the princes were indeed missing from their chambers within the Tower, and that naught was known of their whereabouts, but was generally acknowledged that they must have suffered to murder, and that Richard must be knowing of such a deed, and as such did not bode well with many lords and nobles. But the king swore to bring to trial the persons responsible for this most foul of deeds and did agree with the fact that murder must have taken place. He pledged upon his crown to bring to the light the bodies of such children, that they may be given a most regal and royal burial as befits all princes. And to bring closure as quickly as he could, for does it not sicken his stomach that such vile persons abide in this Realm. He painted the picture upon the large canvas with the thick brush and the bright paint. But only a pen's line upon a scrap of parchment would be all his effort. Time he drew to his side, for within it, all would be forgotten of the evildoings, and, as was his will, naught would come of his endeavours to bring to trial any persons.

Richard was losing confidence in many of his nobles, and so brought in laws to ease the burdens placed upon his common people, and to improve their wellness, making the masses more eager to bring their allegiance to the king if troubled times did come. Richard made it a treasonable act to apply any taxes upon such people to finance any warlike activity, or to fill any loss to the landowners of their income due to faults not of their own fabrication. All these things making the king goodly in the eyes of his people but not so to lordly eyes; but all such happenings did fade the princes' murders into the misty time.

The warming summer days went there way, and in its stead the chill October winds come blowing over the Realm of Richard, with the cold rain cutting the skin of any within its reach who would wander into its searching path. The darkness of the evening brought more trials to the peasants who still worked the fields, and to any who travelled in such dire elements. And so 'twas with Richard's subjects. All it did seem stirring against him like the driving rain and darkness that did creep about. Not seen yet as any rebellion but creeping more into the dark as the days passed; troubled nobles, not inclined to Richard's demands, all of a whisper amongst themselves. The royal murders to them had not faded and still hung over the king's head like a waiting scaffold. Still he continued upon his path, well aware of the growing storm against him. His spies constant in bringing to him all news of impending plots and intrigues. Richard continued laying as much goodness upon the lower classes as he could, to retain all loyalty.

He went on many journeys away from his residence at Crosby Place, as 'twas on this autumn day, making his way into the Midlands to show his presence there and to bring more of his countrymen into his fold. He rode with his brightly-clad musicians. His brave soldiers of the royal guard at the head, and at the rear, gaily bedecked were their horse with bridles that gleamed from the hostlers' polish, their regal bearing showing through the dark rain that tried to dim their day as they entered into the castle at Nottingham, that was to be this night's stop on their journey to York. They pulled into the courtyard of the castle high upon the rock that overlooked the town below, its dulled lights whimpering in the rain. The black smoke floated high from the houses below. The castle stood liken to a giant hawk hovering above them, as the fireplaces burned in each home the wood and peat for cook and warmth. Soon they were inside with the devoted lords and earls seated around the royal table; as they supped 'twas clear that one devoted to Richard was not at his seat, the seat at the king's right hand, the seat of Buckingham, and our king was not pleased at the slight. The nobles were talking and laughing amongst themselves while the king was perusing the morrow's doings, of visiting the market people and the small outlying hamlets. And to give out tokens of his affection towards them.

Buckingham was also taking victuals at this time; he though was residing in the castle at Caernarvon, deep in the wooded hills overlooking the valleys of Wales, he as governor of the principality granted to him by Richard. But all was not well with our Buckingham as the thoughts of rebellion against his long-time friend tumbled within his mind.

The passed months had brought his mind to change, from the devoted to the despising, moulded such by the sly Bishop of Ely, who had been placed in Buckingham's keep after the bloody doings at the Tower. Started he most gently at first with such words as, "My lord, you are of such fine and upstanding bearing, I wonder why you are not standing equal with our most loving sovereign, Richard?"

"Morton, I serve him as humbly as I can, for he has, in all his goodness, looked upon me as his brother, and as such has treated me with much love and with riches abound, and such a thought as you offer has never been with me."

"Aye, my lord, our Richard is such a fine man, and is indeed most generous." And there would end the conference until another day, a time to let the tiny seed grow but just a little so it would not be noticed. And then, when Buckingham thought that any intrigue in his head was gone, the bishop would come again with his little worm to wriggle about in the lord's sanity.

"What thoughts have you, my lord, upon the state of the princes?" Morton knew well of the bitterness held in Buckingham's bosom upon this topic, and brought it out as cutting open the healing wound with the dagger.

"I am, my dear bishop, most grieved at the thoughts that enter my head, and wish not to think of such that doth pain me so. But comes nagging at me like some fishwife chastising her husband, and will not stop, for, as time goes on, the more I hear doth place Richard's hand in the mix, and has come to the state that I have to depart from his presence, for to be so sickens me deeply." Slowly the bishop continued his relentless act of turning the pleasant Buckingham into a most hateful man, and treasonable acts soon were in his frame. Though he was not fully unagreeable to the suggestions that were being made to him.

"You are by far a more noble fellow, my lord, than Richard with his stumped shape and evil manner. You would be a far better king to lead this great land."

"You may be right, my bishop, but would be a fearful trip I would be entering." The worm had grown now and was eating into the swelling head, until all was the bishop's worm.

Then, in time later come, as the bishop let his worm work, came the next persuasion.

"My lord, you have many followers in this land who will come to you, more so than Richard could muster, for his pleasing is low. And would not all of your wild Welshmen follow your banner?"

"I think all you speak is most truthful; am I not of good royal stock, and not soiled by intrigue?"

"Yes, Buckingham, you carry the image of true honour. Take upon you the crown and all its riches, take arms and become king, and end this life of the blood supper and child-killer. Let us rid this Realm of the bragging boar that with its tusks raises everyman's skin."

"I will, my bishop, and will do so straight and to tarry not, for I am burning within, as some mighty force sends me to end this madness that stalks with humped shoulders."

At last, over many weeks, Morton had turned the troubled Buckingham into rebellion against Richard. The bishop thought with evil mind upon his deed, for if Buckingham were fortunate to take the crown then would he not be in favour? If he were not fortunate, there would be one less noble to worry the Church, and would not the power of the king be diminished, now that his friend was a traitor and no longer his ally?

The fire's glow was all bent and misshapen, as it reflected from the single eye, wet and blinking, peeking in disguise from behind the drapes that dragged the floor in the darkness there; for a while it did so watch, until then 'twas pulled into the folds as all to see and to hear was now but naught.

Buckingham went forth to gather his soldiers and his friends, and his wild Welshmen, to do battle against the King Richard. With long striding steps of determination quickly trod to raise his army in much secrecy went the Lord Buckingham, to risk all against his once friend. He had been pushed from the crest to the side he willed best …

"My lord, a messenger in much haste wishes to speak with you." One of Richard's guards informed the king of the arrival from London. He entered on being beckoned by the soldier, all a-huff and red of face came he, tired and dirty from his ride along the rain-soaked highways he had travelled.

"My lord, King, I bring you word of the Kentish men from the Weald marching now to the city, bent upon plunder, and to say that they are coming to test your worth as king. They burn villages as they come and are bringing much distress to your people. My Lord Norfolk requests that you come to dispel these robbers."

"Aye, so," Richard spake as he lifted himself from the table. "Make all ready; we go straight to dispel this rebellion," talking to the officer of the guard, who, upon saluting, went with haste through the hall doorway to make ready for their quick return to defend the capital. Soon all were outside and mounting their unsettled horses, who pawed the ground and pulled their reins with much mischief, most disturbed at this hour to be saddled again. They trundled slowly through the castle gates, which stood black above the heavy mist. Below the rock, neither fires nor smoke could be seen; the mist had laid its sea all below the castle, which stood as a ship, anchored upon a ghost sea. Richard's party made its way down from the high place and was soon enclosed within that sea of mist, and all left was the movement of them as they clopped and rattled, some of the guard talking lowly, horses whinnying, wagons rolling over the uneven cobblestones, all came to ear, but no sight showed more of the soldiery that went their way. The pace rose quickly as the track levelled, and soon they were turning their gait toward the London way; with haste they rode the journey to the city.

The drying weather made the track faster as they increased their pace even more with frequent horse changes and little stopping time, bringing them by the following evening to the narrowing streets of London, sounding about their chorus of a royal army against the close buildings that hugged the way.

Norfolk showed from out of the evening dusk riding forward from the army of soldiers that was his command, standing still with their pikes and bows to hand, their arrows quivered and bulging with the number, to greet the King Richard he came.

"My king!" He addressed Richard from his mount with a bow as best he could from the saddle.

"Norfolk, so what of this uprising? Where are these Kentish men that we may show them some steel?"

"We indeed, sire, went forth to confront them, but when we reached the place of their march, they had stopped coming forward and disbanded, and are now returning with dismay back to their homes. It seems they had no stomach on learning of your hasty return to the city, and have given up their plot rather than face you with the rabble that is their army."

"And what of their leaders? Do you know who they are who bring such trials upon this land?"

"Our agents are within them, my lord, and deem it will be soon that we will know who commanded them."

"Inform me, Norfolk, upon receiving this information for we must take them to task. I wish to bring peace and prosperity for all within this land, but seems some do not want it so."

There was no more conference upon the matter, as all he could do was await the news from the agents and then all would be done who schemed against the Realm. He turned his steed to the way of Crosby Place, and all followed their king at a slower gait, realizing how fatigued they really were, along the winding trek where they could rest a while and fill their empty stomachs.

Richard had just removed his heavy riding coat when he was approached by a dark figure that came to him from the dim recess of the passageway; 'twas his watery-eyed agent who came close and whispered into the kingly ear of that which he had heard within the house of Buckingham. In short time the message was delivered and the king spake into the ear of his agent in secretive tones, heard to no one whose ears may yearn, and then, with his black cape clutched about him, he slithered away as he had come.

Richard was in no frame to rest and if he did not rest then neither would others. He called for all his nobles to meet with him in the conference room, where food and drink were laid, to sup and confer at the same hour. Richard stood still somewhat mired in his journey's dirt, but still imposing in his royal attire, muddied and bedraggled though he was, he stood above all in his demeanour.

"My lords, seemingly many persons are causing this Realm to come into conflict, and I say to you, my lords, we must not have to bear such treasons. We will by the sword end all such devious acts to bring this Realm to peace. Firstly, we will start with that rebel and traitor, our Lord Buckingham, of whom I have heard many whispers of disloyalty. But within the last hour, I have received information that he indeed, at this very moment, in most sinister secrecy, is forming an army to usurp the crown from our most royal self." The room was all of stillness, the only thing that dared move were the candles' flickering flames; no word was uttered from any mouth, with many that gaped in awe at the words that Richard had spoken. They waited for the next words that would change the silence. All had heard of the grumblings and the unrest of Buckingham, but none thought that such things would bring this end. As they were sat uneasy in the conference room, for what is their worth? they pondered; if the king had such hatred of his dearest of friend, who had fought beside him and together had brought Richard to the throne, their lives, as such, would be as worthless as a dead horse.

"We must withstand this malicious purpose. This Buckingham, the most untrue creature living, his mind washed by that evil bishop of his keep. There are plots against this throne urged on by the Countess of Richmond, and the Duke of Buckingham, who, if he cannot take the crown, would put forward as king the countess's son. Make no mistake, for a fool I am not, and all of which I speak is known to me as fact. More devious acts are about to incite the commonalty to revolt. All this has happened in the small space of time from your Richard becoming king. Ne'er forget, gentlemen, my spies are amongst all and any who desire to end my kingship will be known to me, and I will end such with the bloody sword!" These words spoken by Richard dampened any thought of revolt that some may have pondered, and all were pledged to the king who stood before them.

"And this Buckingham who chooses to see me trodden into the mud, as he stalks like some heinous devil about my person, will be brought to a swift downfall, as all who would treason against me; mark such as I speak, for I am in a most disturbed mind and will see the end of this matter in haste. We bide here until we receive course of Buckingham's move. My new adviser, now that Buckingham has turned, will be Sir Thomas Ashton, and as such has all authority to judge all traitors without noise or formality of trial, and without regard to any appeal whatsoever, and to proceed with the utmost execution befitting traitors."

The low conference that was about the hall during Richard's tirade was of complete silence, for stood now before them a despotic leader; cold was the air and the feeling within the chamber; the fire did crackle bright and warm but all else was of chill. Death would stand about them all, no matter how innocent their act may be. The only course left to them was to succour the king, and to bring to him no thought of discontent.

'Twas the end of October. Fifty tribal leaders of the wild Welsh hordes entered now the courtyard of Buckingham's castle, their long black hair hanging down to the waist, their beards swung before them, uncut and unkempt, almost dragging the ground. The bush that was their eyebrows, hung in large clumps over their eyes, all a-curl and awry, bringing to them a fearful and wild look. Hairy they were with such abandon showed that these were indeed the leaders of their tribes. And to see such, as they made their way, reminded those who gazed upon them the stories of the cave people from ages back that had been passed down to them; the black teeth, unwashed and dirt covered, ragged cloth about them, and the smell from their rancid bodies reaching the doors and windows of the castle, long before any sight of them came to view. Some of the castle staff mingled in the yard wishing to see the strange band that entered their civilized state, but quickly cringed back from the smell and felt they could see the fleas and lice jumping from one to the other as they tramped by. Some wore crude sandals afoot, some wore nothing. A short skirt or breeches of leather, or rough woven cloth was tied at the waist. Most were bare-chested, except for the straps of their sword belts that crossed the bushy hair upon their upper body; all were scarcely clad but feeling no cold from the chill October. They had come from the hills and the mountains of Wales where cold and ill conditions were their way of life. This valley where they gathered seemed warm and pleasurable to them, and held but little discomfort.

They lopped to the platform that had been placed in front of the great doorway in the cobbled courtyard, and stood below it as Buckingham came out and stepped upon the stage to plea his request to them. As he stood he could hear the tribal warriors who awaited outside of the gates; over two thousand strong were they, chanting in their high voices that blessed the Welsh with their songs of battle, feet stamping in time with the beat of the drums, that dull thud that pained the ear in its incessant rhythm—that was increasing to a battle frenzy; that sound that would bring the terror of them to burn, pillage, and rape. But then the beat steadied and did not rise any quicker, and continued so with its bump, rattle, bump in the drizzling morn.

"My lordly chiefs," Buckingham began his play. "This day I bring to you no riches and no wagons laden with good victuals to bribe your great force, but ere the morrow and for every day after, you will plunder all you seek. For I bring to you conquest upon this journey to end the reign of that despot Richard, who holds the crown in his evil grasp. We will plunder and crush his towns, and lay them to waste in our path that will take us to his den. And on the journey we are promised many allies from our loyal nobles, who will join our mighty brigade on its victorious march to London and to the crown. Our great friend Richmond is at this present time at sea from Brittany with many ships that carry an army with the same passions as ours, and they will strike on the southern shores of our land, and with haste make a joining with us at the capital. And, my mighty warriors, when I become king, you will be bestowed with much wealth and such lands to satisfy your needs. I ask you all, as your leader, to follow me in this quest of great beginnings. What say you?"

The leaders, with the sound of the drums and the chanting of their followers that rattled all about them, brought on such fever in their heads that they were taken up in the honeyed words and unseen riches that were so promised to them, and all as one shouted to the question.

"Aye! We will follow!" They raised their clubs and swords above their heads as they shouted the words that rung Buckingham's ears, as the sweet song of the birds in the meadow would please him. Calling loudly the cry of the mountains as the drums hastened to the sounds of their chiefs' rant, and in fervour madly danced about as Buckingham and his soldiery mounted, and made out from the castle to take their place at the head of the army's march. Mounted high upon his black steed, fully harnessed to do battle was he, with his black metal as black as the horse he sat, his chest armour overlaid with the crest of his family, surrounded by his shield of honour as a knight, the only thing about him that shone brightly of proud gold. Splendour only nibbled at what he was. Loyal troops rode behind him, five hundred mounted officers, eight hundred soldiers of the foot, two hundred bowmen, and aback, the Welsh chiefs with their disarray of wild followers. They moved off to the command.

"May God be with us!" As they marched away from the Welsh land and headed toward the plunder of England, the beat of the drums carried them forward with its incessant rhythm, marching on through the rain that deemed never to stop. Over the Bristol Channel were they ferried upon the flat barges, pulled by horses upon English soil, as around the capstan they plodded to bring the cargo to land one after the other. After a night's rest they were to the road again as the weather came with more kindness upon them. They were approaching Trowbridge, the first of the small towns of conquest. It stood in the flatlands of Wiltshire; 'twas not large in size but victuals would be there, and the plunder of some good riches from the church and from the abbots who resided in the monastery close by.

"They come! They come!" The ringing shouts passed along the road to the little town. The scouts who had been warned of the coming army had spied them as their dust and cries drifted along the peaceful track.

"How many? How far are they?" The town burgher questioned the breathless runner that hasted with the news. Many townsfolk running to them to crowd around and to listen to what was being spoken.

"One day away at their pace, and fully three thousand armed men with many rabbled Welsh amongst them," he bleated out through his gasping breath.

"Call all the councillors to the hall!" spake the burgher, as the runner offed once more to seek out the councillors; he jogged and dodged around the bustling townsfolk, as they busied about the task that had come upon them, as such had done many times before, and all knew their duty this day. But the many who were coming hastened them along. With all about horses and cattle, pigs and sheep, wagons and carts being laden with all manner of chattels from the homes and shops within the town. Soon the councillors in their ones and twos, hastened to the town's hall to seek the burgher who awaited them. Quickly he told them the number of plunderers that were approaching and to their distance away.

"I suggest, my friends, with the heavy rains that have fallen, that we should use for our cover the high ground of Markham Forest that lies to the west of the marshes where we have some hides in place." The burgher made his suggestion to the assembled parties of his councillors and the many businessmen, all standing side by side with the shopkeepers, the trades people, the farmers, and all others who all had much to lose; all trivial disagreements were put aside as this peril loomed upon them.

"Aye," came the agreement from the floor as the forest of Markham was made their choice.

"Derrick! Derrick Barker!" The name was called from the burgher, whose eyes sought about into the faces of all assembled looking for the man, Derrick.

"'Ere I be, sire," came the deep voice as the Mister Derrick Barker came through the crowd that stepped aside so that he may pass. A stocky man showed himself; dark, unkempt hair hung about his ears; heavy boots clumped along the wooden floor; he as tough as his boots, showing his broken teeth through cracked flaking lips, a man looking as if he had never spent more than one hour inside a covered dwelling, but had slept and made his home under any tree that was close, summer and winter mattered not, for the coddle of a home was not for him.

"Derrick," the burgher spake quieter as he came close, "use your men at the east side of the marshes for your tactics, and Derrick, do them much anguish."

"I will so, sire." Few words came from this man who talked with his crossbow and his plundered sword. Retained by the town was he to disrupt any that wished to do injury to the people, and to wreak what havoc he could against them; with him a small band of townsfolk, all young and eager men, ready to do what hurt they may to such as came this day. Derrick gathered his men who stood at the door's way, and made off with haste to his place of hide to the far side of the town where lay the marshes.

The burgher spake once more to the assembly, as he had done so many times before in such straits.

"Each gather your group together and make sure nothing is left for our invaders. Go, my friends, and may God be with us all." All dispersed from the hall and made their different ways to the departure posts, where already gathering were some of the townsfolk, eager only to depart from the coming intruders. Their carts full with their belongings, and all about was turmoil with carts and children and pigs and tables, and all that made life to them, made to their meeting posts. And soon they were prepared to desert all that was left to the plunderers, as they made their way to the safety of Markham Forest.

The sun shone bright, but the track they struggled along was still rain-sodden as the carts trundled with their worldly cargo. Dogs ran barking and yapping about the wheels, while their masters with their wives and children tramped through the mire. They slowly made their way to the higher ground and the way became drier of foot. They prayed for safety as into the thick woods they went; dark and cool, the branches covered their being, along the known tracks that climbed even higher, making hard the conditions that faced them, but each helped the other as they pushed at the carts and pulled at the horses to make through the close trees and steep ground. The lay then levelled and each group went to its set post within the forest; branches and sod had already been made into crude shelters from the times previous when they had made the reluctant trek. Soon they were tying up their horses, and putting their stock into the roughly-made pens so they would not roam. No fires burned, for the flag of smoke would show of their hide. The night would come and cold would be upon them, so they gathered what they could to wrap the children and prepared to huddle together in their shelters, to shiver with cold and to shiver with fear during this night as the dark stillness came about. Wolves would howl and owls would screech, and the coughing from some dark place were all that would be heard.

The dawn had come to the town that stood so still on this day of October, as it waited for its intruders to come. The steam rising from the horses that trod the muddy roadway gave the first sign of the plunderers coming; the army that marched in their thousands bent on usurping the throne from that fiend Richard were coming, stretching out far along the winding track that was their way to Trowbridge. The leader, Buckingham, was almost at the town whilst the last of his army were still two mile aback; the last stragglers not in any marching order, jabbering in their tongue of Gaelic.

Thud! The arrow came in all silence until it ripped into the chest of one of the lagging invaders. With all the power from the longbow it had come, now it showed sticking out from his back; with blood and anguish did it arrive, as the warrior stumbled into the mud like a broken doll. The stragglers were being repeatedly struck from the woods about them. Derrick and his men peering through the thick bushes as each took a target and did not miss, for they could not fly as the partridge but sat as the docile duck. The soldiers closed together trying to seek some protection, and to see from where the sniping arrows came; but they could see little as one by one they were felled on the mired track. They still moved on in their defensive state, not wishing to be cut off from the rest of their comrades. They cowered under the arrows trying to defend themselves with the small round shields they carried, held in front at first, but to no effect as the bowmen still cut through them with ne'er a wasted shaft. They held their shields high but were struck at the knees and stumbled to the slop, where they were picked with ease as they flopped in helpless state. They lowered their shields but were then struck in the eye, with the arrow searing into the brain; some tried to pull the shaft from their bloodied sockets only to rip their brains upon the barbs and blindly stagger about, falling into the ditches and crashing into the heavy trees as blind, crazed bulls, as still the cutting arrows came and the ground flowed bloody at their feet.

Buckingham's outriders discreetly went into the town ahead of the army, to see if any resistance was forthcoming, but they found only silence. They broke open the doors of shops and hovels but found nothing, nothing to plunder, and nothing to satisfy their appetites. And so it went as they furthered into the town, as forgotten dogs barked and yapped at the intruders as they continued their search. The more they searched the more they became angry at finding naught, and taking out their frustration by slashing at the animals with their swords, and chased after the whining, scurrying dogs from their sight. But no sooner had they done so, that they were back again with their rasping barks like mocking townsfolk. They made to plunder the church and battered open the thick oak door, then stepped into the emptied sacred place, as all about them came others of the army who had seen what the town offered them, and had come also to rob the church. The Welshmen about were becoming raged, with no plunder and no victuals to satisfy them; their hunger was creeping from stomach to brain. Buckingham was trying to calm down the Welsh, with sugary words of the bounty awaiting at the next place they were to come upon, a larger town this time that would yield to them abundant food and plunder. He with much pleading at last calmed them down, but they were desirous of razing the town for its doings against them. Some of the Welshmen went out with clubs and swords to catch the yapping dogs so that they may eat this night, but as they stalked about no dogs did they see. Fled were they as the townsfolk, for they too knew the whiff of danger. Though a few of the buildings were fired, Buckingham managed to stop most of it happening, for in his mind he knew, if all did not go well, he may have to seek some aid from some unlikely places.

"There they are!" came the Welsh voices from the lagging army, as three of the town's bowmen were revealed a short distance from the roadside;

the arrows had stayed and they were able to look about amongst the thick bushes. They left their brothers marching the road as they charged after the bewildered bowmen. Fully fifty enraged Welshmen who had watched their comrades cut down were now out for a bloody revenge, and came they with seething rage towards those hapless peasants.

With swords swinging high above their heads, and screaming the wild cries of their land, the hair upon their crowns blowing about like the wings of hawks, they ran toward the frightened group, who upon seeing the raging surge coming toward them, picked up and fled with cries of fear as the screaming wild men came after them. Across the open field they ran in a terror that shook their knees. The three ahead of the fifty, keeping ahead of them by their knowledge of the land. Down a slope went they as the lay dipped causing a stumble here and a trip there, but with one helping the other they were able to keep ahead. They ran on, still clinging to their precious bows, through some trees and bushes, and made toward the swamp; they became unsighted for a moment as they went through the trees and the raging mob came closer. The three townsfolk cut sharply to the right as they disappeared behind the bushes and dove under a branched cover that waited to hug them to safety. The Welshmen went straight on through the scraping bushes, and saw three of their prey standing but a hundred paces from them. They stood and fled no more, but faced the Welsh. The band swinging their plundered swords above their heads, the blades swishing and glinting, making themselves easily seen, and easily heard with their mocking voices. "Come, you sons of pigs! Come, you smelly bastards! Come, if you can!" All such words were bandied about to rage the enemy, and they were raged and teeming with anger. The Welshmen charged forward with their bloody screams for the pleasure of cutting down these peasants who mocked them. They rushed down the slope and strode across the ground, but quickly did it give way beneath them as they were strode into the mud-sucking swamp; and in the rage that consumed them, they still strove forward until they could move no more, all trapped in the sucking mire. No bows hung about them, only useless swords to hand; their razored edge would cut naught this day. Rising from their hidden crouch, the bowed townsfolk stood before them, with Derrick at the head looking down from the higher ground at the floundering plunderers.

"Raise!" called he, as his true shooting men lifted their bows and engaged their arrows, raising them to sight along the quilled shafts to the floundering Welsh at the pointed head. Such skills did these bowmen have as to choose where the arrow would strike; one shot was all they needed to kill, but this day chose to let the invaders suffer by using them as practice.

One in the shoulder, ripping the muscles, then into the other shoulder, severing nerves as it went straight through. Then two or three ripped the stomach to bleed with spurts of life, an eye gone now with a crunch as the arrow cut. Then on to the next floundering target, as the more they struggled in the mud the more were they held there. "Finish them!" came the order as the targets had become stilled. And they saw their fate as the arrows cut through them with sickening rhythm. The screams became less and less, as the marksmen shot and replaced the empty bow with another arrow and watched it sail to thud into another helpless body. The mud of the marsh was now red with pumping blood being spread into it. Then, at last, all was still as fifty wild Welshmen were wild no more.

The small band moved over their hidden walk of logs to the bank where the plunderers had crossed. Derrick placed a guard so they would be secure, and they began throwing out their noosed ropes, soon to drag from the mud the tombstone-like bodies, they sticking up at different angles where they had been struck. All were needed upon the rope, as the first pulls were very difficult until the legs were released from the sucking mire, and after would drag with much more ease. One after the other the bodies were dragged out, not for any compassion was this done but to retrieve the arrows that stuck from the flesh. They were pulled, and then thrown into a pile to be taken back to the town, where they would be sorted, for each had his mark upon the shaft and would be returned to the bowmen. Belts were taken from the fallen, with swords and daggers pulled from the cold, stiff hands. Rings of crude silver were pulled from fingers, and anything of use was taken to be the shared spoils of the day.

A shout from the posted guard rang about, and it seemed that trouble was making again its way, echoing then in the still air as all looked up from the grisly lot toward the cry, but then the signal came that all was quiet. A few of the Welshmen's brothers had come to search for their comrades and had followed the fateful tracks to the marsh. Six of them only had come, but had been quickly cut down by a group of bowmen from the camp at Markham's wood who had banded together for a little sport. The guard could see that the still warm bodies were being stripped of their possessions, and as would happen in the swamp area, the now naked bodies were dragged into the trees and bushes at the side of the way and left as carrion for the harriers to do their work, and in short time only the white bones would be left; soon they would be scattered and gone, as if no enemy warriors had ever passed through this space of England.

Buckingham marched on toward the promised town of Newbury, where its gold and suckling pigs awaited them. His Welshmen, though, straggled at the rear with no joy about them. They made toward the meet with the

Lord Salisbury, with his soldiery over one thousand strong, all promised to the cause on the day after the morrow, with many others coming from smaller estates whose finger they wished in the pie of the spoils. On until dusk fell did they march, to settle for the night on the banks of the river Thames that twisted its way to London as it flowed seaward. Little food was there where they rested; no fish would swim their nets, and no game would enter their traps. All for the hungry Welsh and soldiers of the lord were a few wild berries and some poor roots. So they settled under the clouding skies as rain threatened them once again at this most dismal of times. The Welshmen, with their stomachs empty of food and of faith, and of little hope that their fortunes may improve, decided that they would stay longer and pray for a much better fate on the morrow. Buckingham sat in his guarded tent dimly lit by one candle, as he with no guilt supped his wine and ate his cold meat and bread, to rest into a broken sleep with his thoughts of the morrow fluttering his mind.

The morn came wet and dismal; the rain had fallen during the night but had stopped at this early hour; the day, still dark and wet, as the soldiers and the Welshmen stirred and rose from their steaming rest. Most rose and stretched their weary selves, but some on the outer places of the camp did not. Soon comrades were gathered about the still heaps that did not answer the call, as laying there upon the wretched ground were twenty of their brothers, with bloodied blankets and slitted throats. They, silenced in the dark of night; the villagers had come, and with their knowledge of the land, came in much quietness to the sleeping wild men, and with silent slash and a slight gurgle ended them as they lay in sleep, the sleep where the dawn would not show. The comrades were in screaming rage at the sight, and cried their pagan oaths with waving arms at the sinking moon, pledging revenge upon the evildoers. They took the weapons from the silenced group and left them as they lay, to join the army that was starting to move away. Still calling for revenge upon anyone they could get their thick hands upon, with blood-red eyes and aching stomachs, they trudged behind the band of soldiers that marched its way to the town of Newbury.

Through the rain-filled tracks they slopped, many were still being cut down with arrows from the dark woods that sided their track. Some still marched on in some reasonable order, others were so enraged that they ran with curdling cries into the thick bushes and trees to strike the taunting enemy. Their shouts became quickly silent, and they where not to be seen again. Soon they learned of the uselessness of this act and stayed within the ranks, or they would see no more of the sun's rise. As they marched 'twas seen that when their brothers were cut down from the silent shafts 'twas best not to render any help to them, for they would surely end up in a bloody heap. They carried no full-length shields as the Romans carried; small and light were their guards, and were of little use against the wicked arrow that came in the devil's silence.

The day went through many hours, and it seemed cursed were they as the heavy driving rain had started again, and through it the arrows began cutting into the soldiers of the guard. Between the bottom of the helmet and the high chain mail, only of an arrow's width, showed a small gap of pale, exposed skin, but over the neck vein did it tempt. Firstly, closed then opened again, as it moved with the march of the feet. A soldier lifting his head a little too much as he peered to keep his leader in sight was all that was needed. Then a numbness as his head was pushed to one side from the arrow's impact; it entered, severing the vein and bouncing off the neck bone, sticking through fully three inches as it showed on the other side breaking out at a strange angle. The blood pumped out from the entry side, with the soldier not as yet knowing the severity of his wound. He placed his hand over the flow but life pumped through the stumpy fingers he held there; all was numb and no pain did he feel, only the warm blood as it filled his doublet and to run down his legs, filling his boots. Faintness then took him over as his brain fogged, and blurred became his eyes, soon to stumble and to fall onto the muddied track. Those who marched close to him did manage to step clear of their fallen comrade, but soon trampled down as the many behind marched over him. Gone to ground, as many others felt the shaft of death upon them during this day of such misery.

They came soon to their town of plunder, as the Welshmen more joyed upon the sight shouted in great anticipation, for they saw the smoking chimneys below them, as they came over the hilly, furrowed land that lay before the town. For was it not a good sign that the fires were burning below? Was it not that the townsfolk had no idea that they were about to be pillaged? Was it not that they were baking their breads and cooking their meats for Welshmen to sup? Thoughts of victuals, of plunder, of murder, and of rape again filled their savage thoughts. At the noon hour they came, the wild cries of the Welsh rang once more, as with their chiefs they ran past the Lord Buckingham and his guard, who with little heart tried to slow the rowdy mass, but 'twas to no avail, for they were bent upon their task. Down the hill ran they where the lazy town awaited them at the bottom. All ran in much disarray as they slipped and slid upon the muddy underfoot, but came quickly to the road and the first small houses with the lazy curls of smoke coming from their pots. They saw though a bigger prize, for the tavern stood but a short distance away, beckoning them with its still open door and the bait of ale within. They burst in with hearty cries that would place fear upon those who waited innocently there, their swords waving above their heads, angry men all bent upon mischief. They tumbled in, but soon were all stood still and in silence, as they saw their dead comrades, who had been seated about the place in grisly fashion, with empty tankards clutched by cold hands, and with eyes of glass that looked out from them but saw naught. No persons here to murder, no victuals here, no bounty to steal, no maidens to rape—all gone as before, just comrades sat and waited at this place. They ran from the tavern as others went in to see of the gory lot; others were coming from the houses empty of all profit. Soon all the town had been searched, and all gathered with emptiness and dismay, for the only thing this day had brought was the sickly display from the townsfolk that mocked their pride.

"Be steady, my fellows; all is not done." Buckingham was in the midst of his disgruntled allies trying to hold his army together, to come again with his honeyed words. "We meet with our Lord Salisbury this day who brings with him many followers to our cause. Then, upon the morrow, we all will join with our beloved Earl of Richmond, who at this very hour is marching with his five thousand Bretons to rendezvous at our place of meet. We then—" Buckingham tried to continue, but was silenced by cries of anguish and disappointment from the Welshmen. All were now frail, and they would hear no more of these false promises from this Englishman who had brought upon them only death and hunger, and, who as others, had lied to them. The rain being the curse put upon them, and until it ceased it would be so, for with the rain all evil would fall upon them. They clutched their pagan necklets and wailed to the black sky, and as the rain splattered upon their heads and bodies they followed their chiefs to desert Buckingham, and to leave him without strength in the middle of Richard's domain. They left the rain-sodden army that stood with Buckingham, and returned to the track that had brought them, to enter what perils may come as they went their way back to Wales, and from the curse of Buckingham's rain.

He waited the long day through for the Lord Salisbury to bring his army to the place of meet, but ne'er he came and once more this day he had been deserted. It meant that Buckingham would have to move his small army to unite with the Earl of Richmond. He waited no more and was soon underway with his loyal troops; he plodded forth to unite with the men of Breton to usurp the usurper. Into the ride less than one hour were they when a spy of Buckingham's came through the late mist; as the rain had stopped, the ground next gave forth the fog of the land. The rider stayed his horse at the side of Buckingham and, as the army stopped its march, he brought to him such sad tidings to put the lord in grave state.

"My lord, forgive me, for I bring you tidings of much distress to your cause. The Earl of Richmond has not made his landing upon the south coast; the stormy sea has forced him to return to Brittany with the loss of many ships and of many men."

"My God, I am done," softly did speak Buckingham with a broken voice of sadness and despair as rain trickled his face. "Is there a ransom upon my head?"

"Yes, my lord, a tidy sum has been placed for your capture of one thousand pounds."

"Then I am not completely worthless; 'tis good to know I am regarded in such high esteem."

"I bear much distress in bringing to you such details, my lord; please forgive me that I had to do such work."

"It matters not, my man, for my time is of little consequence. Begone before you are caught in this noose that closes about; disperse yourself from me."

"God be with you, my lord." And with a reverent nod he was supped into the thickening mist and soon was afar.

Buckingham turned his troops around, taking the road back to Newbury, and soon pulled into the stables at the rear of the tavern, in the place that all thought they would not see again this day. They made secure quarters in the taproom for the night. Buckingham supping upon the little that was left of his cache. The troops were set about the town; some at guard against the townsfolk, others at desperate sleep.

As the night came and the bats flew, a lone figure on foot slinked away from the silent town; unseen was he in the black night as he ran quietly upon the empty track that led to the town of Reading. Still running until the sound of a stray horse brought him to a walk. Many such horses were about—some lost from their master, others about who had bolted, or their rider thrown or murdered—but a timely meeting indeed. The dark shadow quickly cornered the animal, and, with a little sweet talk, soon was mounted and rode on the broad back to the sheriff's quarters at Reading.

'Twas still in darkness as he clattered the empty streets of the town. A lowly paid servant was he, come to claim the monies pledged for the capture of Buckingham. Knowing his master was doomed, he entered the only road he knew to gain some reimbursement for his lowly duties and meagre pay. He came to the iron gate that showed to be the place of the sheriff, and was soon slinked into the darkness of the gothic doorway and up the old stone steps, which brought him to the bench and table that were placed there. Slumped against the wall close by, there the duty soldier in light slumber nodded his tired head, but stirred quickly as he heard the clicking footsteps of the servant as they closed to him.

"Pardon me, sir, I have some information for the sheriff."

"He is at rest at this time, and is only to be awakened to important matters. What is your case that you come at this hour?" the guard answered with barbed words and ill breath.

"Sir, I have knowledge of the whereabouts of the Lord Buckingham, who is sought by royal decree as a traitor."

The soldier came closer to him, making sure the words he had heard where indeed the words that were spoken, as he looked deeply into the servant's face. "You are sure of this? For I wish not to bear the wroth of my master if I awaken him and your story is nothing but that of a fool."

"I am sure, sir, and speak with truth. Why would I come at this hour when even a fool must sleep?"

"Stay then and I will fetch the Master Sheriff." The guard left through the doorway that hid in darkness where no door seemed to be, leaving the servant nervously stepping from one foot to the other, as he awaited in a state that was not his custom, and was feeling some distress at the position he had taken, and thought to flee from the trial he had placed upon himself. But soon the sheriff entered followed closely by the guard. He came all red-faced and a mouth full of yawns, still dressed in his night cloth of linen, and his sleeping cap a-flop upon his greying hair. He sat sour of face and grumpy in his manner at being awakened, which, thought the servant, was probably his demeanour at all times.

"So you know of Buckingham's whereabouts?"

"Yes, sire, I do." And meekly added, "There is a reward for this information, is there not?"

The sheriff picked through some scrolls that lay upon the table, and finding the one he needed spake the written words aloud to the informer. "On capture of the traitor, the Lord Buckingham, there is a bounty to be paid of one thousand pounds." The sheriff then added the words for his own pocket. "Subject to taxes and some levies to be applied from this office, where you will receive your reward."

"I can lead you to him as he sleeps, less than three hours away."

"You are sure of this, are you not? For 'tis no time for falsehoods or missed trails; life in his Majesty's prisons are full of sorrow, be sure of that."

"On my life, I speak truthfully; I am Buckingham's servant and I know where he is rested, for was I not the one who prepared his bedding?"

"I will ready myself, and then we will see what rabbit we can catch this night." And then he was gone through the dark door that hid in the corner.

The guard ran about awakening the soldiers, fifteen in all did he gather for the journey to capture the one they sought, the traitor Buckingham. The guard had passed orders to the stable to make ready the required mounts needed this night. "This way," came the shout to the servant as he followed the soldier down the stone steps once more to the sheriff and the assembled party that readied in the courtyard. The servant mounted the fresh horse given to him; he was saddled and ready to ride out, with many different looks coming his way from the gathered soldiers. Some of doubt, some of envy, some of betrayal, and he knew through all that was to come that his trust must be in no one, for many would have different reasons to see his throat slit. But at this time, until they had the lord in their keep, he would suffer no harm, as on the sheriff's bidding, he took the lead to ride the way to Newbury, and to the place where Buckingham, in uneasy mind, drifted his sleep.

They dug their heels into the soft horseflesh, as all urged forward into the dark night. The rain was not falling now, but moonless and drab was the way. Slowly they started, but soon had picked up their gait as they jingled along the track that was familiar to them. On they went with good haste and, in less than three hours, the town came in sight. They stopped their panting horses high upon the hill that overlooked the shadowed buildings below. And, on directions from the servant, they made their plan to secure the tavern, and to capture the Lord Buckingham in discreet fashion while he slept. On foot and all in quiet, they moved down into the town cloaked in the cover of the black night; ghostly figures in the hanging mist they closed to the place of Buckingham's repose. A lone sleeping guard slumped at the tavern's doorway was all that barred them, and he knew naught as the hand went to his mouth, and, with a deft slash across the throat with the trusty knife, blood poured through the attacker's fingers; once again a poor fellow's life had gone before any struggle could come from his stricken body.

Three bootless soldiers slinked quickly inside, being most careful to make little noise for many soldiers slept the room. To the dark corner, near the window where they had been directed, did they step. The rustle of the rushes came to ear as they left the sawdust of the bar floor to the sleeping shape that was upon the softer lay. They bent low over the warm breath that was drifting up and knew the whereabouts of his head, and with quickness had his mouth gagged. They cuffed the shoulders as they dragged up their catch, tying his hands aback of him as he struggled like some grounded fish; they carried him to the door and passed him to the rest of the party who awaited without; they stumbled him onto the roadway, still in the fleece of blackness they knew not yet of their prey — whether servant or prince. They pushed the prisoner before them as they came to the last of the buildings where silence dwelled, and slipped down the kerchief that stopped his mouth, curious to hear if their catch had any rantings to make.

"Release me, you madmen! How dare you place your peasants' hands upon one such as I! Untie me, now!" he raged as he tried to release himself from his bonds. The tone of the voice amidst them gave some thought that they may have the Lord Buckingham in their hold, as they gagged his rage again.

"Quiet, fellow," one of the guards rasped closely into the ear of the captive. "If you are not whom we seek, you will be released in short time. Move on." As a rough hand shoved him once more into the darkness, he was pushed and dragged in the slop until they came to the higher ground, to the sheriff, hidden with the rest of the soldiers behind the thick bushes and trees. A spark was struck, and soon a pitch torch lit the scene of the faces of the muddied lot, who closed to view their captive. The light was brought closer to their prize, to show a dishevelled mud-splattered fellow all of red face and in some rage. One of the soldiers stepped forward and untied the cloth that held the blasphemous words at bay, and upon its removal did they come tumbling out in polished tongue.

"In God's name, do you not know who you are violating here?" came to the ear more reasonable words as the foul words gave way to a speech more clear. "I am the Lord Buckingham with whom you toy, and if a single part of me is abused you will reap the king's wroth. I demand that you release me at once that you may flee from your transgression."

Laughter rang from the dark behind the torch but slowly quieted as the sheriff stepped into the lit arena.

"My lord, if I may use the word—you, sire, are in no frame to demand aught, for you are naught but a traitor to our dear Richard, the king, and as such you have no rights, you have no land, you have no properties, and no treasures. You, sir, are bereft of all and of a peasant state, so do not vent your lordly tirades upon those of us who are of a more noble state than you."

Buckingham broke away as he heard of the state in which he was placed, stumbling into the forest with hands strung at his back; shoeless and muddy without regal dress he entered the darkness outside of the torches' reach, and was lost into the thick forest about him with branches cracking beneath his feet as he strode for freedom. Torches he glimpsed at his back; with heavy feet gaining upon his struggling tread, he looked forward again but too late was he, for out of the blackness stood the thick trunk of an oak tree, and with much force he bounced off it and was stunned to the ground with split head and twisted leg, to look up into the leering faces of his pursuers, as they pulled him to his feet with mocking words, and marched him back to the waiting sheriff.

"Fool, you! Do you think you have any safe haven awaiting you within this land? For you do not. I warn you, if you try to escape again, you will be maimed." The lord, still recovering from his ordeal, did not answer, but just gazed in defiance of this lowly person who did threaten him such.

"Where do you take me?" Buckingham asked.

"We are to Salisbury, where the writ is lodged for your execution."

"I am no traitor!" shouted Buckingham. "My aim was only to rid this land of a child-killer, and to do such is not the act of a traitor, and I will strive for that end though I may not live past my trial. I will speak of the evildoings of this Richard who walks the kingly way, but each step he takes is of an evil man. And my words may turn many a man against this killer so that justice may come to him."

"Trial!" with some amusement in his voice; "Trial?" the sheriff repeated. "We mentioned not any trial. There is no trial. All that was spake and has been writ is execution. You, my lord, have been a-slumber these past days. Do you not read your dispatches? There is no hearing for any who oppose Richard. It has been decreed all such persons are to be executed at once; that is the reason for our journey to Salisbury, for the executioner's axe and for naught else."

Upon these words, and in much despair, Buckingham fled once more into the darkness. Slowly the party lit more torches, and with bored features made their way with little haste into the forest to retrieve Buckingham. The lord ran quickly with the drive of desperation, but once more was stayed, for soldiers who had gone into the woods to relieve themselves were returning to their lay, and were placed in the path of the fleeing Buckingham who ran directly into them, and with little effort he was bowled to the ground once again.

"Please, release me!" he pleaded. "I will make many riches yours. Please, help me." He lay upon his back in the seeping mud, praying for some show of compassion, but none came to the once proud lord. The sheriff stood glaring over him, as with the torches lit about he was brought back to the small clearing, and watched as the lord was laid and held in a prone position before him, and then spake the sheriff those chilling words to the hapless lord.

"Turn him over! Did not I warn you, sire, not to flee? Now you will never run the ground again. Hockle him," came the command, with fear struck into the face of Buckingham as he heard the order bandied. Bodies fell upon him and he was rolled to be face down in the stillness; across his back and upon his legs, strong hands were holding his struggle. One of the soldiers pulled a narrow-bladed knife from his belt, and kneeling in the mud and the branches, cut into the flesh of Buckingham between the anklebone and the tendon. When his blade showed through the other side he quickly, with a sliding and upwards pull, severed the tendon to a muffled cry from Buckingham mouthed in the mud. To the other leg went the blade, once more through the flesh. And then with the slashing cut, both tendons had disappeared up into the higher part of the leg, never to be joined again. Little blood showed in the flickering light, only flopping feet they saw; Buckingham would never move alone again.

They picked up the floundering lord, and took him to the waiting horses where many now stood ready to depart. The sheriff pulled three soldiers to one side.

"Make a litter for our guest," he ordered. "For he seems somewhat handicapped." They quickly gathered two long branches and lashed them to some shorter crosspieces, and in little time had fashioned the frame for Buckingham to journey upon. Soon 'twas tied behind a horse to drag the prize away to a more miserable sight. As this was proceeding, Buckingham was as if on display, for the soldiers came to gaze and blaspheme at him, spitting upon the wretch at their feet and urinating over him with much pleasure. He lay silently under the abuse that was upon him, and when all had somewhat stopped he opened his stinging eyes to see his manservant gazing upon him.

"You! Do you see what you have done to me? You have murdered me to jingle but a few coins in your pocket. Mark me, no bright days will come of this evil of such deeds."

"Aye, my lord, indeed I have murdered you, but if it were not me then another would do the deed. For you were dead once you took sword against the king."

Buckingham spake no more and quieted to await his fate, for he was done as a lord. He was placed upon the litter, and they took the road that led to Salisbury. The arms of the litter dragged in the mud as it bumped its cargo along the track, leaving behind the trail of a traitor. The lines upon the ground were soon gone, trampled down with the hooves of the horses that came behind. No mark left of the once mighty Buckingham, not even two tracks in the mud.

The following day in the light of the early morn, they trundled into the market square of their destination, with few people about to see the happening. A farmer with his cart, two tradesmen passing through on their way to work at the manor, a few washerwomen with their bundles making to the river was all that would see aught of the dealings this day.

They came with Buckingham to the gibbet whose rope swayed gentle in the morn's breeze. He watched close to a smaller platform, used only for beheading, with a few small steps worn and black that led up to it. Upon the oak frame, stained wooden planks lay, coloured with the bloody aftermath of the executioner's axe, who was at the ready, standing discreet in his black garb. The officer from the court stood close by, clutching the writ for the execution, and upon his ruling 'twas decided that the execution would be by the axe only. The lord was not to be hung, quartered, and then beheaded, as was the general rule for such treasonable acts. For he knew that, in all his anger, Richard would not wish his once friend to bear such a degrading act. The carrier of the writ having some feelings to the noble state of the victim.

The end would soon come to Buckingham, as he was pulled from the litter and dragged through the muddied ground, with a soldier upon each arm as his flopping feet scraped the mud behind him. He was bumped up the few steps with little care to the platform, and, as his head came level with the planked top, the bloody block came to his gaze. He was saddened even more so now, as he knew all was to end for him. When once not too long ago he had more than any man in England, for Richard was generous to him and treated him with the love of a brother, and did ply him with all he may ask of. But the turn had come, and he was pulled along the grisly planks as his head was placed roughly onto the place of death, and quickly as he was placed there two booted feet came close to him. The voice above him spake, and sounded such that 'twas a dream floating his ears in a misty dullness.

"Be still, my lord, and all will be quick for you."

"God—" came the words to the lips of Buckingham, then no more as the edge cut through flesh and bone, spurting the lordly blood to add more mire to the deck. A few twitches, then the bump of the head as it came from the body with one blow, and then showing upon the floor with its sickly gaze of bewilderment. One more act was to follow to finish that which had been writ: the quartering of the body; and with sharp blades and hatchets 'twas cut, as the still warm blood flowed all about the platform and dripped upon the ground beneath. Each quarter was soon labelled and ridden off to its corner of England. The head was piked, as horse and rider took it to be displayed on the bridge at London, with all the other tyrants who swayed there. The officer of the court riding out from the bloody scene to inform the king of the duty done, still saddened by the sight that he had seen many times before, for he was an honest man and seemed to like less the tasks that were placed upon him.

The servant, goodly-horsed, came to his appointment at the town hall to collect his reward. Up the steps went he, no shame in his heart; riches only were on his mind as he made to the treasurer's room and scratched his name upon the receipt. The bag was fetched and at last 'twas in his soiled hands, with a joy he had not felt before, lived in his mind the life he would lead with the bag he clutched. Outside he came and to his horse strode, placing the monies into his saddlebag and securing it most carefully. He mounted his horse and with steady gait made way from the town, and took the way that was to London.

A last gulp of ale slopped from their tankards, as the two leaned against the tavern wall and watched as the servant left the treasurer's office and was upon his way. The ruffians mounted their horses without rush, for time was aplenty, and they need only lumber some distance behind the rich traveller. A day of good fortune for them came to their minds as they trotted along; their daggers clean and bright tucked under their garments lay hidden for now, as they came closer to the servant and his moneybag. And soon, when they are atop of him, he may well remember the words spoken by the Lord Buckingham: "No bright day will come of this evil deed."

Chapter Nine.

Oil of Poppy.

The officer of the court tied his steed to the ringed post that lay in the courtyard of Crosby Place and made way to Richard's chambers with echoing footsteps along the empty passageways. He followed the royal guard striding ahead of him with boots that were quieter, for such were deemed to be worn in the hollow place where the king abided. Soon they were at the great door, robustly made with iron decoration and large black hinges that almost completely traversed the oak timbers. The guard rapped upon the door, which opened slowly and only a little, just wide enough that only a mouse could squeeze through. A few whispers were all the messenger heard, as the guard spake through the small gap in discreet tone. As he pulled his head away, the door was slowly closed to click shut. They both waited upon the manservant to inform the king of the requested audience.

The door opened once more and the messenger was beckoned in, leaving the guard at wait outside for his charge to return. He entered into the high ceilings and bedecked walls of the king's meeting room, where around the table there sat nobles and lordly persons. The table he saw was in much disarray with books and papers strewn about, and the drip of the candle thick and shiny upon the wooden top, with flagons of malmsey and many goblets all about. As he came further into the chamber, there, seated at the head of the table, sat the King Richard, seemingly dwarfed by the high-backed chair he was encased in. The messenger fell to his knees in front of the regal set, and bowed lowly down to the rush-covered floor in a most benevolent manner.

"Your Majesty," he said with loyal tone.

"Rise, fellow," Richard beckoned him. "What say you of your task?"

The messenger stood but still with head lowered, so as not to gaze into his king's face, and to bring him the dire news he did carry. He was careful in his task, for he would not want to bring more upon himself than it did warrant. "Sire, I bring to you word that the writ placed against the Lord Buckingham has been carried out, and that this morning at six of the clock he was beheaded at Salisbury. He was quartered, and his head was sent to be displayed at the bridge of London. All so done as to your Majesty's directives."

Silence arrived for a short moment as the gathering awaited the king's reaction to the news. Worried of the effect it would bring to Richard, that his once greatest friend had suffered death through his own hands.

"Good, that the foul traitor has begot his end, the heinous one gone to his devilish home."

Relief fell upon the gathered nobles that rage or remorse did not plague Richard. Though at this time, a pang of sadness that did not show without passed deep within him, as once this man was tall with his king. Then, with a goblet of wine, bade goodbye, with a swill that washed the dryness of his mouth, and deemed to himself that the word of his Lord Buckingham would part his lips no more. The clerk of the court was dismissed, and made his way from the chamber with his tall guard pacing afront, to return to acts less displeasing, and yearning for the mundane.

Richard turned back to the task of bringing some order to his kingdom, as for all his efforts it seemed that some uprising or other was needed to be quelled, or some tyrant executed. All was not well within the land; rumours abounded with Richmond rebuilding his fleet, and gathering some mighty force to take the kingdom from Richard. And whispers did abound of the princes escaping the Tower, to leave the King Richard in nervous state, that he was deceived, and that amongst him were those who bore no allegiance to him and waited to strike him down. The year was fourteen hundred and eighty-five. Richard had been the king for almost a year, and had he not passed many goodly laws, and hung many evildoers to bring his subjects closer to his bosom? But still they chided him with their needs, and drained his coffers of every penny. The nobles would have to pay even more for their deceiving ways. This rooster will crow.

"Bring forth to me that surgeon!" The weak but defiant voice came from the shape that lay upon the oak settle; lying atop the mattress filled with goose feathers, puffed and soft, and the pillow of the same rested the head, the body covered partially by a linen cover and a worsted blanket. Our Queen Anne lay in some sickly state, pale and weak, resigned to remain in her chambers. "Do you hear? Bring him to me now!" came again the voice from the frail body, the hair grey from her dilemma, falling out more each day, to leave balding patches upon her head amidst the sores bursting from her skin. Her wigs lay close at hand, all preened and powdered upon their stand, but she rarely wore them now, as the discomfort of such an act made it too painful even to pamper her ego.

"You called for me, your Majesty?" 'Twas the barber-surgeon, who had been fetched by one of the queen's waiting ladies to the chamber where she reposed. A thin man was he, dressed in the tweed cloth all of black, which seemed to be making him itch all of the time, and 'twas wondered why he suffered himself so. With the finger pulling of his neckband, the scratching of his arm, the brushing back of the imaginary hair upon his bald head. Five feet four inches of nervous demeanour stood before his queen.

"I need more of that worthless brew that you keep feeding me, though it seems to be a concoction with little result."

"Your Majesty, the dose so given to you is the one that is recommended, and to increase it may bring results not so pleasing. I feel, your Majesty, that if we continue with the dose prescribed every day, you will soon regain your strength; and I can see that you are improving as the days progress."

"Fuddle," came the reply; "I feel no better than I was six months past. I wish you to give more to me now, for it seems the only thing to relieve my misfortune."

"My lady, it is of very strong and potent herbs, and I am feared that I may overstep its effect."

"Will you not do as I bid you! Would you sooner be plying your trade in the street? There are many more purveyors of witches' brews who will do my bidding, and with whom I would not have such strife." She need say no more, for he wished not to enter the world of the poor, for much was for him in this state. His hand went into his leather bag, which when he was seen 'twas always to hand, and from within he withdrew a small crock sealed with a leather bung, and a small drinking vessel of fired clay. Carefully he unplugged the brew and tippled a small amount up to the lower mark upon the cup and handed it to the queen's thin trembling hand, who quickly drank back the black liquid, and remained with her head back and the cup to her lips as she drained all of the relief-giving brew from the vessel. The surgeon leaned forward to retrieve the cup, but the queen was not ready as yet to give it up, as she wiped it clean with her finger, and placed it in her lips to suck the little drop that glistened there. She handed back the cup to the surgeon. And with some contented sigh laid back into her warm covers, and closed her eyes to let the brew relieve her dilemma. The surgeon packed his medicines away, and, strapping his bag closed, left the dozing monarch to her dreams.

His bag clutched, he left the queen's chamber to return to his closet where he practised his medicine. As the surgeon for Crosby Place he tendered all within its walls. Only a few steps had he taken when he was stayed in his progress by one of the king's personal guard.

"Sire, his Majesty wishes to have council with you in his cabinet chamber."

He followed the tall harnessed guard, stepping three steps to one to keep pace with him, soon to come to the small annex attached to the royal chambers wherein discreet councils were hatched. The tall fellow at the front rapped upon the solid door to gain some entrance. 'Twas duly opened by the king's manservant who beckoned in the surgeon. As he was entered in he was given the sour look of disapproval, which it seemed was the requisite for a manservant of the royal house. He looked the surgeon firstly up and then down, as if searching for some part of him that he could reject, and to delay him from the council's meet with his master. But of course he could not, being, after all his haughtiness, a mere servant. He knocked upon the door of the closet, and, though all was silence to the surgeon's ear, the servant seemed to hear from within that he could enter, and did so holding on with much authority to the latch handle. And, with a last show of his high position in this household, he pushed in the surgeon through the narrowly opened door, he having to turn sideways to make through the gap showed him, and just retrieving his sleeve before the door closed behind him to the spring's click of the lock. He looked straight before him, and stood there the figure of the king at wait, standing in the light from the window in his coat of black, which he most often did wear, and showing his regal doublet of blue beneath. A stern look was upon his face at this time, and seeming not to be in a pleasant manner, as he acknowledged the bow of the underling with impatience twitching his neck.

"So, surgeon, what is the latest word on my Anne?"

"Sire," he began as he took in the room about him, of the dark table and benches there, the rushes upon the floor smelling sweet with there newness, the grey stone walls with the snuffed torches upon them, awaiting the darkness to come to fire again their glow. Very sparse was the cabinet, a place made for brief council and discreet chat. "She is, my lord, making some progress in her health and in time I believe we can bring her back to wellness."

"I see her and I do not see any progress; I see only more sickness overcoming her. I see her rotting away with such a smell that it reeks through the whole palace. You must end such vile things as a blade would put to rest the sick dog."

"My lord, we can bring her back to good health, and she will be as before."

"I differ with you, surgeon; do you not see what pain I am in to have to endure such sickness? Do you not see that I am in a dilemma that she has to be so cursed? I pray that, sir, you do not wish to see me suffer so. I wish you to make all haste in seeing to her departure."

"I wish not to see you in any distress, my king." The surgeon realized that Richard would only be satisfied with one outcome, and that was the one he willed and no other; this was not a council of discussion but a council of orders. "I will do as you command, sire, for your word is my desire."

"And, surgeon, make all haste to dispatch her Majesty, and do so without distress to her. Good day to you, sir."

"Good day, your Majesty." The surgeon bade the king as he backed out of the room with lowered head in respect for his sovereign.

Soon he was back in his chambers, his coat now removed and thrown with some disturbed feelings upon the wooden settle, creased and crumbled as the surgeon it did lay. Hands upon hips he looked at the shelves of herbs and medicines before him, standing as soldiers in their labelled crocks, awaiting their next command to do good or to do evil; it mattered not to them as they stood in rank. He selected one of the crocks and pulling it from the shelf, he viewed the label once more. Tincture of lead. He measured a selected amount from the vessel into his mixing beaker and replaced the crock back into its rank. He reached again. Oil of poppy. And dripped the measured amount into the beaker. Then two drops of arsenic he tipped. But, in thought, added two more for this brew, as he took his wooden spatula and stirred slowly the mix. When all was blended he gave a sniff to the beaker; the aroma was not pleasant. To the shelf again he went to bring down a large pot. Dried flower petals. A good measure he added, then replaced it upon the shelf. He measured some water to make the brew thinner, for 'twas of a thick blend. Then, a final stir and a sniff that proved to be more to the pallet. The beaker he then emptied into the crock that he carried in his bag of medicines. He strapped it closed and pulled on his crumpled coat, and, leaving his chambers, made way back to the Queen Anne's abode. Along the passageways went he; dark dwelled in some places, light broke the windows in others; the sound of his steps echoing back to his scraggily ears as he took his path of intent, the path of Belial doings to his queen.

He tapped gently upon the door, clutching his bag with both hands as he waited between the two guards who stood the entrance. The queen's waiting lady answered the rap, and upon seeing 'twas the surgeon opened the door more fully so he may enter.

"Sire," she said quietly, her head slightly bowed as she spake; but he saw the face beneath the bonnet, so full of sadness because of her queen's dilemma. She bade him inside and closed the door most quietly behind him.

"How is your mistress, madam?"

In tones most gentle she answered, "She seems, sire, to be a little improved; some colour has returned to her face, and her demeanour is more pleasant. In my humble opinion, sire, she seems to have started her journey to good health. At the moment she is at rest; though not asleep, she is quite calm."

"Good," returned the surgeon's comment. "I will take a look at her. Have you still more of her remedy?"

"No, sire, she drained the last drop at three of the clock this afternoon; I was about to call upon you for a further supply."

"After I have visited with her I will leave you with more before I depart."

"Thank you, sire, for your kindness."

He entered the queen's chambers and saw her at rest upon the settle. Her eyes were closed, a placid look was upon her face, and truly her colour had returned to improve her appearance remarkably. She stirred a little after hearing the surgeon's crocks rattle in his bag, as he placed one upon the table that stood aside of her settle.

"How are you, madam?"

The queen's eyes fluttered half open as she recognized the surgeon's familiar voice. "I am sickly, sire," she bleated in a whimpery tone. "And I am in need of some of the worthless remedy that you keep plying unto me."

"I will indeed give of you more, your Majesty, and we will increase your dosage, for I know it will please you and it does appear to be helping your malady." He unstrapped his bag, and felt around in there, to come out with the crock that contained the new potion. Carefully in the dim candle glow, he poured out an amount that came up to the second mark upon the drinking vessel, and passed it to the waiting lady who watched over her mistress. And she, with her gentle manner, held her queen's head with one hand as she passed to her lips the vessel with the other. The queen sipped slowly the liquid through her dry lips, and soon drank all, savouring the last of the liquid upon her tongue, as it slid down her throat into the heartbeat of her being. She was soon asleep as the surgeon and the waiting lady quietly left the queen to her dreams.

Out of the queen's ear the surgeon gave the crock of brew to the lady; gently she cupped it in her delicate hands, believing this was the elixir for her mistress's recovery. She gazed upon the surgeon with all faith in his skills to bring her charge back to her usual manner and charm. The surgeon saw the honest gaze upon him, the gaze which hurt him more than the act of murder he was enacting.

"Increase the dose to three times daily, my lady, and increase the amount to the second mark upon the drinking vessel. If you need more, please call upon me and I will give you your requirement. Are you well, my lady?" he asked with some concern in his voice.

"I am feebly tired, sire; the queen's demands have drained me of all my strength."

"Let me give you a tonic to help you in your most difficult of times," he spake as he poked about in his bag once more. "Pray, what is your name, my lady?" he asked, though his mind seemed more occupied with his bag's contents than the lady's title, but 'twas but a device to seem a little interested.

"I am, sire, the Lady Cecily Barnett, daughter of the late Earl of Northumberland." He did not answer, but handed the lady a crock, which she gratefully accepted.

"Remember though, my lady, to take only three drops daily, for more may bring some effect to you." As she reached for the crock from the surgeon, he discreetly touched the back of her hand between the thumb and first finger, lightly and almost unperceivable, but she felt it and withdrew from it clutching still the crock.

How dare he? she thought; he may have some education but is he still not a commoner—versed in the cropping of hair and in the knowledge of medicines—who should know more than to touch a lady? For even if he were a prince, he would be of no attraction to me.

She shrinks from me, he thought, this lady who I shall have, this lady that repulses me for my commonalty, but soon she will be as meat upon the spit for my pleasure.

"Good day, my lady."

"Good day to you, sir."

He left her with her thoughts and made his way to his chambers, not knowing yet the effect of the brew given to the queen, whether death would quickly come, or whether she would linger in some state. But as he walked a twinge of a smile crooked his mouth, knowing that the tonic for the Lady Cecily would soon bring to him pleasurable times. For the taste of the poppy oil could not be resisted and she would be bent. He mulled over again the brew he had given the queen, and to what end the different ingredients would produce. The tincture of lead given in a small dose was to bring out all the poisons that lay in the body, but 'twas not known if 'twas the correct thing to use, and only time would show such. But the dose given to our queen was not a small amount, and the fear was that a large amount would bring more of the open sores to her head, making her hair more to fall, and in time she would become insane. The arsenic would kill all her organs, and much bleeding and pain could be expected. The oil of the poppy would bring a craving to have more of the brew. In all, a cruel drink from hell, as he entered his chambers moulded to the act. He who begets the devil's work himself becomes the devil.

A call came once more requiring the surgeon to attend audience with the king. He picked up his bag and made his way through familiar passageways toward his meet. It had been a fortnight since he had started giving the queen the extra doses of medicine. She was in a dire state but still lingered, of which the surgeon could not understand, for she appeared of death but still did breathe. He was entered into the closet to await the king's coming. As he sat, so entered the king from the inner chamber, set to purge the surgeon once more, who stood and bowed in the most royal presence.

"Get thee up!" Sharply he spake, and not in good humour it seemed. "What of my Anne, fellow! What of her?"

"She is in dire strait, your Majesty, and should surely be out of this world soon."

"Soon!" he shouted. "I am most grieved of this lingering. Will she never die?! Do it, surgeon! We cannot wait longer."

"Yes, sire, I will dispatch her."

"You had better dispatch her, for I am in a maddening state. Do it now or there will be two bodies on the morrow for the cart." He spake no more but turned and left through the door by which he had come, where the smell of perfume and the glimpse of satin came to the surgeon through the open door, then he was gone.

The surgeon picked up his bag once more, and made his evil journey along the familiar way to the chamber of the queen. Alone went he through the dimly-lighted arches of Crosby Place, to be once more at the door that was his task. No feelings had he for the wretch that lay inside; 'twas just another act of his life and 'twas irrelevant. The purveyor of the potion came tapping upon the oak face of the entrance door. Silently 'twas creaked open by the waiting lady, this lady who smiled a distant smile to the surgeon as he entered, and then closed the door behind him with the dull thud of the oak. He looked at the Lady Cecily who appeared to be not the same as she was but two weeks past, now dishevelled and not groomed as before, and seemingly not caring in her misty state, dark of eye, her dress top carelessly unhooked to reveal a small temptation. She sidled closer to the purveyor with things other than the queen upon her mind.

"Did you bring me more of the tonic, sire?" she asked as she touched his arm.

"I think your manner is a tidy abrupt, my lady, and should you not be curtsying before me? I do not know if I have more, madam." He spake sharply as he pulled his arm away from her hand and her face took the look of puzzlement.

"But you must, sire … you must."

"How badly do you need it, my haughty one?"

"I need it most badly … I need it to keep my sanity."

"We will see then after I have dispatched the queen."

"Thank you, sire, thank you." She picked up his hand in hers and kissed it. The surgeon slowly placed his other hand upon her thigh, feeling the warmth of her body through the thin cloth that stretched there. She did not push it away knowing her fate was writ. He released his hand from the soft warmth, and went toward the queen's chamber followed by the lady, liken to a dog that follows its master for any tasty morsel it may beg for.

"Wait outside," he said, turning to her. She did so and closed the door upon him to wait impatiently outside. The surgeon went into the chamber where lay the queen. The draperies were pulled over the windows to subdue the light, and to keep out the blowing wind that still puffed them away from the opening. The flames in the fireplace had dimmed for want of fuel and a decided chill lingered about, but 'twould be a waste of logs to fire it to life at this hour. The grey, damp granite of the walls were wet and sparkling from the lone tallow standing on vigil near the queen. No one watched over her frail body now; the coverings that lay atop of her made her hardly noticeable, for she was so emaciated as to cause no shape to the covers. The surgeon, curious to see the effects of his medicine, pulled back the covers a little to reveal her hairless head, with clumps of hair laying around her form. He saw the bleeding sores, now exposed, covering her head and face, and further he did not look, for he knew all her body was the same. The smell from what was left of her was overbearing, and was making the surgeon, who was used to such things, sicken and retch. For a moment her eyes seemed to flutter open , but the lids were swollen to the extreme and she could not. A feeble whine came from her split and bleeding lips but 'twas meaningless, as she soon would be done; no more medicines or potions would wrack her frailness now. He reached for the bloodstained pillow on which she had laid, and was seen laying by her side. He lifted it over her, and placed it gently upon the once handsome face, which was now of a grotesque state and longing for sanctuary.

"Fare-thee-well, my dear queen," he whispered quietly. There was no struggle, only cold stillness as he placed more weight upon the pillow; he held it so as the tallow flickered its light upon the scene. The fire for a moment brightened with a whisper of flame lighting the room briefly, then 'twas gone to dimness and not to return, as was the life of the Queen Anne. The foul undertaking was done; the queen to suffer no more.

He placed the pillow back upon the settle, and went from the chamber into the closet where stood the waiting lady in her shivering state.

"Your mistress has gone, my lady. 'Tis best you prepare her for the mortician so she may be seen in some better state, and to ease the task so he may remove her to the chapel to care for her seeing."

"What of my brew?" 'Twas all she cared now. No duty to her queen, just her need misting her befuddled brain.

"Brew!" answered the surgeon, his voice in some mocking surprise. "Of what brew is this you speak of?"

"Sire, you said you would see to my need."

"Oh, did I? Let me see." He fussed around in his bag as the lady slavered over the search. "Ha, is this what you seek, my dear?"

"Yes, sire. Please do not let me linger further."

The surgeon tippled just two drops into a drinking vessel, knowing that this amount would only keep her satisfied for a short while—for was not the lady taking a full six drops? "Here, my lady, take this, for you must have some wits about you to ready the queen."

She lapped every damp drop from the vessel, and then handed back the dry crock to the surgeon with pleading still upon her face, for she also knew such a small amount would not suffice for long. She stood before him liken to a linen cloth, not knowing which way she would be ripped next.

"If you come to my chambers at nine of the clock this eve, I will see if I have any of that which you desire."

"Thank you, my lord," she said with a demure curtsy.

"Is that as low as your reverence to me can bend?" the surgeon asked of her. She lowered her head and her body even more to satisfy his desire. "That is a little better. May you need to practice somewhat before you visit me this eve, do you not think?"

"Yes, my lord," the whispered voice came.

The surgeon turned away from his stricken lady and made directly to Richard, to inform him of the passing to the Lord of his beloved queen. He came to the outer door of the king's closet, and after some little council with the king's manservant gained entry to await the royal convenience. The manservant hurried into the king's chamber to inform him of the surgeon's presence. And in short time the king entered into the closet, in anticipation that his order had been carried to its end and that the queen was delivered from her ordeal.

"So, my surgeon, is all done?" he asked as his agent stood from his homage to the king.

"'Tis done, sire; her Majesty the queen died this noon hour as she slept in peaceful mind."

"Good!" No compassion came from the lips of Richard to honour his once beloved Anne. He stood this day as cold as the sword of steel upon the block of granite. "Arrange the details of the funeral with the house master, and then we can all place this sad occurrence aback of us." These cold words did not sit well with the surgeon, but such 'twas this day, being just one more vile action from this king, which one day may add up to destroy such evil endeavours as he preaches. For when justice comes he will have to bear many pages writ against his royal person. He likened him to a bird keeper, who on finding one of his birds to be not plump enough for his table simply disposed of it and acquired another.

"You may be gone now; your service duly noted."

The surgeon bowed to his king and backed out solemnly through the closet door, with the servant guiding him in his exit.

Richard returned to his inner chamber, leaving the cold sparse closet behind the shut door, and stepped into the soft luxury that was the king's residence. The royal blue curtains of draped satin hung over the draughty windows. Bright tapestries of knights in battle looking all of honour and valour as they straddled their muscled mounts. Scenes of the villages owned by the royal house, with their cottages and church spires wet with rain in the painter's mind. All manner of nobles shown seated before their mansions and properties, with the prize horses they owned paraded about the cropped grass. Castles standing high upon English rock, bearing strong and unassailable. Scenes of victorious battles fought, with the proud officers shown routing the evil enemies of this land. All hung upon the cold stone of the walls to make a fine chamber. Fresh rushes covered the flagged floor, where upon stood benches and tables of rich oak, dark with their aged colours. Silver goblets placed upon the blackened tops with flagons of wine ready to fill the shining vessels. Breads and meats, apples and pears, all for the comforts of his Majesty. The fire glowed with a regal brightness, giving out its warmth to those who were within its fingers of warmth. Tallows burned in many numbers, all to bring a pleasurable web over the many fine things that bedecked the chamber of Richard.

The king fell upon the great bed that stood hidden behind the many painted screens around it, and let forth a great sigh of all troubles departed. He seemed alone as he lay upon the soft down-filled mattress, the lavish covers and pillows piled around liken to mountains and valleys. Hills and trails within the folds twisted their paths about. But then a stir from beneath this landscape came; first the soft hand and then the delicate arm. Showed next with a gasp the head of Elizabeth, out from the hidden warmth of her coverings, her face all aglow from the silken den that kept her, her bosomy charms bared in her release. At last to romp in the royal bed she rolled atop of her regal lover; she naked except for her knee stockings, he encased in her legs, teasing him with their warmth and seductive silk. Soon she had him within her charm and his clothing was quickly strewn about the chamber, and he was drawn into the warm flesh of the ever-obliging lady. They caressed and rolled and fell, and entangled themselves in their passion, all in the flicker of the tallows, and the bright fire's glow that waved its dance upon them, as flesh mingled with silk, for a new time had come to them now that the queen was of demise. They lay side by side most tranquil upon the soft covers to gaze at the pleated canopy that hung above them, a night sky, windless and calm, to stay as such forever; then all became silent, and the breath came with little effort and the heart did not pound so strong as before; then, in this bliss, Elizabeth spake to break the serenity.

"Dear one, I must take leave of this place." The words softly came. Part question, part answer. "For, without a queen in residence, I would be viewed as naught but a whore, which would not bear well to you, my lord."

"I fear so, my dear, but our encounters will become less clandestine, and will be most frequent. For the present time I bid that you reside at Sheriff Hutton castle, which is but a short distance hence. And as you know within that place is still detained there my nephew, your cousin, Edward, the Earl of Warwick, who is long kept in honourable captivity at my pleasure. For he has not of yet begged any forgiveness for his misdemeanours against my laws, and I am beginning to think he never will, for seems to my eyes he relishes the state he is in. You may, my dear, be able to alter his views upon the wrongfulness of his actions. But, if you do not, he will still be of much company to you, and there at Hutton you will be close for my call."

"How long must I reside at that place, my lord? For I wish to be placed someday with you, not hidden by walls."

"As soon as the repairs are finished to the mansion I have promised you, we will be together; but the work seems slowly to be done, and much labour is needed, for I wish this place to be a fitting one for one so rich in all attributes."

"You coddle me with your loving words, my dear."

"You well know if I could make you queen it would be so; what I do is little enough for the joy you bring to my world." They caressed once more and then deemed that the time had come that they must part. Soon, helped by their servants, they were dressed and the Lady Elizabeth said her short goodbye to Richard. A gentle kiss and she was gone, tripping her way down the dark passage to the waiting coach that would take her and the entourage that followed to Hutton castle.

As the door closed behind the lady, another door in the same darkened passageway she had just left opened, and a waiting lady of demure stature looked about both up and down the way. Then, with light of foot, she left her chamber; her head and body covered by the black-hooded cloak she wore; her white hands showed all of tremble against the black cloth as she candled her way to the surgeon's place. The ninth hour struck upon the land as she came to the door of her fate, and with gentle rap knocked her presence upon the oak door. No one came to give her entrance; she knocked once more, then yet again. She could not depart, for her need overcame such. She stood being toyed again, and waited for some time without knocking, and then the latch moved and the door was opened, but only slightly did it jar, with only the half face of the surgeon showing.

"Yes?" came the questioning voice from within. The reek of medicines and potions floated out into the grey passage, as the lady was washed in the overpowering aromas. Yes? said he, as if he had no idea as to whom stood there, or of what was their coming.

"'Tis I, the Lady Cecily, calling at your request, my lord."

"My request? I fear I do not remember such a conversation. What do you seek, my dear?"

The lady was becoming to bear not a fair state, and needed most desperately to obtain a dosage of potion to relieve her symptoms. "I need, my lord, your tonic to return me to sanity."

"And are you offering anything in return, my dear lady?" All this conversation being offered between the passageway and the slit in the chamber door.

"I offer whatever you wish, for I am done and in the devil's grasp."

"You offer your body to me?"

"I offer whatever you wish; if it is my body, then that is what I give."

"Show me what you offer, for I have seen naught as yet." Once more the surgeon chastised the wanting lady as he nodded toward her skirts. She stood in a state of dilemma, and with furtive glances along the passageways lifted her skirts up to her waist so the surgeon may see of what she offered. He opened then the door to its full width. The light from within shining for a moment upon the light colour of the stockinged legs before him, then her skirt she dropped once more to her ankles and they showed no more. He did not yet bid her to enter, but stood a little to one side so she may glance into the chamber. She saw there a woman of the street, all glassy-eyed and scantily clothed. A dark shape lurked about from within; some lordly gentleman it seemed, seeking out some fresh body to ravage. But then was seen to her eyes the large crock that stood upon the table there, with the small drinking cups full of brown liquid, the candle glow sparkling the fare of the pleasure awaiting. "If you wish to whore yourself for some sips of my delight then come in." She stood and yet did not move. "Does your allegiance lie within your chastity or within my brew?" he asked. The choice was not hers as she brushed by the surgeon and entered this chamber, this den of misfortune, to hear the door close behind her and to leave her befriended by only one: the small drinking vessel with the brown liquid that sat upon the table. That, lit by the candle, where the shadows stirred.

Chapter Ten.

Hutton's Fool.

The carriage of Elizabeth was bound to Sheriff Hutton castle, a mere trot of one half hour, carried along the cobbled way by two white stallions, both struggling to go at a faster pace than the one asked for, whinnying and head tossing, they went under much duress. The guards mounted afront made set the gait that all were to follow, and at the rear the foot soldiers ran their steps in steady rhythm to keep pace. All were of the royal guard, dressed in their blue and gold livery. The large standard with the White Rose fluttered aloft as they went their journey through the lanes and roads of London. They clattered along as the way rose to higher ground and they came to the castle that would be the place of stay for Elizabeth, though she knew not the time she would be tenured there. Rattling and rocking came they blustering through the grand gate that brought them to the torch-lit courtyard.

The castle before them, draped in the night, was not large, and so thought Elizabeth as she sighted the dark shape. But then 'twas size enough for the keeping in good stead of two noble people. The shouted halt brought the wheels to a stop outside the many steps that climbed to the main entrance. The horses showed their proud breeding, still kicking and most unruly like spoiled children at the fair, as our lady was helped down from the carriage and escorted to the steps. House servants and maidservants, butlers and boys, bowed to greet their new mistress; all lined upon the entrance in orderly state they stood, as she, with proud bearing, lifted her skirts ankle high to step the high stones. Her waiting ladies were there by her side, and went quickly to Elizabeth's bid to help her, as she went up to the high door of the entrance. Standing there to greet her was her cousin, Edward, the Earl of Warwick, confined to the grounds under the edict of the King Richard.

A young man just a few years older than Elizabeth, gaudily dressed in rich clothes of red velvet, with lace collar and cuffs showing, he stood clean of whiskers, with well-kempt auburn hair, his face bearing a scrubbed look. His shoes shone bright with gleaming buckles. His hands soft with nails filed and clean, with one hand resting atop a tall silver walking staff. By all Elizabeth saw, a most handsome fop, a womanizer, brainless and vain; he had changed not since the last time they had met.

"My dear cousin." His greeting smalmed in the much refined voice of breeding.

"My dear Edward," said she with her flashing eyes, which was her natural way of greeting.

"Most delighted to see you, my dear." He bowed, and reaching toward her offered hand, brought the delicate softness to his lips and lavished it with a lingering kiss. She offering no reaction to the tongue licking between her fingers. "Follow me, missy," he spake, smiling through his rouged lips, with the smell of attar all about him, as he floated in front of the party and they entered the castle, waving his arms, first to one side then to the other, as he showed off his knowledge of the various parts of the residence.

"Edward, whereabouts are my chambers?"

"This way, my dear," spake he, as he bowed and beckoned her forward to the high staircase that led to the upper chambers. She came forward and started up the stairs, sided by her ladies as the earl followed in step behind them, Elizabeth knowing full well why she was beckoned to go up the stairs before the earl, for in doing so he was able to glimpse her ankles as she reached from one step to the other, which brought to him great pleasure with his little game. Elizabeth gave a sly look over her shoulder to notice the earl was accepting the offering. And, with a wicked smile to her ladies, she pulled up her skirt more than required to instill him further. On went she up the great stairs continuing her play. The boots she wore were clearly seen, and her ankles showed her white stockings clinging tightly. Then, in the clatter of boots, came about a yelp and a rattle. She turned to the commotion to see that the earl in his rapture, and paying little attention to the steps before him, had stumbled and fell to the oak treads, his rod tumbling free down to his manservants following below, one of whom picked it up before it could rattle to the bottom of the stairs. Elizabeth gazed at the sight and was overcome with laughter, as the pompous earl floundered as another fish thrown upon the riverbank. Arms flailing, legs trying to find some solid ground, his face red with anguish at his fall from grace. The rest of the ladies could not contain themselves any longer; as Elizabeth's laughter spread about them they began to giggle and become unsteady; with watered eyes they had to cling to each other to remain standing. The manservants of the earl stayed silent, giving the impression 'twas a regular occurrence, and nothing to lose any manners over, as they helped their master to his feet. The guards about were much challenged to remain quiet, but their duty curbed such humour.

"Damned steps," said the earl. "Damned castle. Nothing here is of a level state; it all should be knocked down." He ranted a little as his manservants brushed him down with their hands and straightened his shiny cloth. "Carry on, carry on then," he called as he waved his hands about to move his helpers away, and beckoned his cousin to continue, as he moved ahead to show the way once again. The party moved on with Elizabeth receiving support upon her elbows by the waiting ladies. She so wracked with laughter that her legs were like the gelatin from boiled bones, shaking and useless were they. The earl stood atop the stairway awaiting his guests to catch up to him, and as they reached the landing he moved off waving his arms again, and pointing to the different doors and passageways upon the way, talking so mumbled that no one knew what he was about, then clearly they heard.

"These, missy, are your chambers," and with flair did open the door and bid her to enter.

She stepped ahead of her ladies in a much calmer state, more befitting such a lady, and went first into the receiving cabinet and saw 'twas most finely decorated, more so than others she had entered, which were mostly austere and ill kept; this though was bright, and draped with silk and fine cloth and with pleasant murals.

Further in went she, followed by the earl, followed by the ladies, followed by the manservants who placed down the baggage upon the rush-covered floor, and began to rub their hands together to relieve the crink and ache that came from the heavy load. Elizabeth opened the next doors, which revealed a small cozy chamber, ideal for tapestry and for reading she thought. Thick comfortable chairs were about and a couch of some French design, a bench and a table also there most apt for chattering meals. The logs crackled and sparked, locked in their granite fireplace, and then spied upon the floor, and only seen in the most refined of places, a floor covering of wool and hemp. Subtly painted with the dyes and colourings that were of the land, earthy shades of browns and greens and autumn reds. Elizabeth was most pleased by what she had seen, as she went down the small passage that led to the sleeping chamber. But before she reached it, a small door, coloured all of a shiny black wash, came to her eye. Pulling it open she peered tentatively inside and saw the most delightful privy, the wood all scrubbed so clean it appeared to be almost white, making it most inviting, and not the usual smelly dirty room most often found, where one would spend as little time as possible. She saw 'twas brightly lit with many candles about. A good double bench with two copper lids covering the openings; a most intimate and in all lovely place to chat. Clean cloths were hanging with water bowls placed upon a small bench; again she was well pleased. She went on as her ladies followed, peeking into the privy as they passed, they most happy that their mistress was pleased and in good spirits. Two larger doors came before Elizabeth, and she pushed open both to reveal the charming bedchamber. Lighted by discreetly-placed candles she could see the windows and the starry night gazing through, and could well imagine the morn's sun breaking into the chamber. The fire burned its brightness, with the warmth from the big logs filling the room with much pleasure. The walls covered with tapestries and paintings and more fancy coverings upon the floor. 'Twas so pleasing to her that she slipped off her shoes and trod her toes into the soft wools that hid the stone floor, and she was in delight in doing so. The bed there seeming to sparkle in the fire glow with its white linens and thick cushions. The high posts with net draped over charmed our Elizabeth. She then, whilst facing the bed, slipped off her cloak and let it fall to the floor, and turned to face the earl and the assembly that had followed her. Her dark green dress of fine velvet contrasting her ivory skin unmarked from any pox, she seemed immune from such disfigurements; the dress cut low to display ample amounts of her bosom, which caused the earl once more to become fogged, as he took a step back so he might drink in the vision he saw. That such a divine creature would be under the same roof as he brought much pleasure and desire to his thoughts. She fell backwards upon the bed and sank deeply into the soft coverings.

"I am so happy," said she as the ladies started to busy themselves with the baggage. She then sat up with eyes bright. "Bring to me the housekeeper."

Outside the chambers stood waiting the maids and the housekeeper, all lined neatly in their crisp, clean uniforms. She was beckoned in to the presence of Elizabeth, who saw that she was younger than anticipated for a housekeeper, more of her own age, and, by her manner, obviously an educated lady, another who had been deposed from her normal lifestyle; as one ruler displaced another, hardship could not be avoided. "What is your name?"

"Mary, my lady," she stated with a delicate curtsy.

"What is your other name?"

"The Lady Mary Montagu, my lady."

"You are the daughter of the Earl Montagu?"

"Yes, my lady."

"All was lost to you, was it not, at the change of the monarchy?"

"Yes, 'twas, my lady," she spake with lowered head now, as if there was some shame to her position, for she knew not of Elizabeth's demeanour. And her place now was to be of service.

"Be not sorrowful, my dear, for you will be well fared in my tender here, Mary. I wished to thank you for the most careful way you have kept these chambers."

"Thank you, my lady, for your kindness."

"Please convey my thanks to your staff. And I hope, Mary, that we will be able to converse more."

"It would be my pleasure to do so, my lady." Another dainty curtsy came as she dismissed herself, with much relief after meeting the new mistress to find that she was such a kindly person, and bringing a more happy state to her circumstance. For she knew naught of the new lady and dreaded that she may be some pretentious madam who would treat her with ill. But the lady who had come was not such, and the day turned to be most pleasant. As she passed to her maids the message from Elizabeth, they, with giggles and blushes, stood to the praise, for such tributes rarely came to such as they.

"My lady, may we expect you to dine this eve?" Edward asked Elizabeth as the manservants left the chambers, and just two of the waiting ladies were still present.

"I have to decline this eve, my lord. I am to rest, for I am somewhat worn this day. But I should be more than pleased to do so upon the morrow."

"I quite understand, my dear. I look forward then to the morrow. Sweet dreams, missy." He turned and left the tempting rose behind the closing door. His intentions would have to wait a little longer as he went toward his chambers to leave Elizabeth with her ladies.

The earl entered his own rooms, which were quite well adorned with many paintings and tapestries, a similar chamber to Elizabeth's, but more of a manly state of leather and oak. He tended himself in his private room, wishing no one to attend him at this hour. He began to remove his foppish garb, and hung it carefully in his clothing cupboard closing it shut; he stood only in his white linens to unfasten the hasp upon another cupboard, and took from it clothes that were of less frivolous state, to become him more of a manly nature and not the foolish fop that he played, for it did suit his position in many things to appear the clown. But one play seemed to mix with the other, for the clown would show when the cloth was not the clown's, and the clown would sink into verse most serious, when he should stumble and fall for the jovial crowd. As he pulled on his black breeches, most tight and awkward they seemed as he forced his legs into them. He struggled and was felled to his bed causing him to roll around upon it, oft with his legs high into the air as he tugged and twisted with dwindling strength at the unyielding leather. The clown had showed once again as he finally stood the victor, and cried out as such. He then put on his doublet of dark blue, plain and without any pattern; a far cry from the cloth he had removed. He fastened each tie neatly, then stood close to the candle so he may see all below his chin was secure. He had taken great care to wash the rouge and cream from his face, rubbing and scrubbing with his hands to release every dab, splashing and gurgling like a man overboard from a fishing boat. He had rubbed his skin briskly with the drying cloth and his face glowed with the mischief it had received, but soon it had come to its usual pallor. He pulled on his boots, not of any shine but dull and unpolished; he still using the act of bed rolling to bring them to fit. Soon they were snug upon him and he stood again before the looking glass, running his fingers through his dishevelled hair; no difference came from the effort. But the look he received back from the glass was of satisfaction, as the handsome earl stood as he was, and not the fool he played. The long heavy coat next he donned, with leather as black as the night, tying it secure with the wide belt. To pull next his brimmed hat over his ample hair, and then with springed walk went to his door that entered the passageway. With care he opened it and stuck out his hatted head, then glanced both ways, to show that no guards stood about. Silently he went out into the passage, and gently pulled the door closed behind him, and then, like a fast-moving cloud, black and silent, he went to the end of the passage, looking first one way and then the other to place then the worn and twisted key into the door there, to exit from the chambers' passageway, and locking it behind him to wend down the dark spiral steps of a small stairway, with echoes sounding about his ears as if in a stone well. He went with no torch to show the way, and feared a stumble would leave him to lay alone where no one could seek him, and to be left to die in the cold and the wet. His fear stayed with him only for a moment as sure of foot he was, gliding down those steps with room for only one person was its narrowness, but soon he was at the soily bottom. He chose his next key and unlocked the dripping door before him, and opened it into the trees and bushes that were clumped at the castle wall. The stars above his head, the sound of the owl in the distance passed over him, as he locked the door and secured his key.

He was only a step away, as there in the shadows he saw a guard stood his post, only seen when the moon allowed. Close to the wall he hid but seeing all about him, then quietness came over them as they gazed at each other. The jingle of coin mixed with the hooting owl, as the bribe was dropped into the thick grasp and pouched as quickly as it came to hand. 'Twas almost a nightly event, for being confined was not all the word spake, and the earl was able to take his pleasures as he may in the near town, as long as he was returned to his chambers before the first inspection of the morn, which was at eight of the clock. He sidled through the close trees and bushes to the black steed that was tied at the broken oak. Ready to ride was she, with all the brasses and all of the metals covered with leather, so no brightness shone, and any jingle and rattle was dulled by the wrap. He soon was mounted and went his misty way.

The town was but a short ride, and quickly he was upon the road that was brightened by the torches burning in the houses, and in the shops showing him the way. The laughter and smells came to him as he trotted past the dancing folk, past the jester and the lute player with their jeering crowd, to come to The Old Mare tavern. Tying his steed to the horse ring that hung there he brushed the dust from his attire as best as he was able, batted his dusty hat and kicked off some of the dirt that clung so heavy to his boots, and went to the tavern door, which he opened to a stream of light and laughter, and then made his way through the benches and tables, through the folk all jammed close together coughing and spitting, pushing and clowning, until he spied a table at the back, signalling to the barmaid as he made his way, she acknowledged the gentleman and picked his usual vintage from the bar shelf. With the wine in one hand and the goblet in the other, she was soon over to the table, where the duke had disrobed and was just seating himself amongst his group of card players.

"Your usual wine, my lord?" she said as she placed the wine and the goblet upon the table. He placed some pennies in her hand, and as she turned to the bar he slapped her rear with whipping hand, and with a loud squeal and a giggle she was lost in the throng.

"How fare you this day, Edward?" one of the card players asked with a well-schooled voice, and obviously of some noble stock.

"I am in a most happy mood, Charles; all this day has been to my liking."

Others at the table joined in the chat and showed that all were men of some significant means, landowners and gentry, who with their wealth were able to bet high monies at the game. As the cards were passed about, the wine bottles less full, and the coins laid upon the table, the cards were revealed with cursed remarks and joyful cries of the winning hand, as more searching became the idle converse.

"You spake of a guest coming to your abode the last time we met … Remember, you told of the skinny young cousin that used to win your childish games, and you cared not for her bratish ways? Did she arrive as yet?" The chat continued as the cards were played

"Yes, she came this eve, my cousin Elizabeth."

"Richard's mistress?"

"Aye, the same. And now I find she has grown into someone of pure beauty and manner, and it leaves me in some state that I cannot believe that she would bestow her endowments upon such a grotesque figure as our dear Richard. He with his hump, his withered arm, and limped leg."

"One shilling I wager that she is far younger than Richard."

"There is without the need for wagering, my friend, for you would have no takers; indeed, she is many years younger and is of barely twenty years. But, my friends, she can hold good conversation upon many subjects and bears such a mischievous nature that it almost matches her demeanour."

"You seem struck, my lord."

"I am so, though it has been but a short while that I have had any converse with her. I am truly attracted to the lady, and methinks from her to me, for with much flirtation does she act when I am in her presence. But the shadow of Richard floats about me and dulls my advances. I hate that braggart."

"Be of care that which you speak, Edward, for spies abound and you need no more misfortune."

"I will be of a most discreet nature in this matter." He spake, as stifled laughter was all about from himself and from the others who sat the table. "It seems I have won again, my friends," said the earl as he laid down his cards.

"Not again. I wish you would tell of your secret."

"'Tis no secret I hold, so I will tell you, my friends: it is only with buffoons that you can take such gains. So play with fools." Laughter again rang out from the fellows around the table, and so the night drew on to the late hour.

"Looking for some pleasure, my lord?" One of the bar women had sidled up to the earl, her scented water folding over him, she knowing at this late hour he was usually ready for a romp, and more so that he was most generous in his gratuities.

"My tempting maid, I am afraid I must resist you this night, for I am dire to return to the castle. But here, slip this into your purse."

She took the offered coins and placed them in her secure pouch. "Thank you kindly, sire; you are always the gentleman. How about you then, my dear." She swayed up to the next one at the table.

"I have a wife awaiting my return, dear. Though you are most tempting, I will not."

"Come, I have room all ready for you."

"No, mistress, I will not."

"I will accompany you," the one most drunk called to her as he swayed to his feet, whilst holding tightly onto the unsteady table.

"Come then, my dear, let me strip you of all your troubles and take you to heaven." She clasped his hand so he would not fall, as the swaying hips of Jenny the whore took her catch away.

"You must be struck, Edward, for 'tis not often you bed alone."

"It is as you say, my friend, but only time will tell if my amorous feelings will be returned. But time is I must return to my prison," he spake as he guzzled the last of his wine from the goblet and reached for his hat and coat. Soon attired, he bade good night to his friends and started to the door. "I will be engaged in other matters on the morrow and will be unable to join you, but it will give someone other than I a chance to fleece you of your monies." With a mischievous smirk he waved a short goodbye and strode out through the thinning crowd into the roadway. He untied his steed and mounted to return along the track to the castle, with thoughts of rapture flowing from one side of his wine-soaked head to the other; but 'twould take more than a wine bottle to lay him helpless.

He tied up his steed and passed by the sleeping guard to enter the entrance to the back stairs and the narrow flight. He locked fast the door behind him, and made his way back to the floor where lay the chambers. Went he inside the passageway, as he again locked behind him the door of his adventures and quietly went to his chamber door. He entered the key but did not turn it, as he glanced down to the chamber where Elizabeth did lay, his mind turning upon the way to tread. "Be patient, my friend," he said to himself; "'tis too soon, for upon the morrow the apple may be riper for the picking." He turned the key and entered his chambers; disrobed, he fell onto his warmed bed, and with thoughts of ecstasy within his head he fell to slumber, coming under the spell that was the sweet Elizabeth as he dreamed in delight.

The dawn came as clear and bright as the lady peering at it through her open window. She lay in the most comfort, dreaming of her next liaison with Richard and wishing the time would soon come. The teasing of her cousin brought a wicked smile to her angel face, that poor boy who thinks she is naive of all lovemaking, and eyes her as some novice in its art. What a divine little man to twist and foggle* he will be.

"Come, my lady, 'tis at the nine of the clock hour. Time for you to meet the day." The voice of the Lady Helen, Elizabeth's most loyal companion and friend of many years, broke into her mistress's open-eyed dreaming.

"I am awakened, Helen," chirped she as she jumped up from her bed and danced Helen around in a circle, she more than happy to twirl with her friend, until they both were overcome by the room that spun about them, and had to rest for a moment upon the swaying bed.

"Come, Liz, time to make ready. Would you liken to go into the town today?—'tis not far and the sky looks for a clear day?"

"I would love to. Let us seek out some clothes that will be suitable.

---

* *foggle* [coined] ruffle

What is best for visiting towns?" She took Helen's hand and skipped over to the cupboard where all Elizabeth's attire hung.

"What of this, Liz?" Helen held up a demure dress made of fine cloth with a high neck and of a grey colour.

"That is not very fetching, Helen. I think my mother placed that amongst my fine things; she hints of my style to be not befitting a lady. But here—this looks more to my liking and well suited for town visits." Elizabeth pulled from the rack a slim-fitting dress, deep purple in colour, with a revealing neckline.

"You hussy!"

"Yes, I know; is it not devilish?"

"Yes, Liz, it is devilish." With the help of Helen, our lady had discarded her sleeping attire, was washed, and had pulled on her white linens and her white knee stockings. Her boots of leather were fitted and she was ready to slip on the purple dress; her slim body was fastened into it by Helen. The long hair was brushed, and some light rouge was gently applied to her lips, which was all she desired for her complexion's need was naught.

"Let us partake of some victuals before we are away. I do hope Richard calls for me this eve." Elizabeth spake thoughts as they came to her mind.

"Yes, my lady." Helen answered both queries from her friend as they left the chambers and went stairwards to the ground floor, then entered into the warmest room of the castle. The cooks and maids were taken aback by the surprise presence of ladies in their kitchen, for 'twas not usual to be so honoured.

"Good morning, my ladies," the head cook greeted them with a curtsy whilst still stirring her pot. "May we serve you this morning with victuals?"

"Yes, you may, my dear lady, but we will eat here. We wish not to be in the cold of the dining room. Please do not feel any formality is required, for it is not; we have stepped into your realm and will follow your ways." They both sat at the table laid there and ate heartily with the maids and the cooks, each asking about the others' families, with the ladies completely absorbed in the strange dialect that some spake, and the strange words they seemed to use as the chatter and laughter abounded. Soon they left the cheery lot. "Goodbye, ladies." Not your usual lady, this Elizabeth, they thought, with her cheery ways and the pleasantry she showed to such as lowly as they.

"Goodbye, my ladies," was echoed from the voices of the kitchen, as Elizabeth and Helen stepped back into the lower hall, to make their way to the cloak cupboard, which stood afar from the kitchen and close to the great doors of the castle. They each helped the other with the ties and clasps, as they donned the fetched garments.

Two more of Elizabeth's waiting ladies now joined them, bringing with them baskets for any purchases that may be made. The happy group all of gab went out through the great door, which had been opened upon their sight by the high butler, who seemed in haste to rid the place of this party, who broke the tranquil he so deemed appropriate. And as soon as he was able, he closed aback of them the heavy door to be rid of those forever chattering maidens. They continued down the high stone steps of the castle toward the readied coach that awaited them. Elizabeth waved away the guards who were ready to accompany them into the town as was their task; but the ladies would have none of it, for this day was their adventure, and it would be no adventure to be watched over and saved if need be. They were helped reluctantly into the coach by the guard, for they were not quite able to climb in without any assistance.

"Away," Elizabeth called, and they rattled away to the yard gate to take the way that was to the town, leaving the puzzled guards behind seemingly in some quandary of what next to do. But they were not so, for as soon as the coach turned the corner to become unseen, they mounted their horse and followed the laughter at a distance, they too not to be seen.

Soon the wheels bumped along the cobblestone as they came to the bustling, smelly town, a joyful change from the sedate life they led at the palaces and castles they frequented. But to tread into the commonplace may bear them good stead, for was it not the way all people trod, with twists and turns and downs and ups, a king one day a beggar the next? They called the coachman to stop, and stepped down upon the dusty road of the town as the young boy who was the coachman's helper placed the stool for them. Elizabeth ordered the driver to wait for them at the nearby well; he acknowledged her request with a touching of his brimmed hat with a single finger, and a, "Yes, my lady."

The group stepped along the street, past the beggars slumped near the walls of the leaning houses; some deformed and unable to work, others with missing limbs from the wars they had served in and unable to do battle anymore. Others blind from illness, or for some law-breaking that caused their eyes to be put out. Dirty children ran free amongst the horses that clattered along. Men and women of all classes roaming from one place to another with baskets and animals tied. Many would stare at the roses amongst the mire. The roses went into the bakeshop and came out full of giggle, each with a moon pastry,* that soft fluffy bun filled with fresh clotted cream and crushed strawberries. The giggle was for the faces creamed with the white heaven, and redded with the juice of strawberries,

---

* *moon pastry* [coined] soft, round pastry

as they now eyed each other with their jester faces. They jaunted along the street, stopping as they cleaned off each other's face paint. They found themselves outside The Old Mare tavern. Elizabeth was already upon her way to the calling doorway, but her ladies grasped her arm and urged her back, for 'twas deemed most unlike a lady to enter such a place, even escorted.

"I wish to enter. It sounds so mischievous. Come, follow me." But they would not release her arm.

"No, my lady, only whores go to such places alone." She stilled herself as her ladies requested.

"I can play the whore," said Elizabeth as she began to unfasten her cloak, and pulling it back she brazenly pushed her bosom more out of its nest, far more than 'twas already, much to the delight of the gawping gentlemen who were about.

"We know, my lady, of your fine talents," — spoken with a little mirth in the telling, "but trouble could come and we are but gentlewomen, and could offer little assistance to some foul fray."

"You, of course, are right in your advice, but one day, I promise you, I shall go in." She then tied her ribbons and clasps to cover her brazen fetch. And with laughter again they moved along, 'twas hoped to a place of less intrigue; the ladies still not knowing if Elizabeth had any intention of entering the tavern, or if she was playing one of her teasing games to make them fret so. Arm in arm they continued, as the two guards who were at watch over them relaxed, for they were at the ready to move if Elizabeth had continued her play, but were rested again for it seemed the mischief had passed.

The haberdashery had caught their eye, and as they entered the tinkle of the door's bell rang their welcome. The small shop was full of brightly-coloured cottons and wools most suitable for the needlework they so loved. Some cloth of worsted they fingered but settled upon the coloured wools, and some yards of muslin, and some of cotton. 'Twas soon sheared by the old shopkeeper who doddled her day there, and was delighted that the ladies from the castle had spent in her shop. They paid for their wares and promised to return, and left with a happy "Good day" to the shopkeeper.

"Good day, my ladies. I look forward to seeing you soon."

They deeded to return to the castle and sort through their purchases, so returned along the way whence they came, past more tempting shops and the smelly tavern. Helen held tightly onto Elizabeth as they passed to refrain her from making toward the doorway of intrigue.

"Come, Liz, do not falter; we have to return now; there may be a note from Richard awaiting you." Helen using any means to alter her friend's tack.

They came to the beggars as they made to the coach that stood await and dropped pennies into their alms cups, with a "Thankee, ma'am," from those who still had a tongue. And also to the raggedy children who gathered about them, placing halfpennies into the grubby begging hands.

The coachman clambered down from his seat, as he saw the ladies approaching, and opened the doors to the coach as his boy placed the stool at the ready. Soon they were all inside and seated as the coach lurched its way, all chatting of their most happy of days, and noticing naught of the journey that took them back to the castle. Inside the chamber of Elizabeth, the waiting ladies were putting away the town clothes and busying themselves with all manner of duties, as our lady searched the baskets to see again their buys, as all was strewn upon the bed in her seekings.

A note had been placed upon the table, resting against the candle holder there. Elizabeth soon forgot her buys as the straw-coloured letter was pointed out to her. Many things tumbled off her bed, as she jumped up with excitement upon seeing the red wax of the royal seal placed upon the inviting correspondence. She picked it up and with dainty fingers broke the seal and read the penned message—the request to come to the chambers of Richard at six of the clock this eve. A carriage would be sent to the castle to bring her to Crosby Place. She waved the note around the ladies as if it were a fan, so pleased was she that she was to see her love this eve, and that her desires would be filled.

A light knock upon the door stilled the dance.

"Enter," called Elizabeth, and in came a maid looking of very few years, giving a most delightful curtsy.

"My lady," she said with the voice of a child. "The earl wishes to know if you will be dining with him this night?"

"Oh, my goodness!" exclaimed Elizabeth, with the hand still holding the royal note placed upon her lips, as she remembered the half promise to the earl made the prior day. "Please send the earl my deepest regrets, for I will be unable to keep my promise to him, due to a previous duty, which had slipped my thoughts … But please relay my love to him, and I will make amends for any disappointment I may have caused."

The maid gave one more of her perfected curtsies; the most delightful seen outside of a royal household it seemed. "Yes, mum," she said as she turned and went out from Elizabeth to deliver the most disappointing answer to the earl.

"Oh, that poor fellow, he must be out of sorts now, for he seems to be a little smitten, do you not think?" Spoken with that mischievous smile upon her lips. "I will have to make Edward forget his sadness somehow," she thought on as the ladies began to ready her for her meet with the king.

Bathed and dressed in her green gown of velvet of pleasing cut, laced at the cuffs and the neckline, her hair brushed and shining in the early light of the eve, such a beautiful damsel, thought the ladies, a fine and elegant gift for a king. Some rouge now was laid upon her lips and she was readied, with a quick glance in the glass showed her well pleased.

The little band of lady soldiers escorted their mistress down the stairway to the hall cupboard, where Helen picked out the blue cape that Elizabeth so loved. And with clasps closed and hoods up the servant opened the door for them. The cold evening air blew strongly into their faces, as they ventured out to see the royal carriage awaiting them at the bottom of the steps. Six guards in presence stood in their regalia, all fully harnessed, their shine showed by the lamps of the coach flickering and dancing in the wind. A most handsome escort to be sure were they, all unflinching in their forward gaze. The blue and gold of the carriage stood ready, with its painted White Rose, and the royal crest bright in the dimming light. The stallions showed they were restive, as Elizabeth floated down to the open door with her ladies at her side. The grey castle walls stood aback of them, with lights at some of the windows and seen maids and servants peering down upon the royal sight, all longing to be the one to make such a journey.

Another window showed little light but to be seen lurking was the unsmiling head butler, wishing to see, but not wishing to be seen to have any interest in such goings-on; so slyly did he peek with his ingrained sneer upon his face, unable to show any other emotion. A further window was watched from; this one bore no light, but a face of disapproval and sadness hung there deep in its longing for Elizabeth. Edward watched as he saw his desire step inside the coach, as two of the ladies straightened the rich dress that had been disturbed upon entering. The door was clicked shut by one of the officers of the guard then quickly he was mounted. "Forward" was heard loud in the air as it echoed all about the yard, soon helped by the trundle of the wheels and the clatter of the hooves. They were away as the sun began to spend its last minutes this day as it lowered toward the far hills. In the courtyard the noise turned to silence; only the last birds of the day chirped their song to break the still. The yard dogs barked their last of the day, as the kitchen scraps were thrown out and they filled desperately their wild hunger.

At that one window the earl did still gaze into the darkness, to the place where he had last been able to see them, dreaming that the coach would turn and Elizabeth would come a-running back, but, alas, she did not. He left the view that was of no comfort to his soul, and in dismal state returned to his chambers, to ready for a journey to town to drink his trouble with his friends. No Elizabeth for him to charm and entice this eve.

The carriage raced into the yard at Crosby Place; the horses had been given their head upon the journey and frantic was their gait, to bluster and prance as they stopped with much indifference to the coachman's commands; 'twas so far from the entrance before they stilled, they had to be taken by the bridle and turned to come to the stepped manor way. The officer in command opened the carriage door.

"I must apologize, my lady, for the hectic ride. I regret the coachman is still in learning, and the horses took little heed of his orders. I do hope you are in no distress."

"We are in no distress, sire, and wished he could go faster; may on our return he will try harder." Elizabeth placed the situation upon a calmer level, for she wished no one to be feared and all indeed did thrill to the running in the blackness. The officer was thankful that the Lady Elizabeth was such in her ways, and showed she feared little but enjoyed such thrills to ease her ladylike demeanour. He helped all within the coach to foot the ground.

"Good night, my ladies," said he with a flairish bow.

"Good night, sire," they harmonized as they restrained their giggles from the handsome fellow, gazing at his face discreetly as they tripped the wide steps to the opening door. The usual sour butler entered them.

"Good evening, my ladies." His haughty voice and his ill-attempted bow bringing the mischiefs of the ladies to the rise once more.

One of them sidled up to the creaky man and, bending a little, whispered in confidence into the oversize ear. "My dear, when you have finished your duties, would you not like to spend a little time with me within the closet of the king's chamber?"

He looked most disturbed and knew not which way was best to step, but before aught came from his lips another voice spake.

"No! I am the one to entertain such a handsome creature. Both of you are skipping by me, for did you not both take the last one to your chambers? So I think now 'tis my man you seek."

The butler became red of face and scurried away as fast as his old legs could take him, leaving the ladies to fend for themselves in his haste. They hung up their capes with mischievous giggles, as the under-stairs door slammed closed with panicked pull.

"You wicked, wicked women. Shame should seek you out and turn your faces scarlet; you are shameless." Elizabeth spake in her most stern voice, but only for a moment, only until the spreading laughter claimed her also. They made their way, passing through the dank arches of the passages toward the chamber of the king. The ladies came in sight of the senior guard who stood his place at the royal door, opening it gently just as the king's guests arrived at the entrance, who entered without slowing a step into the closet. The great door was closed behind them most quietly, as the waiting ladies fussed about Elizabeth to prim and to make neat her clothing and her hair, a splash more of perfume behind her ears, to then be lightly guided to the door of the king's inner chamber.

The Lady Helen rapped gently upon the black door. A strong voice bid to enter, and Helen opened the door, pushing it wide so that Elizabeth could sweep in. After she entered, Helen, without a glance inside, and with her eyes lowered in respect to the king, closed the door upon her lady.

"Richard, my dearest,"—the voice coming from the rosed lips of Elizabeth as she moved quickly to her love, placing both arms about his neck and kissing him with much affection. Richard responded with much desire. Their lips parted, their bodies parted, as they stood gazing at each other with each hand clasped in the other's, held so neither could escape the other for one moment.

"Are you well, my dear?"

"Yes, Richard, I am in good wellness. I have settled most comfortably at the castle, and am most pleased with all things."

"Good, good. And the earl—how does he fare?"

"He fares well, my lord; though I have not yet had time to make further his acquaintance."

"A strange fellow that one—ne'er mind. Come, my dear, let us sample some of the table's offerings." The room lit with the candles' glow showed them to walk in hand, as Richard guided Elizabeth to her seat, and upon her comfort, lifted the silken hair from behind her neck and placed most gently a kiss upon it. She smiled at him as their hands parted and Richard sat his place at the full table. Silver goblets showed the candles' dance, bottles of French wine through which the fire burning could just be seen glinting through the red offering. Upon platters lay wild rabbit with blackberry sauce, stuffed quail with a dressing of herbs. With fresh clotted cream, soon to lay its richness o'er the fresh berries that lay in the sweet wine from the near monastery.

The table soon was of disarray, the bottles sealed no more as half-filled goblets showed the wine's end, some spilled and slopped upon the table's boards and to drip upon the floor below. The rabbit half gone, the quail partly eaten, the bread broken, the bowl did now show little of the cream and the berries that once piled there, all scraped and bare of its offering except for some idle drips and dribbled slop. The flame came clear now through the bottle's face as the two relaxed from the table's fare, and laid back upon the oak settle, each dazed by the wine they had supped.

Soon Richard made his amorous advances to which no resistance was offered by Elizabeth, and in little time they had moved slowly to the softness of the bed, as the moon shone through the window upon them, mingling with the fire and the tallows' light as arms and legs and lips and bodies tangled through the rapture. They lay then aside each other drinking in their minds the ecstasy that had been, slumbering now a little with honeyed thoughts, but still holding nakedly close in their own worldly heaven.

The ladies awaited in the closet, chatting and sewing as they passed the time until their mistress was ready to depart. Further along the passageway more pleasant quarters were available to them, but they preferred to be close to their mistress and stayed in the sparse closet.

"Are you ready for some victuals, Jayne? For I think our lady will be some time yet."

"Yes, Helen, I would so."

"I will send for the maid to bring a tray to our room,"—rising as she spake.

"No need, Helen, for I am in some need to stretch my poor legs, and will fetch a tray from the kitchen."

"That will be nice." Helen spake as she went back to her sewing and Jayne made toward the door. "Bring some of those strawberry pastries ... The ones topped with cream."

Jayne smiled with a nod as she left for the kitchen, along the jiggling passageway, down the great stairs, across the hall; a little breathless in her haste she entered into the kitchen, that bustling place beneath the stairs that was, as always, the same no matter which stately place one resided, with water always on the boil.

"Madam?" The cook gave a little curtsy upon spying the lady, but still stirred her bowl of mixture, for it seemed there was never time to have less than one hand at work.

"I wish to take a tray to the king's chambers for the waiting ladies there, if I may."

"Please do, my lady. Take all you desire; the table is always at service."

"Thank you, madam." Jayne picked a large tray and entered into the heady fog of delights that drifted from the full table. She began to pick such foods that would both suit Helen, and the other ladies, when they were returned from the jaunt that they had undertaken. Jayne made sure there were ample pastries as requested and that the cream was piled high, some meats and bread she also chose, with a jug of cider, goblets, small platters, and a few knives and forks jingled upon the wooden tray.

"Thank you, mistress cook," she called as she tripped her way back to the closet, across the hall, up the stairs, and down the evening's darkening passage. Around the corner she came with tray a-jingle in the stillness, to hear only her footsteps as she made her way. Bump! She came to a stop into the stomach of the guard officer, who, struck with some unknown force, staggered back from the blow, the back of his hand upon his forehead as if severely stricken.

"Oh! I am so sorry, sir. Are you injured?"

He had slowly recovered his balance, and came as close as he could to Jayne with the tray between them, and his handsome face dangerously close to hers. "You seem to be somewhat at a disadvantage, my lady; your arms are of little help to you now."

She trembled, but a warm tremble, not a feared one. He came even closer, with his cheek almost upon hers. She could do naught but close her eyes, and felt then his full lips pressing heavily upon hers for an eternity it seemed. She helpless as she clung tightly onto her rattling tray. Then the heavy lips but soft left hers, and she opened her eyes to the wickedly smiling face before her.

"I am uninjured, madam, except in my heart, where you have wreaked such havoc I know not if I may recover." He kissed the shaking hand at the tray, and with a curt bow left the Lady Jayne all a-quiver and flushed. She dragged her shaking legs to the closet doorway as the guard gained entrance for her there. She, all in nervous state, rattled the tray upon the table with all the strength seemingly drained from her.

"Heavens, Jayne, what ever is the matter? You look so flushed and distressed. Are you feeling faint?"

"I am not fainting, Helen," she spake as she took the offered fan from her friend, and briskly brought the cool draught of air over her blush. Helen sat aside of her, holding her hand in comfort.

"Come, Jayne, tell me what ails you," she spake as she gazed into the face of her troubled companion whose colour was at last returning to normal, and she was becoming more composed.

She told of the happenings that brought her to the state of her dilemma, with a little smile coming upon her lips as the story was told, of the bump in the dim passage, the rattling tray, the stolen kiss taken by the stranger that left her helpless. All burbled from the mouth of the Lady Jayne, who was no longer in shocked state, but realizing the fateful event had left her with more than tender lips. 'Twas the ache in her bosom that was the hurt.

"Do you know his name? … Have you seen him about?"

"I may have seen him about, but he did not give me his name before he took advantage of me."

"The blaggart."

"Yes, he is," answered Jayne as she started to laugh, with Helen adding more mischievous remarks to the situation, as she saw her friend was most happy with what had taken place, and seemingly a little smitten. "Helen, he made my whole body so weak I nearly fainted; the tray and myself could all have been laid down upon the floor was I so in a dither."

"Well, it may be the next time you may catch him in some helpless state, and you will be the one with the advantage, then what would you do?"

"You know very well I would not dare do anything; we are not so forward as our Elizabeth, are we?" They hardly able to speak with such laughter that bubbled within them.

A crash followed by a scream came from within the royal chamber. The two ladies glanced at each other, one pale, one still a little flushed, they moved not for they knew those playful screams too well. Elizabeth, naked, running from the wicked Richard, all snarling and growling as he played the wild man chasing his virgin prey. She throwing plates and trays as she tried with all her might to ward off the evil ravager; then, at last reaching the bed, her screams muffled as she piled the covers atop of her. But beneath the spreads, she could still hear the snarls as closer to her virgin body came the madman as she huddled herself together, and tried to still her shivers hoping the thing would be gone. The cool air flowed over her body as the covers were ripped from the poor maiden's hide; she was revealed except for her head, which remained covered. Her subdued screams, useless, as the wild man took his trophy. Soon she blustered out all red of face and gasping for air. Richard lay aside her, a king spent.

"My lord, you are a brute!"

"Yes, but I have riches for you."

"What do you have for me, brute?"

He pulled from under the mattress a garter, all of diamonds and precious stones a-glitter in the fire glow, a thousand sparkles shining upon the walls of the chamber.

"Ooh," said Elizabeth, "what a royal treasure."

The king rolled sideways as he clipped it onto her left leg just above the knee.

"It looks divine, my brute, thank you." She kissed him most amorously for his loving gift.

"So, now you may tell all who try to take you, that any who pass this garter will be in dire straits, and will lose all bodily attachments to my blade, for to me you are pledged."

"Yes, my lord, you are my true love and it will be as you state."

"Do not let it leave your body, Elizabeth, for if turmoil comes upon this land times could be hard for those who live on, and as long as you have such jewels you will be secure in a new life."

"Do not speak of such things, my love, for we will not let such things happen. They must not."

"I must speak of such, for turmoil comes across our land, and there are many uprisings against my rule. I fear soon that some army of usurpers will soon be at me and a battle for this kingdom will surely come. To be sure, as well there are about murderers whom I must guard against, for who knows what discreet guise they wait in. When the arrow strikes naught is heard until the blood spurts."

"I wish you not to speak of such terrible things. You are an honest and goodly monarch."

"Many say so, many do not, and many still think that I have some knowledge of those two dear princes that I loved so dearly. They still think I am guilty in their demise, and truth be that I am so innocent of any knowledge of such acts, I would smite myself down if I were tainted in such doings." She held him close to support his words.

"I know, my dear, you with all your kindness could never harm such sweet things, and time will show all the doubters that they did err in their thoughts, and all will come and rally to your banner."

Richard had now dressed, for he had most urgent matters to attend, but still found it most difficult to depart from the Lady Elizabeth with her giving charms. Yet soon she ushered him out to tend his papers. The romp was ended until the next meet.

Elizabeth pulled up her skirts to reveal to the ladies her gartered leg. "So divine. So lovely," they cooed at the beautiful band. They were then tasked to bathe their mistress, taking the warmed water from the cauldron that hung at the fire, and soon drying her with the soft towels that hung all warm and ready for her comfort; they dressed her with care then brushed her long hair. Rouge was painted upon the lips that now had none; she was as perfect as whence they came, though still a little unsteady upon her feet from the wine so dutifully drank.

As they tripped down passageways toward the doorway, Jayne related to Elizabeth the mischief that had happened towards her, and by the time they had reached the stairs they were all giggling once more, this time at the antics of the unknown officer, and passed amongst them various lewd remarks to even further the gaiety. Soon to the steps they came, where outside waiting to return them to Hutton castle stood the royal carriage. They tumbled in and it wended its way quickly back to the castle along the black road, and in little time they were within their chambers.

The evening passed quickly on, as the ladies chattered it away into yesterday. The late hour came as Elizabeth went to her bed and the ladies to their quarters close by their mistress. A lone guard paced the passageway, and as he went by the dark corner, a figure passed amongst the shadows, neither seen nor heard; the guard's movement was at a distance, far from the sight of the shadow that had slipped about. A light turn of the latch and the silent one was within the closet of the Lady Elizabeth; another click and into the bedroom he went.

Stirred by the noise of the opening door, Elizabeth sat higher in her bed. "Who is that?" she called in her most stern voice.

"Fear not, my lady; 'tis but I, Edward."

"Edward, what means this?"

The fire glow bounced off his silent shape as he came closer to his desire. "I could not rest with such thoughts of you within my head, and I could wait no longer to see you, for my need of you torments me so."

"You naughty fellow; we have had such little acquaintance. How can you have such thoughts of me?"

"I see you from my constant search for you, at every chance to glimpse more of your person."

"You do, my earl? ... How quaint. I have seen you spying my ankles; you are really a most devilish man."

"You seem to drive me to frenzy, and I know by your glances that you must desire me."

"Well 'tis fresh to me that I have any desire for you, but let us see some of this worship you pledge." Elizabeth pulled up her covers to reveal her bare feet, so dainty, and teasing her cousin more, pulled higher again to reveal her naked ankles, white and trim. The earl was in rapture's grasp as the teasing continued. "Would you like to see more, my cousin?"

"Yes, I would, my dearest Elizabeth."

"Then remove your breeches and then I will." He did not take his eyes away from her, as he fumbled with useless fingers to untie the straps and clasps of his coverings. But soon, as he danced around upon one leg, and with a stumble and grasp upon the table, he had them off, with only his linen cloth to hide his lower parts.

"Good boy," she said as she slowly pulled the covers to her knees. The earl had become pent with desire, and fought to contain himself, for he wished not to move upon Elizabeth without her consent, for his day then would surely be done and another may not come. The temptress lured him on. "Take them off," said she, pointing with her finger at the discreet coverings. "Then I will show you all you wish." He tugged and pulled at the tie that held up his cloth until the knot fell loose and his meagre coverings fell to the floor to leave him exposed. "Bring your clothes to me," she ordered him in her sternest voice. He picked up his clothes and placed them upon the bed beside the perfumed angel who watched mischievously at every step he took. "Step back now, go on, further back, further," she teased him as she waved him to her satisfaction, so that she was more in a dimmed light and even more desirable to be half seen. She then lifted up her knees and with her legs apart, she slowly pulled up her covers until they had reached her waist, to display her charms to the bewitched earl, who was entranced by the sparkle of the band twinkling bright in that fire's flame. "You may go, earl, for you have seen my jewel." She spake through her smiling lips as she covered herself. He stood befuddled, with no words of his own to rebuff those which she had spoken, and deemed to retrieve his clothes to make a scolded departure. "No, sir, they stay in my company. I would hasten away, for my cry could bring the guard with haste. But if you depart with mousey step I may entertain you further at another time. Quickly now, begone." He left with buttocks aglow as the flickering light played upon his proud skin. The doors closed behind him, as with furtive glances he raced down the empty passage to the safety of his chambers. He shutted,* with shivered hands, the door behind him, still dazed at what had befell him, but yet, did he not live for another day? For, after all, she did not rebuff him.

Elizabeth was wickedly pleased, and fell to slumber with the glint of mischief upon her smiling lips.

The teasing continued as the days fleeted to weeks. To our lady 'twas played only as game. To our earl 'twas no game he played, for the deepest of desire was over him. The time did come when Elizabeth would let the amorous earl go to her sparkling band and allow him to place his hand upon the soft skin below it.

"The king will be most displeased if you pass by his token, my lord"

"I care not for the king; I despise the king that has your body and I do not."

"He is the king, my lord; I love him and I will not refuse him."

"I care not for his wrath, for I will pass that band of his false desire." And at last he took all he desired from the king's mistress and feared naught in the doing. And so it went, as many times as it could be discreetly arranged. The times were such that Richard had been called upon to visit many places in England's north to pacify the makers of troubles there, and 'twas many months before he would return, leaving the pleasure to the earl. Elizabeth's feelings towards the earl were not of love, but of her wanton ways, and hoped that her gift shared would make Edward more agreeable

---

* *shutted* variation of shut; closed

to the king. But 'twas not so, and worsened so that jealousy loomed, and he pledged he would not share Elizabeth with any man or king.

Came the day when Elizabeth entered her chamber to find at last the greeting of a note sealed with the royal stamp; her king had returned and the note placed upon her table, leaning against the silver candlestick, as was requested. She opened it with joy and found once again the request to Crosby Place. But further tucked in there and tied neatly with a ribbon, another message showed from Richard; Elizabeth took it out, and after glancing at it felt she had to read the words aloud to herself, as she sat upon the edge of her settle.

"The sleep of night comes, but not for me as I lie awake when slumber should fold me. I wish not sleep, for awake I can still hear your voice and see your face. I rise at the dawn through those long hours without you, as into the day go I, a lost soul. I await that eve when my eyes are cast at last upon you, my Elizabeth. Comes then the hour of our meet the clock slows as it nears time. Your sight lifts my heart as I gaze at last at my Elizabeth. I lay a rose beside you, but which is the rose? For are not the petals as coarse cloth? Is not the softness as ungiving as stone? Is not the scent given forth that of a wretch? My Elizabeth, your love covers me now. The time is gone, raced as the swift winged swallow. And again I am alone, my heart gone, left once more to the night, lonely, waiting again for my love, Elizabeth, upon the morrow."

She folded the love note with wetted eyes that gazed upon it, and placed it as a newborn child into its crib; she laid the message inside her private casket under lock, and secreted it to its keep. She called the floor maid, and bade her to inform the earl that Elizabeth would not have meet with him this eve, for she has been summoned to sup with the king. Soon Elizabeth and her ladies made way to the waiting carriage and quickly rattled upon their way, once more bound for Richard, who had at last returned to Crosby Place.

The maid was given entry to the earl's chamber and spake the message from the mistress Elizabeth. By the window stood the earl, as he watched in anguish as his desire climbed into the royal coach and sped her away. He watched the happening as the message was spake. The maid tripped away to her tasks; he stood alone and had come to the end of his patience. "I will rent such wroth upon that king that he will rot and beg for Death's mercy. I will use our love, Elizabeth, to destroy him." His mind became twisted with much evil bent. He made ready his clothes most suited for such nightly activities as he was to pursue. Riding through the clear night with much purpose in his being, he came to The Old Mare tavern, and soon was seated there drinking with his friends, until the hour was late and the bar whores still were displaying about, but they were not such as he sought this night. He bid good night to his friends, for he had to return to the castle, was his tale.

Donning his cloak and his hat he went into the bustling street. Dark was the sky, but lit with stars bright and the now-and-then moon. Along the cobbled way he stretched his legs where, plied their craft, strolled the street whores, so low in their esteem they were not allowed within the tavern, placed even lower upon the scale of degradation than the tavern whore. Most unclean and infested were they, with fleas and lice, and raggedly clothed, emaciated with the continuous starvation they bore. But still our earl had not seen one rife enough for his act. He walked on and close to a side alley he saw who may be the one he desired; younger than the others, though still showing unclean, her hair long, greased and dishevelled, her teeth black, her skin blemished with the mark of the pox, with open blisters and unwashed face she stood. He came to her in the shadowy light; she, sighting him as he neared, straightening herself to bring more to her feeble appearance. Not the type of person, she mused, who would likely entertain such a wretch as I. Peering at her face as he came closer, he could smell the odour from her unwashed body, and 'twas not pleasing to him, but he needed to go on, for what he was to do was not for his pleasure, but to destroy the one he despised with all his being: the King Richard.

He took her by the elbow and guided her into the alley, but not too far, for he wished to still have some of the light that was given from the street torch to show upon his choice.

"Lift up your skirts," the earl spake to the girl, and in the discreet alleyway she did so, lifting up her skirts to the waist, revealing her black stockinged legs, with the holes showing the white flesh beneath. He leaned forward and peered closer.

"Remove your linen cloth," he said as she slid them down to her ankles, and, bending over, removed them, and held them at her back, as if they held some secret power that no one should cast their gaze upon. He crouched low and looked at her most carefully; the legs at the top he looked over from the torch's light, and showed to him all that he imagined of the lady, of the pox, rife upon her skin, weeping in its ravage, with some white powder showing where the herbal treatment had been applied to try and alleviate the condition, but seemingly failing to do so. The girl, through all this searching, was most puzzled by the earl's antics, but remained quiet during the activities, for if this was all he wanted then he must be a strange person indeed, and many strange persons had she been acquainted with.

With his mind so disturbed with jealousy, he decided that this was the whore he sought … the one most rife with the ailment. He guided her backwards into the dark of the alleyway into the black, smelly corner of urine, excretion, and bile. The earl untied his garments and released himself from them, to be then amongst the open sores laying their evil upon him. Soon he was done with the silent whore and her diseased baggage, and returned all to its lair and fastened up his breeches. He placed three pennies into the small hand, as she finished pulling on her tattered clothes and lowering her skirt.

"Thankee, sire," she said. "Come see me again if you so desire." He did not answer her but proceeded to the open end of the alleyway. With his head down he made sure he was fastened properly as the light bettered, but bumped straight into a strong body before him.

"Excuse me, sir," — it said as the earl looked up from the blow, and saw that he had engaged with his close friends from the tavern. "Edward! … What, pray, are you doing here? Did you not return to your chambers as yet?" As they spake the urchin came out from the dark entrance, to the notice of the group who had also seen the earl leaving the same place. "What game are you playing, sir?" His friends gathered about him, all concerned about his being.

"I do what I have to do, regrettable though it is."

"What say you, Edward; have you been with that rife whore?"

"Yes, my dear friends, I have."

"You talk as if you have lost all your sense; to do such a thing is against all common reason."

"To you it may seem so, but to me it is not."

"You know full well the whore is filled with the Lues* and any man who entertains her is set for the same terrible malady that it brings. All you can do is pray that you are one of the very few who may not get infected."

"But that is it, my friends, for I wish to be infected."

"What!" In unison his friends, with arms raised, appealed to the heavens, unable to understand the thoughts that ran through the head of Edward. "Do you not know of what ills will be forthcoming to you if you have the disease?"

"I do."

"I think not, sir. You may say you know of such that may happen, of the weeping sores and the fevers, and we talk not of the insanity that comes. You say you know of this yet you choose to embrace it all. Sire, I wash my hands of you, for are you not already of an imbecile? You are a fool, and the time will come of tales spoken of Hutton's fool, and you will

---

* *Lues* Lues venera; an old name for syphilis, pronouced Lou-ease

be the one of the tale told."

"Tell us," spake another of his friends who was not of angry tone, and asked calmly, "why would you do such a terrible thing?" They awaited the answer, as they stood in the night in the middle of the roadway with many people about, but so concerned were they, the speaking came as if they were in private quarters. "You have done this act that will not only affect yourself, but will affect all others who may come into such contact with you."

"That is the very reason I have done such a thing. I most detest the King Richard, who takes my love from me and ravishes her with much insult to me. I will therefore infect my Elizabeth, who will in turn infect the evilness that is Richard and bring him to his doom, and will take all happiness from him. For when he sees that he is infected he will be rid of Elizabeth, the whore, most quickly, and the only one who will have her will be this earl."

"You, sire, are completely mad," the most enraged of his friends continued. "The disease will kill you long before Elizabeth infects Richard. So why would you pursue this further if you are not a madman?"

"I care not as long as I have Elizabeth and Richard does not." His friends stood with heads shaking, unable longer to bear the situation, and unable to bring any sense to the earl, but they continued to try.

"If you love Elizabeth so much, how can you, in God's name, bring such a vile act to her body? You fool yourself if you think there are any treatments for such an ailment, for there are not. You have brought upon yourself such devastation and degradation, you must not even think of inflicting this curse on such an angel as that lady, who is of such joy and kindness, and whose beauty you must not scar."

The earl had heard all he wished, and pushed by his once friends and went his way, bent upon his evil plan.

"I will kill him!" one of group shouted, and went to draw his sword to end the foulness that walked from them. They held him so that he could not move as he struggled to overcome their concern.

"Hold yourself, my friend, be not of haste, for yet he has done naught but talk of evil; and would not the law see that you have murdered an innocent man? 'Tis not worth the suffering you would bring upon yourself."

The sword was slid reluctantly back into its sheath as he shouted his last remark at the far earl. "You are not the earl that plays the fool, but the fool that plays the earl!" They gathered themselves and with hearts that were heavy returned to the tavern's glow.

A time of ten days had past with both the earl and Richard taking Elizabeth many times. The earl examined himself most frequently, and oft wondered if he should have another encounter with a street whore, for time it seemed was drifting by, and no sign of any disease did he yet see. But this morning he awoke with an irritation that caused him to scratch, and 'twas such that he could not stop scratching. He saw now that he was indeed infected, with much blood upon his fingernails, and in seeing such felt his stomach turn with both fear and anticipation. He continued over the weeks to lay his evil curse upon the Lady Elizabeth, and was most careful to only engage in such activities within the dark, and within black places he chose.

The earl's once friends tried to warn Elizabeth, but found it most difficult to put such evil to the quill and even more so to speak of it. And by the time they had the way, so much time had passed that they deemed it now useless to pursue it any further, for the poor lady must be in a frantic state, and must know from whom the evil had come.

Pain was within the body of the earl as he gazed at the rife pox, being seen in a most advanced manner, full of weeping sores spreading over his legs and stomach, and making it so that he was becoming unable to pursue his amour with Elizabeth. But still, even in his sickening state, he continued to ply the scourge upon the lady.

The year was in the month of April. The earl once more visiting the Lady Elizabeth within her chamber, and, as he was wont to do to delight himself, asked to see her ankles as she lay abed.

"You naughty earl," she, as always, playful said. "How is that for you?" she asked as she lifted her gown to reveal her white, tantalizing skin to him. "Do you wish to see more, earlie?"

"Yes, I wish so, my dearest." Then came the gown slowly pulled to her knees sending desirous quivers through the earl. "Show me all now," he said.

"Sir, I will not. Do you think I am but a whore?"

"Please, do not tease me. Show me all." He spake with some hint of a frantic tone within his voice that she had not heard before.

"Very well then, if you are in such a mood to see, but stay your distance; I want you not close."

"I promise, my love." She again slowly lifted her gown above her waist; without any linen cloth showing there to hide any of her modesty, she opened wide her legs. The earl stepped forward a little, only for Elizabeth to tightly close her legs together.

"I told you, earlie, no closer."

"I will not touch you, my dearest; I just wish to gaze at your loving body. Look, I place my hands clasped aback."

"No touching then?"

"No touching, I promise, my love,"—as he came within arm's length of her, she teasingly opened slowly her legs as he had wished, and he put not one hand upon her. With the fire bright and the tallows ablaze, the place of Elizabeth's abode was lit with ample light for the earl to see the effect of his evildoings. He stared close, blinked and stared closer, his heart turning and twisting in his chest as the sight he saw brought much anguish to him. For Elizabeth lay as the newly born child, with pure white skin, unblemished, soft and clean. No earthly afflictions showed to make it not perfect; the skin showed of that of an angel.

"Oh, God!" he cried in anguish. "I have to go," was all he said as he made with much haste toward the doorway.

"Edward! Come back and make love to me. I was only teasing you. Please, come back."

But he had gone; the door banging in despair behind him.

"What have I done?" she shouted to no reply as the earl was making toward his chambers, treading unstable steps as he went, recalling the voice of his friend, who had said that the earl may be the fortunate one of many who do not get afflicted by the cursed disease. But, as fate had played its game, 'twas Elizabeth who was the blessed one and could not become infected; her purity remained intact.

He fell to his bed and sobbed the tear of despair. Knowing now that he was the only one who had the disease, and his life was ruined because of his envy and rage. After a short while he gathered himself and made ready to pay a visitation to the barber-surgeon at the close-by town. He stood before his looking glass, cloaked already and tying his neckband. As he was doing so he saw a slight rash coming up from his chest, and with his heart heavy realized the disease was spreading toward his face, and would be of sight to all if 'twas not stopped. He went with heavy tread to the steed that awaited him, and cantered away from his folly to make toward the town, hopeful of some relief from the surgeon there.

At dusk he arrived at the house of his need, with all about the bustling townsfolk, who seemed never to find a place to stop there activities. The earl tied up his horse to the wall ring and rapped upon the door. He read the brass plate of the barber-surgeon placed above his knuckled hand— Joshua Bloom—as he waited for some notice of his knock, hoping that the surgeon was about at this hour. Then the door opened a crack, and a small lady poked out her white-bonneted head.

"Can I help you, sir?" The little one was the wife of the surgeon, most pleasant in her manner was she.

"Yes, madam, is the Master Joshua Bloom in residence?"

"Yes, sir, he is; I deem you wish to have council with him?"

"I do, madam."

"Do, please, come in." The slight woman pulled upon the door as if it were a runaway horse. The earl helped the entry with a helpful push of his own to move the heavy entrance door, and stepping inside helped the small lady to close it shut. "Please be seated, sire,"—speaking as she led him into the hallway, and beckoned him to a bench placed there for those who waited to visit with the surgeon, Bloom. "May I take your hat and cloak, sire?"

"Yes, madam." He handed her his hat and untied his cloak. Softly he handed them to her, being careful not to drown her in the heavy cloth.

She struggled away with the load, and asked upon her way, "And may I ask your name, sire?"

"I am the Earl of Warwick, my lady."

"Thank you, my lord," she, on turning her head, acknowledged the class distinction. The earl sat upon the bench close to one end, which rested against a side table there, upon which lay a Bible. He picked it up and opened it where it may and looked directly at the middle. "He who sows evil reaps evil." He read no more but closed the book and placed it back upon the table, and sat waiting as many others had done upon this bench, they as much tormented by their ills as he and as fearful of the surgeon's hand. The flickering candles were his company, it seemed for a long time he watched the fat drip, but 'twas not long he dreamed in that flickered light, for now came the person of Joshua Bloom, the barber-surgeon.

"Good day to you, my lord." He bowed before the earl. A tall thin man was he of sallow features and sunken eyes, over which he wore seeing glasses that covered the hollows. Dressed all of black, except for his stiff collar of white, looking able to sever his neck.

"Good day, Bloom."

"Please, come into the surgery." He beckoned the earl to follow him, as he strode with overly long strides upon his black stockinged legs, to outpace him as he turned into the black open door of his workroom; he held it open for the lord to enter. "Please, be seated," he said and closed the door as the earl entered and sat himself upon the seat that was before the table. The surgeon placed himself at the seat that was behind the table, where upon were many books that the earl spied with disturbing titles. Potions and Herbal Remedies. Limb Removal for the New Surgeon. The Treatment of Mental Sickness. And many others, so worn the title could not be read. Papers lay about, and also, there opened at this day's date of the eighteenth day of April, fourteen hundred and eighty-five, lay the ink-splattered yearly ledger.

A quick sight about the room brought to eye the shelves of jars and bunched herbs. Heavy brown crocks stood upon the stone floor. A table of dark wood where laid upon it were the instruments of the practice: dental pliers, clamps, leather straps, knives of different sizes, bone saws, and all manner of strange metal pieces. A flat table covered with a cotton cloth, with a pillow set at one end, and rings at all four corners for restraining straps.

"Is there something ailing you, sir?" Bloom broke into the earl's gazings.

"Yes there is. I have, from what I have seen, become infected with a pox."

The eyebrows above the seeing glasses raised upon the words spoken. "You know this without doubt?" Bloom queried the earl.

"I believe I am not mistaken, sir."

"We will take a look at you, my lord. Please, remove your clothes." The earl, with a most steady demeanour, removed his coverings, and folded each piece neatly upon the seat he had been resting upon. Bloom watched his movements from the seat he occupied at the other side of the table. His brows still raised as he glimpsed the scourge in the light of the candles' flame. The earl stood aback of the chair, trying hard to hide his affliction for as long as he could, for shame had taken his mind. Bloom had risen and was lighting his bright candle. A large wicked tallow placed in a holder, with polished metal upon one side, curved to reflect the light, and a sturdy wooden handle, making it easier to shine the glow to the place of the examination. He came around the table and eased the lord away from the chair so he may see more of the affliction. Bloom lowered the light to brighten the area before him and became somewhat aghast at that which he saw, but made no outward sign of any emotion. The lower body of the earl was in a most advanced state of the disease, the rashes increasing in severity as the pox progressed. "How is it, sir, you have let the affliction go so far before seeking advice?"

"Reasons gave me no chance to do so until now."

"Lie upon the table, please." The surgeon beckoned toward the cotton-covered table as the earl climbed upon it with a resigned sigh. "Open your legs and lie still, please." The lord did as he was bid. The surgeon picked up his metal nips from the close-by tray, and with his light in one hand and the instrument in the other he chose one of the more serious looking weepings, all swollen as some kind of boil. Then, with a swift movement, pulled off the scab that had formed. The earl subdued his cry of pain with watered eyes and bitten lip. Bloom looked closer at the scabless erosion. "You have the advanced Lues disease, my lord," he said as he stood up from his examination, and looking straight into the face of the earl, "and, sir, I do mean it is in a most rampant stage."

Red of face, the lord with much rage blowing out of his cheeks ranted at the surgeon. "Of course it is! I know that! What I need to know is what can be done about it?"

Bloom turned away and related to the earl the measures that had to be undertaken. "The top parts of all infections must be scraped off to reveal the new flesh beneath, and then a paste of sulphur acid is applied to burn off and seal the wound as if cauterized. This not only applies to the outer skin, but to the urine tube, which must be cleaned with the drag wire." Tears had overcome the earl, as he crouched with his hands holding the weight of his head, and he was in a most disturbed state. "And then, if all proceeds as it should, further treatments, at fortnightly intervals, should eventually bring the disease under our control. Now, my lord, the question is, do you wish to engage in such a treatment? … I can give you some remedy to relieve the discomfort that will befall you, both during the procedure and afterwards. The monies to cover such treatments are not for the poor man. I tell you now, this is the only method to rid you of such a dilemma."

"The choice I have does not exist; I have only one option, and further, I can pay whatever the cost, sir."

"Good. Then do you want me to begin now? For I tell you, my lord, more delay and all hopes of recovery could be lost."

"By God, Bloom, do what you have to do, for am not I in your hands like the potter's clay?"

"I will give you some remedy that will relieve you of most of the pain during the surgery." Bloom stepped away and went into the darkened area of the room to his crocks and jars, and poured from one of them a full two measures of the amber liquid into a drinking cup, and brought it over to the earl who was now seated upon the table. He took the liquid down in one gulp and gave back the vessel to Bloom. A shiver ran down his body, as the remedy went to spread its effect through the warm blood. A shiver from the cold of the room, and a shiver from the fear of the purging that was to come. In a short time the liquid had relaxed him, and he became somewhat drowsy, and felt little as he was laid back upon the table; his head was lifted so that the pillow could be placed beneath his head to support it. Four hands were around him as the lady-wife assisted her husband. She fetched the leather straps from the display table and with skilled hands strapped the body tight to the table. A bone with ties upon each end was placed into the earl's mouth, and were then pulled back and fastened behind the head. "Let us begin, my dear." Bloom spake as his wife passed to him the razor-sharp blade. The glint of light from the bright candle danced upon the steel, as the surgeon began the long task of scraping off the raised areas of the skin. The resting eyes opened wide now, wet with the water of pain that was wracking his body. The earl shook and groaned but could not move; he tried to scream, but could not. The surgeon scraped. The legs, the thighs, the manly parts, all places were being stripped bare, as the surgeon went about his task. The lady of the house applied the sulphur, as then the sharp pain of the knife gave way to the burning pain of the acid, and he knew not which was the most bearable. But soon it calmed as the paste dried, and all that was left upon the skin's surface was a white powder, which when dry crumbled away.

The earl eased his muscles as the pain lessened, and he felt the rim of a vessel upon his lips as more of the remedy was trickled into his mouth; he gulped it down past the fastened bone, and again he was calm as the fear he had felt had once more left his body. But yet more was to wreak upon this frame as Bloom's wife returned the drinking cup to the table and brought back with her the draw wire for the next purge. A thin wire with a length of two feet: at one end a wooden cross handle, to give a stronger grip to the instrument, the rest of the wire barbed. With little resistance to its entry, it slid into the required hole with much ease. Withdrawing it though was a different matter; coming out, the barbs would rip the infection clean, as 'twas pulled slowly with the wooden handle.

She handed the instrument to her husband, and then held the earl's manhood upright, and with two hands tightly grasping, steadied the patient for the intrusion. The earl lay still in his calmed state, and felt little as the surgeon gently guided the wire into the hole. He had gauged a mark as to the depth he wished to go and, on reaching it, he nodded to his wife that he was ready to purge the tube. She readied herself, tightening her grip even more for the removal of the vile disease to begin. The surgeon with one hand upon his wife's to steady his pull, and with the wooden handle clasped between his fingers, began to withdraw the cleansing wire. The earl shuddered, and was able to scream through his gagged mouth; but the surgeon heard naught of such anguish and continued to finish the treatment. The cries of the earl lessened to a whimper, and then to silence as faintness detached him from any pain. The pull continued as the wire came out, covered in blood and flesh dripping onto the clasping hands below; then, with a slight whip, it came out throwing the blood from the wire as it did so. Once out, the wife released her grip upon the earl, and took the bloodied probe from her husband, laying it upon the washing tray to be cleaned with the other used instruments. She wiped away all the blood and flesh that had sprayed about from the earl to the table, the floor, and the wall. Then both washed and wiped their blood-covered hands, to move on to the next procedure.

The sulphur liquid was made ready to be induced. The lady brought a small metal tube with a bell mouth upon one end to receive a poured liquid; she handed the tube to the surgeon. The wife once again held the earl firmly as Bloom started to feed it into the urine hole. The depth was reached and, leaving the tube protruding, the surgeon went to the mixing table, bringing back the small vessel that had been prepared of sulphur acid. He held the bell mouth and poured a measure of the liquid into it and waited for it to drain empty. Slowly he removed the tube from the detached earl, and all was finished as the wife took the instrument and laid it with the others in the tray. They wiped away all traces of the procedure from the earl, and laid across him a clean cloth for his comfort when he awoke.

While they waited for the earl to awaken they washed and dried the instruments, and laid them back in their order upon the table. Soon the earl began to stir, and in a little time was awake as the wife removed the bone from his mouth and gave him water to sip. He then raised himself as he gazed at his lower body covered in white powder, and saw that 'twas smoother and with less discomfort than before. He was helped to dress, and began moving about more easily.

"Thank you, Bloom, for your service," spake the earl as he readied to depart.

"Sir, here is some of the tonic for you; it must be taken twice a day." Bloom placed the small crock into the earl's hand. "Our note of charge will be brought to the castle by our manservant. He is well trusted and you can make your reimbursement to him. If you need further tonic, we will be pleased to supply your needs, and in a fortnight we can see what further treatment may be needed."

"Very well, Bloom. I bid you good day, and good day to your lady-wife." He was gone into the night walking away with only slight discomfort from the ordeal, and imagining that it should be worse, was it not for the tonic he had sipped.

The door closed, and they looked at each other, Joshua Bloom and his good wife.

"What say you, my dear?" she posed to her husband.

"My wife, he is a dead man. Too far diseased to have much time to live."

"How long do you think, husband?"

"Long enough, my dear. Yes, we have time enough to drain the pompous fool of every penny he has. The disease will take him surely, but the poppy oil he sups every day will keep him to us, and, my dear, the more he needs it, the more so goes the payment. We will supply him with whores, for it seems he has a weakness for such activities, and they will make certain that he takes his tonic in goodly amounts." Their smiles crossed as they made to their private chamber, and together supped the wine, as thoughts of the earl's dilemma mingled their heads with the fortune to be made, with ease, from Hutton's fool.

Chapter Eleven.

Masquerade and Madness.

"Where is that damned earl?" Elizabeth half asked Helen, who knew of no answer to give. But then Elizabeth did not need an answer. "He has gone to see his whore; that is where he is—with his trollop. Well, if that is what he prefers, she can have him, for I have had my fill of his amour. I wish not to play anymore his childish games, for I desire only one lover; Richard is all I desire. So he may pester me no more, for I wish to be free of him. I will write a note to him letting him know of my intentions, and that will be the end of it."

"Yes, my mistress."

Elizabeth's demeanour changed somewhat from the angry rant to that of gladness that she had only one lover, and one lover who is king. Silence then played in the chamber where they sewed; for a lengthy time was it so, except for the quiet singing that lilted from Elizabeth.

"Helen?" Her little-girl-scheming voice came now; not the voice of the mature lady, but of the mischievous child.

"Yes, my mistress," the reply came, patronizing the child.

"Helen," she repeated, "you do remember the tavern in the town, do you not?"

"Yes, I do." Anticipating the words that were to follow, Helen did not yet look at Elizabeth but gazed upon her stitch.

"Helen, will you accompany me there? For I have never been to such a place, and when we move to the mansion Richard is preparing for us, we will have no opportunity to do so ..." She talked on and on to press her argument into one sentence so Helen could not speak against it, until she had used up all her persuasions.

"If I give you my advice, Liz, will you heed any of it? For if you are inclined not to, I will stay my words."

"Of course I will, dearest Helen; as long as it is the right advice." The twinkled eye showed itself, as Helen looked into the face of her friend.

"Mistress, if we did this, we would need a nobleman to escort us to such a place, would we not?"

"Yes, Helen, we would." Silence came once more upon the chamber, as Elizabeth toyed with the question from her friend and in time spake once more. "If I can sway such a person to escort us, will you be game?"

"I say yes, my lady, for you will be unable to find anyone for such a task; without Richard's permission there is no one who will risk his ire for such a fling. There are no such people about; so rest your mind from the idea."

"Well, I think I can persuade someone who may take such upon themselves."

"Very well, Liz, do as you may. For you are so set upon this play that I am of no persuasion."

"I love you, Helen." Elizabeth jumped up from her seat, and with her arms around Helen's neck, kissed her most playfully. "If you were but a man I would show you of my love."

"You shame me with your words; you know you are brazen, do you not?"

"Oh, yes, my dear, I know, but I use only words to show you of my affection."

"And you know you are quite mad. You sew without thread in your needle."

Elizabeth shivered with laughter at her friend's humour bent. "Oh, my dear Helen, you are such a joy to me, for you know more of my soul than I do myself."

Helen began to tidy away the sewing, picking up from the floor the stitching Elizabeth had dropped in her enthusiasm.

"Helen, ask Jayne if she would wish to come with us."

"Yes, mistress," Helen answered as she started toward the doorway.

"Mary Montagu—Helen, ask her to come to visit with me. I will be in the privy; ask her to seek me there."

"Yes, mistress." And Helen went her way down the passage, duty bound.

Elizabeth to the privy went, and removing to her ankles her white linens, sat over one of the holes and gently relieved herself in a most ladylike fashion. A light tap sounded upon the door, and with a "Come," Mary was inside, with Elizabeth to close the door behind her softly.

"Please, sit my dear Mary; relieve yourself." Mary pulled down her undergarments, lifted her skirt, and sat herself upon the hole next to Elizabeth. It had not been since she was removed from her home in a destitute state that she had shared such companionship, as she now most demurely relieved herself.

"How fare you, Mary?"

"I am most well, my mistress."

"Mary, please call me Elizabeth, for you are no servant to me, as one day I hope I would not be to you."

"Surely not, Elizabeth, for it hurts me so to think of such matters."

"It does seem that Richard bears some concern and fears that a war against him is being plotted. Who can see into the future of what may occur in such changing times—but enough of such maudlin talk. There are happier things about this world than troubled times and I am most anxious to seek them out."

"If I may say so, Elizabeth, your reputation for such things precedes you."

"Yes, I believe it does, does it not, for I cannot sit for long in the hard chair of life … Mary?"

"Yes, Elizabeth."

"Are you one for sitting upon the hard chair, or are you game for some adventure?"

"Well, yes, I believe so, for I have not engaged in any such plans for many months now."

"Does the devil rise within you at times, to seek excitements and frowned-upon games?"

"I know not of yet which games you wish to play."

"Have you ever been to a tavern, Mary?—in the barroom of a tavern?"

"No, I have not."

"Would you not be excited to do so?"

"I supposed I would … with the proper escort."

"Oh, yes, of course it would have to be a most fitting escort." They were standing and washing themselves with water from the bowl there. Elizabeth had a little time to mull what words next she would use, as they dried themselves and started to pull on their clothes.

"Mary?"

"Yes, Elizabeth."

"I cannot find an escort."

"Oh."

"Mary, will you play our escort?"

"Pardon, my lady," came the reply with unwilling tone.

"No, Mary, please listen, nothing will occur, for we will be in the tavern but a few minutes, and then we will leave. I promise you … I have some lord's clothing in my cupboard that we can make fit, and no one will know that you are not a gentleman to escort us. Please, Mary, please say yes."

"Elizabeth, I cannot be as a man … I have no tact for such a masquerade; please do not ask me."

"But you can, Mary; we can make you look a likely noble, all fine and pompous. Please say you will, Mary; you are our only hope."

"Mistress, I would die God's Death in fear. Do you not see me shaking at the very thought of it?"

"You will have no fear, Mary, for you are a brave soul. You have endured much this past while, and for you to have some happy adventure, instead of the sadness you have suffered, will lighten your heart, Mary— Mary?"

"Very well, Elizabeth, I will try on the clothes and see in the glass, and if then I feel I can do such a thing then I will, but I cannot promise so."

"Mary, I knew you would." They both hugged and kissed. Elizabeth with the devil's happiness, Mary with doubt. They both left the privy, hand clasped in hand, with Elizabeth holding the tighter, more to stop Mary from fleeing than aught else. They came to Elizabeth's chamber and waiting for them there was Helen, who said firstly that Jayne would not be accompanying them.

"Why ever not?" Elizabeth asked.

"She is smitten with her guard officer, and wishes to remain here so she may contemplate her dilemma."

"Oh, poor dear," answered Elizabeth.

"I suppose you found no suitable noble for your adventure?"

"Far from it, Helen; I did so find someone."

"Pray, tell, who did you find?"

"She is standing here, clasped at hand."

"I beg your pardon, my lady, for I do not understand your rhyme."

"It is simple, my dear Helen. Mary will dress in the garb of a noble and be our most noble of escorts."

"Elizabeth, what in God's name did you say to her to agree to such insanity? And Mary, what do you have to say in this matter, this boggling matter?"

"I told our Lady Elizabeth that I would agree upon seeing that I would not be seen as a lady, but as a man, and only then."

"I am in absolute awe at the game you have undertaken. You know you will fool no one."

"But, of course you will help us, will you not, my most dearest of friends?"

"Yes, I will, of course, my lady, for if I leave it to you, a clown will stand and a noble will not stare from the glass,"—Helen smiling a little at the thoughts of the daring adventure to come.

All three ladies went to the cupboard, as Elizabeth opened the door and, kneeling, pushed around the clothes and the shoes, until she found that which would be the most suitable.

"Take off your dress, Mary, and we will see how they fit upon you." Mary did as she was bid and removed her outerwear. The two ladies then pulled on the breeches, which lay more than a foot along the floor past the dainty feet of Mary. Elizabeth took the shears from the tapestry basket and cut them to a more suitable length. Next they slipped onto her the velvet jacket. Her hands were out of sight as the sleeves were at a dangle to her knees. The shears cut once more to reveal the white hands from their guise. "You are looking most fine, Mary."

"I think not, Elizabeth. You only try to deceive me with your sweet tones."

"Wait, Mary, please wait until we are finished, and then you will see your splendid self."

Ladies black boots came from the cupboard, most suitable for a noble to wear. Then they sat their Mary down, and started to transform the face from pretty to handsome. A wax pencil they used to darken her eyebrows, then pulled the hair from one of the wigs that was not in the fashion of the day. And, using the gum from the sewing basket, stuck to Mary's face a moustache and a beard. "Sit still, Mary, whilst it dries," they told their unlikely lord. Soon the shears were cutting again as 'twas shaped by Elizabeth to a manly style. "Woo," she said as she stood back to admire her barber's work. "It looks divine." Though Helen commented not. They stood Mary up and placed upon her head a most rakish hat. Both began to tuck Mary's hair under the band so that 'twas not seen, then pulled a black cape over her shoulders and clipped it closed at the neck, as she now was becoming manlier. A walking staff was placed in one hand, which Elizabeth thought could become a weapon if needed, but she did not offer such words to her companions.

"Close your eyes, Mary," spake Helen as they guided her to the looking glass and primmed her a little before she was to gaze. "Open your eyes Mary." She did so and gazed at the stranger before her as she stepped back a little.

"I feel faint," she said.

"No, you do not," said Elizabeth. "But what say you of the guise?"

"Well, it does not look of me. But I do not walk or talk as a man."

"Try … Say … say: A flagon of ale, and gin for my ladies, wench. As low as you can speak, Mary."

"A flagon of ale, and gin for my ladies, wench." Mary did keep trying the line, but the voice, though a little deeper, was still more of a lady's voice, and was not improved by the constant speaking of it.

"We will try the voice later; let us see the walk now, Mary. Take strides that are long, too long for your legs as a man does."

Mary strutted along as directed by the ladies and seemed to master it most quickly.

"I will surely die, Elizabeth. I fear I cannot continue."

"You can, Mary; you look most manly."

"I do not know; my knees shake and we are still in the chamber."

"Here, sit for a while; let us sup a little wine to fortify our bodies."

The three sat and gulped at the full goblets that Elizabeth would not let be empty. And soon all believed that Mary was as close to a man as anyone could wish. Hearts of the brave came from the wine supped.

Helen and Elizabeth donned their cloaks, and, with hoods raised, the trio left the chambers in secret and whisked down the passageway, dresses rustling as they went with the heavy overstepping boots of Mary, clopping their song with the rustled sweep. Using the rear entrance of the castle, so as not to be seen, they were soon outside as past the sleeping guard they slinked, and climbed into the small carriage that Helen had arranged with the castle hostler. They closed the door, and quickly the coachman had his horses at the gallop, to wend through the dust-laid track to the town where lay The Old Mare.

"A flagon of ale, and gin for my ladies, wench"

"Yes, Mary, that is sounding much more sincere," was the praise given so that Mary would be able to continue her roll. But the fact was, as Helen and Elizabeth glanced at each other, the words were no better in their coming, and they had to gaze to the windows to subdue their mirth; they could not gaze upon each other for fear that Mary would see they were not sincere, and may flee from the task.

They climbed out upon unsteady feet, each wishing to return most quickly to the safety of their chambers, but each not wishing to be the one who failed the shoot. They closed the carriage door behind them as Helen told the coachman to wait for them at this spot, and not to stray from the place he was set. The three waltzed their way to the tavern through the tumbling crowd around. Both holding tightly on to Mary, more to support her than any other need, for her legs would not move as she desired. They pushed and stepped through the humanity—shouting, laughing, fighting, sleeping—to the door of their journey, the light and noise coming from within, on and off it went as the door was continually opened and closed.

"Come along, ladies," Elizabeth said as she dragged her companions to the handle of the door. Click it went as she pushed it open to see all she ever thought it may be. The smell of sour beer mingling with sawdust played her nose, the pies and cheeses upon the tables added more. Urine smelled at one side of the room, where 'twas used for such activities. The noise then seemed to dull the smell, as the shouting of ruffians rang about as they goaded each other. The laughter of men and women, brash and loud from the lewd jokes bantered about. Dogs barked and fought, a mayhem of life in one small room. Elizabeth, awed by the spectacle, her eyes sparkled, for was not this the most exciting place one could ever wish to enter? In they trod, pushing the shaking Mary into the lead; to the backbench they went, as 'twas seen empty at this time; it invited them to sit and they did so, with the two ladies slightly hiding their faces, and their escort sticking out the bearded chin. 'Twas all a new experience for them and they wished to feel the vibrant room little by little. They pulled the table close to them and told Mary to place her elbow upon it with one hand under her chin, as men were wont to do. The ladies lowered their hoods a little to view more of their intriguing surroundings, looking as a child upon first seeing a chicken.

"Mary, catch the eye of the barmaid to bring us some gin, so we may look as if this is our usual haunt." Mary tried most bravely waving her arm toward the maid but she would not take the notice. "Call her, Mary; I think you have to call for the wench."

"Wench!" called Mary to no avail. Now standing, she called once more. "Wench!" This time she came over to them. "A flagon of ale, and gin for my ladies," came the words from the mouth of Mary, with even less manliness than she had practiced. But seemed no matter, for the wench left to bring to them their request. As they waited they looked more about, reaping in the life about them; they had never seen before life such as this, as real to the lower class as 'twas to the nobility. The life they saw was brash and crude, loud and obscene. They absolutely loved it.

The wench broke their trance. "One ale, two gins, nine pence." The drinks were placed upon the table and the hand was shown for the fare.

Mary looked at Elizabeth and Helen, still with hand under the chin. Like an oak tree it seemed unable to move. "I have no coin," Mary gruffed through her clenched teeth to her companions.

They both looked at Mary, and, in their minds, said to each other, of course she has no coin; she wears manly clothes and is unable to carry a purse.

Elizabeth put her hand to where she kept her coin purse, but with the excitement of leaving she had not picked it up and could still see it in her mind, sitting lonely upon her dresser, begging to be part of their game. Mary and Elizabeth looked at Helen, their last hope, as the barmaid did stand impatiently with hand on weary hip. Helen indeed did have her purse, to the decided relief of her two friends. She took it from her side, unclipped the silver catch, and peeked inside, helped in her quest by the eyes of Mary and Elizabeth, who were most interested in the outcome of the search. But 'twas all to no avail; only two pennies lay in the bottom of the silk, tucked down there with dust and fluff. Not enough for their fare. They all looked up to the wench but she had soon departed. Gone she to the innkeeper to relate that no monies were forthcoming from the table she was pointing to … of the gentleman and his two ladies, whose eyes were meeting those of the innkeeper. He started over to them in a state that was not happy.

"He is coming toward us." Through the teeth of Mary came again the frightening observation. The shadow of the innkeeper fell over the table, followed by the smell of the unwashed body, then the unshaven face of stubble, of unkempt hair and grimed teeth. The dirty stained apron was thrust before them. Two thick fists were rested upon the table as the ale-washed breath of the hosteller came over them, all before the words were spoken. Though held he some mischief in his bearing.

"No one sups 'ere without payment."

Mary stood then, being the man of the party and deemed 'twas her place. "My good man, we will pay you on our return to the castle of Sheriff Hutton where we are lodged. We are sorry for our lack of coin, but you will be paid and with gratuity to boot for your inconvenience."

"Sit down, come with such jibber when your voice is of a man and not of a maiden." The innkeeper pushed Mary down onto her seat as a small crowd of ogling drunks gathered around the table, pushing and shouting and egging on the innkeeper. "If you are penniless, my ladies, then we will take payment from your virtue."

Elizabeth now stood … 'Twas time. "Touch one of us and you will forfeit your life. You know not who you are in conflict with—"

But before more could be said, the innkeeper had reached forward and pulled open Elizabeth's cloak revealing the ample bosom of our lady, always dressed for enticement wherever she stepped. Crack! Down came the staff swung by Mary across the hand of the villain with all the strength she could summon.

Loudly he cried, releasing his grip upon Elizabeth and holding his pained hand with tears swelling his eyes; 'twas not pain that he showed there but rage, and stunned by the hurt placed upon him by the slight fellow, but only for a moment was all in wait, as he grabbed the staff of Mary and began to pull it from her little grasp, with Helen helping her to hold it so the madman would not take it, for they feared he may wish to use it upon them. Elizabeth joined the fray as she pulled and tugged at the fat fingers that battled her ladies.

The hand came over Mary's shoulder, strong and masculine, the clean cuffs of linen showed, the hairs, black and curled, upon the back, the nails clean and fine, the hand's voice spake behind Mary. "I think that will be enough, landlord." The voice as strong and clear as the hand it belonged to.

Mary and Helen released the staff as the hand pulled against the landlord's hand, and Elizabeth stopped her tugging at the landlord, as they all looked to see who the handsome officer was who had come to their aid. A saviour indeed, not uniformed, and, would have it, was spending a social night out with his friends; his evening though had turned to the task of rescue, after he had been watching for some while at the ladies' dilemma and their stubborn fight.

"Your intrusion will not be enough, sir! I am owed monies, and will be paid by coin or flesh." The large man clutching the other end of the staff still showed his anger, more 'twas to be abused by wenches than aught other.

"What is their payment that you are owed?"

"Nine pence."

"Here, my good man, take this shilling and let things return to calm."

The black fingernails snatched the coin. "I will take it this time, but if they show their faces in here again, I will take my flesh," he growled at the ladies, making them step back in some fear.

"I do not think they will return again." The officer retrieved the staff from the landlord and noticed the wicked twinkle in his eye as he did so. As the landlord, with raunchy words, strode away to his counter, pushing past the drunken oglers still around the table.

"This way, my ladies," the officer bowed and beckoned the ladies toward the door. Elizabeth yet did not move but picked up her paid-for gin and downed the lot with ne'er a flicker. Helen saw the move to be made so she followed her companion and drank all down, until every little drop was supped. Mary wished to follow and also to show her fire, but 'twas a tankard that stood before her as they watched to see what she would make of it. The masquerade was over, as relief brought her tiny hands to the tankard of ale. She upped it to her lips and drank away at the cold, bitter liquid, appearing not to breathe but did so inside the tankard that ringed her head; soon she had drank all her frame could take, and with a smiling face, which had not showed upon the fair skin for many moons, placed down upon the table the half-supped ale, and, feeling most brave, shouted over to the landlord, "Good night to you, sir!"

"And good night to you, my lady," he replied.

The officer held the door open, so the ladies could leave their adventure with dignified ease.

"My Lady Elizabeth," he bowed, and she nodded to him as she passed. "My Lady Helen," he bowed again and was acknowledged once again as she passed. "My Lady Mary," he bowed again, but no acknowledgement did he receive, only blushed skin under black whiskers swept past. He followed them out, bidding farewell to his friends.

"Farewell, sir. Do not tire yourself," they replied with loud laughter.

He was outside and but a few steps aback of the ladies, as they walked in the comfort of their twined arms and engaged in much conference. He soon came up to them as they neared the waiting coach and, stepping before them, courteously opened the door.

"Thank you, sir," said Elizabeth as he held her hand to ease her into the leather seat.

"Thank you, sir," came from Helen, as she was also helped.

"Thank you, sir," came from Mary, as she took the helpful hand into the carriage.

"'Tis my pleasure, my good man," the officer smiled, delighted more as Mary's knees gave a little as she fell into her seat. "My Lady Elizabeth, may I be so bold as to inquire why there are only three of you in this intrigue, for does not one more lady belong to your entourage, a dark-haired lady full of such abundant charm?"

"Do you know of this other lady, sir?"

"I have had the pleasure of meeting her but once, in the passages of the castle, my lady."

"'Tis you, sir? You are Jayne's officer, the one who bedevilled her whilst she was unable to offer any modesty." The other ladies also spake with surprised tone.

"My lord—Jayne's officer. You blaggart," they smirked.

"'Tis your fault, sir, she sits alone in her cozy, smitten to distraction by your devilment."

"Oh, my ladies, I do hope I have not caused her too much distress."

"We forgive you, sir, and we know that our dear Jayne does. And, pray, what is your name, sir?"

"Steven Moran, at your service ladies." And gave he his most loyal bow.

"Please follow us to the castle, Steven, for we owe you so much, and indeed are indebted to you for the sum of one shilling."

"Do not trouble yourself, my lady; 'twas well worth it for the sport, for I have spent more and gotten less."

"No, sir, we insist. Please, follow us."

"As you command, my ladies. I am your bewitched servant." He closed the door upon them, then banged the palm of his hand onto the side of the carriage there to summon the coachman to make to the castle. The trio trundled away, and as he turned to mount his nearby steed, the laughter from within the coach lilted over the darkened night, wafting about the trees and roadway; so much joy flowed, bringing lightened heart to all whose ears it befell.

In the mooned sky, came to sight the castle of Hutton, rising black from the dark hills where it lay. Silent were the carriage wheels as it stayed at the rear entrance. Silent were the shoes of the rider's horse as all stopped in the shadow of the wall, all heard was the baying dog. The officer dismounted and, horse tethered, opened the small door to the carriage, helping once more the ladies who alighted upon the black ground. Then, past the knowing guard, they went into the dark entrance, and stepped the still, dark stairs to the passageway of their chambers. Inside was laughter abounding once more as they spake of the ordeal they had encountered, and to the best time they had ever had. Amused with all fear gone, they had stepped into the den of lions and had survived a mauling. The officer stood at one side to let the ladies relish their moment, watching the brave souls relive their time.

"It will not come off! I tell you, it will not!" Mary, he heard, pulling at her whiskered face.

"Of course it will," Elizabeth said as she gave help to Mary by pulling at the gummed hair.

"Ow-ow-owww …" came the painful cry as the whiskery evil would move not a hair. "Am I forever to look like this!"

"Wait a little, Mary; I am sure it will loosen soon," came the comforting words of Helen. Though her words were spoken with much compassion, she had much difficulty in speaking them.

"Oh, I am most sick," spake Mary as she flopped in despair upon the settle with heavy sighs at her plight. Elizabeth left Mary alone and, with Helen in hand, tried to silence their laughter as they left their bearded friend reposing and came to Steven.

"Stay right there," Elizabeth said to the officer. "Stay there and watch over Mary, and comfort her if you have to."

"Where are you going ladies? if I may ask." He somewhat puzzled why he was the one left to watch over Mary, for was he not a soldier and certainly had no practice as a nursemaid.

"We are still indebted to you, sir, and have to compensate you for your endeavours, do we not?" Before any answer could be given, they were gone. The laughter soft was the only reminder of their being, and 'twas soon faded.

"Jayne! Jayne!" Into the ladies' waiting chambers they entered, all a-bluster, calling as they went.

"Goodness, what is it?" Jayne queried.

"We have a gift for you."

"Oh, how nice of you. Please, show me."

"First, we have to prim you." Bewildered a little by the excited ladies she stood as her friends brushed her hair, rouged her lips, and daintied her eyebrows. Elizabeth stood back to take a more interesting look at Jayne. "No bosom," she said. "I see not enough bosom." She came close to her and gently eased down the dress at the front to reveal more of Jayne's breasts.

"What are you doing, mistress?"

"Just do as you are bid and you will soon know, my sweet one."

"You only call me with such affectionate names when you have some scheme to hatch, my lady."

"Oh, how can you believe such, my dear thing? Come." Elizabeth and Helen both spake as they eased Jayne along the passageway to the waiting chamber, and nearer to the door that stood beckoning. "Close your eyes, Jayne, for your surprise." Jayne did so with a resigned sigh, as Elizabeth stood with her eyes open wide with delight, and waited with heart a-patter, holding tightly to the hand of Jayne. Helen entered the chamber alone.

"Sir, we have a gift for you, but we wish you to close your eyes so you may open them with much pleasure to your sight."

"Very well, if that is your wish." His eyes closed as he was bid, as Helen stood with him hand in hand.

"Come," beckoned Helen, and Elizabeth brought in Jayne with guided step, and brought her to face the officer standing as bid. The warm hand of Helen was eased from the hold of our officer, and the cold hand of Jayne was slipped into it.

"You may open your eyes, my dear things." The eyes opened and tranquility drifted about them, as the voice of Helen was faintly bathed over them.

"Jayne … Steven. Steven … Jayne. You are no longer strangers."

"Kiss her, Steven, kiss her," Elizabeth urged. "Bring heaven upon her." Steven leaned forward and kissed gently upon the lips of Jayne, who closed her eyes once again in the rapture of the kiss. She stepped back with face flushed and, as discreet as she was able, pulled up the front of her dress to a more demure state. Bringing a heavy sigh and some disapproving looks from the brazen one. "We will wait in the bedchamber with Mary and chaperone you from afar." They left them to see of Mary's state, leaving the two with hands joined, and gazing into each other's eyes.

Mary sat with reddened cheeks, still trying to remove the curse upon her face, but naught had come of her efforts and the beard remained the same.

"'Tis late, Mary; better for you to sleep now," Elizabeth spake most seriously. "For we have to awaken early upon the morrow."

"Where are we to go on the morrow?" Mary asked.

"We have to visit the fair that has come to village."

"You puzzle me greatly, Elizabeth. Why to the fair must we go? And why so early? Have you not seen my plight? How can I go anywhere?"

Elizabeth could not continue the conversation, and stood with her hand covering her mouth to contain herself.

Helen continued to explain in the same dull tones as Elizabeth. "We have to be there early, Mary, for they are seeking a bearded lady for their tent show and you deem to be most suitable." Mary stood for a moment as the two teasing ladies fled the room with stumbling laughter; then the screaming Mary, in hot chase, rushed after the fleeing wicked women, to come upon them skulking behind the brave Steven, who had risen from his amour upon hearing the loud screams and raised voices.

"Out of the way, Steven! Let me at those witches!" she shouted with her snarling voice and catlike clawing. But upon reaching Steven she placed her arms about his neck with an unyielding grip and kissed his lips; her soft lips came tender, then the hawthorn brush she rubbed and scraped against his shaven softness.

"Away from me," he begged. "Release me!" he cried, overplaying his agony as he managed to remove himself from Mary's hold.

"What in God's name has happened to you, Mary? What is that upon your face?"

"This, my dear Jayne," spake Mary, "is what our Elizabeth has done to me with her witchcraft. A guise to visit the tavern that she wished so dearly to enter, and, had it not been for dear Steven, believe my words now, we would all be dead in that place of evildoers."

"Is this true, Elizabeth, that you have tormented this dear lady so?"

"Yes, I am afraid it is so ... 'Twas all in fun, and once we remove her whiskers, gone will be her fret." Helen giggled in agreement.

"Helen, I am surprised at you for letting this happen—Elizabeth I can understand, for I fear the insanity on her father's side has at last reared itself, but you?—I thought you were morally bound, but I fear I have been mistaken, and led upon the path of goodness that does not exist."

"Yes, Jayne," they answered with lowered eyes from the admonishment that Jayne had dealt them. But seemed she had not yet finished.

"So, ladies, do you wish to hold her down whilst I pull off the whiskers, or do you wish to do the pulling, my dear Elizabeth?" They all laughed and gave their saviour rewarding kisses.

"Unhand him. He is not to be subject to the affections of crazed ladies." Jayne stepped in between the kissing maidens. And, just before she placed her divine lips upon his, said, "He is not for you, my dear ones."

All were most happy with the laughter affecting each other, except Mary, who tried to be as happy as her friends but was still feared her beard would never fall. And so, after all calmed about the chamber and quietness loomed, 'twas Mary again who spake. "But how will I ever be rid of this affliction that hangs about my face?" All thoughts were spreading with much kindness towards Mary. As her new friends came about her and comforted her in her sad tone.

Steven stood, though to the one side. "I have a suggestion," he said, "that may help you, my lady."

"You do, Steven? And, pray, what is it you suggest?" they rhymed together and looked over to him in some anticipation of a remedy for Mary. But strangely, Steven moved away further, to give some distance from the ladies. He then spake with serious intent, as eyes searched his voice.

"On the morrow, I will send over my barber to shave off the beard that bedevils Mary. I think that is the best way, do you not agree?"

Silence befell the chamber, a silence that delved the words that had been spoken, the words given with such sincerity that showed no such pledge. The ladies all with gleeful rage, ran at the fleeing officer who, with little courage and no cover to delay them, curled up in the far corner where the darkness may help his dilemma, as a kitten, with closed eyes, seeking any help he could muster and awaited the reprisal to come upon him. He felt then the warm bodies about, as dainty fists gouged his ribs, and caused the humour within to show itself, as laughter wracked his body, and under much duress he was able to cry, "Enough, ladies, enough."

"You are most sorry then for such an evil remark?"

"Yes, I am truly sorry for my remark. Please stop, for I am beaten, with all strength gone."

"As long as you are sure of your repentance, you are forgiven."

"Thank you, thank you," came from the tear-wetted mouth, as he composed himself a little.

"But remember the retribution that will come if again you tease our Mary." And they, after releasing him, piled atop again to give final satisfaction to their hurt.

"No more—please, please—I am done of all reprise."

"Very well then, sire." They as weak as he from the turmoil, climbed off the still shaking Steven and sat upon the boards, gulping in large breaths of cold air to relieve their gasping lungs. Soon the ladies were risen and dragged up to his feet the limp Steven—that weak kitten—as they sat him upon the bench of the chamber to regain his composure.

"Come, Mary, let us remove the curse you so bravely carry. Some hot water will soon soften the gum and then it will come easily away."

"Thank you, Elizabeth," said Mary as they left with Helen into the bedchamber.

"Sit down, dear Mary, you have suffered long enough, let us now relieve you of that unwanted hair." She sat upon the bench beckoned to her and, in the warmth of the chamber, she waited as Helen ladled out some hot water from the cauldron there into a pewter pan, the steam rising, and dampening her hair as she brought it over to the small table aside of Mary. Then with wetted cloths, and mindful not to place it too hot upon Mary's skin, they began to bathe at the haired face. Slowly and with care they dabbed at the black whiskers; at first it seemed to make little difference, and once more it seemed that their Mary would indeed be so cursed. But then, with the constant wetting, it began to work most quickly and, to Mary's relief, the miserable hair began to tumble off, and soon only reddish skin showed where the hair had laid. She smiled again, her most perfect smile, not seen for some little while, and all were glad to see its return. The looking glass was held to her so she may see for herself the whiskers all gone.

"Thank you, my ladies." Most happy at the face shown in the glass was she.

"Mary, we find you have such spirit and joy, we would be so pleased if you would consider becoming one of our waiting ladies, would you, Mary? Please, say you will."

"Of course I will. I have never been so happy as to be with you, for sisters are what you seem to me." They hugged together as the thought of Mary amongst them was truly a blessing for all.

The lovers were at last alone, but shadows in the candlelit chamber in which Steven's soft tones did fall.

"My dearest, I have not had long acquaintance with you, but I wish to tell you that you are the one with whom I beg to have by my side for all time, and for no other do I hold such desires."

"My dearest," replied Jayne to Steven's pledge, "I am within my heart tumbling as the jester, for since our first meet I have been smitten, and prayed that some day I would look upon your face again and tell you of my love for you." They kissed in a most heavenly fashion, as their bodies weakened with the pleasure, and all other states were floated away to nothings.

"My love, I tell you of my feelings at this time, for time is little that I may stay with you, for within a short spate I have to leave with Richard's army. My orders are to be at the ready by the morrow's morn. Revolution is rearing itself and there are many mongers about. Armies are rising in Kent and upon the Welch borders, and such the time has come for the sword."

"I wish you were not a soldier, my love, but you are a brave soul, and I see you are duty bound to our king."

"This life I chose was my destiny, but, my dear Jayne, you have become that destiny, and when I return from this war I will soldier no more, for I would not be apart from you ever again."

"My dearest, I am most fearful for you whilst you are away from me." They stood and held comforting hands.

"My love, I will return, for no matter what is whispered or what is written, I will return; never think I will not. For if not soon then months later I will come; never have any doubt; I have not waited these many years for your love to have but a few hours with you, God would forbid it."

"I promise you, Steven, I will never despair." They stood and held close to each other for an eternity, each not wishing to let the other go.

"'Tis time I must depart,"—as the embrace at last was broken. "Goodbye, my love, my Jayne."

"Goodbye, Steven."

"Goodbye, ladies," he called into the bedchamber upon his departure.

"Goodbye, fare-thee-well, Steven," came the loving call of the voices from within.

Steven pulled the ring that hugged his small finger. "Care for this, my dear. You may return it to me when our eyes meet once more."

"Yes, my love," she pledged as the gold band was placed in her dainty hand and hugged forever close to her bosom. The misty eyes saw him depart, a strong, proud man gone to war …

Jayne went to seek the ladies, and to help Mary if 'twas needed. But the whiskers had gone, and she saw only the red cheeks of Mary where once that beard sat, and the captivating smile showed once more.

"So, Jayne, are we to expect Steven to return soon?" Elizabeth inquired, as all waited with much interest as to when her love would next visit.

"Oh, Elizabeth, I know not when I will see him again," she spake as tears welled her eyes. "He has gone, summoned to ready himself for some enterprise with Richard."

"With Richard!" Elizabeth stood upon hearing what may be forthcoming.

"Yes, Elizabeth, I am told there are some troubles about, and the time has come to repress them. Steven spake of the time, for the sword had come upon them. I am so worried for such little time we have had." The ladies gathered around her to console her teary words and dry her wetted eyes.

"I must go to Richard." A concerned Elizabeth began to gather herself, and started toward the door.

"Please, lady, wait," said Helen. "Richard will send for you when it is the proper time. He will not delay seeing you, but he must be in much conference at this time."

"Yes, of course, you are right. I will only distract him from his task, so I must be patient. He will send for me when he is able."

Elizabeth did not sleep this night, her head filled with thoughts of ifs and whens; restless she turned one way then the other. The creeping morn came at last to awaken all. The birds' twittered flight, the cock's crow, the neigh of horses, and the rattle of wheels … The rattle of a carriage? Elizabeth was fast risen as the pheasant from its hide. Pulling the cloth of her nightgown to her knees, she scurried to the window and peered at the courtyard below. The coach with the royal crest all bright twinkled back at her. Came then her ladies, all fussy and excited, with their making ready of Elizabeth. A light knock came upon the chamber door.

"Come!" Helen called as one of the maids entered.

"My lady, a coach has arrived for the Lady Elizabeth," she curtsied as she gave the message.

"Inform the coachman, my lady will be down shortly."

"Yes, ma'am," came the maid's reply as she left to her duties. Elizabeth was soon dressed. One of her most favoured gowns adorned her body, with a pearled necklet and dangled ear pearls. Dressed as she desired, she went out with her ladies into the passageway to make to the waiting coach, but stayed herself and did not yet continue.

"Firstly, I must see that the earl is well. I am most concerned of his demeanour, for I have been unable to converse with him for many a day. Please wait, my ladies; I will be but a moment." Elizabeth walked her dainty way to the earl's chambers whilst the others waited for her return. The door was not guarded, which seemed unusual to the lady. She tapped quite loudly upon the blackened wood. But no answer came. Again she knocked whilst opening it, and calling, "Edward … Edward … Are you about?" Still no reply came as she looked about the outer chamber, which seemed to be in a most untidy state and smelled most disturbingly. She moved on to the partially-opened door of the bed chamber, almost thinking she could hear some noise. "Edward?—" she softly called again as she pushed wider the door to enter the chamber. Though the morn was bright only dusty shafts of light chinked from the draped window; the room was most dark, a place lit with only two candles burning. The fire lay now nearly all of ashes with no flame about its embers. Clothes and platters she saw tossed about without any order, and a stench lay making it difficult for the Lady Elizabeth to draw breath. She pulled her scented kerchief from the sleeve where 'twas hid, and placed the fine cotton over her mouth and nose. She was sure now that she heard some slight groans as she came closer to the bed. "Edward?" she quietly called again, then a rustle so lightly did she hear, but the darkness of the chamber prevented her from seeing aught. She picked up the candle that flickered close by, and felt the cold of the metal upon her warm hand as the wax dripped. With steps softly trod, she stepped closer to the faint movement. The odour was beginning to make her retch. 'Twas too strong for the tiny cloth she held to her face. By the candle's glow she saw the crocks of tincture; as if for a sickness, so many were there upon the small table; some stood with stoppers, some lay upon their sides, empty of their contents. A score of them were scattered about, as Elizabeth picked up one that was empty to read the label of its contents, but no label showed, nor as she waved her candle about, upon any of the other crocks. She bravely moved the kerchief from her face to smell the dregs that were left, but found it difficult to place the aroma to anything she was familiar with. Sweet like a flower did it smell, but it meant naught to her senses. She placed the crock back upon the table, and her cloth back over her nose. Closer to the bed came she with the candle's light, the sound of something stirring as a head came to view, almost hairless was it, a few wisps of hair was all that clung. Then the head turned its eyes toward her, a face hardly known to Elizabeth. Covered with boils and sores that weeped, the lips cracked and broken, but she could see the face was something common to her. The hot tallow dripped upon her fingers, but she felt no discomfort there as she probed further.

"Edward?" she said, a question with an answer already known, pressing the kerchief even tighter to her face, as the smell brought her almost to faint.

"Go away," croaked the once young and mischievous voice. "Go away."

"Yes, begone, leave us be," another voice came from the bed to settle upon Elizabeth's ears. She moved her candle over, to light upon the red hair and painted face of a trollop that laid abed with Edward. The thick flour paste upon her face could not hide the deep pox marks and blisters that lay there. "Leave us be," it said again.

"Edward, what have you done?"—Elizabeth playing the candle back onto the earl. She had been told of the sight of Lues, and knew that Edward had been struck by it, and she knew its evil.

"I did it for you, Elizabeth," the croaking voice broken with sobs came from the shell of the man that laid there.

"You are with insanity, sir!" She placed the candle down with shaking hand, and hitching up her skirts ran quickly from the chambers into the passageway.

"All for you, Elizabeth … I did it all for you," she heard the croaking voice calling faintly to her, as she came to a breathless stop away from the door, leaning upon the stone wall and breathing deeply, trying to regain her composure. The waiting ladies saw her plight and came quickly to her, offering all support in her state.

"Whatever is it, Elizabeth? Is the earl struck with some illness?"

"In there," she pointed to the earl's chambers. "He is raged with Lues; it is terrible." The ladies peered into the dim chamber but could see little, wishing not to enter as the vile smell drifted from within; they closed the door upon the vile escapade, wishing to see no more.

"God's Death, let us depart most quickly from this place," Mary spake as they all helped Elizabeth away from the sight that chilled her so. They stopped further down the passageway where a window brought to them some light, and the breeze blew freshly o'er them as they dabbed their lady's flushed face, and broke away the hard tallow that was upon her fingers. Elizabeth was beginning to recover from her ordeal and spake with more reason.

"He once was a fine man, but that once proud ship that sailed upon the pleasant sea lies broken upon the rocky shores of jealousy. In that chamber does lie madness full of stink and rot."

They moved away, consoling their friend as they went toward the stairway, and stepped down to the bottom where the cloak cupboard stood. Elizabeth was quickly recovering, her spirit rising once again. "I wish never to return to this place again after such has met my gaze. I will bed on the common before such I bed here, for evil spirits prance about these towers."

"We will try and help all we can," said Jayne with a reassuring look into the face of her mistress. They were soon all cloaked, and went out to the coach that awaited them. Richard's guard officer helped them step upon the stool, and soon they were settled. A cantor was their gait as the wheels, rattling along, played its drum. The armed guard added to the noise as the party, with royal banner flying, made track to Crosby Place. The morn, still bright and cheery, seemingly more so to Elizabeth, for this morn she had been to the gates of hell, smelled the brimstone, and brushed with the devil's disciples. Even the slums and beggars they past in such squalor seemed heavenly to the eyes that had seen such vile madness.

Chapter Twelve.

Journey to War.

Elizabeth was completely herself now as the coach stopped its ride in the courtyard of Crosby Place. The disturbing confrontation of the morning was fogged as thoughts of Richard came more to mind, more important than any jealous lover could ever be. Soon they were inside the royal residence, their cloaks hooked, and being escorted by the maid up the wide staircase to the chambers there. Elizabeth bid goodbye to her ladies who made to the chambers provided for them, close to where their mistress was to be entertained. They smiled at Elizabeth as she departed, and lovingly blew her a kiss to send her to Richard. The guard stood tall at the chamber door as our lady came close.

"Good day, my lady," he bid her as he bowed in respect.

"Good day to you, sir," the light-of-heart Elizabeth replied; she came as chirpy as a free bird. The guard knocked upon the door, and the unsmiling one came to answer.

"What is it?" spake the head manservant, by his manner shown, another who had never smiled from dawn to dusk and all time between.

"The Lady Elizabeth, sir, to visit with the king."

"Come in then." She entered again with much trouble, as the manservant, by some ancient law of all manservants, would only open the door to a certain width. Elizabeth surmised that the more respect you obtained the wider the door would open for you, and decided upon herself to use her guiles to see if such was so.

"Cloak?" said he with little respect, and waited for the lady to unclip it herself. She did so and handed the garment to him.

"May I ask of your name, sir?" said she in her most appealing voice.

"Blackstock," was all his reply.

"And what, pray, is your given name?"

"Jeremiah."

"Oh, Jeremiah, thank you for taking my cloak." She stepped closer to him so her perfume he could gather, so her bosom was more enticing, so her hair was close. And then, to his surprise, she kissed his wrinkled cheek. He said naught as he turned to hang the cloak upon the peg, as the red of his neck showed above his stiff collar.

"This way," he said as he walked, with Elizabeth following, to the inner chamber, being most careful he to keep his eyes from meeting hers. The rustle of the lady's skirts and light step upon the rushed floor were the only sounds as they came to the chamber. The servant rapped upon the door, at the same time opening it. "The Lady Elizabeth, my lord,"— lowering his head as he spake to Richard.

"Enter her, my man, enter her." The servant opened the door wider to let Elizabeth enter, as she posed to herself that the door seemed to offer a wider gate than was normally offered to her.

"Thank you, Jeremiah." Only to him did she whisper, as she brushed her dress against the arm of the manservant. The door closing quietly behind her as she knowingly had made another conquest, and, as the door clicked, came the shape of Richard over her as he kissed her lips. She could smell the rosewater upon his skin, far more appealing than that odour she had drawn but one hour ago. As the kiss lingered she felt the fine leather, and silk, velvet, and cotton, the crisp lace and soft wool, all these pressed against her from her royal lover. Dressed most fine was he this day as his hand unsighted moved about through the cover of her dress, to bring her heart to pound more so at his closeness. Then he broke the meet with tender greeting.

"Are you well, my dearest?" said he as he held both her hands and looked into her face most tenderly.

"Yes, my lord, I am in goodly spirits, and most happy to be in your company." She heard movement within the chamber and some rumbling chat. Richard came aside her as her gaze plied upon the nobles gathered there. She recognized Sir William Stanley and the Earl of Norfolk, standing amongst the other lords.

"My Lady Elizabeth." Although they all spake and bowed as one person, the mode of dress they wore was strikingly different from one to the other. Most attired in clean fashionable clothes, others dressed in lordly clothes but not too clean, with stains about their fronts and worn boots about their feet, and smelling of little cleanliness.

"Good day, sirs," replied Elizabeth with a short curtsy.

"I must leave you alone for short while, my dear. The lords and I are in urgent conference, which has lasted for a longer time than expected, but 'twill soon now be ended." Richard brought her over to the fireside, and sat her down in one of the booth seats, which faced the table they were all gathered about.

She half gazed at the flames dancing, and half interested in the table's gathering. Richard was over to where the nobles gathered, his wide shoulders and the hair over his neck were all she saw of him; his back was to her, but his voice, commanding, aired around the chamber. If not for the urgent conference occurring, 'twas a most regal place, delightful for evening sup and dimmed play. The candles brought about a softness to the stone walls with many of them flickering upon the gathered table; she saw maps and charts laying there being pushed and poked about, as if each at the table had his own order that they should be in. The faces glowed with some bearded and mustached, some shaven clean. Some hair cropped, some long. Bright white teeth, black dull teeth. Some faces red, some pale, some grey. From high voices to low voices played over the table.

"So we may rule then that first the town of London will be defended by the troops of the Tower garrison." Richard waited for the ayes to pass the plan that was tabled. "Aye," it came. "Second, not yet knowing the place that Richmond will land, the main army under my command will go to the centre of our Isle to move more readily upon the course it necessitates."

"Aye, sire," came the agreement.

"Thrice, that Stanley will join his army to the northern force with much haste, and then 'twill be known the place of our encounter for us to move quickly against Richmond, before he may bring others to his evil cause."

"Aye, sire."

Elizabeth's ankle showed discreetly as it bathed in the light from the fire, catching more than one of the nobles glancing at the tantalizing flesh that was the same colour as her knee stockings, trim and alluring it showed there. Elizabeth it seemed as always having some gift to offer. She knew of the glances fleeted her way but was demurely looking away, as if not being aware of her enticement but knowing all the time what she was about. Many eyes were discrete upon her; she moved her head not but flashed her eyes to meet the stares, and with instant movement the eyes at watch glanced quickly away, as Elizabeth smiled so slightly to her satisfaction.

The voice of Richard was still flowing, until she heard at last the words that she had awaited.

"'Tis done then, my friends, on the morrow, which be the first day of August, we will go forth and press our royal forces against any who try to usurp this crown, and we will be victorious in our endeavour." They grasped hands and solemnly bid their oath to the king and to victory. They bid Richard a good night, and to the Lady Elizabeth good night, each kissing the back of her offered hand, as she stood beside Richard, a queen, albeit not in name.

They had all gone from the still brightly-lit room, the table still laid with maps and written papers, all black and white they lay. But soon the only colour that would come from those drab sheets would be the red of blood spilled.

"Come, my dear, let us to the bedchamber and lose all thought of such doings that hatch about this room," — Elizabeth holding Richard's hand as she pulled him inside the chamber. Soon Richard's fine clothes lay strewn and crumpled upon the rushes as she pushed him onto the tester bed, and with the mischief that seemed always to erupt from her, she now frolicked about him half clad, he soon befuddled by her spell and charms. Soon as one body they both played the ecstasy that filled them, and spent, lay in deep tranquil until the ecstasy misted and they both returned to life's reality.

"I gather, my lord, that you must leave me upon the morrow?" Elizabeth, lying atop of Richard, posed to him what she had heard at the conference.

"Yes, my dearest, it is with saddened heart so, but the time is nigh to show these pretenders that I am the only true king, and no other has right."

"I fear for you, Richard, the thought of you in such peril tears me asunder, and it is so difficult for me to bear."

"Fear not, dearest, for I have been victorious in many a battle and so shall I be this time. I say this though, my Elizabeth, you are stronger than you know. God forbid that I may perish, but if it is so, you will go on, for you have so much joy in life and you will grow stronger. And do not forget, my dear, if that rogue, Henry of Richmond, does usurp the throne, he will look to you as the only person who can unite the White and the Red Rose, to end for all time the conflict between the standards of York and Lancaster. You, my Elizabeth, will be the prize sought."

"I am in shock that you speak such, my lord."

"Do not be so; face all; do not let emotions sway the facts. Fly as the arrow, straight, and bend for naught."

"You are so much stronger than I, my lord, for I look through the eyes of a woman at all things, and have not the will to battle."

"You will see, my love, the strength you hold that has not shown. But this is but council we speak and aught else but full of ifs. We will have our love for much time to come." They loved, they slept, they loved. The night stars blinked through the cloud to bring close the morn that Richard would depart. Awakened, Elizabeth thought it the proper time to relate to her love the state of the Earl of Warwick, who dwelled within the castle where she had residence. And so described to Richard of his dire position and his sunken depths into a diseased state, and of the fact that life had little time to dwell in such a body so wracked.

"We will leave him to murder himself, my dear." No remorse to his prisoner was shown by Richard, for did he not decide upon himself which road he wished to tread. *If you show the lion your hand, will he not bite it off?* "But, my dear, as fate may have it, I have a most pleasing gift for you, even more pleasing since you have related to me of the circumstances that abide at the castle." He reached from the bed where he lay and leaned over to the small table placed close, and from the box thereon brought out a jingle of keys all shiny bright. "There you are, my dear, the keys to the mansion I did promise you, at last ready for your residence. As you know it is close upon the road to the heath at Hampstead, and it is to my favour that you will be closer to me." He let the ring of keys drop into the white hand of his most dearest. The hand held the keys with such tightness the knuckles paled even more.

"I am so happy, my lord, happy that I will be closer to you, and happy I do not have to return ever again to that castle where that evil doth dwell." Embraces folded once again with loving warmth in each other's arms. But Richard was soon about his readying, as his manservant came within the chamber busying about his royal task, making ready his king for warlike days. The King Richard was washed and then, after he was dried, rosewater was splashed upon him. His barber came to shave the royal growth, and 'twas soon the scrape of the blade that gave Elizabeth a concerned look, for she wished not to see the blade slip upon her Richard's skin, as the barber with deft strokes flied his blade about. But soon was finished with ne'er a scratch. The white linens now upon him and his doublet was fitted and hooked. The breeches were next pulled and tugged tightly upon his legs. His soldiering boots pulled to fit and then laced. Light chain mail, not for battle but for safety whilst marching, was also fitted, though with much difficulty for tight 'twas about the neck. His helmet was placed upon his proud head and then clasped under the chin. His harness buckled to carry his sword and dagger. He then stood almost ready, far too quickly for Elizabeth, for she wished him to dally for a while longer. Richard forced his hands into the chain-backed gloves, and, when fully fitted, clipped them to the arm mail so no gap showed between hand and sleeve. For horse was he ready, as the manservant and the barber stood well aside so as not to offer any discourse to his exit. Elizabeth stood before her most handsome knight, he standing in such magnificence there, ready for the battle's call.

"Fare-thee-well, my dear Elizabeth, for with my heart filled with such love for you I must depart."

"Farewell, my king, my love. Return quickly to my side. I await you from the moment the door closes upon you." He kissed her and held her tightly to him, the cold chain pressed against the warm face leaving the dimples of the steel upon her cheek. And then with a swirl he was gone, through the open door soon closed, to leave her alone within the silent chamber.

Alone she thought, but then thought no more, as her ladies came to ready their mistress, and soon, ringed by her devoted trio, they washed her and were dressing her when through the chatter she broke. "Look what I have," she sang in lilting tone, her finger through the ring of keys jingling as they swung about.

"Oh, Elizabeth, is it so?" Jayne asked.

"Yes, it is so; the manor is ready for us, my dears."

"Oh, happiness, you are mine," Helen full of joy spake her thoughts.

"We do not have to return to the castle, and we will go straight to our new abode, no more that cursed place to set upon our eyes. Jayne, I wish you to make arrangements to have our chattels fetched, and I must ask you just one more time to go to the castle and to use your sweet charms upon the cook, and see if you can persuade her to come to our new home, and any of the staff that would wish to service us, we would be most pleased. Edward will not have need for any servants, for little is his time left to his wracked soul."

"Yes, my lady, I will do my very best," Jayne replied, most happy for the responsibility that Elizabeth had placed upon her, and knowing she was doing such to keep her mind from dwelling too much upon the danger that Steven would encounter.

All sparkling and happy, they left Crosby Place to be driven to the new mansion at Hampstead; 'twas but just a short distance away to rattle up to the adorable residence. And as the coach stopped outside, war and strife were as far away from their minds as the bright moon. They stepped down with help from the coachman, and as the coach drove away they stood and looked at their new place of residence. The stone that was once dirty and ill kept had been scrubbed clean by the masons. A new slated roof now showed as black as the Welch quarry where it had been fetched, where before 'twas covered in wooden planks that had been driven to rot, and to let water upon all within. The chimney stood tall, letting forth its wooded smoke; straight up this day it went like an angel to the clouds, mingling with the other angels from other chimneys about. They went up the new steps made of good stone and not in the crumbling state as that 'twas before. The manor being of little space from the roadway, as to be most convenient for the waiting of horses and coaches and for social activities.

The shiny door was not locked as they entered to the hallway, all new and clean it showed. No rushes were spread upon this floor but the newest coverings from France. *Always the first to bring decadence to royal residences and palaces were the French, luxury and splendour were theirs; while others still had bare floors, or rushes to soften the tread over the stone that lay beneath, they trod upon the soft silk of the carpet.* And so was the tread in Elizabeth's manor, bringing such pleasure as they carefully walked their way upon it. All about they explored now: the kitchen and pantries, the woodshed, the fine living chambers and bedchambers, the places of easement, and the gardens, which delighted them more, as the month of August closed to bearing the fruits of autumn.

A single maid took care of their needs, whilst they awaited news of the staff from the castle and of dear Jayne's return. The day closed upon the household all worn from the time of unexpected excitement, and slept they the sleep of babes in their new home. So deep a slumber, that 'twas not until the birds sang from the trees and bushes and the bark of a dog echoed about did they awaken. They all dressed quickly, eager to explore further, when a rap came upon the door. The breakfast had arrived. Mary went to the door to enter the laden maid, as she opened it there stood Jayne with a smile as wide as the tray she was holding.

"Come, Jayne, come," they beckoned her in, helping with the awkward tray as they did so. She entered to join the happy friends that greeted her with such affection.

"When did you return, dear Jayne?" Elizabeth asked.

"Just a short while ago, my lady."

"And what of the outcome of your journey?"

"All is well. Cook is coming. Most pleased was she. Her kitchen helpers are coming too with cauldrons and pots and all manner of vessels piled upon a cart, and indeed are making their way at this present time, and but a short distance away. Oh, yes, the floormaids and the two butlers are also bound."

"Well done, my Lady Jayne, you have done goodly service."

Breakfast was all supped as they stood looking out of the large upper window, but still sipping their drinks from their cold goblets were they as they stood, four in line, looking across the heath, still misty this early morn, but far could be seen, even to the oaks that stood so proud upon the far edge of the grassed common.

"Mary?" The three took sly glances over the top of their goblets at each other, for the voice that came was of that childlike pleading tone that they all so well knew, of some mischief afoot or of some not-quite-to-the-law task.

"Yes, my mistress?" Mary spake with wary answer to Elizabeth, knowing that something was about to be broached and would be trouble for those who agreed to it.

"Mary? ... Have you ever been to a foot-the-ball* tournament that is played upon the common?"

"No, mistress, I have not," spake Mary as she quickly looked at the smiles hid somewhat behind the vessels, though now empty still remained in the sipping place.

"Would you not so much like to go amongst the ruffians down there who shout and blaspheme at the players, and enter into all manner of discourse upon the common?" The excitement seemed to be bursting out of her mistress, as she seemed to be having much difficulty in restraining herself from the intrigue she imagined.

"I would so, my lady, but this time I will not be wearing any whiskers and no escort will I be; send me to the dungeon if you wish."

Elizabeth stood as if pondering. Her face she tried to make of serious intent but 'twas becoming harder for her to fight back her laughter, but she did manage before she was overcome to offer one last suggestion. "No, Mary, I would not ask of such a thing from you, for this time it will be Jayne's turn to play the escort." The goblets flew as Elizabeth crumbled to the floor, her humour draining all strength from her body as the ladies plied their wrath upon the frail madam that curled beneath them, as arms and legs were flailing about and all the kempt hair was in disarray, their fancy dresses all twisted and soiled; but they cared not of their style, and soon all strength was gone and the laughter and frolic at last played out as all were breathless, and no play was left in their helpless selves ...

This same day, Richard, a true knight, readied for his campaign. They were well upon the road and had passed the small town of Dunstable, and were plying north to Northampton. Far ahead of the army could be heard the sound of their fife and drum, and all about knew of their coming. The incessant beat gave warning to those who may wish to try their skills against such an army as they, but many would take to the call, for to do battle with a king who taxed them to the hilt they would relish. Richard rode at the head of his troops, his light riding armour as black as a moonless night. A glint now and then showed as the sun made a star upon the metal. Proud and noble sat he, his white charger stepped beneath him plodding the dirt road, the horse's bridle all at shine from the hostler's labour. A white cape edged in deep red was draped about the horse. The king rode tall, over his black armour were draped the colours of the House of York with its White Rose proudly at show, his sheathed sword clapped his side to the beat laid down. His personal guard flanked him, they all true and battle-tested officers, with Steven in the midst and close to his king, as all spied

---

* *foot-the-ball* [coined] expressing games played at this time

alert of any enemies that may try to take this monarch's life. The guards wore full battle armour, such worn to be more able to protect Richard if the need arose. Armed they for warfare, with heavy broadswords aside their belts adding to the beat. They all helmeted over the chain-link that covered their heads and necks, as each did display the White Rose upon their chest with pride. Two score in number were they all pledged most so loyally to their king.

Aback of Richard, more officers came dressed in battle finery, all field tried, all true warriors of Richard. The red band carried around the helmet was all that separated these officers from the royal guard. For in battle the royal guard did not brandish such for the less shown of your rank was proven. *The arrow brings down first the deer with the largest antlers.* Five score were there of the officers of the field; close to Richard's flank they rode. Mounted cavalry, ten hundred were they all armoured with honed sword, with a rattle of harness and horse trap, they came noisily, strong in battles past, devastating whilst fighting from the mount, all eager to prove still that they were the elite of the soldiery. Pledged to their king, and feared must be all usurpers and rouges who cross before them. Infantry came bobbing along on foot keeping good pace with the horses, they able to travel great distances without rest, carrying heavy baggage as they did so. Many carried the long-flagged pikes held high, a fully ten feet in length were they sharpened and fired. Their swords and daggers closely swung by their side, sheathed in leather to protect them from the wet about, and all carrying the long shield to defend against the bowmen's arrows that may sprinkle from the sky. Another ten hundred were they; they too believed they were the heart of the military that strutted this day. The archers next came, no armour did they wear but loose and free in their skin jackets with worsted breeches, green and brown, liken to the woods and forests they oft fought from. Bows slung across their backs, their quivers full as they gaited along, a full nine hundred of them deemed they the finest soldiers of the military. A total force of three thousand men, far less than he needed, but on the journey Richard hoped to increase his army with the Englishmen who, as always, would fight for their king and country. Far back from the army came the loaded carts of food and chattels, the cooks and peasant workers, the blacksmiths and bowmakers, and many others of the royal upkeep, all atrack upon the road that led north. A massive marching band with dust flying from the horses' hooves that blew constantly over the unmounted troops, who, with kerchiefs tied to their faces, marched it seemed with little heed to the discomfort; though the colour of their dress changed with the different dust they passed through, they still marched as one.

The army trod for many hours in the day, warm and bright, through villages and hamlets, with small groups gathered to see the king with his army pass their way. Mostly in silence they stood, as the dust cloud came closer and dusted them over, then continued on. A few cheers were shouted intertwined with some jeers, and voices from some discreet place cried out "Baby-killer!"—more than thrice was it called, but 'twas not seen who shouted such—showing the thoughts of the Towered princes and their fate had not yet faded from the minds of many. Richard was not pleased; the calls from the people gathered about were only part of his displeasure, for no Englishmen were coming forth to join with his army, and he did not hide his anger at this outcome.

"Where are the bastards?! Why are they not with me?" he shouted about, but no one came forth with any answer. Richard was in too much rage to be offered any reason, for no matter the words, they would all come forth as the tongue of traitors.

A dust cloud approached; a single horseman, spied afar, came this way toward the army of Richard. Soon to view he came with that cloud of dust twisting behind him. 'Twas one of the king's outriders. Bringing himself close to his Majesty, with unsettled horse and grime whisked about, he stopped.

"Sire," he said with kingly respect, but was stayed from more homage by Richard.

"Stand not upon any ceremony, my man; these days only war is king."

"Yes, sire," he continued. "There are many archers ahead, my lord, they all covered in branches and clay, lying in wait within the fields close to Fenny Stratford. But three miles hence does it lay."

"How many?"

"We see two hundred, but there could be more."

"We will be prepared," spake the King Richard, for he had time to make ready his action for that which lay hidden upon their path. The outrider was dismissed and rode again the way he had come, spreading the dust cloud once more. Richard called his leading officers to conference, still upon their horses, still at march.

"Bring the infantry along each flank, readied to join shields for defence of our sides, for they will strike when we are within their midst, and, after their first flurry has been shot, we will form a circle fully shielded. Soon after, they will flee as if in some disarray, but no man must break rank. Fit this into their heads: no man must follow, for they will lure them into the swamps and mantraps, and bring fear to those who wait. One officer and one bowman will chase them to fell one of their lot, and to bring him back as a prisoner to our camp, for as yet we know not who these villains are who lay and wait. Then, make our circle larger and collect all the arrows that have fallen, and take them to the bowmaker's wagon to repair them for our use. After we move on, these rogues must find in that field not one single arrow to use against us again, for if they have but a few arrows they can do us but a little harm, but if they have no arrows they can do us no harm. Issue straight this command and be ready to form circle upon my command."

They closed to the fields that were about Fenny Stratford where lay the ambush; the track was flat and level with the fields at both sides; no hedges or fences broke the land. Bushes afar they saw that seemed of a false presence, standing may of two hundred paces away and swaying in the slight breeze. 'Twas quiet all about, except for the rattle the army brought. No birds seem to fly in the field that was their stage, bourn to flight. Richard's eyes shifted about for he knew well the signs of ambush, and the signs he had seen. No birds did flutter, no rabbit scurried. The crows in the trees at the far distance, sitting high upon the dead branches with some strutting about as if disturbed. The swaying bushes did not sway together as one breeze. He knew of these things but his hand did not show. He went on and on deeper into the bushes false. His troops, though ordered to eye straight forward, were inclined to gaze sideways, for they knew the enemy was about and were fearful they had trod too deep into the circled rope that lay about these fields. Though their gait had slowed, the scraggy track still threw its dust all about.

"At them!" was the cry heard from afar of the bushes that fell as if struck by an axe and showing, in their stead, stood the roguish archers, all standing in a circle around the army of Richard and quickly they were all ready to fire as one. But 'twas not quicker than Richard called his order.

"Defend!" he shouted, strong and clear the words came. The army stopped as their shields went up high and pikes showed like a hedgehog with its spines. The mounted dropped to their feet and crouched in low stoop, to hear the first shower of arrows come whistling over their heads cutting through the warm air, pointing their way to death of all whose path came before it, ready to rip into flesh and kill. Metal clanged metal, as the deadly armoury ended, dulled and broken, upon the meadow that lay, as they bounced from the shields and fell wasted there upon the cradled grass so soft. After the first flurry, and as the archers once more filled their bows, Richard cried the next order.

"Circle!" shouted he so that all heard the words, and his officers, as they had been trained, brought each of their platoons into position, and quickly the army was in defence and safely shielded. The tight circle of steel was all about them as the next shower whistled its way, but failing once more upon the shields as again the arrows fell softly to the ground. No more in heavy showers did it rain but in free shooting, which made effort for a long half of the hour, but naught could help as ne'er all shafts had been loosed and the fat quivers were empty of their weapons, and no soldiers lay bloody about.

Cries and shouts echoed from a distance, as two hundred screaming warriors came running with swords and shields raised, clapping them together as they ran toward the south side of Richard's troops, to bring them much terror with their savage screams and foul cries. They knew they could not breach the tight ranks with their small force, but came they to lure the stubborn soldiery to panic, and to gap the wall that stopped their slaughter, to draw the ranks into their terrain, and to destroy some of their foe and spread discourse to others. They came in rage, the two hundred, and beat their swords upon the defenders. Clang and crash went the blades as they came upon the shielded, but naught came of their efforts except the dulled blades. Soon there were cries of fear bandied about as they took to heel and ran from the fortress of steel, stumbling and picking themselves up and taking slyly glances back as they fled. But only two of Richard's army had broken rank and the shield had already closed behind them. One bowman and one officer came from the right flank tasked to bring one of the fleeing rebels to the king. The officer brought his bowman into the open field; no cover befriended them but all to sight were the fleeing band. The officer called for a stop, and gave quickly directions to the bowman who had sighted the lone target along his shaft, as he pulled back slowly his longbow … The twine twanged by his ear as the whistling shaft flew with deadly accuracy from the English bow. "Aah!" the cry came in the dusty air as the straggler was cut down with the arrow through the knee, dropped as the hunted grouse was he. His fellows, not aware of his plight, ran on in their conjured terror. The officer and the bowman ran to their prey in crouched haste, and soon had the struggling fellow in their grasp and dragged him back to the safety of their stand, still fighting and struggling for freedom was he, as within moments they were breathlessly inside the circle. A blade glinting came to the throat of the prisoner as his raged account ended and he was borne to silence. The officer and the bowman were upon their knees, gasping for the sweet air that would bring back life into their taxed limbs that dangled there but seemed not to belong to them, as they recovered from the draining encounter placed upon them.

The rouges had stopped their fleeing, and saw their baiting had not lured even one soldier away from the army across the field. As they looked to see what would be the move next that would come from Richard, they bravely stood in their hundreds, jeering and blaspheming; they jauntily stood well out of range of the bowmen's arrow. Waiting they that Richard would soon depart this stage, for the quivers they carried were empty, and they waited to go into the field to reclaim their shafts. But, as 'twas, Richard moved his circle wider to cover the arrowed place, and all the arrows were harvested and placed in the bowmaker's cart to be repaired, all except for a few that were so broken they could not be used again. Two thousand shafts were reaped from the field, and, almost as they came, the bowmaker and his apprentice boys were repairing them, sitting in the carts as they moved along. The army had formed to rank, collected their weapons, and duly were an army on the march once more. Forward had come the order, slowly at first but soon in gait most suitable. Within the hour they had left the place of the skirmish and did continue to their stop for the night in Northampton. The dust of Richard's army was far to the eye, as the rouges came to the field to seek their arrows. But, as they sorted around, kicking into the grassed soil, they found naught except for one or two arrows that were not worth a dog's chew. The enemy had picked clean the meat bone. They left dismayed, for many hours had they laboured to make such straight arrows, as they trudged away quivers empty of all armoury. 'Twas belittling to be a bowman without even one single arrow. They went their way, empty cauldrons with naught to sup.

Richard's army was piping their way into the town of their stay; many subjects watched as they came through the narrow streets, but still few cheers rang any welcome. The people of the town were low in spirit, for three thousand soldiers were to drain them of the little they held. The officers and Richard made way to the burgher's mansion for their stay, as the common soldiers, with a few officers to keep some order, spread into the town. The residents had some ways of eking out their modest food supply, wishing not in any way to use their own victuals; they used such that was ready for waste or to feed the animals. The dogs would sup little this night.

Large cauldrons were set upon the roadways standing outside the houses and shops, a score or more coming to the bubble over the blazing logs, throwing its heat upon the metal above. Peasants all about busying themselves. A small table there with some of the women cutting and chopping in their grubby attire, bonnets no cleaner than the rest of their clothes, with hair that hung greasy and dishevelled over the steamy brew. Unclean hands grasped the wooden paddles as they stirred the victuals within the pot. They dropped in the meats that had been readied, the rats that had been skinned, their heads and tails removed, the internals cleared and the rest quartered were thrown into the pot. Any cats they could catch that looked like rabbit when skinned, any meat that cost naught was thrown in, a rotting animal of any kind, stinking turnips and old vegetables were thrown into the fine stew, most fitting for our royal soldiers. The odd spit of phlegm as the women vented their displeasure at the added task that was placed upon them. "Floater for the child-killer!" they would shout as they laughed and stirred it about. A swig of gin from the crock that they all carried helped somewhat to ease the burden, making them more jovial and more drunken. The gin of much strength brewed in the cottages; "Drunk for a halfpenny" was the creed. Mouldy bread upon the tables with the green cut away to make it more edible. Soon the soldiers came with their victual cans and their drinking vessels, some running to be the first in the wait, and desperate in the need for some nourishment. They had trotted for many miles and were in need to replenish their strength. They stood in rowdy lines pushing an jostling to get at the rat stew. The peasants slopped the victuals into their offered pans, another handed them a chunk of bread, and another poured spoiled ale that had been revived with a little honey and "'twas now most pleasant." They sat upon the roadside with their separate groups of comrades leaning up against the shops and houses, and with noise of eating and wind letting, it appeared they were well pleased with the victuals that were before them.

He dipped a ladle into the cauldron and, bringing it to his nose, smelt the stew. He did not offer any comment to its smell, but gently sipped a little, giving again no remark to the taste. He moved on, this officer of the day, seeing that the soldiers were cared for as deemed by Richard. He felt the bread and with a look not pleasant placed it back upon the platter. He picked up a small goblet and poured into it a little of the ale and gulped it down, and winced his face with the taste. He stepped back again to the bubbling cauldron.

"What have you got in there, woman?" he asked, not too pleasantly.

"Nothing but fresh rabbit and pork killed but this morn, sire, with good vegetables and drippings."

"It does not taste as such—" he turned as he spake. "And where are all the menfolk? And where are all the roaming farm animals?" asked he as he looked about.

"My lord, those usurpers of Richmond's ilk came in all bestiality, two hundred of them there was, they just came a-plundering and a-swearing, and under death took all the animals, dragging them pigs and cows on ropes behind them, the chickens tied they onto poles, their heads a-dangle, and away they went to leave us with naught."

"So, where are all the menfolk?"

"After they stole our animals, sir, we all came out of our 'iding, and the menfolk, our 'usbands went with discreet distance after them, and that during the dark 'ours they went to get back our animals from those vile gypsies, and they 'ave not yet returned. We 'ad little left, and did kill all that remained to victual our most 'onoured guests. But now we 'ave no food and no animals to sell, and of such we 'ave no monies to pay our coming levied taxes, and, sire — " She tried to continue with her heartbreak but the officer waved her away having heard enough of her unlikely story and marched away to more pressing duties. She watched him go, the one she had converse with, and when he was no longer sighted, she laughed through her worn teeth with the other peasant women that stood by her side her; they smiled at each other then dipped into their pockets for their crocks and supped another splash of gin, and laughing to have fooled the officer. The menfolk had left the village for to remain they would have been forced to join the army, which they could not bear for they would not pledge their life to a child-killer, and they were becoming a little prosperous and would not leave their animals to be taken by the king's men. So they had took themselves away to the woodlands with their stock until the army had left and they could return. Some of the peasants stood at lookout, as others tendered the livestock and fired the gin stills and picked the berries of the sloe bush to add to the fermenting grain. Time was well played out, and was rewarding as they awaited the call to return.

Richard was in the burgher's mansion, dining with his nobles and personal guard, they all sat at the banqueting table there. The high walls all adorned with paintings and tapestries, the table spread with silver goblets and plates, all it seemed with the coat of other houses etched upon them, some stolen, some bought, some given in payment for some favours given. Flagons of French wine and jugs of ale were splashed about, with the most desirable of foods piled upon the table of banquet for all to feast.

"Enough. We have all supped our fill. Let us hear what our prisoner has to say to our waiting ears. Go get the louse, John," Richard called upon one of his guards for the awaited task.

"Yes, sire," the officer answered, eager to go and bring out the captive for some sport. His heavy boots clomped out of the echoing hall and then through the kitchen with passing stares upon him; he made his way to the wood store where chained to a horse ring crouched the subject of his order. The two guards leaning against one of the posts straightened up from their talk and saluted the officer. "We need him … Release the chain and bring him." They unlocked the chain from the ring. "Follow me," he said to the guards as they pulled the captive up from his crouch. Not easy did he come, but began to struggle as some wild man in his chattering chains, pulling and grunting at his bonds like a bear from the forest, with the blood still flowing from his injured knee as he did so.

"Come on!" shouted one of the guards as he pushed at him to get him on the move. The prisoner snarled and lunged at the guard, flailing with his chains, trying to take some revenge from his plight. The guard, though, with a quick swing of his arm, took him down with the clang of his armour upon the head of the prisoner. Stunned, he stumbled back and sat his rear upon the floor. They pulled him up once more and guided him to follow the waiting officer, who had watched the fracas with some humour. The prisoner was dazed and showed little of his anger, as he allowed himself to be pushed and pulled through the kitchen, where the disturbed staff backed away from the path of the soldiers and their prisoner. Soon he was being prodded into the main hall, past the nobles and officers seated there who measured up the ruffian as he passed them. Unable to walk with good stride, for his shackled legs brought him only stumbling steps, he came and was stood at the table head. The chains upon his cuffs were pulled tight by the guards upon each side, who tightened upon the chain so he was unable to offer any resistance, and could show no danger to any who came close. He stood and saw he was facing Richard, who, half sat upon his chair, turned to more face the ruffian. With the other table dwellers seeking a closer look, some stood behind their seated comrades, swigging their ale and wine as they did so and in a most sporty mood were they. The prisoner nodded his head to Richard, in reluctant reverence to the king.

"Has he had victuals?" he asked toward his officer.

"No, sire, he has refused all."

"Do you want a drink of ale, my man?" Richard rather out of character queried. He answered not but lowered his head and took to gaze at his boots. "Get him a flagon." Richard pointed to the barrel that stood at the table's end. One of the officers of the guard picked up a tankard and filled it with the cool brown liquid, with its heady aroma so filled to the brim that it flowed over onto the floor. He brought the slopping drink around the table and handed it to the prisoner. The chains were slacked so that he was able to hold the drink with two hands, with the officer, the guards, and others watching intently, wondering whether he would drink the offering or throw it upon someone—they prayed it would not be Richard who took the gesture, for he would no longer be the affable king he was playing, but would become the enraged lion. A sigh; he drank it, gulping it down as quickly as he was able, for his thirst had not been at satisfaction for the most part of the day. It ran from around his filled mouth, down his bearded chin, over his coat and his breeches, splashed his boots, and then dripped in a pool about his feet as he emptied the tankard; "Ya-a-a!"

The officer looked at Richard who nodded his head toward the barrel.

The officer took the dripping tankard from the man and overfilled it once more, bringing back the spilling contents to the prisoner's grasp. Once more he drank like a victim of the asylum with thirst insane, until, once again, the tankard was emptied, and was drained mostly to his thirst, as the officer this time did not engage Richard's time, but took the tankard and filled to the brim again the brew that would loosen the prisoner's lips easier than the thumbscrew or the brank.* The tankard held out in front of the guard once more, as he lopped to preserve his uniform and the slipping through the river already laid, 'twas replaced into the eager hands that grasped the grog, but more slowly he lessened the tankard's gift. He was not too steady afoot, as no victuals he had eaten for the longer time, and none would this soldier obtain.

"So, fellow," Richard in due time broached the prisoner, "to whom do you render your service?" The prisoner looked at Richard, a puzzled look veiled his face, for he understood not the question asked. "Who … sent … you?" Richard separated each word so that it may be understood.

"We received orders from up the north."

"From the north?! Only Stanley is in the north and he is no usurper of my throne. I ask again, who sent you?"

"Sire, a rider came to us saying that he had ridden from Durham over many days to give us our task. He paid us well but we knew not who had sent him."

"And why were you plying your arrows against my army and my rule?"

"They paid in good coin, sire, and told us we would be welcomed into the new monarchy." His mouth was overrunning like the ale he had spilled, and was giving more than he need, and 'twas not good for his well-being to rant so.

"Are there more of you?"

"Yes, sire, there are many paid to hamper your progress and to take as many lives as they are able."

"Take him away!" Richard was much enraged at the demeanour that had been shown to him, and saw that respect was not within this man's body. "Sever his head!" he shouted. "Sever it off—now!"

The prisoner was hastily removed from Richard before his anger spilled onto others that stood about. The oglers at the table cringing to become as unsighted as they were able, to avoid any mud that may come their way, for a Richard in rage was not the one to befriend on the day of his madness.

Through the kitchen and through the woodshed was dragged the

---

* *brank* head restraint; torture

rogue, and out to the back of the manor, struggling with his captors as he went; they stopped in the wooded place, with the trees' branches almost touching the ground, where upon the scene was played. He was pushed to kneel by the two guards and his head pulled forward so his neck showed white, and before he could stir his drunken eyes the officer's sword had made its flight through the air, swift as the arrow did it come, and was through flesh and bone and into the air again as all resistance went. No more the birds would he hear, nor feel the warm sun upon him, nor tread the lands of his ancestors.

"We seem to be fighting ever-increasing opposition. Why is this so when I have given these peasants more freedom than ever before, and taxed them less than ever before? We have no countrymen coming to join our fight, when but a short time ago they would bide our side without question. Come, give me an answer ... Can no one relate what is wrong?" No one gave an answer; all could, but they wished to live longer than this day. To stand and declare such folly as:

My lord, I know why. 'Tis because they will not fight for a child-killer, and because of the new laws you have passed, they have more valuable things to occupy them, their time is of value now. To fight for a king, I think not, my lord, for to win or to lose would bring nothing but pain, and discomfort to them and their kin as it has been for all time. We have seen these men of England return from the bloody wars. Without limbs, and worthless, unable to work, unable to keep their homes and wives and children, beggars thrown with no reward for their loyalties. Yes, my lord, they will come in their droves to fight by you side, and will do so when you become God.

Many liked to speak in honesty, but could not.

"Do you think I am an imbecile and do not know wherein lies the troubles? And all my brave ones stood here to show me the backbone of the worm!" Richard raised his voice and angered red. But soon he was calmed for he knew all too well that none dare risk the truth that would blacken the king. "No matter, no matter. So, my advisers, what can you relate to me upon the state of our position?" The subject changed to the task before them. The commanders all came together to offer their counselling, they grouped together with the officers and nobles standing and sitting about the great table, ready to listen with great interest as one of the council took to speaking of the situation.

"We know, sir, that that heinous traitor, Henry of Richmond, left by boat with one thousand armoured men, leaving Harfleur on the first day of August, the sea being calm and has been most calm since, and because of the calm waters there is a heavy fog about this land's shores. It is now the third day of August and no sighting yet has been made of any vessels. So, sire, it seems he is not landing upon the southern coast, for he would have made land by this day, and seems most likely he is coming more northward to make his landing. The castle at Nottingham seems to be our most favourable position, as already our chosen place to bide until we have a true sighting."

"Good. We will steadily our way to Nottingham and abide at the castle until we hear of Henry's place of landing; we will then form our offence to rid us of this slithering tyrant."

The eve with all its trials had past, and all residing at the mansion made way to their chambers, to rest and to be at the ready on the morn to take to their horses once more. The soldiers and the few officers within the town slept also, but their sleep came with the shouts and noise all about the narrow streets as ale and gin brought out such riotous pleasures. The soldiers huddled by the side of the roadway, their coats wetted with the heavy dew, the owls screeched above them in the blackness that was. But long asleep were they, to snore and belch, and let wind, with others spewing up the foul meal they had eaten. But, as night came late, all were in the land of their dreams awaiting the morrow and of what may come. Only the guards were awake as they stalked the lonely path around their sleeping army.

The dawn came, too soon for some and too long a wait for others, as the army stirred; the pots were a-boil once more, as the peasant women threw in more scraps from the yesterday, and stirred up once more the less-than-tantalizing victuals. The early morn went its way and all supped who were still able to stomach the offering. Officers and nobles were well content with their meal, though mostly leftovers from the night of yesterday, they were good leftovers. Richard was soon out amongst the mounting horses, one of the first to see that his steed was in good state, and ready he was to ride for many an hour; he felt pleased with the overnight stop and content was he. The cry of "Mount up!" came and the fresh horses were straddled as they fussed and became restless, until "Forward!" rang out and they calmed into their pace as the army struck from the town. They travelled on for the next three days each day much the same as the day before. The stops during the days under bright skies; the night stops with the rotting food for the soldiers of foot, and the rich food for the king, his nobles, and officers. Small skirmishes came upon them, but naught came to distress the army in any way, and all attempts to do so came to naught.

Upon the fourth day, at the noon hour, there came into view the sight of the town of Nottingham. Through the hilled forest they had come and, as cover was broken from the trees, the castle could be seen afar, high upon its rock. That rock placed there by some act unknown, it stood alone, with flatland all about it and with no other rocks within a hundred leagues of it. No doubt placed there by some divine power so one day a castle could be built atop its towering cliffs. It stood there peering back at them from its perch high, close to the clouds it must be, for did not its grey stone glisten from the sun more than any castle ever gazed upon? It waited for its visitors to come to its towering portals. The army seemed to step more proudly as closer they did come, perked were they with the sight of the town that showed ahead. The banners fluttered higher, the horses pranced more, the riders taller in their saddles. This could be a stop of a few days as they awaited the coming of Richmond's army, which seemed to be time yet far away. The town's welcome was no better than the others they had passed. Crowded about were many people, but mostly stood in silence, curious, they had just come to see the army of Richard that, foretold, was making to their town. Some were to cheer, some were to boo, others to murmur the voices of unrest. The army passed by, with many from the ranks looking about for able-bodied menfolk to join their cause. Some grey-bearded fellows watched with grumpy faces and missing legs, balancing upon their rickety crutches, their fighting long done. Some baby-faced boys, still milk-fed it seemed, but naught else was about, no one who could pull a bow or wield a sword. Those able, fled to the forest at Sherwood were they; long gone from their stead, away from the forced time serving a master they despised.

The army stretched far; with drums banging and pipes blowing, they came along the castle way, up the steep roadway that circled its side to the bridge that o'er the moat did lay, and then to the entrance of the courtyard and the great castle doors. The leading officers clattered over the bridge with its oak planks, and iron straps, and the lifting ropes lying loose at each side. The king followed his officers as the nobles came close behind him, and all nobility and all officers of high rank circled into the courtyard.

The officer of the day, leading the soldiers of foot, wheeled them past the gate, to take them to their campsite but one half of the mile away from the main castle entrance, to the grassed slope there that was the common. There they made ready the camp that was to be their barrack until next they moved, the move that would take them into conflict with Henry of Richmond, the red-rosed upstart that they despised. Eager they all to do battle with this Lancastrian and to be done with that red banner that did wave. In little time the soldiers had the poles placed which would take the heavy canvas and would be their shelter, each cover large enough to take eight soldiers and all their chattels. The tents soon raised as they stood proudly in lines straight as the archer's arrow. Some fetched wood from the waiting pile and began to light the fires for cooking, for in a camp such as this, rations were provided so that they were able to cook food for themselves. Rations were one sack for each man every day, and usually contained a small loaf of bread, two apples and some blackberries, two pieces of fowl, one piece of pork—"low upon the hog," two pints of ale, and some butter churned fresh. Other days would find a different ration of fresh vegetables, some oats ground for porridge, and a variety of nuts. A far better fare than had been eaten during the past days. Soon they were settled into a routine: eating, sleeping, cleaning and repairing their weapons, sewing their clothes and boots. Then life at dusk in the town spread below; came now the taverns, the wages placed on cockfights and the card games, and always the street women, all too eager to take what money was left. The military it seemed was one of the few callings that were paid with any regularity.

The castle stood high upon its rock, wherein for many years the caves and passageways that riddled its stone had been used for dwellings, and indeed still a few families made their abode inside the dank chambers. Above this riddled rock, a suitable gated storeroom showed itself within the castle's walls, and 'twas there most busied, as all manner of soldiery brought the armaments of battle to be stored in this secure place, being ushered by the bowmakers and blacksmiths in whose care they were placed. The bringers of the weaponry were shown where such items had to be placed, for some were to be repaired and others were in fine metal, and each put in the desired place and stacked in good order. Soon the line of fetchers stopped as all weapons were secure in the stone house. Apprentices lit the torches in the darkened chamber, and, as the light lapped about, they set about their task of making good all the weaponry that was battle-worn. Blade was heard scraping upon the stone wheel as 'twas turned, picking up the water to hasten its grind from the well it sat in. More than one was at the task as many weapons were bloodied dull. The tradesmen showing the apprentices the guile of the craft, so one day he will not be lighting the torch, or turning the stone's handle, or pumping the bellows, but he would be as his teacher and skilled well to enter the guild. The blades of knife and sword and of pikes were all dried from the wheel's cut, then well-oiled and placed carefully into the travelling boxes and lidded secure. The bowmakers were the busiest in their task, for, with one thousand archers within the soldiery, each would carry two quivers, with twenty-four arrows in each quiver, would bring forty-eight thousand arrows to be readied. The archers would care for their own bows, all tinkered to their own liking, always kept close and guarded with much zeal. The arrows all had to be viewed one at a time, and a small army of apprentices were used with the craftsmen overlooking the work. Some were sharpening the heads as the feathered flights were given their special need, held over the pipe pots that steamed its water upon the bent and returned them to straight, the feathers stroked together and made uniform under the heat, and then, with deft hands, a slight twist was put into them, which in flight made it to spin and whistle through the air, bringing strife by its sound upon the enemy as it glided over and, upon striking, would render a far more serious injury to the victim. Ne'er fifty thousand arrows were stored within the secure cavern, a most tempting prize for an enemy in need. A guard was stood without, and was dutied to make but short security to the other storage areas. But the castle was under close guard with many at watch about the outer walls. And, because of its position upon the rock, was a most difficult place to gain entry, even more so to leave with a cart full of weapons.

Richard felt all was in an orderly state, and his troops in good frame to do all that may be asked of them, and so came he from his viewing of the activities, to meet with his generals and noblemen and leading officers, they all in high spirits to do such royal duty. In the great hall they joined, to a map of England painted upon a canvas, that was laid upon the oak eating table, as the victuals and the flagons were pushed to one side. They all gathered about, the canvas held down by a tankard at each corner to stay its curl. In the flickering light that danced, the map showed all the noted towns and hamlets that had been recorded. The king was picked from the chess set and placed with much cheering upon the town of Nottingham. Another hand passed the knight to Richard.

"Here then is Norfolk, awaiting his orders just ten miles north at Southwell," as he placed the piece upon the village. The rook came secure into Richard's hand, for he much cherished this one. "Ah, … our great ally, Stanley, awaiting our call at the northern border." He placed the rook within the county of Durham, for he knew not the exact place he was now moved to. "Now, my friends, do we have a devil upon the board to place for our friend Richmond?" Laughter flowed the gathering as they joined their sovereign in his joviality. He picked himself the piece to stand as Henry of Richmond, and held it 'twixt his thumb an his first finger; small in stature to the other pieces chosen, he showed it to the nobles about. A pawn held there, a piece that was the lowest ranking upon the board, a piece given up with little respect that others may survive, something used to others' advantage. Richard, with smiling face, shook the piece within his hand like a die to be thrown, and looked about the map considering where would the place be that Henry may show his colours. He placed it to the southern part of Wales, and upon the town of Newport he set it down. All looked to where it had been placed, leaning upon each other so they may see more clearly the place where Richard thought the threat may come from.

"Well, my comrades, there for this time we must leave it, but soon we will know for sure to which place we may bring our armies to do battle against this usurper. A game of patience is all we can play, and not until the news arrives will we then be able to finalize our campaign. So, my gallant ones, enjoy all you can—the wine, the ladies, the sleep of kings—for this one battle will see us free of the last of those who think they have a right to this crown, this crown of England that we all hold so dear. Just one fight and all in this land will breathe the air of peace."

"Three cheers for Richard!" was called for, and all assembled gave to the king their pledge. Most departed from the conference and made their way about the chamber, but still a few gathered around the map to further press their thoughts amongst each other.

The castle fireplace threw out its warmth and its bright glow about the hall; many candles stood all about to flicker in the draught that passed. A place of knights and of nobles and of riches. Romance arrived with the glow as the courtesans came a-mingle with the lordly lot, and the goblets were filled with good French wine, and clasped with ringed fingers of gold and jewel, and bangled bracelet that clinked upon the silver vessels. 'Twas soon that laughter and lewdness spread the hall, some leaving entwined to chambers await, fondling and drooling as they floated away upon their misty clouds. Others stood close to the shadows of the draped walls, standing there then seen no more, as they drifted into the dark folds that hung, their antics now unseen. The one so drawn took her waltz to Richard, seemingly more alluring than of the others. As if a special gift for the king, her demeanour breezed o'er him with the perfume of the French court, deep and musky did tremble him. The breasts displayed before him as if untouched by the world, the lips, painted thick, hovered close to his face. Her dress rustled in the temptation as her warm leg pressed his, and she filled his goblet once more with the heady wine, and placed the cold metal rim upon his lips, gently tilting it back until the red liquid trickled slowly into his mouth. He gazed the rim and saw her long, slender fingers wrapped around the vessel, and her fingernails filed to desire, tapping gently upon the metal side. The ring upon her finger was close to his mouth, glinting its own fire from the glow about; as he sipped he felt the cold stone upon his lip as the wine flowed about it. Not too often did the brave soldier crumble, or his knees shake, but 'twas so in the seductive charm of this madam who knew all about the games played, and played them with unseen bonds.

"Am I to your pleasure, your Majesty?" came the husky voice with the French tongue, as the warm breath breezed about his ear.

"You are, my dear, most enticing and your art is well-taught."

She placed the goblet upon the table and, with Richard's help, she turned around the chair he was seated in so the back was at the table, then lifted her silk gown to straddle him; facing Richard, with her arms about his neck and her breasts, plump, beneath his chin, she softly pulled his head back and pressed her red lips tight upon his. He felt the warmth of her as she sat upon him, and then some desire to release her lips as he tried to speak. She felt his slight struggle and released her lips from his, though still squirming about upon him was she.

"Enough, my dear, enough."

"Do you wish to bed me, my lord?"

"Yes, I wish so; time is done of this dally; let us make to my chambers."

She lifted herself off her lord and then, with gentle care, helped him from his seat. They walked slowly together, her arm about his waist as they upped the stairway and into the bedding chamber went. As they approached the bed she began to remove the clothing from our most royal king, and in little spate he was in his most humble state of nakedness. She laid him back upon the softness, as she began to reveal the creamy skin that once lay hidden in the silk, the skin as fine as the cream from the urn, a true tantalizing delight hovered before him. Then she was atop of him as the pleasure flowed within the candles' light, and the pillows and covers of silk rolled and were in disarray about the bed. After much time and frolic, sleep came over them and led them deep into the night.

The monastery clock rang from distance far and was not easily heard in this slumbering chamber. Three of the clock in the morn did it speak. Richard lightly felt the silk cover move a little, and the bed to rise somewhat. He remained still as if he in sleep still was held within its tranquil; though he did not move, his eyes were not at rest, but searched about the chamber as best he could in the light that played dim about. But then the moon broke its cloudy covers, and he could see the goblets and the jugged wine and the clothing he had worn strewn about the floor. The dress of the courtesan tossed upon the covers he saw. With the light from the waning moon entering the window, he saw the slim hand with the nails filed to desire, the rings upon the fingers sparkling the moon's light, as it moved toward the jug and gently poured out two goblets of the rich wine, the good French wine. He sensed her turn toward the bed and closed his eyes to slits, but were soon opened a little more with the glint that crossed his sight. The small vile showed in that light held in the slim fingers as it trickled a liquid into one of the vessels, and dripped it to the last drop; the stopper was replaced in the king's sight, then 'twas gone. The bed then lowered and the silk gently moved as the whore turned to the warmth. The courtesan, whore, murderess was beside her king, the vile plot turning in his head: That she would think that he would be so unwary as to be seduced to Death's gate—I think not, my dear.

The dawn lighted the room, and the courtesan stirred with yawning arms as if this was the night's first awakening.

"My lord, are you awake?" Her seductive tones still at play as she lay only in her short white linens and her black stockings, as now she sat upon the bed coverings and looked over to Richard to see if indeed he had awakened.

"Yes, my dear, I am awake." As he too lifted himself up aside her, awaiting the next device that would be cast his way. A fish he, awaiting the hooked worm … it came.

"I will soon have to depart."

"Yes, I know."

"There will be a token for me, will there not, my lord?"

"Of course you will receive a reward, for are you not, without any doubt, a most unusual lady? And you will receive all you may expect from the talent you have displayed."

She smiled at him and kissed his cheek, her smile of amour, her mind of murder, her voice came of seductive lure, as she played then her highest card against the king. "Drink with me one last sup, to bring to close the most splendid of times that I have spent with you." Her slender fingers came before him again, this time not with love's games but with a poisoned cup. Richard took it from the pale hand and awaited for the murderess to bring close her own vessel. "Here's to you, my king, in all health may you reign for many a year." She clinked her vessel against his with naught but affection in her demeanour. She drank as her dark eyes looked over the goblet at Richard. Over the other goblet was seen the eyes that looked upon him, peering over the silver as she waited for him to drink. The painted lids closed to join the lashes, then broke again to show the black eyes, and then closed again, then opened, that she did not wish to be seen looking in so much anticipation. Richard, though, in less haste, brought up to his lips slowly the tainted goblet, and tipped it upward as if taking a gulp, but his action was not so, for he supped naught, drawing it back from his lips and lifting his kerchief, he dabbed the liquid away that dwelled there, to gaze at the satisfied smile displayed before him.

"Now, my dear, you must do one last thing for me."

"Anything you desire, my master; I am but yours to will."

"We have shared our bodies, have we not?"

"Yes, we have and so delightful was it." All coldness came from her with no emotion to show anything was amiss. Will he die straight, or will he linger? Will I be afar before he is gone?—thoughts within but shown not upon the fair skin.

"As I am always inclined after I have bedded such beauty, that as our bodies were shared so then must our wine." And he, in much deftness, took the goblet from those slim fingers and placed it within his own, curling his fingers around the vessel so it would keep safe, and in the same moment swilled the wine he had gotten, empty now that cup, the sweetest cup he had ever supped. He placed his own goblet carefully into the hands that seemed not as sure as they were but moments ago. Then he looked at her with face close to the murderess. "Come, my dear, drink it down."

"My lord, I cannot." She trembled as Richard's face pressed against hers.

"*My lord, I cannot?* ... Who am I, pray, that you say to me thus?" Anger was passing his lips as he stepped away from her. Thoughts then plagued the mind of the mistress that all was awry—Richard knows of the plot against him; it started to rent her inside and despair began to shiver her body. "Answer me, am I not the monarch of this Realm?"

"Yes, sire, you are, and I am made humble before you, my lord,"—as all the strength left her legs and she was almost no longer able to bear her lost self.

"Then, madam, drink from this goblet!" His voice raised in shouting tone; his whiskers rubbing her soft cheek.

"Sir—" she started to speak once more but could not continue, as tears and terror struck through her trembling body, for she knew that Richard was well aware of her task this day. She crumbled to the floor as shot by an arrow through the heart. Richard clothed himself and made ready, whilst the whimpering heap shook.

"Get up, woman!" shouted Richard as he pulled the consort up to her shaking knees. "Guard!" he shouted, and almost immediately the guard came to the call.

"Yes, your Majesty?"

"Get all within these walls to assemble in the great hall immediately," he ordered the guard as he held tightly the wrist of the fainting woman.

"Yes, sir, your Majesty." And, with a salute, backed from the door and hastened about calling upon the other guards to help in the orders so given, as soon mayhem had embraced the normal peace of the castle. Like the ferret down the rabbit burrow did it happen.

"Get thee down the stairs, woman, and remember, do not open your mouth one lick, unless I order you to do so!"—Richard glaring at her as he held her wrists and raged into her face.

"Yes, my king," meekly she spake, as Richard removed his grip upon her wrists, now red and bruised from the harsh treatment. She made to move as if to retrieve her gown of crumpled silk that still lay upon the bed, for her cover was little.

"Leave it!" came the brash voice from Richard, as she flinched back from the bed, startled, and knowing the clothing she wore was all she could expect. He roughly took her arm once again, and, picking up the goblet of poisoned wine with the other hand, dragged her from the royal chamber, crossing the cold passageway and then down the wide staircase to see below the hall, almost filled. All those assembled there looking at the sight of the king in much rage, he fully clothed, and the courtesan with him wearing such clothes as a common whore would wear. They came down the stairway, she pulled along by the king, and they did not stay their step until the centre of the hall was reached. Still holding tightly onto her wrist, he spake to all assembled.

"This bitch, my lords and gentlemen, some little while ago did heinously try to poison your king." The group assembled rumbled with words of disbelief and of horror, and stepped back for some reason to widen the stage where stood Richard and his accused. "With this goblet of wine did she try her evil task." Richard held the very vessel at full arm's stretch so all could witness it. "This goblet with wine and nightshade's deathly berries. This, my lords, to be given and supped by the master of this Realm. My friends, I wonder where she may have gotten such designs. One word that pains me, and is beneath the slimy worm, that word is spy! I feel that such a creature of deceit is in our midst: this wretch before you!" He held high the hand of the doer who had to rise upon her toes so she would not be lifted from the floor. "She does not have the guile, nor indeed the means to bring such an act to fruit; she is just being used in this deadly game. And deadly is the game, for I pledge to you, death will strike swiftly this morn, and will not come easy as upon doves' wings and feathered pillows, but will come as hell bent with lingering strife and unheard pleas. Though a pawn in this act, she is, nevertheless, a carrier of death." He spake in some discreet tone to one of his bodyguards, and after short converse the officer withdrew his sword from its scabbard, and placed himself behind the courtesan the point of his blade, dimpling her back. "Go now, woman, amongst the people about this hall, and point out the spy to us who did buy your soul." She looked at Richard with puzzlement upon her face, for she knew of no such person beholden to her task. The king, with his eyes blazed, looked into her face, and she was reminded with the look to say naught and to obey all commands.

So she slowly and unsteadily stepped forward amongst the gallery. She no longer the proud brazen one full of charm and manner; dressed in such finery was she no more, but seen the lost waif; shoeless, small, and humble she did walk, already dead was she. All looked as she came close to the gathering, most of them were innocent, others not so pure as they stood awaiting pointing fingers, some were fully dressed, others stood in their nightclothes, the lords not so lordly in their flopping nightcaps, dishevelled and unwashed were others as they all waited. The courtesans all stood together in a group by themselves, standing with hands clasped in fear for their sister. She made her way slowly, the black eyes looking into the faces as they parted to allow her to pass; she looked but did not know for what, as on she moved to the far reach of the room. Richard from a distance watched her as she moved about, but also he watched the faces as they looked at her passing. The ladies of her ilk held out their hands to touch her as she passed them, in a show of sympathy and of compassion to the stumbling coquette before them. Had they not warned her to play only the games she knew?—but the jingle of lucre was louder than they could shout. Past them now she made her way to a group of officers standing staunchly as they were wont, and was again to move further to another pride of loyals when from the back of them some anguished movement came. The officers parted themselves to clear the scene of the commotion; they stood back from one of their kind, who it did seem had gone mad with a violence that had overtaken his body. Richard moved quickly closer to see the cause of the disturbance. The officer had drawn his short sword, and, standing in full gaze of Richard, and before anyone could subdue him, shouted loudly, "God bless Henry of Richmond!" And, as the last words departed his lips, he, with two hands upon his sword, plunged it into his chest, almost to the hilt, with sickening thud and splurging blood all about as he fell to the stone floor. Richard stood as he saw the fatal act close to his face, as gazing also upon the grisly scene the poison-bringer stood, she not of this world but in some other state. A spy was gone by his own hand. He who chose the blade, for he could not bear the rack. Flushed out with false measures, for none knew of his being; his own fear of discovery ended his vile deception.

"And so, for all to see, such ends all who practise deception against this Realm," spake Richard, as two of his guards stepped toward the death that lay upon the floor as to remove him from sight. "Leave him!" shouted the king. "All the blood to be spilled this day may not yet be done. Move!" The king began to push the courtesan in the small of her back once again; it seemed only one bloody heap was not yet enough for him, as he moved her on further to the quest. She moved on with the guard following four paces back, with steel shown, as she continued around the hall. Soon she had walked all about and no other words had come to ear, as she came to the face of Richard. "So, my lady, now that you have seen death, tell me straight, who sent you to me with this evil act? ... Be sure of your answer, for, if it does not suit me, you will lay also beside that bloody heap." He clutched her hair from the back as he searched for the truthful answer.

"My lord," she sobbed, hardly able to utter her words so feared was she, and was unable to contain her functions as she wet upon the floor with splash upon the stone. "I know not who bought me — 'twas done most discreet — the word coming down from a rider who had travelled many hours from the northern borders."

"*The north?* — From the north! Why is it all I hear is 'From the north?' — like Judas thrice those words have been bandied. Am I doomed? ... I think not." He released his grasp upon the hair and then stepped away. She saw his nod to the back of her, as then with a deft thrust through the shoulder blades the guard pushed his sword into the soft flesh of the helpless lady. A gasp went about the gathering at the terrible sight they had beheld, a cruel and unwelcome demise. Through her heart went the steel to protrude out at the front, as the life fled the eyes that were looking at Richard, who watched with little feeling towards such as she, someone bent to murder a king. The sword was withdrawn as quickly as it had entered, and the body piled to the floor. Richard tipped the goblet of poisoned red wine over the heap, the good French wine, its contents trickled about upon the stones, as atop came more red as the blood too mingled about. "Clear the mess!" Richard ordered as he dispersed the gathering. "We will meet again here at my desire when news of our adversary is gotten." With no more words, the king stormed away toward his chambers, leaving the murmurings behind him. Groups gathered about, some in council, some peering at the bodies that lay there. Ladies sobbing and distraught. The king's door slammed shut and he heard no more ...

The days drifted along and all still awaited word of the enemy. Darkness had fallen at this eve, the air warm, the bats in flight, the moths fluttering, flying as if blind, landing in hair and eyes as the group moved along as silent as they were able. They came dark from the forest to the base of the blackened rock, which held high above them the castle, so high it could not be seen. Six in all were they, grubby of face and unshaven, with straggled hair tumbled down. Black coats over ragged clothes of green worsted, bringing itch to their thighs, close-fitted caps pulled low, booted and broad of shoulder; no arms did they bear, for they did not look for fight but bent upon some thieving of much-sought goods, which, if they were successful, would bring much reward to them, for unpaid taxes had to be paid, and roofs were in need of repair. Local peasants were they, used to soldiering for their king, but not for this king. This bloody monarch was not to their liking, and they had pledged together to do no battle for Richard's pomp.

The bushes at the rock side hid from sight the cave that they sought; they knew well of its place and were soon in its black hole. A place of shelter many years past, but now no longer used for such, for the dank, dripping cavern was no place to live long. They lit their pitch torch in the raven-like blackness; it lit quickly but was soon spitting and sparking from the drippings that fell from the ceiling. From the light they could see well their way as they made toward the back of the cave where a great rock stood. They took a good grip upon its rough face, and, though slimy wet, the six strong bodies began to urge it from its place as it scraped and squeaked upon the floor, uttering its defiance as 'twas moved like a piglet taken from the sow. Soon 'twas to one side. They pushed their torch into the hole they had freed, musty and little used except for such rogues as they. Always known as Mortimer's Hole, it seemed from far back in history 'twas so, and the name still clung. In they went with one following the other into the narrow and low roof of the passageway. The leading man carried the torch ahead as the floor began its steepened climb upward, and soon was as steep as the hills of Yorkshire, where they had hunted often to poach the king's deer. The necks stiffening with looking high to the torch ahead, with slipping and stumbling upon the slimed stone beneath their tread, they went on. Many passages they passed going to other places; some they knew of, some they did not, but the one they trod was well known to them and they would not be lost within the rock upon this way. At times a small shaft of moonlight would break through the blackness to show that they were not hell bound.

"Come on, lads, come on!" the torch-carrier urged his men as up and up they went, with legs seeking some rest as the pain made them groan in their task, but they struggled on. The passage somewhat levelled for a while as the ease came to their aches. The bats began to fly about their heads, disturbed by these intruders that had entered their domain. The peasants flailing their arms about to ward off the creatures that swooped about them, for were they not known to tear out the eyes of any who trod their way? Squealing sounds about their feet was heard, and things brushed against their legs with oft softness underfoot as they made their way; rats were everywhere, the level was infested and none could tread without the crunch underfoot. Then they were climbing once more and the vermin were left behind. The legs began their ache again, as the slipping and sliding went on and they struggled to the top of the rock. Then, at last, they stopped and rested, for they had reached their place of entry into the castle. They leaned against the walls that were dry in the air that came about. After a short rest they moved toward the square stone that was lighted ahead of them. The torch-carrier dug about with his boot into the soft soil to rattle upon some iron levers that were hidden during their last visit. They all gathered about picking up the bars that clinked together, as they pulled them from their hide. Little was spoken, for all knew their task and talk was not to help. But later in the tavern, amongst the filled tankards, 'twould be all talk, albeit whispered amongst the laughter and comradeship. They began to pry at the stone; using the levers made it an easy task, as seen was a little light that did enter from the loosened rock, and so the torch was snubbed and laid to wait. The stone was soon away and pushed to one side, the opening large enough for one man on his stomach to crawl through. The leader went first, the one with the key that swung about his neck, the key that had been forged and filed by the blacksmith, made from the master key that had been discreetly borrowed and then returned to its hook. He squirmed his body through the opening in the thick wall and met with a stack of old hay piled high and thick; pushing it aside, he was soon standing within the stone chamber where the horse feed was stored. The piles of hay hid the gape in the back wall; all then gathered there, but still hidden behind the stacked hay and bagged oats therein.

"Right, lads, wait here whilst I see what's about." The leader crouched with his men behind the hide as he whispered to all his next move. He pushed his way through the hay to make toward the door, the rats about scurrying once more as his boots came down upon their nests, the pink hairless creatures crawling about with eyes not yet opened crunched beneath his foot. The other men helped in the venture, stomping their boots upon anything that was afoot. Came the door close to the hand of the leader; he peered through the iron bars that covered the opening. In the moonlight he could see clearly: all seemed calm and quiet, seeing only but a single guard leaning against the pillar that was the armoury … The place they sought, the place where the arrows were stored, all sharp and ready, a cache that would be lucrative, quiet to move, light to carry, ideal for the peasants to sell. The leader moved away from the bars and made back to his comrades to whisper once more his findings. "Just one of them. I'll call you as soon as he moves."

Away he went again to spy from the door. As the moon passed the castle tower, the bell from the monastery rang the hour of the night, and the guard stretched himself and went slowly upon his way to secure all about as he did every hour upon his watch. Soon he had reached the corner of the main buildings and in the shadows was lost to sight as he went his path.

"Come on, lads." The call low and whispered to his friends. The door creaked open and they were soon in the shadow of the wall, slinking along to the armoury door with hearts thumping within their chests. The key slid into the lock and turned the latch as easy as if 'twere the real key; inside they went and in the darkness with the door closed behind them they stood in silence, breathing deeply. They waited to become more accustomed to the little light that entered the chamber. Soon they could see more and gazed about, still not yet moving as the swords and the armour came to their sight, the pikes leaning high up against the walls. Some bows there with the twine only attached to one end, like fishing poles they stood and not weapons of war. Baskets of gauntlets and boxes of daggers. Then they spied the bundles of arrows; they were stacked neatly and piled high, in their thousands were they, all tied readily with twine, ready to be carried to the army's wagons. *Like the wasp 'twas the archer's sting*—but just as easily carried by robbers to market. In the dim light two of them began to gather the bundles together, then carried them quietly and stacked them close to the doorway, as the others took them, making their way within the walls' shadows, they piled them within the hay room. One of the group was placed at watch for the guard's return. Chosen to be the watchman, he was told, because his teeth were the blackest and would not be seen in the moon's light. They had many arrows moved to the hay room in little time, but the group were becoming concerned of the guard's return, though no signal had yet come from their comrade, whose dark shadow they could see peeking around the corner to spy his coming. Soon, though, was the signal as the watcher's shadowy image came to them.

"He comes now. Come on, quickly!" In whispery voice came the cry. Calmly they gathered the rest of the bundles that lay at the armoury doorway, pulled the door closed, keyed the lock, then scurried to the safety of the horse feed room; quickly inside with the door pulled closed, they stood amongst their booty and began to look into each other's faces, and all could not stop but to smile their smile of intrigue. The amount that lay about even awed those who had stolen it, to make them revel in the task ahead: to bring all to the bottom of the rock and to sup soon the ale that awaited their parched throats. Through the piled hay they went, carrying their bundles to lay them inside the passage, then to fetch more, till all was in the tunnel. They pulled the hay back to cover the entrance and then pushed the stone to seal the chamber once more. The torch was lit, and they were piled, each with many bundles, but they were unable to carry all and would have to return for the others. Off they went, all following the torch that led them down the slippery blackness. The bats still whirling about their heads, as they hugged the bundles in their arms with other bundles tied to their backs. Easier was the task to go down; they felt little of pained legs, and after some slips and slides, and with their cut elbows and grazed knuckles, they had reached the bottom of the way. They piled their burdens to one side, and rested themselves with their backs against the cave wall, readying for the climb once more. As they stood, the crock they had brought with them was brought out and soon the smell of ale soaked the cave's air. One after the other, they gulped down the cool liquid to ease their dry mouths. The ale brought more grins to their faces, for the monies they would bring from the weapons would enable them to buy some livestock, and some tools and timber to improve their lot, if all indeed did continue to unfold to their dreamed ends.

Quenched and in good spirits they went for the last time up the hole's sapping climb and to the stash. They quickly loaded all the remaining bundles within their arms and upon their backs as they made again down the dark way. Breathing heavy, as at last the bottom was reached, they sat again to reap their strength; with a few more swigs from the crock, and some banter between them, they were most pleased at the night's work. Time was to load the cart that awaited in the forest. The leader went to the entrance and pushed his way through the covering bushes, then made into the thick growth to see the cart and his horse tethered to the twisted oak; still chewing some greenery, the horse looked up as he approached, the bridle brasses glinting too brightly in the shafting light. He untied the animal and stroked its forehead to keep it calm, at the same time whispering comforting words to it, as they moved through the trees as far as he was able to the cave opening. The backboard was lowered and the leader rolled back the canvas ready for the bundles.

"Stay there, me beauty," he said to his horse as he ran back to the cave and his friends. "All's well, lads. Let's load 'em." They were glad to hear the words at last, for waiting alone in the cave they had too much time to think of what could go awry. Soon they were moving as quietly as they were able, backwards and forwards between the cave and the wagon, placing the booty under the canvas, for eyes may pry upon their short journey. They turned the filled cart and the horse was led back into the oak forest from whence they had come; the leader pulled at the reins to ease it through the close trees and branches, the others pushing upon the wheels to keep it moving along the uneven ground, over logs and low washes, bumping and twisting it went. The pathway then showed, and smoother was the way that wound through the woods to their homesteads close to the hamlet of the Meadows. The wheels were rolling in the ruts left by other travellers, and all was quiet as they lopped along each side of the cart under the starry sky that soon would bring the morn's light. They came to their cottages in the dawn's light and to its safety they did seek, for six men with a cart draped in canvas seen before the cock's crow was not a sight oft seen. They were rattling in the alleyway where the cottages sat, but were soon at the back where the stables and a low barn lay. They stopped close and the horse was unhitched from the cart and led off to the stable; yet, as water and oats awaited, the animal no longer needed to be led but was the leader. Once inside, the stable door was closed and the six turned to the cart. They did not unload it but pushed it into the barn as far to the back as it would go, and then 'twas covered all about with stacks of hay and straw, until 'twas unseen, and the doors were closed upon it.

"We meet at the tavern at noon, lads." The leader spake as he made toward his cottage, and then called back to his friends as they left, "And don't be late." Their voices calling back, "Aye, aye," and then only quietness; all was left to the bats and the other night creatures …

"What is it?" The presence of the officer of the day had been requested by the armoury guard; he stood before him to hear the reason for being called.

"Sir, we are missing some armaments." The guard reluctantly the one who had to bring the observation to his superior.

"What do you mean, soldier?" The officer talking as he came over and pushed open the door to the armament chamber, followed by the troubled guard.

"Sire, when we made our daily count we found less than yesterday's tally."

"How many less?"

"Well … more than two hundred bundles of arrows, sire."

"What! You must be mistaken in your count. How can anyone enter this castle and steal such an amount without being seen? No, my man, you must be wrong."

"I know not how, sire, but we are sure of our tally." The officer, determined to show the underling he was wrong, took one of the lit torches from the wall and paced back to where the arrows were stored, and, in the flickering light with the black smoke swirling, poked about at the arrow stock, and he could see even without a count that many bundles were indeed missing.

"Who was on guard last night?" he posed to the guard.

"That would be Anthony Miller, sire," the guard answered with but a little thought, for he knew the roster well.

"Go and bring him here in all haste, for I would be most interested to hear what story he has to tell."

"Yes, sire." Away went the guard at a fast trot toward the camp, up the slope to the brow of the common, and then down the other side he ran through the morn's still misty blanket, to the tent of his fellow soldier who was sleeping soundly after his night's duty. "Anthony ... Anthony," he called as he entered the tent, and, looking about, saw only one man in there wrapped tightly in his blanket, but stirring from the noise about.

"What is it?" he asked, only yet half awake.

"Anthony, you're wanted at the armoury. There are some bundles of arrows missing."

"Arrows missing? I know nothing about any arrows."

"Well you had better get your story straight, for the duty officer is in not too good a frame, and is looking for some likely soul to be faulted in this matter."

He was up from his blanket now, that warm place he did dwell, and had soon tied his boots, and with hat placed upon his head, he was already upon his way, for all the camp slept with their uniforms on, ready to be called at any time. Soon he was running up to the castle with his breathless friend behind him. Within sight of the officer they came through the gates and made across the yard. He stood impatiently at the entrance to the storage room with angered eyes staring at the coming guards.

"Sir," said Anthony, saluting the officer as they stopped breathless before him.

"So, what do you say of last night?—Miller, is it not?"

"Yes, sire, I am Miller. Sir, all was quiet. I saw and heard naught; the only time I left the door was to carry out my hourly security. And all night there was naught about and nothing amiss."

"You tell me this, Miller, yet how is it that two hundred bundles of arrows can go amiss without anyone seeing or hearing naught but the still of the night? I know not what to say, for they must have had a cart to move such an amount, but there are no tracks and the way to the armoury is well spied from the tower. I am deeply puzzled and pray you had no doing in this act."

"I did naught, sire; I am of no guilt. I cannot say more, for I know nothing of it." The guard was most concerned that he would be suspected of the intrigue, for some heads must roll and was he not but a humble soldier.

"Go now and finish your rest. We will have to look further into the theft."

"Sire," he saluted and walked away somewhat disconsolate, and, with head bowed, he trudged back to his tent in some nervous state; he would have little sleep to ease his mind.

The officer left the other guard to his duty at the armoury whilst he went to report the matter to the castle commander. Across the courtyard he went and stepped inside the castle's doorway, then, with long strides, he headed toward the commander's chamber. Two guards outside the entrance stood to attention at the approach of the senior officer.

"I wish to speak to the commander; it is most urgent." He made known to the guards his reason for the intrusion.

"One moment, sir." One of the guards advised the officer before he knocked and entered the chamber to present himself to the commander with the request for council.

"Bring him forth," came the answer with boomed voice. The guard saluted and returned to the waiting officer, beckoning him in toward the black table where sat the commander. An old soldier was he, with his fighting days behind him, as his grey hair and his wrinkles had brought him to this position to plan and organize. Gruff and knowing, his arrow always shot straight.

"Sire," the officer saluted the commander.

"What is it you wish to converse with me, sir?"

"There has been a theft, sire, of two hundred bundles of arrows from the armoury. This happened during the night of yesterday, and we are unable to find any way to trace them, for there are no tracks and naught was seen. The guard carried out fully his dutiful orders and appears to be innocent in the matter. I come to you for some guidance, for I am somewhat distressed at the outcome, and for the wrath of Richard, who will not be pleased."

The commander leaned back in his chair and brushed his hairy chin with the quill he had been writing with as the feather played a tune upon his bristle. He stayed silent for a while after the officer had finished his report. "Sir, there are many entrances to this castle, not just the ones with iron gates and vigilant guards. We know little of these tunnels and I would not waste my time seeking them out, for many hours would be spent to finish your day with only ifs and buts. The first thing we must do is replenish the store as 'twas before. I suggest you double the guard so that someone is at the door at all times, and, upon each hour, enter the chamber to see if all is in order. There must not be more pilfering whilst we seek to replace those weapons taken. We must beg, steal, or buy as many arrows we can without malice, for, believe me, our enemies will do the same for such a cache, for their need for arrows is as great as ours. Be not feared of Richard, for if his armoury is full by whatever means, he will be a happy sovereign. But time is short. I will give you a docket that you may obtain the required monies from the bookkeeper to purchase our required lot."

"Thank you, sir," he replied to the commander, gratefully acknowledging the plain facts and action he had given, given without the frills of noble lace.

"Take six men with you, you should need no more, and do remember, no malice, for we may need such contacts as you find for further use in our endeavour. If violence should come upon these fellows, they will not deal with us again; they will deal only with those who bring no threat to them. I cannot stress more, for we are in readiness and it is a most urgent matter that you are required to close." Whilst talking his quill was scratching upon the crested docket before him, stopping for a moment as he dipped his pen and pondered a little, no doubt estimating the amount of coin that would be required for such a purchase. "Three shillings for a bundle of twenty-four—" he said, half to himself and half to the officer. "Two hundred bundles is … six hundred shillings is … thirty pounds. I will make the docket for thirty-five pounds, which should suffice for your purchase." He passed the paper over to the officer.

"I will do my utmost to bring the matter to an early close, sire." The commander waved him out with his quill and was nosed down within his books as the officer left for the keeper of the monies, who was but a short distance away. As he made his way across to the entrance, he made arrangements with one of his fellow officers to bring to a place near the gate his soldiery requirements, and a nondescript horse and cart with canvas cover to be readied for the stated morn's hour. The door to the chamber he sought was open, so stepped he inside to place himself behind two more officers both clutching dockets. They stood before the table where sat the bookkeeper, he with saddened face and miserable demeanour, giving out monies most reluctantly and sadly, it seemed, against his religion.

"And what is this for?" he was asking the first officer.

"Three horses have to be purchased for the royal guard."

"Huh," was the reply, as from his money box he divided out the amount stated upon the docket; he counted it twice then placed it before the officer at the table. "Sign," he said as he placed his book forward and gave his quill, ready dipped. The officer quickly signed his name, scooped up his gains, smartly exited the chamber, and was gone to the cry of: "Do not forget your receipt! It is needed for my records!" But there was no answer. The other two officers came closer to the table, as the one in front placed his docket into the stretched hand before him. "What is this for?" the bookkeeper asked the same question once more.

"Officer's supplies."

"Exactly what kind of officer's supplies? It says naught here upon this paper." The bookkeeper had no choice but to pay what was writ upon the dockets, but it seemed he had to play the same game every time, and so the officer joined in, though his features and his voice were of a most serious nature.

"We need four whores, two barrels of wine, and a small amount of nightshade." All were stated sincerely to the bookkeeper, who looked up and with sneered mouth and saying naught else, counted out the monies and placed it down upon the table, pushed his book toward the officer, and handed him the quill. But unfortunately in doing so he dropped a spot of ink upon the officer's white cuff.

"Oh, so sorry, how clumsy of me, sir," the bookkeeper spake, he also with sincere words.

The paper was signed, the monies were handed over as the officer turned, giving a smirk to the one remaining, and then departed. The next docket was handed over.

"What's this for?" came once more the terse remark.

"Armaments."

"Armaments! You always seem to be buying armaments."

The officer remained for a little while calm, as the sneering remarks continued, but soon no more was in his stomach, and he felt that one more remark would overflow his bucket. *The farmer knows naught of the blacksmith's work.*

"Are you daydreaming? Did you not hear me? Of what armaments?"

The officer then leaned over the table in a menacing frame. "Sir, it matters not to you what items are purchased, and I would in all haste pay me, for I am in need to quickly depart. And, sir, do not drop one spot of ink upon my person or this dagger I carry will pop your eye like a winkle from its shell." He then calmly stood up, feeling most satisfied. The bookkeeper said naught as he went through his process. The book was signed and the monies handed over to the officer, and with a "Good day, sir," he departed from the money office. The bookkeeper, though, was fazed not by the officer and seemed to enjoy the confrontation.

Two mounted officers stood at the cart, two soldiers sat upon the board, and a sergeant mounted at the rear made up the party; all were at the ready in the great courtyard of the castle, in which many activities were being engaged. Groups of soldiers being drilled, bowmen on one side practising with their targets, horses being led to and fro. Groups of officers were about, some in converse, others with swordplay pranced about, shouting and laughter mingled the yard as the guard officer reached his men. In a close group he related to them the task they were engaged in, and impressing upon them, as he had been ordered to do so, that no reprisal must be taken upon any persons that they may deal with.

"Are your orders clearly understood?"

"Yes, sire," came the reply of all the soldiers. He relayed then to each officer in turn their duty in this matter. One of the officers, as requested, was not in uniform and was to be the main contact, dressed as the gentleman he was, and, as would have it, this officer was of the personal guard of Richard.

Out they trundled through the open gate and past the posted guards; the day was at nine of the clock in the morn. They rattled and clopped down the lane of Castlegate and past the tavern there, then on toward the market square where the stalls were already set out; buyers and sellers fingered their wares, animals shook their pens, vegetables stacked the tables high, children ran amok. The party stopped to one side of the square around which many taverns and inns lay, and 'twas agreed that such places would be the most likely to find what they sought. The officer in gentleman's garb stepped from his horse, this officer was our Steven Moran, who began to visit one inn after another, but so far had made no suitable contact, until he went to the inn of The White Horse. A lively place sounded as he entered, for 'twas close to the noon hour and many throats needed to be quenched, and many stomachs needed to be filled. The landlord caught the gaze of Steven as he approached through the jostle.

"Sir, are you the innkeeper?" he queried.

"Yes, sir, I am such."

"I have a request that you may help me with."

"I am at your disposal, sir." They moved to one side in a dimmer area of the crowded taproom.

"To the point, I must come straight, for I have no time for fiddle-faddle. I seek a large amount of arrows, I have ready monies for such, and quickly is my need. I give also my word in this enterprise, as a gentleman, that no one will suffer any reprisal in such a transaction. Do you know where such a purchase may be made?"

"May, I could, sire, but I know not that which you speak to me is the truth. You may just be bent upon some revenge and I could not place such persons to come under such circumstances."

"Sir, I repeat to you, I am a gentleman and a man of honour, my words are spoken in all good faith to you, and to all others I pledge the same. I can say no more but show you by my actions that I am to my word."

"Wait here, sire," was all he spake as he drifted into the crowd and was then unseen. He came back shortly with a rough-looking fellow following behind him, dragging a lame leg, smelly, and not at all a friendly person.

"Aye, sire," his rough, ale-smelling voice drifted across to Steven.

"You know what I seek?"

"Aye, I've 'eard whispers of such things."

"Come, my man, have no fear of me. I am most urgent in my quest."

"Well, sir, I do know who has such as you seek."

"Can you arrange for me to meet such a person?"

"I can, sire."

Our officer gave the man a florin. "There will be another for you upon your return, but you must have with you the man of whom you speak."

The words brought the toothless grin to view. "Wait here, sire."

"How long must I abide?"

"Within the hour, I will return."

"Be with haste, my man, for time is not in my pocket."

He limped away and was gone. Steven left the inn shortly after the limping man had gone, and made his way to the cart at wait.

"Were you able to find any information, Steven?" the guard officer asked as he came close.

"It went well, a contact I had converse with has gone to bring the seller to the inn, and in good faith should be back within the hour."

"Good, good," the relieved officer answered.

"I will inform you as soon as I am able as to the outcome of the meet, and let us pray all goes well." He left his comrades once more and returned to the inn.

Sat he supping a flagon, he awaited the return of the limping man. Then, close to an hour, he came.

"'Ere 'e is, my lord. Thomas Smith,"—who now appeared from behind the ruffian.

"Good day, sir." He a peasant too, but of a more likeable ilk, dressed fairly well, and clean-shaven. Though grubby from his day's chores, he seemingly with more of a brain than the other fellow, for which a pimple may serve. Steven passed over the promised token into the held-out hand before him.

"Thankee, sire." And with a finger to his unseen hat he was gone.

"Now, my man, I gather you have arrows for sale?"

"I may know who has them, sire." Steven beckoned the barmaid and she put before Thomas a flagon of the best ale. Steven placed in her hand some coin as then she waltzed upon her way with her jug slopping. Up went the flagon, like the fall of water into a pond went the ale.

"Look, Thomas, I wish no harm upon any man in this bargain, all of interest to me are the arrows, for I am duty bound to purchase such as soon as may be. I ask you to please bring this matter to light so I may return to my other duties. What say you, Thomas?"

"I say, sir, may God be with you if you deceive me, for many friends I have who will look upon such an act with glum sight, and they will not rest until all is wiped from the slate … I have the arrows."

"Good, and what will be the cost to me?"

The flagon was downed and the lips wiped with his hand's back, a sly look about the place he gave, more to toy with the price he may be able to get for the stash than to see if he was being watched. "Twenty-five pounds is the price, with no quibbling."

"I have no argument with that figure, and to show you of my good faith I will pay you thirty pounds, but I must see the arrows before any money is given, for bent or broken arms would be of no use. Further, to make all truths known to you before we continue, I am an army officer and there are two more officers in our party, also we have a cart and three soldiers."

"I do not like the army being involved in this."

"What say you then that only I and the three soldiers meet with you. Will that make things less fearful for you?"

"I am fearful to be of truth."

"But, Thomas, if you wish to sell these armaments you will either be selling to an army or to rogues, and I tell you there is less to fear from me than should be feared from the others, do you not think so?"

"Very well, I will sell to you." He spat upon his hand, as Steven did likewise, and 'twas clasped together, the bargain sealed. "Meet me in the forest at the Trent where it passes under the bridge at the cross … Do you know of this place?"

"Yes, I know this place, but I will be carrying the crown's monies, and so we must have a hostage to secure our safety, for the darkness of the woods could bring us much grief and we would be easy prey for robbery."

"To show my good faith, I will let my loved wife ride with you, for a token more valuable I have not. I have seen your cart, also I have seen the people you describe, and I know you speak to me the truth, and so I will ask her to go to you straight. We will meet then one hour from now, at the bridge forest."

"Good. Thank you, Thomas."

"Aye, sir." He left hastily, still with worried features, for it seemed this was not his usual trade and it bore upon him heavily.

Steven returned to the cart and relayed his converse with the waiting party. "He was very much edgy, and I had to promise him that only the three soldiers and myself were to meet with him, but he has given us a hostage to show his pledge in this matter, that being his good wife, and one can give no more than that ... She should be here shortly. The price paid was thirty pounds; a good price, do you not think?—even if they are our own arrows."

"Yes, Steven, the price is well, and to make such an amount of arrows again would be too far from our reach, for soon I think we shall see Richmond. But be with care in your endeavour, for the dark forest hides many things."

The small lady came to the cart, a scarf covered her head, a black dress of worsted cloth and a white apron she wore. A young wife, a devoted wife was she, who would do all for her husband who loved and protected her, and she knew he would let no harm befall her.

"Excuse me, sir, my name is Jemma Smith. I believe I am in your entrustment for a while."

"Yes, Jemma. My name is Steven Moran; I am an officer in our Majesty's army, and I will treat you with the utmost respect and care." He offered the slight lady his hand as if she were a gentlewoman and helped her into the cart.

"Thank you, sire," she quietly said as she sat upon the board; the two soldiers sat with their backs to her as they steadied the horse. Steven and the sergeant mounted their horses, and the party gently sidled out of the market square and headed for the bridge at the river Trent. The officers watched them as they went from their sight, and then left to wait at the tavern for their return.

The travel was at a steady pace as it left the crowded town and headed toward the thick forest that lay dark ahead. Soon to sight came the bridge as the officer and the sergeant rode close each side of the cart, with rocking and shaking along the rough track.

"Are you well, lady? for the road is rough," Steven asked his keep.

"Yes, my lord, I am well," Jemma answered as she clung as best she could to one side of the cart. Clatter they went over the old stone bridge, with its wooden track beneath the wheels rattling through the cart. They pulled to a stop as Thomas stepped before them from the thick bushes.

"Jemma, are you well?" was his first thought as he looked into the cart.

"Yes, my dear, I am in good stead."

"If you bring your cart this way, sire, you can view the arrows, and, if all is to your liking, we can finish our bargain."

Steven dismounted, and spake, as he did so, to one of the soldiers sat at the board, relaying his message in a loud tone, so that any who skulked about in the forest would know he came not to play games. "Soldier, get in the back with the lady; if there is trouble, you know your duty and on my command it will be done."

"Yes, sire," said he as he came from the board to place himself at the side of Jemma.

They moved off but a short distance, as Steven led his horse followed by the sergeant into the darkness of the forest. Brightness came within the dark as the sun came through the high branches above their heads, sometimes making it difficult to see, was it so bright. Came then the sight of the loaded cart; the canvas still covered its hide. In the clearing, five men standing around the booty came to view, all wary of the strangers Thomas had brought, as they looked at their coming with their black eyes, made so by the forest's light. No doubt the other fellows of Thomas's group, who had much interest in the outcome, came the thought to Steven's head. One of them with naught said pulled back the covering to show the bundled arrows stacked therein. Steven went closer so he may see that which he had bargained for, and indeed saw that the arrows were in good readiness, just as fine as when they were stacked in the castle's armoury. He was looking to see if all the bundles were the same when, from behind him, a scuffle began. The sergeant, on seeing the goods were the ones stolen from the castle, had surprised Thomas and thrown him to the ground; astride him the soldier was reaching for his dagger to finish him off. Thomas shouted out for help, but as his friends made haste toward him, a cry of "Hold!" came from the other cart that still held all in sight; the soldier there had his knife at the throat of Jemma, and so the friends became as helpless as the newly-hatched bird. Steven had turned and in quickness threw himself upon the sergeant, and was able to knock him over and hold him down as he was about to vent his justice upon Thomas.

"You—quickly—hold him down!" called Steven as two of Thomas's friends came running over to assist their leader and fell upon the soldier, who, now pinned, lay helpless, another chick in the nest. Steven was upped. "Leave her!" he shouted to the other soldier who still had his blade to the throat of Jemma, and though he seemed unwilling to do so, he released her and sheathed his blade. "Are you in any distress?" asked Steven as he went over to see if Thomas was injured, who sat upon the leaf-covered ground, his hands were clasped about his knees and was still recovering from the skirmish.

"No, I am well, much more than you, sire."

Steven looked at his arm, which was bleeding, being cut by the sergeant's dagger as they fell about, but he felt it not. "'Tis little, Thomas; I will tend it soon—"

"Jemma!" they both called, "Are you well?"

"Yes, I am well; do your business," she called.

"Pull him up," Steven spake to the two who were holding the sergeant, and dragged him up with heavy hand. "Sergeant, what were your orders upon this journey?"

The sergeant answered the question not, but then raged, shouted his anger. "The peasant is a thief and should die for his act, at the least we should take his hand!"

"Your orders were of no such act, and you disobeyed my order, now 'tis you who must face the punishment."

"He is but a swine, sire, and should be within his sty!" Shouting and still raged, the soldier vented his anger.

"At least he has some honour in his dealings; I would sooner have him stand at my back than you, sir. Bind his hands and tie him behind the gate. You—help them," Steven called the other soldier down from the cart, and they bound his hands securely and roped him to the back, as our officer, holding Jemma's elbow, helped her down from the cart, and talked to her as he walked her over to Thomas. "Are you harmed, Jemma?"

"No, sir, I am just very frightened, but I will be recovered in a moment."

"Do not be feared, lady. All is well." She was then in the arms of Thomas and felt at last safe. "I give both of you my deepest apology; you were to be treated with respect and I failed in my duty to do so."

"No harm was done, sire; 'twas one rogue who was evil, not you. Let us load now, for time is not idle." Thomas left his wife, who sat leaning against a tree still recovering from the excitement. "I will not be long, my dear … All is well. Do not fret."

Many hands, except the disgraced sergeants, began to load the bundles of arrows and in short time the task was done, as soon the canvas was covering the bundles within the army's wagon as unsighted they lay.

"Here is the agreed payment, Thomas." The thirty pounds were counted out into his hand, as the others looked upon the monies and counted along with each coin and note; his band looked with gleaming eyes and grins of black teeth at more monies than they had ever seen before. They grouped around Thomas as he divided it out amongst them, all with an equal share into each hand, and then to be stuffed carefully into their pouches. "Be careful with your monies," Steven reminded them. "Do not show it around, for there may be questions asked as to whereby you came to such a large amount. Beware the taxman and watch your backs, for there are thieves abound everywhere." All smiled for they did know the humour in Steven's remark.

Jemma was with them now, and without any ado she was pulling up the sleeve of Steven's shirt to care for his wound, though deep, was not bleeding too much. She pulled a piece of cloth from her clutch bag, wetted it from the horse's bucket, and then, with caring strokes, wiped clean the wound.

"'Tis not a serious cut, sire, but it should be wrapped when you return to your camp."

"Thank you, Jemma," Steven replied whilst his sleeve was pulled down with gentle care, as some of the blood she wiped from the cloth, and then fastened it with the ties. Thomas then lifted his Jemma into the cart, as the others of his band climbed on also. Steven put his hand forward to shake the hand of Thomas; a most unusual act from one of a rich, privileged family. He with great pride trying to be chivalrous; the other, a peasant, trying to survive in the world of nobility, to have as much dignity as he was able. They both felt that there was some small bond between them, but neither knew what 'twas. The hand that Thomas went to shake was strong but pale with clean nails and no rough skin or warts. The gold ring showed from the white flesh with the initials: S. M. The hands were shook with the strong grip of friendship in this uneven world, and naught was spake as Thomas climbed onto the board seat.

"Goodbye, Jemma," Steven spake as he stood by the cart where sat the good and courageous wife.

"Goodbye, sire; 'tis not often one finds kindness and chivalry in one person, but you are such a person. Hold it with courage, for 'tis a precious thing, and kindness is to the like of throwing a ball against a wall." And the wise words and the cart trundled away to their abode.

The cart of the army slowly pulled to a stop in the square of the marketplace, which was even more of jumble with bodies than when they left. Steven left the two soldiers sitting upon the board, with the sergeant, bound, sitting in the back with the bundles of arrows beneath the canvas, like the sack of grain, lumpy and uneven. Went Steven through the beggars, the thieves, the shopkeepers, the jesters, and the swaying stalls to come to The White Horse. A-shouting and a-singing came to his ears as he entered and made to the taproom; his fellow officers he spied sat cornered awaiting his showing. They beckoned to him as their eyes met.

"How went it, Steven?"

"All went well; the barter was thirty pounds, and here is the remainder,"—which he placed within the hand of the guard officer, who quickly had it stashed within his pouch to return to the bookkeeper. "We do have one small problem though; I regret to say our sergeant in the midst of the situation did not remain calm, and in doing so disobeyed my orders and had to be restrained."

"We will charge him upon our return to the castle but for now a flagon for you, my friend, you have done well." The ale was poured for Steven, who drank it down with ne'er a breath, so much of thirst was he. They gathered themselves and left the inn together, making way to the waiting cart and the riderless horses. They were soon mounted and in short time climbing the gate road to the castle. They entered into the courtyard where much activity was underway, and the feeling within the returning party was of the impending undertaking. They did not dismount, but rode to an old wooden door, which was being used to display all orders that were issued, and there, nailed atop the old papers, displayed was the latest command: at six of the clock upon this day of the nineteenth of August, fourteen hundred and eighty-five, all nobles and officers are to assemble in the great hall. They looked at each other in anticipation that the awaited battle was at last coming about. Then they went their different ways to perform different duties. The sergeant was placed in one of the castle's cells to await the military hearing that would be brought against him. If found guilty, which in this case was certain, he would be subject to twenty lashes of the whip, and reduced to the rank of the common soldier. The arrows were unloaded into the armoury to bring the quantity to the written amount of the inventory, the horse was settled within the stables, and the cart returned to its place. At last, all the buying and bartering was done, and 'twas the time come for soldiery and the journey to war's endeavour.

Chapter Thirteen.

Two-Headed Cow.

The time had tripped to the sixth hour past noon. The officers were spruced and dressed, ready for the meet. The nobles, all fussed over and preened, stood awaiting the hour, with the servants still hovered around them, never to be finished. And then, as from some unknown signal, they all moved as one to the great hall, with mumblings and laughter drifting about. Some streamed from the officers' quarters, some from private rooms; others came down the wide stairway from their chambers close to the king. The hall was soon filled with all who were beholden to Richard, as then a murmur seemed to rise from the far of the hall, giving notice of his presence, and as he came close to the table set there, "My lord … My lord," could be heard as each paid their respect as the king passed by them. He came with proud step to the head of the table, with all his people before him and with all eyes upon him.

"Gentlemen," loudly he spake so that even those at the far reaches of the hall could have no doubt about the words that were drifted . "Time is nigh for us, and word has come that Richmond has landed his armies at Milford Haven but four days past." Some low rumblings could be heard about, for no one, not even Richard, could have predicted such a place for Richmond to start his enterprise. "And, is duly making his way to do battle with us at some close-by field. It is we who must lay the place for this battle and not for that tyrant Richmond to choose. He has some days of travel before him, which gives us time to ready for him in a most deadly vein. We must choose a place that is the most suitable for our plans, and, in doing so, we must bear in mind the prospect of rainy weather, for the sayers have received many signs that such may befall the land in the coming weeks. It has been suggested to me of a suitable place and from what I have been told of the lay, and of the wetness that may be upon us, it seems a most royal arena: the field known as Bosworth is the chosen place. The maps of the area are displayed here upon the table before me." He waved his hand across the table to express more regality to the words he spake. "If anyone has any knowledge of the named place, and if indeed anyone knows the lay of the common, I would be pleased if you would speak with me, for all trifles that seem of little use may add much to that which we know of this place."

The king stepped away from the table to let any who wished to view the maps to do so, and indeed a crowd did gather about to do such; shoulder rubbed against shoulder as the maps were poked and the details pointed out from one to another. Some of the generals came to converse with Richard as the meeting became more informal, they posing many questions to their leader that troubled their minds. Of what number was the approaching army? How many were mounted? How many archers were in their command? But little more could the king relay at this time, for the messenger's arrival was still awaited, and was little known when next he would show his face. "We still await such news, my friends; we must be patient and gather ourselves to full readiness so we may end this insidious act against us."

An officer made his way from the table, where he had been viewing the maps that were laid there, and made through the gathering of generals to the place where stood the king. "Sir," he saluted in coming close to Richard. "My lord, I was born at Litchfield, which lies close to Bosworth Field, and over the years have visited the common, as both man and boy, many times; I have indeed ridden across and all about the area of your fancy, and I know well the lay of the land at that place."

"Good. Come, lad, show me upon the map all you know of these fields." He took the officer by the arm as if he were some long-forgotten friend who had returned to the king's fold, and urged him through the parting group to return him to the table and the maps that lay shuffled there. "Show me all you know of this place." The maps were looked over by the officer one after the other, until he came to the one that was the most meaningful to him; he stretched flat its curling edges and gazed upon it most carefully. "Are there any wooded areas where the trees and bush are thick upon the common?"

"Yes, sire, there are." The king passed the readied quill to the officer and beckoned him to mark the places where lay the lots. He marked three large areas of trees, as the king peered over him to see where he had made his mark, and seemed to be pleased at the placings.

"Are there any ponds or streams?" he added to his searchings.

"There is a stream, sire, but far north to the edge of the common and does not run through it; there are no ponds there."

"About hills or valleys?"

"Not to my recall, sire; as I remember, all was of fare flat, a meadow of short grass, for many goats at times do graze there but do so mainly in the late spring."

"The soil—what is the soil?—do you know? Did you ever ride when the conditions were wet?"

"Sir, I cannot say of the soil, but in the time of rain, the water laid about in puddles, and 'twas slip under the horse's hooves, making it difficult to turn the steed quickly."

"Sounds like the clay to me, for the water will not soak away. Thank you, my man; your words have brought good service to our plans."

"Thank you, sire. I am always at your command." He saluted his king and then drifted off amongst the gathering to his group of fellow officers, they pleased that one of their kind was able to contribute something more to the plans being formed.

"Gentlemen," the king interrupted the room full of murmurings. "Time is that you must organize your separate duties, and make ready for the noon hour upon the morrow, for that is the hour when we will depart upon this most royal of battles. I will have more reports by the time of our depart, which you will be made aware of … Oh, I must add before I depart your company, that I was most pleased to hear that we had retrieved all the bundles of arrows that were recently stolen from our armoury." A little smile he showed of his guile as he left his place, to let all know that very little escaped his knowledge, and to remind all in their dealings that spies were about everywhere, and mostly for the king were they.

Ordered for a duty that eve by a secretive meeting with Richard, two of his personal guard were given the task to move a number of wooden boxes in a manner most discreet, to be undertaken when darkness fell about the castle's walls, when all was a stilled night. One of the officers was Steven Moran; chosen often for the service he did render to his king with such devotion and honour, he was at the right hand through intrigue and through war. They had been taken by Richard himself at an earlier time to his locked storage, and had relayed to the officers the four large boxes that were the subject of the matter. The night had come as they waited within the darkening chamber; the boxes they stared at through the bright and now the dark. The contents, within the oak with its royal crest upon the side, was not known to them at this time, except in the thoughts of the two officers, who had sure ideas of what those four black boxes held, but one dare not whisper such to the other, only to see in each other's eyes the glint of knowing. Though 'twas dark about and not one thing stirred, thoughts of a spy's ear to the wall would keep them in silence. Told they to bury the boxes at the back of the storage where the horse feed was stacked. "Do you know of this place?" the king had asked the officers, who at that time stood before him. "Yes, sire, we know of the place where the feed is kept." Then they had been pledged under all secrecy and solemn oaths to perform the duties so entrusted to them.

With much vigilance and care, carrying one box at a time, they toted the locked cargo close to the shadowed walls, taking ways about to keep themselves out of any eyes' reach, and to lay them secreted within the horse feed. With the last box they carried, they brought with them two shovels, then with the closed doors at their backs, they dragged away the feed that lay stacked against the back wall to clear the ground underfoot, caring not for the rats that scurried from their boots. The floor was of soil; dry and dusty, it crumbled as they dug in their shovels. Only a little soil had they moved when the strike of rock clinked their shovels; they looked at each other in the gloom of the chamber, as they, upon their knees, began to dig with their hands, to pull out many stones the size of a turnips; they pulled and tugged out all they could find and then began digging with their shovels once more, until the clang and clink again shook their arms, and they had to pull once more at the stones that seemed to have no edge to hold on to. They had little light to see their task, except now and again the moon would shine its light through bars of the door. Came the time, after much toil, the soil-banked hole was seen large enough for the boxes, which they slowly placed in—stamping and jumping upon them to push them as far down as they were able, filling them in with the loose soil, and then some stones, and continuing such until 'twas more than full, as then they stomped it down again, jigging about as if they were in some tribal dance, to bring it to firmness, and to make it look as 'twas before they scratched its grime. They stacked the rocks they had left over neatly in the dark corner; then, bundling the straw within their arms, they placed it back from whence it came, and all seemed to be untouched and showed as 'twas in the earlier light. Somewhat worn from their labours, they rested, leaning upon the stone wall to regain some strength.

"What do you think about the boxes, Steven?" came the question from the other officer.

"My friend, I would rather not speak of such, but I believe our thoughts are much the same—'Tis the kings doings and no man will cross him."

"Yes, Steven, 'tis best it be forgotten this night." They were now recovered from their task, and through the cool night they drifted back to their quarters, the guards still not about, for some orders had taken them to other tasks for a while. Soon they were at sleep with thoughts of the morrow: the rattle of metal, the smell of horse, the sound of the pipes.

Henry Tudor, the Earl of Richmond, the usurper of Richard's throne, the most hated enemy, was upon his journey to the place where would come the battle. He had left Harfleur after his time was spent in Burgundy. And had been, all his life, dealt the hand of misfortune, always under some oppression from one source or another. His enterprise to take the crown seemed to be of little value, for he had no monies and had to rely upon other parties to finance his lifestyle. No power had he and found it most difficult even to be employed; his sway at court did not exist, his past reputation was that of a philanderer and waster, he was much disliked, and lastly, above all of this, he had but little right to the throne. His mother was Margaret Beaufort, Countess of Richmond, and the wife of the Lord Thomas Stanley. Henry, her son, had been exiled to Brittany for his activities against the crown, but he was in constant contact with his mother, who indeed was much involved in his act of gaining the throne. In Henry's name she was trying to call the communities of England to revolt against the king. The King of France was helping Henry in his endeavours but had little faith in the outcome, though did supply him with arms and some military and some small monies, for he did not want to extend his treasury more than was needed. But if the unforeseen did happen and Richmond was victorious, then France would be closer to its goal of invading England, a dream the kings of France had long savoured.

He had sailed upon the calm sea the morning of the first day of the month of August, with three thousand Normans, rogues and vagabonds — the king was pleased to be rid of this soldiery. But Richmond had more support than could be gleaned from afar, for Richard, so involved in other occupations, had not guarded his Realm against the rising Lancastrian party. He sailed with more might than anyone could see, except himself. Horses, arms, and food all dipped and swayed upon the tiny vessels as they crossed the Channel. Then, with the white cliffs showing as England came to sight, he changed his course and swung his boats to westward, around Land's End he went, and then to steer north again up the coast of England to the land of Wales, and made to the harbour at Milford Haven. Taking them six long days at sea in the small boats, causing much sickness from the rolling sea, the weather had changed from calm to heavy during the last hours before they anchored. The land sighted upon that sixth day was a joyous sight to the water-washed soldiers. They stepped ashore upon legs that were still rolling with the ocean and swayed them about like the wind-blown corn.

Richmond had landed, and was soon greeted by the Welsh lords. Large, hairy men came toward him with animal skins to clothe their bodies, with swords tied upon their belts and clutching spiked chains in thick hands.

"Sire," they greeted Richmond with as much reverence as could be expected from the Welsh, who held little truck for Englishmen and less for Frenchmen. The Welsh leaders were schooled in the language of the Realm and were able to converse with Richmond. He shook their hands one after the other, dismissing the odours drifting to his nostrils, and the lice and fleas about them. They all moved to the village, passing many small abodes upon the way, with women and children peering out from the dark holes to see the strange people who had come, dressed so brightly as gods they seemed, with a strange tongue that bore no rhyme. To the main hut the party came; large tree trunks and thick branches were its walls, all tied together with some kind of hemp, and then the roof, with thick branches across and woven together with the supple willow, to be covered with grass sod, making a hill-like mound. An opening at the front was the only entrance, and 'twas very low and narrow, making it most difficult for any who could bring arms against them to enter, for they would have to crouch down and turn sideways, and would be in no position to wield a sword. Animal skins swung over the hole to keep out the cold winds that seemed to be always blustering through the hills and valleys of this Wales.

They entered into the chamber, which seemed like a warm cave. A crude, rustic table, made with little skill from tree trunks and logs, hacked to a near flatness upon the top, centred the floor, and could well seat a hundred warriors. Some benches were placed around it, each made from two stumps with a split log atop. An open fire blazed at one end with its sparks spitting about as the smoke drifted upwards to a hole in the roof, with its black swirl lingering there, waiting to escape. The floor was of dirt, with rats and mice scurrying about with their fleas in the blackened place. Only a few pitch lamps were lit and with the fire's glow 'twere all that broke the dark in the dim hut. But soon the eyes of the comers mellowed to the darkness as all could see the activities that were about. In the fire's light could be seen womenfolk toing and froing, plying the embers with fresh wood and peat, the sparks spitting and flying from the new feed. Some brightness came from the licking flames, and Henry could see the women stirring their bubbling pots, dressed as in rags with animal skins draped over their shoulders, the bobbing heads covered with a scarf or a cap tied beneath the chin. He could see they wore no shoes, and their faces glistened, blackened from the fire's smoke with their hot-rosed cheeks spying through the black. They bustled about, some staring, some just glancing at the menfolk about, and chattered in their archaic language that the Englishmen understood naught, the talk now and again pierced with a strange laughter, sounding as if even the laughter was in a foreign tongue. The white and black of their teeth seemed to show in the firelight as Henry looked about, a pile of skins upon one side caught his gaze as it seemed to have some stirrings within them; 'twas the place where they all slept, close together they laid with the warmth from one body to the other keeping away the cold of the night. The stirrings showed to be one of the womenfolk with two of the warriors, showing little shame as they frolicked about in the tumbling skins, with grunts and groans as of a farmyard.

A shallow trench lay at the other side with a most odorous stench drifting from it, scraps of maggot-ridden meat, green pieces of bread, dead rats, all were thrown into this hole, as well 'twas used by all to urinate and to excrete until 'twas full, then 'twas covered over and another was then dug. The mangy dogs were running and sniffing about, chasing rodents and any other thing that was game, barking and howling incessantly but to yelp and whine oft as they were given a goodly kick, or a crack with a staff as revenge was taken upon the hound, but no matter how many times they were to suffer it made little difference to their continued song. Naked children it seemed ran with the dogs, dirty as mudfish; some ran, some still could only crawl, all in the dirt with the rat droppings and the grime, laughing and shouting in their games, then tears and yells would come about as disagreements came to show, or they had taken a swat from someone who had heard enough of their screaming games. The flies and mosquitoes buzzed their song around the heads of all, living splendidly upon the rotting mire in the trench and the ripe flesh. All this activity and noise was within the timbered walls of the hut, but then from the outside could be heard the beginnings of chant and drum beating, as the Welch warriors gathered outside the chief's hut, the pounding came and the Englishmen knew it would not stop, and would only get louder and faster as time wore on, dulling the brain with its enchanted rhythm. The animal warriors, the pagans of the hills, rearing for battle and looking for some bloody act to calm their wrath.

Food was brought to the table by the womenfolk and placed before Henry and the Welch lords; though of no appetizing fare, Henry, in respect for his allies, had to eat heartily with his lords of the hills. The stew-like victuals were slopped into the waiting bowls, the ale was poured, and the bread was broken. As they started to eat with wooden spoon and licked fingers, the lords ravaged the bowls before them; Henry, though, took a more cautious approach, but with a spooned mouthful, a bite of bread, and a sup of ale, found to his surprise the food was most favourable, but his mind did not dwell upon the ingredients and to what was caught to fill the pot.

The victuals were ended soon, and then, amid the wind-letting and belching, the leaders started their conference. Henry stood so he may be seen to the far of the table where darkness hung its shade.

"My lords, I have with me monies to wage both you, my lords, and your warrior bands. Also, I bring food and supplies enough for ten more days, so we will not have to scavenge for bread and ale. I believe our envoys discussed such things with you, my lords?"

"Yes, sire, that is what we agreed—a set amount of monies and victuals for the journey." One of the council answered for all to Henry's query, and they were satisfied with the dealing that had been proffered.

"Good," Henry nodded to one of his officers, who placed upon the table a tied bag, singing a jingle as it sat heavily before them. The monies were paid, as the leader untied the hemp and tipped out the contents a-rattle upon the dim table. Eyes saw it and hands squeezed it and let it fall from high to rattle its song once more; they were pleased with the sight and that the words proffered by an Englishman had been kept. 'Twas not all true that had been spake by the sayers, with the stories they told by the fires that crackled in the dark night, of mistrust and betrayal. "I wish on the morrow to move away from here, for I must engage Richard as quickly as I am able; he has had more time than I would wish to give him to set himself at the ready."

"And, of his whereabouts, sire, do you know where he is camped?" The Welsh leaders wished to know how long they would have to march before they could avenge themselves and spill some English blood.

"He is at the moment camped at the castle of Nottingham, and seemingly the place he chooses to do battle will not be many days march from there."

The Welsh lords went out from the meeting place and upon their sight the chanting of the wild men came to a stop, and tranquil came o'er the land once again so they may hear the voices of their lords, as they spake in the tongue of the Welsh with its lilting tones. They were told of the monies that would be paid to them, of the victuals promised, of the rewards from the battle to be gleaned, of weapons, of horses, of loot that would spread upon the field of battle; rings of gold, tokens of much value, coats and boots would all be theirs. Came then wild cries with shields and swords raised on high, as they greeted that which had passed their ears, and with great noise they rose—a far more agreeable army than the one that had deserted Buckingham. 'Twas called out to them that upon the morrow they would make to their field of prizes, and to prepare themselves to march for three to four days to reach the meet of their battle. The Welch lords then prepared to return to the hut, as the drums and the pipes started up once more to bring forth their chanting rhythms, the sound again soon drumming their ears and to make the dogs howl once more. Henry wished a good eve to his Welsh lords, and, with his officers, made his way to retire for the night in his tent that was raised upon some drier ground.

The dawn came at last to leave the restless night behind them. The drums seemed to have not stopped for one minute and were still droning at dawn's light. Henry and his officers ate their own victuals that morning, as they sat about in their leader's tent, eating their bread with cooked bacon dripping upon the top, and drank the hot mulled ale that shivered them as it cut into the coldness of their bodies.

"I feel, my friends, that from the Welsh we should muster from one to two thousand warriors." Richmond was speaking of tactics as they were finishing their victuals. Most of his officers, and himself, had little or no experience in the art of warfare, and were relying far more upon the numbers of soldiers that would do battle for them, than for any plan they had of tactics. "Though these Welsh are peasant-soldiers they may cause some terror to Richard, and at least they are expendable like fodder to the horse. Our three thousand Bretons should show some fight, for us as well as the many Englishmen who will join us, for to the teeth they are filled with this Richard. Also, we will gain even more of an advantage, for there will be other forces who will join us as the time nears; they not yet seen by ourselves or by Richard. So the least we have will be of five thousand men, and even to six thousand."

"Do you know, sir, of the numbers of Richard's army?" One of his officers asked the needed question, as another of the other officers took it upon himself to answer by numbers of what force Richard commanded.

"Sir, if I may state the numbers I have gleaned from information passed about, it seems that Richard will have one thousand mounted soldier, one thousand archers, and one thousand common soldiers, which would bring his army to three thousand standing army; this does not include they who may join him, for Norfolk has fifteen hundred at his disposal and the Lord Stanley having two thousand men—"

"Do not count the armies of Norfolk and Stanley; he still only has three thousand under his command."

"Yes, sire, but we must consider them for—"

"Concern yourself not about those two nobles, for they will make no play for Richard upon the day," Richmond interrupted the officer once more, now to silence and to his seat he sat. For the first time came to light some plot against the King Richard. "More will be to our knowledge as we closer get to the day of our fates. We have been engaged in a long journey and it has been wearisome, but soon will come the fruits of our labours, and at last to rid ourselves of that child-killer that puts upon himself the title of king."

With spirits high they left their tent, and all mounted their horses that awaited them, and took themselves into the fog that drifted about as they went on to the moors. Naught yet could be seen and only the rattling of their trappings made it known they were about. The horses drifted through the mist that lay, like some Greek stallions stepping through the high clouds in godly fashion. As they came to higher ground they began to see but six paces before them. They rode in their light armour as no danger yet was to threaten them. The foggy dew wetted all they wore and dripped from them, running down upon the already-wet horses and onto the muddy 'neath. All about them, but not seen, were other horses rattling along their path.

The drumming and chanting came to their ears as closer they came to the Welsh who were ahead of them. Then heard the shouting of the Welsh lords came calling in their Gaelic tongue, and bringing their followers to some form of rank. For the present, Henry's horses were led by the stable lads so none could wander off into the mist of the moor, and become easy meat for any who wished to prey upon them. Henry was to lead the army, but until they had passed by the thick curtain draped over them, the Welsh lords led, as the farmer who knows where every stone and every fallen tree lies, they knew the valleys, and it seemed even with closed eyes they would be able to smell their way. All had left the village below, as the horses' hooves dug into the soft ground and made the track all of slop.

The tents of Richmond were being taken down, and the carts would soon follow the churned way before them, carrying the tents, their supplies, and many arms. They came steady from the village with children clinging to the back of the wagons, dragging their feet upon the mud afoot, the dogs barking and yapping as they ran beside the wheels, needing to join the game, but soon all were left behind as the carts moved on to follow the sound of the drums that beat from far ahead of them. The army moved across the hills for more than two hours with only the back of the soldier in front of each to be seen. On they went, the ghostly army, and then, like some saving beacon through the fog, came the bright-burning light of the sun breaking through the cloudy mist, slowly burning away the curtain that covered them like a cloak; then, as it lifted, first to be seen about them were the hills that showed, grass-covered and bright with sparkle from the sun and the clinging dew. Raggedly, Welsh came from their hovels to see the strange men with their strange language passing by, as they spied from the sides of the trail. Horses were not yet to be seen as the fog still drifted low and covered their bodies; only to be seen were the soldiers who rode upon their backs, rising now up and now down along the grey river, that was the army, as bobbing apples at the fair, ghostly and mystically they rode along. They rose from the wash of fog and came into the brightness that was close to the noon-hour sun, and as they came to the valley that pointed their way, so then did Henry of Richmond move to the lead, with his officers about him as he deemed it his rightful place, and as he did so he turned in his saddle to look to the rear, and could see the many miles of soldiery and wagons that trailed him, with some at the far distance still coming out of the low fog. Richmond seemed stirred by the vastness of his army, and the red-rosed banners that now showed waving high against the white clouds. And, as he looked forward again, he saw many more Welsh warriors coming in groups to join his force, more bent upon plunder and rape than any thought of a crown at stake. Oh, but were they Englishmen and not pagan savages that would come to his aid, were the thoughts of Richmond as he saw his army grow. But, no choice do I have, and if it means the crown, then so be it, for I would have dogs fight for me if it meant victory.

On they went, marching for a full three days through many towns and hamlets, all deserted except for barking dogs and howling wolves to greet them, as no one wished to be about when this army came with their mad Welshmen. All had fled to the woods, the farmers with their livestock, and the monks with their valuables, and there stayed until the army was about no more and they could return to their homes and monasteries. The wildmen, though, were not pleased, for there was no looting or ravaging to appease them, leaving them in a sour mood and itching to do battle, as they reached the empty hamlet of Cannock, close to the last sighting they had received of Richard's position. The mass of Richmond's army were taken to rest at this place, stuped by ale and full of stomach, for they knew that in the next two days their fate would be written; but on this day they would not know how the pages would be writ, to whether be heroes or to be vanquished …

Richard, upon the morn of the twentieth of August, moved out from the castle of Nottingham. His well-trained soldiers left their camp filled with confidence; they were well-rested and were led by the most feared field general of all the land, a master of tactics and fearless in battle; no greater man could they have to lead them.

Cloudy was the day as they came down the hill from their camp, and soon made their way over the bridge at the river Trent to make their way to Leicester, along the old road still steady and level, that road the Romans had laid far back in another time. They reached soon their destination to make rest for the night, and saw the advanced party had raised Richard's tent to greet his arrival. In short time they were in the midst of their victuals, and talk around the table was of tactics and news of Richmond's forces.

"My soldiers," Richard spake to his officers who sat about the table, still eating and drinking but listening most intently to their leader. "Richmond has three thousand Bretons of good fight and they all are battle veterans.

The rest of his force is of Welshmen, that rabble of savages that number two to three thousand, who can be routed most quickly with our arrows. I meet soon with Stanley to acquaint him of our tactics, and to place before him the time and the place we wish him to join the fray. The common where we will defend our crown is flat but prone to mud during heavy rains, which will be part of our plan, for we will be a stationary force as the ground dictates. The soldiers with pikes will be at the first line, behind will lay the cavalry, and aback will be our archers, who will be our main offence. We will set all so that we are two hundred paces from the copse behind us, where will lay our ally, Stanley; in secret will he be until the horn be sounded whence we will divide in two, making for him a tunnel to break out with his fresh soldiers and cavalry; when he passes through, our mounted will join him to rout the enemy, and put an end to the bloody mess. No breaking of ranks must occur before the horn is sounded; this is most urgent to our plan. Finally, I repeat once more: Do not move from your rank!"

"Yes, sire," came the reply from about as all seemed pleased with the play of the battle and felt victory creeping their bones. The day slowly faded as sleep fell upon the waiting camp, all secure and to rest easy as the guards about watched vigilantly over them.

The morn of the twenty-first day of August broke to the readying army, soon clattering through the narrow streets of the town, in the cloudy, broken shine of the sun, to make with steady pace to the common at Bosworth. Through small hamlets and villages they went; still the sounds of cheers and jeers came as they rumbled by the sparse watchers, and on down the narrow tracks made by the wheels of the farmer's cart, across narrow stone bridges and across wooden bridges, the clatter dinning the waters below, as disturbed from their tranquil the ducks that busied themselves there began to flutter about, squawking and quacking until the noise had gone, and they were able to suckle the weeds once more, with tails bobbing and their pink-webbed feet splashed about. The woods thickened as Richard led his army on with many more clouds about that dulled and dampened the day, and with the sun it seemed not wanting to look upon the bloody outcome of the next days. The black trees were close to them with the branches scraping as they passed through, for a mile 'twas such as the bright armour and the banners carried broke the dim light. The sound of their march echoed back and forth as they broke into an open meadow; the corn shone its yellow heads as it swayed in the August day, then to ride on to the fields of barley awaiting the scythe. As they passed it by many thought of who would be left to eat the bread that the corn would give, and who would drink the ale from that barley that rustled about the fields of England. On they marched until the late afternoon, coming then to spy the common of their fate; and, as they marched into the grass, found that 'twas steady underfoot and not soft or muddy but firm pasture.

To Richard, all looked as it had been described to him; the ground as yet had not taken much rain and stood most suitable. He sat his horse alone, well ahead of his officers, who awaited him as he viewed the field; for a full five minutes did he look it over, from front to back, from side to side, and to then slowly gait back to his waiting officers. He stopped before them and pointed to the positions where he wished his troops to be placed, and to the place where his army should be camped. He viewed too the wooded place at his back, and let it be known that the camp should be one thousand paces from the woods to the fields beyond, so there would be little interference with the gathering of Stanley's soldiers.

"I leave you to your duties, as I will await at the abbey of Mirival for this night."

"Yes, sire," the officers acknowledged Richard as he rode away with a group of his personal guard, to pray and make ready for the morrow. The officers left at the field went about their duties to prepare the battle site. They dismounted and went forward to the area that had been pointed to them, they followed by foot soldiers, who carried poled flags and heavy wooden mallets that would be used to mark the lines for the soldiers; straight lines would be set to the woods each side where no danger would come, for all that would come would be ahead. They began knocking in the markers, but after a while stayed their mallets to the sound that came of a distant horn from the far field. Then, into view came six horsemen where the leader could be seen clearly, as he showed more regal than the others beside him. Richard's officers formed themselves into a defensive position, with hands placed upon their sword hilts at the ready as they looked and waited. Closer they came with banner held high, and sighted was the Red Rose at flutter and flap, as they galloped forward to Richard's officers standing ready. The lieutenant went forward from the others to face the newcomers, ready for a fight if need be, until he saw they were not armed and was but a delegation, and indeed headed by Richmond himself, coming to make some compromise with Richard no doubt.

"Sire,"—the lieutenant was most chivalrous to the earl.

"My good man," the earl returned with a nod of his head in some respect. "I wish to council with Richard. Can you arrange such a meet?"

"Yes, sir, I can, if you will just bear with me for a moment whilst I dispatch a rider to inform the king of your coming." The lieutenant spake to one of his other officers, who, with haste, mounted his horse and rode off at a fast gait to inform his leader of the coming of the earl, Henry of

Richmond. Richard's lieutenant mounted his horse and led the party at a slower gait toward Richard's place of rest, leaving the other officers there to carry out the given orders. The party passed through the wooded area and through the camp that was being prepared for the night, and in doing so Henry discreetly looked about to glean some idea of the military force there, and if it indeed was paired with their own information. They came very soon to the abbey at Mirival, which was almost in sight of Bosworth Field, and tied up their horses to the ringed post there. Richard stood awaiting them, forewarned by his officer of the guard. Standing was he in the receiving hall, in that place where the monks would meet their spiritual leaders. Stood he there in all his majesty to council with the usurper of his crown. In they came all of bustle with their cloaks flowing about their necks, revealing the polished armour that gleamed beneath, and the glimpse of the Rose of Lancaster, bloody red and not a pleasing sight to Richard.

"Your Majesty," Henry bowed his respect as he spake, and followed all the same by the others of the delegation.

"Sire," answered Richard with no movement except for his lips, most aloof in his dealing. "And, pray, what is your presence here that I am disturbed?"

"Your Majesty, we wish to bring to you some way that we may stop the morrow's bloody day."

"And so what do you offer me to do such?"

"If you surrender all your forces to our cause, we will bring no reprisal to you or your dearest ones, you will keep all your lands and properties, and all your treasures, and you would be welcome at court."

"Sir, I will offer you the same, except for one thing, in that I will firstly take your head. Do you think I would believe all that drivel you honey about? Your words are liken to the rain that falls into the stream, which can be seen most fine and clear as it falls, but once it hits the water it is as if it 'twas never there."

"There is no council on this matter then, sir?"

"No, sire, there is not. I do not council with usurpers and rogues. I wish you to depart with haste, for you will need all the time you can muster to bring your army to any threat upon this crown—but then a thousand years would still be not enough."

Henry bowed without further word, turned with his officers, and, with capes swirling and heavy-booted tread, left the meet through the door they had entered with some hope, but naught did show this day. They mounted their horses and were escorted back from whence they came. The officers of Richard, and some soldiers of little rank who worked the field, watched as the six riders galloped over the common, the rear of the horses bumping up and down the riders as they misted out of sight; the last to show was that rosed banner on high, 'twas then gone.

Richard was alone in the abbey in prayer at the high cross; the sun, on its down, left its last light breaking the dark within, then 'twas gone, bringing the candles now the only light to view aught. Soon his homage done, he left the holy place and made his way to his chambers, where stood at wait for him Norfolk, still muddy and dishevelled. Richard's eyes brightened as at last he saw an ally of his own virtue.

"Norfolk!" he spake as he embraced his comrade, for it had been many a day since they had met, and quickly the time for battle was upon them.

"My lord, are you well? … May I be of any help?" Norfolk asked the frowned Richard.

"I am well, sir, but of troubled mind, though your coming has lifted me heartily. My mind is filled with things that are but mine, and help can only come from myself. I pine most desperately for the sight of Elizabeth and have never been struck so before. Knowing she is in the same state as I twists me cruelly. Then there is the morrow's confrontation, which disturbs me greatly, the fact that I keep hearing reports of some major force from the northern counties, that in this matter has some great play. The men I hoped to join us as we marched has proved meagre, and I fear 'tis all to do with the rumours that abound, that the princes are not dead but alive and awaiting their time to reclaim the throne, which could be disastrous for whoever rules this land, for many would rise against the Realm and sidle up with the princes. When this battle is over I must once and for all end this false chatter, for this land will not rest until all are appeased. These are the things, my friend, that weigh heavily upon me and will do so for some time yet, and, as you hear my words, it is so spake that no one can bring to me any solace. No matter, Norfolk, what is to mind is how you fare, and how is your soldiery?"

"I, and my men, are ready, sire, and wait only for your command; we, all eager and for the crown."

"The battle plan still remains as you have viewed it, my friend, and all I expect of you is to bide upon my left flank until the sound of the horn, and then to bring your force upon Henry's men, which will, with Stanley's strike, be an end to that braggart."

"I will do as you command, my lord, and bring to you all you desire upon the morrow."

"Good, Norfolk. Be upon your way now and make the morrow your most blessed day."

"Aye, my lord." And with shook hands he left to his army at wait.

Richard, with much ale supped, slept most sound till the cock crow afar did awaken him. He looked from his small window and with face smirked saw the rain coming with steady force, as then he was washed and readied by his manservants. This day his battle armour cased his frame, this black metal that he had worn undefeated since donned. His helmet was placed upon his head and the field crown, gold and shining, was then fastened over his helmet. The vest, with the White Rose upon it, was pulled over his metal and tied secure with the blue ribbons. His black battle cape was tied about his shoulders to be tugged and straightened. All tucked and fussed, he was ready for Henry. Outside the abbey among the busied officers, he stepped upon the mounting stool and slung himself upon his charger, his great white steed of much affection, an animal of faithful deed to his master. He rode from the abbey with his personal guard at close ride, as they muddied their way through the rain, not yet heavy but drizzling lightly.

"Hold, hold!" one of the guards cried out, as a small dark shape came close to the party, bringing the ride to a stop with his call. "Move away, woman! Do you not know you are delaying the king!" Little could be seen, only the voice of the officer heard and then the dark shape spake her reason.

"Sir, I am a sayer from the village anon, and I wish most urgent to speak with his Majesty."

"We have no time for such. Move yourself away."

"Bring her forward, my man; let us hear what words the sayer speaks," Richard called, and waited for her to come close to him, his guards most vigilant, looking about for any intrigue that may come upon them. Richard's horse in its finery pawed at the ground anxious to be away.

The hag came close; with ragged clothes and limping leg she came, helped along by her gnarly staff, her back bent and her face hid by the draped hood of her black cape. "My lord, I come with dire happenings within the village yonder, for this very morning was born upon the church's meadow a cow, the cow 'aving two 'eads, its eyes—all four of them—searching about for some evildoings. My lord, 'tis an omen: do not go to battle this day, for the monster must be killed at midnight and in the darkness its parts scattered far so the evil cannot spread more. And, my lord, the cow was as white as snow—as white as the Rose of York. The signs speak, my lord; hold yourselves until the evil is scattered, and battle not this cursed day."

"I hear your warnings, woman, but this day is set and a two-headed cow will not delay it. Take your musings with you and upon the morrow you will see that this omen you bring is but idle prophecy, and but the ramblings of old women who have little else to occupy them. Go back to your hole and upon the morrow bring to me your falsehoods."

The hag shook her head and mumbling some ancient tongue hobbled off into the drizzled forest.

To their tent that stood at the battlefield they came; the commanders waiting there stood and greeted their leader as he dismounted. The King Richard and his guard went amongst them and made toward the field of battle to review the placings of his army; all were standing as ordered in the exact positions stated. With the drizzle dripping about them they stood, the mud drawing at their boots like the surgeon's leech; at each movement they made, deeper went the boot. The common soldiers stood at the fore, pikes at the ready, swords sheathed but close to hand. The cavalry stood next, with unsettled horses stomping upon the softened ground, and the mounted officers pulling upon the reins to steady their steeds; all in armour were they, rattling as kitchen pans swinging from their hooks as they itched for the fray. The archers stood aback the mounted horses, quivers full, bows at rest with the strings hanging loosely until ready for the strike. The rain falling upon them had turned heavy, but seemingly gave no discomfort to them, as all to mind was the coming battle, though throughout the knees quivered.

The eyes searched afar, but as yet no sign of Richmond showed. Messengers rode back and forth bringing news of the happenings that were out of sight. He was there on the far side of the field, and Norfolk had been seen close by, but as yet he was not in his position. Stirrings came from the far side of the common that brought to sight the army of Richmond, still draped in the misty rain and but ghostly shapes toing and froing, no doubt making ready his force and with some anguish trying to control the rebellious Welshmen, who, like the bridled horse, struggled to be free of any master and any command. They would be the first to test the metal of Richard's resolve, with their fearless rage and fatal acts, they would try to the full to bring fear to Richard and panic to those who barred their pass.

As was chivalrously apt, a delegation from Henry rode from his camp and slopped across the meadow with their leaders, as banners dripped the rain from the colours hanging; like the washerwoman's cloths, it flapped its best in the driving wet, as they came to Richard's appointed lot, and faced one of his commanders await.

"Good day, sire," came the voice of Henry's mouthspeak.

"Good day, sire," came the dripping reply.

"Our Henry wishes to offer a truce to your Richard in that he will be pardoned of all acts if he will abdicate his throne to our Henry, and all his armies will be given free passage away, under no abuse."

"I will relay your proposal to my king; if you would tarry for a moment whilst I convey your Henry's message, I will bring to you his answer in most haste." The officer turned his horse in the quagmire and rode toward Richard who stood awaiting this formality, which meant naught to either side, but had to be entered within the book of chivalry and taste, for neither wished to be seen as a barbarian. The message was given and the answer was received in but a short moment, and the officer was quickly back to face his counterpart. "Sire, my king, in much respect, declines the offer made to him."

"Thank you, sire, and may God be with you upon this day."

"And with you, sire." The party turned with the rain bouncing off their armour as they raced back as fast as the ground would bear, back to their leader to give the undoubted answer to Henry. The rain continued, the skies darkened, no brightness would fall this day upon the bloody encounter to come. The crows in their high perches looked down. All other birds that hovered about had flown, for did not they sense that this was one field not to be fluttered over this day? Only the evil one watched about from his lair … the devil … the only one that gleed at the sight that was to unfold.

Richard readied his officers to meet with Richmond, and as they did so and took their orders, the drums of the Welsh started their beat; far in the distance came the sounds, throbbing through the wet morn, reaching the ears of all who prepared at Richard's camp, reminding them all of the terror that these heathens could bring. Leaving behind the safety of their camp, Richard's delegation rode forth into the slop, hoping that Henry would have some control over the warriors who stamped and shouted in mad tones. They closed after a short while to the far as the drums came upon them loud, and the ground seemed to shake from the beat. Henry's party stood at wait before his army. The Welshmen were chanting loudly and began slapping their broadswords against their shields in rhythmic beat.

"Sire, I bring a message from my king, Richard," the officer spake his ordered lines before his adversary. "He wishes no battle with your Henry, and states that if your leader retires from this field of Bosworth he will allow all members of his force, and indeed Henry himself, to depart back to your ships in all safety, and that your Henry would, under oath, not avail his usurping tactics to cross our border for all time. He sends these words so that the bloodshed that will undoubtedly be thrust upon your Henry of Richmond may not come about."

"Sire, we will convey your message to our leader." Henry's officer turned his horse and made way to the field tent where awaited Richmond to listen to the hollow words. The words so labelled from Richard came from the officer. The head shook as the message was passed and the answer so given, as bowed went the officer back to Richard's party. "Our Henry thanks you for your most generous offer but reluctantly has to decline."

"Sir, then I will return to my master and relay to him your Henry's answer. The time of the battle has been deemed to be upon this midday. Will that be suitable for your Henry?"

"I, in confidence, do agree that noon would be a most suitable time to begin. I also understand your Richard will be taking a stationary position upon this day?"

"That is so, sir, as defenders of the crown our right to choose has been exercised."

"That is so, sire. I then wish you good day, and may death be quick." Away from the enemy came the last officer to ply for some peace upon the day, but to no avail came the quest, and all that was left was the day of trial to come.

Eleven of the clock came soon upon that twenty-second day of the month of August, of the year fourteen hundred and eighty-five. The last battle for the crown of England that would be fought upon the soil of England. The last battle that would see such chivalry, gone for all time. No more, because of this war, would the pledge of a knight be honourable, but would become shallow and without truth for deceit did show.

The drums and chanting became louder as the battle time came close.

"What of Norfolk?"—the king laying the question upon one of his scouts.

"Norfolk, my lord, has just reached his position and is now in concealment at our left flank."

"And of Stanley?"

"Stanley, sire, is not yet in his position, but is making his way quickly, from the north, and will be in his place most shortly—within the next hour." Richard glanced with somewhat of a querying look over the words that came to ear, that Stanley would be so late in his orders, and those words "From the north" that had so concerned him for many a day, but he quickly dismissed them from his head knowing that his most loyal friend would act with knightly honour, and would be at the ready when the call of the horn came.

"I will speak to my men now," Richard stated to one of his commanders, as he was lifted to his steed and made way from the battle tent toward the army's front, the ground slippery as his horse splattered mud about the legs of the officers who stood close. The heavy rain had stopped now, as only a light misty drizzle fogged the readied common. "My fellow soldiers," Richard started his speech to the dripping army before him, but saw no fire coming from their souls as they listened to such words he could bring to them. "This day will bring to us all much glory and fame, and for all time we will be shot of all usurpers who rage against us. If we are not victorious in our efforts then under the rule of this infamous Henry our days to death will be few. We will lose all we have gained in our prosperity, and we will lose all of the laws we have passed that made this great land a better place for all to live, the new laws, that have brought such goodness and fair treatment in the courts for all who dwell on this Isle, be they rich or be they poor. Now is the time to bring forth all the might we can muster so this day will end in our victory. Think all of your wives and children, and of your blessed England that we all must defend with all our force and bravery. Be strong and this day will be ours. Fight as if you are all kings and knights. Retreat not, and fight with honour, for this land that is ours, our native land that is the most sought place in all the world's kingdoms, for its riches and for its honoured people. May God be with you this day and to shine the bright sun upon you all, to warm your bodies and to make them feel no coldness and no despair, and to bring to you riches, more riches than dreams can hold. For our country … for God … for your king!" he called loudly now. His horse rising upon its rear legs as if scripted, Richard raised his glistening sword above his head and swirled it about in defiance of his enemy, rousing his troops to do battle with the ferocity he knew they held within their breasts. They, in that field of Bosworth, waved on high their weapons, and called out their allegiance to Richard's cause. The fife and drum started up its stirring tune in the drizzled air, as Richard took his place of command within his soldiers' wall. They made final their positions. The bowmen chose the arrows from their lot—the arrows that would be the first to strike the foe. Some licked the cold iron at the point of the shaft, for in doing so they knew it would fly clear and straight to its target—and strung their bows. All was ready as the drumbeat stirred their resolve, and the time did close to the noon's hour. The chanting they could hear from afar seemed to be reaching some frenzy, as the battle was soon to begin. Only the word from Henry was awaited to clash the armies together, and as the noon hour came so came the anticipated word.

"Now! Release your warriors!" The Welsh lords shouted to their followers to start the move to encounter Richard, and, at last, the Welsh were released from their unseen shackles and started slowly, at first, to the meet they had longed for. 'Twas time for battle as they moved forward. The crows flew high from their nests atop the overlooking trees, cawing and chattering, disturbed by the movement so vast below that broke their tranquil, fluttering and diving about and leaping from their perch, as below the black form moved across their field. The butterflies were no longer settling their wings upon damp patches, gone they to seek the dry of a far place. The sweet smelling meadow flowers, once bright and young, were trampled underfoot and mashed into the mud and grass. Boots and bare feet and the hooves of horse, making the green and bright common that was full of life into a desolate piece of ground, and 'twould lay such until the blood had washed away, until the rain had stopped, until the sun dried, and all would live once again at another time in that sweet meadow of England. On they came those two thousand Welsh savages, the beat quickening as they made halfway across the common, and came then the command to start beating their shields with the broadswords. With their black hair flattened to their heads, long and sticky in the drizzled rain, beards glistening, arms and shoulders shining as the wet washed away the grime from their bodies. Strong the legs picked up the pace, and all was mud and slip as they raged closer to the ranks of Richard, chanting the battle chants of the ancients. The foot soldiers that raged against them stood steady and did not flutter an eye, as they peered past their shields at the devil that came before them. They were feared by the sight but stood unmoved, with some unable to control their bodies, released themselves in the terror that was coming closer toward them, but still they all stood their soggy lot. The Welsh were but five hundred paces from the enemy line that awaited them. They quickened their gait again, coming like a tidal wave of the living. The field, as far back to where the mist dwelled, seemed covered with the screaming enemy.

"Stand ready!" Richard's soldiers heard from behind them as the orders to the bowmen were made. The first row at four hundred paces, the second row at four hundred and fifty paces, the third row at five hundred paces. From the call, though unseen by the bowmen, they knew exactly how far the enemy was away. The archers stood two hundred paces back from the front line, as the Welshmen were within three hundred paces and coming, mad, toward the army of Richard. Steam could be seen rising from the mass that tumbled before them. Two hundred paces now as eyes were met, and Richard's men would run if they could, but they knew they had to stand upon legs that knew no such word.

"Fire!" At last came the command, and, like a thousand birds fluttering to flight, the arrows were let. As they left the twang of the bow, the archers were already pulling their next flights. The shot arrows fluttered across the heads of the cavalry, their sight then lost in the dark sky but heard whistling as they reached their speed in the misty air above. O'er the soldiers and o'er piked men they went as they reached their height, and whistled down, wet and heavy, striking at the enemy who came thickly at two hundred paces, with already the next flight cutting its way through the air just as the first shot was landing upon the bare heads of the Welsh. No armour did they wear, and so were cut down heavily like spiked fish in the pond, into the mud they stumbled and fell with arrows sticking from them in grisly fashion; they cried out in their anguish, trampled, behind them the unscathed still coming in their dire rage and blind eye, trampling the bodies of their comrades underfoot, as then the next volley landed and did bring the same horror upon them, but still they came with many closing to Richard's first line of defence, and being too close to be struck by any arrows were they. Screaming in their droves they came upon the soldiers, laying their heavy-bladed broadswords upon the pikemen, they ravaged with clang and bang as blades hit shields and swords. Many of Henry's men hung from the pikes in the first rush, gurgling and crying out as they hung helpless, unable to escape. The pikes could not be pulled from the bodies, and so the sword was brought to play against those who were still coming over the piled soldiers. The two armies were clashed in close battle; arms lost, severed heads rolled in the mire, gutted stomachs spraying their innards all about, as the arrows still whistled above their heads. Higher piled the bodies from both camps. More of Richard's soldiers came into the fray, both of horse and of foot, and with great strength threw back the crazed Welshmen. Bitter losses they had taken and very few remained who could fight; those left stared at death with no hope of victory, and ran from the bloody scene to regroup under Henry's banner. The army of Richard watched as they fled but did not break their rank. Many staggered in the gore that was piled about their legs, almost unable to see over the bodies before them to the field beyond.

Richard stood in his stirrups upon his white charger in the midst of the scene; his blade dripped the blood of the enemy. All quieted now except for the agony of the wounded sounding out to the crows that circled above their heads. A group of soldiers came out from the safety of Richard's lines and began their task of dragging those of their own that still lived back into the confines of the army. Those who were in a hopeless state were quickly dealt with to end their misery. The Welshmen who still moved about in distress were quickly beheaded where they squirmed, and ended was their day. The cries of anguish all dulled as the bodies were piled before Richard's first line of foot soldiers. Henry's soldiers would have to climb over the pile of death to attack, making them easier targets as they slipped and slid over the glistening limbs and body parts of the hill.

The lull in the battle lasted close to half of an hour as each side readied for the next onslaught. Henry's three thousand Bretons, joined by what remained of the Welsh warriors, came out from the mist, the rattle of the drums urging them forth to where Richard stood, jogging over the bodies that had been struck by the arrows that had fallen far into the field. Soon though they were upon the gruesome pile, the mud beneath their feet squelching red as the blood mixed with the earth and splattered all about; the arrows had fallen but did less damage than upon the first rush, as armour covered the Bretons in this coming surge. They clashed with furious cries and shouts; the foot soldiers at Richard's line with the cavalry, fighting with their king who was midst in the fray, holding their line against the outnumbering force with fury and bravery, and with great resolve turned them back once more, as they dragged their wounded with them, hacked and battered by the more skilful soldiers of the king's army, back once more to regroup for another charge. The numbers of men they had lost was far in excess of Richard's losses, and whilst forming to attack once again they knew this would be their last chance of victory, for they were in some sorry state. Richard knew of their plight and saw his men in good stead as they awaited the coming of their weakened foe; victory, it seemed, almost within their grasp as they stood with fogged breath and bloody hands. The king shouted further orders to his ranks, pulling his front line back twenty paces so the hill of the dead would not be atop of them; for he did not wish the enemy to look down upon his close lines, which would give them some small advantage.

"Norfolk is steadied at his position!" Richard let all about him know of the situation. "And of Stanley?" he queried one of his advisers.

"Stanley is most ready, sire, await in the cover of the trees," came the reply to his question.

"Good. Then all is placed. Henry will come with his weakened force shortly and we will repel him as before, and upon the sound of the horn we shall split our ranks and let Stanley through to finish them all … God be with you, for the field will soon be won."

"Aye, sire!" came the cries from his able men, though cut and battered they still had much fight left within them.

Came the sounds in the distance of the coming army. The Bretons and Henry's English followers, and the few Welsh that were left, who, with their barons, had taken the most out of Richard's army and had brought Richmond to this final surge. Behind them, standing fresh, lay Henry's cavalry, all burning with pride to at last do battle. And so they came across the field hoping some event may turn the lost cause into something victorious. O'er the bloody pile they came running at Richard's line with all their fury, only to suffer once more heavy losses, as they were held in check again in that wicked place between the wall of bodies and Richard's soldiers. The king made full use of his fighting skills, hacking from his horse with his broadsword, dealing much havoc upon the enemy who were slowing in their endeavours. Although still stayed at the rear, Henry's cavalry had not yet joined the fray, they twisting and turning their horses to keep them ready, but impatient in their wait as they watched their comrades falling to the metal of the King Richard. All was well for the king as the onslaught was almost coming to naught. The signal was called for the sound of the horn. It came, shrill and clear, in the late afternoon, heard clear over the cries of battle. And, as ordered, the field commanders split their forces in two as Henry for a moment stalled his attack and called his soldiers back from the line. Cut about and battered, they came to the banner, all await for the coming move that would end this bloody day. Richard stood await for Stanley to heed. Henry ordering his cavalry to ready for the charge. Richard waited still for the sight of his friend and prayed soon he would show. Then, through the wood, at the back of Richard's stage, came the dark mass that was the Lord Stanley's army ... come they from the north to engage this war, and now it came at a gallop, till full the mid of Richard's divided troops were they. Then, from the sound of some unseen horn that was about, they turned sideways, half to the left and half to the right and started to attack the army of Richard, cutting down his unwary cavalry like corn in the field. Stanley's fresh troops coming with no fight against them, began running through the unprotected archers with much devastation, leaving all in tumbled bloody heaps as they were ravaged by the sword.

Richard, devastated by the happening so grisly before him, and most embittered by the fact that, of all the signs that were shown to him of some treachery, he ignored them, could not now believe the trust he had placed in Stanley without spying upon his activities ... Richard had been bought and sold and was as naive as some young maiden in the ways of the world, bought and sold like some farm animal at the market. He feared his brain had lapsed into that of some low creature, and feared the end would soon be upon him. To then hear the cries from afar as Henry's cavalry made its move, charging into the bewildered troops, they still fought from two sides, but in vain was their struggle, as the fresh armies were upon them. The king rallied from his musings and called his personal guard about him and made a last stand in the middle of the massacre. Oh, for a Buckingham beside me this day, his mind wished for his old friend. Richard then, with much ferocity, fought on with the last of his troops, now just a small circle, as they were chopped down one by one. They were completely surrounded by Henry's men in the midst of that Bosworth Field where the flowers once grew. And upon this place, were it not for the saddened treachery, Richard would have won the day, and would have taken himself with pride to the meet with his dear Elizabeth. But nays would be yeas if 'twas so. He looked about and saw that Norfolk did not enter the fray, that loyal knight whose deceit with Stanley would end with others that solemn oath of knights. The closest to Richard did fall; his personal guard were his last hope, but were mingling upon the ground with the others who so lay. Steven Moran stood by his king, but a deep arm slash and a stunning blow with a mace to bend and dint his helmet, fell him to the thick of the heaped bodies. His brave horse cut from beneath him, Richard still swung his blade with all the valour of the knight he was. Then, above the terror, a horn sounded, and for a moment the carnage ceased and the troops of Henry stayed their act. As then, above the steam and the stench that laid upon the common, the voice of Henry loudly called out to Richard.

"Yield the field, Richard! You will be tried fairly in my court if you lay down your weapon and pay homage to the new king of this land."

"How can I be tried fairly with such as you? I make no such pact with usurpers and those with traitorous acts. Do what you must and let no one say I did not die a true and noble king. I will give to no man such pleasure as to see me disgraced with lies and falsehoods at some dishonourable place. I will yield no field to you, sire, who is but a pretender followed by treacherous lords. Come then, do your deed, for I am in no fear, as the Lord doth know of my goodness,"

"Then God rest your soul for here Death comes to you." And Henry with a wave of his sword sent forth his men to finish the king, who, with the last few of his devoted followers, fought for longer than all could believe. Until the last one stood, Richard, still flailing with his sword, still taking many lives as he cut and hacked about him, until his legs were almost chopped away from him, but still upon his bloody stumps swinging his sword and raging his mouth, then he was finally cut down and made still for all time, he the last of the most noble warriors was gone …

The cheering floated o'er the blood-soaked ground as Henry's men cried out in great joy and pain. "The field is won!" carried the shouts all about. "The field is won!" Sadness though filled the heart of Norfolk, for he had failed upon the day to honour his word, for he knew Richard would not do such, but face him and tell him close if he had any other scheme in mind. He would not have cringed like some weakling. Stanley was not so reticent in his thoughts; he did his deed only for the fact he hated the king for many things, but mostly because he had caused the murder of the innocent princes, and that would not leave his soul. One of Henry's personal guard went to the heaped bodies where the last stand had taken place, and, grovelling about there, pulled from the bloody mess the golden crown from Richard's ogling head. Then, as well as he was able in the middle of the field, he wiped it clean, and, with much reverence to Henry, was allowed to place it upon his soon-to-be king's head, as the cheers of "God bless King Henry!" rang about the messed field.

Came then the task of saving the wounded of Henry's soldiers, and ending the lives of those who were beyond any help, and to finish all of Richard's men who lay floundering so another day would not come upon them. The quick slash of the dagger brought many cries about, as the unsavoury task was carried out to the far reaches of the common. And so it went until darkness came; lamps lit the scene, as they continued to search about for any armaments and valuables that could be taken from the stricken bodies. Other torches glowed, shining upon the dead as the army searched about, blinking from afar of the field. Anything of some value was brought to the waiting carts, which were piled high with armour and weapons and all kinds of loot. They scavenged all that they could in the flickering lights, and trundled away, leaving all behind them for the body carts that would show early upon the morrow, and with them other scavengers would come searching for any valuables that were unfound.

Richard was stripped of what was left of his royal garb, and all naked was tied across the back of a mule, like a sack of flour, to be taken in much degradation to the abbey near Leicester; and, as they did so, and they left the field behind them, the old hag stood at the roadside with two more hooded women, four men, and two children. And, washed clean with a ribboned ear, stood with them a newborn white cow, with two heads showing, to be taken to a far field at the midnight hour and its body parts scattered afar.

The evil eyes that looked would be burned out so no more vile things could come from its devil's gaze. The old sayer watched as the king's body in tattered skin was paraded by. She pulled back a little her hood to reveal her crinkled face and broken teeth. She said naught but shook her head in dismay at the fool who would not listen to her words. He who would not wait one more day, now rides alone to his grave. She pulled back her hood to cover her face and made away now to the far field.

PART THREE: KING HENRY VII

October 1485 …

Chapter Fourteen

A Common Knight.

Through the towns and hamlets trotted the mule that bore the king. The crowds grew along the roadside as word of the coming spread. Torches burned all along the way, with the light showing the grisly scene. Some stood in silence and gazed in awe at the sight of Richard passing before them; women wept and children gawped; others jeered at the naked body, hacked and battered, that was paraded for all to see. Along the way to the abbey, the people gathered about to see the last of their king upon that late hour. They came soon to the abbey of Leicester; and brought there to the waiting abbots came the body of Richard, as they, in all reverence and with gentle hands, took what remained of him, carried him upon a litter into the resting place, making him ready with wash and white shroud, and laid was he within a box made of English oak, ready for burial, to be interred without ceremony as decreed by Henry. But they did as much as they dared to treat him most respectfully. Then, late upon the following morn, he was carried out to an unmarked grave, where many people stood silently about watching all the happenings, as the mist still drifted about them. They dispersed only with the sound of soil that bounced off the hollow-seeming box at the bottom of the dug hole. And came to an end such; the brave soldier rested near that abbey at Leicester, laid in the damp soil, filled to the level as the sun shined through the leaves, patterning the ground where he lay as it will for all time. Henry and his followers left the scene of their notorious victory, and after resting overnight made way to the palace at the Tower of London, wearily was their plod as they came their way to the crown and to the rewards it would bring …

That same morn did brightly come over the common at Bosworth. The sun lit the scene now that the devil's dark work was done, coming over the far hills, making the mist to rise as its warmth dried the sodden ground, and then seen all about were the body carts as they moved into the carnage that lay there. The drivers dressed all of black to show their trade, their hats stood tall, and they as black as their coats as the sun bounced its sparkle off the clinging wet upon them. Their unsmiling faces peered from beneath their covers as white as the dead they sought. They came with boys bouncing about in the creaking carts, all raggedy and dirty;

these poor souls would drag the bodies and load the carts for their masters, who would watch over them with stern face and whip in hand, as the boys searched about for any valuables to be found upon the twisted bodies, their eyes never leaving them, for all that was found was to placed into the hands of their masters and not slipped into grubby little pockets. The whip cracked loudly in the air to remind them of any deception, and fear made it there would be none. They picked, yet like carrion themselves, they fed the hand that held the whip. The bodies and parts would be taken to a mass grave that was being dug but two miles hence from the common, and there tipped into the hole, to fill where the soil had once been and covered to show but a mound, with no stone and naught writ to show of the brave souls who lay there.

Into the field that early morn came other carts, scavengers they, seeking no bodies but come to find whatever they could among the remains scattered about. Fights breaking out all about as finders and keepers clashed. Another body in the heap mattered not, but would lay just another pebble upon the beach. The crows and the ravens that had been first to take from the scene, fluttered and screeched as they were disturbed and frightened away by those with two arms, but some still pecking and clawing at the piles of flesh. Rats scurried about, unmoved by the activity about them; too many in number were they, for a hundred killed would leave room for a hundred more.

A single cart pulled close to where the last stand took place. A man, in the peasant's rough clothes, climbed down from the board where he had sat for many an hour, his old mare drooping as she waited for her next move, the grey hair upon her mane giving her age to the sunlight. The peasant started pulling at the heap, at the bodies and the remains that lay in the deep pile of the dead. Searching for ringed fingers and money pouches, gold teeth and silver buckles, but finding naught at this time, he moved more bodies about. But shame he felt upon himself that he had to stoop as low as the rats that scurried about, all this to bring some small token to his purse. Teary-eyed he lifted and pulled at the hands and the arms that stuck from the mire beneath, and in doing so thought of all the wives and children, all the mothers and fathers who would be at wait for their return that would never be. He was saddened as he placed himself in the same state as these forgotten heroes who stirred no more, and knew what sadness would come to the one he loved and who loved him ... His devoted Jemma.

A glimpse came of a shiny object in the mess of blood; he delved deeper into the bodies and was able to pull at the hand, and lift it far enough out so that he could see the trinket that glittered. A ring of gold he saw—a mighty find amongst the hell. He moved to pull it off and held the wrist in one hand whilst he turned the ring that stuck the finger; he looked at it closer, then dropped it as if he had been burned, his move so quick, a grass snake turned to an adder. "God!" he cried in a whisper to himself, but recovering he lifted once more the hand that bore the ring, and looked again at the writ upon it: S. M., he saw clearly. "Steven Moran," he breathed the words as once more he released the hand, and began to pull away the bodies that lay upon the top of the officer. He became more frenzied as he saw the body was in one piece, and it seemed to have been little harmed to his quick sight. Most was cleared away and so he pulled upon Steven's wrists to drag him clear of all that clinged, and in doing so he was sure that he felt some movement from the hand he held. Yes, life still ran through his body. He dragged the heavy bundle closer to his cart, and removed carefully the battered helmet from the head of Steven, and then unbuckled his body armour, and threw it to one side, into the red mud amongst the bodies. He tugged a cloth from his belt and wiped the blood and dirt from the face rested in his lap. The eyes opened to see, and a mouth he heard whisper.

"Thomas, Thomas, by God's grace, it is you. I do not know if I am in death or still of earth bound."

"You are still in this damned place, my lord."

"How are you here upon this day and at this place?"

"I know not, but seemingly fate was my eyes. How do you fare, sire? How does your arm feel?"

"I can still move my hand." Steven lifted his arm a little higher so he may gaze upon it more closely. "God must have looked over me upon this common. Of Richard—need I ask of the outcome? for I remember a little that we were in some dire strait."

"Richard fared not well, sire, for with much bitter fighting he lost the field and stood he alone at the end. The cause then hopeless, and the usurper finished him to take the crown."

Steven had gone into some lapse, and looked a breathing corpse as Thomas pulled him to the cart, and, using all his strength, lifted him onto the boards and covered him with a canvas. He then retrieved some bloodied clothes that were strewn all about, and made a support for the limped head, so it would not rattle upon the journey to come. He seated himself upon the board, and urged his faithful mare out of the grime and the blood of the field, to make to the track that would lead them back to his small cottage at Nottingham. He trundled the roads all that day, only stopping to give a some care to Steven. Fetching a little water for him from the close streams, and to rest and feed his horse. The groans he heard as they went on gave some comfort to Thomas, for at least life was about in the cart as it wended along the winding track. Night came but Thomas did not tarry, for he knew the road well, and was able to make his way through the dark lanes and fields, and through the forests, black and foreboding. Dawn came upon the cart, the day starting bright as the old mare plodded on, she needing no one to show her the way. Thomas stirred from his welcome nod, glancing back as he did so in concern for his companion. Soon the noon hour came upon them, and afar could be seen the town of Nottingham, its castle standing black at the sky. Through the local woods he came with his cargo, and down the slope to the smoking chimney that puffed over his home, bringing the mare to a stop close to the cottage door, whereupon, seeing her husband arrive, Jemma came from her kitchen, most happy that Thomas had returned, and safe, to her.

"Are you well, dear husband?"

"Yes, Jemma, I am of good stead."

"Was your journey worthy?"

"Well, my dear, I come with a find, a find you would not believe." He took her hand and led her to the cart, then gently he rolled back the canvas, as Jemma peered into the dark folds that lay upon the boards. Her breath was short as upon the sight she stepped back with her hands covering the gasp from her lips.

"God's grace, is it not the gentleman who bargained for the arrows? … Steven Moran?"

"Yes, my dear, it is him, found upon the battlefield and almost left for the body carts."

"Let us not stand at prattle, Thomas—bring him inside and let us comfort him." She was already making her way to the doorway of the cottage, her skirts hitched to aid her step as she went to prepare for their visitor. Thomas called for his sons to aid him; soon they came from the old barn, their bare feet running.

"Take care of Dolly," he spake to Robert, the youngest one. "Give me a lift with this brave fellow," he spake to the eldest, John. And with one holding the shoulders and the other holding the feet, they lifted him out, and, with laboured step, they took him into the cottage, as Dolly was led to the stable by the younger boy. Steven was laid gently down upon the table that Jemma had covered with layers of cloth, with a bolster placed at one end for his bruised head. Thomas fetched some hot water in the wooden bucket from the steaming cauldron, ready for Jemma to wash the face, and to bathe the wounded limb that was of their care. The face stirred a little from the cleansing water, though as yet the eyes did not see. Jemma looked at Steven's head where he had been battered by the mace, making his hair stick out from the large swelling. His helmet had been bent into his neck and 'twas cut deeply, but in all it seemed not a serious wound. She cut away the cloth sleeve that was his shirt, and saw that his arm was indeed seriously injured, the cut gaping wide and looking infected from the mud it had laid in. She was quickly upped from her gaze.

"Remove his garments and wash him Thomas, but remember to keep him wrapped warm, for he must not chill," spake Jemma as she made toward the door of the cottage, pulling on her head cloth as she did so

"Where do you go, Jemma?" Thomas asked, as his son peered from behind his father with queried gaze.

"I must go quickly to old Peggy's croft, for we need some remedy for that arm of Steven's; it is not in good state, and, unless we can do something, it will have to be taken."

"Then take Robert with you, for you must not be alone within the forest."

"Yes, my dear," she answered, and she was gone, leaving Thomas and her eldest son to tend Steven. "Robert! Robert!" she shouted to the other son. A boy of twelve years, tall and mostly skin and bones, he came from the stable at the call.

"Yes, Mother?"

"Come with me. Have you your dagger?"

"Yes," said he, as he placed his hand upon his hidden belt.

"Then come with haste." He did come with haste to his mother's side, as they made their way down the track that led to the forest, and did wonder about the things that were not of normal place.

"Who was that wounded man, Mother?"

"He is a gentleman who fought at the side of Richard at the common but two days past, and there he has suffered severe wounding. That is why we are on our way to Peggy's croft, to buy some herbal remedy, for his wounded arm is in some dire strait."

"Come then, Mother." The son took Jemma's arm to help her along the rutted track; so uneven was it, he was feared of her stumbling in the mission of haste she had undertaken. They went from the track to a narrow pathway that wound its way into the forest's cool air. The trees and bushes were close to them, with little room even though one followed the other. Overhead the branches closed to dim the light as through the green, sweet smelling tunnel they went, and came to the clearing that gave view to the croft where Peggy dwelled. They went toward the low door that hung rickety there, as Robert looked all about as they crossed the clearing, taught such by his father to be always vigilant and to care for his mother at all times. "Be ready," he had always said, "for when all is calm and of peace that is the most dangerous of times. The hidden villain will not crack a twig while he awaits his chance." But no danger showed here as his mother rapped the old door and entered.

"Wait there, Robert; I will be but a short while." He stood outside upon the order, dreaming of being a soldier on guard duty whilst his queen was in chambers; stiffly he stood as a soldier would, his hand upon his dagger, ready to stand before any intruder who may show his face.

"Peg! — 'tis Jemma — are you about?"

"Jemma Smith … Oh, yes, Jemma, how do you fare?"

"I am well indeed, Peg, but I call for some remedy for someone in my care who is suffering a deep wound."

The voice of Peg spake from the far side of the room, lit only by the fire that burned in the grate, and gave about the shape of a small person as hunched as only an old woman could get, and with a crackle of voice it came. "Wounded at the common, aye?"

"Yes, he was … How did you know of such, Peg?"

"Ah, my dear, Peg knows things only the birds know; they fly about telling their tales for any who are able to listen." Jemma looked at the dark figure that spake the words, unable to understand such a gift as was professed. "Right arm, is it not? Deep and infected from the soil of the common?"

"Yes, that is so," Jemma answered, now somewhat given to the fact that Peg did know all. She had befriended Peg many years ago and oft had bought remedies from her and she was always most pleased to have a visit from Jemma Smith. Her other powers she had only heard whispers of, but this day she had heard them for herself.

"Let me see then." The crooked woman moved slowly her stick, clicking upon the stone floor. She moved to her shelves of crocks and lifted some to the fire's light, to peer into the liquid within. She kept the one that she deemed suitable and placed the others back to their place. "'Ere, my dear, three pennies for this." Jemma took three pennies from her pouch and placed them into the bony hands of Peggy, who clutched them to herself as she gave Jemma the gallipot. "Now, do exactly as I tell you: wash down the wound with water, well-salted, clean out all the dirt you may see. If any of the wound is on the turn to black, you will have to cut it away, for any you leave could bring the flesh rot, then spread the remedy all over the bloodied flesh. You can use a needle, can you not, my dear?"

"Yes," answered Jemma with some apprehension.

"Get someone to hold together the wound, then, with your sharpest needle and some good gut, stitch it like you would a feed sack as neat as you can, then wrap it in the leaves of a plantain weed, and wrap that again with a cloth binding. Keep the arm raised upon some bolster so the blood will not puddle. If you do all I have told you, the wound, with God's help, will mend. If it does not, come to see me and tell me of the state."

"I will do as you say, Peg, and bid you a good day, and God bless you."

The bony hand with its long nails waved her out. "And give that boy of yours some bread, coated thick with meat drippings, and some pig scratchings, every day; he walks as a garden rake soon to disappear," she called after Jemma as she went to gather her son, but she knew meat would soon come to his bones.

"Come, Robert," Jemma spake to her son as he lolled on the wall of the cottage.

"Did you get it, Mother?"

"Yes, I did, let's to home now." And soon they were cracking their walk over the still lying summer branches, as they went through the woods and back once more to the track that led to their cottage and plot. The door creaked its welcome as they entered their warm abode. The latch clicked as they closed the door behind them to see John standing beside the table where lay Steven.

"How is he, Thomas?

"He is still the same; from time to time he has stirred a little, but still lies as if in some faraway place."

Jemma placed the gallipot upon the sill whilst she removed her shawl and placed it folded upon the cupboard shelf. "Well, let us take look at his arm." Jemma gently lowered Steven's arm from across his chest and placed it close by his side, then began to peel back the cloth that covered the wound. She saw the large gash still gaping open, with the blood still dripping from it, but 'twas cleaner now and Jemma could see what she had to do. "Fetch me another bucket of hot water, Thomas." Before he could, one of the sons had already moved to the cauldron; both sons had stood aback from the table watching all that was taking place, and were only too pleased to help in the cause. The water was brought, as Jemma was returning from the pantry with a bag of salt that was used for curing their winter meat. She ladled two full scoops into the hot water and gave it a long stir with her ponch*; dipping then her readied cloth into the salt water, she began to wash gently the open wound. Jemma felt the arm pull away from her as if in some pain, but the eyes of Steven told her he was still in his coma, and though he stirred, he felt little of any discomfort. After more washing, the wound looked cleaner except for some blackness at the edges of the skin; she reached for her shears, placed handily by, and

* *ponch* T-shape-handled, wooden implement

with Thomas holding the limb, Jemma snipped off the dead flesh, to the stare of the wide-eyed boys, as they grimaced their childlike faces at the sight, and the black was cut away and dropped to the floor. A groan and a little struggle were all that Steven could muster in his fogged state. The cutting was finished, and, with Thomas still holding the arm, the crock was unsealed and tipped onto the wound. The green, slimy liquid that was of Peggy's brew, was spread onto the open gash and wiped all about so no place upon the arm was not green. Thomas gently pulled the wound together, ready for the stitch; as he did so, the red blood and the green remedy mixed together and oozed out from between his fingers. Jemma, with her readied needle and gut, began to sew her neatest stitch, first to one side then to the other, wiping away the bubbling fluids as she went slowly and carefully until all was gutted together, and then was wrapped in the plantain leaves and bound with cloth tied securely. The arm was raised slightly onto a bolster as they stood back to see their friend lay in the arms of God and await his judgment. The boys, at last relieved of their stress, sat like bumps upon the bench; Thomas sat with them able to do little else except to wait. Jemma picked about all that lay, and threw upon the fire the bloodied cloths and black skin …

Three days had passed; Steven had stirred at times and was given sips of water when he did so, but then he would lapse away again into his healing sleep. Five days came and went, as Robert, with sucking breath, came a-bustle into the cottage.

"Mother!—Mother!—"

"What is it, Robert?" The boy was red of face and little able to talk. "Be calm, son; take your time; take some deep breaths ... There now, tell me, what is the matter?"

"There are soldiers coming this way from town—they have been searching for any of Richard's followers that may be sheltering about—and, Mother, any they find they are putting to the sword and firing the homes of those who hide them. Mother, it is terrible, I am feared of what may—for they are but two miles away and come along the track that leads to us. Where is Father? We must warn him, and he will tell us what best to do."

"Robert, he is at the market with John and will not return until sunset." Jemma was taken with fear, for Steven could not be moved, but quickly she rallied herself. "Son, do as I say, be strong as your father would see you. I wish you to lay beside Steven, as he would be your father. We must say you are both with sickness and pray we can make them believe such."

"I will do as you bid, Mother, though I look not of a sickly state, and if they look me over, they will know that I suffer no sickness."

"I will make you look as if you have some malady." Jemma fetched from the pantry a crock of vinegar of the wine. "Be strong, Robert, for this may hurt a little," spake she as she dipped a cloth into the crock.

"As long as we can save Steven, I care not for some little pain," bravely he spake as his mother kissed him gently upon his cheek. The soured wine dripped from the cloth as red as the grape it had come from; she held her son's head back and squeezed from the cloth the vinegar that dripped into his eyes, making him pull away with discomfort, but he whimpered not once. His eyes were slits and running tears as the liquid ran down his face, now red and blotched.

"My son, sip some of the remedy that is left, and try and hold it in your mouth for as long as you are able." He did as he was bid and closed tight his mouth, as the liquid trickled from the corners of his lips in some sickly fashion. He looked more like a stricken wretch in some last throes of his life. "Under the cover now, Robert, but leave your face to view." His lips and face were swollen as he slipped under the covers aside of the dreaming Steven, who knew nothing of the antics that were happening about him. Robert's face showed above the covers, but only the hair upon Steven's head did peek from the drape. *Bang!* came upon the door, quicker than thought. Jemma looked at the two who lay, and, taking a deep breath, she slowly went to the door and gently opened it, only to have it pulled from her grasp as three of Henry's soldiers in some vile temper burst in.

"Are you hiding any enemies of the King Henry, wench?"

"No, sir, we are not." The squeaky voice unknown to her came out from her mouth, unable to talk properly for the fear that possessed her.

"God be with you then, woman, if we find you are in league with such." As he spake he pulled from his pouch a writ parchment and gazed upon the names before him. "One man, one woman, two boys. Who lies there?" The sergeant of the group pointed at the two abed upon the table.

Jemma strengthened and was able to speak more clearly. "That, sir, is my husband and my son, both stricken by some malady of which we know not."

"And where is your other son?"

"Sir, he has this morning taken the horses to the smithy in Nottingham."

The sergeant stepped forward with some authority about, as he came close to peer at Robert, who indeed looked full of some illness, sickly and bloody, and with much sweat. The sergeant then moved toward Steven and reached for the hair that showed above the covers. Upon which Robert, as if in some fiendish dream, sat up most straight, his eyes wide like the owl with green slime dribbling from the corners of his mouth, his face all red and blotched, his eyes teared. He screamed and pointed with his thin finger into space. "The devil comes! ... I see the devil about ... He comes ever closer."

The sergeant stepped back with his sword rattling at his side, somewhat startled by the boy. Two more soldiers, who had started searching about the stable and the barn, came running into the cottage to see about the troubled cry. Jemma came quickly to her stricken son.

"Oh, Robert, my Robert, pray to God it is not the sleeping sickness that wracks your mind."

"God save us, the plague is about this place—Out! Out!" the sergeant shouted to his men in some distress, who needed little help in fleeing the cottage; they dallied not as the word they dreaded most washed their ears, and went for their horses, and they offered no last look back. The sergeant, though, shouting as he ran, still following his orders, "And forget not, madam, your taxes must still be paid, even without your menfolk."

"Yes, sir," answered Jemma as she closed the door behind the intruders. "Shush," she whispered over to Robert as she waited leaning upon the inside of the door, her heart thumping like the rabbit that had slipped its trap. She heard talk without as the group still looked about the farm and rattled about in the storage shed. Then, with some mumbled talk and the jingle of the harness, they were gone, and outside all was of stillness. Jemma moved away from the door that was closed upon her fear, and sat with face in hands trembling from the encounter she had suffered. Robert, on seeing his mother's plight, was quickly up from the table and, with arms about her, consoled her fear, to bring her strength from his own. Soon after her sobbing ceased she returned to her usual self, kind and generous. "Let us look at you, Robert; we must wash your face." She sat him down upon the bench, and, with warm water from the pot, washed away the stinging vinegar and patted his face dry with her softest linen, until he was of more comfort; and, as she dried him, she praised him for the bravery he had shown during the intrusion of Henry's soldiers. "Your father will be most proud of you, Robert. You were a man this day and did manly things." He smiled through his blotched face and was heartened by his mother's praise, but he thought he was not the bravest one in this room, not nearly the bravest, for the one who wore skirts, she was the bravest of all.

They helped the still Steven to lie more comfortably, for he had laid such for many an hour. Gently they rolled him upon his back and, whilst pushing his bolster to fit his neck, his eyes opened as he was wont to do, but no moaning came from him this time. They gave him some sips of water before he lapsed again, but this time though he did not, and his eyes that were closed for many a while now stayed open. He moved his head slowly, and saw the face that looked upon him, gazing into his eyes—the eyes that asked the questions the lips could not speak, quizzical and needy.

"How are you, Steven?" His brows furrowed as she spake, for he knew not yet of his circumstances. "This is Jemma … the wife of Thomas Smith."

"I remember you, Jemma." Steven's brain had caught up to his mouth as his hand tightened upon hers. "Am I whole? Do I have all my limbs?"

"Yes, Steven, all of you is with us, but you do have a severe arm wound and 'tis almost six days since we doctored it. Can you move it?" Steven looked at his wrapped limb and gave it a little movement at the elbow.

"Can you move your fingers, Steven?" He looked at his hand that stuck from the wrappings and wiggled his fingers to Jemma and Robert's delight. "I think you will mend, thank God."

"I think, thank you, Jemma. For the ball has bounced back." They sat him now and supported his arm with a shoulder cloth and made a pad for his back.

"Get some stew," Jemma said to her son, who fetched from the pot a bowl of hot, stewed rabbit. "This is my son, Robert, who has been most brave this little while."

Steven held his hand with a friendly shake. "Hullo, Robert," he said with a look into the blotched face that greeted him, and wondering of what mischief had been put upon him.

Jemma gave rest to his thoughts as she scooped the stew into his hungry mouth. "Soldiers came but a short while past searching for any of Richard's followers that may be about. We managed to give Robert the look of someone with a most disturbing malady, and, when they saw him, 'twas the plague that came to their minds, and so went their way most quick."

"You are so brave, I know not how to thank you, to have taken upon yourselves such an endeavour, for you know but little of me. And what, pray, of Thomas? I do have some memory of him finding me upon the common, amongst all that mire where I had been struck down."

"That is so," spake Jemma. "He managed to lift you into his cart and brought you to our care." Steven sipped the stew as it still was spooned into his mouth, and listened to all that was told and of which he had little memory. "Thomas has been at the market all day and knows naught of our soldiery visit."

"I will be pleased to see him once more," he spake as he gently slid down into the warm covers, and closed his eyes a little to rest.

Six of the clock came as Thomas clattered the cart into the yard with John by his side. Jemma peeked through the small window to see his coming, and to see if the pigs he had taken to market had been sold; she saw no large animals there and was pleased that they had been sold. She saw some slatted boxes at the back, with the heads of chickens clucking in and out of their cage. Thomas was talking to John, and, with a back pat, left him to see to the horses, and to take the chickens to the barn and free them in there. As he hurried to the cottage door, noticeably he was in some angst. Jemma opened it as he came closer and his worried face lifted.

"Jemma, are you well?"

"Yes, Thomas. Be not concerned, we are all well."

"I was in some distress, for I did hear at the market that soldiers of Henry's army had been searching for Richard's followers in these parts."

"Yes, Thomas, that is so, they did come here, but we were able to keep them from discovering Steven."

"How does he fare, our companion?"

"He has been awake and talking; he seems to be recovering, though it be slow."

Thomas came close to where lay Steven, and saw his face more at peace than the last time they were together. He looked over to his younger son and saw the marks red and blistering upon his face. "What in God's name has happened to you, Robert?"

"Thomas, we had to make him look sickly so that the soldiers thought he was with the plague, and they were indeed in haste to depart upon looking at his features." Jemma then told the entire story to her husband, who listened with more pride as the tale was unfolded to him. "Robert was so brave; 'twas through his actions that they abandoned their search and quickly went their way. I was so proud of him."

"Well done, my son. You are a credit to this house."

"Thank you, Father. I enjoyed the act so … 'Twas most exciting. I would one day like to become an actor."

They both looked at him with a humorous glance. "I think not," they both said to his boyish talk.

Steven then began to stir and looked around to all who were gathered about him. "Thomas!" he croaked, as joyous as he was able. "I am most pleased to see you, for you have saved my life." He hugged him close with his one good arm, as brother would hug brother. "I would have died if you had not come upon me."

"'Twas naught, sire; 'twas my duty."

"Do not call me sire. In all ways, you and your family are far more noble than I to wear such a title. A common knight you are, but you are not common, for you are a brave lord, and Jemma more of a lady than those born such, with two boys who will grow into more than has yet been spied. 'Tis I who should call you sire and honour your words. You are a brother more so than one from the flesh. Please do not shame me by such words."

Hands were clasped and tears welled.

"Yes, Steven."

The days passed, floating into the September harvest with the fields bright with the gold grain, all ready to be cut. The fruits hung from the trees. The swaying flowers luring the passing bees to taste their sweet offerings, as the warmth of this month made others fill with envy. Steven was strengthening from his fevers, his arm well upon the way to being of some use again. He walked about, but still he was he weak, though growing stronger day by day, and, as some caged bird, seemingly unable to wait to be set free. The evening came upon this day late in the month, as all supped at the table spread with the fields' offerings. 'Twas as if God had looked upon their kindness and had bestowed upon them the fruits of which they had laboured.

"I must go to my Jayne," Steven spake as if he had received some unseen message, moving his food about upon his platter in some melancholy.

"But, Steven, you are not strong enough yet; you must wait longer."

"Even until the days turn colder," added Thomas to the persuasion.

"I cannot wait, for she will be of such fret that I ache to stop her hurt. She must see that I am well."

"We do understand, Steven, but you are in a weakened state and are unable to travel far. There is that to consider, as well, there are still many soldiers about who are seeking Richard's followers to bring you into further danger. For you know they still vengefully seek their enemy," Jemma pleaded with him to think carefully upon his actions.

"Do I look as if I could be of any danger to the crown?" He stood shakily, his hair long about his ears, his beard covering his face. Peasant's coat and breeches hung ill fitting from him; a raggedy man he showed. "More liken to a farmer than a warrior," he smiled as they all looked at him and indeed he looked aught but a soldier. And, as Jemma and Thomas glanced at each other, they knew, no matter what, that he would go to his Jayne.

"Then I will take you if you have such a strong desire," Thomas spake as he placed his hand of someone who understood upon the arm of his comrade.

"I cannot place you in any more danger, for you have bore enough already. No, just give me a horse and I will make my way."

"Steven, I will take you … If you do not agree, we will tie you to the table, and nowhere will you venture until all your strength has returned. What say you now, my friend?"

"You will take me, Thomas, is what I say, for I have no such desire to succumb to such dire straits," Steven spake through his half-smiling lips.

"Can we come, Father?" the boys queried, for they had never been further than the towns that were marketing towns, and they longed for a more exciting journey.

"I am afraid not, my dear boys, for I must rely upon you to take care of your mother, and to tend the animals. You have proven in your bearing of late that you are now responsible sons, and I can leave you with great faith knowing you will do all that is right."

"Yes, sir," they gloomily answered, but knowing they were about to be responsible for more than they had ever been before, they were hearted with pride.

"I will be no longer than seven days, I promise you. All is well with you, Jemma, if I take upon us this journey?"

"Yes, Thomas, for I would not rest if Steven were alone. And I will pray for your safe return, Steven, and for the safe return of my husband."

"Then all is settled. We will early make our way to your Jayne."

"Good, for I am most anxious to do so. Till the morrow." They clinked the mulled cups and all within the cottage were warmed by the feelings about them.

Came the dawn, which showed the cart already laden with straw and hay for rest and for horse feed, and Dolly, all brushed and fed, stood between the shafts, with Robert holding the bridle, stroking her nose as she waited. John was helping his father to bring Steven toward the waiting cart, where stood Jemma; most concerned was her face, but 'twas not shown when their friend was brought close, and she managed a pleasing smile.

"Goodbye, Steven," Jemma spake as he came and kissed her cheek, as she, upon this, lowered her head demurely and turned to hide the tear that tickled her eyes.

He then whispered in her shown ear, "Jemma, you will see the ball has not yet finished its bounce." He squeezed her hand and then climbed onto the cart with help from Thomas, and sat upon the board seat.

"Goodbye, boys … Take good care of your mother."

"Yes, sir," they both replied brightly as their responsibility came near.

Thomas leaned from the seat and kissed Jemma. "Goodbye, my dear wife."

"Goodbye, Thomas, be of great care." As slowly they left the yard, and with a last twisted wave, they started to a trot as they made to the lane that would take them to the road that was to London Town. Thomas's family all stood close, as they watched the cart fade from sight behind the bushes and trees that covered the track's twist, till all was lost in the woods' cover.

Chapter Fifteen.

Elizabeth and Jayne.

Through the window once more peered the wetted eyes of the lady looking down upon the courtyard that lay within the mansion's arms. Waiting with hope these many days for some sign of her love, resonated the words so softly spoken as if of only yesterday: "No matter how long, I will return to you." To and fro was Jayne to that window, many times a day; when she was not there, others watched for her, for she would not leave unless someone stood to vigil. The arms of Mary and Helen always consoling their friend in her wait that seemed would have no end. This day, after some while at watch, and with Mary left to her gazing, Helen took Jayne and went they to the inner chamber where rested the Lady Elizabeth, so they may both sit with her in her own saddened state and aching heart. Her loved one would not return. Richard had gone to his peace and would no longer cloud his love about her. But Elizabeth, always of strength, knew the time had come to shake the flour through the sieve, and start a fresh the new dawn. For she had known, even before Richard's death, that one day he would succumb to some treacherous act, and she was prepared. As the saddened ladies sat, she jumped up from her cot and became hidden behind the doors of her cupboard where within hung her gowns. And soon she showed dressed in clothes more to her ilk. She then sat beside Jayne and placed her arm about her friend who was so troubled, and spake to her of many things, and though still showing great faith that Steven would return, she offered advice so she would be more prepared for any news that may be grievous.

"Jayne, my dearest, be of strength that Steven may not return, for it has been many days since the battle, and there has been very few stories of any who have survived."

"I know what you are saying, my dear Elizabeth; you are trying to soften the blow that I may receive, but Steven said he would return to me, and, in all faith, I know he will. I will wait in vigil as long as I must until he comes back to me, for there is naught else I can do; without him, I wish no more of this life."

"Jayne, we will always be by your side whatever conspires, and we will stand with you in wait." Elizabeth kissed her forehead with tender love.

"Enough of me, Elizabeth—of you, dear one; what are you to do now that Richard is not about?"

"As yet I know not, but fate will come again to tap upon our door." The words had hardly left the tender lips, as the personal guard of Elizabeth did tap upon the door, and each looked at the other at the omen that sounded its timely coming. "Enter," she called.

The bow came, and then he was again standing straight. "My lady, a courier awaits from Henry who wishes council with you."

"Enter him," Elizabeth nodded her request. The guard bowed once more and then opened the door to enter the visitor. The ladies all stood about their lady, as she sat of regal bearing upon the chair awaiting the words of the messenger.

"Lady Elizabeth—" A small thin man dressed in black, his hair greying, and hands that clutched his twisting cap, lowly bowed to Elizabeth.

"What message do you bring, sir?" she said even before he had finished his act of reverence.

"The soon-to-be King Henry wishes you to attend council at the Tower palace at the noon hour upon the morrow, and that he will send a carriage for you and your entourage at your pleasure."

"Please, tell the soon-to-be King Henry that I will be honoured to meet him as he so desires."

"Yes, my lady, I will relay to him your acceptance of his request." Then with a deep bow to Elizabeth, he departed the chamber, as the guard there reached the catch and closed the door upon the ladies who were engaged in some quizzical chatter.

"What do you think he wants Elizabeth?" they queried to their lady.

"I know not for sure but he seems to have some offer to make to us; we will see upon the morrow what his scheme may be. But whatever game he plays, do I not have charms that I may dangle before him? Do not be of concern, for times will not be destitute. He will be as a bird feeding from my hand, wanting much but only pecking at that which I offer him."

"You are a wicked lady, Elizabeth Plantagenet."

Restless was the night spent at the manor of Hampstead with the thoughts that begot Elizabeth of the morrow's meet. Unsettled was the bird of sleep as it nodded and fluttered through the starred hours. Jayne lay with saddened heart, she restless and awake to all sounds hoping that one may be the sound she sought.

The bells of the church rang the hour at eleven of the clock, as Elizabeth in her finery left the chambers, with the ladies of her wait following her down the wide stairway. The rustling cloaks dragged the flagstone floor as they clipped their heels toward the opening door, and out into the bright day's light. The roof of the regal carriage glistened as it awaited their pleasure. Four armed soldiers stood the front with their red-rosed banner carried aloft. Four more soldiers stood the back, their black armour showed from beneath their royal capes. Two black horses as pompous as their masters hoofed the rough ground in their wait. The coachman opened the door with due respect and helped the serene ones into the plush carriage. They all inside now, a thick coverlet was eased over their legs to secure them in comfort. A loud shout came about, as then the jangle and rattle of the royal carriage moved with much regal ado on its way to the palace at the Tower, a ride of one half hour. They entered through the guarded gateway and looked about, as they came near to the tall grey towers that held much agony, gazing their black openings upon the bright party that was below. Through to the far entrance went they to stop with rattle and snort at the door that lay there. Flunkies came from the opening doors and pranced down the high granite steps to the carriage, a stool to hand as they made their way to assist the ladies that were within. The door was opened and they gently alighted from the carriage, helped with hands at reach, and stood together at the foot of the stepped entrance with an air of anticipation. Elizabeth quickly, with raised skirts and clicking heels, was up the stone steps and at the tall-standing doors followed by her fussing ladies. The flunkies came trying to keep pace with their wards as best as they were able. Into the darkened passage they went, the way cold and chilling, holding no warm welcome for them as they rustled along. Elizabeth paced on to the cardinal who stood at wait, his regal cloth of blue and black skirted to the floor, his many rings glinted in the glowing candles, his arms folded before him, protruding thin and white as they showed from the drooped sleeves of his garb. He stood clutching a thick book—though 'twas not the Bible—to himself as if to bring some comfort. A little cap atop his head, placed more to the back than the front, upon the hairless top as would be a chicken's egg.

"My dear Elizabeth," he creamed as the lady upped to him close, with cape unhooked and displaying its bosomy view to him. His legs quickly unsure as he was put immediately at a disadvantage.

"My dear cardinal, are you well? pray, for you look a little flushed"

"Yes, my lady, I am, by God's grace, well. You were called this day, madam, by the soon-to-be King Henry, to relay some of his desires upon you, and when indeed we have come to some agreement, he will grant an audience with you to convey his pleasure. Please follow me, my lady." He half bowed and beckoned her forward, as she moved the way shown to the appointed chamber, with her ladies gracefully behind her. "My lady—" The cardinal stopped the group by stepping afore Elizabeth. "My lady, this conference is for your ears alone, and no others must be present."

"Sir, I wish my ladies with me; they must, for my sake, hear that which I hear for words can be bent, as the smithy bends the iron to a different shape than when first seen fired."

"No, madam, you alone must accompany me."

"Cardinal, I do not cross words with you. My ladies, come with me, or I with haste depart and leave you to Henry, the soon-to-be king, to explain my dilemma."

The cardinal stood still, except for his neck and shoulder that showed displeasure at the words stowed to his person, and come upon him was an uncontrolled nervous twitch from beneath his cloth, and a coming reddening neck. "This way, my lady," was all he spake, as Elizabeth, with a face that did not glimmer a smile, passed by him with her ladies at follow into the counselling chamber. An oak table with benched seats about 'twas to be the place of the chat. The ladies removed the black cape from Elizabeth, and sat her at the head of the table before the cardinal could gain the place, thwarted was he in his quest to be at the head. Elizabeth sat in her bare-topped dress, striking in her beauty to unsettle the cardinal once more. He sat close to Elizabeth so he may whisper some things he wished to hold in some secrecy, but then moved a little away, for he knew our lady would suffer no such desires. The waiting ladies sat, further down the table their seats; fidgety about their manner most urgent, they waited with small patience to hear of the proposal that was to be offered.

"My lady, Henry—"

"Soon-to-be king—" She could no longer resist but speak the words to jiggle the dagger into the side of the cardinal once more, amidst the palmed smiles of her ladies.

He did not suffer to listen but carried on with his message, aloof of all jibes. "Henry ... wishes it to be known that he, with all parliamentary law, wishes to take your hand, Elizabeth Plantagenet, in a marriage of convenience. To become, with Henry, the queen of this England and to bear him children, so to, while continuing your Plantagenet line, begin this new line—the House of Tudor, and so ending all strife that purveys this land, in as much the House of Lancaster and the House of York will forever be as one. What say you, Elizabeth, to this proclamation?"

The ladies of waiting looked at each other as the proposal came to light, looked they with eyes that bulged in the words they did hear, looked they now toward their Elizabeth who had been asked to be the wife of the new king, and awaited the yes.

But Elizabeth did not give a reply straight, for she was in mind of Richard's voice, as even now it seemed that he was beside her to whisper most secret in her ear: "This is the only scheme that Henry can use to bring this land into a peaceful state, and you, my dear Elizabeth, are the only one in all the Realm who can bring such to happening. You, the only one with the bloodline. You, who would bring to her state many loyal people. You, who are of a young age to birth many children. You, Elizabeth, are in the position of power. Use it, my dearest one."

"I will do as Henry wishes," she spake at last the words all wished to hear, but 'twas Elizabeth who spake the words, and she was some way yet from finishing her acceptance. "But before I do so, some things for my sake must be writ, or I will be unable to fulfill the request so placed upon me."

"And what would that be, my lady?" The cardinal waited, quill in hand and ready to scratch the bargaining upon the parchment curled before him.

"First, I will not reside in this place of evil; I wish to stay in the manor at the heath of Hampstead." He scratched. "Further, what allowance am I to receive in my position of Queen?"

The cardinal sat down his quill, and searched through the book that the future king had beset him to write, searched he as if he had no recollection of the amount, but Elizabeth knew he was well aware of the figure writ. "Ah, here it is, my lady, the king has most generously placed the most regal amount of five hundred guineas per annum for your upkeep, and I feel that he is being most benevolent in this respect."

"You may think so, my dear cardinal, but I do not. Am I but a muffin seller seeking pennies?"

The twitch returned to the neck and to the shoulder, as once more the cardinal squirmed his displeasure. "What figure then do you consider of reason, madam?" he spake as he dipped his quill without any glance from his parchment, awaited he the reply from our lady. The cat had the claw upon the mouse.

"I could not possibly comply with the request without the sum of one thousand guineas per annum."

The pen slipped from his hand, as the strength in his fingers left but did nothing to strengthen his knees. "But, my lady, the king cannot bring such to the table; his coffers are in dire strait after his long efforts to gain the crown. No, madam, he would not be for it."

"If he is so poor then he has not the means to keep me as his queen. My time is wasted this day. I will have to seek my future elsewhere." She stood as if to leave, her ladies standing with her, though somewhat bewildered by the events.

"Please, sit, madam, I pray." He picked up his splattered quill, dipped it, and was ready to write once again. "I will put forth your request to Henry."

"Sir, it is no request; it is a demand that must be met if he wishes me to be his queen."

"Yes, my lady," with resigned tone did he come to speak. "Is there anything else you wish?"

"Yes, there is. I would ask, in all of Henry's compassion, to pardon all of Richard's followers. For in doing so he would be seen as a great leader, and would he not want such brave fellows for his army? I wish him to spare their lives, and to restore all their lands and fortunes so taken from them, so they may be close again to the folk that they love."

Scratch and squeak went the quill as the ladies sat quietly, watching the doings and listening with much intent.

"If you would excuse me, my lady, I will place your requests — ahem — *demands* to our Henry."

"Thank you, sir." Away he went with coat at swirl to be gone to the chamber of Henry. The ladies, all close and chatting, sipped a little wine that was laid for them upon the table. Elizabeth sat seemingly cold to the barter she was engaged in. Serene and unruffled, she sipped and waited. Soon the cardinal was back with them to sit with his book and manuscript.

"Now, my lady, the king-to-be has agreed to all your requests except for one, that being that he will pardon all that were against his cause, but they will all forfeit their lands and fortunes with no exceptions."

"I do not feel such an Act is in good grace for the king of this Realm," Elizabeth replied to the worded manuscript.

"I have indeed tried, madam, to sway the king to yours and to my request, for in this matter and for the good of the Realm I am in your court, but he is most adamant in his position, for he states that he must have the revenues from such properties he has gained to fill once more the depleted treasury. But, madam, if you wish to broach the matter with Henry, I will in all faith give my view to be as yours in such a meet. If you would follow my humble self, my lady, we will take audience with Henry."

She did step in due respect behind the cardinal toward the chambers of the king. She had not answered any statements by the cardinal in respect of the lands and properties that would not be returned to their true owners, for she had thoughts to change the matter by her own designs. Down the passageways they wended their way, to come to the soon-to-be King Henry's chambers. The guards stepped to one side as they saw the coming party making to the entrance. The doors opened somewhat mysteriously by the flunkies pulling upon the iron handles from within. The cardinal and Elizabeth entered the chamber without break of step.

Many lit candles were about, brightening the drab walls with their flicker. The regal person that was Henry stood awaiting their presence. A slight man was he, dressed in the most frivolous of clothes and far different from the bold, strong person of Richard. He stood before them in the effeminate stance of the fop, prinked up, indeed. The greetings between Henry and Elizabeth were most pleasant, for this marriage would be not for love, and attraction mattered not. Though Henry desired her more than words that had been writ, and was taken much by her, this strong, proud woman that soon would be his queen. He would show to all her beauty, as she rested upon his arm. Elizabeth though had no desire to give one tot more than was agreed.

"My lord, in respect, I have to appeal to you in regard to the return to full compensation for the returning soldiers of Richard—" But before Elizabeth could proceed any further she was interrupted by the stern words of Henry.

"In respect to you, my lady, I have to say that I cannot adhere to any such request in the matter. The funds are needed from these properties, for we are deeply debted, and I am most adamant in so doing, and that must be the end of the matter, for I will hear no more."

"Thank you for your consideration, my lord." But Elizabeth knew that soon the king's desire for her would alter many a spoken and many a written word, as she flashed her eyes pleasingly toward the monarch. They both in turn sat and scratched their agreement to the contract, which would be placed before the Parliament for their approval, but 'twas already stamped with the king's seal.

"My lady, Elizabeth, this document will be passed by the Parliament when sitting in five days' time. Upon such, my coronation date will be set and our marriage date will also be set, when you and I will be King and Queen of this land, and our two Houses will be as one."

"Thank you, my lord, for your most benevolent doings in this matter." She stood and gave to him one of her most lowly, bosomy curtsies to plant once more her mindful seduction. "My lord," she said, as he kissed the dainty offering that was her hand, as then she took leave of the soon-to-be King Henry, took leave of the sly cardinal, and was escorted to her ladies by the tall guard with gentle step. She entered into the chamber and most quickly sat, and looked about as if in some relief that the ordeal was over.

"Are you well, madam?" the ladies asked, as in some concern they gathered about her.

"I think I am well, but heavy were the hours just past."

"You were very strong, Elizabeth, and we are so proud to be by your side."

"'Twas good I appeared so, and good that I wore many skirts, for my legs were at such a tremble I was feared they may be heard."

"And what of the soon-to-be King Henry, madam? Is he of noble bearing and likeable nature?"

"Ha! Henry is but a powder-puff. With his French lace at dangle from his sleeve, he reeked of excess, a man I feel will bend nicely to our ways. 'When the clay is thrown upon the wheel it can become whatever the potter desires.' And are we not the most skilled of potters?"

"Elizabeth, you are a wicked woman, but we have told you so many times, have we not?"—as they giggled once again at their ladies' antics.

"Come ladies, time for us to depart from this place of intrigue." Elizabeth stood and they began to gather their cloaks, and hatted their locks, soon to be stepping through the menacing ways of the Tower, and to be then outside in the bright day. Their coach stood ready, the flunkies with the open door and the readied stool awaited their coming. Their shoes clicked upon the wooden step set for them, and they were soon all seated. The cover was placed over their legs and the group were on their rattling way once more, as Elizabeth spake then with light heart.

"How say, ladies, that we stop at the heath, and there join in the watching of the foot-the-ball with the common?"

"We think not, madam, for Elizabeth, the soon-to-be queen must not display herself such," came the happy reply from the ladies. And so to the mansion. Sport will have to wait another day, thought Elizabeth.

They were happily back in their beloved reside and to their normal pastimes: the stitching of tapestry, the sewing of cloth, the making of music, and the playing of the cards. And most to their minds, the consoling of Jayne with tender care and compassion. They stood with her long at the window, the window that was the view to the hope that she did cherish...

The cart travelled long, and was many a mile from the cottage that lay at Nottingham, as it trundled its way southward to London Town. They both sat at the board as the swaying and rattling played the hours. With the late afternoon coming upon them, Steven, who was now feeling stronger but lapsing into long sleeps upon the way, spake to Thomas of what must be done to ease their way to London.

"We need to obtain some monies, my friend. When we reach the next town, I must seek a moneylender and give my ring in lieu." Steven looked over at Thomas to see his state at the suggestion.

"Steven, you should not give up your ring, for you will get little of its worth."

"'Tis wasted wrapped here around my finger, more good would it be if it were to purchase our victuals."

"But it has been a good ring to you, do you not think?"

"Yes, it has, but may one day I will buy it back. My mind is made, Thomas, at this time it will be of more benefit to us than the bauble it is." As the town came into view the agreeing answer was returned.

"Steven, you must be very wary when we walk in the town. Remember to act as a peasant; be not proud, but bent and submissive, do not take a stand on any dispute you may encounter, but make haste away. And do not talk with that tongue of education that flaps about."

"I understand, Thomas; I will do all that you say, no matter what is pushed upon me. I will be of a blade of grass growing in a field of grass."

They stopped at the town that came upon them. Market Harborough, the rickety sign pointed. Dolly was tied up to one of the posts near the lane that led to the marketplace, her bag of feed hung about her neck as they shuffled along down the way. Into the open square they came where all about businesses plied their trade. They walked together like two farmers of poor state, jostled and bumped as they searched their way to the lender. They went by the sweet smell of the baker's shop, by the roasting chestnuts at the fire, sounding their cracking shells as they passed, their mouths wetted with the aromas. The sour–sweet smell of the tavern with its noise and gaiety spilling into the street. Then spied a little ahead the swinging sign of the moneylender. They made to the worn steps that led to the grimy door. They pushed it open, as the bell swung about and the door creaked; the dust spun in and around from the seeking wind; a musky smell filled the small shop. They padded their soft boots to the counter. Unseen was the top, for 'twas covered with this and that, of papers, of books, trinkets, and daggers, as all of mankind's troubles it seemed did lay there each with a tale to tell.

"Yes?" the grey-haired man asked, his long beard reached down his front almost to his waist, with traces of his last meal still clinging to the curled hairs. A black cap hugged the back of his head, his clothes also black, made with a course cloth to last long and to keep out the cold that chilled.

"I have a ring of gold I wish to sell." Steven using his educated voice to deal with the lender, hoping for some respect in the transaction and a better price.

"Let me see it," creaked the voice in the whiskered cover. Steven pulled it from his finger, and dropped it into the shaking hand covered in a mitt, which darted close to the lender's chest as quickly as it dropped.

He turned his back to Steven and Thomas, as he pulled his glass from its pouch and peered at the band. "H'm ... H'm ... Poor, poor gold," he whispered to himself, but making loud enough his comment so that the sellers could hear.

"Not that poor, sir, as you can see by the legal stamp inside, from the guild of London, and dated with good karat."

The lender moved closer to the smoky window. "Ah, yes, I see now in this better light." His scheme did not work to someone who was aware of its value. "One guinea, I will give you." The lender set his price.

"Make that price of two guineas, and it's yours, and a bargain too."

"You sound a true gentleman, so I will give you thirty shillings; that is my final dealing."

"We will agree to that figure, but soon will be that I may return to purchase this same ring, and pray that you bear in conscience the price given."

"Of course, sir, I do not stay in business without honesty." He then counted out carefully the coins into Steven's hand. "Twenty-eight, twenty-nine, thirty."

"Sir, would you please recount your coins that lay in my hand, for I believe I am one coin amiss."

The mitted fingers poked about in Steven's hand, moving the coins from one side to the other. "Oh, yes, sir, you are indeed one short; I do not know where my thoughts lie these days,"—as from his pouch he picked out another shilling and dropped it into the rest that lay in Steven's palm.

"Thank you, sir, that is correct; I am sure as the moon rises at the morn 'twas an honest mistake." The comment flying over the lender as a breeze would through the trees. His mind bent upon the ring that was his, and grasped in the grubby mitt. They left the moneylender to his greed and to his dust, and made down the crowded way to the tavern.

"We sup well tonight, Thomas," Steven spake as they pushed their way into the taproom. Musky, dark, smelly—they made their way through to a back table. Steven called for the barmaid in his untried peasant tongue, and a good place to give forth the practised words. "Over 'ere, ducky," he called, as Thomas tried to contain his mirth, but more was to come and he felt he would not be able to bear it, as the maid came over to where they did sit.

"What do you want, dearie?" she asked.

"We'll 'ave a pie of pork, a loaf of bread with some butter, a big onion, and two flagons of ale, thankee, my ducky."

Thomas had to turn away from the conversation, for his laughter was spilling from his mouth with tears that ran his cheeks. The barmaid left with a puzzled look upon her face, for she understood what was said, though 'twas not the way 'twas usually spake. Steven turned to Thomas, for he seemed to be in some state of choking.

"What is the matter, Thomas? … Are you ill?"

"Yes, I am stricken, stricken with laughter's tears that I cannot stop, and makes me that I am unable to breathe; please, talk no more such, for next I will writhe upon the floor."

Steven laughed, as he could well imagine the strangeness of his speech, laughed for the first time in many moons, and happy that some lightheartedness had splashed over his body, for he thought he may not know of such again. Came soon the sup they had ordered. The coins were pressed into the hand of the maid, and, as she left, they ripped the bread and spread it with the fresh butter, and, with a thick slice from the onion, stuffed the delight to their mouths; they bit the crusty bread and crunched the biting onion. The most wonderful banquet in all of the world's banquets. No talk was offered as they ate and supped their ale, for it had been long since food had nestled their stomachs. Chunks of pork pie were cut, the herbs from the meat passing their noses with its desiring aroma, and into their mouths with dribbling delight, fulfilling their hunger's promise. 'Twas well past an hour before they had eaten their fill, and, what was left upon the platter, Thomas bundled into his cloth, for hunger may come to them before another meal showed. They moved out into the darkening eve with the townsfolk, it seemed all out from their houses, and partaking in the street goings.

"Mark my words, my fellow Englishmen, now that our dear Richard is no longer the king, that ponce Henry will levy even more taxes upon us to pay for his excess." The troublemaker spouted his words as he stood upon his box in the middle of the roadway, ranting his anger to the many who were only too willing to listen to such words of truth. "Be wary, my friends, of the lands that Richard in all his wisdom did give to us, to release many of us from the burdens we did carry, to take us away from such laws of serfdom, and all of this that Richard has so generously given could be stolen away from us by the greed of that usurper, that bloody Henry. We must, my friends, be ready to unite, to stop such actions against those of us who have so little. Stand with me and let us do mischief—" His words then stuttered as pushing through the crowd came soldiers of Henry, with clubs and sticks did punish all about those who listened to such rebellious jibe. The speaker picked up his box and made a run through the gathering, brushing past Thomas and Steven into the narrow alley at the side of the tavern; many of the crowd that were fleeing followed down the alley away from the coming soldiers and their swinging clubs, and dragged our pair with them into the cold black way. The soldiers did hastily follow the mob, as Steven and Thomas hid themselves behind one of the side pillars. Dark there, wet and smelly, they cramped into the corner, as peasants and soldiers rushed past them into the gloomed alley. The footsteps sounding less as they went further from the hid pair.

"Two here." ... "Where?" ... "Here in the corner." Words echoed about as they huddled, thinking: Not us—we are well hid.

Two soldiers, the last of their group, had spied the hidden in the dark of their cover. Except for the two soldiers, all had gone and only the breath of haste coloured the alley.

"Get out from there!" The soldiers cuffed the two at the neck, and pulled them roughly into the light that sprang from the entrance. "In that crowd of villains were you?"

"No, sir," chirped up Thomas. "We were passing by and were pushed inside by the crowd. We are true and faithful servants of Henry." The heavy stick came down upon the shoulder of Thomas, making him pull away with the pain.

"I think you lie. And you who say little, I take it you are of the same following as your stricken friend?"

"He is, sir," Thomas interrupted, which cost him a further blow upon his arm, causing him to cringe in some pain, placing Steven in some anguish as he tried to contain his feelings.

"Can he not speak for himself? Be thee silent or the next one will be in the mouth, and you will have no choice but to be of silence." Thomas could do little as the soldiers started to make Steven their target.

"He speaks the truth, we were innocent passersby."

"Innocent? Ha!" The club swung at Steven, cracking him upon his shoulder, but he suffered the blow and contained himself, for they may soon have had their sport and wend their way. Thomas moved forward to assist his friend in his injury, for he was grieved that it may be the injured arm that had taken the blow. "Get away from him! What are you, some nursemaid to render such affection upon him?" Crack! The club came upon the head of Thomas, giving it a bloody gash; then the club was raised once again to strike.

"Enough!" came the voice aside them, the coming strike stopped in air at the disrespect that was laid upon them from the mouth of Steven. "Leave us be; we have done naught." The club was raised once more, this time to strike the speaker with his insolence. "We are in the pay of Henry—spies, in effect, entering the rebels fold to bring out their leaders." Steven's voice of education and commanding state stopped the attack. "You have interfered with the free duty of Henry's bound officers. This disguise we wear is worn with the honour of the Lancastrian, and you have endangered our actions with your tactics. I need to know from you the name of your commanding officer at once, for punishment for this act you have purveyed must be brought about."

The soldiers took a quick glance at each other, then, as one, they dropped their weapons and ran with shaking knees the way of their comrades, leaving Steven and Thomas looking to see them blend into the dark alley. They wanting no more doings with such as they, for the punishment to come they wished not to bear, and fled like thieves from a robbery were they.

"Thomas, how are you?" Steven helped his friend up from his knees and was most concerned of his state.

"I am bloodied a little but it is not severe. And you, Steven, how fare you?"

"I am well; 'twas good they did not strike my injury. Come, Thomas, let us make back to the cart." They helped each along through the milling crowd to where Dolly stood at her post, the mare's big eyes seemed to sparkle as she saw them close. Steven untied her and brought her over to the trough so that she may drink. The horse slopped at one side, whilst at the other Thomas bathed his wound.

"Let me see, Thomas, how deep you have been cut." Steven parted the wet hair. "It is a deep cut but it is not bleeding now. Sit upon the cart, Thomas; I will fetch some balm from the herbalist, for it must be tended." Thomas sat, his head resting in his hands, whilst his friend once more made through the throng to the shop he had spied, the smells that drifted told him of its place. The bell rang its cheer as the door closed upon him, and he dimly saw the rows of crocks that sat upon the black wood of the shelves.

"Good day, sir?" He was greeted and questioned at the same time. The woman looked into his eyes as she spake, she red of face and of a jovial nature it seemed, where others of her ilk were usually sombre and gaunt.

"Madam, I have a friend who has suffered a deep cut to his head and I need some remedy for him."

"Is it still of a bloody state?"

"No, lady, it has stopped." She turned toward the dark shelves and selected one of the crocks from the many that sat there.

"Here you are, sir; this will stop it from going bad, but you will have to rub the wound first to bring forth fresh blood, then, after it is bleeding, spread the remedy thickly over all the bloodied flesh, and within a few days all should be healed."

"Thank you, lady. How much will that be?"

"One penny, sir." Steven delved into his pouch and, picking out the desired coin, placed it into the outstretched hand, and took away with him the crock.

Thomas was still resting his aching head in his hands, as Steven returned with the cure to his side. He did not ask him of his state, for he could see he was pained; his face showed of the strife he was in. "Here, Thomas, let me see your injury." Steven gently lifted away the hands that seemed to bring some relief to the discomfort. He looked again closely at the wound. Congealed blood lay upon the live flesh beneath. "Thomas, I have to wipe the wound clean before we can apply the herbs."

"That is well, Steven; do what is needed."

The rip of the cloth came loud to the ear as a piece was taken from their stash. Steven, as quickly as he was able, rubbed the wound until it bloodied once again. Thomas's grip tightened upon the cart but he stayed silent. Then he felt the cold balsam spread o'er the red flesh, and in little time all his wound was covered and he felt the pain did drift away.

"There, Thomas, you should be well again most quickly."

"Aye, Steven. Shall we depart and rest for the night?"

The cart rolled into the starlight as they made to the river that lay close by. They released Dolly from the shafts, and let her graze and drink from the river, where the banks were low to the waters' edge. The two travellers of such weary state climbed into the cart, and laid down their aching frames upon the warm straw. Though heads throbbed, they most quickly went into peaceful sleep, deep and sound …

She spied her youngest boy scurrying over the open fields, in some unusual haste was he; she left her chores and went toward him, coming flustered and breathless to his mother's side.

"Mother!"

"What is it, my son?"

"'Tis Peggy—at the croft—she is not of good feeling and wishes you to come to her—the lady who chores for her has sent me with the message."

"Come then, let us see what her need may be." Jemma placed her shawl about her head and with Robert made haste to the croft of Peggy.

"She has asked for you, Jemma; her health is not of a good state." Peggy's helper stood waiting outside the old cottage, talking to Jemma in the quietness of the garden there. After she had listened as to the state of Peggy, she made through the borders of fragrant herbs, and entered through the open door into the dwelling.

"Where are you, Peg?" Jemma called, for in the dark room as yet she could see very little.

"Over here, Jemma," came the weak voice from the far side of the room.

She saw her now laying upon her low couch, covered with a rough blanket, the grey hair in view and the crinkled hands at clutch to the cover. "Peg, my dearest, how fare you?" Jemma asked as she placed her warm hands upon the cold ones that were Peg's.

"I fear, Jemma, that my days of seeing the sun rise are few indeed."

"Do not fret, Peg; you will not fade so soon."

"I mind not, for indeed I am weary … I wish to give to you the most cherished thing I hold, that which has been my life. I wish, Jemma, for you to take my herbal book, for you are the only one that is gifted with such compassion and inner soul, you care so much for others, and are the one to carry on after I am gone."

"Peg, this is your life you place before me. I feel so undeserving of such a gift."

"Jemma, I would burn it if I knew there was none worthy of such. But you are, and you must do as I wish."

"I will do as you wish, Peg."

"Please, take it now, I can remember all the brews so written and can continue without the written page. I give it to you, my friend, for I wish it not to fall into any other's hands, those who wish only greed and profit from its words."

"I will do as you desire, Peg, and will cherish and care for your book, and use it only in good faith as you have always done."

Peg pointed to the shelf where lay the life that came in the guise of a book. Jemma upped and lifted the dusty bible to her bosom and held it close and secure.

"You can go now, Jemma, for I am in need of some rest. I will call for you when my time is close upon me."

Jemma pulled the cover that kept the frail Peg with some warmth as she lay in the dim room. "Is there anything I may do for you now, Peg?"

"No, Jemma, I am content now that my book lies safe in your keep."

"Then I will return on the morrow and visit with you, and will so do every day after to comfort you." She kissed the forehead that was beneath the greyed hair and both spake their goodbyes until the morn. Jemma left the small croft hugging the book closely to herself, with someone's lifelong journey held in her arms. She walked holding her son close, as tears welled and thoughts were all of her dear friend Peg …

"How are you, Jayne?" Helen besought her friend who stood as she seemed always to do so, peering across the courtyard from the manor house of

Elizabeth.

"I weary much, Helen, but I will not forgo my vigil. For only Steven can make this pain depart."

Helen put her arm of sympathy around her friend who rested her troubled head upon the comforting shoulder. "I will wait with you, Jayne, and one day your joy may flow over me when Steven shows below this window."

"Thank you, Helen, you are most kind to me in my need."

They both stood until the night came and the yard was dimly bathed below, for only then would Jayne sup and sleep, longing for the morrow to quickly come, for the new day may bring her vigil to an end, in the sought happiness of Steven's return.

Elizabeth was oft away from the mansion in meet with Henry, as was his wont. Dates were set for the coronation ceremonies, and a date mulled for the wedding to come. Henry, during this time, was enacting new laws to be passed by his Parliament; taxes were to be increased and other laws were to be repealed—many of the laws that Richard had enacted, the laws to relieve the lower classes from their burden. Henry, in doing such things, would bring much anarchy to the land. He also instituted a commission to seek out all knowledge regarding rumours of the princes' escape from the Tower and that they were still about. For any princely male of the White Rose would be a most decided threat to Henry's rule. Elizabeth, at this time, was plying her unlimited ardour on the soon-to-be king, stretching his marriage of convenience close to a blind desire. She soon would be the puppeteer, pulling the strings and mouthing the words to this killer of her Richard …

The morn came once more upon the cart as it made its way bound to London. One more night upon the track as then the following day would bring them to the manor and to the waiting vigil of Jayne. They moved at a steady gait but did not press Dolly more than she could offer. Close to the midday hour they came to the town of Luton. The grey spire there lofted tall above the trees, as dark it stood against the blue sky. They clopped down the tree-sided track into the valley town. All green and gold stood the fields about, await they for the scythe and the flail. The beets ready for harvest fresh and green were they, to be pierced and boiled in the field kettles, then rendered down to the sweet liquid that would dry to the crisp sugar, so sought for the bakers' and the land's kitchens.

A market day, this day, as they came to the stalls, and to the pens and paddocks. Animals of all kinds noised about, all auction bound. The two travellers tied up Dolly to the inn that stood close to the auction's shout. They sat this day at the table set outside supping their rich ale and munching their newly-baked bread. The noise of the crowd drifted about them. Stray dogs, scraggly and wild, came sniffing about them, seeking any scrap that may come. The yelp and bark rang as the passersby gave hefty boot if paths crossed, seeking some unknown revenge. Children, dirty and hungry, came to beg, and Steven, in his ache at the sight, gave half pennies to all whose grubby hands were about, soon to scurry away with their treasure. The two left the inn and made toward the laughing shouting crowd that were about the horses' paddock, some standing high upon the rails there, waving and cursing at some disturbance that was out of sight to the travellers. Steven and Thomas were able to find a space that let them see why all about was so fussed, and it appeared the auction was in some turmoil, as two stable lads and two men of horsely bent were trying to bring calm to one of the sale horses. So full of fire was it, seen kicking and snorting; its bridle held by two long reins, with one each side, by a stable lad. The other two trying to bring the animal under some control, but, as yet, none came to the disturbed one. The auctioneer's voice could be heard from somewhere within the crowd, though he could not yet be seen, shouting above the din, making his plea to calm the animal, and to lay down the price upon this steaming terror. But it would have naught of any calm, and was bringing more distress to the other horses that awaited the hammer. The travellers stood upon the rail, as the laughter and the jeers bantered about the square arena.

"You know, Steven, that is a fine horse with good breeding, its only problem is that it has been abused and trusts no man. And see?—they are not treating it in any way that will pacify the animal; they will only make it worse. This mistrust is like a pebble under its saddle; it will not calm until the pebble is eased away."

"Two shillings for this fine animal," called the auction man above the rant.

"Ha ha … You will not get two pennies for that knacker's meat!" came the call as laughter caught the mood.

"C'mon, gentlemen, give me a shilling; come on, sirs, one shilling; 'tis little for this fine horse."

"Give me a shilling and I will take it off your hands," a voice cried from the crowd to more laughter and derision. Steven had been watching Thomas, and saw the look upon his face as the antics continued, and knew that his friend had much knowledge of horseflesh, and saw he the look of compassion for the frightened animal, the look of a need to help.

"Buy the horse, Thomas," he spake at last.

"Pardon?"

"Buy the horse. You need another horse, do you not?"

"Yes, but I am penniless."

"Well, I am not, and for the price of such, 'tis very little, and the bargain has not been struck yet. You say it is a goodly horse. Be not shy—take the money—buy the horse. One day, if you need to, then pay it back, but it matters not for the moment. Care only for that horse."

"I will, Steven." Thomas climbed higher onto the rail, and above the noise and banter, and the noise of the horse's distress, he shouted louder above all. "Sixpence for the animal!"

All stared at where the voice had come from, and the noise stilled for a moment.

Then, with: "Where is your jesters cap? For indeed you must be some kind of fool!" the laughter and ribbing rose once again. "Take it to the knacker's yard! They will give you a penny for it on a sunny day!" … "Pull its teeth and make some token from them!" … "Food for your dogs!" … "Make a nice coat for your missus!" All rife and riddle washed about.

"Take the damned thing then!" The auctioneer was glad to see that tail away from this circus. "Sixpence, sir. Pay me now, for I wish to see how you will take away the animal without slitting its throat."

Thomas jumped over the rail and paid the six pennies into the thankful hand. He turned then toward the fired animal, all steam and sweat, lips curled and teeth snarled, kicking and prancing from the two tethered reins. He came closer to the rearing animal that stood giant above him.

"Run!" … "Get away from it whilst you can!" came the cries of fear from the milling throng. Hushed then was the crowd, the only the noise was of the dogs' bark, the penned cockerel sounding, the sheep and lambs, bleating about their pens. The horses were pulled away, neighing their tune to the song. Could be seen that Thomas was talking to the horse, though no one knew of the words he spake, but talk he did.

"She's like your missus … no matter what you say, she will take no heed!" The quiet broke again into laughter, but soon stilled once more, for all wanted to see what game was being played in the arena, as then some slight whispers of Thomas's words could be heard as he still continued talking to the pranced animal.

"Easy girl, easy. Do not be afraid. I am your friend and I will bring you no harm. Easy now, easy," he whispered. She calmed a little and came down to four legs, lulled by the sweet tones of the honeyed voice about her ears, calm and warm as it laid inside her. She still snorted. Still pawed the dusty ground. "Easy now, my dear, easy girl, good girl, good girl." The crowd were no more bantering but quiet in respect of such happenings, and watched so to see what would come next. She calmed even more under the spell of Thomas, who, reaching forward, began to stroke the nervous nose that was before him; gently and with soft talk he rubbed the warm, bristly hair that lay on her, and, after one or two pulls, away, she fell to the caring hand so soft. Thomas then placed his cheek upon hers, and spake in low tones to her for a full five minutes. In all quiet and calm about did he continue his spell. The ears of the animal flicking back and forth as if catching each word that was whispered to it. She lowered her head and slacked the reins that tethered it. Thomas lifted his head and, whilst still talking, unclipped first one and then the other of the restraints that held it safe. The animal stood most tranquil as Thomas moved slowly, stroking her neck, then along her back and to her rump, as he made his way to the rear of the horse. He stroked tenderly but firmly down her rear leg to the fetlock and the hoof; she looked back at him as he continued his sweet talk and gently lifted the hoof to be sure she had not suffered any injury to herself during the distress she was in. Placed gently back down, he went to the other leg. The horse turned her head to look the other side as Thomas wiped the hoof clean and then viewed the fetlock, to place it down with gentle care. He moved with caressing hands to the front, the horse was, it seemed, in total trust of its whispering friend. The front legs were lifted one by one with no move from the animal of any anxiety or fret. He was front again, stoking and patting with his cheek close to the horse, talking again for some time. The horse was as calm as the sea under the windless day. He slowly took off her bridle, which left her free to go where she may, but she did not stray and stayed close to Thomas's side. Our man started his slow walk toward the paddock gate, two steps he took away from the horse, when it began to follow close behind him, not tethered in any way, with its head almost over the shoulder of her friend in front. As he went the crowd shouted and clapped at the pleasure of the sight before them, happy as well that the auction man had at last lost out on his dealings. To the gate where Steven waited they went, his face full of respect for this horse doctor, as a little twinkle in his eyes showed some thoughts in his head of future dealings. They walked away together with their horse at back seeking Dolly and the cart.

"What did you say to the animal, Thomas?"

"I just told her I would be her friend, and that I would protect her and shield her from all harm."

"Just like us, Thomas."

"Like you say, Steven, just like us."

"What shall we call her?" spake Steven, as the horse's head was hanging over their shoulders.

"Only one name, aye, Steven?"

"Yes, Thomas, only one name." The joint cry came loud: "Sixpence!"

To the tethered Dolly they came, giving a pleasing pat to the waiting horse. Sixpence nosed by the two travellers to seek the other horse; the two mares sniffed each other's heads as Thomas came amidst them, with his own head talking and whispering to both horses and seeking to bond them. But as he looked at them he saw 'twas not needed for they had come to their own trust. Steven brought over the bag of feed and placed it open upon the ground so that both horses may feed, which they did in a most placid manner as if they had been together for a long time. The bucket was dipped into the trough, and the fresh water was brought over to the animals by Thomas. The two then sat at the back of the cart as the animals fed.

"I see from your looks, Steven, that you have caring feelings for such animals."

"Yes, Thomas, I am most interested in horses, but I have not the gift you have shown this day."

"'Tis naught I do, I give them trust and that is all anyone can do."

"No, it is not so, for you have something in your soul to be as one with them where others do not." A smile was all the reply. They supped and ate at the cart as the day drew its close, another day that Steven learned many things of the ways of other folk. They lay as two poor peasants, smelly and dirty, with unshaven faces resting upon the straw, and slept contented the night. Steven's heart filled with joy for the morrow.

The mist-filled morn came with the sun low, trying to break the curtain of lace that covered the awakening travellers. They both washed the night away from their faces in the horse trough as the mares moved in to lap at the cold water from their night's wanders. Thomas and Steven dried their faces upon the rough cloth they carried, rubbing away until the skin glowed. They harnessed Dolly and, with Sixpence trotting along beside her, moved away from the market town in that mist, upon their rattle-bump way. The morn cleared its veil but cloudy came the sky; no sun this day would bring its warmth through the blanket cloth that hung o'er the land. On they went, close to the noon hour 'twas as they came to the town of London, now in the drizzly rain that fell. Heavy mud splashed under hoof, as they neared the heath at Hampstead. Donned in their canvas coats and hooded hats, they crouched on the board together as the rain seeped all about them. The gates of the mansion came to sight as through the misty drape they came. The leaves blew from the trees and stuck to their coats like misplaced medals upon a warrior. As they neared, joy was filling Steven's heart, so much was it that he could think of Jayne no more for fear he may burst, and had to fill his thoughts with other things to ease the bubble. Heavy was the rain now, and little to see for the face that gazed through the window of the mansion.

Jayne with squinted eyes looked as best she was able, with Elizabeth and the other ladies about the chamber, still giving her comfort as she stood again her vigil. She stood as she had done for many days, leaning upon the stone of the framed window. A shape it seemed was coming closer to the gate. She straightened from the wall and leant with both hands upon the sill, so her face could be closer to see who came. Closer through the murked light two horses she saw, then a cart with two shapes at crouch, they dark and unmoving as they sat upon the board.

"'Tis Steven," she whispered.

"Did you speak, dear Jayne?" Mary asked her friend as she looked up from her stitching.

"'Tis Steven,"—a little louder now but still a whisper, as if the words would not fit her tongue. The cart was almost through the gate, and still only two dark shapes did show, as the ladies put down their sewing and came to Jayne at the window, for it seemed she was gaining some excitement from the happenings in the courtyard below. They saw torches lighted and closing towards the cart and its people. "It is, it is Steven, I know it is." Louder now her voice, with welled tears misting her view even more, but she wiped them away and recovered somewhat her composure.

"Be calm Jayne, you know not for sure who holds those shapes in the dim."

"My heart tells me it is him. I must go to the yard." But they did not move yet, as they looked at the lit stars that came to the cart, stopped inside the courtyard. Voices raised carried to the window.

"What do you seek here?" One of the guards, holding the torch close to see who had come to the yard, asked; he shone his light upon the bedraggled faces and wetted garb of the two travellers. "Get away from here! The likes of you are not allowed in this yard!" From the window they could not hear all the words that were bantered, but could tell from the actions they saw that a confrontation was in the making.

The unheard voice from the cart spake calmly to the irate guard. "I wish to speak to the Lady Jayne, she—"

"Do not bring such to your speech. Best to move from this place before blood is spilt about."

"Guard! Guard!" Elizabeth shouted to her personal officer who came at the beckoning call.

"Yes, my lady?"

"Go thee down to the yard in much haste and end that fracas that is about. We will follow you as quickly as we are able."

"Yes, my lady," came the fleeing reply, as the guard was already making quickly to the yard and its troubles.

"Come, Jayne, put on your cape and let us see indeed who is about."

They all donned their cloaks with hearts beating fast and made toward the corridor that the guard had taken, to see the door that led to the courtyard open wide, swinging in the wind and rain that withered against it.

"Sergeant, we mean no—" was all that Steven spake before the heavy stick swung by the soldier journeyed down toward his arm, as Thomas came quickly to place himself in front of the blow and was knocked to the muddied ground. Steven was then stumbled to the yard trying to avoid the swinging stick that was coming to strike again, whistling through the rain it slashed. A hand, strong, held the stick from its travel.

"Hold!" shouted loudly the mud-splattered guard sent to quell the melee. The blow was stopped, but the angered soldier was still filled with rage and tried to pull away the battle stick from the strong grip that held tight.

"Let it be. These rogues need teaching a lesson." A loud crack came in silence as Steven had upped and swung his good fist upon the jaw of the mischievous one, to send him spinning into the muddy slop; close to where the horses bristled and stamped in the disturbance around them, he lay bent in some unconscious state.

The ladies had made their way to the outside steps, in stockinged feet ran they, their shoes left tumbled at the door, not neatly laid as was their way.

"Hold onto us, Jayne. Do not stumble." They guided their charge to the safe that was at the bottom step. There she—muddied up to her ankles and her skirt dragging in the slop—moved closer to the shapes with fear and joy mixed as one in her heart. The backs were to her, as she came within an arm's reach of the tall, canvas-covered shape, rain-sopped and mud-splattered. Her white, slender arm reached out, her thin delicate hand closed to the canvas, her rings sounded with the rain's splash.

"Steven?" she quietly asked as she touched the shoulder of the man before her. The head moved to turn, her heart stilled, the world stopped. Whose face would look upon her? She knew it would be the one she prayed for, but a fearful spell came upon her, all jumbling and tossing her mind. The face came around with the turn of the body, all whiskered and wet and full of mud, and not, it seemed, the face she sought, for under its growth 'twas seen weathered and brash, and not the skin of a gentleman; her heart sank …

"Jayne," the voice said all she wished for, and she breathed again; she knew now her love had returned as he swore he would, and her wait had not been in vain; her knees weakened and she was almost ready to fall into the mud. The ladies who stood at the back made a move toward their friend, but 'twas not needed as the wet arm with canvas dripping came about her, and pulled her tight and close to the warmth that came through the coat he wore; she regained her strength and fought off her faint as she was secure in the arms she had longed for. She looked up into the eyes above her, as the lips through the whiskery blanket did kiss her longing mouth, both rough and soft were they that closed upon hers. Her knees weakened once more as the ladies were with them, holding Steven, holding Jayne. Steven lifted his head and, with watery eyes, looked to his friend. Thomas was standing and was no worse from the blow he had taken.

"This is my most dearest friend, Thomas," he spake as he looked over to his comrade. "Without him I would more than once be at rot in some field. Come, Thomas," he beckoned the reluctant Thomas.

Two of the ladies took it upon themselves to kindly entreat him. "Come, let us take you inside and tend to you." They walked him on each side, he shakily still from the blow he had taken, but would not speak of it, as toward the mansion steps they went, followed by Steven and Jayne as one. Elizabeth stood rain-drenched, her hair no longer the hair of a lady, but of some ragged farmyard animal. Stood she with hands upon hips tolling her displeasure to the recovering guard.

"Sir, you know your duty, and that is that all comers must be treated with respect at this place, no matter what acts are used elsewhere, and your orders do spell such. If danger is present, then an action against it is approved. But to attack two helpless persons is not to our liking. Guard!" she called to her personal officer.

"Yes, my lady."

"Take him away and rank him to common soldier ... And if you mistreat anyone again, it will mean the lash for you. Do you hear my words?"

"Yes, my lady," the dripping scarecrow managed a shameful answer.

"See to the horses!" she called over to the standing watchers from the stable, who seemed to be in some kind of melancholy. "Am I the only one with a head in this yard?" Still at anger, she hitched up her wetted dress and slopped to the manor door to enter the hallway. Maids and manservants were fussed all about as they removed the dripping cloaks and coats from the sodden party, drying them with warm towels as much as they were able, the hair rubbed and dabbed to soak up the wet, and then to wrap them in blankets to keep out the chill. They at last were able to look each at each, and as Elizabeth looked about she began to laugh, the laugh of Elizabeth as catching as the fever it came, until all were caught in the spell that was cast upon them as they squirmed with the pleasing pain. "We look not unlike a flock of farmyard hens dipped in the trough." Elizabeth was able to cackle out between her teared eyes and reddened face. The laughter weakened her knees, making her sit untidily upon the floor, and then visited by others who could stand no more.

Soon they were able to rise and, with some outbreaks from time to time, they went, each helping the other as they did so, to the upper chambers. There the two men were ushered to one of the washing rooms and the ladies to the other. The ladies were bathed and dried, then powdered and dressed most finely for the meal they all would share, and to hear all of the doings of Steven and his friend Thomas, to all at last be of happiness, and to see Jayne radiant once more. The two men likewise were bathed and dried, as into the chamber came the barber-surgeon, called by Elizabeth to see to any injuries that may be of bother. In converse with Steven, the surgeon had learned of the threatening wound that he had suffered. He jingled his surgeon's bag upon the floor and sat before his charge. Young was he for the position he held. Elizabeth had chosen him, saying that she felt he was the one for this position, for such was in her heart, and the older surgeons shown to her were of the old school, and would be unwilling to try new remedies, and so had placed her trust in the bright caring man who sat before Steven.

"Sir, may I see your wound?"

"Yes, of course." Steven held out his arm, still covered in canvas. Into the bag dipped the gentle hand as he peered into the instruments, to bring to ear the rattle of metals as he searched for his small shears. Out they came, bright and shiny, looking as if they had never been used; he snipped through the canvas to the cloth beneath.

"How long have you had such a wound, sir?"

"The day of the battle of Bosworth Field was when I was so struck."

"That is a long time without care, do you not know?"

"I was treated as in the olden times, with herbs and salves from the woods, ways long forgotten I am told, and was told not to remove the coverings, but to let it drop away."

He snipped through the cloth as he listened to the words spoken, and came to the blackened rot of leaves that showed. "What is this?"

Thomas leaned over to see what the surgeon was poking at. "Oh, that is the leaf of plantain."

"The leaf of plantain! What sort of witchcraft has been practised upon you? I dread to look further."

"See the wound first, sir, before you judge whether witch or saint."

The surgeon pulled away the rotted leaf to expose the arm—all black and discoloured did it appear. A cloth was very wetted in some warm water and the surgeon began gently to wash the held limb. "Do you feel any discomfort, sir?" he asked.

"No, I do not, it feels as an arm should feel."

The surgeon continued to bathe away the black that lay there, and in little time in the light came the showing of clear, fresh skin—a skin that was healed; he rubbed with more vigour as Steven felt no pain from the ordeal, and soon all the blackness was washed away as two heads gazed at the arm. One of Steven, and the other of the surgeon, for Thomas had no need to see, for he knew it would be healed.

"I do not believe what my eyes clearly see. With all my medicines, I could not bring such a wound to this, so much repaired, it is like a new limb." The arm had completely healed, showing only the thin scarred line with the small spots each side where it had been sewn, the gut rotted away leaving naught for the surgeon to do but awe at the work. "Whoever did this has far more skill than I can ever hope to have. Yes, sirs, there is no witchcraft here, only saintly doings."

"Yes, I know she is a saint," came Thomas's reply.

The surgeon's helpers came and showed their work, as they clipped the two beards as close as they could with the singing shears; then, with the soaping brushes, they rubbed into the left stubble, bringing the whiskers more to softness for the shaving blade, honed to the devilish sharpness upon the stropping leather. They both sat back upon the bench with heads against the wall as they were shaved with much deftness by the helpers. The haired faces soon showed the sheltered skins beneath, rubbed dry with the washing cloths, until they showed clean and shiny like the newborn's face. Clothes were brought and they soon were dressed, with the traces of lavender sprigs still clinging its scent to the cloth as 'twas donned. No fancy, puffy clothes did Steven ever wear, just practical attire more suited to a man of business than to the son of a lord. Thomas was fitted likewise, and not for many a moon had they both felt the net of cleanliness upon them. Though Thomas, being of peasant class, was always, through Jemma's guiding hand, kept in cleanliness, both in his body and in his clothes, so unlike many of his ilk.

"How does that feel, Thomas?"

"So good, Steven; like floating upon a white cloud above all that is real."

"Come, my friend, let us sup the sup of kings," Steven spake as put his arm around his comrade and ushered him along. No more did Thomas step in the shadow but stepped as an equal, his confidence rising by the hour as he drew from his friend. They came from the washing room, in like grubbing pigs and out like fine horses, all a-shine and brushed.

They came down the broad stairway to the kitchen, which was still the most favoured place to eat, more used than the dining hall, which, except for kingly visits, was too pompous. They traced the floor to the kitchen entrance. The laden food drifted its enticement to Steven and Thomas's hunger, the aroma mingled with the laughter and the chatter of the ladies bantering with the kitchen folk, as they brought a homely feeling to the cozy kitchen. "Come, come," they beckoned to the men upon their entering. The ladies all dressed most elegantly as was their wont.

"What a handsome pair you are indeed. Come, Thomas, sit between us, we want to know all." Mary and Helen reached out their hands and helped Thomas to sit. "Here, sir, a flagon of ale; you must be overcome with thirst."

"Aye, ladies, that I am." His coarse speech and class mattered naught in this house. They knew they had been blessed by their births into rich families, but they too had known some hardship, for they had been thrown into the street with naught, and but for a different bed they could have been born into to such a different world, and they knew that one day all men would be equal, and as such felt no reason not to treat Thomas as their brother. Thomas guzzled at the flagon, joined by Steven, both having saved their thirst for this event or so it did seem. Jayne sat clinging to her loved one's arm, afraid to look away for that he may vanish.

Steven stood. "A toast, my dear ones, a toast to Thomas, who saved me more than once." They drank with an "Aye!" … "And a toast to his wife, Jemma, who recovered me from such an evil wound and brought such strength to me." … "Jemma!" they all cheered, as Thomas's beaming face was with much happiness. They sat and drank to fill, ate till no more be done, talked and cried and laughed, until the lateness of the night called out rest to them. Then, together, they walked up the stairway to their different chambers.

"On the morrow, I must be away, Steven," side-by-side upon the way, Thomas spake.

"Yes, I know, my friend, you must return to those who are most anxious for your return. But, Thomas, I tell you this, that when I am fully able and have completed some dealings, which should be in the coming spring, I will come to you at Nottingham, for I will have much to discuss with you, have no doubt, Thomas, as I speak, I will indeed come to you."

"Steven, if the words pass your lips then I know them to be true, and in the spring I will look forward to greeting you once again."

To rest they all went to their separate places. In the dark night the heavy door creaked and closed most quietly, as Jayne came to the chamber of her loved one, and slipped in beside him, into the warmth she had longed for, feeling more safe and secure than she had for many a day. They slowly closed to each other's nearness, until no space did show in their togetherness and slumber sweet painted over them.

The dawn bright did come with the rain gone its way, as the cart and horses stood at the ready with Steven and Thomas standing with the ladies. The goodbyes came, most reverently to Elizabeth, the queen-to-be, but an unlikely demeanour for such as she kissed the cheek of Thomas, filling him with much pride and teared eye. The ladies followed and gave him the most loving attention.

"Goodbye, Thomas. I will see you again."

"Yes, Steven, until we meet again." They shook the hands of comrades and then Thomas was up upon the board. "C'mon," he called to Dolly and Sixpence, as they rolled out of the yard and into the laneway, with a wave from Thomas as he wended his way. A wave from all then of goodbye, and he was around the corner and unseen, only the echo of the clop heard as it went quieter away till naught broke the stillness.

All were within the mansion as Jayne and Steven walked through to the far side of the chamber, to enter the garden that was all awash with the brightening sun, and seated themselves upon the bench that was hugged by the thick bushes and trees, the flowers giving off the last of their bloom and aroma, as the bees flew about them and, as if in some ritual greeting, buzzed about their ears, on the way to and from their gather. Their hands held clingingly together as they looked at each other in the bathing warm.

"Steven, what will your plans be now that you have lost your king?"

"As yet, I know not fully; much depends upon Henry's proclamation regarding the officers and soldiers of Richard's army. But I fear that any who opposed Henry will lose everything; the only thing we may be allowed to keep would be our heads, and I fear for all else he has in mind."

"From what I understand of the contract between Elizabeth and Henry, it is so, that all lands and fortunes will be forfeited to the king." Thoughts would trace the face of Steven, as he saw that which he feared had come to pass, and he would be without any means. "You think deeply, my love. Will you return to the army and serve the king?"

"No, Jayne, I will not fight any more the battles of any king. And more so not the battles of Henry, who took the crown with treachery and little honour, and did murder a most loyal knight and king. He is a little man who wears this day a big coat, but he will always be a little man."

"What will you do then, Steven, without your fortune and your lands?"

"Have little fear, my love, for with God's blessing, I will have the means to become once more prosperous. But I must be sure of that which I seek still awaits me. I talk in some riddles of that which I must relay to you."

"I care not, Steven, for such fortunes of gold and silver, for I have been with aching heart for a lost love, and have found I need nothing more. If you walk in rags, I will walk beside you."

"Thank you, my dearest Jayne. 'Twas the thought of you that gave me the will to live when death was all about and suffering came with its awe. You kept me from the gate, for I had to see you once again even if only for a moment most fleeting."

They gently kissed and held each other close upon that bench cradled by the greenery, warmed by the sun in that intimate corner. 'Twould be little time afore the winter would come and lay its frost and snow upon this isled land, with the sea to blow and storm all about. They sat longer as their thoughts searched ahead to what may be.

Chapter Sixteen.

A King's Fortune.

As the days passed, Steven was feeling stronger, with an itch inside him that he knew was his future. To breed fine horses would be his calling. He knew the English horse was strong and able to haul all manner of loads great distances, but the needed speed was not present, and in modern battle speed was more and more desired. He had heard about a stallion, and then later had seen the horse which had been brought back from the crusades, but this was many years ago, and since that time had never seen another. The memory was always with him of the speed that animal had shown, the most quick horse he had ever spied, though 'twas only able to maintain its speed for a short time. Steven wished to obtain such an animal and to breed it with the English horse, to give strength and stamina to its quick.

Steven rode about into the country to the north of London, and did so for many hours and for many days, then after much time had past in this endeavour he took his Jayne upon the journey into the rolling countryside he had searched.

"Come, Jayne, come!" Steven, looking back from his mount, called to the lagging Jayne.

"You are in haste far more than I, my love."

"Oh, Jayne, I am sorry; in my exciting path, I run too fast."

"We will, I am sure, be there soon, Steven, wherever it may be."

"The road to a palace is as pleasing as the palace itself. I do hope you are enamoured by this place, Jayne. I will be most happy if it is to your liking."

Along the winding lane they went until no lane went further; the horses began hoofing through the long grass as they went the gentle slope ahead to rise to the top, then to stay their horses and to behold the placid valley low in the hills' fold, and there stood in quiet grace a large manor house of grey stone, standing strong amongst the green hills.

"What say you, Jayne, of this place?"

"It looks most handsome; how did you come by it?"

"'Twas placed for sale at the land office; the owner has lost possession of such, being killed at Bosworth fighting for Richard. The place now empty, his wife and children fled."

"How sad, Steven."

"Yes, it is, but that is the way until the kings of this land come with more compassion. Come, let us look closer."

They rode down the hillside toward the manor's place, o'er the logged bridge above the washing stream, and made way to the oak entrance; they dismounted and entered the large cast iron key into the door's lock to release its bonds. Steven pushed the door wider and entered Jayne gently inside to the bright sunlight that flashed upon the settling dust, to sparkle its mist as they moved about, the hall sounding all hollow and empty as it echoed their walk.

"Steven, I love it, and it can be made most delightful. Let us see the kitchen." Hand held hand as they found first the pantry, and then the large kitchen; all empty and of quietness it stood, but could be seen the pleasantness that lingered there. They upped the stairway and searched each room, their pleasure abounding. Saw they from the windows the rolling lands, and far in the distance the farmhouse that was also within the lands' bounds. The roof of slate peaked above the bushed and treed 'scape, awaiting some family to bring it to the life and joy it once protected.

"The soil is good for the horse and I know of a wizard who can charm such animals."

"Thomas is the wizard, is that not so, Steven?"

"Yes, he is, and if I can obtain our fortune, and with dealings from the aristocracy and with Thomas's skills, we could make a very good life for ourselves at this handsome place."

"But, Steven, I know not of the fortune you speak."

"It will come, my dear. I believe it is waiting for us at the castle at Nottingham. Jayne, two days before the battle at the common, another officer and myself, under the most discreet orders of Richard, did bury several boxes within the walled fortress, and I am the only survivor of such knowledge, for all others have gone by the board. It is also the reason that the king's coffers are empty, and that he thinks Richard squandered all the monies upon frivolous things. As Henry has taken all we possess for being loyal to our king, then I feel it is only just that such fortunes go into the pockets of those so slighted."

"But would not these treasures contain the royal jewels that are still missing, that belong to the king who is in seat?"

"Yes, those gems would have to be returned to the crown by some covert means."

"And how, pray, would you manage to uncover such treasure without being sighted?"

"Ha! My dearest, that is where Thomas comes to play." Jayne's eyes widened even more so. "You see, Jayne, our Thomas knows of some way to enter the castle as a cloud in the mist; I know not how he can do such, but I know for certain that he can."

"I fear for you, Steven, to undertake such a quest; you have only for a short time returned to me, and again you must go forth into danger once more."

"Be not so, my love, for I will not undertake any plot that would not return me to you."

"Well, it does seem shameful to let it rot in some dark corner, does it not? Come then, my dear Steven, let us return to the manor of my Lady Elizabeth, where you may go about your business and see if you can secure this divine place for us and your horses."

Within the next day, as Jayne attended her lady, Steven rode to the purveyor of lands to see if some bargain could be struck; being without funds, Steven needed all the devices he could bring to mind. *Purveyor of Lands and Titles to his Majesty, the King* was writ o'er the door, all red and gold it stated the office within, and, no doubt, thought Steven, of pompous and stately keepers of book, with snoot and demeaning words as was always with the legal doings of the courts. He entered within, as a long hall met his gaze, lit well at this time with daylight shooting its arrows through the high windows, piercing the dull interior. Many tallows stood about, awaiting the dusk's call to be brought to life again with their flickering charm. He came to the chamber of his need and saw many benches and tables about, each with a clerk sat, all appearing to have the same mother it seemed, with black clothes and caps, their rat-like faces half hidden as they worked at their tables. Some person sat opposite them, squirming and unsettled, treated like some tad from the pond, nodding and shaking heads as they answered the many irrelevant questions put to them, as the feather flicked its ink and scratched at the legal parchment before them, tabled flat as the notations were writ. Long benches where placed inside the door, where a score of people sat awaiting the shout of their name, and then to walk the uneasy walk to the table of their call. Steven sat, arms at fold, as the lad took his name and placed it atop the pile of those who waited. He sat uneasy for his inquisitor with the others upon the same mission, shifting and twisting their documents. Names were shouted about as some left and others entered. There were many dealings this day, when many properties were changed from one who had lost all, to others purchasing the spoils. The seats were not empty for long as the to and fro continued.

"Moron! … Steven Moron!" came the call. Steven upped and made to the bench where he heard the voice call, and not sure to which he had to go, but an empty bench he saw and made toward such. He sat, as before him perched one of the ratty clerks.

"That is Mo-*ran*."

"What?"

"The name; it is Moran."

"Oh. What did I say?"

"You said Moron."

"Oh, did I?" No apology came, both knowing well what was said, but the clerk in his position started his demeaning early in the conference. "What do you wish?" he tiredly asked.

"It is to purchase property that is in Hertfordshire, which at the moment lays empty."

"Papers!"

Steven delved into his pouch, and thought that he had little chance to persuade this person before him to offer him any compassion in the dealings. He brought out the scroll, rolled and tied, and passed it to the creaking hand afore him. "These are the documents I was given regarding the property."

The clerk pulled on the ribbon and laid the parchment flat, but no sooner such than it rolled up again. The deepest sigh of despair came from the lips of the clerk at this effrontery to him of the rolling scroll. But before aught else could be uttered, a dark figure came to whisper into the ear of the scribe, and moments later he upped with some papers, and left the table as the dark shape sat. Another clerk sat before Steven but lo he had a red and cheery face. How did such as this man obtain a clerk's position? for he appeared not sour and agitated but of a more accommodating air.

"I am sorry, sir, but our Master Scrowl has been called away. My name is Martin Mallory," he gave a smile. God save me, thought Steven, the walls must be about to tumble. "Now, let us see, what do we have here?" He opened the rolled document and held it so it would not curl back. "I see you are interested in the Hertfordshire property—a very desirable piece, if I may say so. You have seen the price asked, have you not, sir?"

"Yes, I have, and I am willing to pay the price stated, but my tale is that after fighting for Richard at Bosworth I have lost all to the state, both my lands and my fortune have been taken and 'twill not be for a full six months that any fortune will come to me; I therefore ask for a note of intent so I may secure the property for that time."

"I see … You have at the moment no support?"

"That is so, sir. I live in the good grace of the Lady Jayne Brownley."

"Where is your abode whilst you are in this temporary state?"

"I reside in the manor of our Lady Elizabeth Plantagenet at the heath of Hampstead."

The clerk's eyes lit as he mulled the answer. "You are then, sir, at the moment in residence within our future queen's abode?"

"Yes, sir, I am betrothed to the Lady Jayne, who is one of the waiting ladies to the Lady Elizabeth. If need, I could bring a letter of recommendation from our lady to vouch for my honour."

"I think that will not be required," he leant forward and spake quietly. Steven also leant toward the clerk to hear the lowered tone. "Anyone, sir, who stands upon a battlefield to fight beside his king needs no letter of honour, for honour is beheld with your courage." He then did lean away and sorted through some legal readings to pull out one particular sheet. "Note of Intent" 'twas headed; he scratched at it with his quill, and shortly signed the note himself, and then slid it over the table to Steven whilst handing the dipped quill to the waiting hand; Steven signed the note and handed back the doings to the clerk, who then shook the sand from his shaker upon it, and blew it off carefully, away from the faces about. He then folded it neatly and handed it back to Steven.

"Thank you for your understanding, sir," Steven spake as he offered his hand to the clerk, who shook it with some sincere warmth. "If I may say so, you seem not the usual person that works in such a position as this."

"You are right in saying such, for I did hold some high position within the court of our late king, but I was shuffled down to the only work available to me after his demise. But at least I am employed as many are not, and indeed I do not have to live upon the street. But as always the wheel will turn. I must to my duties now, sir, but I must relate that payment can be made in monies or gold, whichever is suitable to your good self, and if through circumstance you need a little more time, please come to see me and I will extend your request. Please ask for Martin Mallory, Head Clerk; any of the pages will direct you to me."

Steven took his leave, thanking once more the clerk for his kindness …

Jemma made way to the croft where Peggy did dwell; a basket upon her arm, she walked the path that wended its way past a poorly built shelter made of branches and trunks of trees with an old tattered cloth covering the crude opening that was the entrance. Smoke leaked through the small hole in the roof. Two grubby children played about in the dirt. Their mother, a peasant, worried inside as she tried to make some victuals with the little food they had. A most poor family who had naught. Jemma called at the entrance.

"Marge? Are you there?"

"Yes," came the reply as the mother came out into the smokeless air. "Oh, Jemma, are you well?"

"Yes, my dear, I am, and how are you?"

"I am well."

"Is your husband still away?"

"Yes, he has work at the ore diggings near Gedling. I pray he will return to us for a short while soon." Jemma knew Marge suffered much hardship and loneliness whilst her husband was away, but at no time did she ever complain of any.

"I am sure he will return to you soon. I have brought you a little food; it seems more was made than we needed." She handed the basket over to Marge.

"Thank you, Jemma. You are most kind."

"'Tis little I do; wished I that it could be more. Here, take this." Jemma pressed two pennies into the reluctant hand, only able to do so by holding the wrist and making it be taken.

"Thank you, Jemma." She did not refuse it, for it would be wasting her time as Jemma would not leave until the coin was taken.

"I will see you soon, Marge."

"Yes ... I will return your basket."

"Thank you," came the leaving voice as Jemma stepped toward the croft of Peggy.

A young woman stood at the doorway awaiting the coming visitor. She, the niece of Peggy, and, as agreed, would be willed Peg's property upon her death. "How is she?" Jemma asked as she closed toward the doorway. Tears were seen, held back from the trembling lips 'neath.

"She is in a dire state, Jemma; I am most feared for her."

Jemma put her arm around the woman's shoulder, she another whose husband was away at the mine. "Sit yourself outside here for a while, Isabel. I will see how she fares." Isabel solemnly sat as Jemma went into the cottage.

The couch in the corner showed little as Jemma went to her friend's side. "Peggy—are you there?" No answer came. Fearing cold skin as she did so, she touched her hand upon the white one that was now at show, happy to feel a warm squeeze upon her fingers, which held gently with a friendly touch. Jemma sat herself at the stool beside the couch and held the hand ... until, in time, it went cold and all was done. "Dear Peg." Jemma kissed the greyed head at the bolster, and gently pulled the covers over the small body; it would keep her safe until the women from the village would come and make her ready for the morrow, and the mourning rites, upon the day, Peg would not see.

Jemma came out with her eyes wetted and saddened, and took herself to console Isabel, the closest of blood to Peggy. "She has gone, my dear; a long and blessed life she had; do not shed tears but be joyed, for she is with her maker and far into happiness." She held Isabel tightly and rocked her as she sobbed until her tears lessened, and she gathered herself for the duties that befell her.

"I will fetch the womenfolk to make her ready."

"Yes, do that, Isabel, and I to the church will go to make the arrangements." They kissed and parted their sad ways and went to their duties.

Two days had passed, Peggy had been put to rest, and Isabel had moved into the croft. But to Jemma fell the vigil for her dear Thomas to be returned. She prayed nightly that soon he would safely come, and wished that the future for them would be happy, and that they, through hard work, would become prosperous, if only enough to help the less fortunate that were about. For Jemma believed the more kindness that was shown, the more it would bring rewards that were far more lasting than a sack of pennies could ever buy. She waited with her sons for the return of her husband, and their father.

The dawn came upon this day, misty thick with fog and damp that hung about the banks of the river Trent and spread all over the lowlands and marshes hiding all within its clutch from the gaze of each. Thomas came at last toward the cottage where at wait were his wife and children. No highway was needed to guide the way; Dolly, the eye that needed no sight to find her home, came through the gateway to the yard. The fog not only making things unseen but dulling all sound with its cover. Thomas climbed from the board; all was still about.

"Jemma! … Jemma!" he called. A misty light came, the door had opened with the firelight, trying to fight its way through the blanketed air, but little did it gain. A shadow across its rays flitted.

"Thomas!" came the cry of joy as Jemma ran from the doorway to the sound of the call and made toward the voice that was her love. The thick fog still covered and, though she heard the voice, as yet Jemma could not spy him. "Where are you?" she called, as then from behind her came the two strong arms grasping her tightly, the arms that blissed her, and the kiss longed for was placed upon her neck.

"Jemma, I have deeply missed your loving self these past days." She turned and kissed the lips of her dearest.

"Father! Father!" shouted the boys as they came to hug the one they had waited for, nearly felling him in their quest.

"My boys, it is a most happy day this day that I am at last within this fold. Come, see what we have, my sons." He took all to the new horse, now only a dark outline in the murk but as closer they came 'twas seen more clearly.

"Father, where did you get it? … Can we ride it? … What a fine animal! … What is its name?" All bubbled out as they stroked the mare and looked her over.

"Her name is Sixpence."

"Sixpence?" the children replied with some glee. "How was she named so?"

"That, my boys, was the price paid ... Stable them, my little men, and we will sup and I will tell my adventurous tale of such doings that even I can no longer imagine. You know I supped with the soon-to-be Queen Elizabeth."

"Father, you did not."

"Oh, but I did, my sons, yes indeed I did."

The boys took the horses as Thomas and Jemma armed into the cozy of their cottage …

The winter came with windy blow striking its freezing snow and rain to all corners, and drifted high were the snowy banks to stay the traveller home, the farmer to his barn, the lord to his fired chamber. Fourteen hundred and eighty-six loomed but spread no cheer as winter's fingers held all in its grasp.

The months slowly went past, no more to be of coming soon, but lost, as all others, in the ever-thickening fog that was time. Came the month that the fingers of winter warmed and let free all it had held, slowly and with drip did melt away the binding state …

Riding from the yard of the mansion, where dwelt the Lady Elizabeth, came with steady gait the gentleman, Steven Moran, and wayed he toward the town that was Nottingham. The weather warmed and was more clement to his journey; the waiting could no longer be braved, and naught but to seek out his fortune was within him. No storm nor activity, no ruffians nor blaggarts would ever 'ter his quest. Through the early morn he rode ere the sun could ray its light upon the land. Too much excite was he to lay abed; to be out and away was all to mind. North he rode, stopping only for a little sleep and a bite of victuals at the inns upon his trod way. The journey blurred, the days melding to one, the end was all that mattered. Tiring little, he rode many hours, changing most frequent to speed his way. Soon he was to spy the nearing castle upon the rock, as quick through the cobbled streets he did trot, and up the gate road he went, steep with slip under hoof. Close to the castle gate with its high wall he came and made about it close to the wall. The guards, dressed finely, watched the rider clop by, peering all about as he went. Turning to the back of the castle he came, riding upon that same green that was the place of King Richard's fruitless gathering.

It stood still now, except for the crows that strutted. No thousands were about here this day but burnt grass and ash in tidy step, pieces of wood for the fires stacked, the flame long gone with the soldiers who carried it. A broken arrow, a shaft, twine, and gut lay here and there, but 'twere all that would tell of such brave fellows that readied and rested at this place. All the cries and shouts had gone. The lutes stilled, the laughter and the songs silent, all gone to cold graves. Steven looked up at the walls high as he softly foot upon the grassy 'cline, leading his horse as his creaked legs stretched their bones. Then up he saddled once more having tasted the past to savour or to spit, and to what might have been in those days gone. He pulled then his horse to the roadway, the road that would take him to Thomas and the enterprise to be offered.

Along he rode; the trees and brush hung thick at his sides, branches brushing horse and rider, whipping against the shiny leather saddle, snapping and springing against the horse's haired flesh. The holding came afore him, a chimney he saw with smoke curling and blowing from behind the hiding trees; soon he was in cleared ground and slowed to stop, to mull that this was the heart of someone's life, quiet and tranquil came the scene. He saw the horse at graze, heard the pigs that grunted in the unseen sty, the fields afar all black and tilled, and thought: Would I be the one who would change such, to these folk who live here in such peace and love? But to them may it is not so, for my eyes only see the bright paint upon the outside and not the twisted boards beneath. For lay there oppression, treated as inferior and with much disrespect, taxed beyond their income and always in fear of one or another lord. Then, yes, they would leave this behind with no thought. He moved on to the holding, still unseen except by the barking dogs that called their displeasure to the stranger at dismount from his steed, who knelt and beckoned them to him. Brave they were with bristled hair and showing teeth, still at bark as they came close and sniffed at the hand gently offered. The stranger had no fear of them, he is a friend; soon the wet nose and the wagged tail were about him, the licked face sealed the pact, as he rose with them fussing about with jump and joyful bark. The noise brought forth with puzzled face a boy from the gloom of the barn; he peered to see what the fuss was.

"Come here … Come,"—the voice commanding and father-like.

He came from the barn to the voice heard, and the bark of the dogs. "Sir!" With joy he came skipping as he saw who 'twas who had called upon them. "'Tis you, sir, are you well now?" he called as he came over at a quick pace with the dogs at scurry about his ever stride; he came and shook the offered hand of Steven, as his mother had taught him so to do, for she wished he would not have to be a peasant worker when tallness reached his bones, and with manners taught would better himself with God's willing hope.

"Yes, I am now well, Robert, and how are you, my son?"

"I am in good stead, sir, thank you."

"Steven!" Another face from the cottage door did show; with skirts hitched and a hurried run, she came with joy to the friend that had shown. The dogs at bark again as the excitement spread to their faithful waggers. Jemma opened her arms to Steven as she closed; he lifted her light body and swung her around with a kiss upon the glowing cheek. "Steven, Steven, are you well now?" she breathed the words as she hung onto the leather coat, not wanting to let go.

"Yes, Jemma, I am most well; your doctoring worked like a prayer upon the Bible."

"I am so happy, Steven," she spake through her crying eyes and sobbing breath. Down upon the ground again he gently placed her, still held though by the warm grateful hand of Steven.

"I will fetch Father and John from the field." Robert was ready to speed away in his excitement.

"Let us all go," Steven said. "Let us surprise them."

"Yes, yes, they will be surprised." Robert tugged at them to move more hastily. They walked the way hand held in hand, as the dogs, more excited than anyone, led them fussing into the meadow. At the far side, close to some bushes, two figures worked away at the soil; only the horse lifted its head, looking to where the barking was coming, and seemed to join the dogs' mood by striking its hoof against the ground—thump, thump. The figures turned to see what had disturbed the horse, and saw to whom the excitement was about. John threw his rake to the ground, and ran ahead over the uneven ground, stumbling as he did so but not falling, as he waved his arm high in greeting. Thomas came from behind, striding long strides, trying to make some time to his son, and pulling along the horse as he jumbled across the land. A hug around Steven came from John, then Thomas was there, clasping arms around his comrade once more.

"Your wound is still well healed, Steven?"

"It is as good as when I was a young man," he jested. "And your head, Thomas, how does it fare?"

"It is well and soon did heal. Come, Steven, let us sup and tell me of your travels. Come, Jemma; come, boys. All to the cottage—no more chores this day."

They drank and supped around the table in the cottage kitchen, where the large fireplace made it warm and cozy, filling the place with its treats that the land had blessed them with. Simple food they ate but in Steven's mind far in excess of any banquet's givings, the company more pleasurable with straight talk; no lies nor falsehoods were spake at this table, no deception, no intrigue; honesty was all that dwelled here.

"Thomas, Jemma, I have something I wish to ask you, and also I would like your sons to listen too, with your agreement."

"That will be well with ourselves, Steven. Speak on."

"Before the battle of Bosworth, Richard gave to myself and my fellow officer the responsibility to hide some certain boxes of Richard's personal account. My fellow officer and our dear Richard were both lost in battle, and I am now the only one who knows of their whereabouts—I who survived because of you."

"And the boxes that were hidden, do you know their contents?" Thomas asked the question the others also wished to know.

"Well, I have heard stories that many have been searching for them, but, as yet, they have not been found, so all seems to the reasonable fact that with so much effort being made to recover them, it must be Richard's own fortune that is within the boxes. And that the royal treasure chest, which contains the jewels that belong to the crown, must be in one of the boxes hid." All at the table were somewhat stunned by the revelation of Steven, and though the boys and Thomas were enthralled by it all, Jemma had many doubts and worries that such a worldly happening was within their midst, but she remained silent until all the facts were shown.

"Steven, I cannot believe that which you speak, but I know you are telling the truth of the happening. So what do you want of us?" Thomas asked.

"First, my friend, if we can retrieve the personal treasure of Richard, to my mind this should stay with the finders, for, if we disclose it to the king that we have the treasure, many questions would be asked, and I fear strife would come upon us, and no reward would be forthcoming to us, the finders; all would go into the coffers of Henry to be frittered away upon fanciful things, and all soon to be gone like the chaff from the grain blown in the wind. I fought for my king and to what was I bestowed? Naught but the loss of my lands and fortune, my mother and father thrown to the streets, all because I showed loyalty to my monarch. And you, Thomas, because of your birth, you are treated like a slave with little hope of your children bettering themselves. Fate should show better to you. The royal treasure is another matter, and this should be returned to the king, for it is our heritage, and all future generations must be able to look upon its history.

"I mean to seek this fortune, if indeed it is such, and I need you by my side, Thomas. Are you willing for such a task? But before you answer, there are many things you must consider. You would no longer be able to reside here, for the monies coming to you would bring too many questions and would peril your life. I tell you this now, for you must know what it would bring to you."

"You say to me, Steven, that we will share in some of this fortune?"

"Yes, you will. Your share would be the same as mine; one half to the each of us, for I know where the boxes lay, but I need you, for I know not how to reach them, and you do."

The family looked at each other in some state of disbelief, that such a proposition could be offered to them, and sat intrigued by the words so bandied.

"What do you mean, Steven?—that I know how to reach these boxes so concealed?"

"Shortly before we met, I believe you entered the castle in some discrete way to obtain the bundles of arrows stored there. The boxes lie within the castle, and a way to enter I need unknown to all about, but I know not how without grave risk; but, Thomas, I believe you know how to enter unseen."

"I can enter the castle unfound and to the place you know, for I am most familiar with its lay. If all is well and we do retrieve the boxes, where would we settle ourselves? for we have little knowledge of such doings."

"That is the next thing I bring to you, but please forgive me if I presume too much, for I see a future bright for us all, and what I say is only a suggestion, for you will reside in a state that you may do as you please. At the moment I am in the midst of purchasing some lands that lay just to the north of London. On such lands I wish to raise horses, the best horses in the land, and I need someone to partner me in this endeavour, one who is well versed in the ways of the animal. It is you, Thomas, whom I need, someone with the gifts you show, someone who is my brother. On this land is a fine farmhouse, which would be most suitable to your needs, but all this remains with you and whatever you may wish." Thomas and Jemma looked at each other, before Jemma spake.

"I am most concerned that this dealing is not lawful, but then the law has never given us justice. The treasure should go to the king, but he will abuse it. If others find it then no good will come from it. For my children and their future, for the good that will be done with such riches and for our future, we cannot refuse. Though I will pray to the Lord each night to forgive me, and to guide my hand in such matters that it may bring upon us."

"And of the farmhouse—would we own it and pay no rent?" John asked.

"Yes, you would own it, and your mother and father would have enough monies to do whatever they pleased … There are good schools about for the boys where they could learn much to take them through life. Jemma, there is nothing you would not be able to afford. But, if you do wish to join this endeavour, all of us must be most secretive and naught said to a living soul."

"What say you then, my children, to this gesture? Are you for such a journey?" Jemma asked her children. The boys looked at each other with toothy grins, and no words were needed for their answer, but it came with a loud "Yes! We would be so happy to do so."

"Then it is all agreed, Steven; we are with you come whatever may cross our stride."

"I am so pleased with your decision, that you have put such faith in me. We pray that the boxes are still intact and have not been plundered. When do you think would be a goodly time to do this, Thomas?"

"The guard does its change at eight of the clock, and just before the hour they do a walkabout, when there is no guard for one half hour as they change, for they are not in a state of war and lax in their ways have become. If you agree, Steven, 'tis best we go now, as six of the clock nears and there is little to gain by dallying."

Jemma looked at her husband, for it seemed that only a short while ago that he was trodden down and bent of back under the burden of his peasant's life, unable to give to his family all he wished he could; but, since his encounter with Steven, she swore he was two inches taller, and as confident in his dealings as any schooled man. Her eyes misted with the proudness and love that welled within her.

"So be it; we go now. The boys, Thomas … We do need them," Steven wheedled to his friend, for he wished them to join in the intrigue, that in their older years they would always remember the night when their mother and father let them partake in such an adventure, the night when they were given such responsibility and faith, the night that indeed would live with them and make them stronger. Steven still thought the thoughts of a soldier, which was to make men of boys.

"What do you say of such, dear wife?"

"I will be most worried until your return, but they must go, it is time. Guard them well, my husband."

"I will let no danger befall them, my dear. Boys, go and hitch Dolly, and place many branches in the cart as we would use for to start the cooking fire; it will give cover for the boxes and look, through eyes that may pry, that we are gathering wood for the cottage."

"Yes, Father." The adventurous boys quickly went to their task.

"Jemma, pray, would you find some old clothes of mine to bring Steven into the fold of peasantry? He is dressed a little too fine for this task."

"Yes, my dear, I will sort something most suitable." She went to the storage cupboard and rummaged about until she came upon the desired garb. Steven took them from her with a thank you, and, in the outer room, dressed himself into the world of the peasant.

They were soon readied, the cart with many branches loaded as Dolly calmly stood between the shafts, and Steven standing with his farmer's hat upon his head, pulled down so far his ears showed curl under the brim, a fool's look indeed.

"Be most vigilant, my men," Jemma urged, "for I cannot live without you." She spake to the four straggly that were her heart.

"We will be of care, Jemma," Steven spake. "Have no fear, for we will all return safely."

They gained the cart and took themselves toward the rock that stood beneath the castle. Through the dense bushes and dark trees that wooded up to the base of stone they came. The boys tethered Dolly close to where they would gain their entrance. The four went then through the green and brown of the leafy cover, with Thomas ahead to guide the way, to come to the place of enter, which seemed not so to the others, but looked a solid wall with no opening, until, with some squirming past bushes and trees that hugged the stone, and the removal of some branches that were placed, the black hole came to sight. "This way," he quietly spake, and beckoned them forward, to come to the place that, but a short while ago, was to all no gateway.

As they entered into the dark, the only light was of the dusk that showed through the opening they had entered, that let the outside spread some of its glow into the dank chamber. The boys ogled about the cave they were in, seeking any shape they may recognize. Thomas held out the torches that they had brought with them, and they were lit by the older boy, John; the light then showed more clearly the walls, black and a-drip from the wetness that ran from above. Thomas kept one of the torches and went to the front.

"Be wary of your tread; the floor is like the goose grease, and pray be as silent as you are able, for sounds in this chamber carry like the wolf's howl."

They went up through the blackness; disturbed bats fluttered about their heads making their rickety cry all about the chamber. Up they went as steeper became the steps that would bring them again to some light. Thomas stopped ahead of them and turned his torch upon the group to see of what state they were in, and whispered, "Is all well? … Are you tired? … Do any of you need to rest? for we can sit for a while if need be."

"No, Father—Go on, go on." Their hearts beat fast, and with blood at rush from the act they were engaged in, none needed to rest.

"Very well, we go on," Thomas spake as he gazed at them to be sure they were suffering no hardship. He pulled his torch ahead again and continued the light that cut through the chill and darkness. The squeak of rats that scurried beneath their feet 'terred them not. They came to what seemed a solid wall before them, till closely spied the stone that was the gateway to the chamber that would take them to their seek. They rested for a moment and gathered themselves for the entry. "Steven, do you recall of which storage chamber we seek?"

"Yes, I do clearly, it is forty paces from the guard's quarters, within sight of the spire to the right hand." They pried the stone slowly and with as little noise as they were able, until there was a spying gap. Thomas eyed through the space, seeing only piles of hay that were mounded to the opening, for of more sight there was none. Only silence did hang within the spied chamber, like the midnight's still, it all seemed with peace. They pried harder at the stubborn stone, able to dig their hands through the opening, to force it to open enough so that entrance could be made. Hearts were beating, it seemed, even more loudly, for if the chamber indeed held some persons in silence then a ruckus could come, which the boys did not relish, for still green were they, at their young age, for such doings.

"Stay a little," Thomas spake. "We will wait until the spire sounds its bells, for eight of the clock must be near." They sat still as they waited within the cave, cold and dripping wet, their heads bespattered with bat droppings; steam rose as they stayed, but all were of good heart. Soon the dull clang from the distant tower rang its bells of eight, and as the last tone struck and melted away, and all was still again, they moved themselves into the storage chamber, pushing away the hay and straw to make room for themselves. Thomas hushed, and all listened in the calm. All was still quiet within, but voices afar sounded the air; soldiers, duty bound in some act at the far side of the yard, scuffled about, and then stillness came once again. Thomas dared a peek over the hay, pushing it lower so that he could see more of the chamber. Light filtered through the iron bars, flickering from the torch that hung upon the outside wall, showing the oak door and the rusty lock and the hay-strewn floor.

"'Tis clear, Steven. C'mon, boys." They all rustled through the storage chamber to gather at the doorway with each trying to spy through the small grill at the same time. Thomas spake. "No one close to the door ... but a group at the far end of the yard in some conference ... but all appears calm. Come, Steven, spy out and see where the chamber lays that we seek." Thomas beckoned his friend closer to the bars as the boys stepped away so that Steven could find his bearings. He peered alone through the bars, taking some time to assess his position, then he turned his head to look better at the chamber they were in. With both hands upon the door, he turned his head once more so that he could see outside again, then turned to face the trio before him with a strange look that the others, as yet, could not fathom; his hands still rested as if nailed there upon the door.

"By the grace of God, Thomas—This is the chamber, this chamber ... This is the chamber."

"This is the chamber?" Thomas asked, hardly able to believe of the fortune that showed their way.

"This is the chamber," replied Steven once more, his hands released from their fastening upon the door. They, all with face of cheer, looked at each other, for they could not believe their fortune. Steven led the way through the piled hay to come to the wall where they had entered, and the boys began to clear the straw and chaff from the floor area where Steven directed. Hard was the lay where they first began to scrape, but then they moved a little away to where the ground was softer and loose. They all dug hastily, flailing at the soft layers of soil with bare hands, soon dirtied with nails broken and full of grime, as they clawed with much ardour at the deepening hole, until the wearing nails scratched upon wood, as to their eyes came the shape of a chest that did lay fairly shallow. They scraped around it and pulled it out of its cradling soil, placing it down upon the chamber's floor, then brushed away with their hands the thin layer of soil that still covered the top of the box; a small show of white they saw, and brushing more came to view the White Rose of York that showed faded upon the lid. With bulging eyes, the two boys looked at each other again, awed by the rose they saw. Thomas fingered the iron lock, rusty from the dank ground, then went through into the cave to retrieve the bar that was used to pry the stone from the opening.

"This should make entry for us, my fellows." He placed the bar under the hasp, and, with one strong pull, jagged it open, splintering the wood that showed, bright and clean.

Steven knelt upon the grubbed floor before the box with the wondering eyes of his comrades looking over his shoulders. He slowly lifted the lid, all with hearts a-pound and fear in their stomachs. Then, to all's gaze, the box full of coins, of gold and silver, shone in the dim light. Naught was spoken, each overcome by the sight that befell their eyes, then they dipped into the coins, like water, cupping it up and then letting it run through their fingers back into the pool below. Up they shot as one, arms linked dancing about in circles, their mouths shouting in silence, as they jigged with tears falling for their good fortune. They grubbed some more and soon pulled out another box from the clinging ground. Again the bar pried it open to show full of coins once more, spilling its bounty as the lid sprang open.

"There should be two more," Steven spake, and indeed two more came to light. The next one they opened was filled with diamonds and precious stones, of gold rings, chains, and bracelets. They dragged the boxes into the cave chamber. The only box that remained unopened would be of the royal paraphernalia, was his thought as to its contents— The door rattled with a key and creaked open, filling the chamber with the brightness of a held torch at the open doorway; though they did not enter, voices carried about from the outside.

"… Put it in here, stack it at the back, and make haste with the task, I have more things to do than spend my time watching over you. C'mon, get moving …" Then, through the doorway, came a peasant carrying bundles of straw and hay for the horses. The pile he carried was high in front of him, hiding the steps he took and the way ahead of him. The group slipped into the cave and huddled beside the wall, all in there except for Thomas, who had no time to move without making noise, and lay hugged close to the wall, partly hid by the hay about him. The peasant threw down his load, and was about to fetch more when a glint from near the dark wall caught his eye. Bending over, he pulled away the loose straw and chaff that was about, to show to light the face of Thomas, fingers at lips to relay silence to the intruder. Thomas lay still.

"Bloody hell!" the man exclaimed, the words spilling before he could stop them coming from his mouth.

"What's the trouble in there?" the guard shouted whilst waving his torch into the chamber.

"Nothing, sir, I was just shouting at the damned rats ... Get out!" he barked as he kicked his boot about into the straw at naught but air.

"C'mon then, they will not harm you; get the other straw and let us go to our places."

The peasant went to his laden cart and carried in more stock piled high in his arms. "What are you doing, Thomas?" the peasant whispered upon his return.

"Luke, be of silence, I wish to leave this place without any to-do."

"What scheme are you up to now, you rogue?"

Luke was one of Thomas's close friends. Who, a little time ago, had helped him steal the arrows from the castle. He remained silent as he went

to and fro with the bales of feed; the guard stood impatiently by the cart
and did not enter the chamber, too busy was he swigging a drop of rum
from his concealed crock. Soon all the hay was piled within the chamber
and stacked high against the back wall, hiding anyone who may secrete
there.

"Fare-thee-well, Thomas," came the whisper as his friend left. The
guard came no closer than just a step inside the doorway, and with a quick
glance about at the piled load in there, he groped for the handle and pulled
closed the door to all who waited in some nervous mood within. Still they
kept until all sounds had faded away and only stillness was about. Then,
when all was deemed safe, they came from inside the cave and pulled the
hay off Thomas, who was breathing more easily as he would when no
cares laid his person.

"Come, let us quickly look at the last box and return to a more
peaceful place, for I fear fortune may not smile upon us much longer."
They pulled from the black soil the last box that had been placed there,
and soon cracked it open with the bar. The last lid was lifted and the dim
light showed a fortune glinting there. The royal treasure lay before them:
glittering rings with the royal crest, chains of office dripped gold and
jewel, princes' crowns and queens' bangles shone into their eyes. Things
of ancient times passed down through royal ages from one monarch to
another. Never to touch or even to be gazed upon by such commoners as
they, upon death, upon agonizing death. There was no temptation, for one
jewel taken would be the end. Too much danger would plague them to
deal its lot. Enough they had, more than a thousand lifetimes to sustain.
Thomas closed the box, upon a sight never to be seen again, only tucked
away deep in the mind, far away. Steven came to help Thomas as 'twas set
back in its rest. They knelt and covered it, with some reverence, with the
loose soil; all the holes were levelled so they did not dip from the floor,
then thrown upon the top was chaff and straw to make all unseen. Like the
grouse at lay in the meadow, to look as if naught was about. They were all
gathered together in the cave, and did ready themselves to push and pry at
the stone, to set it back into its hole, to seal once more the out from the in,
and the in from the out. By the torch they set their way, the boxes carried
'twixt one hand to the other, as they stepped themselves down the slip of
black cave, wishing for the view that would come of the starry night above
that lay the heavens. They stopped oft to rest their weary arms that ached
from the heavy load, but excitement above all carried them forth to, at last,
the bottom cavern that was their sight. They rested for the last tread they
would have to take in this dark hole, for the cart was at wait in the wooded
night. All were ready as the torches were snuffed, with only the light of the

night guiding them to the opening they had sought.

Out they came secretly of step, still in the guise of the close bushes that hugged the stone. They placed down upon the ground their treasure as they covered over the cave's entrance with stones and branches until all was concealed as before. They quickly upped the boxes, and with more haste made toward the waiting Dolly, who gazed at their coming as they loomed from the dark mist of the woods. Lifted onto the cart with grunt and puff, and dragged close to the driver's board were the three treasures, quickly covered with the branches and twigs they had brought with them so naught could be seen. The two boys sat upon the branches that covered the boxes, whilst Thomas and Steven rode the board; all dirty they sat with the wet drip and bat droppings, muddied from head to toe, hands crusted in dirt; a steamy, smelly group, but all with beaming faces and with smiles that would not go, no matter if they wished to try, they would not go; they were victorious, proud, and fulfilled. They came to the dark passage of trees that led through the forest's path. Toward the cottage that lay ahead they came still unsighted from their road, but they knew the chimney would be at smoke, the candles alight, a restless mother awaiting within the warm close of home.

Through the trees and into the clearing they came, and saw their stead as its hands of light and warmth drew them close. The clouds thickly came to cover the stars, bright. But as the dim spread about bringing its blackness, the cottage light grew brighter with the coming, like a wilderness torch, it shone its guide. A look from the window as the dogs barked their warning. A shadow flitted across the yard and then moved away, as Jemma, now shawled, came to open the door, and cast her shadow o'er those loved ones who came. Then, outside was she with hasty step, and as they stepped from the cart she hugged each with the special affection she felt to them. She need not ask the outcome of their adventure, for their faces showed more than could be spake. But she did so, for the joy she knew it would bring to them to relate their lot.

"Come, Mother, come and see," came from her question, "How did you fare?" The boys took each hand of their mother to the cart, as Thomas and Steven stood close with them. "You will not have seen such as we have stowed here, never ever will you see such." They pulled away the branches from the black-crusted boxes as she peered into the cart.

"Lift the lid, my dear," Thomas urged her. Jemma looked at the faces about her before she did so, as if in some state of such a fearful task that was upon her. The tender hand shaked as it came to touch one of the boxes, and then did gently lift the lid as the flickered light of the yard splashed upon the gold and the silver that lay. She stilled for a moment, taking in the sight, and then, as gently as it had been opened, she closed the box. And began to cry with sobs that were uncontrollable; her eyes ran the tears that dripped about her face, as she began to cling to Thomas for some support in the weakness that possessed her body. "We do not deserve such," she spake between her heaving bosom. "We do not."

"Yes, you do, Jemma," Steven spake. "You are good people, you are kind and helpful to others. And with your remedies and herbs, you are gifted, and will be able to ease many a suffering with such; so feel no guilt in this matter, for you deserve all you have gained, and in little time your heart will fill with joy, for the goodness that your fortune will bring."

She could not answer in words, for her sobbing state would not let her, but hung her arms about Steven's neck to gain what comfort she could from the words he had spake, and she knew well, 'twas the honest way that it should be seen.

The boys led Dolly and the cart to the stable, unhitched her, then brought fresh feed and clean water, all to end her day's labour. The cart was pulled to the corner and rested under the dark eaves of the barn.

They all stood in the light that was shed from the cottage, talking closely of their movements to come upon the morrow.

"We must not leave the cart without guard," Steven came with his military rules. "So, if you are in agreement each will take a shift of three hours."

"We will be first," John said with agreement from Robert.

"That is good; then Thomas and I will take the next. Take with you the cowbell, and, if danger shows, shake it with all your strength and we will come with haste."

"I will bring you some sup that you can eat at your watch."

"Thank you, Mother," they chimed as they left for the cart to give their duty to the cause. The others went into the beckoning cottage to sup and to plan the morrow's doings. They ate and they drank until content of their fill, and made their play for the morn.

"Jemma, we have to go quickly upon the dawn's break; we can not have this fortune to lay about."

"Yes, I know, but I will find it difficult to leave this place. Ne'er the less, the net is cast. But early I must go first to do some business, for this place cannot be left to rot."

"Do whatever you have to do, my love," Thomas agreed. "And, whilst you are gone, we will load the carts with that which we cherish the most, and, upon your return, we will soon be upon our journey."

The turns at guarding the fortune went on through the night, and ended when the morn came with its breaking light, and they supped well together at the table—soon-to-be hauled upon a cart and taken many miles before they supped once again.

Jemma left the cottage and wended down the wooded path—with her youngest son by her side so trouble would be less to come her way—toward the croft that would always be "Peggy's" to her, though 'twas now in the holding of Isabel. She rapped upon the thick door and called out the name of Isabel. The door opened with that old creak that would not depart; the hands of Isabel's husband showed upon the black board.

"Peter—you are home; how pleasant to see you."

"Thank you, Jemma, it is good to be home. I have some time away from the mine, for some troubles are looming with the new government, and it is not a place to stay until all is settled. Come inside, Jemma. Isabel will be most happy to see you." Peter beckoned her in as Robert waited outside for his mother, on vigil once more was he. Inside she went to greet Isabel, who stood making her bread at the kitchen table.

"Are you well, Jemma?"

"Yes, my dear, I am most well. I come to tell you though that we are leaving Nottingham, for our future we feel lies elsewhere."

"Oh, Jemma, I am dismayed that you have to leave."

"Be not, Isabel; I am happy that it is so; though I will miss my friends from this place, fate lays the path that we must tread. The reason I call upon you is that our cottage will be left barren and, as such, I wish you to have it, for it has more land than you have here and I think it would suit better for you, especially now you are with child."

"What words can I say, Jemma? It is so generous of you, but we are in no state to purchase such."

"It is a gift. I want not any monies but to place it in the hands of someone who will tend it with love."

"We would be most grateful then, Jemma," spake up Peter. "You are most kind."

"There is one thing I ask of you though, that you give this place to Marge, who lives in such poor straits along the lane."

"We will do as you say, Jemma. And when will you be leaving?" Isabel queried.

"We leave today, so you may move whenever you wish. I must now with heavy heart say goodbye to yourselves, for time does press and I must hasten away." They embraced as watered cheeks touched to mingle as one. Jemma went her way most quickly before she became overcome again. "I will mention to Marge of our dealings and will ask her to visit with you for some arrangements," Jemma called as she went her way.

"That is well, Jemma. Take good care of yourself," they answered as their friend, with her arm about her son, mingled away into the forest, and made her way to the poor place that was Marge's lodging, the branched shelter she called home—a home, with naught except caring.

Marge was stood upon an old stone step, as her friend she spied. "Jemma, how are you this day? It is nice to see you."

"'Tis well I am. How do you fare?"

"I am well, thankee."

"Marge, I am leaving today, not to return to this pleasured place." Marge looked at her friend, her face saddened. "Come, be not unhappy," Jemma hugged Marge as she spake, "I have some good news for you, for Isabel is moving into my cottage and I have arranged that the croft she now lives in will be given to you, so you will have a better abode for your family."

"Oh, Jemma," she sobbed, "you are the kindest person."

"'Tis the least I can do for you; but time presses and I must be away, so go you to Isabel so you may arrange a time for your move … And here, say naught." Jemma clinked some coins into her friend's hand as she held it by the wrist so it could not pull away. "You will need some chattels. I must go now." She kissed Marge upon her teared cheek and then made her way toward the lane with Robert in hand. Marge stood and watched her until she could be seen no more.

"God bless you, Jemma Smith," she called, as the good fortune she had not seen yesterday was upon her this day.

The pair walked through woods, heading toward the cottage that lay smokeless behind the trees. Jemma thought more of the words that Steven had kept telling her, that the fortune would spread its joy further than anyone could imagine, and now she knew that it would be so.

The men stood about the carts awaiting Jemma and Robert. Thomas had talked to Steven some little while ago concerning the king's treasure that was buried at the castle, and 'twas decided that they would call at Luke's cottage upon the way and relate to him of its whereabouts so he may claim the reward offered. But, as they waited at the carts, coming by upon his way to the castle with another load of hay, came Luke, who stopped at the gate as Thomas made toward him.

"Thomas!" he called from his seat upon the board. "How fare you?"

"I am well, and how are you, my friend?"

"Can't grumble, Thomas, the hay I deliver is keeping us in stead until the pigs grow to size." He then looked over the head of Thomas to the activity that was enact. "It looks like you are moving away, is that so?"

"Yes, we are; the time has come for us to start anew at another place, to see if we can beget a better life."

"Well, I am deeply sorry ... I will miss your comradeship."

"Luke, I was coming to see you upon our outward journey, but fate has brought you to us in its stead." Thomas came closer to the lowered ear and spake to him in some quiet tones. "We have agreed amongst ourselves that you should benefit from some fortune of our knowledge." Luke's head lowered even more as the words drifted to him. "Where you saw me at the castle, the chamber where you have been storing the hay, at the place where I lay, there is buried, in shallow depth, a box that contains the treasure of the crown lost for these few months."

"My Lord, Thomas, I cannot believe this which you speak."

"'Tis so, my friend, I tell you true. But remember, you cannot take such for your own, for the king's spies abound and you would soon be brought to justice, where you would get little joy from such a find. You will have to state your find to the sheriff and to the commerce chamber, so you may claim the reward that has been placed upon it by the king. The reward is most bountiful, and your mind will be at peace and not under constant fear. You must know of the reason we are leaving, but it is best left in the mind. We leave you in trust, my dear friend." They shook hands and bade themselves goodbye, to each left upon his own journey to fate.

Jemma and Robert came from their quest, and, after one final glance at their home, they climbed to their carts and moved away with some sadness. But joy soon overtook the melancholy as they left their old life aback and rolled out to a new life, that once they thought would never be shown them. They trundled along to the road that led to the south, as the sun shined upon them, this first day of their travel, and made to them a good pace, for many miles did the wheels roll until the fall of night came toward them, and they closed to the village of Wigstone, there to spend the night asleep in the carts, and not to leave them in the evening's coming nor through the night's long. The boys, with Steven, brought victuals back to the others, fetched from the tavern in the village. They supped most heartily with joy and laughter in the cooling air of the night, and soon, with tiredness overcoming them, they all into slumber did drift. The morn came and they set toward the river that lay close, to splash the cold water upon their crusted faces and to stir themselves fully. They went on once more until the late morn, when time came that they should stop to partake of some victuals and to rest for a short time. The small town of Lutterworth came upon their tread and they pulled their carts into the stables there, which lay upon the road that snaked through the town. The stable boy took the horses to feed and water them, then to the blacksmith, for new shoes were now needed. The carts they cornered to the dark shadowing side of the yard.

"Time, my friends, before we sup to purchase for ourselves some new clothes. We step into a new life and so must we also become new, like the cygnet to the swan."

"But, Steven, we are not such to wear frivolous things," Jemma spake her thoughts upon the matter.

"I mean not of things such, Jemma, for I too do not bow to such dress, but to clothes of good cloth and leather, of new sturdy boots, and strong shirts of cotton, all to a practical means, and clothed such we will gather more respect in our movements, for as you know the garb that we wear will show our state in all places we may venture. I speak with all due respect to you all. I beg that you trust me in this matter, for you will see in short spate of what I speak."

"As you say, Steven, for are we not just babes at this game."

"What say you, Thomas?—that Jemma and I take the boys first whilst you remain with the carts, and then upon our return, I will stay whilst you buy whatever you need?"

"That is well, Steven. I will stay here as you wish."

"We must take some monies to buy our goods, if you agree, Thomas?"

"Of course, Steven, let us sort this matter." The two climbed into the cart where the boxes were stowed, pulling back the branches and straw from around them, and then with a quick glance about, and the boys peering over the side to take in another look at the treasure, they lifted the lid to the glitter within, full to the top lay the gold and silver coins. They each took equal amounts to jingle in their pouches. The smile upon the face of Thomas was if it would come in 'twixt, was he so of delight with the jingle he heard, for never before had such wealth crossed his palm.

"Come, my dears," Steven spake as he beckoned Jemma and the boys toward the street with its ever bustle. They left Thomas with cheerful farewell to enter the town's roadway. No respect was allowed them in their peasant's garb as they passed many shops, being bumped and jostled upon the way with foul words laid upon them. To the shop of the clothier they soon came, as Steven helped Jemma up the steep steps that led to the door, with the boys at follow they went. The door jarred before they could hand the latch as two flouncy ladies of silk and lace and perfume came out, all of bustle and laughter until they sighted the party who awaited to enter, when their demeanour changed, and the lilt of their gaiety stopped, as they put kerchief to mouth and to nose to squeeze past them without touch, as if plague lay before them. Jemma lowered her eyes and her head as was the way, and then stepped back to give room, and the boys pulled close to the wall. Steven moved out of the way and, with much anger in him, shook, for such treatment was against all his morals, but naught could he do against such acts, and for a little while longer he had to stay a peasant, with no rights and downtrodden was he. The prinked ladies passed, and in doing so their laughter returned as they, arm in arm, strutted their way.

"Come, Jemma." Steven held to Jemma's arm and ushered inside the clothier's shop; all inside, the boys closed the door as the bell tinkled its call.

"What is it?" The rudeness once again raised its snake's head. "Moneyless peasants to buy a button?"

"We are here to buy some clothes."

"Oh yes, and, pray, will this be in exchange for a bale of hay and a pig?" The last words were too much this day, as Steven boiled over his rage to the ignorant shopkeeper.

"Sir, if you do not alter your manner and treat all here with respect, I will see to it that you do not have the fingers to sew one more stitch of cloth." Steven spake loudly, his rough-bristled chin almost scraping the shopkeeper's face as he vent his anger. "There are no pigs, there is no hay; we pay in hard cash and I pray, for your own sake, that from this measly shop you can give of change!"—as he clicked a gold sovereign upon the counter. *Because the peacock does not show its plume, it does not mean it is not a peacock.*

The throat apple upped and downed, as the keeper realized his mistake, and had this time brought his ire upon the wrong person. More so was the fear that he may lose a good customer with coin at the ready. "Yes, sir, I sincerely beg your pardon."

"Beg your pardon to the lady, you oaf."

"I beg your pardon, madam, I meant no disrespect to your good self." Jemma did not answer, and was not pleased with the situation that had been placed upon her.

Steven came to her, for he could see the distress in Jemma, which had unfortunately been pushed upon her natural kindness to others. "Be of faith, dear Jemma, soon this upheaval will come to a close."

"Yes, of course, Steven," Jemma answered and returned more to her usual self.

"Now, sir, clothes for the boys, some good strong boots, and some thick stockings—not your poorly made ones shipped from another land of God knows where," Steven spake.

"Yes, sir, English-made stockings, certainly."

"Breeches of fine woollen cloth, cotton shirts, and cover overs, cowskin jackets, and two good caps … Oh yes, canvas capes, good canvas capes."

"Yes, sir, I will fetch my wife to help." To the backroom through the curtained opening he went, as the buyers perused more the shop's wares. The shopkeeper came out shortly through the swinging drapes followed by his plump wife, bustling at his side. "I will take care of the boys, my dear, if you will tend the lady and gentleman."

"What may I get for you, my lady?" Her politeness showed that she had been groomed to be of good manner to the lady and gentleman who dwelled their store.

"What do you think, Steven?" Jemma turned to her friend for some guidance, for she was in a strange, unaccustomed position.

"Good ladies' shoes ... not fancy, but your best." Steven glanced at Jemma, for fancy she would not bear. She smiled her approval. "Ladylike stockings, and ... ladies' things, which you are more aware of than I," he spake with some embarrassment. "And that ladies' dress you have in the window ... the grey one, and a good coat and bonnet, I think. What do you say, Jemma?"

"That sounds well to me, Steven." Jemma went through the swinging curtain to try on the clothing, and, except for the womanly talk that drifted from within, all was quiet. Steven looked about, sorting for himself as he saw the boys were still being fitted. He saw a good pair of leather riding boots that suited his fancy, a pair of leather breeches in a mossy colour, a thick wool coat he pulled over a new shirt, a brimmed leather hat, and a goodly cape. He tugged and pulled at his buys until he was satisfied with the attire that was more suitable to his station; not for many a day had he been comfortable in his clothing, but now he was, and his confidence did rise again. He went to oversee the boys as to their state, as the caps were being placed upon their locks to finish their outfits.

"Ah, boys, do you not both look most splendid, and more a manly bearing do you carry."

"They do feel so fine, sir." Both boys most chirpy over the clothing that was carefully fitted to them. The old, dirty and worn attire lay in a heap upon the planked floor, solemnly drab and tatty. The ringed curtains then rattled back as Jemma came out from the fitting; she showed pleased features as she stood dressed in a most rich cloth.

"Jemma ... The look of a woman of means you bring. What fine cloth you have chosen."

"Yes, Mother ... You look so different."

"And you do so too; all the most handsome of men."

Steven turned to the shopkeeper to finish his business. "Make your bill, sir, and we will be away. In short spate there will be another gentleman who will require the same service, whom my good Jemma will bring, and

I trust he will be well respected?"

"Yes, sir, of course, it will be our policy to do so." The shopkeeper now an obliging keeper of goods. He writ the bill within the quietened chamber as the pen scratched the totals, finished with a flourish then sanded and blown away to leave the dried ink. "There you are, sir, methinks all is correct."

Steven looked carefully at the bill. "Yes, my man, all is well."

The keeper clinked the change into the hand of Steven.

"Good day to you, shopkeeper," Steven spake as they made toward the door.

"The old clothes … Tie them together and I will take them upon my return; there is still some needy who can use such," Jemma spake, she now with little meekness seemingly not about her tongue.

"I will see to it, madam, and have them readied for you."

Ching! The door chimed behind them, as they came down the worn steps to the chattering roadway. They squeezed through the folk; hither and thither, the crowd twined. A small bump of contact was made to Jemma in the thronging group. "Sorry, madam," with a tip of the hat. A step upon her toe. "Excuse me, lady," came the quick apology and then gone into the crowd. The bustle somehow seemed to leave space for them as they moved along. As they did so Jemma looked at Steven, for she saw what was taking place. The cloth she wore painted a different picture, but she felt no different within herself, and she wished to tell all about her that she was Jemma Smith and no different then when she was clothed in peasant's attire. But who would believe her? No one would, so she would use all that her station would offer, to causes that would lift her heart and the hearts of others. She would no longer stand by and watch unjust treatment. She would be more like Steven in her actions, to bring justice and fair doings in a ladylike manner … Yes, that is what this Jemma Smith will do. She smiled back at Steven, a stronger smile now.

They took their way back to the stable's yard as Thomas stood at the cart in his wait. He saw them coming around the corner to light his face like a candle in the dark, all glowing and bright and filled with joy was he at the sight of his loved ones.

"My dears, you look most handsome, I hardly know your sight." Thomas circled around them to take in the changes that had come over them, and to look at their most pleasured faces.

"Come, Thomas, let me take you to the clothier to fit you with such." Jemma took Thomas's hand and guided him to the lane beyond the yard, her confidence abounding. "We will return in short time," she called as she guided her willing husband to the store, and in the same manner he was dressed most handsome within the small shop, looking most prosperous and with proud stance. They paid their bill and bid good day to the clothier, to come once more down the stone steps, with Thomas holding Jemma's arm as she clung to her tied bundle, and upon taking to the street it took her little time to find needy persons. An alleyway they came to was the home of such a family. Jemma went alone into the dark way, for 'twas her doings and needed little help for such. She saw them huddled there in that cold place, looking destitute with no warmth coming. The clothing they wore was of a raggedy state and offered no comfort.

"Take these, my dear," Jemma spake to the woman crouched there as she handed to her the bundle. She smiled at Jemma as best she could through her crumbling teeth.

"Thank you, my lady, you are so kind to such a poorly one as I."

Jemma fiddled in her pouch, sorted two coins out, and dropped the pennies into the woman's hand. "Buy some food for you and your family; but for another stride, I could be sat in your place."

"Thank you, my lady, may God bless your kindness."

Jemma left the alleyway with welling eyes, and came to Thomas's arm and hung tightly to it as they made their way back to the yard.

"Father!" cried out the sons as they jumped from the cart. "You look verily as a squire."

"I must say it is a most pleasant feeling that has come upon me."

"Well, my friend, a look most suitable for you do I behold. Come, let us find a place for some fare, and a goodly chamber to rest ourselves."

Away from the bustle and to the outside of the town they went, to slow their gait outside the stage stop with the lights from the inn beckoning them. Steven jumped from the cart with the boys at follow as it rumbled to quiet.

"We will see if they have some accommodation for the night," he called to Thomas and Jemma, who sat at the other cart and cheerfully waved them on to their task.

The door opened at their coming as they came to the innkeeper perusing his ledger. "Good day, gentlemen," he spake as he saw the arrival. "May I be of service to you?"

"Do you have chambers for the night?" Steven asked. "We need three rooms, if they are available."

"We do, sir, the next coach does not arrive until the morrow's noon hour. There is food at your ready, if that is also your need."

"Then we will take the rooms, and when we are settled we will take advantage of your fare. Do you have entrance from the stable yard into the chambers? For we have some chattels that we wish to have in our keep."

"Yes, sir, the entrance for tradesfolk will take you up to the rooms, and if you require anything further just call for Liz—the biddy will take care of your needs."

All was of pleasantry at the inn; the boxes were stored secretly within the rooms and the door locked securely as they ate their sup and drank their ale in the warm inn, and then slept, deep sleep, upon the strawed mattress.

Time had passed upon the road, and 'twas soon that Market Harborough showed upon the sign.

"At last," Steven spake as the carts pulled to a stop within the town. "This is the day when with some fortune I may regain my pledged ring, for my finger is deemed a lost digit amongst the others without it."

"We will obtain some victuals whilst you are at your business, Steven," Thomas, climbing down from the other cart, spake his intentions.

"Tis well, I will eat with you upon my return." Then he was gone with cape aflutter as he made to the street of the broker. 'Twas not market day on this cool late morn, and less people roamed the streets than were about the last time he walked the way. To the lender he came and up the steps to the black door, still as 'twas from the beginning of time it seemed, covered in dust and mire and ne'er a wipe clean in all this while. He was soon inside, clumping upon the wooden floor with his well-heeled boots, not the soft patter of the peasant's shoe he had last trod. "Good day, sir," Steven spake to the back of the man, who crouched at his table before the small window's light. The black-capped figure, with his bushy grey of beard, turned his face.

"What is it you wish, sire?" came the voice from the unseen lips.

"I have returned to repurchase my ring, left to you in forfeit."

He was slowly upped and floating about behind the table that separated his self from all others. "Can you describe it?" he asked, for it seemed he had little knowledge of its whereabouts.

"Yes, it is initialled: S. M. A ring of gold, hallmarked."

"I know of it ... Now, let me think," he said as he picked and scrabbled about his boxes and trays. "Here ... Here it be." A gold piece he picked from the tray, and, as he stepped toward Steven, rubbed it upon his rough cloth to bring to it more glitter, for in his mind 'twas the more did it shine the more was its value. *The feathered hen sells for more than the one that has been pecked.* He held it under the gaze of Steven, twisting and flashing it as best he could in the dim light.

Steven picked it from its fluttering flight to see indeed 'twas the ring so pledged. "Yes, this is my ring. What price do you ask?"

"Three guineas, and well worth it to be returned to its owner."

"I will give you two guineas to relieve it from you, for laying about in your den it is worth naught in your pocket."

"You are a hard man, sir, to someone who can only manage a mere crust now and then."

The banter continued.

"Do not sever my heart a-'twixt ... I see your wine flagons and your goblets and your left pork cut high. Do not break me so."

"Two guineas and ten shillings then."

"Done!" Steven counted out the coins and slipped his treasure back to its place. "Good day to you, sir," he spake as he left the lender and closed the door behind him, as if closing a part of his life that had seen much pain and anguish. But the past was done and he moved his way toward the cart that awaited his coming. They saw him from a distance, he waving the back of his hand, well seeing that he had regained his treasured possession and that he was complete. For all the time he had longed for his ring, at last 'twas upon his finger.

They trundled away from the town, and soon were upon what were once those far hills.

"Soon, my friends, only just a little further to our new abode." They wound the rutted lane as light sprinkled through the leaves that branched overhead. Full light came upon them as they made toward the hills' brow. All sky it seemed was to sight, until they came to the top of the rise when they were able to peer the valley that lay below. They saw the grey mansion nestled there, and further away the brick walls and slate roof of the farmhouse, flashing its windowed eyes to beckon them home, as they stood beside the carts to take in the scene. "There it lies, my friends, awaiting our love to bring it most fruitful."

"Steven, it is so beautiful my heart is to break with such solace," Jemma spake as Thomas placed a caring arm about her, and then his other arm about Steven, as they gazed for a moment at the sight of the valley before them. Chimes from the Newmarket Town, a distance away, they could hear, its spire above the forest that spread about.

"Thank you, Steven, for your considerable act, we are all overcome by it all," Thomas spake as they lingered.

"All to you, my friend, all to you; we would not be at gaze here if were not for you." The boys were already running down the hillside, whooping and shouting like young warriors to the battle fought. "I look to the day that my boys will run with yours upon this land, strong and free." The wheels rolled once more as they went slowly down to the estate that was before them. They saw the boys far ahead making toward the farmhouse, and then quickly hidden by the whispering trees. Soon they themselves came upon the house, the boys swinging and shouting as they balanced upon the fences and pointing out to the newcomers the objects they had seen. They came into the yard and with the horses stayed, Jemma was helped down from the cart, and, with skirts hitched, must to make her way to the kitchen. She was gone through the door's opening welcome, and was soon to be seen peering through the window. "Come, come!" she called, beckoning them to move more quickly and see the delight she saw. They came in under the low doorway and soon clomped upon the stone floor of the kitchen. The iron racks stood as they had been left, neatly stacked over the now unlit fire with dust-covered cauldrons still placed upon them. Jemma hugged each one who stood there; one at a time she squeezed, with such an embrace the breath was gasped from the body as she tearfully showed her joy.

"John, Robert," Thomas spake, "go and see if you can find the woodshed and bring wood so we may light the fireplace and bring more cheer to this place—our home."

"We know of its whereabouts, sir," they called as they left in all adventure to pick the fuel.

"My friends, I must be away, for I have business to complete, and to visit my dear Jayne, to relay to her the past days' outcome. If you would care of our boxes until my return and then we can share our lot to each."

"Yes, Steven, we will secret them in some safe place and take care of them until your return."

"If all is well, I will return on the morrow, when I can take you to Newmarket so you may buy your wares and victuals, and the market there has many animals that you may need to purchase."

"It is not needed for you to do such," Jemma spake, her esteem rising by the day. "You have much to do and we are most capable of fending for all we require, but we thank you much for your consideration."

Steven felt a proudness within himself, for he knew Jemma was seeking new horizons and neither wanted nor needed help in these matters. "Thank you, Jemma, I am most pleased that you are to undertake such, for if I am able, I wish to seek out my mother and father who were cast into the streets for following loyally the King Richard. I wish to bring them to this place and give to them the caring they have given others."

"God bless you, Steven." A kiss from Jemma, and a shake from Thomas freed him to his directions. The horses were unhitched and Sixpence stood with saddle ready. He called his goodbyes to the boys, and waved his short farewell to all. He guided then that most tranquil animal that was but a short while ago naught but a wild thing. No more was he hidden as he bypassed the treed way and made toward the manor at Hampstead and to his dearest Jayne's close.

With fast horse beneath and skilled ride, he made sure time to the place he longed. Quickly he dismounted in the courtyard as his fine steed was led away to the stable's care. He stepped through the door's entrance, and no sooner inside when came those sweet-laced arms about his neck and the perfume of rose and lavender drifted his nostrils. The heavenly voice laid itself upon his ears, as whispered were love tones, to then close his cheek upon as Jayne melted to her love, long awaited. "My dearest," he whispered, his lips close to the soft cheek, and then most gently and with such softness did he kiss his beloved's lips, even more delicate and softer than he remembered. They sat, with hands to hold, upon the seat that was at stay in the well of the bright window. Then, when hearts were less to flutter, came talk of earthly things.

"Did your journey bear the fruit that you sought, my dear one?"

"Yes, Jayne; all was laid there as the day we placed it in the ground. We took three boxes of coin and jewel, and left the box that contained the state's treasure, for such cannot be brought to market. No man should set his hands upon such splendour that lays within that box, matters not to which House he bears allegiance. We did, though, give notice to another soul of its whereabouts, who will reveal the knowledge to the sheriff, and shall reap some reward for his findings."

"You are right, my love, for no one's hands should soil such heritage, and, from what you tell me, fortune enough for all is reaped."

"I wish you, my dearest, to come to our new home where one day soon we will become man and wife. And, until God blesses us with his joining, I will stay at Thomas's house."

"Steven, I will come straight now; it will take me but little time to arrange for some servants, and it will take me little time to ready my chattels, for, if need be, I will come without such trivials."

"I will arrange for tradesmen to be at your order to bring our chambers of that which you desire. But what of Elizabeth? What will be her thoughts upon this endeavour?"

"She will be of all happiness for me … and to wonder of such long time taken by that handsome Steven Moran." Jayne smiled at her mimicry of Elizabeth.

"Firstly, Jayne, I must be a short while away once more. I will at our manor stay this night and then to pay off the note of debt upon the morrow; I must also seek out my mother and father and bring them more to an abode that is in keep with them … which will give you time to arrange your business, and to say your goodbyes to your loving friends who dwell in such harmony here."

"Your mother and father will be most comfortable at the manor, Steven, as we discussed, but, on thought, it would be even more suitable for them to have the south wing to themselves, for they would have all privacy there."

"That is such a kindly thought, Jayne; I will offer to them such. On the morrow's eve, close to six of the clock, I will return and we can dine at our leisure, and be peaceful for as long as we wish and to discuss the date of our marriage." Jayne kissed the cheek of her loved one and then he bid at last another farewell—a farewell that would be his last parting for some time.

He rode his rested horse through the town of London to spring his flight to the mansion that was his place. He settled for the night in the stable upon the straw that was about, and slept with no worry to render him awake. At dawn he did rise to wander the path that was to the farmhouse, and to the smoking chimney that gave thought to the hot bread, and cheese, and dripping beef upon the spit, cracking and spitting about the fire's hearth. Welcomed like a lost son upon return from some long journey so far away, he was greeted with warmth and care. Then, with belly full, he waved his farewell, and to see them again this eve when Jemma could meet his Jayne.

To the purveyor of lands he rode to a meet with the Martin Mallory, Head Clerk. He came once again through those black doors of the purveyor's office, and entered the chamber to see the clerks still at their tables, and the benches of waiting folk, fidgety and in some restless state in their strange circumstances. Steven caught the look of one of the pages that were about, with the red caps that bobbed telling of their station. He came to the wave, a young boy attired appropriately for his position, but grubby of face and of hands. A farm boy earning monies as best he could to help in his family's poor income it seemed.

"Yes, sir," came the high, questioning voice of the youth.

"Pray, tell the Master Martin Mallory that Steven Moran wishes a meet with him," slipping a halfpenny into the boy's hand as he spake.

"Thankee, sire, yes, sire, straight away, sire." And away he bustled, securing his coin deeply into his pocket, as he, betwixt the tables and the clerks, did speed his way, with a whack coming at him now and again for his insolence at bumping slightly against a clerk, or a table, or anyone who stood about, any excuse it seemed to have a little sport upon the scurrying rabbit if he came within reach. Far at the back now was the bobbing hat as Steven peered over the jabbering lot, and mused about the stories spilt, both truths and lies bandied. He felt the tug at his sleeve and looked down at the red-capped face below. "This way, sire," the page led Steven through the maze of tables and benches and folk. Never to find the way back to the safety of the outside, crossed the heady mind of Steven.

"Mister Moran, sir, ... And how fare you?" his friendly clerk greeted him.

"I fare well, sir," he answered as the page left from the desired meet. "Thank you, boy," called Steven to the disappearing youth. "And, sir, how do you fare?"

"I am indeed in good spirits, thank you. And how did your venture fare, sir?"

"I fared mighty well, thank you, sir. I have brought the monies promised to pay off my debt to you, and I must thank you for the kindness you did place upon me in this delicate matter."

"'Tis all the thanks I need that you are satisfied with your purchase," said he.

Steven placed his moneybag before the seated clerk, to rattle its gold one upon the other as it settled upon the table. "Here, sir, is payment in full to close our transaction."

The clerk untied the twine that held all safe and tipped out the clinking coins bright upon the black wood; he then, as often he had done, did count out the monies in clear tones and in quick deftness. "That is correct, sir," speaking as he slid the payment into his safe drawer and locked it securly away, he then tugged further at the handle to be sure it had latched. Papers from some cover were displayed. The clerk scratched at the legal scrolls, his feathered quill flicking and moving like the stinging wasp. "Sir, here is your signed receipt." He pushed one paper toward Steven who glanced over it to see that it had been signed and dated. The fifth day of May, in the year of our Lord, fourteen hundred and eighty-six. "And here is a docket that gives you legal right to the property; the full deeds will be sent to you by rider when they have been prepared, to be of three to four days. It has been a distinct pleasure to serve you, sir."

Steven, always looking for honest people to help manage his enterprise, dared to propose to the clerk some inquiry to this end. "Martin Mallory, I have a question for you."

"And what would that be, sir?"

"I would ask, sir—and please forgive me if I am a little blunt, for I am a straight man, and will not chase the rabbit about the field when I can await him at his burrow—this property I have purchased ... I am in mind to breed upon it some fine horses and also to be engaged in other interests, therefore, there is much clerical work to be done, both for the manor and for the new enterprises. I have little time for such, and look for an honest man to take care of these things. One who will treat our servants with respect, and even to the stable boys to show some caring. I look not for a bully nor of someone with a sour nature. From our dealings this past little while I believe you, sir, are the person I desire for this position. Is there any interest to you in this venture? There is plenty of room at the manor for you and your family if you wish to reside there, or to whichever circumstance may suit."

"I am surely taken aback, sir, for, though I am well pleased at this work, it can become a fickle game; however, as you well know, and always it is wondered of the future, for whoever rules the land almost always says who is to be employed and who will be so engaged at this office. Although I have little to complain of, it would be of great pleasure to work at a more secure and generous place, where fields and woodlands would be within my scope. To your question, sir, and in due respect for the position I now hold, I would deem it a great honour to ply my trade with you."

"Good, I am well pleased," Steven answered, and shook the hand that was held out. "This is my bond, sir, that binds my words, but feel you are not so bound if circumstances dictate otherwise. I will need a fortnight to ready things at the manor, and by that time you may name your wage and to let me know of your living requirements, and then we should have a meet to finalize the agreement, and of such please bring with you your family so they may see the position you are entering."

"I then look forward to our next meet and wish to thank you for your trust in me."

"It is well my pleasure, Martin. I bid you good day."

"And a good day to you, Mister Moran."

Steven made his way toward the doorway, and, on coming close to it, as if by some wizard, it swung open without his touch. The red-capped, smiling face had beaten the move. "Good day, sir," he said. 'Twas the same young lad that had greeted him on his coming, the same lad that Steven had taken a liking to for some reason he knew not. He did not think 'twas pity, for many such boys were about, and he did not know if 'twas but for the grace of God, but 'twas something that the boy was blessed with.

"So, you are a farmer's boy, are you not?"

"Yes, sir."

"I take it you are of poorly state, and that you have to work so your folks may survive."

"Yes, sir," he said with lowered eyes that showed the sadness of his state.

Steven took the boy's chin and lifted it with his gentle hand. "Be not ashamed, boy; stand tall, you are doing all you may for a little tyke. If you wish, I can give you work at my farm … Paid work, which I guess is more to your liking than this den." The face held in the hand lit like a candle at the words heard. "Let your parents bring you to the old Taylor estate—do you know of it?"

"Yes, sir, I do, in the valley near Newmarket Town."

"'Tis so. Come with your parents and I will tell them of my offer to you. My name is Steven Moran; I am the new owner."

"Yes, sir, Mister Moran, I will do as you say."

Steven left the blessed child and wondered if his heart was becoming softer and more liken the milkmaid's skin, and if every sad-eyed wretch he met, he would be inclined to save them from their ills, and did it not seem his soldier's heart could be gone to soft endeavours?

He went to more pressing things, as of his mother and father, who had been given shelter at the cousin of Steven whose cottage lay but ten miles away. He set Sixpence upon the road and trotted with hopeful heart to his parents' abode. In fine weather and on dry road, the miles were behind quickly as he came at noontime to the place of his kin. He skipped from his horse in some mind of anticipation to may see his parents once again. The door was not fully closed as he stepped toward it, his hand ready to rap upon the wood at the same time it opened. The lady stood there with only boots spied from her lowered head. He stood with only the top of a cotton bonnet to view. Slowly the head lifted, hardly wishing to see the face that may gaze upon her, for was not her son killed at Bosworth common? and was not this insane to hope the face shown would be his?

"Mother," he spake as the full-teared eyes gazed the face.

"Steven!" She fell into his arms with joy, and with weakening body almost to faint as upon his chest she sobbed. "We thought you were dead, my son … We thought the rest of our lives would be without you … We were in such a sorrowful state."

"Do not fret more, I am here and will take care of you."

She pulled away a little so she could see more of her beloved child, and recovered somewhat from her heart's leap. "'Tis well you are come, for our future was indeed of bleak set; though your cousin has given all he has to us, he has little left after caring for our needs; he is a good man."

"Where is Father? Is he about?"

"He is at the manor, close to the village."

"And, pray, what is he doing there?"

"He is engaged as the butler, for he had to find work; we could not survive without the little he brings. But I fear, each day he dies a little more, his heart broken when you were seemingly lost in the battle, and the lord at the manor is no treater to kindness and demeans him most dishonourably."

"You will not have to endure such any more. Where is my cousin?"

"He was to market this morn and should be returned here most soon."

"I must go and take Father away from that place of servitude. While I am gone, make yourself ready and gather your chattels, for upon my return we will depart to a place more suitable to your needs." He kissed his mother's cheek and leapt upon his horse with much determination, realizing all his strength had returned and his heart could do battle if needed. The warrior was hid for a little while but had returned with fired belly.

He rode at haste for his speed would belay the treatment his father would otherwise suffer. To the village he came, the grey stone of the manor leered at the rider that approached from the dusty fog that bellowed about as if upon a hoofed ship. He was soon up to the yard; its gate there hung open wide, held with heavy boulders to keep it such, as carts and peasants carried wood to the store hut; some with livestock hurried one way, others with horse feed hurried the other as all at bustle was the yard. He slowed as he came to the manor's door and slid from his steed, tying his trusty one to the ring that rusted upon the wall, and patting its rump as he went duty bound to seek his father. He stepped up the short reach to the door, which was not latched; he quietly pushed it open to feel the chilled interior upon his skin. He saw no one, as in all silence did lay the entrance. A lone, loud voice from the far end of the hall he heard, coming from the chamber that showed its way to him. He made towards the voice that seemed in anger risen, and pushed wider the gaped door, to see some lordly person of large stature pacing afront a line of feared servants. Meekly of state they stood as the loud person ranted his displeasure at the trodden lot. Behind his back, clutched there a leather whip, black and with sweat it dangled.

"Two cut-glass goblets have been broken. The person who did this malicious act must show himself now! ... or you will all suffer the punishment." He struck the black whip upon his palm with a loud clack to echo about the high chamber. Not one soul moved, for all it seemed were innocent. "Very well then, if that is your wish, then all will suffer from the crime and each will be obliged five lashes." The young pages in their short cut breeches stood in shivering fear, often cuffed about the ear and given a hastening kick at the rear, but never subjected to such a cruel fate as was to be laid upon them.

"How much the cost of those goblets, sir?" Steven's voice bounced the echoed chamber, as the party lined up tried, with twist and stretch, to see who had command of the voice. Steven's father could see naught from his place of wrath, but something in the voice he heard tempted his mind to hope.

"'Tis naught to be with you … whoever you may be."

Steven came forward and placed himself afront the lout who raged his temper upon the innocent. "Sir, it is so to be with me when my father, a most honest man, stands in this line."

"Steven—" the whispering voice came, unable to speak louder for the joy that stuck his throat.

"Father," said Steven as he saw where his pater stood, and looked longingly toward him, for to hold him he needed, but the time was ill met for a moment.

"Silence!" came the rant from the lord. "My guards will end this frolic that you have enchanted these serfs with. Guards!" he called, and then again with louder shout, "Guards!" But none came, all at sup it seemed in the guards' hut, their ears far from the cries of their master's orders, as the ale and the merriment dulled all that was about.

"Come, Father, come," Steven spake as he made toward his embittered kin to place a comforting arm about his shoulder. The other servants closed together in some form of unity as he did so.

"Stand back, sir, away from my servant, or you will feel my lash," shouted the lord loudly, his neck bulging, red and ripe. Steven looked at the lord with disdain in his eyes, cold and menacing, to speak naught, but a thousand words went unspoken to cut down the bully as he stood with whip raised, his backbone now melted to a gibbering snake and he became no more of any threat. Steven taking no heed of the lord brought out his father from the gathered servants, passing in front of the fuming bully as they left the chamber, to wend down the passageway toward the light that showed through the main doorway, and then to hear behind them much noise and disarray from the chamber they had left. Sounds of revengeful acts mayhap, he knew not nor muddled his brain with such, but lifted his father upon his horse, untied the animal, and led his kin away from his grovelling existence.

At last words came to be spake to Steven; in the last short while he was unable to do so, was his father so overcome by the events. "Steven, we thought you gone at the battle of Bosworth. What a blessing to see the son I thought was dead. God surely has looked upon us this day."

"God, it seems, has smiled upon me for some while now; after that dreadful day upon the common, an angel has stood by my side and guided me through many strange circumstances to bring us all to this place. I have seen my mother, and have told her to ready herself, for, upon our return to the cottage, we will all make away to our new abode. Have you heard news of my brother since you all had to part?"

"He took out to the north to seek a new life after we were bound to the street. He has sent messages to us to say he is well, and is now betrothed to a lady from Cumbria, and he tells of a visit to us soon."

"'Tis good he is well; we must send a letter to him of our whereabouts." The chat continued almost without stop, all of news unknown and intrigues played, and quickly it seemed did they come to the sight of his cousin's cottage. And could be seen Steven's mother and cousin awaiting them at the doorway. They came to a stop close to the cottage as came to Steven another greeting from his mother, who was with such joy at the sight of her son with his father. He shook the hand of his cousin and greeted him most lovingly. Turning now, he helped his father down from the high saddle; more handshakes came, more embraces clutched as much joy lay upon them this day. They went inside to the warm kitchen and supped ale betwixt them, and ate some good cheese and crusty bread.

"Cousin, will you be joining us at Newmarket?" Steven queried.

"No, Steven, I am most comfortable here, but thank you kindly for the opportunity."

"We must thank you though, for taking in my mother and father when they were in such dire straits."

"'Twas my duty, Steven, to do such, and no thanks are needed."

"Nevertheless, I am in your debt. If any time you need anything at all, call me, and I will come direct."

"I will do so."

"There is one more thing I may ask of you, cousin, and that is to supply us with the loan of a cart."

"Yes, I can do as you ask. I have one that is not in need; you are most welcome to it."

"Thank you, we are once more indebted to you."

"'Tis naught, Steven."

"Come then, my dear ones, let us depart to Newmarket." The parents stood and bid farewell to their saviour who had cared for them in their need; the shook hands and kissed cheeks came and went as they climbed to sit at the board. With Sixpence in the shafts and a few chattels at the back, the three made way toward the laneway, to give a last cheery wave to the young man who had given them much kindness ...

"Good day, my dear. I am Jayne, the betrothed of Steven." The fine lady spake after Jemma had answered the tap upon the door.

"Come in, Jayne, what a delight to meet you at last."

Jayne opened her arms as she came forward, giving Jemma a hug and a caring kiss as one would do so to a long-lost friend, a dear friend. "I am so delighted to at last see you, Jemma, for my debt to you and your husband can never be repaid—if 'twas not for you, I would have died by now of a broken heart," she cried upon the willing shoulder of Jemma, overcome with happiness she hugged her closer still.

"One man worth saving, Jayne, was your Steven; he is a blessing to us all. If we had not done our duty to him, we would not be in this place with a future now for all of us. We are well enough paid." They did talk and laugh, and cry some more as the friendship between them quickly grew.

"Jayne, I must ask you if something is of concern to you, for I feel some worry within you. Is your health as it should be?"

"'Tis little, Jemma, that I should trouble anyone about it."

"Please, tell me what it is, Jayne. I may be able to help you ... It is your arm, is it not?"

"Yes, Jemma, it is ... How did you know such?"

"I do not know, it has just come upon me as a bird that whispers. A dear friend of mine this past while passed on and she told me that I was gifted, as she was also gifted, to know of things that dwelt in the far reaches of life. But, until I held you, I had never known of it. Now I can see at last such things that I could not before. Tell me of your arm, Jayne."

"Jemma, it is but a rash and seems little cause for concern, but I am a little worried, for I believe that the plague can start in such a way." And in telling Jemma of her feelings she unclipped the sleeve to her dress, and revealed her arm that showed of much redness and discomfort. Jemma gently held the offered arm and quickly reassured her new friend.

"Do not fret, Jayne, it is little to be worried about. Sometimes if you have been close to a dog or a cat, this rash can occur. I will give you some balm and it will soon be gone, but be wary when you handle any animals, for it could return—but quickly can we make it once more be gone."

"Thank you, Jemma. You have eased my mind of all bad thoughts. You are, indeed, a gifted one. What a joy it will be to live beside you in this most pleasant of valleys." They talked some more, and 'twas that each knew they would be the greatest of friends. Until at last 'twas time for Jayne to depart, for she wished to be at the manor perchance Steven should arrive with his parents. They knew not that she had come to the manor, but to wait longer she could not bear, so she had made her goodbyes and had come quickly to her new home, and began to make it comfortable for her coming guests. She bid goodbye to her new friend and was soon again at her new home. The fires lit and burning brightly, pots at the kitchen hearth starting to bubble the cook's makings, the candles flickered, and warmth flowed, journeying all about the cold chambers that lingered still within its walls.

The late afternoon passed as the cart made toward the homely stead. The road was rutted and dusty, and the hills seen far were soon each side of them as they came upon the manor, its grey walls dashed with pink as the low sun cast upon the stone. A low mist came about as they entered the courtyard, and all seemed in darkness and did not seem to show any welcome to the newcomers. Steven lifted his mother down from the board as his father climbed down from the other side, then guided them both to the heavy door that opened without touch; 'twas Jayne who had come to greet the visitors and to surprise Steven with her presence at their home.

"Jayne, I did not expect to see you here. What a joyous surprise to us … This is my mother and father, who I found in the care of my cousin."

"Good day to you. It is with great pleasure I greet you, Mister and Missus Moran." Jayne kissed each upon the cheek to greet them to their new abode.

"'Tis good to meet you, my dear. Steven has talked of you most of the day, and seems to have left nothing amiss, though you are more charming than he could convey."

"You are so kind; please, come in." She held Steven's mother's arm to help her inside and to befriend her. "You are most welcome in this house; please, make it your own."

The manor had become a home. Steven's parents were settled into their own wing, and thoughts of those hard times past were gradually fading for them, and joy was within them—for was not their son close, and proudly did he not stand? Thomas and Jemma brought joy and happiness into the farmhouse. Steven now was recovered, after many long months of trial and upheaval, his life threatened more than once; from the day all suffered upon the common and until his return to the manor at Hampstead was he turmoiled. But he began to settle into the life he had longed for with his beloved Jayne.

The old cart came upon the track to the manor, and Steven, who had been engaged in some outside duties, saw the parents with the scrubbed boy between them upon the board. The pageboy from the land office had come as asked, and, after some chat, 'twas agreed that they would leave their son in the care of Steven, to learn more than could be taught at the poor farm from where he came. 'Twas also agreed that half the monies earned by the boy would be sent to the parents, and the other half would be given to the boy; the arrangement most agreeable to all.

Jemma and Thomas had hired a farmhand to give more help to their labour, and a housekeeper was needed, for Jemma with her independent ways was oft to the villages and towns about, helping with her remedies and her caring ways to the needy and the sick.

"Mister Blackberry … Do come in, sir," Jemma spake as she entered the tall young man, now seen all garbed in black as the light from the farmhouse glowed upon him. Steven and Thomas nodded politely from their table to the man who had come, and then continued upon their business of horse, both aware of the nature of his visit but leaving all to the pleasure of Jemma.

"My lady," he bowed to Jemma as he stood beckoned to the warm fire.

"Mister Blackberry," she answered with a small curtsy. It is pleased we are of your visit. Is there something we may oblige you with?"

"Thank you, ma'am, there is something you may help me with." A tall polite man was he but showed somewhat nervous with little worldly show. "I know not if word has travelled far, but I am the new surgeon for this area, old Mister Click having retired. It is but a small practice, but one that is growing."

"Please sit, sir," Jemma beckoned him to ease his uncomfortable state. "And please state what service we may offer to you?"

"Well, 'tis a very awkward question to put, ma'am."

"Be not timid, sir; spit out the words," Jemma urged as Thomas and Steven glanced over their papers at each other with amused faces, for Jemma was once again showing her new-found standing.

"Well, my lady, it is that I would wish you to join with me in my practice." Mister Blackberry spake with little breath between his speech, and sped them quickly from his lips in haste, it seemed, to rid them from himself as he continued his planned words. "I know of all the skills you possess, of the herbs, and of the ways of the old folk to cure many things not of science. I have not the skills for such, but I know it is needed, for many are poor folk and do not always need the surgeon for their cures. That is what I have to say, straight. If you need time to mull that which I have spoken, I will leave it to your good selves."

"Time is not needed, sir, for all here know my being is to help those who need me, whether rich or poor. I will do as you wish—will I not, Thomas?"

"Of course you will, Jemma, for you are blessed for such." Thomas gave his will to the request and Steven's smile showed his way.

"But before I do so I have one request to place before you. That is, many folk have little or no monies and cannot pay for the help they need, and as such I have to treat such people, whether they can pay or not. When such situations arise, I will take no wage for my service to these poor folk. If you do agree to that, I would be most pleased to join with you."

"It is agreed, Jemma, for I too would offer some service free of any dues, and I believe many of the rich clients would give freely to help in this endeavour, for would they not sooner have a healthy staff about them than a sickly one? Yes, Jemma, I think we will do just fine. Would you be able to come to the surgery tomorrow?"

"Yes, that will be convenient; and at what time would you wish me to be there? For I can come to your convenience."

"Would nine of the clock be of suit?"

"Yes, Mister Blackberry, that will be just perfect."

"Then I bid you all good day, being most obliged to you all." Mister Blackberry donned his cap, and left those about to mull the good fortune that had once more looked upon them.

"I must away, my friends," Steven spake, "to rest soon this eve, for we tomorrow make to the far lands across the Channel—do we not, Thomas?"

"Yes, Steven, may the morrow quickly come so we may bring closer our future, for I am in some pleasure to see these fine horses you have spoken of." Both were restless as itch came to foot, wishing they to breed the fastest and the strongest horses in England.

"I bid you good eve and upon the light of the day to come we will journey on, and whilst we trod through those far lands across the Channel, we may hear more of the rumours of the princely twosome who may there still roam about." Steven's words faded as the door closed aback of him and he took his way to Jayne and to the manor, this third day of the month of August, fourteen hundred and eighty-six.

PART FOUR: PRINCE RICHARD

1484 … / November 1491 …

Chapter Seventeen.

Master Osbeck.

The little boat guided by Josh vanished into the dark swelling water of the Channel. The stars' blinking set their way to Portugal. Tyrell and the princes lay at rest in the hull, their heads giddy from the dunking boat, their stomachs squirmed and unsettled. Richard had not yet fought his battle at the field of Bosworth, and Steven was still at guard by his side. The blackness of the night did not slip, as the oak bow made away from the cliffs that white no more did show. Vigil came about as they neared one mile from the coast of England, the line where the king's ships guarded the coast, stopping all who had no warrant to cross the dipping waters. The crafts boarded and searched, the cargo taken as bounty to swell the king's coffers, and oft the crew and the ships were not seen again but to rest all upon the black bottom. Silently the boat slid through the dark waters, unseen and unheard, like a leaf washed down the stream of the night's dim.

Two hours had passed as the little craft made away from the king's watchful ships and into the safe but turbulent waters of the mid-Channel. The little boat was thrown about in rhythmic sway. Rain came in the brew about, lashing into the eyes of Josh, as he was troubled much to see his way for the stars were not showing, relying only upon his experience to guide all in the way of Portugal. Blackness hung as they lurched about.

"Ooh … I am full of sickness."

"What is the matter?" the Prince Richard asked of his queazing elder brother.

"I am of sickness; I must go to the deck, for air I need within me, and to rid my stomach of such ills that churn about within my body."

"Be careful, Edward, it is very wet on the deck and slime is upon the wood," Richard warned as his brother made in some haste from the safety of his rest. Tyrell, in all the uppings and downings, was able to sleep as a babe rocked by his mother. The older boy struggled along holding onto the sides of the shelter as he groped about the blackness for the canvas that was the cover to the opening. He found it and pulled it to one side and, in his darkness, met the other darkness that was without. The canvas flapped to close behind him; he could not stand for his legs and his head were of some other state, so he crawled and gripped the slippery deck with his fingernails, tugging himself along in the rain that still lashed upon him, and to find himself at the edge of the boat, where he placed his head over the low board there and retched his stomach out into the surging waters. The victuals he had eaten during the past fortnight seemed to pass from him as his head spinned, the rain washing upon his neck and upon his face like a thousand tapestry needles. His blond hair all at wraggle, hanging down most straight and dark.

I hope that he is all right, came the thoughts to the younger prince as he could hear naught but the waves' crash and the winds' howl. Thoughts filled his mind, to him alone known, to other places and to other things, as a dozing came over him with the boat's lilt like a cradle to bring repose to the muddled mind.

The deck was awash with the salty wet, as still the boy huddled over the edge in the sickness of the sea. A figure made closer to the retching prince; the wet canvas black and dripping from his flopped hat to his seaman's boots, he neared with steady legs upon the waltzing boards, those sea legs that carried him as if he walked upon the land. The shape lowered, and then, with a swift movement, grabbed the legs of the sickly one, but the grab was not to pull him to a safer place, but in its stead pulled up the legs and flipped the boy into the black waters. The tossing of the sea made all of silence and no sound other could be heard. A bob up, a gasp for air, his hair then floating like a weed upon the swell. Then, with no cry, he was gone as aught had never been before. It stood still, that shape of canvas, to sure the deed was done, and then turned back to his rudder place. Josh, sitting with head low at the till as the water did drip from his brim, by his station, seen to have not ever roamed. An evil spy he, paid off to do dirty works.

The lurching of the boat had not stopped as Tyrell stirred. The water's drip from the canvas and wooden planks above his head, splashing his hair and his face, running into his mouth, the salty wet, thirsting his throat as he croaked his words to the Prince Richard. "Where is Edward?" he spake as he eyed about the shelter.

"Pardon, sir?"

"Where is Edward? I do not see him about." Concerned was the voice's tone as it came to the ear of Richard.

"I know not, sir; I was at slumber. He had gone outside to be sick and I did fall to dream before his return."

Tyrell upped in most haste, his nails at tipped finger, clawing at the dripped boards as he made his blind way toward the canvas draped. He pulled it aside, but with no more light to show, then he was upon the deck. The figure, dark over the till, moved to edge his face to the lord; a light glint of eye was all that showed from beneath the black drape. Tyrell looked about the deck clinging to the shelter's frame; in all he saw naught and knew quickly that there were only three souls here upon this vessel.

"Did you see my eldest boy?" Shaking the shoulder of Josh to bring him to the fact.

"What say, sir?" he shouted, and showed he could not hear the lord for the rampant sea's crash and whine.

"Have you seen my oldest boy?" Tyrell repeated this time with gesturing movements. His hand flat above his eyes. "Have you seen—" the hand next placed to his shoulder with the palm facing down "—tallest boy?"

"No, sir, I see naught." His head lowered once more and all converse ended. Tyrell slumped with wilted shape back through the canvas flap to the inside of the shelter, all dark and wet, the wind wet and blowing through the slits between the planks making a place of drab tidings. He sat broken next to the young prince, readying to bring the saddened outcome to Richard. Cut was Tyrell; all the guile and lies, all the intrigues and the murders had been washed away with a high wave and weeded water, and, with that, all hope for a king's return had gone, left washing to and fro at the sand bottom; soon the shrimp and the crab would nibble and suck away the flesh of a king, to leave only bones that could be but of a peasant for anyone's eyes would see no king, just the left bone.

"You look sadly engaged, sir," the Prince Richard broached to Tyrell.

"Yes, my dear prince, I am in some distress."

"Is it for your boy lost?"

"Yes, it is … What mean you, sir, with 'your boy lost'? 'Twas your brother, the rightful heir that lays at the sanded bottom. What riddle are you letting from your mouth, sir, that you speak such?"

"'Twas my brother not, my lord, but one of the boys brought to bring some gaiety to our drab."

"My mind is lost in some turmoiled fog with these words. So then where is your brother, the Prince Edward?"

"I know not, sir. In the day's light, after our sleep that night when you took us from the evil Tower, I saw the boy who clutched my hand was not Edward."

"Why in the name of God did you not say such to me?"

"We were frightened, sire; we are only young boys, not enlightened to the world's wicked ways, and so 'twas we played the part for we feared for our lives."

"God's Death … Then Edward was still in the Tower when we left?"

"Yes, sir; we saw him not again."

"What terrible act have I laid upon us that through my intrigues Edward is no more and but done by these shamed hands?" Tyrell looked down at his wetted hands seen all black and evil in the dark of the shelter. "'Twas these that pointed and ordered the devilish act against an innocent babe, the one I wished to save but ordered to death in its stead. I am done ... I have ended the life of the king, to no more be a Yorkist upon the throne."

"Be not such in your ill to yourself, for am I not here? Am I not of princely state, and am I not the next royal to reclaim such as seems lost?"

"How know I that you speak of truth, that you are who you say you are, and not some lecherous boy upon a quest, shooting to me slanted words dipped in honey to hide the falsehoods you chatter?"

"I am such as I say, my lord ... And do not I have some question of you, sir? Was I not asleep when the boy was gone, leaving you to pursue such dirty games that you may play?—for you have murdered before and must now be most trivial to you."

"What say you, that I would kill a king purposely after such arduous tasks to keep him lived?"

"I know not to your mind, sir, but to be on some vessel muddled in the sea there would be no eyes to see aught." The young boy stood defiant, for life or death he stood and carded all to Tyrell.

"You have the pride of a royal, I give you that, but such means naught to me as yet, though if some other has done this day a murderous act, then it falls not upon either of us, for I have committed no crime." The banter did quieten somewhat as thoughts about their state fluttered mindfully. The morn's light placed its lines through the planked gaps, and laid them with its dark and light across their shapes to where they sat. The sea had calmed as passed the blackness of the night to drift away to another place. They pulled back the canvas to flood themselves with the light of morn. Josh was not at the till as Tyrell scoured about to seek his place. He saw him then, the small man pulling at the sail to catch more wind. Far ahead the black line of land showed to be, with hope, the coast of Portugal.

"Is that which I see the land of Portugal?" Tyrell called out to Josh.

"Si, sir, si, 'tis Portugal," he called back to the lord. The sea was as if by some spell calmed, the air warmed, the body warmed, the heart, though, cold still.

"See the land ahead, my boy," Tyrell spake in kindly tones to Richard.

"Yes, sir, I see it clearly."

"Go to the bow, my boy, and there sit to see the land come upon us." He then quietly stated to only one ear. "Do as I say ... and fear not."

"Yes, sir," at whisper came the retort as Richard moved past Josh to the front of the vessel.

"I shall be at the shelter to prepare some victuals and ready our chattels," Tyrell called to the boy as he made to the edge of the boat.

"Yes, sir," called the meek voice of Richard, sat, as asked, with one hand placed each side of the bow's low rail. He watched the water as if cut by a hot knife, as the boat closed to the eyed land that lay upon the sea's far sparkle.

Inside the still dripping shelter went Tyrell, stepping about and moving such chattels that barred his way until he was within the bow. The light from without first played upon his chin, then upon his nose, and then upon his eyes, as he peered through the slit between the boards to see all before him. The boy at the front crouching and peering ahead, a shape there pure and innocent, a worm that dangled upon the hook. The Josh at the rope, pulling and straining, his small body filled with evil intent mayhap. Then he saw him turn and peer at the shelter, and seeing no eyes at watch upon him, he made slyly to the boy who gazed at the land closing before him. Tyrell could see him talking to the prince, who sat at the bow, he all of trust and faith. Josh, pointing to some mark upon the landfall, the prince peered to see the mark, and stood to better look along the crooked pointing finger that hung out before him. The prince stood but for a little, while seeking with squinted eye the spot that did hide from his gaze. As then the short canvas-covered arm came swift, to push with force into the boy's small back, and thrust him into the cold wave with flailing splash. He yelled loudly his plight and struggled to keep his head above the swell, and prayed he would not be left a-bob in the brine, for his strength was not enough to make that landfall. At slip and slide came in haste the shape of Tyrell, a rage of rush and fume. He pushed the ugly shape o'er the side, sending Josh spinning with arms at flail as he was dunked into the churn. Tyrell looked about for some suitable weapon, for his sword would be of little use in this play. A heavy docking pole he saw a-lay upon the boards; he lifted it from its place and with all his strength wielded it above his head. Josh, still floundering with face to the shore, saw naught of the retribution that swung behind him. The pole came, brought with all the force its wielder could bring, with a loud crack; it came down full upon the haired mop that bobbed about that sucking sea, cracked atop he like a broken egg, skin and bone a-fly as the blood spurted and the brain forced itself out from the skull's case and gurgled and leapt to float upon the water's top. The arms still flailed, not yet knowing that 'twas dead, as the salted water poured into the gaped shell like a goblet dunked into a bowl. Then, in little spate, all that remained was the bloody mess atop the frothing wave, and the pale brain parts afloat upon the black waters, done he like the headless fowl. Richard, treading in the swell, watched from a short distance the grisly scene that played before him.

"Hold this, boy!" shouted Tyrell as he laid the bloody pole toward the prince, who pushed himself closer, and clutched with numbed hands the pole, his life held by the shaft that hung before him. Tyrell pulled his ward back to the lurching boat, and dragged the sogged shape to deck with its coughing and spitting at the brine, and the bloody mess that had gained the mouth and lungs. Tyrell pressed upon the boy's back and forced out much of the vileness that was within, and soon the splutter stopped as then the prince rolled over to his back and gazed skyward to the white clouds that floated above, as he sucked in the cold air that for some time he had but little. Soon, with Tyrell watching over him, his breathing returned to its normal state and he was able to conjure some words.

"Thank you, sire, for saving me from such a dreadful state."

"Yes, young sir. Is this the act of someone bent upon your demise?"

"No, sir, 'tis not; my voiced object to you was wrongfully laid and I am indeed indebted to you … once again, it seems." He was then up with the help of Tyrell's sure arm.

"Now, sir, you have seen my loyalty, now all that remains is that you prove to me of yours. Come sit with me at the till and we will sort this for the last time." They both moved to the back of the boat and untied the rudder, and placed their hands to guide the craft to the place of their commission. "You say to me, sir, that you are the Prince Richard; I wish you to give me some proof of your words, for the royal garb you wear under your canvas is no proof, for all of you within the Tower were dressed such. So tell me of the Tower palace and its doings, and be mindful, for I know it well."

"Firstly, my lord, why was it that Josh had such evil intent upon us, he being just a fisherman whom we had done no harm?"

"Not 'just a fisherman,' my boy, but someone paid by the king's agents to murder anyone leaving England with two small boys, for odds were they were of princely nature and if they were not, 'twould matter little anyway. You must always be vigilant, for they are game to seek you out. But enough of this, tell me of the palace and all the things that it does hold."

"The Great Hall has walls all washed white; there is a tapestry at the far, placed near the great stairway—"

"What of this picture, what does it depict?"

"It tells of the crusades, sire, of King Richard the Lion-Heart and his journeys to the Holy Land."

"And what, tell me, of the meeting chamber, when the king, your father, was at sit; who stood aback of him?"

"On the right side of my father's hand stood the Lord Buckingham, and on the other the Bishop of Canterbury."

"And, sir, tell me of your father, I need to know from you what I know of him and his personal acts, which are known."

"Young though I am, I know of the debauch he carried about. The whores of the town often visited him and I saw many young boys ushered to his chamber as we were supposed asleep. I ashamedly know of this, and of the lines of young maidens who stood awaiting him, and this I cannot yet speak of, for in many things I am naive, and wish not to dwell upon such things. My father did spend but little time with us and showed no tenderness."

"You seem to answer my questions with some deft, and your knowledge of the palace and its activities is indeed a true reflection of it, and so I must give you that you speak truthfully. But I must repeat to you that anyone who wished such could learn of these things."

"Mayhap, sir, but I give you truly my state, that I am the Prince Richard, and I may remind you as such that you are no more than a servant to one of royal blood."

"I will for now believe that which you have told me, dear boy, and I will, with all my strength, do all that I am able to bring you to the state that you will be shown as the rightful heir to the throne of England. But, I tell you this, I have been dangled before upon the twine of trust, only for it to be cut and fall me to the ground, and leave me as a fool to all others' eyes. If ever I find you did not speak to me with words of truth, I will cut you down with most pleasure, to spill your evil blood about and sunder you no more. Do you hear what I speak? You have a crafty fashion about you with which I am not well pleased. This is the time for you to be gone if lies are spilled from your mouth; you can go without malice, for I will do you no harm. But do such now, for never again will such chivalry be shown to you. And, as for being your servant, be not so bold, for in this land, at this time, you are my boy and to survive, that is what you are. If you wish to be master and I your servant we will not see the morrow's dawn."

"I have no need to flee your side, my lord; you will hear no untruths in this matter, and I wish you to forgive me for my brash ways; it is sometimes difficult for me to go the way of the worldly man when one has been pampered from birth, to be only of royal bearing and honoured titles."

"Then 'tis done, you have my complete devotion, my prince, and my honour will always be for your good, though, from this day, ways may be strange to you, they are the only path we can tread to survive. We are but one mile from the land of Portugal, for I know the lay well. There is a small cove to the left of that peaked mountain where we will tie off this vessel."

"Why do we make head for such a place, sire?"

"We need a secluded place, for we have to burn all things that have any royal bearing, for whilst we are in our learned state, we must not be of a princely state."

"Yes, sir, I understand," answered Richard, knowing times indeed would be changing for him.

The small craft floated upon placid waters silently to the small beach; surrounded by large rocks, it lay hid beneath the high cliff and was seen only from the sea. The bow slid from the water and sliced onto the beach where it stopped, dragged to still by the heavy wet of the sand. They trod the soft underfoot to tie up the craft to one of the rocks, gathered wood, which was scattered about, and then, with some cloth soaked in oil, did strike a spark and soon they brought the dry wood to flame, quickly to be crackling and spitting about its smoke, drifting high to the blue sky.

"Boy, take off your prince's trappings; we must throw it to the flames." No reply came to Tyrell's request as the boy, Richard, began to disrobe; the last shred of his regal bearing would soon be gone. Turning his back a little so sight was not to Tyrell, Richard, with his small dagger, did cut off one of the royal buttons from the doublet, and as he placed the cloth upon the sand, he slipped his memento into his breeches' waist pouch, secreted most carefully, for naught else had he to remember his days past, knowing well in time to come, when things were bleak, that when he looked upon it he would remember his calling, and the royal heart that beat beneath the common cloth he may wear. He picked up all his discarded clothing and, with Tyrell's assist, placed them upon the reaching flame, to feed upon the new fuel to its like. Soon the flame dulled as the thick black smoke upward went. He slipped over his skin the canvas coat he had worn; except for his breeches, 'twas all he possessed to cover his body.

"We will obtain for you some more suitable cloth to better your state; there will be many shops in the town we seek." Tyrell spake words to ease the saddened face of Richard.

"Yes, sir," he answered, trying to bring some lightness to his drab state.

They waited until all the cloth was but smoke and ash, then climbed aboard the boat. 'Twas then pushed from the sands clinging as a mother to her child, but quickly freed when the sea lapped its willing boards and it cut through the foaming waters with the wind pushing past the face of the new land to come. Only one half of the hour did they sail to the southwest and arrive to a place oft visited by Tyrell. A small fishing village, it lay close to Lisbon, tucked in a sheltered bay, a place where they could roam without fear. They drifted into the shallow harbour, the old sign windswept and sea-washed could hardly be read, but was called out by Tyrell.

"Cascais, at last!" They drifted upon the warm breeze to the timbered dock's side and tied up the little craft, which had been of all evil and little good. They stepped gratefully upon the boards, with the small fishing boats bobbing in rhythm with their own craft. The clear sky was all blue with naught to paint other upon its sheet. The sun beat down upon the heads below, far hotter than Richard had ever known before. They walked through the throng of jabber and shout to reach the market close. Little shops of all kinds lined the place of the crowded lot. Strange were the build of house and chamber to Richard's green eyes that had not been shown another land nor blinked or teared at such. The folk, all of darker skin than he, and most of smaller stature, busied about their day. He had some schooling in language and could pass some converse in French and Spanish, and of the chatter about him he knew many of the words bantered.

"Come, Richard, this way," Tyrell beckoned him to an open door of one of the shops that was a seller of clothing. Inside they went, to be met with the heat of the day that could find no escape. Breath seemed hard to get in the laden air.

"Yes, sir?" The small swarthy keeper of the business came from the dingy back to greet his customers.

"Good day, sir; we require some clothing for the young boy here, something apt that is the normal dress here. Nothing frilly though. You know of my needs, do you not?"

"Yes, sir; how do these suit?—good breeches of English worsted, and this shirt of imported cotton." He showed with much flair his wares to Tyrell. "We have a nice coat here made of deerskin. Feel its softness; you would never wish to part with a garment such as this."

"Yes, yes, they look suitable; have you a place he can dress?"

"Yes, sir, here through this curtain," he waved toward a blue drop at the rear of the shop, and, pulling the drape back, did show a small dressing closet, with a sitting bench snug in the corner. Richard was ushered inside and the drape closed upon him.

"We will need some boots and stockings," Tyrell spake as he sifted about the shop, picking through the goods that were displayed.

"Here, sir, here is a good pair of boots made in Lisbon, and these stockings are sturdy and will last for many years."

"They will do well. So, how much is the bill? I only have coins of silver or gold; I have no escudos."

"Your gold coin is of acceptance, sir, and half a sovereign will cover the cost of your purchases." Tyrell picked one of the gold coins he carried and dropped it into the shopkeeper's hand.

"Thank you kindly, sir, for your business."

"Boy, how do you fare in there?" Tyrell called through the thick drape.

"Almost ready, sir," Richard called.

"I will await you outside, for I am stifled within this chamber."

"Very well, sire, I shall be but a short time," called his charge.

Tyrell stepped out into the cooler roadway and stood at gaze of all about; the bustle and noise as in any town and in any country seemed always the same. He leant upon the wall of the shop, next to an alley, damp and musky, so narrow the bright day could not broach its dark. And lapsed he there, almost to close his eyes as the burdens of the past weeks drifted away, and left him with a mind free of troubles replaced by his restful pose.

With such swiftness from the dark of the stone passage, an arm, most powerful, was about his neck and he was dragged back from the brightness to the dim within. A big brute clung to him with heavy arm tight against his throat, making the air difficult to reach. Another shape showed, and lifted the sword and the dagger of Tyrell from his belt, so that he held no weapons close.

"Where are the two boys?" the husky voice from the darkness croaked, the face came close to Tyrell's cheek, the garlic fumes played upon him with spit and fume.

"I know of no boys," Tyrell managed to force out an answer from his crushed pipes.

"You bloody liar! I ask you one more time, if you do not tell us of the truth, I will kill you, have no doubt about it, I jest not." The spit and spray splattered his face once more from the rage behind. "Speak now!"

"I know not of what you speak, sir—" The words had not fully left Tyrell's lips when he felt something cold slipping inside his stomach, with no pain to come with the sensation, but to feel warmth running from his body as hot blood began to spray over all; done with a short sword was he, as then he felt another slash and a pull as his innards slopped upon the cobbled way. He felt them frisk about him, still held standing by the strong arm that bulged his neck. With Tyrell still alert to all the happenings about him, they took his moneybag, which held all his goodly worth, all taken except for a small pouch well concealed. He was dropped then to the ground, amidst his own seeping life; left floundering as his head lightened and he became vague …

"Sir! My goodly lord, what in all God's sight has happened?" Richard spake as he gazed over his master, watching the life run away to the gutter's edge and down the drain grate to mingle with other of life's waste. Tyrell summoned all the strength he could, to clutch at the boy's garb that hung over him, and to pull him close to whisper his last words.

"Take the money from my purse and flee from this place … Evil spies are upon us and they will seek you out. Be gone now and lose your regal ways in the humdrum of some small town. Do not show of your features until the sun browns your fair skin … God be with you, Richard."

"And with you, my Lord Tyrell." The grip that clutched at the boy's cloth loosened as the hand fell; pale 'twas as the trickle flowed no more, and life was done. The worm never saw the coming of the sparrow; alive then quick dead in two minutes. From the sun upon the face warm and comforting, to the cold and nowhere black. Richard pushed about his hand in the bloody mess and groped about to bring out the dripping money pouch; small pittance did it hold but to naught was rich indeed. He removed the monies from the soggy leather and threw it into the dark of the alley, as then with care he placed the coins safe in his own belt. With glance first hither then thither up and down the roadway, he was alone, away with jig and jag amongst the throng, to be seen not, as he went a-mingled, lost in the roads and amongst the dwellings, the narrowed alleys and wiggled pathways, a foggy lost was he … Gone.

The moon and the sun flittered their flight of night and day as on went the year of fourteen hundred and eighty-six. Richard the Third, time ago, gone to his death at the field of Bosworth. The new king, Henry the Seventh, sat upon the throne and in seek of the princes that were fled from their Tower of intrigue. His spies about at all places to watch and to wait for some tongue's blab. But, as the years passed and the prince grew from boy to youth, naught was gained from the agents that still waited, until it seemed that all was mayhap, just hearsay and blemished tale, painted green when red was the colour …

The striking figure of the tall youngish man now showed, having some commanding presence about him. The skin darkened by the high sun, the hair light of sun's fade upon tussled top. He came up the narrow street way that was steep in its lay; the ocean glinted at his back, as he journeyed the way through the calm that was of Lisbon, hid to all who may so wish. Dressed as some learned scholar with books hugged close under arm, he wended toward the bishop's keep, which lay close to the royal palace, high and regal. To the abbey courtyard he strode of firm step and high chin.

"Good day to you, Master Osbeck," the gatekeeper spake as he beckoned the visitor to enter.

"Good day, Signor Santos." The words of Portuguese flowed with ease from the full-lipped reply to the keeper. He strode on across the slate flags, his wood-soled shoes to click-clack as he made toward the bishop's entrance. He went through the old gateway built ago by the Moors, still standing strong as it towered to greet the sun, then into the cool air of the thick-walled chamber, where little of window showed. The sun's hot rays, best to be kept at bay from the inner sanctuary, making the need for candles and torches forever lit. In some far chamber rang the chanting voices of monks at prayer, droning their rituals into every corner of the building, to seemingly flicker the candles' glow with its passing.

"Good day, Master Osbeck," one of the learned monks called to the sight of the coming student, and beckoned him into the chamber, wafting the lit candle as he made to sit and await the coming of Piers, striding as quickly as he may behind him. The table was as usual piled with manuscripts and heavy books of much learning laid upon it, with a space between master and pupil so each could be seen. "Sit, Master Osbeck," the monk proffered.

"Thank you, sir," politeness folded Piers's reply, as he sat before the placid monk all hooded in sack-like robe.

"Have you studied the Latin verse as I asked?"

"Yes, sir, I have."

"Then open your book at the mark and read to me of your lilt."

Piers chose the book's place, and read aloud to the ringing chamber his words at bounce from one stone to the other. With ease the Latin did spill from his mouth with creamy word, as he spake with only quick glances at his script, to others seem as though at speak with no prompt.

"Very well; now the Spanish ... Read to me from the Spanish lesson."

"Yes, sir." The pupil began from the book of Spanish. With ease again the words did flow as if the mother tongue he did speak, with again ne'er a glance to view the verse.

"Thank you, sir. If you would study the calculations before you, I will return in but a moment."

"Yes, sir," Piers answered and stood slightly, in respect of his tutor monk. As then, with hands unseen within the sleeves' folds, he shuffled away upon hidden feet to the far of the chamber. There stood the elder monk, viewing the schooling that was at different tables within. A dark grey habit did he wear, distinguished from the brown of others by his title, his hands also lost within the sleeves' folds, the robe's hood nestled his head. He saw Piers's tutor making way to approach him, and shuffled to meet his coming.

"My good Monk Bernard," the elder monk spake to the tutor.

"Good day, Monk Peter."

"What pleasure do you bring with your greeting, Bernard?"

"I wish to speak to you of the certain young man Piers Osbeck."

"I pray he has not disappointed you in his schooling, for he seems indeed a most industrious student."

"Far from such, Monk Peter, for he seems to possess more knowledge of books and of more worldly things than I, his elder by some forty years. And, if I may say so, without any vainness, I thought of myself as a scholarly person with much to offer someone of few years. But this Master Osbeck has such a grasp upon languages, and with such ease of tongue, that it seems he was born in many different places and leaves me as some mindless yokel. And, above this, his English is without flaw and sounds of a most genteel nature."

"What say you then, Monk Bernard, that our Osbeck seems more than he divulges?"

"Yes, Monk Peter, he is of a different breeding from that which he states."

"When his lessons are finished bring him to me, and I will chat with him and see if he will reveal his situation."

"Thank you, my good monk, I will do as you suggest and bring him over when his lessons are completed." And with a gentle nod only seen by the elder monk, his respect hid by the robe's hood, he turned and made his way back to the table of the seated Osbeck, diverse in the task placed before him. The tutor monk sat quietly so as not to interrupt the thoughts of his student, for he seemed to be far lost in his endeavours. In short spate Piers spake.

"Sir Monk, I have reached the end of my calculus; would you wish me to do further work?"

"No, young sir, your tasks for this day are done; I will give you further studies before you depart if they are required. But before you do so, the elder Monk Peter, who awaits at the far end of the chamber, wishes to have some converse with you."

"It would be a pleasure for me to do so, sir."

"Come then," upped the monk as Piers spake. They walked over the flagged floor, and as they did so, it seemed that only Piers's shoes made any noise with their clatter upon the echoing stone. The Monk Bernard floating as some saintly being without noise or breeze as they made toward the Monk Peter.

"Master Osbeck, sir, how are you this day?"

"Well, sir Monk," Piers replied to the query. Whereupon a stream of Latin ensued from the lips of the elder monk, fast it came like waters rushing the stones, a-gurgle and a-slop, it licked the words and then to quickly stop came, to direct its blab to Piers. Much had been spake as the monk from beneath the guised hood quizzed the face before him, seeking to beguile Piers with his chant. The reply came from the Master Osbeck, playing the scene as some jest, in Latin, with all ease, with ne'er a false word to answer the tricked jibe of the monk. Then quickly to English the monk switched his tongue, speaking not in his native Portuguese but in his best English; though broken, 'twas still heard in clear fact. From Osbeck came the English words, pure as the morn's milk did come, with no taste of falsehood tainting its rhyme, but clear and with great bearing back to the monk. The elder again spake in his native tongue to query the Piers.

"Sir, your manner and knowledge seem far in excess to your station. A fisherman's son is your claim from the small village of Cascais, which seems far from your learned state; what say you to this; are you in fact some atheling?"

"The truth, sir, for me to say at this time, is to say naught, for my life would be in such danger to do so."

"You, sir, are to me more than you act; you are full of riddles. I feel you belong to some upper reach of society, and I suggest to you, my dear boy, that if you have such blood that flows within you, to go and seek out your heritage, for rest will not come to your state until you do so. I speak of this for there is no doubt your knowledge and education is far in advance of that which we can teach within this Holy place. It is, as you say, not possible at this time to enlighten us of your position, but I presume because of your grasp of the English tongue, and your deep knowledge of the ways of that land, that it is to those Isles you must go to seek out what you must. I say this, for in Lisbon, living close by, an English knight resides by the name of Sir William Bray; to his particular residence, I know not, but gather he is within the cathedral's shadow. He may be able to offer you some advice in the matter you hold, and to guide you to some road that will take you to your desire."

"That is most benevolent of you, Monk Peter. Thank you for your kindness. I will go forth straight and seek out the knight."

"God be with you, my boy; may He bring upon you all the riches you deserve."

"Thank you, my good monks; my thoughts will oft be with you and of the deep kindness you have shown to me; your teachings will bear me in good stead, and I pray for each one in this Holy place that God will bless you all for your goodness." He upped his books and took his steps from the cool dark chamber that was filled with peace and tranquility, and stepped out into the other world that was beyond the cloisters.

Chapter Eighteen.

The Emerald Isle.

Bright and hot the sun beat upon his cool head, as he squeezed and scraped once more amongst the throng that milled about the narrow streets and covered alleys, stepping with much care o'er the sleeping lots, they who rested within the cool shadows, shielded kindly from the searching sun. Richard went on through the mingling until he came to sight the towered steeple of the cathedral, standing black against the drop of the clear blue sky.

"Excuse me, sir, I seek an English gentleman by the name of Sir William Bray. Do you know of such a person about these parts?" Richard asked the storekeeper who lolled in the cool shade of the narrow way.

"Yes, young fellow, I do know of such a man, he lives but a short way along there." He pointed further along the road that Richard had not yet trod. "To the bootmaker's shop go. The gentleman you seek resides upon the upper floor. The sign of Alfredo's Shoe Repair will guide you to the place."

"I am much obliged to you, sir. May you be well."

"And to you, sir."

He was away between the narrow walls that cramped all with there closeness, clutching tightly upon his moneybag—the bag held little, but would soon be lifted by the scoundrels that flitted about these close places, if 'twas swung freely and not coveted. *Alfredo's Shoe Repair*—he saw the sign as he loped closer, and saw also the high steps with its rusty old rail that led to the doorway. Even with his long legs, Richard found it most difficult to climb the stairs, and thought that all the customers to this place must be giants, for no person small of stature and certainly no lady would ever manage to gain entrance. But then he noticed a bell swung upon the wall, with the rope dangling to the way below, where a pull would bring the shoemaker to its call; though he still to mind that 'twas a most unlikely place for such a business. The door he opened slowly and gave him entrance to the shop. Its sweet smell of cured leather and polish oils played its scent upon his nostrils. He saw off to one side another door, hid in the shadows beside the piles of leather, with the name Bray etched deeply into the black surface, the fresh woodcut showed clearly the carved name. Richard opened the latch and pulled wide the door to the high wooden steps that twisted up so the end could not be seen, and one man's width alone to tread as up he went, the way curving around as he climbed to the upper floor, to be faced then with another doorway that led to the chambers of the knight he sought. A trio of raps he laid upon the door's grunge and grime, his knuckles acquiring some onto his skin, as loud and echoing about the chamber went his rattle, the only noise in the small place to hear.

"Who is there?" came the booming voice that broke through.

"Sir, my name is Piers Osbeck and I wish to have audience with you."

"Enter; the door is not shackled."

Richard pushed upon the door, which was stiff and heavy to move at first, and then, springing free as a bird from a cage, pulled Richard inside; he released the handle before he fell, so as not to make himself of a foolish entrance, for gentlemanly airs were his companion upon this meet. He stepped most assuredly inside. The room was hot with the tiled roof above their heads spreading the heat within. The open windows that showed each end eased the oppressive warmth a little, with the breeze from the ocean wafting through the dusty sparkle. Sir William Bray sat before him; a large seat hugged tight to his ample body, a larger man Richard had not seen. He sat there, but showed even at seat he would stand well over six feet tall; he had broad shoulders and his muscular arms dripped with sweat. His beard was short. With one eye peering at the visitor and the other covered by a black patch, he looked a man not to be trifled with.

"What do you think of this then, laddie?" The gruff, common voice raised across to Richard as the knight lifted up the eye patch to show out his missing eye, all sunken and scarred, a gruesome sight to offer as some greeting, and to place the seer at some disadvantage. There, craggly below, a deep smile bloomed as he took much delight from his repulsive affliction. The knight then flipped down his patch to cover again the scarred gape. "Well, what say you, laddie?" He would not lay his greeting to rest, as Richard stood before him with little-shown fluster.

"A most attractive scar, sir, a true knight's wound; I have no doubt, you must be most proud of it." The bludgeoning laughter rocked the room, as he savoured the answer that was played upon him by the Master Richard.

"Come, laddie, sit." He splayed his hand to a small bench that was placed beside him. Richard sat aside the bawdy knight. A knight not blessed from birth with such titles as lord or sir. But a commoner who had gained his place by his valour in the field, by his gallantry in places where none need be given, and, in reaching such esteem, he could not be denied a knighthood; the only thing the upper class could do to delay such was to place a high purse upon the honour, but seemingly he had overcome that obstacle too; so, this gruff, ill-mannered giant was now indeed Sir William Bray. Richard sat hoping to keep more than an arm's distance length from him, for even a comrade's hug from such a frame could prove most hurtful. "So, laddie, what do you ask about this day?"

"I seek you, sir, that you may bring to me more knowledge of the day-to-day life that is present within the palaces and castles of England, for I know little of such, for I was of early years and my memory of many things has faded, and wish, in respect, sir, to regain it once more."

"And laddie, why do you wish such? For you show me a young fellow who is not rich in dress but far more in words and education, and in your bearing, more than should lay beneath such cloth ... Pray, once more, your name?"

"Piers Osbeck, sir."

"I say to you, Master Piers, I am a true and loyal knight, sworn to the most highest of honour, and to silence so when required ... Though it seems since the betrayal of Richard there are few left who can claim such, for the word has become tarnished by unworthy acts. But I tell you, sir, I am not one of those who play make-believe and act with disgrace; I am a true and loyal servant to whoever rules that land. Though I am exiled, I am still loyal to the king who stands. So, to me, state without any foggy plot the truth, for it will stay within me as my soul is such."

"With all trust, I will tell you, sir knight, of my state, and after such my life will be in yours, cupped. I am, my Sir William Bray ... the youngest son of the late King Edward IV. I am, sir, the Prince Richard, heir to the throne of England."

"Ha!" came the response with guffaws of laughter, once again ringing about the chamber. "Please, Piers, do not jest more," the knight managed to jabber out the words through his mirth. "My heart cannot take more jest this day."

"'Tis the truth I speak, sir; I was rescued from the Tower by Sir James Tyrell, who, through his misfortune, was killed by the King Henry's spies. I managed to elude all who tried to secure me, and have made all use of my time by following as much learning of books and of language that I could. For when the day came, I would be of a scholarly mind to rule that England. Not under the guise of some usurper, but under the name of the true heir, I am pledged, for the only colour of rose that should reign ... the White one."

"So, tell me, laddie, of such as you recall from your early years within these palaces."

The knight listened with some intent to Richard's recollections. The humour flitted from his head, as indeed he saw this person was bent upon his quest, and showed naught but the truth to that which he spake, and stepping not one foot off its path. Then, the tale ended; with little doubt it seemed that this young man had frequented such palaces as he stated.

"I wish to hear more of your mother."

"What more do you wish to know, sir knight? I have spake all I can recall."

"Tell me of her hand."

"Her hand?'

"Yes, laddie, her hand, her left hand, tell me of it." He wagged his thick finger at Richard as he spake.

"I — 'Twas the most delicate of hands."

"A thing of beauty, you would say, Piers?"

"Yes, sir, an exquisite hand, most beautifully kept, with many rings to adorn it."

"Why do you play upon me this fiddle-faddle? ... You, sir, are an imposter!"

"Sir knight, I am who I say and speak to you only of the truth; I am hurt that you ply me so."

"I wish to know, sir, how it is that all the people in that blessed Isle, from royalty to peasant, know that the queen, your mother, has the first joint of her small finger amiss? If then you are the true Richard, her son, why would you not know of this?"

"Tender were my years and spent much in play and costume and games, not at sit to examine faulty digits. I never saw such as you say; only perfection through a child's eyes did I gaze."

"Your jibe is full of lies, and I do not bind myself to any who cannot the truth tell. I must do all I can to see that you do not spread your evil ways upon others who may be more gullible than I."

"But, sir knight, I do speak the truth, and I have not stated to you one falsehood." Richard pleaded with the knight, but it seemed 'twas going to be to no avail, for 'twas stuck in his head and the truth was not reaching his ears. There seemed little Richard could do to gain aught from the meet; 'twas coming to the time when another course would have to be struck, if he wished to continue ... "I implore you, please, let me continue with my quest."

"I told you, laddie, at the start of this converse, to the truth I will bring respect, but I have no time for such mischief as you bring, and will, in all my honour as a knight, do all to belay this deceitful act you unwind. I give you warning fair to leave this place. Begone. I will speak to you no more."

Richard slowly upped with the impression of sadness cloaking him.

He shuffled to the back within the knight's shadow and stooped as if to retrieve his books that he had laid upon the small table there; they lay beneath the dusty picture of some proud knight, with sword held high upon his prancing charger, an invincible giant he glared with such mad defiance. Richard's hand was at his waist, not seeking his reading, but to the long dagger that glistened at his belt. He drew it in all silence, for this stroke must of sure strike be, quick and deep, for the man of mountain must not be able to bring his wroth upon the Richard, young and lithe was he, but no match for such a warrior, for death would surely come from those brutish hands and Samson arms. Quick it did come, the bulged vein at the neck showed where to cut, and Richard plunged with all his might the razored blade. The dagger no sooner in than blood spurted all about from the severed skin, but the blade was forced on and even deeper did it cut until it came to show from the neck's other side. A gurgle came as the blood flooded the throat, coming so fast it could not clear as it drowned the lungs.

"I am not your laddie, sir," Richard gruffed as he twisted the blade. The thick hand clutched the one that held the dagger, and with strength still surging within him, the knight pulled out the blade with ease, letting more life spurt all about from the wound, as the weapon slipped from his grasp and rattled upon the bloody floor. Richard pulled his hand from the weakening grasp and picked up the dagger once more; his knees shook and his strength ebbed from the frightening act he was engaged in, and fearful that the knight would find some strength to overcome him. With the blade clutched in his hand, Richard saw the knight gathering strength from somewhere as he attempted to stand, but before he could fully reach his height, the dagger came fully from high and plunged into the good eye of the knight to have the anguish show but a gurgle to the act. He was writhing upon the planked floor, twitching and pushing forth his blood. Richard pulled off the covers that lay upon the sleep cot and placed them upon the floor, rolling the bubbling body onto the cloth to try and stop the seep to the floor below. The heart had ended its fight for life and was stilled and bloodless. He searched about, the prince, to tip and pull and to ransack the room, seeking any fortune he could, for his funds were low. In haste he plied, for he wished to be gone from this place before he was found with bloody hands. He moved to the seat where had sat the knight; he tugged then underneath, pulling at the tattered skirt to drag out a wooden box, which showed with iron, black strappings and a strong lock, to rattle as if some treasure did lie within. He moved over to the blood-soaked roll and groped about the still corpse to find amidst the gore the belt of the knight come to hand, and, with another slash from his blade, Richard was able to slide it out and to hold it up, for there at dangle, keys with a bloody dull rattle did swing. He pushed one and then another into the lock, as then he heard the click as the box gave up its lid, and lifted enough so the eyes could see within that many gold and silver coins, heavy rings, and trinkets lay. Not the fortune he did seek, but still a tidy sum for the prince to continue with his quest. He slid and slipped upon the seeped mire as he crossed the chamber. To the draped cover he went, pulling it to one side to see before him the knight's attire, hung like bats awaiting the dark, once most regal and bright but now dull and lifeless, some so worn as to show their bare threads and grimy braid, but some he found in goodly weave, and some good boots of fine leather. Upon the floor a rough-woven sack with a rope tie did lay. Richard took the best garments he could find, and with boots and hats pushed them without care into the bag. He wrapped the wooden box in a cloth and forced it on top of the clothes therein. Into the bloody mess he groped again, searching for the right hand to slip with slimy ease from the cold finger the ring that was the knight's seal. Richard then washed himself clean at the water bowl, and dried himself with the hanging cloths that, befouled, hung there. He picked up from a small table, which had not become splattered by the blood, some reams of paper that were marked with the knight's arms, and some letters that lay about; he did fold neat and place them within his books of study, secured by the leather strap that he swung over his shoulder, then picked up the bagged loot, glanced quickly about chamber, and started to make his way from the slaughter place, cold and unmoved was his state, for no one would keep him from his rightful place, and if he had to murder, then he would do so.

A peeked gaze from the doorway, then back again, and then another look—clear was the stairway. He was shaking again; his demeanour changed once more as the fear of discovery wobbled his legs. He crept down the stairs as silent as he could, and as he stepped he remembered that little noise did echo the narrow passage as he went up, but 'twas not so on the coming down, for every tread tweeted like a bird, and all noises came from about him as he made toward the freedom door—squeak, rattle, rustle—as down he came to the small entrance that led to the bootmaker's shop, he who would soon be suspect to the dripping blood that would shortly splash about his leathers, and with thickly goop lay its red lines of stain as the boards' cracks let drip the magly* gore. A creak came from the once silent door as he took chance and saw into the small entrance; all of empty did it show, and quickly he stepped to the door that reached the roadway. Richard laid his hand softly upon the latch to ease its sound

* *magly* [coined] thickening or congealed blood

and opened it most ghostly as the sun's rays lit bright, down first upon a face, and then upon a body that was about to gain entrance. A gentleman of some means stood before Richard.

"Good day, young sir," said he as he opened the door and beckoned Richard out.

"And a good day to you, sir, and thank you for your kindness." All composed and at his most guile. "'Tis another fine day we have, sir."

"It is so, sir." The gentleman in all grace stepped inside as Richard left with a glance over his shoulder, to see the visitor make to the door of the stairway and to the chamber of Sir William Bray … Deceased. A quicked step came as down the rickety way he went, for haste away was to mind; too many knew of his meet with the knight. The monks, the storekeeper, the gentleman visitor, and all else who knew that Richard did not. Still many people did bustle about the streets all to help Richard guise his way, as along twisted alleys and cool, dark walkways he trod, again a weed in a field of weeds. Soon he came to his small abode that wedged itself upon many others such. To breathless, half fall, half stagger through the doorway, as the cool air that greeted him bathed his fired face, gulping then the bottle of wine that had sat upon the cold slab, drinking and at gasp for air at the same time.

"What ails you, my friend?" The voice came from the far side of the chamber, in the bright corner.

"Let me breathe, Alphonse. I will relate all in a moment, but for now I must recover."

Richard's friend for many a year was concerned at the sight that lay a-gasp upon the stone of the floor. For strange 'twas for him to see his friend such, for Richard was always composed and aloof from such mortal games.

As the cool room refreshed him and security calmed his mind, he raised his slumped frame to sit more upright, though still seated upon the floor, he then leaned his back upon the doorframe and clasped his hands around his raised knees, as if in some state of ritual known not to other beings. The room still watched in silence awaiting some response from the prince. At last …

"I murdered the knight."

"What say you, Richard? My ears must falsely hear your words."

"No, Alph, you hear the evil truth; the knight did not believe that I was of royal blood; he did not believe that I was Richard, and did most vilely state that he would expose me as an imposter. My choice was to suffer his betrayal or to end his rant, for he was fully set upon mischief and I had little choice but to end it. But now I must flee this land, for my time would be little if I tarried here long. You will be safe, Alph, for innocence is your staff."

"Where you travel then I too will travel; where you tarry, there I will tarry; I will not desert you, my prince."

Richard raised himself from his respite and embraced his comrade. "Thank you, Alph, you are a friend indeed to give me such devoted trust, and I swear to you, when my day comes, you will be at my side, and you will be blessed with all that I can offer you. But we must hasten away, for soon it will be that they will come for us, and I believe there were many people who did see me flee from that place. I was able to find some treasure at the knight's chamber that will enable us to continue our endeavours and for passage away from those who seek us."

"Where will we go, Richard, that we may be welcomed?"

"We cannot foot to England yet, for our words have not yet sung their song, and until we can count upon some following, time must go its journey. So, methinks to Ireland we will take our journey ... Yes, to the Emerald Isle we will go, for there are many in that land who do not have affection for that usurper Henry, and, most surely, more will come to our cause at that time. That is it, Alph—to Ireland."

They gathered such possessions from their abode that would in ease travel with them. Richard untied the roped bag and pulled out the wrapped bundle, placing it upon the table between them. The cloth was peeled away to bring to view the wooden box, then to turn the red key in Richard's hand, and to spring it open. Alph raised the lid in some anticipation as then to see the glint of coin that was within, and to smile his sallow cheeks.

"'Tis a goodly sum, my prince," spake he, as the nature of his smile to Richard showed more of intrigue.

"Tide us it will, my friend, until we reap more from those who will rally when the time comes." Richard dipped into the coins and laid some upon Alph's palm, and some to jingle in his own pouch. Then the box was closed and locked securely to be wrapped once more in the red-blotched cloth and replaced within the looted bag, then tied tight with the hemp to swing upon the back of Richard, and, with some other chattels hugged under his arm, he led out from the chamber. Alphonse followed behind him, clutching another lot slung over his shoulder, with a thick leather bag grasped in hand.

As they came to the alley, the light had dimmed and the sun downed its fiery head. Chatter and bustle was still about as they went their troubled way, seen groups at talk as they passed their by, and caught some of their garbled chat. "They hope to have the murderer shackled by day's end." A glance back from Richard to see if Alph was keeping pace with him as more tattle fell. "They know who did the foul deed and are in search for him." On they did scurry, trying to remain as the normal folk about them, to be seen not in any haste—legs wanting to trot, brain to not. The crowd somewhat left behind as the road sloped its way to the dockside, and the cool breeze from the ocean hung the air with much pleasantness. The flowers at eve giving forth their heady perfume as it mingled with the sea's salty waft. To the dockside they came as another world opened before them. Not of murderous gossip, not of bustle and shove, but of laughter and nautical jibe, of crates and boxes, ropes and nets. Seafarers of all manner with tasks to hand, at shout and grunt, as they pushed and lifted and worked their day to be gone.

"Come, Alph, to the tavern yonder; we may find there the ship we seek."

In they did venture, pushing through the drunks and ruffians; many sailors filled the tap with flirty maidens all about. The sweet–sour smell of the ale and wine drifted from the sawdust that covered the floor. "Two goblets of wine," Richard called to the serving wench. Quickly two goblets showed and the pure red flowed tempting from the pitcher, splashing to fill to the brim. They paid her with the soiled monies as she left them to their pleasure. Both gulped the cool liquid as the goblet gave up half its juice. "Stay and watch the chattels with good eye, Alph; I will seek the sailings list." Richard left his friend and pushed himself through the filled room, to the narrow wall that was beside the doorway, to spy there the sailings posted. Some ships names were crossed out as having sailed, and others who were deemed lost at sea. Other ships and destinations were being added as time went by. He fingered down ... Ireland, he saw ... Sailed yesterday at noon. Further down went he. Ireland ... Tomorrow morn at high tide, eight of the clock ... Going to Cork ... The blessed vessel *Turbot* ... Captain Jonas Rodriguez ... Tied this day at mooring twenty-one. Richard took to mind the writings and pushed his way through the people pressed in the small tavern room and back to his friend, who, with one hand placed upon the roped sack, awaited him. Hidden from all, he sat in the sheltered corner. "Alph! There is a ship leaving on the morrow's tide journeying to Cork." Richard was in high spirits, for such a sailing would take him away from the hunted situation he was in. "Let us drink up and make our way to see the captain, and obtain such a passage." They dribbled the last of the wine down their throats, and left through the throng that filled the tavern, to the outside where the revellers had spilled from the tap and onto the street; with drinks in hand, they laughed and scuffled about in merry voice, blocking all view of Richard and Alphonse as they made into a narrow alley that pointed the way to the moorings.

As they took their way with baggage in hand, from the far side of the crowd they could hear the drums of soldiers in close formation. Led by a pompous officer they stamped their booted feet nearer to the crowd. No doubt at search for the villain who they believed, in a most gruesome way, had murdered the knight, Sir William Bray. They made for the tavern straight to question and to poke their swords about. But the crowd that did frequent the docks had their own ways of dealing with blaggarts, and had no respect for these tyrants who posed in their uniforms and dealt little in chivalry; there was no thought that they may pass.

"Stand aside, we bring the king's business!" the officer shouted to the taunting, unmovable mob. "Go home to your mother's milk … Come again when you can grow whiskers." … "Your wives with their hairpins are more frightening." Remarks and laughter plagued the soldiery as the crowd revelled in the confrontation.

"Move away or swords will be drawn," shouted once more the officer, feeling not secure anymore as the mob took little notice of his title.

"Let's 'ave 'em, lads," came the cry from some seafarers who had chided against the military. And before a weapon could be drawn, the brazen mob charged at the small group of soldiers, who tailed and ran panicky from the scene as quickly as their whimped legs could take them. They stumbled and fell as they made their way, with swords and belts flailing about as they scurried and tumbled. No help came from those who where passed by, those who were not in the mob, but did all they could to impede their escape. A leg stuck out here to trip, an elbow hung to catch a chin as it passed. Bloody knees and thickened lips were all they gained this day, as the jeers drifted behind them and they made to safer ground. The laughter heard from afar as they lay and lolled in a cool alley to regain their strength. No more this night to search and poke, but to march back to their camp and to talk of the brave acts they had done, and the adversaries they had overcome, losing not one soldier in the fracas.

Mooring twenty-one came to sight as Richard and Alphonse made along the way of the dock. The waters splashed and slapped against the sides of the tied boats, the gulls squawked overhead as came the night, with the twinkled sky come to chase the sun's bright away. Torches showed more of their flickering light, with smoke, black, rising to dim the stars' coming. The ship showed misty and dark amongst the torches' glow, many lit upon the dock but few upon the ship. The plank from ship to shore bent and creaked as cargo was being humped up and laid upon the deck, as then other bent shapes moved it further to teeter close to the open hatch. Heads and arms showed through to clutch the bags, and then were quickly gone like mice peeking from their hole then to scurry back. A sturdy ship, it stood may forty feet from stem to stern, appearing clean and not rotted in any way. They joined the labourers plod up the plank and placed their feet upon the lilting deck.

"Where may we find the captain?" Richard asked one of the seamen, who seemed to have some rank over the others, he shouting about orders, spying over the cargo as 'twas laid upon the deck, then checking from above that 'twas properly stacked in the hold.

"Down there, sir … The red door." He managed directions with a wave of his hand without breaking his trusted labours.

"Thank you, sir." The two went forward to the stated cabin, hugging still their chattels close. Richard rapped his strongest knock upon the weathered door, the thick red paint flaking off, as the sea had played heavily its salty wash upon it.

"Enter!" reaped the knock almost before the knuckles left the cold wood. They both entered, stepping over the threshold that stopped the waters swill on the deck from flooding the cabin. "Close the door, lads," came forth the cheery voice from the whiskery fellow. Short and wide was he, never to be pushed over, never to lose footing upon a gale-swept deck. He stood upon the swaying boards as if nailed by a horse's shoe to the wood. "So, lads, want to go to sea, do ye?"

"Well yes, sir, but only as far as Ireland; we do not look to make it our lifetime occupation."

"Do you have money?" No waltzing about the garden from he, but straight as the bowman's shaft.

"Yes, sir, we do."

"The cost will be one guinea each, to be paid now, and you will have to work for the rest of your passage. You can work, can you not?" he added as he looked them over. "But by the look of your meatless carcasses, nothing too heavy, eh, lads? The galley, I think … Can you cook?"

"Just a little, sir. Yes, sir, just a little," they both answered.

"'Tis done then. Pay now, lads." Richard placed the asked for coins into the rough and weathered thick red hand. "Go below and find yourselves a bunk. We sail early morn, so both of you be with the cook at five of the clock; these lads of mine will need feeding afore we float."

"Yes, sir," they replied, as with unsteady gait they made to the cabin's exit.

"Running from something, lads?" the question came from the captain, and thoughts were to mind of how to answer it and to what tale to tell. But before some story could be told he continued. "Worry not, lads, half of the crew are away from something. Just do your job and we won't 'ave to put you adrift." The wickedly smile gloated upon his ruddy face as he turned, and 'twas unseen by the "lads."

"Yes, sir," answered they once more to move quickly to their place. For they wished not to be abandoned upon the rolling sea. Richard's mind oft drifted 'twixt man and boy. Able to murder one day, and then fearful of a jolly captain's words the next. They closed the door behind them, and were met by the cool air that blew along the dockside. Down the narrow stairway they went, almost sideways so as to move freely and with heads bent, for the room above was painfully low. They groped the dim way to the wooden chamber that lay upon the keel; the boards showed wet beneath their feet and the ocean's sound played upon the hull about their ears. This would be their stay for many a day, and, though not to their custom to be castaways, 'twas indeed a cozy place. Two bunks, one above the other, came to their eyes. No sacks or bundles lay upon them to claim their owners, so the chattels they carried were stowed beneath the bottom bunk upon a raised board there to protect them from the searching waters. They made as ready as they could for the journey to come. Odd people were about, coming and going the chamber. Old tars strode along in their seafarer's gait, their shanties rang; young boys quickly, about their own state, seeing naught of what was about them. Richard and Alphonse laid their buzzed heads upon the restful bunks, scratched and tickled at first by the straw they rested upon, but soon to lay still and reap the warm nest, for they needed to gain as much rest as they may afore the early morning wake came.

Clunk, clunk. Upon the red door rapped loudly the knoddly[*] stick, swung by the officer afore his party of soldiers.

"Come!" the gruff voice rattled from the Captain Rodriguez.

Came first in the officer, pompous he, standing lordly inside the cabin, followed by his sergeant—quickly to be laid face down at the feet of the captain. The threshold claimed another lover of the land, to not know the ways of the sailor, he fell the jester. Quickly though he jumped up, little worse for his adventure, except for the cut of the officer's gaze. The leader of buffoons was he, spake his blank face.

"How may I be of service to you, sir?" spake the captain, seemingly ignoring the fateful entrance.

"Sir, we are seeking a young man who has committed the most heinous crime of murder. We are searching all vessels that are sailing shortly and could harbour such a person; your ship, sir, is one of those vessels. Do you have anyone aboard who has sought passage with you this day that would fit who I describe?"

"No, sir, I have not, but, pray, if you wish to search my ship then I have

---

[*] *knoddly* [coined] a rough stick with a knob on the end

no objection, but I must state to you that aboard this vessel there is some kind of sickness about, that I pray soon will be gone."

"Captain, your words may speak truthfully, but you must know many times such things have been spoken of to avoid a ship's search, and oft there has been no sickness, and as such is used to deceive the king's search, and, upon this, when no scourge has been found, I must warn you that the vessel in question has been seized and held to ransom. Do you wish to alter your statement without recourse?"

"No, I do not, for I tell no lies, sir."

"Very well then. Do you have someone who can show us about?"

"Yes, I do." The captain stepped over to the door and, opening it to its widest, bellowed his voice outside—the voice that could be heard above the crashing of waves and the howling of gales. "Georges! … Georges!" he shouted, loud it came to frighten the birds from their roosts and to flutter them up in disturbed squawk. He closed the red door to await the coming of his shout. "Georges has the illness of which I did speak, but I would deem it kindly if you would not show any revulsion to his sight."

"We will do as you desire, Captain," replied the officer, but his head was somewhat troubled by the captain's request where before none had existed, such was planted in the minds of these soldiers of the king by the Captain Rodriguez.

No knock came upon the door but a loud "Captain!" rang from without.

"Enter!" the captain called in his first mate.

The hulk entered, sideways he came, for the door was not of sufficient width for any other coming. In now he closed the door and faced the party who awaited him. Close to his captain stood the sergeant needing no distance from his own ilk. The man stood wider than he was high. Once he may have been taller but his legs had become as bent as the horseshoe, appearing to be on the edges of his wide body. But that showed his goodly shape, for the rest of him was of some ogre. His skin lay covered in weeping boils and festered spots, his nose bubbled with the ooze that seeped out and dripped upon the floor. One eye was closed, swollen by the blisters that grew about it. The back of his hands and his arms also of a cringed state. Not one hair showed upon his head, and but a few teeth seen from the black-holed mouth. "You called, sir," he mumbled through his broken lips, spraying some green liquid as he did so. The officer and his sergeant were taken aback by the gory sight. The meaning for their quest this day was quickly deserting them, and they had no will to continue, for the captain indeed had spoken no falsehoods to them but had stated the grisly facts. They had no wish to stride the ship guided by the hulk before them, for how many more like he may dwell below in the creaking hull? And no desire had they to breathe the foul air that pumped from the rotting mouth, for did they not have wives and children awaiting, upon whom they would not wish to bring such a plague?

"Georges, the king's military wish to be shown about the ship—"

"No matter, sir," the officer interrupted; "you are an honourable man and your word is all we need."

"'Tis no trouble, sir; Georges will be most pleased to escort you about the vessel."

"Yes, sirs, I would be most pleased," Georges beckoned them.

"No, no, 'tis a late hour; I fear our day is done. I bid you good day, sir." The military wished to leave the cabin with some haste, squeezing by Georges so as not to touch any of his being, and with a stumble over the board they in blackness melted into the night's grasp.

The door closed. The captain looked at Georges, the blotched face looked back as the mouth moved wide and then wider, to show fully the gapped teeth, laughter then spilled from the mouths of each with uncontrollable reach. They laughed as they had done many times before. But this time was the most satisfying, for the military showed in complete fear of coming close to the stricken Georges. The captain's arm was closed about his mate as they gasped for air in their rolling state. The vessels they held in their hands shivered and shook as they tried to sup some of the rum that had been slopped into them. But soon calmness came about and they were able to drink heartily their rewards of the day. The mate was an educated man and, but for his skin's affliction, would have been an imposing figure of some prominence, but as fate would play its game, the only place that peace would come to him was upon the deck of some vessel lurching about in some far sea. For just two days upon soil he would succumb to his affliction. But, as God would have it, two days at sea, with the salty splash and the howled wind aface, his skin would rekind and all his disfigurement would wash away; with the sea's mystic ways he would be of smooth skin and in no revolting state, but no soil must tread his foot for the cursed would wash about him. A curse he had, but a life he loved and could not change …

"C'mon lads, stop your laying about; 'tis almost five of the clock, c'mon."

Richard and Alphonse struggled to awaken; the light rock of the ship had lulled them into a deep repose, to be warm and cradled back and forth as in their mother's arms.

In the darkness, they made along the narrow way to the small cabin that glowed some light; a metal box there held the fire, with loose bars across the top to balance some pots. The heat from the fire swathed their faces as they came to serve the ship's cook.

"C'mon," he spake his most favourite words. "C'mon lads, you get the sack of oats." He pointed to Alphonse to bring over the sack. "Help him to tip it into the water." He spake to Richard, who, with his friend, lifted up the bag and tipped the contents into the boiling water, bubbling and splashing about as it did so. "C'mon, c'mon. Get it stirred." He handed them a large spoon and soon, with their efforts, the mash had thickened to a gruel. "Put it in the bowl … Over there … C'mon, c'mon." They ladled it out as the cook fussed about, until then twenty bowls were filled, and with bread and ale the first meal was readied for the always-hungry crew.

The same acts were repeated day upon day, breakfast then the noon meal, another at six of the clock; the work seeming never to end from one sup to the next. The time spare they had for themselves was spent with acicular* and thread and the snip of shears, as they cut and sewed within the dimly-lit cabin, making the fine clothes of the knight to fit upon a prince. Richard tried them on from time to time, to pull and tuck with the help of Alphonse, bringing the cloth to a more suitable drape, and to soon deem that 'twas the best they could hope for with their little skills in the craft.

The flicker of the oil lamp within the cabin was seen glowing upon the white parchment paper, retrieved from within the learned books that were carried. Writ the pen's black ink scratching with most sure strokes. A letter with the heading sealed upon it of *Sir William Bray,* and so being writ as his hand would write. Bestowing in the reading that the carrier of this document, "Piers Osbeck," after due and thorough investigation, was indeed, as he had claimed, the Prince Richard of York, and was, therefore, the rightful heir to the throne of England, which has been usurped by that heinous Henry, and prayed that any who read this statement would in all faith follow the prince, and they fill his coffers so that he may regain the crown to be placed upon the only true king. Richard writ three such letters, for he knew not yet how many he may need, but to ready himself for all circumstances. He folded each with care and, with taper, dripped the red wax of nobles onto the parchments' join, and whilst still warm did seal them with the signet of the knight demised. The letters he then stowed discreetly within his books; they were wrapped and returned to his chattels' bag for use as may be deemed.

"Land ho!" came the stirring cry, high from the mast above the cutting hull. The calmed waters showed clearly the land ahead … The land of the

---

* *acicular* needle

Irish, they most loyal to the White Rose. And to most detesting the King Henry with his heavy taxes and his heavy-handedness, and of his wicked ways towards them. With arms at rest upon the bow's rail, Richard and Alphonse gazed at the dark line that marked the sea's edge.

"What folds for us ahead, my friend?"

"Time is the only one that knows such, my prince."

They continued to gaze at the coming land as they pondered what happenings lay.

"Let us pray our kingly quest will soon start to bear to us some rich fruits, that we may continue our journey to our awaiting kingdom."

They looked with others at the closing land, for none had seen the sight for many days, all peering ahead, all seeking different adventures upon its soil—the soil where foot would at last press some ground that did not sway. All was well, except for the first mate, Georges, whose smooth skin it seemed to him had already started its lumpy crusts, and aready to burst out, though the land lay still five miles afar. The grey hills could be seen veiled atop with a misty lay, and soon the emerald green, brighter than all other greens, covered over all they could spy. And with less than one mile to the dockside, they lowered their sail and brought out the fluttering flags that waved to the harbour ahead.

"Alphonse, when we make land I wish you to go from me, and to spread about as much as you may, to as many folk as you can, of my presence in this land," Richard spake to his friend in a most serious manner. "Speak to them and tell them that the Prince Richard, son of the late King Edward, does indeed tread their soil, and that I was not murdered in that bloodiest of towers, but am of this life and ready from this land to start upon the journey to become the rightful king, and will, in all my gentleness, bestow much caring and written laws to bring good to all the people who live on this blessed Isle."

"Yes, my prince, I will do such with all my endeavour and bring many to your rally." Alphonse had listened and spake with much commitment to pledge his prince.

Soon the harbour at Cork embraced the little vessel. Its bay lay like cradled arms welcoming its son. Sails were all stowed to drift in quiet time to the mooring place, where their cargo would soon be carted away and replaced by the bounty from this Isle, the goods loaded by the lowly paid stevedores, fetched and carried from lands that they would never set eyes upon. The creaking plank was put down as the captain's orders rang about and gave passage to all those that were to shore. The first to bustle down the way was the Master Alphonse; in much haste was he to spread about the word of the prince's coming. With coat flying and voice shouting out the news, he ran into the town's square to spread that the time was nigh to go to the dockside and greet the come prince. Crewmen and travellers tottered upon the rickety plank to set their swaying bodies upon the still land and to go their set ways. The crewmen made straight for the tavern, their purses itching to open, to bring to them ale and wagering, and loose women, until all was gone and their purses tipped up to rattle naught. Back to the ship was all that would be left, to then fill once more the small purse at another journey's end. The travellers took to horses and to carts, to clatter away to all places about. The captain watched for a little while, and then, with his crusty mate, went to his cabin to sup some rum and chart some maps.

The harbour became a little calmer, the boat lilting, almost empty of life except for the unloading of the hold where life still busied. Small groups stood at chat upon the harbour's deck, and stalls with produce showed as the bustle departed. To this sight Richard came. He stood upon the ship's deck and readied to step upon the plank. A deep breath he took as if he may never take one more, to relish the cold air that lifted his mind and gaze all about at the land before him. Richard stood, donned in the garb that was the knight's, altered as best could, it did show ill-fitting, but rich enough for a prince with its gold and silver braid, and a fine hat with swirling feather topped the proud head. Good strong boots upon his feet, looking a might big but not to appear so to a layman. The prince in name came down with sure steps the slipped slope of the wooden plank, then from the lilting ship to the firmness of land to step upon the soil, little different to other lands, but a different step indeed to the journey that may start upon it. The small crowd stared at the stranger who had stepped upon their shore, and as others came they stepped closer to Richard, to may hear the message that Alphonse had told would be spake. The handsome, richly dressed Richard seemed all of a prince, as some then began to cheer him as they looked upon his sight. "God bless you, Richard!" shouted about from the faces around, some with teared eyes as they saw that he had not been murdered, and had chosen their land to show himself. Some were for him, but others about were doubters and called out such to his ears, jeering and shouting, "Imposter! Go back from whence you came!" … "Take your troubles away from us, for we are laboured enough." But gradually more called out the name of Richard and over-cried the dissenters, their thick voices dulled them out, so only those who were for the prince could be heard.

"Thank you, my good friends," Richard raised loud his voice to speak to the most eager crowd that milled about him. "I hear your welcome and I am joyous with such." The hecklers still shouted out their mistrust of him as he tried to bring them all to his fold. "Those who shout disapproval of my words I shall dissuade, for upon me I have letters of proof that I am no imposter, and stand here as your true prince." And he with a flourish waved the sealed letter at full arm above his hatted self. All about could see the letter with the red wax, now brittle upon the parchment's soft white, waved about liken to some royal banner seen against the blue sky. "I come to this Ireland, this part of our great kingdom, to reclaim the crown that was so evilly taken from us. For murder was to mind when I was secreted in the Tower, was it not for some loyalists who took it upon themselves the greatest of all dangers and escaped me from the evil clutches that did scheme to destroy me. To your land I come before any other place, for you are the most loyal to my rose. And to here raise an army, and, in time, when other forces have been gathered, to march upon that madman, Henry." Cheers and cries of good stead filled the air as proudness and allegiance played upon their hearts. For Richard, with his great charisma and compelling voice, raised the crowd to such affection. A quietening came over the throng as from the back the crowd began to part as someone with authority, though not yet seen by Richard, was let through to step close to the prince who stood proud. A well-attired individual with a large hat of some expense first showed, bringing along the jingle of a thick chain rattling about the neck, and seen clear the heavy links of gold that dangled a large medallion at its drop, and as the dappled light glistened upon it, showed there the coat of arms of the town of Cork. The mayor elected stood. A small round man, well troughed, and with little hair left upon his head, he came red of face, with a breath of recent ale wafting about his person, wishing to gauge for himself the truth of this visitor to his town.

"Good day to you, sir ... The Lord Mayor John Atwater at your command, sire."

"Good day to you, Mister Mayor, sir. I am the Prince Richard of York, the only remaining son of our beloved Edward. For reasons of my safety, I have in these times had to use the name of Piers Osbeck, for my real state would have brought my destruction. But one day, I pray soon, will come a time to our liking when I will, under only one name, be known the Prince Richard of York, soon-to-be king." He laid words upon the mayor in a most bewitching fashion, to captivate another to his fold, hoping some assistance may come from the mayor, John Atwater.

"I see you wave about a letter relating to the fact that you are the true prince; may I have the privilege of perusing such a document?"

"That is true my lord, I do have such a letter, and indeed it would be my pleasure that you scrutinize it." Richard brought out the letter once again from the folds of his braided coat, and once more in a flourished manner placed it gently into the eager palm of the mayor.

The mayor looked at it, doing so with seeming a knowledgeably eye, turning it first to one side, and over to the other, then this way, then that way, to squint then closely upon the red seal. A seal of a knight, and clear of mark, there was no doubt 'twas a legal document. "If I may ask, sir, I would deem it most kind if you would accompany me with this letter, to place the sealed script into the hands of the Earl of Desmond, who, with great itch, looks forward to a conference with you, and would be honoured if you would reside with him during your stay at his castle … The castle of Cork."

"I would deem that most pleasurable, sir."

"Then we will away. I will order my man to bring around the horses."

"I see the castle is but less than a mile away; I would wish not to ride there but to walk, so that I may take my steps with these good folk who have pledged to me their loyalty."

"That is well, sir. Come then, let us away." They moved onto the pathway that led to the castle, standing grey upon the hill and gazing down upon them. The crowd flanked the prince, proud to be in step with one who was royal. Richard knew of the many ways to gain others to be loyal to him, and to walk with peasants was one of them. The mayor stepped in front, a leader of rabble was his stride, his large hat a-flap in the sea's blow, his coat billowed out, his long staff tapped the stone at his feet making his tread more sure. Richard, striding with his followers close at back, marched with his braid coat and his silk shirt blustering about him. His boots, too large, flopped as he trod the path. Alphonse had rejoined his friend and was astep with the party as it made its way. Happy he that his endeavours had borne so much fruit. And as they walked, his prince gazed at him, and Alphonse knew that in the face that did so, Richard was well pleased with the outcome of his persuasion, and that some rewards may be forthcoming to them. The march was becoming more of a joyful occasion than some inquisition. A young boy taken by the delight had run to his closeby home and brought forth his father's dusty old drum, the drum that had laid silent in the horse barn for many years, for there had been little occasion to stir the air or to rattle its marching sound, but again 'twas within the throng, and beating its steady beat to the step of the boy's army as to the castle they marched. A reed flute came and joined the drum as another boy caught the mood to twitter his chirping sound. On they did go as some of the crowd were caught in the music's waltz, to have them skipping and dancing the street ways as the train lengthened, with all manner of folk wishing to be part of the event. Came two farm workers to join in, acting as jesters, they rolling and shouting about, taking tumbles and causing much joy, as their baggy clothing wafted the dust about as they did so. The crowd indeed was full of laughter and mischief, as the tail of the throng thinned to the raggedy children that paced at the back, dancing they along to the lilting sounds, shoeless and without care, they kicked the dusty ground about in their glee. Blackened teeth showed from the wide mouths; with lungs a-cough, they skipped along, showing their delight.

To the castle came the front of the parade through the last of the narrow streets, to the great gate that reached high above them. The mayor with Richard and Alphonse were entered in, to be followed by the councillors of the town and other notaries. Many dignitaries were lined up within the yard, all greeting the young man with bow and scrape. For if he was the prince then favour would be more to come to them; if he were not the prince then they had lost naught but a short grovel. The common were not entered, as the great iron gate was closed upon them and they awaited outside for the outcome, gleaning what they could from the shouts of the knowing that would ring from the open windows high upon the castle's walls, to tell all below of the happenings from within those cold, select chambers. Though locked from the meet, they were all in a joyous mood, except the few that were still at doubt, and rendered their thoughts of an imposter about to any ear they could persuade. A shouting, dust-covered throng mingled outside the leering castle, all it seemed full of parch, and thrust with pains of hunger, tormenting those who could not without victuals go for more than a few short hours; those with large stomachs seemed to be the worst to suffer with their growling worms needing to be fed. Then some enterprise came about with many barrels of ale being brought from the tavern and the tankards sold as quickly as they could be poured. Hot pies appeared, as the baker brought from his shop the steaming delights, with the hungry lot to soon jingle their monies into his cup. Quickly an hour had flitted by as the enterprises reaped unforeseen bounty, and the crowd frolicked about the high gates.

The party, pompously led by the lord mayor, had clattered their way into the castle's arched entrance and along the passageway into the great hall, where awaited the Earl of Desmond seated upon his high chair of state, four steps up to sit was he. Grouped about him his advisers stood, all with an unsmiling air and lordly pomp watched the coming. Nobles mostly, they gifted with fortune and state. But in their midst stood tall and dark one man not of their loin. The Bishop of Cork with his religious agenda, stood he with menacing eye upon these intruders who may not be of his faith, and may not be any advantage to his aims, they who would be seeking monies from the nobles and giving naught to the Church. He stepped forward and did speak first before all others, his voice booming about the echoing hall, as if in his cathedral chastising the sinners who lingered far back in the cloisters.

"The good arrow of truth flies straight and veers not and never failing. The evil arrow of lies becomes bent and misguided, returning the black devil to whoever is the shooter!" He held his staff forward as if some weapon, pointing it at the visitors, with his eyes glaring into the eyes of the Richard, then did step back to his place without releasing his gaze as if to cast some spell upon him.

As if naught had been spake so then did speak the earl from his high-backed seat. "So, you are likely the prince?" The smooth upper voice flowed from the painted lip. He sat in the most refined of clothes, with a silver-laced staff in hand, imposing his figure to all about. "So, tell me, why should I trust your words?—though I see you of some fine features and resemblance to our beloved Edward. Time is that you convince me of your state."

"My dearest earl," Richard spake with much eloquence to the inquisitor, "it is deemed a great honour to me that I am asked to place my case before such distinguished gentlemen, for I know after which there will be no bent arrows alie about this place." He placed his first words toward the bishop, for he knew 'twas the bishop he would have to persuade more than any other he stood before this day. "Firstly, I place this letter upon your plate, written and sealed by the good knight, Sir William Bray, who did write such before he was so evilly cut down to his death by the spies of Henry."

"The good knight is dead?" Surprised were the voices that spake from the platform. Unknown to them was the knight's demise and sad were they of face.

"On behalf of all assembled here, we are most dismayed to hear of the death of our good knight, Sir Bray." The earl offered his sadness to Richard as some sympathy came to the young man before them.

"Thank you for your kindness, sir; he was a devoted servant to his country and a most dear friend to myself; I shall indeed sadly miss his guidance."

The letter that had been placed upon the tray of the flunky was then opened by the earl's manservant, and with bowed head was held before his master so that it may be read. The earl read the document and commented only with the wave of his kerchief, as the servant moved from one to the other, so that they may read the script and examine all of the document as the inquiry continued. "Tell all of the life whilst in the palace with your father and what was about that place."

Richard began to speak again the lines that he had spoken many times before, and would speak many times to come until left were no disbelievers. Of the most detail he spake, his mind speaking the words as if from a book. The inner chambers of the palace, its rich tapestries and to where they were hung, of the furniture and to where 'twas sat, of the servants that were engaged there and to what their duties were obliged to be. The name of the head butler was asked, the name of the cook, of the housekeeper, and any of the maids he could recall. All queried to Richard, who without fail answered all the questions as quickly as they were asked.

"Of your schooling, *Piers*—tell us of your schooling." The booming voice of the bishop broke the civilized air as the pertinent question was posed. Calling he "Piers" as his name, to show as yet he saw no prince before him. Richard came again with his book of answers, speaking of the teachings of Latin, of French, and of Spanish. The names he did state of the teachers who gave him such council, and of those who taught him of mathematics, of geometry, and of the planets. Then, to no reason, from the lips of the bishop came a stream of Latin, spoken quickly to trip the unwary, with mumble and feign he burbled. The chamber became silent from the storm, and all there at look awaited the answer from the inquired. Out came such with the most eloquence of mouth, of fine pronounce and of clear tone and of answer true. To the French language the bishop flew, flitting as some bird from one tree to another, hoping to lay some droppings upon the head of this pretender prince. The answer in French did come with much ease, and then to the Spanish word he did answer in fine tone. The eyes of the bishop seemed to change as from the hawk to the sparrow he did go, as all others there in judgment jumped upon the bishop's wings, seemingly convinced that indeed the Prince Richard, heir to the throne, was stood afore them.

"We are, sir, in deep respect of your presence here amidst us," the earl spake out for all that were assembled in the inquisition. He stood now, and bowed at the royalty before him, a deep bow not, but a bow of some respect to someone they believed to be the prince, wishing though to see some move toward the crown before they would grovel. Straight of back and the clutch still upon his staff, he spake his say. "It is deemed that you, sir, are the speaker of truthful words, and that you, after all letters have been considered, and after our interrogation has been completed, are indeed the true Richard of York, son of our late King Edward. We will offer to you all assistance within our power and will join our forces with you at your command. We must say though that there are many of our countrymen who have yet to be convinced, and, until they are, there cannot be total allegiance to your cause. You will have to convince them with your actions, whatever they may be. You in your own person will have to devise some means to do this, for they will not trust our findings, and only you can sway these disbelievers to your side."

"My lord, I am deeply indebted to you, and with thankfulness for your belief in me, and I will, in all haste, sway these disbelievers to come to my side. I again thank you and your lords and the most learned bishop, for your faith in someone who was but a short while ago a stranger to your land." Richard took his leave to deal with the task that was placed upon him and, with Alphonse by his side, strode from the great hall of the castle of Cork to step across the courtyard and make toward the milling crowd that awaited outside the gates there. Dusk was bringing its eerie light to the time when the bats' flight would begin. The sun gone behind the green hills, only the redded glow showed the way …

"What say you, sir?—the pretender has escaped your grasp?" Angry were the words that raged in the court that was of Henry VII. Its walls cold and not inviting to the spy that had left but a short while ago the warm and pleasant Lisbon. But choice was not his; to relay the news was all he could do, and pray that his head stayed to his body. The king's chief interrogator stood close to his king as he poked and queried the spy.

"Tell me, in exact words, the way this *Perkin* awayed without being spied."

"We know not for sure, sire; one minute he was within our grasp, then the next a crowd had blocked our way … and the next known was that he had passage upon some vessel."

"And do you know now of his whereabouts?" the king's man asked as the king watched and listened to the story being shed.

"Yes, sire, he is at the present time landed in Ireland, to the cove of Cork was his passage, and is engaged in his act of prince, to try and persuade the Irish to join him against our King Henry."

"I take it then that he seeks this assistance from our Earls of Desmond and Kildare, and their cronies?" the king spake as the threat to him was disclosed, and his nature was not shown of patience, but of rage contained in a spider's web, thin and soon-to-be rent all about.

"That is so, your Majesty."

"Get him away from my eyes or I will have his head!" The guards were quickly in to remove the bringer of troubles; fearful was he as he was ushered along, but the king had not ordered his life taken, and so he was duly marched from the palace and removed to the far side of the gate, happy he and joyous for his head this day was still upon his shoulders, a goodly day indeed.

"Bring to me the garrison captain!" the king rasped out in vengeful fashion.

"Yes, your Majesty," the aid bowed and hurried away from the chamber as quickly as he may, for the mouse that lingers will soon be sup for the cat. Gone was he behind the rattle of the latch. But soon to be rapped on again, and entered by the elegant captain who most humbly bowed in deep respect for his king.

"You summoned me, your Majesty?"

"Get thee and some soldiery to Cork with much haste. At this very moment our prey, the said *Perkin Warbeck,* is at land there. We wish him to be brought back here unharmed so we may determine his state in the matter. And, sir, with you take the royal axeman, for we wish not the eyes of Desmond and Kildare to gaze upon more villainous acts, and any others you my deem worthy. Get ye prepared, the execution documents will be ready at your going. They will all know that others who so try such insurgence against the king will suffer such. Treason will be felled and will not rear its evil head about this place."

"I will follow your commands, my king," the officer spake as he went forth to his duties, to bring back the Perkin Warbeck, and to execute the traitors to the crown of the King Henry …

Chapter Nineteen.

Shielogue.

The torches bright shone upon the faces that gathered about. Some at cheer, others at jeer. The shouting though was laid quiet as they at wait eared for the voice that was of Richard.

"My friends, I seek your faith in me, for I wish to lead you to the usurper of the throne that is, by all birthright, beholden to me. I have laid myself at the feet of your Lord Desmond, and have bared to him and his parties of all the facts that I possess, and they, in their goodness, have called me Prince, for they have taken me to their bosom, and have sworn to assist me in my endeavours. The task upon me is to sway any who still do not believe my words so truly spoken, and to bring them into our hearts. Tell me what must I do to convince you?—for whatever it will be, I will so do. I swear as my name is the Prince Richard."

A dull murmuring began to spread about the crowd, and even as far as the farthest torch it could be heard; to those that stood more than half of the mile away at the old mill it could be heard. The jabber spread about, flowing from one side to the other, like the ocean's tides it ebbed. Richard and Alphonse at each other gazed to await some meaning from the chatter. And then lone voices began to shout out a name, one here, one there, another from far back, others close by. Soon more voices called the name and was picked up by others to call it, until it seemed all the throng in unison called it, the name to which the deed had to be done. "Shielogue!" they shouted. "Shielogue! He must face Shielogue, for only she can tell us the truth."

"Who is Shielogue, Alph?" Richard did whisper to his friend.

"I know not, my prince, but I will in haste come to answer." Alphonse slipped away from his friend and sidled into the crowd, pushing through the shout and wave of arms he was soon in the most noisy part of the throng. He spied a young man standing there who was at this time subdued in his actions, and did query to him. "Excuse me, sir, I am a stranger about here and do not know to whom Shielogue relates."

"You must indeed be a stranger if you know not of Shielogue, for all and sundry know of her." He spake on, his eyes now sparkling bright, his hands and arms gesturing as he so. "She being many things … a witch …

a sorcerer ... a caster of wicked spells ... a healer of the sick ... a prophet. She is all things, but mostly she is a seeker of the truth, for no liar can deceive her. One never has and one never will. So that claimer of the throne who stands in his fine cloth and peers down upon us will surely be found if he does not speak the truth. And the crowd you see will have no remorse for him, and he will be as all others who were liars. This throng will be seekers of blood, and he will be as the lamb to the wolves. So may truth or God be on his side this day."

"Thank you, sir, for your frankness, for surely you have left naught to ponder." Alphonse pushed a way through the crowd to come aback of Richard, who still stood as he was left, as the crowd then began to urge him to follow them. But before he did, his friend closed to his side, and Richard lowered his head to hear the outcome of the query.

"Did you find what this was about, Alph?"

"Yes, Richard, it seems they wish you to meet with this Shielogue, who I am told is a witch, a soothsayer, and a seeker of the truth. And that she will, my prince, seek you out if the words you pass are false. I am deemed somewhat troubled by her gifts, my lord."

"I fear not such from an old crone. I will away with these folk and before the night is to dawn, all will be swayed to our favour, and they all will be good and true soldiers. Come, let us follow to this place of Shielogue." The crowd saw that Richard was moving to follow them, and from the castle's windows high, lighted by the torches within, could be seen the shapes of the earls and the nobles as they watched the crowd below move toward the truth, and did still ponder they whether the young Richard would return, or lay bloodied with his quest done when the truth did out. Away they marched, as all joined once again to the marching step. Washed with drum and flute, they jumped and danced along the way that led to the dark hills, laying but a short journey from the lit castle 'twixt day and night.

Far ahead Richard could see the torches dipping and swaying up the hill's side. He paced along, a boy really with boyish ideas stepping along in the wide stride of a man—to who was he the fool? Did he not understand what his interference would suffer to the monarchy and to the lords that accrued their fortunes from such? And did he not know that all the might that could be mustered would be brought down upon him if he came with a rabbled army to change the state? A boy awaiting to become fully a man walked this path.

The wormy light ahead led to some lay of a witch and her coven; she waited knowing the coming. Torches flickered all about Richard, lighting him as some messiah on a journey of faith. The black smoke wafted and waved above them, as the bats fluttered and dove about their heads, with the torches' light teasing their flight. Strange bats that seemed to be seeking someone out … bats from a witch's cave were they. The lights ahead had now stayed and awaited the coming of Richard. He came through the lit crowd, all quiet were they as if the sound of their voice would bring some devil upon them, and all anxious of the outcome this night. To joy indeed if the witch gave him the nod. To bloodshed if he were proven not. The dark hole of the cave showed before them; it dripped all wet and dank about the entrance. A dim light, spied far inside the hole, flickered and spit, as Richard lowered his head and went into the low cave; only Alphonse continued with him as the other brave souls stood without, and were only brave enough to push their torches a little at arm's length inside the opening, to see as far as they dared. Crouched though he was, Richard moved along with steps of confidence, his aim to bewitch the bewitcher. Alphonse followed his friend's steps, pulled along by his bravery, and, with head lowered, scurried along behind, and deemed if he were alone he would not continue but to flee to the world of the living. The bats still whirled about their heads. A quiver full of followers had overcome their fears and had entered deeper into the cave of Shielogue, drawing bravery from each other, all hoping one would flee with fright so they may follow and not be branded a coward. Muddy underfoot they slopped along as an odour drifted from deep within the cave had Richard and Alphonse retching and seeking cleaner air, but there was none; they clutched to their noses the kerchiefs they carried enabling them to continue. The others who followed knew naught of any smell, for stench was always about them, and within the places they habited their nose did not quickly itch. Into the main cave where dwelt the hag they came. The place that wherein the stench did flower was here. 'Twas lit but dimly by the flickering torches and by the dying fire that was laid in the middle. The whiskers of smoke drifted up to the chamber's ceiling and seeped through the cracks that freed it, the same cracks that dripped down its wetted slime on all below. The witch's coven was this, and all as you would expect such a place to be. A place where all other covens would draw plan to this one. The wet floor was covered in filth. Cockroaches crunched underfoot and things scurried away. A pile in one dark corner barely seen but showed of food scraps at rot, thrown there by the hag to feed her rats. Some stood atop the mound, standing on legs two as they held the food bits at their front, they grasped with tiny hands to munch with whiskered glee. Richard looked further to another place as he placed his kerchief back in its fold, his nose able to breathe as he accustomed himself to the vile. A pile seen again close to the cavern's wall, full of bugs and thousands of flies all buzzing about. A pile of excrement showered with urine and moving as if alive with the maggots that homed there. Then another mound was seen different from the others, and appearing not to be infested by any creatures. The mound seemed to be of thin sheets, all of strange shapes, as thin as a dragonfly's wings were they. The fire burst out a last flame to shine through the fineness, showing them as ogres sat in perfect witch shape atop. 'Twas skin piled there. The crone shed her skin twice in a year like any good witch was apt to do, and piled it with neatness to her liking. The brave lads at the back came no further than the chamber's entrance. Alphonse was sickenly feared of the sights that he had seen, and drew little bravery from his prince, he able to stay within only some little way, but that place was as close as he wished, and he would be gone away quickly if aught of terror came about.

Richard stood well into the den, peering for the witchery shape to show. And then, from the far depths it came, all of black, to be little seen in the meagre light that flickered. But the floating shape closed to the embered fire that quickly burst into some bright flame. The long robe he saw. Long so no craggily feet could be seen, except for the black shoeless toe that peeked out, its nail showed twisted as a cockleshell. Her step crunched and squelched upon the slopped floor. The waist was tied with some old twined hemp. Her arms were folded within the wide droop of the sleeves; black, grimy, and bony were the hands showed as they crossed afront, with long nails that clawed at the peeling flesh of the other hand, and drifted the scales of skin onto the floor's grime. As she closed to the fire her face showed from within the hood she wore. A skeleton covered in a skin was seen, with hooked nose and eyes sunken. Matted hair was seen about the head's cover. Two warts upon the face and blackened teeth at rot. Shielogue was the witch that all other witches would wish to be. A true bringer of evil and fear to those that would cross her. Able was she to speak the words that all would believe, so mattered not if 'twas true or if 'twas false, for, if it came from the mouth of Shielogue, 'twas deemed to be the truth. Close she was now to peer at the Richard from within her sheltered garb, as her rancid breath was laid upon the seeker, like some evil fog it flowed over him. She crackled her voice toward the unmoving face.

"So, you be the pretender to the crown?"

"I wish the crown, madam, but a pretender I am not."

"You speak the truth then? that you are indeed the Prince Richard of York?" She came even closer to him as she perted the questions upon him, so close that one would feel some warmth from the other, but there was no warmth, only striking cold drifted about.

"Yes, madam, that is who I am."

She screamed her high cackling laugh. There seemed little reason for it except to bring some fear to the meet, as indeed those who watched with some dread from their distant place backed further away with a mousy gasp. Richard felt some strange thing brush by his leg, and, peering down about Shielogue's hem, he saw her old cats mulling about. Some were almost hairless, others with matted coats much as their mistress wore. She called loudly some strange word toward her pets.

"*Bagdeble!*" she shouted, and again did shout, her bent old finger pointing to the midst of the rats. The old tom streaked from her side to follow the quest that was called, and with a bound across the floor and a leap, he bit down upon the neck of the screaming rat that was too slow in its scurry away; he brought it back like some hound to its waiting charge. Still it screamed its displeasure as the witch pried it away from the reluctant tom, and held high the prize above her head, its legs kicking and its body squirming as the bony hand held it tight. She brought it slowly down, and with her other hand she drew from her pouch a blade, it twinkling in the fire's light as 'twas drawn, and she split the rat wide open, without ever taking her eyes off the eyes of Richard. She placed down the knife and picked up a goblet that was at lay upon the hearthstone; 'twas dripped with the warm blood that poured from the gape, and when enough was captured she threw down upon the floor the drained rat, which was ripped quickly to pieces by the mangy cats, each running to its favourite place to devour the morsel. Shielogue held the warm cup in her hand, and with some magical deft, sprinkled some powder that came from nowhere upon the red wine of the rodent.

"If you be the prince, you will drink this without wait." She held out the vessel toward Richard, who as cold as a winter's morn took the goblet and without breaking his gaze from the witch, swallowed the vile brew with one gulp, and handed it back to the bony hand that awaited it. The brave souls about recoiled once more at the act before them, and 'twould take little help for them all to flee as one body. Another screech came from Shielogue to shake some weak knees about, and made them all unable to run from what was about them. The lads stood in awe as the witch began to dance and swirl about. The robe she wore billowed out as around and around she twirled, still screeching loudly as she did so. Cats and rats ran from the craze with wild calls and eerie cries. And then as quickly as she had started she was stilled, and drew from her pouch three stones. Each stone had three flattened sides. Upon each flat an ancient sign was marked; each mark was different, each mark a witch's mark. She shook the stones in her bony clutch to rattle their echo about the empty chamber. The stones did rattle or the bones did rattle, to which was not known. She spun about once again and dashed the stones upon the floor, cleared of filth by her swirling dance, and as they chackled* upon the stone she threw a witch's powder onto the fanning fire, which then showered all about with sparks and flashes, and urged the bats to screech and to swoop lower, causing the lads once again to cringe back and to clutch at each other's cloth as they did so, trying to gain some comfort in knowing someone else was adrift in the same boat. No eye could see further back within the chamber's dark hole, but heard clearly were the cackling and cries of more witches lurking there, watching their queen work her sorcery. Shielogue crouched down to read the stones that showed her all she wished to know. Another shriek came out from her black mouth as she viewed the stones lay, and saw the mark that looked from each face.

"Before I pass the word to you, my palm must be played with a coin of silver." Richard slipped from his pouch a shining coin and placed it into the held-out bony nest. She peeked at what lay there as gold showed its bright and not the shimmer of silver. "You cannot buy me, boy," she whispered but still tucked away the money's glint to jingle within her pouch. As she did so Richard grasped the wrist of the witch and held it with firmness. "Release me! For I will rot the flesh from your bones for touching Shielogue. This will be your fate, you deceiver." Cries of anguish and hisses came from the blackness, as 'twas seen by the coven a hand had been placed upon their queen, but all stilled again as they tried to hear the words that Richard closely whispered into the ear of Shielogue. But quietly from the prince came words of lowly converse, so no other could hear that which was spoken.

"Dear witch, your rave does naught to raise my hair or to creep my skin. So belay your threats, for they are idle." Naught could be heard or seen of this, the words all whispered, as the fire embered and the torches almost drained of their pitch. The fretting witches' ears heard naught, Alphonse heard naught, and the lads with craning necks and flapping ears heard naught. With his free hand Richard reached into the reeking wretch before him and tugged upon the chain that was about her neck. The chain came to light and showed the bright bauble that hung from it, the jewel he had spied as she danced and twisted about in her ritual. Saw he the swinging charm and the glint of dark green as it flashed by the fire's flame, showing its colour upon the cave's dripped walls. He lifted it out from the depths of the coarse cloth that held it close. A gold spider hung from the chain, that twisted its legs about an emerald, as large as an acorn it dangled from its clasp.

"I see here, witch, a fine stone, not a trinket for one such as you, not

---
* *chackled* [coined] sound of a stone skipped and clattering across a hard surface

upon your fingers to show, but around your neck to hide from those who may pry." Shielogue would not move away from her tormentor, for she wished not to break the chain that bangled her neck, so did hang there as a caught fish upon a hook. "I know of such a treasure as this, my lady. I remember the tale told and the night 'twas spoken. A night when I was but young, and had crept from my sleepless endeavours to listen to the stories that seemed always about in the Great Hall. That night I did eavesdrop at the stairs' bottom to hear my father, the King Edward, as he did hear the lament of the Lady Beatrice Lumley. She told him of the lost ring that had been handed down from mother to daughter for generations; 'twas missing and feared to have been stolen, and 'twas thought the thief to be the housekeeper of the estate. The housekeeper was brought to torture and subject to much depravation, but no confession came, though she was badly marked from the irons. Naught was ventured from her lips and she was cast out. Neither the housekeeper nor the ring were ever seen again … Until this day, whose wrist I clutch. And with some further search, lady, I am sure I would find some iron's brand upon your witchery self … if I wished. Was it so beautiful that you could not grind it down for its poison? Is that why it still swings about your neck? And would it not be the end of all witchcraft for Shielogue if this story were told? And would not a scheming witch burn nicely at the stake?" He then released the clutch he had upon the bony wrist and placed gently the dangling stone back to its folds. "I have seen naught, my fair witch." Released from her chain she stepped back a little. He saw her black eyes flash beneath the dark hood, all under there that could be seen. Her creaking back was bent over as she uttered curse upon curse for her dilemma. The rich bauble was a noose she had placed about her own neck that she could not escape. And knew she that there was only one way to end this dilemma. A calmed silence came upon her for a moment, as then she cried out in her freaked voice.

"He speaks the truth! Before us stands the Prince Richard of York, son of our beloved King Edward and the true heir to the throne of England. This you heard from the lips of Shielogue, and a curse upon all who doubt my word! God bless the Prince!"

The lads ran to the tunnel's entrance and shouted all about to the waiting crowd that stood. Bringing such news brought joy to those who did believe, and to those who had not. Shielogue had called the truth, and so 'twas for no one to say 'twas not so. Richard looked at the witch who scowled her discontent toward him and made she then to the dark shadows that still cried and hissed within the darkness, where no man should tread his step.

The shadowy shape of Richard came from the dark into the light. The prince, in true name, showed before them, and all marched again to the castle that stood below, pushing its grey towers into the gloom of the night. From the high towers there could be seen the torches, as they came twisting down the hill and soon came to ear the cries and shouts from the followers of the prince. The earls and the bishop with the other nobles gathered and watched the march as it came closer to the yard that stirred below them, and saw they the prince as he waved to the throng, being greeted by beloved cries and shouts of allegiance from his new-found followers. From their window high the gathered there saw that the young prince had been accepted by the people who were ready to rally around him, and to do battle for him, and to become his soldiers against Henry, the king. The earls and the barons were ready also to serve him in his endeavours, for certain considerations that would multiply their coffers.

The bishop stood forward and spake once again to the gathered lords; he wished not to see too much fortune flow from his diocese, for little monies in the pocket would not fill his plates. "Sirs, though it deems most beneficial for us all to follow this prince, I must say, in the true spirit of the Lord, what also may be upon us: the emptying of our coffers to make us poor, which, if you recall, did happen in the last uprising we undertook against our king. Then the loss of many of our hard-working labourers, so that when all was done we had no monies and no labour. It has taken us this fifteen years to bring all to the state it is this day. Our coffers are full, our labourers many, and taxes upon them high. I say to you, my dear brethren, let us not leap from the hole before the ferret is out the bag. Let us send our prince to our ally the King Charles of France, for is not his life devoted to overthrowing that icon the English throne? and to placing their own puppet as king in its stead? To gain back the lands lost to them is all they wish, and to have no one in power that will offer war against them. If our prince can gain from Charles a commitment to supply him with soldiers and war monies, then I say to you, only then should we commit our labour and our coffers."

"Your words speak most sincerely, Bishop, and I do in all agree with you." The Earl of Desmond then spake his piece. "I move that we compose a dispatch to Charles stating the facts of our duty towards the prince, and to give our solemn pledge to deploy all our armies and all our monies to the quest of the Prince Richard. We will bring forth our armies from the west, to press the Red Rose into the arms of the French coming from the east. A meet with the Prince Richard is proposed, that these requests may be brought to fact."

"Aye!" was shouted about as all agreed to the tactic to be presented to the King Charles.

They moved from their council and went they each one to convey their pleasure that Richard had been accepted to all, and did so within the closed doors of the regal meeting chamber.

"We are most pleased, our dear prince, that you have swayed such a following to your cause."

"Thank you, my dear earl." The prince acknowledged the compliment from the Lord Drummond who then continued his address.

"We have further deemed that a dispatch is in order to be sent to the King Charles of France. This to inform him of our intent to place ourselves at your command, and for you to secure a meet with the king, so you may press your convictions to his Majesty and to gain from him a pledge of soldiers and of monies. For the French do abound in riches, and would assist our cause many fold, to richen our humble state." The words of water dripped. "What say you to this, our prince?"

"I say, sirs, you do not want to commit to our cause until I secure treasures and soldiers from some other place. Do I not speak the truth in this?"

"Yes, my prince, it is so, but you must also know our coffers and our soldiers would not be enough to overthrow the might of Henry. With all certainty we must have more soldiers and more finance from other places, and when such is placed we will lay our lives down for your cause, and will, with little stay, strip our coffers bare to bring to you the throne as we have pledged so to do."

"I will do as you wish, my dear earl, but only once can I show my hand, for there would be no second time to play the game, and, once shown, we must win with that card."

"That is settled then. We will to our scribe convey the writings required, and will in all haste dispatch the letter to Charles, so that upon your arrival in Paris he will have been already apprised of your coming. Also, my dear Richard, as a token of our pledge to you, we will finance your needs to the sum of one thousand pounds, so you may be able to conduct yourself in a more royal fashion. As for a ship to France, we have a captured brigantine that lays offshore in wait of a mission such as yours. And this night, my prince, we wish you to rest within the comfort of this castle, so upon the morrow, when the weather is deemed to be fair, you may catch the early tide and make for the French coast."

"I will do as you offer, my lord, and I must add that I am most touched by your generosity, which one day will come back tenfold to you."

"Then all is well, my prince; as quickly as we receive a dispatch from you of your success, we will arm and await your orders that we may do our utmost so that you may regain the throne."

"'Tis well. We will sup with you this night, and on the morrow with the sun's rise we will make to those fruitful lands of France."

The morn's scarlet and purple slashes crossed the blue sky that hung o'er the sea's light swell. The sea that was to take Richard to the country of Charles, and may a chance at a fortune to pay for an army. Clattering hooves rattled through the narrow ways as they made their way to the cove's edge. Few people were about at this early time, for many had been drunken to a late hour and lay sick abed. They stepped upon the ferry boat that would take them to the brigantine at wait. The splash of the oars pulled them out from the harbour of Cork; they travelled a distance of may two miles, with the town showing just a misty promise behind them. Around a rocky headland they came as the boat rocked and lurched in the swell; with the wind coming across the sea, they had little shelter, and were pushed about until they rounded further the head of land. The small brigantine stood awaiting them, black and dull it heaved as it hugged the rocky place. Little to be seen from a ship upon the ocean, all hid by the land and rocks from the shore. It stood in its rocking wait as dripping oars were tucked away, and the little boat pulled to its side, bouncing out of rhythm with the waiting ship, as down they went, as up went it. But a grasp at the rope ladder, and with effort to reach out to the arms of the waiting crewmen, they were hauled aboard the sturdy ship. The little boat was already pulling away to the jumble of rocks, and to be gone upon the swelling sea back to its safe harbour.

Richard and Alphonse stood aboard attempting once again to regain their seaman's legs. No prince and his aid stood now, but two travellers, with one, known by King Henry as Perkin Warbeck, with a memory of a witch in her cave; a sorry creature, he thought ... that Shielogue.

Chapter Twenty.

Traitor's Court.

The ship had been tied up, hidden by rocks and thick bush. The brigantine with the prince had slipped away unseen; as one vessel came, the other went. The riders with flags and banners showing came from the ship, hid, bright and at flutter in the morn's sun they soon to come their way o'er the emerald hills, like butterflies they waved over the common's green. On they came but thirty soldiers in all with sweated horse and muddied garb. The high boots they did wear; no more shiny black as they were but three days past, when they did march to the beat upon the parade ground. All shine and polish were they then, the saddle and the harness gleamed, the stirrups shone. The horsecloth never so clean and soft as it lay upon the steed. But all such was lost in the journey; scraped, wet, and dull was the new picture, except for those butterflies that fluttered above them all bright and heady. 'Twas the garrison captain who had come. Sent he by the King Henry to do his duty, the orders ordained stashed in his saddlebag. In the group rode the axeman, a priest, and the king's interrogator. All that was needed to bring forth royal justice into a traitor's court. They came three abreast from the hillside; the mist had not yet cleared from the low ground as the legless horses floated toward the cove of Cork. But soon down into the stone-laid streets they came, all clatter and steam, snort and whinny blustered they, banners still wafting high as they scurried the narrow way. The stones and rotted apples came like a hailstorm upon them; the townsfolk were awake and showing their displeasure at the sight, for always trouble followed when the king's men came. The jeers and jibes cried out to the soldiers as they came through the town, some already with bloody faces and dinted helmets as they offered yet no reprise. Until no more the captain would take against his men and deemed now was the time to draw his sword.

"Belay them!" he shouted as his men split rank and went for the crowd, which was gone as quick as the rabbit to its hole, to be seen not again until the next lane crossed. Then stood there again with their stones and their jibes. "Shields up!" came the cry, as the stones now bounced away to no harm come. The clang of rock upon metal followed them into the castle's courtyard, but 'twas soon too far to throw their stones. They could cause no more anguish to the soldiers, and so the crowd mulled about outside the gate to see what the coming may bring.

All bustle and shout was about as the ground stirred in the courtyard, and the dismounting soldiers were given their duties. There had been no time for anyone to flee from the castle, as with speed and shadow the king's troop came and all within of lordly brow were caged. The doorways had been quickly guarded and there was no escape from this place. The captain rattled open the high door and strode inside followed by his soldiers at arm; with swirling coat and flying dust they clattered along to quickly face the earls and the cronies in the great hall. Sat they still around the dining table at this hour of mid-morn, to sup of their victuals and discuss the events of yesterday. Startled like maidens they stood as the troop burst into the chamber, and the soldiers at arm caused a circle about them.

"Stay you still, sirs," the commander spake to those who were about the table, they being most disturbed by the coming, but even more so that no warning came to them of the intrusion. "We represent the King Henry in this matter, and I must tell your lordships and underlings that this is a dire situation that has brought our coming." The bishop stood and did start to make some move from his place at the table. "Stay you still, sir; you will remain at your station until ordered to do otherwise."

"But, sir, I am the bishop and have no reason to be counted with those who so await your call. I am but passing through and know nothing of any situation that would bring the king's troop. I am in protection of the Church, therefore you cannot stay me. So if you will part your way, I will to my chapel."

"You will stay, sir; the Church holds no throw over the acts so brought about by this clan. Sit thee now, or my soldiers will make you, for I have little time to bandy any more words with you. I now address the Earl of Desmond." He looked over to where the said earl was seated. He placed his fists upon the table and leant more toward him in a threatening mood. "Where is the person of Piers Osbeck? We know he was at this place, so do not use false words to alter such."

The earl stood shakily and started to speak with a nervous tongue, gone was the strut of his stand and his haughty presence. "I know not of his whereabouts, sir; he came within our midst seeking some assistance in his endeavours. Try he did to convince us that he was the Prince Richard. And try he did to trick us into opening our coffers. But we bought none of his wanton drift and did send him away under threat."

The officer looked at the earl's eyes and doubted he had been told the truth in the matter, but he spake naught at this time regarding such. "The interrogator will speak to you one at a time. You will all remain here and will be brought to us at our pleasure. My soldiers will make sure there will be no converse in your wait." He had spoken all he needed for now, for it seemed that if Piers Osbeck was not about this place, then the duty that remained of their coming had yet to be carried out. The officer and his interrogator, followed by two of his soldiers, left the main hall, they to seek a small, intimidating chamber suitable for their task so given. Soon found and close to the stairway, a closet, small and dark, suitable for their needs. The door was closed with a good strong lock, and musty was the smell from within, as death upon a graveyard's slab. A small table and some benches were brought to their needs, and one lone candle was set upon the table to bring the only glow in the windowless place. To light only the faces of the sitters at that table, as the officer and the interrogator did seat themselves at face to the doorway and readied their documents. One soldier stood at the outside of the doorway, the other within, who held in his hand the key to the door.

"Bring the earl, Kildare,"—was the first to be called by the trumped court. The soldier without acknowledged the call: "Sir," and then stomped away, his booted feet pounding their sound about as he went to the great hall, and at the entrance did stop to call out the name that was summoned. "The Earl of Kildare!" called he. The tall bulky earl stood, then strode, with wide gait and some proudness about his bearing, behind the soldier to the closet. "The earl, sir," he called into the room and then stepped aside to enter the lord.

"Sit," the interrogator spake, but did not lift his gaze from the documents that were laid upon the table there in its meagre light. The earl sat opposite his accusers as he heard the key within the lock. Not so much an action as to be secure, but an action to shut out all hope to the one so seated within this place, and to bring more to fear was its aim. The officer sat silent at the moment, leaving all to the one who knew his job well: the interrogator. Straight to the quick he went as behind the dragon's ear. "Is the person of Piers Osbeck hidden still within these walls?"

"No, sir, he is not," the unnerved reply came short.

"Then do you know of his whereabouts?" The interrogator was leaning across the table and looking into the face of the earl, as if knowing when the truth or when a lie would be spoken. The candle's glow flickered upon the three faces close at the table: one to answer, two to judge.

"I know not, sir; he was told to leave this place in haste, for we wanted naught from his evil intentions, and indeed pledged naught to his advances."

"What would you say, sir, if there amongst you was a spy from the court of Henry—would your song be the same?"

A quiet moment then came about as the earl tried to justify his words, to relive, or so to seem, as quickly as he could in his mind, the faces all about the council of a traitor there, and he could not finger one, for all were true and loyal to their aims. 'Twas a device that he would break and tell truthful words. He would call their bluff and become hostile to their questions, for they had no facts to place him in such a position; their proof was but chaff blowing in the wind.

"Sirs, I am most disturbed by the questions you put, for I deem you have no right to interrogate a lord so ordained by the king himself, such to be only undone by the king or his legal court. And I will only answer questions to such a court and not to some acolyte." He stood to leave, as if his words had rendered all that had been spoken before as meaningless, and moved as if to begone from the closet. "I bid you, sirs, until that is so, a good day."

"Stay, sir!" The officer stood, disturbed at the unwelcome confrontation, and spake with stern tone against the earl's statement, and to his making to leave before the inquiry had finished. "We have all legal right to ask these questions," he spake to the earl, who slowly sat again in his place, for the door remained locked, and there was no attempt left that he may leave without some swordplay, which he declined at this time to so do. The officer removed from his satchel the letter writ by the King Henry and placed it upon the table. The candle's glow showed the red glint of the royal seal in its wafting light, and stared upon by the sat earl in the cold closet. "Here, sir, is our right, designated by our king to bottom the matter. And when all our interrogations are complete, it will be our great pleasure for you to peruse the contents; but, have no doubt, sir, we do have the right." And then the officer, with a heavy thump of his fist, rattled the table, to startle the earl and to more press home his words. "Now, answer the question, sir!"

"That of which I have told you is the truth of the matter." Silence prevailed as the taunting answer was given, and the earl struggled with a nervous twitch that had come upon his cheek.

"For now that is all, sir," the interrogator spake as again he shuffled his parchments, disinterested in the earl's state as he left the chamber to the releasing door. The call then was for the Earl of Desmond, who was brought forward and made renegade by the same questions, and did indeed give the same answers as if scripted. The court required to hear little more of his banter and returned him with the others to the great hall. But soon the earl would look upon the inquisitors' faces again, and they knew the next time he came before them his chided story would ring of falsehoods.

"Bring forward next the bishop." ... "Sir." The call came to the guard as he left with the earl to the waiting party. "The bishop!" came the call into the chamber, as the Earl of Desmond took back his seat there amongst the inquisitive eyes, the eyes that probed his face for information, of which none was forthcoming as sat he with sullen look and bowed head. A shadow seemed to hover above him, for he had some inclination of where he was being led. Each had to depend upon the other, and to not break the chain that would hold them innocent. He feared one link may break, which one he knew not.

The bishop came forth, and shuffled his blessed shoes along the passageway to the closet shown. His religious cap with its gold braid glinted as he entered to the candle's light. A short cape rested over his shoulders, held there by a silver clasp at the front. His arms lay folded beneath his black robe, held together by a thin gold rope tied at the waist. His cross that hung about the neck jingled against the dangled chain. He came close to the table of inquisition with his sour face showing his contempt at the court.

"Please be seated, my dear bishop. I wish to tell you we do have the full sanction of his Majesty to ask such questions as we may, all writ and sealed in his hand." The interrogator started once again into his set play. "Pray, tell us of this Piers Osbeck and of your dealings with him."

"He came, sirs, in pretense that he was the titled Prince Richard of York, but through my deft questioning, it 'twas quickly seen that he was not that which he had led us to believe. He gained no respect from us, and so he was quickly dismissed and bade then to leave this place with the utmost haste, and he did so before he was set about."

"Then no benefits were proffered to him, by you or any others that were in attendance at that meet?"

"No, sir, none; he was quickly dispatched from this place."

"Thank you, bishop; for now that will be all." The bishop upped and left the closet, fingering his gold cross as he shuffled out. "Bring to us the scribe." ... "Yes, sir." Again the soldier took his orders and strode away with the bishop, to enter once again the silent chamber of wait. "The scribe!" called the guard, but no movement showed. "C'mon. The earl's scribe!" once again he called. And then a creaking bench was heard from the far of the room, where others of some lower place were sat. Showed then the called one, he coming slowly with little faith. And even before he was near the soldier who had called him, he was mumbling loudly his innocence in the matter.

"I have done naught," he pleaded. "I have naught that I can say. I just writ what I am ordered." He was close to the soldier and pleaded with him his innocence in any wrongdoing. The soldier stood, unmoved; he could do naught and cared less. "Come on … Come on." Impatience reared and was overcoming the guard with the slow ambling of the scribe, as then he grasped the hem at his neck and pushed him ahead to thus speed his exit. Then, further along the way, another push in the back that seemed for little reason but mischief, which caused the scribe this time to catch the toe of his boot in the uneven stone that lay underfoot and felled him like a shot bird, to scrape upon his nose the rough flag and to split his lip bloody.

"Get up, ye parchment scratcher," the guard jibed as he lifted the little man up and continued to push his fetch along the passageway. To the closet they came, and, with one last kick, the guard pushed the scribe with much duress inside the chamber.

"Sit down, scribe!" the officer shouted in stern tone to the fearful clerk, as he left to stand his duty without. "Soldier, wait outside until you are called and close behind you the door." The other guard was also ordered outside to stand with his comrade and closed the door behind him as he did so. The scribe who had sat reluctantly seemed to plead with his eyes to the soldier to leave him not alone with the two inquisitors, but the door had closed and he was left to fend for himself.

"How fare you, scribe?"

"I am well, sir."

"We regret that you are so injured," the interrogator kindly spake.

"'Tis no matter. I wished it upon myself to suffer some slight abuse, for it brings to my plight more sympathy."

"Then it is well that your wounds are small and no danger forecomes you. We all eagerly await your dispatches from this part of the kingdom, for this Ireland seems all of waving its own banner and not that of the king who dearly loves this land and its people. For a spy such as you brings great service to the Realm, and all know your task is well hardy, and fraught with danger.

"You are too kind, sir, in your praise."

"Relate to us all that has passed in these last few days." The officer and his interrogator leaned more to the scribe so that they would miss not one word of his report.

"Sirs, the Piers Osbeck with his ally, known only at this time as Alphonse, came but two days past, and did duly convince the king's nobles here that he was indeed the Prince Richard. Later on in council he was offered soldiers and offered aid in the form of monies, all on condition that he was successful in obtaining the same commitment from the King Charles of France. And to France he has recently gone to seek such aid. A letter pertaining to this was draughted and duly signed by the earls and by the bishop. I then made a forged copy of the letter and the signatures, and that is the letter that was ridden out with haste to the Continent. No one within the French king's administration would be able to recognize the said signatures, for they know not of these people."

"Do you have about you the document in question?"

"Yes, sir, I do." The scribe then slid out the sealed script from beneath his coat, and placed it into the eager hand of the king's officer, who quickly slit it wide with his dagger. Both the officer and the interrogator read down the traitorous page, savouring every word that was writ thereupon. Pleasing features were upon them as they saw the signatures so placed upon the bottom of the document. The Earl of Desmond. The Earl of Kildare. The Bishop of Cork. The inquisitors smiled at each other, for the meat was cut and readied to be dropped into the traitors' stew.

"You have done well, scribe. His Majesty will be well pleased." The interrogator spake words true, for all was placed before them with no escape from any who may so try. "For a little while your business is done, and we must of course remove from you your property and your possessions, and you will be cast out with the other underlings who were cajoled into this intrigue. You must be painted with the same brush, for we will need you once again in this advantageous position."

"I understand, sir, what my state must be."

"We will reside you in the town of Ardmore until things about are faded, and when a new earl is appointed, he will be under the king's orders to reinstate you as the scribe, and, at such a time, all properties and possessions will be restored to you. His Majesty wishes to keep good stock of this place, for unrest seems to flourish here." A bag of coin was brought from the satchel that rested upon the floor and was placed in the keep of the scribe. "This should cover your service to the king until the next time you are called upon."

"Many thanks to you, sirs, and to our dear king." He slid the coins into his bag that hugged in safety beneath his coat. Upon its security, the officer's voice gruff and with angry tone called out to the guard.

"Sir," he answered as he entered inside the chamber, and stood there once more at his chamber's post.

"Guard, come," the other guard was called.

"Sir," he answered as he came inside the closet.

"Take this dim-witted clerk back to whence you found him; he is of little use to us with his babbled talk." The scribe still sat and did not move toward the door. He waited until the soldier came in some anger to scruff him once more at the neck, and to drag him out and along the passageway to the hall where all were still at gather, and then given a hefty boot to help him upon his way, as his face was greeted once more by the hard floor. All bloody and dishevelled was he, but soon helped with sympathy to his seat by his fellow servants, who tried to console him, and to wipe away the gore from his bruised face.

The time had come to bring the king's orders to their finality. The two representatives of the crown were ready to bring forth their judgment. The crop ripe and all harvested most deftly then piled in the barn to be done with as ordered. Clean was the judgment with no doubt of the guilt of those so charged. But they were already on the block before the signed document was revealed. For had they not held the Piers Osbeck within their grasp knowing full well of his intentions to usurp the throne? For had he not been sought for many years, and did not all of Britain watch for his showing? And then, at last, when he did show, he was allowed to disappear into the mist of the ocean. For this act, they would lose their heads. But some may say that the case against them was grey. But as 'twas writ this day, the case was as pure white.

Outside the iron gate the crowd grew in numbers, as the word was spread about of the intrigue that was taking place within the walls of the castle. Shouts were heard from the high windows from those servants in the know, and they let it be known to the people below of the dire straits of the nobles and the latest turns from within. 'Twas again another joyous time as the ale was again supped, and the hot pies wafted their sweet aroma to tempt the giddy crowd. All manner of folk took to dancing about the dusty way, as jugglers came tossing their coloured balls from one to the other, with the happy crowd awed by their act. The clowns came about with their falling and rolling, bringing the watchers to hurting laughter as they did so, throwing small tokens into their dusty hats that sat upon the roadway. Merriment abounded upon this day. As they learned more from the questions being parried, they grew more in sympathy with the king's men and little for the earls and the bishop. They who jollied about had placed all the trials and hardships they had to bear upon the heads of those who were traitorous bent.

"Bring forward the Earl of Desmond." The call was made to the guard await as the court made ready to deliver its final reckoning.

"Yes, sir." Once more away went the soldier to bring the disgruntled lord to the closet.

"How much longer do we have to wait for your pleasure?" angrily spake the earl as he was beckoned to sit without answer to his question. "I have much on my plate ne'er mind such as you bring to me. There has been no act of aggression against the crown from those confined and I protest most strongly to such confinement." Still naught was spake to answer any words from Desmond. The officer and the interrogator sat calmly and listened to the lordly rant. And when it seemed he had finished, the document slated for the King Charles was slid slowly across the table toward the earl. "What is this?" he uttered as he picked up the crisp, neatly folded sheet. He eased it open and read it slowly from start to end.

"What say you now, sir, as to the fact that this letter proves that you did lie to this court regarding the questions that were put to you."

"I say, sir, that this court has no rights in bringing such inquisition to a lord of the land, and this you well know, and also, as you are well aware, I can only be tried by a jury of my peers." Once again no rebuff of the earl's remarks came. Only came was the sealed letter with the king's stamp upon it, showed under the nose of the earl, Desmond. He placed the first letter down upon the table and picked up the king's letter in its stead. The red seal upon it showed him the royal crest, which he broke with his fingers, letting the brittle wax tinkle its tune upon the table before him. Carefully he opened the dispatch and, as they watched, the dismay within him washed his face as he read the royal script. His mind was boggled as he sought some words for his innocence, but none came and he was lost. Now but a blind man in the forest's night.

"It seems, my lord, you have little left to speak and you have fallen silent in your defence." He answered not; numbed and ill of stomach, and turmoil flitted his brain, as a child lost within a great forest to roam, with no thought of rescue. "As you have read, my lord, the king gives this court all the powers necessary to bring all traitors to trial, and to administer the punishment for such crimes as writ by the laws of the land. Your punishment for your traitorous acts against his most royal Majesty is death by the axeman's tool, and so be it. Take him away guard, and stand by him close, for he may have poison secreted somewhere upon his person. No easy way must be given for such a traitor to leave this life. Await in the passageway with him, until we have the others ready for their fate. All will be done this day, for tarry we will not—Guard!"

"Yes, sire?"

"Bring forth the Earl of Kildare, and upon your return bring forth another guard to stand at the ready. Also, inform our axeman to make ready his trade."

"Yes, sir." The guard marched away silently repeating the orders to himself as he went. "Kildare! … Follow me." The soldier turned as the earl shakily stood to make those faltering steps behind him, he reluctant to leave the great hall, which did seem a more tranquil place than the one to which he was beckoned. He ambled along the passageway soon to come to his ally who stood with a guard close. A sheepish glance was all he could muster as he passed, and fearfully went he into the closet.

"Sit down, earl, we will waste little time here. Firstly, read this letter, supposedly dispatched to the King Charles of France on behalf of the Piers Osbeck, which, however, has come into our hands. And this letter from our King Henry, giving full power to this court over any treacherous acts." The earl looked at one parchment, and then at the other, to place them both with hands at shake back upon the table with not one word spoken. "What say you, earl?"

"I say naught, sires." A whispery reply was all that was told and faint to hear.

"To be taken from this place," continued the interrogator, "and to be executed with haste by the axe … Take him away under guard to stand by with the other that waits."

The earl could not stand, no legs did he have but two useless things as eels at dangle. The guard was beckoned; lifting the earl from under his arms to be dragged out, his functions gave way with excretion and urine running from him, wetting the stone beneath; as he was pulled from the closet and sat down in the passageway, all functions without care, lost to fear, as the mire oozed and dripped about his fine cloth. The other earl who waited with a more honourable bearing eased away from the wretch.

A young biddy was fetched to clean the chamber's foul. A grubby little bonnet she wore atop her head, a handed-down uniform was her code, with more holes than cloth to cover her child's body. With cloth mop and water she began to wash away from the closet the deed left by the earl. The king's court stood as far from the spectacle as they were able, trying not to be overcome by the smell as they watched the biddy in her progress; they becoming more prone to some impatience as they awaited her efforts, for 'twas not a matter that they had foreseen, and they wished to be away from this task. Soon though she was finished, and the place was mostly relieved of the stench that had permeated that little closet. With a polite curtsy, she left the cold closet to finish its bloody agenda.

The bishop, in some serenity, came to the closet. The last of the instigators sat before the court once more, aloof and disinterested in the shuffled parchments before him, disdaining to even peruse the evidence. "Sirs, you waste your time with these accusations." As he spake he pushed away the documents that had been placed before him, leaving them closer to the interrogators than himself, his fingers glinting many rings as he did so. "You know well that I can be only reprimanded by a jury of bishops and cardinals, and by no other court of common men."

"That may be so, my bishop, but in proven cases of treason, of which this case is so proven, the king has all jurisdiction; if a threat is made to end his life, by a first party or by a third party, deems all guilty. And your signature upon this letter places you within that group." The said document was held up betwixt thumb and forefinger like it already dripped wet with blood.

The bishop banged his fist upon the table, as all roads were seen to have closed upon him, and his shovel of faith bent and of little use. "I will not be subject to this!" he raged. "I am the Bishop of Cork and you have no rights to such activities against me."

"We have all the right we need, dear bishop; but, if you do not think such, you may make address to your Church upon the morrow. However, you will be executed today."

The bishop stood as if to place a curse upon those who sat before him, but only spit and bluster moulded his words. "I will have none of it! I am untouchable by heathens such as you."

"You will not be touched by us … have no fear of that, for we would not soil our hands upon a traitor to our king … Take him away to the others and remove all valuables that they bear, and be certain you have all the bishop's finery, for he doth seem little able to move with all that clings to his person. And then deliver the found goods to the keeper of the books that he may record all for our king."

"Yes, sir," the guard answered, as he took away the bishop and stood him with the others who awaited their fate. The soldier then carried out his orders, and with little respect of their previous titles, he removed all the valuables that bedecked their person, and took them away to the treasurer to be placed in the king's care.

The prisoners were marched and dragged toward the outside stage that had been set beyond the confines of the gate so all may see the result of those who dared to depose a king. The crowd gathered about to see the sport to come, though kept a little distance away by the king's soldiers, but close enough for the splatter of blood. The crowd cheered as the traitors came to sight from the darkness of the open door. They paced and they stumbled across the yard, until they were outside the gate where awaited their fate.

He stood tall with his sharpened axe resting upon his bulky shoulder; no fat seemed to make his body, all muscle and strength was all that showed. A proud man he stood, wishing to show to all his handling of such delicate matters. The only thing that seemed to not fit his person was that upon his face and head a black cover he wore that showed but two slits for his eyes and another for his mouth as if to bring some disguise to himself. But a raucous person he was and not bent to any modesty. Many deemed that the reason for the cover was not to hide himself from any living soul, but to hide himself from God, for he believed that he would not be known to the Lord if his face could not be seen. For when he reached the gates of heaven, he wished not his acts to be known, for to hell he wished not to travel for his earthly labours.

They came close, those of guilt, to the rickety stage that awaited them. The crowd milled about, to view the act from a more advantageous place, more so than the one they occupied. The king's guard with the prisoners close stood still at the place designated. A clergyman with his worn Bible stood with solemn face to administer the last rites upon the wretches who, in sad state, awaited their fate. Pushed through to the block came the Earl of Desmond, trying to be proud as he stepped upon the stage, but shaking as if the plague had taken his body. The executioner placed the earl's head upon the block and set it to his liking, then, before anything could be uttered, the axe had taken his head. Like a lightning flash it came down with but a little sound. Only the startled cry from the clergy, who it seemed was little ready for the event, cried out in surprise as the blood bespattered his person and took him from the event in some distress. A young trainee was he, thrown by his elders into the fire of hell, and he was little taken by it. The life of the clergy seemed not as tranquil as he had envisioned. The crowd cheered and laughed as the head rolled from the body. The officer of the execution picked the head by its thick black hair and held it high, as he walked about the stage displaying it so all may see, and they knew that this would be the fate of all those who practised treason. The head still pumped its blood about, the eyes still fluttered as if ready for sleep and not for death. The two who awaited their turn looked not upon the ritual. The bishop turned away and stared at the old castle before him, his back straight and still with haughty presence, as if his turn would not come and he would be saved by the pope. The earl saw naught, for he was just a heap of death upon the dusty track and knew not even the day. One of the soldiers so designated came forward carrying the head pole, and as the officer held the head upon its side, the sharp pole was pushed inside the skull, making the eyes pop open wide and the mouth to grin, to the cries of revulsion that came from those who were close and spied such. The pole was then lifted high and placed in the readied hole close to the gated entrance. Many eager hands came to push in the stones and the sand to secure the bloody idol, still dripping its red upon the yokels beneath. The officer and the interrogator watched on as the verdict was carried out.

The jellyfish of Kildare was lifted to the block, he all of whimper and despair, reeking of his functions as they leaked about him. He was laid upon the block and was seen lifeless already, all still was he except for his fearful shuddering. 'Twas stopped quickly though with one stroke;

his fears were all gone, to be troubled no more about earthly doings. The cheers and jibes of the crowd flowed once more. The grinning head looked down from the pole next to his ally, closer to the earl than he had ever been before.

"Bring on the bishop!" the crowd now chanted, as the bloodied block was swilled off with buckets of water to clear the grim slop. And the bishop did come, still pompous and unbroken. No rings did he finger. No chain with its gold cross swung at his neck. No cape covered the white, soft executioner's neck—for indeed 'twas the executioner who coveted that pale offering. Standing next to the block the bishop called out for forgiveness to all who so did this ungodly deed. But his words did not come clear, for the ranting crowd buried his voice with their own last words.

"Off with his head!" cried they. "Off with his thieving head!" they called out against the scribe of their persecution. That he had committed treason mattered naught to them. What mattered to them was that this man had pushed them deeper into poverty and that criddled* their bones. "That stealer—that moneylender—let him go to his God!" Cries of such that had been kept bosomed rang about, as he was pushed onto the block and the axeman pushed his head into its place. The axe came down no different to its cut, whether it struck pauper or king, the cleft still spurted the blood red, still cut through muscle and bone, and still brought its justice. The bishop's head, still with its religious cap perched upon it, swayed upon the pole, with the grin of death upon its face, bumping and swinging with his ill-chosen comrades.

A day to remember was this, to be passed from parent to child, a day of terror for the three accused and a lesson to be learned. The garrison officer spake to close the book upon the day's story.

"To all who deceive our beloved King Henry such will be their fate, to sway high in the wind and await the crows' visit. Be warned, do not stray from the path your king has laid before you, for he is good and seeks only to bring forth truth and justice to all his people."

Disrespectful were the mumblings that floated about the crowd, knowing nothing of the king's justice nor his compassion, for they were sorely treated. But naught was spake loud enough for the king's men to finger. The officer looked about to point out the troublemakers, but could not find any who showed their disrespect, and so to carry on once again with his written text.

"The headless bodies will be burnt upon the readied fires to at least bring some warmth to those gathered who have suffered from their cold

---

* *criddled* [coined] bedevilled

acts. The others, who remain in the great hall, who were with ease dragged into this intrigue, will all forfeit such lands and properties, with all monies from such sales returned to the care of the king, and they who were conniving will be thrown out into the street to fend as best they may. The kindness of his Majesty lets them remain with no bodily harm from this court." The crowd cheered loudly once again, as the misfortune of others was to be drizzled upon the class they abhorred.

The play was over until another time, and may that time be the time of Piers Osbeck, who it seemed was bent upon his quest to seize the throne with his honeyed rap, and to stir the people to revolt in every part of the land. All these thoughts ran the mind of the officer as he paced his way toward the horses at wait. With haste he waved his men forward to London Town, and for he to report to the king direct. The path they took was of that which they had arrived, that time before blood was spilt, seemingly long ago. Up the darkening hills went they, climbing higher by each trodden hoof. They glanced back upon the town that lay below, with most distinct three fires at burn, bright, fuelled by some blubber and lordly fat no doubt, and seen the dancers with hands joined in circles around the flames, their shadows skipping and leaping upon this happy of days.

Chapter Twenty-one.

Rebuffed.

The brigantine cut through the cold sea taking Richard and Alphonse swiftly away from their Irish comrades to the shores of France in spirits higher than they had ever been, for it seemed their time was coming close and the crown would find its rightful head.

"Fortune is turning our way, Alph. With the nobles of Cork showing their willingness to join our cause, surely the King Charles will look upon us most fairly, for hating the English is one of his sports, and he may with much pleasure bring others to our aid."

"Yes, my dear friend, let us pray our road is of a Roman way." They stood together at the boat's bow with their eyes searching for land. No work was required from them upon this vessel, for all was paid and given freely to speed the way of the prince for him to bring the prize of fortunes to their fold. Fast and sleek was the Brigantine, making quick time with favourable winds and stormless sea. No fear of English ships did they hold, for they knew that well built was their boat, and speed was their advantage; their small craft would billow faster than all other vessels and would outpace any to the shores of France …

"The English ambassador, your Majesty." Lords and ladies, counts and countesses, hangers-on and courtesans all dressed in such finery. For in this court of King Charles VIII all other courts were to shame. Turned they toward the voice that announced the visitor. To see what drab person would enter their chamber, especially from those Englishmen of little manner and less taste. But dapper and mannered he seemed as he came forward, and looked he to be tolerable. Striding toward the King Charles with much bearing in his step, for he cared not, nor did his countrymen, that the French court was affluent and far more sophisticated than the court of England. For all their wealth, they did not have the strength for wars. The English were mightier by the sword than the prinks who dwelled within this court. He knelt, though, in all respect at the feet of Charles, who had requested council from the King of England to avert a war of conflict upon his land, for he wanted naught of it. His treasures were too good to waste upon blood and lost lands. His court the richest in Europe. His ships bringing treasures to his vaults by the load. His courtiers fashioned to shame all others. Rich were his palaces in gold and silks, with fine carpeted floors and all manner of opulence. He wished not to drain his coffers once again. He was not obliged to enter into such a war and would seek some solution not to do so. Why indeed would he wish to suffer such from these ruffians? He had learned that Henry was preparing to invade his land, and had summoned the English ambassador to his palace to mend the conflict, and to preserve his style.

"My good ambassador, how fare ye?"

"I am well, your Majesty. I bring happy tidings from my king to your good self, in the hope we may lay some compromise in this matter of our conflict. He sends you a gift, your Majesty, in his true faith of the outcome. If you would honour him by its acceptance, my lord?"

"I will do so, Mister Ambassador, with deep love and affection to our dear friend Henry." Charles reached out his laced-cuffed hand, the hand so clean it must have touched the clouds of heaven to be so pure. The dainty fingers held the small casket but for a moment, like 'twas a diseased rat, and barely wanting to place his hands upon it. One of the king's aids stepped forward, and, with his Majesty's permission, took the soiled casket from him and did open it for his perusal. The king peered inside the box, his lace 'chief over his mouth as he did so, for it seemed that the odour coming from the gift was that indeed of some dead animal that pervaded his nostrils, though only to him it did so. Two gold rings lay a-bottom upon the velvet cloth of royal blue. The stones shone the eyes of the king, as he nodded his approval and waved away the aid with the trinkets. "We are well pleased with your offering, Mister Ambassador, and such will become part of our treasured possessions. Let us now to business, for I have time to idle away elsewhere than to confer for long upon worldly happenings."

"We bring to you, your Majesty, a letter writ and sealed by my king, as to his intent in this matter of our invasion upon your most tranquil of lands, and to place before you his one desire for a peaceful compromise." The sealed letter was handed over to the king's treasurer, with only a few of his close ministers showing any interest in the matter, for in their eyes the wine and the dance were being fritted away. He opened the royal letter and read its contents aloud to his leader, who it seemed was finding some difficulty in finding much to hold his thoughts. Sighing and squirming about upon his royal seat, his mind seemed spent upon the courtesans who flaunted about at the far reach of the chamber, their laughing and chirping laced with foul-mouthed chat that was bandied about for all at listen.

"Come, my dear treasurer, make haste your way. Others eggs will be fried in the pan before yours are laid. Pray, tell me straight, what price he doth ask for? And belay the faddle 'tween."

"Yes, your Majesty ... It appears, my lord, that for a peaceful end to these pretensions he requires from the treasury of France, gold, jewels, and monies to the value of two-hundred thousand English pounds." The king still looked about the chamber and showed little emotion as the treasurer continued his chant. "Also, my lord, upon his show, the person of Piers Osbeck, who is in pretense to be the Prince Richard of York, must be returned to England, so we may determine once and for all the true facts of his claim ... That, my lord, is the gist of the King Henry's compromise."

"We will draught a letter, my lord treasurer, to the effect that we will pay one-hundred thousand English pounds, and until this figure is agreed, the act against Piers Osbeck will not be in force. Away you all now and make the papers required. I have more pressing matters to attend." The king was soon away to the goings-on aback the palace's chamber; no more tattle this day for Charles, for he was duly stressed with such trivial matters ...

The brigantine showed its sails to the people of Calais, as from a good distance it could be seen coming at speed set for the busy harbour. The word was about of the coming of the prince, and France did wish for such, bringing them an ally of English decent amiable to their own royalty. For the King Henry seemed but a warmonger and was set upon the cause of much mischief in all his acts. They gathered in all anticipation, awaiting they at the dockside as the ship grew larger, and the harbourmaster there could see with his eyeglass the flags upon the vessel waving high. The French flag unfurled in prominence with the ship's jack of St. Patrick's cross fluttering by its side; and there, looking as bright as the morning in all its glory, the White Rose of York showed once more. Brought from its kept box after these many years, and deemed by many never to be shamed again.

Horsed soldiers arrived, all festooned in their ceremonial vesture, with trumpets sounding and drums rattling; they were the royal guard, sent by the king to escort the prince to his palace, where his Majesty was in some interest to hold council with the called prince, wishing to determine for himself the truth of the matter. The escort waited, dismounted, and stood about in groups, talking and laughing, with some time spent calming their restless horses that kicked and fussed about. Closer came the ship to the crowd that had gathered. The mayor, with his chains of office strung about his neck, stood with his council in their most stately robes. Lords and nobles with their bedecked ladies were ushered to the front of the underlings; the courtly leant upon their staffs as they waited with the look of boredom upon their faces. Ordered there by their king were they, and not there of their own volition. Some stood with kerchiefs pressed upon their noses, for there could be some sickening drift from about this common place. Soon the ship closed to the harbour as the dignitaries and the soldiers readied themselves for the prince. The crew upon the vessel could be easily seen now, moving about with some urgency in their tasks of docking the brigantine. Also came to sight a figure standing tall above all others, proud and princely in his rich clothes. A fine feathered hat that flapped about his head was pulled firmly at the brim so it would not be tempted by the sea. Silver glinted about him from his buckle and clasps, his sword held close by his other hand, and all showed as a most princely person.

"See the gathering awaiting our arrival Alphonse?" Richard spake to his friend in tones excited. "Look—See the royal escort to guide us in safety to Paris? Alphonse, this is a most gratifying situation that comes upon us. With the Irish already committed to us, with the French, and soon with hope the Scots, we will soon be a force for that Henry to fear."

"'Tis as you say, my prince, a most gratifying situation. Be of patience though, for I have heard the French king is not one to be chased as a fox, but to be ladled slowly like the thick cream from the churn."

"We will be patient, my friend, for to await the outcome will be of little hardship in the court of Charles."

The summer was giving forth its rich harvest in this year of fourteen hundred and ninety-two. A year that may yet lead Richard to his rightful place, and bring to ground in defeat his most hated Henry.

The wooden hull scraped and bumped the harbour wall as the brigantine was drawn to the waiting throng. The ropes were tied off below the sound of the fluttering banners, and the vessel was made secure; the plank was placed from ship to shore and readied for the prince to embark. The sails were being folded and tied, as to the plank strode the handsome comer in all his finery, waving to the cheering crowd. The pipes and the drums mingled their greeting as he came down the walk most gracefully, to give of himself the most likeable impression he could. The solid wharf of the harbour was underfoot, and the first of the party that had awaited his coming stepped forward.

"Greetings to you, my dear prince," the mayor first spake to make acquaintance with Richard. "I pray your journey was without hardship?"

"'Twas so, my lord, a most delightful journey, and to be at last to stand upon your most pleasant of lands has brought even more delight to it."

"Come, sir, we have many lords and ladies who wish to be of greet with you." The prince was ushered to the waiting nobles who greeted him singularly with grace and grovel befitting a royal. The crowd all about was in a most joyful mood, shouting and waving at every meet. They passed all the lords and all the dignitaries to move along to the soldiers who smartly stood. "And this, sire, is your personal guard, who will escort you with all speed and safety to our king, who awaits the pleasure of meeting with you."

"You are most kind, Mister Mayor, and such will not be forgotten."

"Your kindness precedes you, sire," thus spake the mayor as he left the duties to the troop officer, who let himself be known with his beginning gesture of a low bow.

"Commander Charles Monypeny, at your service, my prince."

"Good day to you, sir," Richard greeted the officer.

"If it is your pleasure, sire, we have taken the liberty for you to ride horse in its stead of the carriage, for methinks you will be glad to saddle again from your coop upon the vessel."

"That will be most admirable, sir; please, lead the way."

"The journey should take of four hours with suitable stops. If you and your servant will follow me, we will attend you at horse." They followed the officer, and then did discard some of their attire to a cart that was to follow with their chattels, for the vesture they wore would not be suitable for the riding of horses, and felt they more pleased knowing that their riding skills would not be hampered. Saddled and upped they moved slowly away with the drums and pipes at lilt once again, to the crowd's pleasure at the most pompous sight. The fleur-de-lis fluttered high next to the English standard of St. George's cross, as the troop tinkled and rattled away through the narrow garland-trimmed streets. "Vive la Prince!" was cried out from the windows, and from the seers upon the rooftops as they passed by. Soon they were to the edge of the town with fewer people about to cheer them, and so the pace was quickened. Into the bright countryside, green and placid as a lake, they came with the gait increased more to a steady gallop along the lane's wind. They made good haste along the dusty tracks and through hamlets, with small groups waving their flags of peace to the prince as they cantered through. On they went for more saddled hours, with only short stops to rest and to change horses, and then to the gallop once more till the afternoon did come, whence a smoky haze was seen that drifted to the clouds, the sign of a large town at some distance. The wind blew stronger as they came to the bridge that was covered, misty in the smoke, almost hiding the slapping river below it. They clopped over the planks that lay, and then the giant steeples of the cathedral were seen above their hide, showing their glory and might to the coming travellers.

For 'twas Paris now seen that gathered itself about the river. Past the city walls and clattering over the stones they came through the outer town. A foul smell was about, to discomfort the riders as deeper into the city they came. Into the streets the open sewers flowed their muck, and into the sparkling waters of the river, turning the clean to brown where 'twas fed. Rats floated by, bloated like the pig's bladder; upside down they drifted with four legs up like the masts of a sinking ship. Dead dogs, pieces of body, rotted food, all emptied into the mighty Seine. The smell seemed to become less troublesome to them, and they continued onward with their noses becoming more accustomed to the odour.

Rich landowners and dignitaries waved their welcome at the passing of the parade, they, fenced off, a good six feet from the lower classes. The reach made so, for 'twas too far for the hop of a flea. They waved and cheered as the prince came toward them, but many rats were disturbed by the commotion and ran about their feet, as the regal party was almost upon them. The peasants began kicking at the vermin with their heavy boots, and, with some luck, one was booted and sent spinning and squealing into the air, scattering the screaming women from both sides of the fence, as they pulled their hats close, case the thing would fall upon them. The menfolk laughed at the goings-on and kicked about even more for the sport engaged, but no more would come to the boot, the rats all fled, and all seemed calmer as they gave respect to the passing prince, who, in return, waved back with laughter upon his face at the sight he had seen, for he had spent many years with the common folk and knew their antics, and once would have joined their fun but now he could not.

Time was soon that they came to the Louvre palace. The magnificent building stood so clean it must have been washed by scrubbing women in the dark of the night so no one could see their labour, for it did appear in the light to have been touched by an angel to stay so pure. The iron fence that circled the grounds was all neatly straight, and painted as black as coal with no rust to blemish it. Guards of the palace stood their duty along its length with one every forty paces, watched over closely by the duty sergeant, who passed along them once every hour looking for slackers and dozers, for the king had to see no gaps at any time within his military. The grasses and the roadway within, cut and raked constantly by a hundred keepers of the grounds, seen as if 'twere a painting that would always remain the same; these walls would not darken and this grass would not grow. The windows would be clean for all time, the painting would always stay as 'twas painted. They rode up the path of gravel to the main doorway, each side stood a flunky dressed most refined in the costume of a royal servant, seen to dress even better than some nobles at other courts. Richard had seen others with their meat- and wine-stained doublets worn without change for week upon week, full of odour and disturbing scent, but here was all clean and sweet of smell, as the richness of the inside seemed to flow to the outside. The travellers dusted off their garb, and then, guided by the officer, Richard and Alphonse made their way up the wide steps to the door that was opened by the flunkies there. The party entered into the foyer of the palace to see the line of waiting greeters before them—though managing some moments to look about at the splendour they had entered. The floor was of grey marble, a stone that Richard had never trod. Carpets lay atop the cold slabs; no rushes for comfort here, stead the carpets lay. Many tables and chairs were about, all richly carved and seated with tapestries, others inlaid with gold and exotic woods. Mirrors so large they showed more than the eye could gather. The walls were hidden by paintings of such size and number that the plaster's colour they had been washed with could not be seen. Windows reached from floor to ceiling, hung all about with draped silks and fancy lace. The ceilings covered in frescoes and gold leaf. Chandeliers hung low as large as a pond with a hundred tallows lit.

Richard, with Alphonse at follow, made way along the lines of bowing nobles and curtsied ladies, nodding with great charm and pleasure, and upon passing the last in line, as if on cue, the King Charles did enter and sat he in all his pompous glory upon his high throne, looking down as the gathered bowed and curtsied their homage to him. Ponced he in laces and silks, his large white wig high upon his head as untouched snow. Stockinged in pink rose with black leather shoes and silver buckles. Clenched at hand his staff of state, he awaited the visitor who came in reverence before him.

"My most honourable king, it is a great pleasure to be called to your good self, and I greet you as a most humble servant." Richard bowed lowly and played his most humbling state about this King of France.

"My dear prince, it has been many a day that I have awaited this pleasure. Come, sit aside me, I am most interested in your story, and wish to hear all you have to relate about your situation." A seat was brought forward and placed beside the king so that Richard would be able to chat in more intimate jargon to his Majesty. The court went about their own activities, with Alphonse amongst them, drinking with all the bubbling wine of France and nibbling upon fine delicate foods, as they laughed and talked amongst each other, doing such in this courtly way each day. "I hear say you have gathered support for your cause in Ireland?"

"Yes, your Majesty, I have been promised monetary assistance, and an army with all support from the lords of that land. But it is given on condition that I can raise more soldiers and more financial offerings. And, if I may say so, sire, I hope that I may obtain some contributions from you. I have already sent letters relating to my position to the King of the Romans and to the King of the Scots, who I feel will side with me in this matter."

His Majesty, though, did not yet seem to be fully taken by the young man, and wished more insight into his past before he would commit one penny. "Tell me of the memories you have kept from the time you did spend in the court of your father."

Richard went once more into that story, with lilt of tongue and practised phrases that came from his lips like water over the rocks, until he had spake all he could remember in his young head. Once again though the king seemed that he had not heard that which he wished, and indeed was needing to hear of more sordid matters hinted by his next request.

"I must ask you, sir, after listening to your story so far, why you did not mention a certain ritual that did happen most regularly at the court of your father? Thus far your story, as related to me, and my knowledge of the court, points to the fact that you are as you state, the Prince Richard. If though you can relate the question posed, then I would be complete in my belief that you are the prince-in-waiting."

"I am at your service, sire; that if at my early age I can remember, then I will so relate it to you, and if you would be so kind as to offer a little more information as to the gist."

"'Tis, sir, the day that was known as the Day of the Virgins. Which, I was related, happened at least once upon every month. Do you recall any of this?"

"Yes, my lord, I recall such a happening. I would spy with my brother through the curtained doorway to the chamber where the ritual was held. 'Twas writ that upon the stated day every month that all virgins of noble birth, if they so desired, would be entertained at the palace and would be taken by the king. The line seemed always to be long, may eighty to one hundred girls stood in their dresses all of white, most at laugh and chat amongst themselves. They would peer ahead to the one whose turn had come, for the act was held for all about the court to see. She was helped in her task by the servants, who lifted her upon the high chair and displayed her properly so the king may have little strife. With legs held high, she was one of many this day to be deflowered by my lecherous father. One after the other they would come, playing it as some child's game. He counting his takings and somewhat disinterested in the act he was engaged in. After the procedure was completed they went to the scribes table to pay their fee, and to receive a writ verifying that they had lost their flower to the king. And, as all did know, no one could deny the king such pleasure. After they had received their cherished scroll, they were free to enjoy their pleasure where and when they may, for to be promiscuous mattered not. And when the arranged marriage would come and the legal documents were exchanged, the loss of the lady's virginity was not a question, and was oft sought by the suitor; to know that the king was the one who had taken his lady before him, she was indeed a prize.

"It appeared that many enjoyed and found pleasure in the experience, and felt little discomfort; some though were in dire strait for being ravished and forced, causing them to bleed unstoppably and would scream and writhe upon the cold floor. And quickly would come the servants to cover the young girl with a blanket and to carry her off. Maids came in the meantime and mopped up the blood that had wetted the stones, with the king standing naked from his waist to his feet, impatient at the delay in the activities and most anxious to satisfy the waiting line. Some were shivered at the bloody spectacle that had gone before them, and shunned were they at the sight of the half-naked king who awaited them. But none left or ran away from the doings, for the signature upon their scroll meant more than a little distress. My father would continue till all was done, and as his servants washed him and replaced his garments; he would always then ask the amount of the monies taken from the fees that he charged for such a service, and was mostly happy at the outcome.

"And, sir, to my knowledge that is all I can recall of the matter, for I was but an infant at the time and knew not exactly of the game being played, then, when I grew older and reflected upon the scene, did I know the true meaning of the acts."

The king seemed to have heard that which he had requested, for his eyes were fiery with some passion. "Your description, sir, and the details you have recalled, does relate to me that indeed you do have some first knowledge of this debauchery, and from all I and my advisers have gleaned, we, in all trust, take you as being the rightful heir to the throne of England."

The king stood and, with Richard at his side, gained some hearing from the courtiers before him by rapping his staff upon the wooden platform where they gathered. Loud and resounding it echoed about the chamber to bring all to silence. For the king did speak and all did listen. "This day of our Lord we have found in favour of our visitor, and 'tis our pleasure to call him the Prince Richard of York, most true and noble heir to the throne of England and all its domains."

With cheers and flying hat the throng shouted and applauded with much vigour to the most joyous news from their king. For this prince was no warmonger to the French but was now a dear ally.

"My prince," the king spake cozily to Richard as the courtiers continued in their merrymaking, "our great friend, the Marquis DeVernoe, is making much readiness with banners and music, and all manner of entertainment in the great hall at his castle to honour you for your visit here with us; he wishes to show you our French culture, with a banquet and a ball the splendour of which you have never cast upon. Would you honour him with your presence?"

"It would be my certain pleasure, sire. I have heard though that the marquis is rather a devilish man with many gibes and cutting speech."

The king laughed loudly, though with an effeminate sound. "That is so, my prince, but I feel you have the blade to parry his thrust, and also to score points with your own tongue. It is just his sport, but he relishes it most dearly and, believe me, he is a master at it, for only to his king has he lost the battle of reproachment. I regret that I will be unable to attend the frolic, for the government has such duties for me upon that day. To stay the night at his castle before the morrow's gaieties start I feel would be most apt, my prince. We will furnish you with suitable attire as you will be treated with much respect in your station. And I will await to hear the gossip of your encounter with the marquis with much anticipation, for I am sure it will be the main topic at court.

"I am deeply debted to you, sire, and I look forward to our future meet when we may discuss my endeavours to regain the English throne."

"'Tis so, my prince, that I also look forward to our council." The king departed the activities, and Richard left with Alph to ready the trip to the castle of the marquis, as the courtiers continued in their merry delights and clandestine acts …

"Alph, Alph," came the half-whispered words from Richard, spoken such in the bedchamber where they had been placed, within the abode of the Marquis DeVernoe. Alphonse came over to where the prince was seated. The day was almost done and drawing to eve, as the royal and his servant were making ready for the banquet. They had spent one night at the castle, and this day had been wasted away with childlike taunting and games. But now 'twas the time to ready for the coming event. "Sit close to me, Alph, so I may bend your ear." Alph sat close beside the prince. "I believe we are being spied upon—Do not gaze about, but I have noticed the painting of that lordly fellow that hangs aback of us, to be seen as bewitched with eyes that follow us about, and then at other times they are still and blank to any kind of movement. I am suspicious of the marquis, who seeks any scandal to fuel his fiery tongue. I would be most interested to see inside another chamber to relate if the same mystery is happening elsewhere."

"I will stroll the corridor, my prince, to see if any of the chambers are empty," Alphonse side-mouthed his whispered action to the prince. "We must, my sire, bottom this cruel jest with haste."

"Please do so, Alph. I will await your return … Be wary, my friend."

Alphonse stepped into the passageway looking most official in his flunky garments, with a roll of parchment clutched in his hand as if sent upon some legal matter. He quickly spied, but four doors away, a group of young ladies of the court dressed divinely, laughing and hugging as they made to the stairs that would take them down to the great hall. Soon out of sight were they; only their laughter did linger about, as Alphonse creaked open the door of their chamber and peeked inside. "Good day!" he called, ready with an excuse if anyone was still about, but no reply came as he closed the door once again, and with haste scurried back to the chamber where awaited the prince.

"Richard!" he called in his secretive, whispering voice, as if all about were not candles or bowls of fruit, but big ears awaiting any words that may come their way. "Come, come," he called, only halfway into the chamber, as he looked both into the room and then into the passageway to spy that no one was about. He stuck his hand out blindly toward Richard, to at last clutch his hand and guide him quickly along to the doorway of the ladies' chamber. The click of the latch brought them both inside like some common thieves, slinking and creeping about upon a foul mission. The heady perfume still filled the chamber with its heavy scent. Clothes were thrown all about. Upon the floor, upon the chairs, and upon the bed they lay, mixed with the bed linens, the cushions, and the cloth covers piled there like some mountain. They looked about for that which had brought them to the bedchamber. And 'twas quickly they saw opposite the bed a large painting of some ancestor sitting in a fine chair with a dog at his feet looking ahead straight. They came nearer to the painting and upon a closer look at the dog they could see that the eyes were not of the painting, but set back, as if painted upon a piece of wood so that it may be slid to one side.

"Do you see this, Alph?"

"Yes, Richard; I see the devil's play."

"He is a peeping Tom, Alph … A voyeur. He must be spying upon all the chambers to gain such things he seeks for his black mind. Come, Alph, let us away, for I am much criddled by such as we have seen." A peek, a breathless run, a click. They were soon returned to their chamber. "Alph, help me spread this bedcover over our peeping lord." Alph helped Richard to drape the cover over the painting to bring some private ways to their chamber.

The banquet had begun two hours ago, with Richard having been sat conveniently opposite the marquis, while Alphonse, as Richard's servant, stood aback from the table with others of the same standing. They stood at the ready to come forward to help his lord or lady in their requirements. The stuffed doves had all left the empty platter. The truffles were but crumbs scattered about the table. The strawberries and the cream left the crystal bowls with only the mist that once abounded there. The wine goblets full then empty again. Cognac flowed like the peasants' wine, as large jugs slopped the amber into the goblets, to spill upon the remains of the meal and down the doublets of the lords as they slurped the contents. The tongues changed from chat that was friendly to barbed snide.

"Tell me, my good prince,"—the marquis led in with his cutting remarks, peering over his goblet, clutched by his dainty hands, his puffed wig curled about his face, his painted lips twisted as in some disrespect, the face powdered white, showing clear his black, peircing eyes—"is it so that the English bathe only once in the month whether they need to or not?" The giggles and laughter rent about the table from the remark that was bestowed upon the prince. All to quiet came at the spread, only heard was the tinkle of a goblet, with heads turned as the answer from the prince was awaited, if indeed he had an answer.

"My dear marquis, you are correct in what you have heard, and 'tis with some honour and chivalry they use this practice. For their enemies of soil foreign can smell from which way they come, so they know which way to flee." Laughter and applause came about all in the prince's favour, for he had outdone the marquis in the first joust. The answer though riled the marquis even more.

"Well said, my prince," he replied, but could not contain his surled lip, as then he continued his search to find some weakness that would rile his guest. "Also, my prince, is it not so that even the nobles wear such drab cloth in that rained land as sack and that worsted that scratches like a thousand fleas?" A hundred eyes watched and waited once again for the reply to come.

"It seems you know much of that itch, sire, but I do not, for I have never become flea-infested and know not of the feeling." Laughter rang again, with many drunken lords having to be helped in their state by their manservants, as they choked upon their brandy and slipped from their chairs. The marquis, though, was not amused and felt subject to much ridicule; with his face of red, stood he from his chair, and blurted out angrily such words that deemed to be unworthy of his standing.

The hawk does not succumb to the sparrow!

And then started he to turn his jibes to more personal daggers, as the normal talk fluttered and fell as a shot grouse. "I have to ask of your mother, sire."

Richard slowly stood from his seat. "I pray, sir, the words you are about to speak of my mother are in gentle tone, for remember, she was a queen … and before you stands the next King of England. So be not of vile words upon this matter. Remember, the soft cat has claws unseen."

With little regard for the warning that came from Richard, the marquis continued upon the road from which he could not return, and to slight the prince was all his head contained. "I did hear such mentioned that your father was unable to satisfy the queen's lust and so she took to lovers … Three of them, I hear." A hush came veiling over the proceedings, as all did know the marquis had overstepped the mark of jesting, and had now entered into words of insult. Richard sat awaiting the final remark that was to come from the mouth so foul. "The only thing was that she bedded them all at the same time!" The marquis laughed aloud at the comment, but his laughter was not joined by any other. The jest was in bad taste, and cries of "Shame!" rang about.

"Well, sir, I know not of which you speak, but I do know my mother was a fine and gentle lady blessed with goodness and compassion. But you, sir, must know more than I, for I assume you have gathered your information, and the information of others through the spy-holes you have in all the rooms of this castle." Richard stood as a disturbed murmur spread about those who sat around the table, all wondering of each if they had been seen in some compromise. "I can well see you with twinkling eyes peering at me through the noble painting that is hung opposite my cot. And to mind comes the slinking about in those dark, damp corridors, with only the flicker of your candle to light the blackness, as you and your mistress skulk about in your devil's cave. And I say to all so gathered within these walls, to cover over these lecherous doings that hang with false majesty upon the walls of your chambers, for you will be spied if you do not."

"You cur, sir!" shouted the raged marquis as his humiliating secret was about. "I must have satisfaction!"

"Satisfaction for what, sir? for I have told no lies; from my lips have come no fables—"

Before more could be spake, the goblet of wine flew its contents across the table to splash upon the face and doublet of Richard, who slowly wiped away the liquid with his serving cloth.

"Calm yourself, sir, I wish not to fight you."

"Coward!"

"I am no coward, sir, and I pray you will calm yourself. The only thing

I require of you is an apology for you actions, and for your slight upon my family."

"I will not! … If you are no coward then do me the honour of obliging my request."

"I feel you will not change your anger, sir, until you have your way, so to it now, sir, if you so desire."

The two at disagreement stomped away from the banquet hall and down the wide stairway, with its ogling-eyed paintings seeming to watch every step as they went by. All the guests with their servants followed behind, with their chattering and clicking shoes sounding all about. The swish and rustle of the ladies' silk dresses called like the sea upon the shore, as all in sporty mind followed the combatants to the spectacle. Any thought of the splendid ball to come was gone from the mind, for far better things were afoot. Past the flunkies aside the great doors they went with ne'er a glance. Past the guards standing with surprised faces as they went quickly by them to the dusty courtyard. Lit by torches high, flickering their smoke and flying sparks, adding to the stars at twink. The blackness, thick and dark, lay outside the arena; like the devil's treacle it stuck to all about awaiting some reluctant soul. The circle formed, with barons, lords, and earls, ladies of aristocracy, ladies of nobility and giggling courtesans. They, all dressed for the ball, with high wigs a-sway and washed in perfume, and wine all mixed in the aroma that was about.

The two combatants stood opposite each other; the swords that were chosen were readily unsheathed and held in sweaty hands. A quick salute came as the blade touched their lips, and then the night was split with sweet ching and chang, as one blade parried the other in the fleeting light, now dim, now bright, as the breeze blew the cloud to decide which it would be. A thrust to show a torn doublet, as the blade of the marquis cut the cloth of Richard with a gasp and covered eyes from the watchers. Richard playing the easy target; he had been taught well, to lure the enemy into some false move that would bring him down. The marquis had seen the ease 'twas to cut this boy and would take his blade to the fool, for he showed he was no swordsman, and would not be able to compete with the master. Richard showed again an open breast, availed to a lunge to finish the game. And, from the marquis, it did come; as he lunged for the spot, he knew the game for Richard was over, and that this prince would never rule England but feed the grass upon some foreign shore. Quick came his blade, ready to feel it slip like silk into the soft meat of the breast that was displayed tantalizingly before him. But naught he felt from his steel as it flailed into the dank air. Richard was aside him now, his blade twisted into the blade of the marquis, and with a flick he aired it from the ungrasped hand, and 'twas seen to fly like a dove against the black sky until no more could it be seen, as then to ground it came pointed to the flags with fate to find the gap there, and to sway to and fro liken to a lance swaying in its target. Off his balance, the marquis was pulled to the ground with a deft hook from the foot of Richard, to plant him dusty upon his rear, to the oohs and ahhs of the circled arena. The blade was then thrust at the throat of the grovelled lord, pushing the skin to dimple, with force played not quite enough to pierce to blood. The marquis lay prostrate, done and at the mercy of Richard. He looked up with glazed eye to ponder of his fate.

"Get up," was the fate shown from Richard. The cold point drew from the vein the dimple gone to flat; a small red frag was all that showed.

"Are you not going to cut me, sir?" the marquis asked as he lay still upon the ground.

"No, I am not; please, get up, sir." Richard put out his hand to help the prone marquis.

"No, sir, I wish you to cut me before I rise."

"For what reason would I do this?"

"For my honour, sire; please, cut my cheek—here." He pointed to his red chub. "For when you become king, I can point to the scar and say 'twas received when I duelled with the King Richard of England."

Before there was any further talk, the blade was flicked and the blood spurted from the struck cheek. Richard had obliged. The marquis took the hand that was reached before him, and then, with kerchief pressed to his cheek, bowed to the prince.

"'Twas an honour to lose to you, my lord," the marquis spake as he dripped away to his chambers. Applause abounded to both of the nobles from the gathered throng, for justice had been done to the satisfaction of all. They all gathered themselves up and went toward the ballroom to end the night that would not be forgotten easily …

The speeding horses skidded and rattled to a stop within the courtyard. Still early of the day with the cockerels bent upon their call, the royal envoy from the court of the King Henry was back to converse with Charles. To come, 'twas hoped, to some agreement on the matter of monies and of "the Warbeck." Held tightly to hand, a scroll he carried sealed with the royal signet, and held secure to present to the King of France. He was brought through the echoing ways to the royal chamber of meet, a closet close to the king's quarters. Sat he the king at wait for the rider that came all of sweat and smell to enter his scented state.

"Greetings, your Majesty, from my royal master," the envoy greeted the king with the most sincere bow and reverence.

"Thank you, sir, and please convey to the King Henry my most devoted affection."

"I will, in pleasure, do so, your Majesty. I have brought to you, sire, an offer from my king that we hope will fulfill both our countries requirements." He held the document toward the King Charles, who beckoned one of his advisers to receive the letter and to make it known to the king of the contents. The adviser snapped open the seal and unrolled the parchment, and after a quick perusal read to the king the gist of the letter.

"To receive from the King of France the sum of one hundred and fifty thousand pounds. And to require that the Perkin Warbeck be handed over for confinement at the king's pleasure." One end of the scroll was loosened as he finished the letter and flew up to its journeyed shape, as all gazed at the king for his voice to the envoy, for war or for peace it would speak.

"My dear sir, we will pay one hundred and forty-nine thousand English pounds in gold to your king. As for the *Perkin Warbeck,* we cannot in true faith give him up to you, for we believe he is of royal blood. And, as royalty, one royal cannot fate the other, nor should not. But we will give some respect to Henry's request by not harbouring the prince. We will ask him, in all respect, to leave our France and urge him to seek sanctuary elsewhere. If your king does agree to such diplomacy then I would say the matter should be closed."

"I believe, sire, your offer is acceptable, for I have been given the authority to sign such documents that are required to bring forth this agreement."

"Then my scribe will prepare the documents with haste so you may soon depart back to your king's favoured shelter."

"Thank you, sire, that will be well suited. May I further request a council with the Perkin Warbeck? for I gather, through gossip, that he is at present within your keep."

"I presume the gossip you refer to is from the agents that Henry has about my palace." The king came with a blunt observation to place before the envoy.

"That, sire, I know nothing of; I am but a devoted servant to my king."

"No matter, sir; spies abound both here and abroad, 'tis a fact we all live with. You are correct in saying that Richard—*Perkin*—is at the moment under my keep. He has just arrived back from some foray, so you are indeed fortunate in your timing. If he agrees then you are, with pleasure, able to see him, for in doing so you will no doubt come to believe in his royal demeanour."

"Yes, your Majesty," the envoy replied in much doubt.

"I will send a message to him of your request, and he will come to you if he is in agreement. You may use this closet for the purpose if you wish."

"Thank you, sire, you are most kind." The royal party left with its advisers and hangers-on, leaving the envoy at wait. Sat he with many thoughts turning in his head. If the imposter does meet with him, to treat him to the dagger would not be apt, but 'twould bring to an end much strife, though his king would frown upon such an action, for a murder within a foreign court would bring out many enemies from many lands where royalty did reside. To council with him then, and may to find some way to bring him to Henry where the matter could be settled without the shed of blood. He looked up from his musings to the sound of the handle pulled, and the rusty creak as the heavy door opened. Stood at the entrance was the so-called pretender, with the dark of the passageway at his back. The light from within the chamber splayed from the window to make the Richard shine like a prince indeed. He showed dressed in regal attire from the French court. A ponce sovereign he wished to appear before this pettifogger of Henry's.

"Good day to you, sire," the envoy greeted the visitor, but offered no bow.

"And a good day to you, sir," Richard replied as he gained the room. A commanding figure with some aura about him, and with features in 'twixt with the King Edward, his reputed father. The thoughts ran again through the head of the envoy to which tack should he take … the road would show itself without doubt.

"Please, sir, let us sit." The seat was beckoned to Richard, which he did not take, for the seat that was shown to him was opposite to the window, and he did not wish to sit in such a place, for the light would show his every twitch, his every frown, and give out more than he wished. So chose he to sit with the window at his back. The envoy sat in the place of the brighter light, which did not suit his tact. "So, you are the gentleman who graces the name of Perkin Warbeck?"

"Piers Osbeck, yes, sir, I am, but the name is used only to protect me from my enemies, who 'twould suit to see me in the throes of death. For I cannot about at this time with my true name: the Prince Richard of York, the last Plantagenet. The last White Rose."

"You believe then that such is your true title?"

"Yes, sir, that is so."

"We have read with much interest the account of your journey from the Tower to this present time. We have read your letters from kings and knights, all to state your legal title, but, as my king decrees, 'tis but drivel, and he will not have it that you are who you say. But, in all trust, he wishes to speak with you, declaring before God of no harm to come to you, whether you be true or be false. If you are true, then he will respect your title, and bestow upon you lands and properties, and will pay you a goodly sum per annum to keep you in your princely fashion. My king wishes no strife to come upon his people by someone wishing to usurp his throne, and so he will keep you in accustomed state to bring you tranquil. On the other hand, if truth is not what you speak, he will pay you a ransom to leave his Isle unharmed, to seek refuge elsewhere."

The prince had sat silent whilst the envoy gave forth his speech, the speech so painted with the brush of kingly deceit, his face not moving with one itch to relay any kind of emotion to the offer. "Sir, I do not have to prove anything to the King Henry; the people of England will decide, and they will know that I am the true prince. As for trusting the King Henry … I think not, for this was the same Henry who, through his devious means and bribes, did cause the betrayal on that field of Bosworth to murder my uncle, the King Richard. *Trust him?* Trust me, sir, your king laughs at the word. I would not leave my dog under his trust. I tell you once, envoy, that I am the Prince Richard, and, until the crown of England is upon my head and the King Henry is subjugated, I will not rest. That is enough of this wasteful chat, for you will never call me *prince*." Richard stood, for the only thing offered to him was to become at best a prisoner of Henry.

"Sir, no matter of my personal view, in respect to my liege, I cannot call you prince."

"Then good day to you, sir." That was all to be said as the envoy was obliged to leave the closet, but the prince could not resist some parting words to lay before the envoy, and to be spoken to the King Henry. "When next we meet, I will be riding at the head of an army so large the king will beg me for *my* compassion, and all those who doubted me will receive their fill."

The envoy had heard all he wished and left the closet to the prince, closing the door behind him for his cajolery lay fruitless. He went straight to the scribe's chamber to come by his promised agreement, and to make much haste to his king with the letter and of the meet with the pretender…

"Please sit, sire." The King Charles and his advisers now governed the same closet, as they sat themselves before the prince. One of the king's advisers spake the words of his monarch. "We talk with little modesty to you, sire. A ransom has been paid to the King Henry so he will not to war upon this land, to which my king is most pleased. Also the King Henry wished to bind the agreement with the seizure of your good self, and for you to be conducted to England and there to be put on trial for treason." Richard sat and listened moving not one finger, as he was able so to do. "Of course my king refused the latter, but to seal the agreement, and to save our land from war, we had to agree that we would not harbour you in this Realm, but to send you out from it. We have sent dispatches to your aunt, the Duchess of Burgundy, who will keep you in sanctuary at her palace at Flanders until the time is ripe for your taking of the crown."

"Do you tell me, sire, that my journey here, and all the promises made to me are all rebuffed and I am once again to my own devices?" The prince was sorely irked at the words that had been said, and could wait no longer to voice his concern.

"No, sir, that is not so, but we do have to tread softly upon this shaking ground, and we must not appear to break any agreement until it is too late for the King Henry to offer any reprise. We hope you see our position in this matter. We will, upon your summons, provide one thousand armed soldiers, and we will finance immediately the sum of five thousand English pounds so you may raise an army for your quest. But all that we offer must be kept confided and only those in this room must know of our commitment. We are behind you, Richard, with all our strength, and will be most honoured to prove ourselves in the field."

"I am deemed most obliged to you for your generosity, sire, and, in time, I will readily call for such as you so offer me. I regret, though, that there are no forces coming from this land at this time that would entice others to my side, so I must quickly depart to take upon myself a different path to the same end."

"On your journey to the Lady Margaret be wary of your tread, my lord, for surely there will be those about who will try to stop your meet with the duchess." The king offered forth some warning to the prince, of the agents that were about who would soon see him murdered.

"We must readily be away then, my king, for delay would bring upon us time for our enemies to prepare against our journey. We bid you all farewell until we meet again when my feet have set themselves upon the soil of England." Richard and Alphonse quickly went to their chamber, and did hastily ready for their journey to the Duchess of Burgundy, for they would feel no safety until they were within her dower. But stirred within them were feelings of betrayal that clouded the promises, and stomachs twisted at the thought.

The dimly lighted passage within the castle, where few would linger, was now inhabited by the English envoy. He stood in the black shadows whispering to an accomplice, who in the dark could only be seen by his even darker shape that quietly yea'd and nay'd in the converse that was being passed. Some plot to hatch, some deed to be done, some blood to slop. Soon the shape was gone and to his waiting ship the envoy went, to ride again the ever wind-blown Channel back to his king, back to the land of his content. But the king would not be a happy king, for he wished this Perkin to be rid of.

Chapter Twenty-two.

Whore's Iron.

"If you are ready, Alph, let us depart this place," Richard spake to his friend as they prepared to leave the palace. They had dressed themselves in drab clothes to mask their heritage and to ease their journey. "Our task here is complete; methinks we have gained all we may from the King Charles, and we must make new friends to add to the pot. The horses are readied and stayed in the dark alley near the gate; the monies are secured in our bags. We must be as the corn in the field and sway with the wind, not a ripple out of place."

Soon all was ready and through the door that was placed discreet they went. The dark was with mist as they slinked about, like black painted to the wall, blended as one and unseen, except for the coin they carried that wished to betray their coming, quietly rattling, knowing not to be silent. The horses at wait were startled as the darkness showed to them the two riders. A whinny and a snort came before the soothing words and the warm hands that patted their hollow brows to satisfy their nervous trait. The pair took the reins, and with no haste led the animals to the outside of the courtyard, stealthily away from the king's palace. They mounted soon in the cover of the forest that lay at the roadway, and went in silent gait slowly until distance dulled their sound and they could not be heard from the courtyard. But eyes did twinkle in the stars' light, peering through the stone arches of the palace to see the two: one a seeker of a kingdom, the other his accomplice, both to quietly slink away to another land to further their aims. They wended further away toward Flanders, to the land of the Duchess Margaret that was held in her dower, and by law a land secure in its borders against all outside factions.

Further into the night the torches of Paris were afar, and then unseen were its flickering lights and oily black smoke. The smell from the sewers no longer hung about the riders, as the clean country breezes blew about them. Soon to a forest track they came that in the night showed no way, except for the moon's light that went from the puffed clouds to the clear sky and then to quickly hide once more. They rode along; quietly was their tread laid upon the leaves and moss of the forest's carpet. No danger to hear, no danger to see, the black night was their shield. They rode until the dawn cragged its light through the mist, and awayed the blackness that had been their cover. To travel only at night was their aim and to rest during the daylight hours. A small town came to view as from the forest they came, to the cleared place that was huddled by a river. In the early morn, few people were about, only some farmers they saw moving their animals along the quiet roadway. Then seen, meats and produce being placed by the merchants upon some stalls that were being readied in the marketplace. Soon the villages from about would awaken and gather this day at the market, for every Wednesday they would do such, with some to travel many miles to barter and bid. The two travellers made track for the yard that was aback the small inn; this was the place they would rest, for weary they were and wished only for sleep. Chattels and horse bags were removed, as the horses were taken to feed by the two lads, raggedy fellows, both tugging and pulling the sweating animals into the stalls, to soon choff* upon the hay golden.

They entered the inn with their baggage — some slung over the shoulder, other pieces in hand. Quickly sorted was the price with the keeper; they fell into their room. The room that had been in mind for much of the last hours of their ride. So fatigued were they that still in their dust and grime, they lay upon their cots and fell asleep, as the street outside increased its sounds to bustle and shout. The calling of wares for sale, the rattle of carts, and the dogs at bark did not in any dream awaken the travellers. This day they did not walk in the sun, they did not shoot game. No lovers' tryst came to light; the time forever lost in slumber's deep. The church clock had struck the noon hour before they awoke, with mouths slimy of taste and smelled garb. To the tub they went, splashing and rubbing until most grime was cleaned away. They dried themselves upon the hung cloths, and put back on the clothing that they had worn for many miles; they stood not in the sweetest of smells, for there was no time to scrub clean the drab cloth; another day would have to dawn before any change would come. They took to victuals in their room and stomached all they could, awaiting the late of the day to shield them from prying eyes.

Richard glanced from the window at the street below, eyeing the mob that busied themselves, mingling about with vendors and merchants. But more he saw as coming from the narrow lane afar ... horsemen, their manner not of local folk, but more with a military bearing they, forcing their mounts through the jostle. They were strangers and were not given any standing by the people they bruised, who blocked their coming in some common cause of dislike; they shoved and shouted loudly as they stopped the riders still. Yes, Richard thought, they were military, for 'twas

---

* *choff* [coined] a combination of chomp and chaff

the reason the crowd were up against them. They had the bearing of some English troop and if they were the orders they did carry it would not be to his liking. He glimpsed the swords and the daggers that showed partly hidden beneath their cloaks and knew 'twas no time to tarry. The two travellers moved with haste, gathering up their bags and chattels that lay about, and made from the haven of the inn's walls to the stable below. The lads there soon had their mounts ready; quickly a coin given and they were away to move from the coming confrontation, to speed with dusty blow all about them, unseen by the murderers who were still bogged by human mud. No hindrance came upon the travellers, as soon they were into the hills that wrapped about them to hide all now from any seekers.

"Trouble for us is about, Alphonse," Richard spake as they slowed their gait entering the forest's track, with cool breezes under the tunnels of branch and leaf. "The spies about must have seen our departure from the palace of Charles; we are under eye, my friend. We must not show ourselves at all and we must stay clear of inns and such, for we will be as a pigeon upon a post, sitting in preening style to be cut down easily by the hunter's shaft."

Slowly on they went, slumping in their saddles as the time wore on. The horses seemingly knowing the way of the path needed no guidance. Upon this way they travelled for two full days, eating what they carried and sleeping among the thick bushes that hugged the trail.

"Methinks, Alph, with the time we have spent travelling we should soon be within Flanders; I have a good feeling it could be this day," Richard spake with some weariness to his friend. "I feel sure we will see some sign soon." They continued upon the winding path that had become a steady climb for the last mile, broke out upon the top of a hill where a small clearing gave them a view ahead, and there in the valley below lay a small town. They stilled their horses and took upon themselves a moment to rest, and to see if they could find some mark that would make known to them the place they looked upon, but from where they gazed naught could be seen.

"What town do you think it may be, Richard?"

"I know not, Alphonse; it could be Arras, but I see no steeple; all we can pray is that it will be friendly to us. Come, let us ride on." They pulled their horses to the downward track and in little time had reached the town's walls. A few peasants sat outside cooking something foul upon the open fire they had struck there. Though hungry, the smell did not tempt them. They came through the open gate and along the dusty track that led them to the many people within. They too set in their own doings to mind the strangers who entered the gate. They warily looked about, and amongst the different folk that busied about, Richard saw groups of soldiers lingering, only lightly armed and seemingly in a time of relaxation; some looking over the goods upon the stalls, others supping ale outside the tavern. But what struck the most was the uniform they wore. Black 'twas with trim of gold, white stockings, and boots of black. All wore the emblemed hat with the black lion rampant, with red claws and tongue showed there upon yellow. The insignia of the Duchess of Burgundy, who did reside in the dower of Flanders.

"We are safe, Alph; this is the town of Arras … See the old church there?—that is the church of the Saint Stephen; we could not see its steeple, for it had burned and has not yet been rebuilt. We can relax, my friend, and sup some good victuals and make some pleasant sleep." Richard hugged his friend with the relief of knowing soon they would be well cared for in the palace at Malines. They led their horses through the crowd that mulled about and, upon reaching the inn, left the animals in the care of the lads there. Then the two sat within the inn, a table of victuals before them with a jug of ale spilling its top. They savoured every morsel and licked every drip, and when they could sup no more, away they drifted to their rooms above. They washed themselves of all the smells that reeked their bodies, and then lay in pleasant, like Morpheus, upon their cots that drifted to the clouds.

The sun lighted the chamber to bring them forth bright and strong, to continue their way. They stopped only one more night upon the journey, and upon the following day made with good speed to the town of Malines, and to the residence of the duchess. Late of the day they came to the walls of the palace, showing tall and white in the rays of the dipping sun. They came around them to find the iron gates stood by guards and, coming closer, 'twas seen the only entrance of the residence.

"Hold there!" one of the guards called out as he stepped from his station and barred the entrance. "What do you seek here?" he queried at the dishevelled pair. Richard and Alphonse both dropped from their saddles to crack their ailing bones, and to stretch a little from their seat of discomfort before Richard answered the guard.

"Sir, I have a letter here from the King Charles … to grant me an audience with your most honourable mistress, my aunt, Margaret. The said lady having received a message by a carrier to the effect I relate." He handed over to the guard's outstretched hand the scroll with its red seal atop. The guard quickly glanced at the writ and then bade them to wait whilst he reported to the officer of the house. He strode away leaving the other guard to stand the gate, as the travellers took this time to stand and loll about whilst they awaited his return.

"My fellow guard will be but a short while, sires; I regret that you have to wait," the second guard stated, trying not to bring too much hardship upon the travellers, for the carriers of royal documents may wield more than they seemed.

The palace rang to the sound of the guard's boots as he stomped his military step into the lavish hall. He made toward a small table of the duty officer who sat with little to do. Two more guards stood at the back of the officer's chair, with a young page nearby dressed most aptly as a servant boy with his white shirt and black jodhpurs, he stood scratching and twitching about as he waited for some duty to perform. Stood he far too long this day, with too many games to play elsewhere than to be so encumbered by some trivial labour. The table was placed there in the shadow of the great staircase, which loomed behind like some giant fall of water. A stairway indeed that led to unseen pleasures and intrigues within its closed doors.

"Sir."

"What do you have, soldier?"

"Two travellers, sir," the guard related to the slumping officer. "They come with sealed letters from the King Charles to our Lady Margaret." He handed over the scroll, which was closely perused by the officer, and, after searching again at the seal, was well satisfied that indeed 'twas from the king. He quickly swung around to face the startled boy who had been dreaming of more important things.

"Here, boy, take this to the duchess, and hasten your way." The boy snatched quickly the scroll and made away as fast as he could muster, as the booted foot swung to miss his rear by a cat's whisker, for the officer took great pleasure in abusing the lad, until it had become some sort of game to him. But his nimble quick had this time escaped the brute. Up the water's fall he ran, pulling upon the high rail to help his way. At the top, all he could see were the legs of the guards, of maids at scurry, at butlers all aloof. Then the regal chamber showed before him, its great wooden door looked as some unclimbable mountain. He gazed up with cricked neck to peer the faces of the guards stood at the entrance.

"Important message for the duchess," he called up. The door was opened and he was admitted in, though slowed now was his step as he came toward the lady's adviser who took the letter from the chubby hand.

"Wait here!" Roughly came the order to the meeked lad. "And, for the Lord's sake, stand still." This time he was not quick enough, as the rolled message was delivered with a loud whack upon the boy's head to emphasize the order.

"Yes, sir," the boy answered with hand upon head as if in some great distress.

The adviser turned with his long coat sweeping the stone floor as he went his way. His long sleeves sloped down to almost cover his hands and to make the scroll almost unseen.

"A message from the King Charles, my lady."

"Read it to me, Simon." The sweet lilting voice played like a harp across the chamber where dwelt the duchess. Sat she upon a high chair. Beauty was a poor name for this lady whose charm engaged all. Her long hair drifted upon her back, like ocean waves it played upon her gown of black, corn ripe upon the dark peat. Her eyes, clear and bright, blessed green and hypnotic to gaze. The white skin of her bosom showed full as was the French style. A tantalizing young woman showed. But cleverly wicked was she with scholarly mind. A dangerous foe, a dangerous friend; careful must be the tread about this duchess.

"'Tis from Charles, my lady, stating more facts than from his last dispatch; he seems most taken by the lad. The letter is an introduction to the nephew of your good self, the said Prince Richard of York. Our Charles deems, that by all accounts of the letters showed and a thorough search for truth, our Richard to be the true and rightful heir to the throne of England."

"Is that so, my lord? He is not a pretender then?"

"Seemingly not, my lady; he carries many letters to the effect of his right. He wails on that, under the threat of the English Henry, he cannot succour the said prince within his kingdom, and deemed him to seek sanctuary in your court, my lady, until the time is apt for him to reclaim the throne, that in all rights is his belonging. That is the gist of the letter, madam."

"Most interesting, my dear Simon. This could be very much to our advantage, do you not think?—for it matters not if he is the heir or if he is not. If enough people believe him to be so, then all who ride upon his wagon will arrive at the fair."

"True, my lady, but I think after we have met him, then we will know what kind of clay we have. If he is naught but some parvenu we waste our time. But if he is liken to us we may help him and fill our pockets in his cause, and aught that we may reap can do us little harm, do you not agree, madam?"

"Yes, my lord, I so agree. If he is true, then well for us, if he is not, I shall teach him all he needs to know to deceive any who may question his claim. Bring him to the blue chamber when he is prepared. For the moment, let him rest and have him bathed, make available suitable garb and plenty of victuals, then we will chat to him. Does he have servants?"

"It seems just one, my lady … more of a companion than a servant."

"Then give to them a maid and a manservant to fetch for them. And Simon—"

"Yes, my lady."

"Keep that harlot away from him; he is for my play and will not be for her enjoyment." The sweet voice changed not its tone but daggered were the words spoken.

"I will do as you request immediately, my lady." With respectful bow and a tip of his stately cap he left the Lady Margaret, and upon his way from the chamber began to push the unhurried page before him. "Go on, boy, go on. What ails you that you cannot move at some respectable pace?" The boy stumbled and half fell from the long-striding man above him; four steps to one was all his legs could muster, as he was poked and shoved along like some sow to the market. Soon they were down at the entrance, where awaited Richard and Alphonse, leaning their wearied selves against the cold wall, more fatigued now that their journey at the moment had ended. "Go on, boy," they heard as the farmer with his pig came close. "Good day, sirs, I am Simon Le Bowe, chief adviser to the duchess. We pray that you fare well?"

"Good day, my lord; we do indeed fare well but are troublesome weary."

"Come then, let us pamper you so that you soon will be renewed. Please, this way, sirs." He led the two toward the stairway.

Two black eyes of allure fluttered from within the high window of the palace, watching the meet below. Resting they upon the proud young body of the likely prince, with sight came the desire to wither his knees, the thought bringing a heave to her bosom and a quiver in her stomach, as another likely noble had come to be lured into the chamber of the harlot. Catherine was she, the younger stepsister to the duchess. Though she did not possess the ravishing beauty of her sister, her seductive air was proving far more of an advantage. Her body was renowned for its softness and allure. As clouds and silk, of thick cream 'twas oft described, and 'twas told that once bedded by this angel, no other would seem as soft, but would be as dry as grass cut upon the yesterday, compared to the charms of Catherine. And whereupon she would be the only satisfaction, and when 'twas so, 'twas others she would then seek, for old loves she would harbour not, but to leave them in muddled mind. Much was the frustration of the Duchess Margaret, who had lost many a lover to the sister in name, and had vowed she would lose no other.

The half-seen figure watched from above until the party could be seen no more. Her black hair swirled as she turned back into the chamber, her eyes sparkling, her lips wetted, her desire surfaced.

"I know of that look, my lady. What have you seen?" Catherine's closest waiting lady queried her mistress.

"'Twas the young prince, so rumoured to arrive amongst us; he strides so handsomely. I think he may wish to bed me; what do you think, Marie?"

"I think, my lady, you should tread most carefully where this one is concerned, for would you not think that Margaret will covet him, being that he may be the next King of England?"

"I care not for my sister. If the charms she offers are less than mine then it is all to amour, and that, my dear, is the case, for I will only have to bed him once and he will be ours." She fell back upon her cot laying her plans of seduction, not to *if,* but to *when* ...

The voice rang about the hall, "Where have you been?" The officer on duty shouting and shaking the scrawny neck of the boy upon his return, finishing his tirade with a loud whack about the head that echoed the hollow chamber as a crow clapper* might. The party glanced back at the sound of the strike, and the "Owe!" from the boy, but continued to their chamber, with the pain he suffered still ringing their ears.

"The blue chamber, sir; one of the finest we have and reserved only for the most noble of visitors. Will your servant be staying with you, sire?"

"Yes, he will, my lord; though he is not my servant, nor to anyone else a servant. He is my most devoted friend and adviser who I wish to keep by my side."

"That is well, sir. We will send to your chamber a manservant and a maid to do your bidding as you may wish, and they will be yours for as long as you are a guest within these walls."

"Thank you, sir; your generosity is most appreciated."

"Then, sirs, eat your fill of the provisions, rest, and bathe. The maid will bring you suitable garments. We can meet in the Duchess Margaret's closet when you have recovered yourselves, and there she will formally greet you." With no more ado he was gone to his duties. As the door closed, Richard and Alphonse perused the chamber that shone in its elegance and brightness.

"Yes, Alphonse, this room is most definitely blue." They laughed together as they flailed upon the beds, laying like angels upon the clouds of heaven. A rap upon the oak door brought in the maid and the manservant, followed by a kitchen skivvy, pushing a wheeled table piled with victuals of the most tempting sort. They gorged upon the meats and breads, and

---

* *crow clapper* two flat pieces of board hinged together to flap and create noise when its handle is shaken

upon the pastries and fruits, all swilled with different varieties of wine and ales, until no more could they continue in their gluttony.

"Come, sirs, may we now prepare you to meet with the duchess?" The servants had stood at their posts whilst the travellers had reached their fill, and were now wishing to perform their duties.

"Not yet, my man," slurred came the speech from the mouth of Richard. "We will sleep first, then we will ready." Near as quickly as the words were spoken was the time they took to slumber, to do so at the place where they sat, for they could not gather themselves to any cot or to any settle. The maid and the manservant looked at each other and decided there was little use to wait, and so moved quietly from the chamber to await without, and to listen for some stirring from the deep sleep they had grasped.

'Twas the morn's light that shone upon them as they awoke, feeling much refreshed as they had had their sleep's fill. They lifted from their strange beds with bones that cracked, for they had not moved for many hours and now complained to do so. The servants upon hearing the stirring sounds came from their nodding rest, and were soon busied about the chamber, bathing and dressing the two visitors, combing their tangled hair that had grown to mid-back in its curled folds. They ate and drank a small amount of food and ale that had been fetched into the chamber. Their mouths were then rinsed and picked clean with the wooden tangs by the servants, who probed and flicked the matter from the teeth of the visitors. They were soon ready in their finery with lace and silk draping their skin; they smelled much sweeter now with the scented oils and powders that had been caressed upon them. A final wipe of the shined boots by the maid saw them ready to be presented to the Lady Margaret. A page had been dispatched to see if 'twas the pleasure of the duchess to meet at this hour, and 'twas deemed so convenient, and that the council would be set for the twelve of the clock.

And as from the far abbey was heard the bells' toll, the troop of Richard, Alphonse, and their servants made way from the chamber of blue to walk the carpeted way to the closet of the duchess. They passed along to many admiring eyes and pleasant acknowledgements from the courtiers who were about. They to be seen and to catch what gossip they may of the man who would be king. Richard stepped along with pleasing face at the respect being bestowed, but the face he looked upon next did not offer such as the others, but offered more without words spoken or curtsy displayed. The black eyes beckoned with enticing innocence, the lips as strawberries; 'twere all he could gather in his glanced passing, but set in his mind was the creature he had spied, and caused the worm of desire to squirm within his stomach. Catherine had begun her seduction of a king.

From a draped cove, eyeing every sign and every movement that the Lady Catherine made, a tall lady watched. Only for a short while did she so but 'twas enough to see the words that were being writ, as then she took herself discreetly back into the hidden folds of the dark cloth, to click the door hid and return unseen to her mistress's closet.

The closet door of the duchess came to view for Richard's entourage. High and wide it stood, all of black oak and rusted iron, and crested upon 'twas the dragon of Burgundy, black, red, and gold, glinting bright in the candlelit passage. A guard stood each side with knife and sword, each sheathed and hanging from its baldric. Held they pike of great length, the blade polished and sharp as it took to the grey walls above. Both were bearded with capped heads and hair cropped at the neck; they looked straight ahead and seemed not to see aught. But upon the party's approach, as if by some magical sign, they both at the same instant pushed open the doors to the closet as wide as they would go, as if two horses side by side were to enter rather than the spindly group that came. They entered to a lavish place of tapestries and rich carpets. Murals and silken drapes hung upon the walls and windows. Heavy oak seats were about, as they saw at the far of the closet the desirable Margaret, sat she upon a most elegant chair that was placed upon a raised platform. The allure of the duchess beguiled Richard at the very first sight of her.

"Good day, my dear cousin, if I may be so bold as to utter such," Richard spake as he with bowed ceremony approached the high chair.

"You may in all pleasure say such if you, in all truth, are my cousin, sir."

"In truth I do speak, and it will be a most joyful task to relate to you of the circumstance that has been placed before me, and knowingly that after such you will, in all respect, call me your dear cousin, Richard of York."

"We pray it is so, my lord," the lady answered as best she could. Alphonse stood aback as Richard was brought a seat and beckoned to sit before the duchess, though 'twas upon the lower level placed and not upon the platform where sat Margaret and three more peoples. "You are converse with my adviser, are you not?" The duchess waved so slightly her hand toward the gentleman who stood by her side. His black robes hid what shape he was. From neck to floor they hung; his glinting rings showed though that he was not all drab.

"The Marquis Simon Le Bowe at your service, sir," spake the adviser, his short bow showed of some respect .

"A good day again to you, sir," acknowledged Richard.

"These are my two companions," the duchess continued as she waved to the other side of the platform in the same manner. "Antonio Bercholi, who teaches me music and song, and reads to me all manner of books, and is indeed most learned." A short swarthy man was he, weighted heavily around the stomach, and dressed in bright colours as a jester might. He seemed not to think he dressed any more unusual than anyone else, and one could only think that he could see no colour from his eyes but greys and blacks. His looks were not appealing, with hooked nose and teeth missing; he appeared not a likely gigolo. Margaret did affirm the observation with words that placed the picture within the frame. "Pray, though, sir, be not concerned on what you see, for he is a prized eunuch."

Taken aback by the remark, Richard saw upon the face of the duchess a wicked smile and the twinkling eyes, as she watched for the reaction that would show. He knew not if she spake the truth, but he wished not to find out.

"So be it, my lady," was all he could utter from his bewitched tongue, as once more the duchess continued on, with Richard at wonder if any more surprises would be unfolded.

"And this is the Lady Marcela De Boer, my most close companion." A fine-looking lady was seen, tall and slender, with straight black hair to her shoulders melting into her black dress, tight and restrictive, making little the need to ponder the shape that warmed beneath. Her hands showed as white as snow against her attire, her nails long, filed and polished to perfection. Her face was powdered white with hinted red upon the cheeks. A strong woman standing decidedly close to her duchess. "The lady is at times my bedded companion." As the most recent intrigue was uttered before Richard, the duchess held out her hand to finger the pale digits that hung from the black cloth of the Lady Marcela. The eyes of the duchess suddenly upped, flashing to Richard once again to seek his reaction, but naught she saw of any, for he was readied for any remark made to disturb his demeanour that may be spoken by his cousin. "We will bring your seat so you may sit close by us." She beckoned one of the servants forward from his half-hidden station, to place now the seat where she directed. He sat, again almost opposite the tantalizing duchess, as she leaned toward Richard that he may search her décolletage, doing so whilst still holding the fingers of Marcela. "Let's to it then, my dear." The voice broke into Richard's stirring thoughts of the desire that welled for her. He knew the act that had been placed upon him was to unmind his head, and the story he was to tell, and to make him stumble. As to pull from the one-legged man his crutch. He withdrew his eyes and composed himself.

"I will relate to you all I remember from my time as a child until all I have gathered to this time, when my eyes have lit upon yourself in your wicked pleasure." The duchess could not resist a tickling smile from the corner of her mouth but did not show more. And so he did chat for time long, with each in and out, of each failure, and of each triumph, until all was told to the querying gaze of the Lady Margaret.

"Your story is most intriguing, my dear," she spake as one would to a chucklehead, and gave the impression of believing little of the story unfolded. "You will not be troubled if I ask of you more delicate questions regarding your tale?"

"Not at all, madam; I have naught to hide."

"You mention not the Day of the Virgins. Do you know of this?"

"Yes, madam, I do know of it. I wished though not to mention it, for it is not one of the most pleasing memories I care for. But, madam, if you wish me to relate it to you then I will." The duchess nodded for Richard to proceed. Her council continued to bring forth as much turmoil as she could to his mind. He knew that this would be the way. "I saw my father, upon what came to be known as 'the Day of the Virgins,' perform his duties upon those young maidens who waited patiently in line for such. And then to grasp, as some deed to a mansion, the notarized papers from the clerk, to skip like children with sugared plums into the debauched world." Margaret offered no remark from the words so spoken but continued on to her next inquiry.

"You talk of paintings that did hang in the palace at the Tower."

"I know of many paintings that hung there, madam; is there any one in particular you wish me to mention?"

"The one I wish to refer to is the one that hangs over the fireplace in the Great Hall. There were dogs upon that picture … Do you recall what kind of dogs were so painted there?"

Richard did not answer straight, but wished to give some thought to the scene that lay misty in his mind. As he faltered, the pouting red lips showed the white teeth, once more conspired to disrupt his thoughts. "I … I … think they were beagles." For the first time the words did not drip like honey from his lips. His mind tried for the truth, but was washed to a blur by the ways of the lady and his own long-discarded recollections.

"They were hounds! Do you really know what was upon those walls?" A coarse tone came to her voice as she teased his bumbled head.

"I was sure they were beagles, my lady."

"Well, they were not, sir!" Her eyes flashing as she spake, and then to sit back in her chair and wait. Then spake she. "Were you there at your father's lecherous dinners?"

"I was not at the table sat, but I was able to spy the goings-on from time to time, and did see some evildoings."

"What saw you?" The duchess leaned herself forward once again so that she might not miss one word spoken. The sweet musky aroma of her perfume wafted about as she came close, bringing her intoxication upon Richard to become more submissive to her ways. The adviser and the lady's companions were all the while looking upon him, most with a demeaning gaze, as they listened to his mumbling jibe that seemed but a tale.

"I was only of a few years old and it seemed to have little reason to me, but parties were arranged and as always the guests were chosen by my father. And being that 'twas at the king's request, then none could refuse the royal invitation; as you are aware, my lady, such a slight against the monarch would bring down his hand hard upon any who so demeaned him. At times I saw him with different ladies, toing and froing to the king's chambers. And only now that I am more of age do I know the happenings played."

"You remember much, my dear, for such a child as you were." The duchess spake for the first time with some kindness towards Richard. "I will tell you such of my dealings within this shame, for I was one of those ladies who was called upon with my husband to attend such a dinner. We accepted with joyous hearts, for to dine with the king was not granted to all, and we felt much honour in being asked. But turned that 'twas not a king with compassion who headed that table, but some vile and lecherous person. I tell you this regardless of any memories of good and happiness you may bestow upon him. For some day you may need to know such as I speak if you are to pass for a prince. For knowing not all things could bring your journey to naught's end.

"All manner of society were asked to attend and all did seat at the royal table; many knew of the king's appetite and waited with much trepidation. My husband and I had heard many whispers of the goings-on, but dismissed it as gossip, for a king could not act with so little chivalry. And then 'twas revealed that at any time during the sup, whether the fish or the meat or the sweet pastries, that the king felt inclined, and to feel inclined he often did, he would point his finger to anyone he desired, and the lady would have to part from her husband, and would have to follow the king to his chamber, whereupon the lady would be bedded and ravished by the monarch to no recourse. After the act the king would be washed and readied by his servants to prepare for another encounter if he wished. The lady was left to care for herself, and to return to her place in such dishevelled state, flustered and embarrassed, to sit by her husband who was as helpless as a sheep, whose lamb had been taken by the wolf. This though was not enough for the king, who salted the wound by describing to the husband the act taken upon his wife, and to rate her lovemaking to his sadistic scale.

"Many invited to such dinners would dress most drably, would not comb their wigs, would wear no rouge upon their cheeks or lips. Their eyes they would not lighten, for they wished them not to be appealing. Spots and pockmarks were not hid but were displayed to all. To wash, they would not, so their odour was much displeasing. But it mattered not of their look or of their smell, for 'twas only the king's pleasure to lift their skirts and then to ravage someone else's property, for no other reason than to show that he could without reprise do so."

"Speak no more of it, madam, for I am filled with remorse and sickness; tears break my eyes with such cruelty."

"That which I speak of is so and did happen to me but once, and I swore it would not happen again, for if we were again called, my husband and I, I would carry my knife and stab him in the throes of it. Then, one day, 'twas in the summertime, when all was warm and of gentleness, we were called to dine at the palace. We would not face the situation again, and so we gathered as many of our chattels as we could, and we then fled ourselves to Flanders. To leave behind all our properties and lands. But fate did strike once again, for my husband was struck by some malady and was soon passed to God's keep. I did then marry the Duke of Burgundy, who, 'twas said, was many times my years, and 'twas soon after that he did not awaken from his bed. And so my state is as you see it. But I still wish my lands and my properties to be returned to me, that which lay in that England close. But until Henry is done I cannot; but, my cousin, you could be the latch to the gate in your ambitions.

"'Tis all true that which I speak, and you must know such detail, for this can be a learning story of God's vengeance upon such acts. For did Henry not reap his justice in the end, ravaged with the whore's disease, rotted away bit by bit as he lived and watched himself decay? All of his debauchery was laid upon him, overcome by the fate that the Lord had metered."

Richard sobbed as a child's toy found broken. His revered father painted as the devil was hard to sit. He bore the remorse for all the pain that was laid upon so many honourable ladies in such evil of times.

The hand, soft and caring, caressed upon his neck. "Do not take your father's deviations as your shame, my cousin, for you have the way to become king, and in doing so you will have the power to show to all your kindness and pleasant state, to be a fine and fair ruler, and able to change laws to better your countrymen. And indeed to show all you are *not* your father." The duchess consoled her cousin with caring affection, and he was now more of a man than he was before.

"Marcela, has the Lady Catherine yet made any more advances to our prince?" The duchess spake to her confidante in the dimly-lit chamber, where they sat upon the same bench in the fire's glow.

"No, my lady, only made was the eye contact yesterday, but I will continue to watch her most closely."

"Please do, my dear, for you know well that if she makes no advances to him it will be for the first time, which I deem will be most unlikely. He is too valuable to us to be seduced by that lady, who will turn him into potters' clay and not into a king."

"She is under watch, madam; we will know her every move."

"Have you had any progress with her waiting lady—Marie, is it not?"

"Yes, madam, that is so. She is most devoted to the Lady Catherine that she finds it most deceitful to break her trust. But I have hinted that her mistress's games will, one day, end in some circumstance where she may be unable to enjoy the company of servants, for her means to do so may not suffice. And, at your suggestion, I did promise that if she gave us the information we desire about her lady, then we would, when the time came, bring her into our fold and to be in our employ, which seemed to reassure her to her actions."

"And of her tendencies, did she seem receptive to your advances?"

"Well, my lady, she did not rebuke me or utter any desire for me to desist."

"So you think, Marcela, that upon her deflection she may wish to join us in our privacy?"

"With a little more time to bend her, I do not see, madam, why she would not." The duchess was cold towards the Lady Catherine, but decidedly warmed at the thought of the Lady Marie.

The morrow had come to see the late afternoon as Richard made to the chamber closet of Margaret. He strode alone along the dim-lit passageway with its dark alcoves and curtained ways. Composed and elated was he with all the evildoings aback of him and some lightness was gained to his stride. The drape before him swayed to catch his step, and seen were two eyes from the dim folds gazing back at him. Two engaging eyes of black showed first, then could all be seen of the Lady Catherine and her fineness.

"Good day to you, my prince. You seem in some haste in your journey. Is there a lover that awaits your coming?" Richard was taken aback, first by the sight of the lady, and then by the bluntness of the question that needed some kind of answer, though hard to come by, under the gaze of the one who stood before him. But an answer to the probe was not needed it seemed, for she continued on in her likely manner. "If you are, sir, upon some tryst, then no matter who the lady may be she will not match my offerings. And, sir, if you are not bent upon such a journey, why not let me offer you some comfort within my chamber. Upon the morrow would be of suit—what say you, sir?" She put forth her hand that he may kiss the pale skin that lay warm in his fingers, and after the softness had blessed his lips he looked into the face of desire. The lady tempted him into the drape's folds, with her warm body pressed against his in the dusty heaven. Her mouth he could resist no more, as he felt the silken lips upon his own, the warmest and softest ever plied to him. The desire was strong but the place was not such to dally. Richard managed to squirm from the entangled body of the lady, and with flushed face stepped away from the web.

"My lady, I beg of you, please do not continue, for I cannot be seen in such circumstances, and may I suggest that you should not also."

Catherine straightened her attire in the hide of the drapes, and came out into the passageway to still press herself towards her prince, having no shame to her actions. "So, sire, will you come to my chamber upon the morrow?—I promise you many delights."

"Yes, my lady, I will come to you. Do you have a time that you wish me there?"

"I will send to you a note with my waiting lady to inform you when it will be the most suitable hour. I look forward to your company, my dear prince." She turned and waltzed her way down the passage, giving one final glance at Richard as she turned the corner. She saw him watching her desired body, and knew he would soon be completely in her seductive cage.

The would-be prince straightened his garb and shook as best he could the thoughts of the liaison with the Lady Catherine. He continued on to the closet of the duchess, hardly believing now the circumstances played but minutes ago. The door of the chamber swung open for him as he went through the closet and into the private domain of the duchess. The heady perfume once more drifted its enticing call that always told of her presence, an intoxicating musk of desire.

"Good day, my dear cousin. You may kiss me." The words of "my dear cousin" meant all he had hoped for, and he was obliged to be known as the Prince Richard within this place turned so dear to him. Margaret called the prince to her closeness; the sullied yesterday, but a minute in life, was misted and gone. He came to her with those eyes of the lady flashing, and her skin of cream and honey were before his lips, as he made to kiss the offered cheek. But the face to be kissed turned of slight and 'twas the soft-giving lips that met his, akin to some succulent peach opened upon a summer's day, all moist and warm it covered his own, but for a moment it did linger, then pulled away, to part from such divine pleasure as the fluttered eyes. "Come, my dear, sit before me." Her hand reached for his and brought him gently to the seat that was placed close. "Let me continue to instruct you, cousin dear, for all that you know, you must know more."

A screech from the antechamber disturbed the moment. Came from there some strange noise; not known to Richard was the sound he heard; a cry in the forest's night. Three cats, as if chased by the devil, came out, shrieking and wailing, as if in some anguish. "It is just some of our cats; please, do not be of concern."

"But there seems to be many of such roaming about the palace; everywhere I tread there seems a cat scurries."

"There were many rats and mice about but a short while past; the cats were brought in to end their free roam, and have in short spate done so. Though we are now blessed with more cats than there were mice." The door to the chamber opened wider, and some discreet person, to silently close the door once again, ushered the felines out.

"Come, Richard, let us continue our teachings. What like is your etiquette?"

"'Tis good, my lady."

"And your attire … We must seek out for you more elegant clothes as suited more to your state." All idle chat, thought Richard; this is not the reason I am placed here this day. But then came quickly the reason he was placed so, and without any falter 'twas put to him.

"And your lovemaking … Is it adequate, or are you naive?" He did not answer. "Come with me … Be not shy." She held out her hand and lifted him from his seat; as he gazed at his divine cousin, her ankles showed, her décolletage dipped to please him, her desire for teaching came to bring all parts to play. She led him slowly to the bed. With most of her clothes deftly shed, she lay upon the silken sheets. "Show me, my dear, all you have learned of the art." He came to the bed and laid beside his cousin still not yet disrobed. "Come, Richard, take off your breeches and play your song upon me." Soon she had him to her liking, and made time slip into its fog as the eve wore to night, but deemed that the prince would need many more lessons to bring him to the state that a prince must be. "We will continue on the morrow, my dear one. You will need all the attention I can give for you to be a worthy lover."

"Yes, my lady," spake Richard, as quickly dressed he made his way toward the door.

"And cousin—" she spake as he opened the door.

"Yes, cousin?" He half turned to answer the duchess.

"The dogs—"

"Yes?"

"They were beagles."

"You witch!"

"Yes, I know," she laughed mischievously, as she closed the door to her chamber and Richard left the lady of the night.

Marcela came softly to the chamber of her mistress, slipping in through the partially opened door, barely wide enough for her body to squeeze through. Then quietly she closed it behind her, to turn toward the Lady Margaret who was seated close by the window. Darkness had fallen, and only the candle that flickered upon the table by her showed her presence there. The waiting lady came closer to her mistress, who saw in the dim light the face that bore little happiness. She had awaited the coming of the Lady Marcela, and knew in her mind the tattle she would bring would not be pleasing to her. Margaret beckoned for the lady to sit, wafting about the candle's flame as she did so. All else was of silence within the chamber except for the cat that would not hush.

"So, Marcela, what joyous news do you bring to me?"

"I regret, my lady, it is not joyous tidings I bring, but of deceitful acts within your roof."

"Continue on, for I have no doubt that I can surmise what you have to state."

"It appears, my lady, that the Lady Catherine has made the most ambitious advances to the Prince Richard, and has brazenly seduced him in one of the dark alcoves of your palace." The duchess sat still and showed at the moment little emotion as the deceit against her unfolded. But the waiting lady knew the quietness was not a good sign to the lady who had taken little note of her wishes. "It also seems that some liaison has been proffered and the poor struck boy has accepted the offer."

"I have told that whore to keep her step from this prince, but she seems not willing to listen." The lady paused for a moment. "Go now, Marcela, and bring her forth to me. I will warn her one last time, and then if she takes my words as false it will all be done with her."

"Yes, my lady, I will go direct." Marcela lifted her skirts and made quickly away to the chambers of the Lady Catherine. Whereupon stating the duchess's request, the Lady Catherine was only too willing and indeed seemed somewhat anxious for the confrontation. They left the chambers and walked the shaded passageways to Margaret's chambers; Marcela, the Lady Catherine, and her faithful lady-in-waiting, Marie, all in close step came.

She sat upon her high chair so she may be above the one she had to call sister.

The Lady Marie and the Lady Marcela placed themselves close to the door's drapes, away from the words to be spoken. There they stayed in the dimmed light, as the Lady Catherine flounced with little shame to the place she was beckoned and stood indignant as the lighted candle flickered upon her person.

"Sister dear, did I not give you warning to keep your self away from the Prince Richard?"

"Yes, you did, dear sister, and did I not say that I would not? … and that amour was all that will decide who he is bedded with?"

"He is the heir to the throne of England and much depends for us that he does so become king, and that nothing alters his path to that end. We cannot have him twisted and lost as to his cause, for if he is lured to your folds he will become some spineless worm to your bidding, and that, my sister, cannot be."

"That is not your choice, sister, nor my choice, but the choice of the prince, and if he chooses to dwell in my company over any allegiance to you then it would not be my doing. For I believe what I offer him is more inducing than fighting in some muddy field far away in the middle of that rain-washed land that is most dull and boring. What, my lady, if you stood in his boots, would your choice be?"

"For the good of my people I would place myself up to the neck in mud if it meant the throne of England. I will say now this to you: you are forbidden to make any encounters with the prince. The liaison you have arranged in your bedchamber will be no more, and you will send him a note to such. I am sure you can come forward with some excuse to this effect. And I warn you—and this, dear one, is the last warning I shall give you: do not harbour him, for you will compromise the possession you cherish more than all else."

"What will you do? Tie me down, straddled and naked, for the rats to chew upon me where they may? I fear not such gossip and will do as I please."

"In mind for you I have far more lingering things than the quick bite of a rat. A life of misery for you; so beware, my fair sister, and heed my words."

The Lady Catherine huffed, lifted up her skirts, and left the warnings within the chamber of the duchess. Flounced then her scolded self back to her chamber, with Marie trying all to keep up with her hastening mistress.

"Bring pen and paper, Marie. I have a note for you to take to Richard."

"Yes, madam," replied her lady and fetched she the things asked for, then did not she say to Catherine any words of caution, for she knew she was bent upon her ways, and if the duchess could not deter her, then a waiting lady would have little hope in doing so. But was coming to the mind of Marie that her mistress was upon the path of destruction, and now was the time to make good the offer proffered from the Lady Marcela, for this ship would soon sink and was coming quickly the time to abandon it. She took the brief note from her mistress, secreted it within the folds of her dress, and made as discreetly as she may to the chamber of Richard. "Come" was the reply to her gentle tap upon the door. She entered and, with a curtsy, handed to the prince the note of her mistress. He quickly ripped it open, for it seemed he was in much anxiety to fall into the fatal hands of the Lady Catherine.

"Please, tell your mistress I will be most delighted to visit her as she so requests."

"Yes, my lord, I will do so," she replied, as she went her way after giving her curtsy to the young prince. Along the passageway she went, but a different way she trod, taking her close to the curtained way that passed by the chambers of the Duchess Margaret, knowing that in such a place the Lady Marcela may lurk, as she was wont to do in her duties as confidante to her lady. Marie slowed and slipped discreetly behind one of the drapes, and would wait a short while in its cover. But 'twas of little time before steps she did hear that came close to where she was hid. She dared a peek, and saw indeed the lady of her seek coming to the doorway of her mistress and readying to enter therein. "My Lady Marcela," she whispered her shout from the dusty hide. The lady stopped on her way to the chamber and came over to the whispering drapes, with a wary glance up and down the still passageway as she did so.

"Marie, my dear, 'tis you."

"Yes, my lady, 'tis so. I have some information for you," came still the voice in whispers discrete. The Lady Marcela slipped silently behind the drape that made them unseen from without, and, as if the space was little, came close and pressed herself warmly to the Lady Marie who did not become disturbed, for indeed she surmised there was but little room for more than one person in this tight place of intrigue. They stood with faces close, the warm breath of one drinking in the warm breath of the other. Even within the dim, one could see the eyes of the other shining with their dewy glow. "There has been a letter, my lady, passed from my mistress to the prince, to arrange a time for the liaison set for my lady's bedchamber.

I know not of the words so writ, for 'twas well sealed, but the prince has agreed to come to the chamber, and it seems by all reason it may be this night."

"I am unable to understand somewhat why the Lady Catherine would place herself in such a position after the stern warning given to her. My lady will be most ruthless in this matter; believe me, she will stand no more." The Lady Marcela spake in serious tones but then changed once she had rid herself of the folly told. "The news you bring to us is most valuable, Marie, and as such bodes of a sacrifice of your mistress. I would take it that once this charade is over you will come to my lady's employ and serve her as you have done so loyally when your mistress was loyal?"

"Yes, my lady, I do so desire to enter with the ladies who care for the duchess."

"Then it will be so, Marie. If you can please continue to bring to us your observations, I will make it my business to be at this place upon the morrow and at this same time, for then you may know more of this night's episode."

"I will do so, my lady." Marie glanced through the gap in the curtain to see that the passageway was empty and made to move back to her chamber, but her arm was stilled by the hand of Marcela, who, with soft lips, kissed lightly the open neck that showed from the dress of Marie. Her knees needed little for them to shake, for she had stood in the lady's warmth for some little while. Her face reddened, her legs seemed indeed to faint, and with eyes that could not look into the face that was but a hair away, she managed to walk, though unsteadily, away from the lady who was overpowering her emotions. She still remained pure and unsullied, but urgings were rising within her that tempted her resolve.

The night black had come, as all to sound in the passageway were the step of the guards as they dutied themselves about the palace at Malines. And also watching from some dark place were the eyes of the duchess—the Lady Marcela. As the guards approached close to the chambers of Catherine, cries and laughter could be heard. Even through the heavy door they sounded, the sounds of frolic and lovers' doings did ring about. The two who guarded looked but a moment at each other and spake naught, for such sounds were oft heard, almost nightly they did ring outside the chambers where Catherine dwelled.

A yawn crept upon the face of the lady who watched, for the hour had turned late. The guards had passed but a short while ago and stillness hung about. The bells from the abbey she heard ring their chimes, but was not sure if 'twas two or of three that were struck. But did raise her from the half state she was in, and then, in short time after, the door of the lady's chamber opened to a discreet wide, and from the dim room came the Prince Richard. His boots held in hand, his shirt open, his hair as a tangled ball of wool. He looked about as he slipped away to his chamber, and was soon out of sight to end his night's jaunt. The eyes of the Lady Marcela blinked from their weariness; she yawned once again as she stepped from her hide, and she, the last one to bed, made straight to her chambers. The morrow would be a day of some retribution, without a doubt.

They came upon their call, the prince and his companion, to the chambers of council, knowing not upon their way why their stride took on that of a military gait, but turned 'twas so as if some strange hold had soldiered them. Even in step were they as they both came to a stop upon the same tread outside the great doors, and to rap upon them they're coming. "Enter" called the voice from within. They creaked the door to gain the chamber, and saw many people gathered there awaiting their coming. With respectful courtesy they greeted the prince who spake to the assembled.

"My lords and ladies, I thank you for your acknowledgement. I feel well at home in this pleasant land." Then the reason for the gathering was known, as from the crowd stepped forward the ambassador to Scotland showing fine in his royal tartan, his emissaries about him, all with the black beard, and skin, red and rough. He began to converse with the prince, but his accent made it most difficult to be understood, till the ear fell more to the sounds and likened soon to good talk. Forward then came the party from Austria; stood they all military proud and unmoving, speaking the German tongue of greetings sincere. A tongue in which the prince was learned. The Lady Margaret and her courtiers looked on at the proceedings.

"Come, sit," she now gestured and beckoned them to the conference table, and to watch as they sipped the French brandy that was jugged upon it. When they had supped a little 'twas the duchess who spake firstly. "The prince has one thousand soldiers promised by the King Charles, and monies gifted for their upkeep. I myself will give to the cause one thousand soldiers with monies for their upkeep. Will the representatives of the King of the Romans and his son, the Archduke of Austria, add to these most generous gifts?"

"We will, madam," came the stern reply as was their talk. "But there is one condition, and that is that all the lands that have been subjugated by the English will be returned to us without any claim upon them."

"Sirs," spake the prince, "I have no reason not to return such lands to you, and, upon becoming king, I will, in honour bound, do so."

"Then, sir, in respect to your cause we will place at your command one thousand and five hundred of our finest soldiery, all battle-tried with arms and monies paid towards your enterprise."

"Thank you most heartily for your generosity, and pray you convey my gratitude to your duke." After the reply from the prince, the Austrian party wished quickly to be away, and would not linger for the hearing of the Scots' offer, for their sights looked upon different hills. The duke's envoys bowed as if in some parade, all in union with ne'er one movement amiss. Placing their respect once more to the Prince Richard, who had vowed to release all their lands.

"And the Scots, my lords, what say you to this prince of kings?" the duchess queried her speech to the ready Highlanders.

"We will, for certain concessions, give to this prince all we possess. But firstly a pledge has to be given that the lands of Northumbria and the lands of Caledonia, which were so deviously taken from us, will all be returned into our fold so that peace may come to this arena, and our countries binded together under one flag. Our King James the Fourth of Scotland will offer one of his kin, the Lady Katherine Gordon, in marriage to the prince so to unite our lands for all. We wish also to state that the said Lady Gordon is of prime looks and a desirable maiden, ripen to childbearing. At your pleasure, upon acknowledgement of these requests, your armies will all be welcomed into our kingdom, and so will be able to strike from the same island against that weakling Henry."

"You ask much, my dear lord, but thought must—" Richard spake as one of the cats about leapt upon the table where they counselled and stopped the conversation abruptly as it stalked about looking for some morsel thereupon. With a quick swipe with the back of his hand, one of the Scottish envoys sent the feline spinning like some child's toy, to send it skidding over the floor and up against the wall, to screech and scurry itself away to a more peaceful place. They all at the table watched the occurrence with some humour, including the prince. "Thank you, sir, for your most couraged act. We may now continue with less dread. More thought will have to be delved before I can say yea or nay. Your lands, which you ask to be returned to you, bear no hardship to me and as such will be done. Such kilted warriors as yours bring terror in the field to their enemies and I would bless their coming. Your generosity of using your lands to strike against our foe, the King Henry, is an excellent scheme. But the one thing that may bring this union to a halt is that of love. For to take into my heart a lady I have not seen, I can make no promise."

"We do have a portrait, sire, brought with us for such an arrangement."

"I offer no disrespect to you or to your lady, sire, but I have seen before such portraits and always it seems they do not do the lady justice, whether for good or for bad. And then, when the flesh is seen, 'twas not what the canvas showed. For the convenience that such a marriage would bring to our houses I readily agree. But love must enter into it, for I will not marry falsely to a canvas. The blind man can take a witch as a beauty, but I am not blind."

"If you then will bind yourself to the other requests, we will agree. Although my king has many more kin for your perusal, some of childbearing age, some as not yet, but all of a fine disposition, with good table manners and many with pleasing features. My king does all this not for his own pleasure, but to unite our lands and put to end all the strife that has befell our nations. And, sir, if naught is to please you, then so be it. He will not on this count renounce any allegiance to you, my prince." The Scottish envoy spake his piece to Richard, and wished that he may hear the right answer to his plea. And the answer was such as he sought.

"Then, sir, if I am not bound to the contract of matrimony, I will in all my humbleness be obliged to the King James and will fulfill my bargain. And upon seeing these ladies you speak of, we may hope indeed that one is to my desire."

"Do you know, my prince, of such a date that this enterprise may take place? for we wish to be well readied."

"My dear cousin, the duchess, has ships at this moment being prepared for sail, and now that we know our true destination, all will be hastened. Within a fortnight the soldiers of Charles and of our duchess will be assembled, and upon such a day, when the weather is kind, we shall set forth. Our soldiers of Austria will then join our ships at such a date, and will sail with us to the haven of Scotland … 'Tis done then, my comrades." The prince stood and raised his goblet, as all had followed his will and all did raise their vessels to shout and to cheer at their unity, and scoffed the rich brandy all drained. To pledge that soon the ever-widening hole in the ship of Henry will be fraught with many more. Far more than he had pitch to match.

They all then moved to their different ways, and in doing so the Lady Margaret brushed her body of entice to that of the prince. "Tonight—my chamber. Be not late my prince," she spake quietly and close into his crinkled ear, to quiver the hairs upon the neck's flesh.

Then parted all with plans drawn and ready for the fray of the war to come. Soon blood and death would be about upon the lands of England once more. The prince could see already his march triumphant into London Town. He could see the banners waved and hear the cheering voices, loud about the throng, waving in their thousands, as the rose so white flew high above all. Wishing mightily upon his dream that soon would come true, he walked along with his good friend, Alphonse, toward their chambers.

"We must bear all of our strength; for this hour we have waited long, and now it is upon us. To deep resolve we must and only be for ambitious acts and not for folly. Only once will this chance show its face; if we do not take it then it will be gone forever."

Alphonse with deep emotion added his thoughts to the pot, after his friend had shed his words. "We will succeed, my prince, for the Lord is with our army, and are we not of true and noble demeanour to bring us in God's eyes to the throne? And you, after all conflict, will become king."

The prince placed his arm about his friend, as a true comrade. "I am proud, Alph, to have you aside of me, for your words bring much wisdom, and when times were hard for us 'twas always you who saw what I could become. You will always to me be a true friend."

Marie readied herself to meet with the Lady Marcela. A letter from her mistress with an invite for the prince lay upon her table. She wore a dress that was more revealing than she normally would. She perfumed herself more than she normally would. Her shoes were higher and her lips were painted more than they normally were. What was she becoming? she thought, as she looked at the stranger that showed in the glass. Do I stumble in my virtue? Her mind could give no answer, for 'twas fogged by some desire. She looked again upon the glass and tugged at her neckline once more to make it less tempting; the childlike act eased the mind that did seem as a child lost to the right way.

The passageway was still and naught seemed about. The spit of the lamps was all that broke the calm. Their glow flickered upon the blackened walls as the smoke drifted to the ceiling above. The folds of the drapes moved but a little as two hands made room for a slit to peer along the dim way and to see, coming along in some discretion, the Lady Marie. She wore her cloak laced at the front with its hood raised to cover her head, and prayed that if she were spied her person would not be known. To the place of her encounter she came, taking one last look about the passageway as she neared the draped alcove. The voice from within whispered her name. "Marie—" … She slipped silently through the dusty cover and into the dark corner. She untied her cape and laid it down upon the grey stone of the floor, for the small place in which they stood was already most warm. She turned as the drape was closed, and before she could settle her breath, the Lady Marcela was upon her, pressing her legs against her own; she felt the body, warm and soft, coming through her vesture and flustering her skin. Her breasts were pressed gently against the black dress that was

Marcela—she who coveted all that was within that small chamber.

"My lady, do you have some writ for my lady?" Marcela whispered into the ear of Marie.

"Yes, Marcela, I have a letter from my lady to the prince that has not yet been delivered." The Lady Marie fumbled about in her folds to find the letter. She had placed it far from any opening so it may be safe in its journey. As she spake, the voice of Marcela seemed to ripple through her body, was it still so close to her own. Her shaking fingers fumbled for the note that seemed to be hid beyond reach. As she waited unhurried, the gloved hands of the Lady Marcela traced figures upon the bare shoulders of Marie, who found it little help in her search. With the hardness of the stitching upon the end of the glove's finger, the lady followed the neckline of Marie's dress from one side to the other, pressing hard into the softness of her flesh, and bringing forth a red welt where she travelled. Marie groaned as she was led down the path unknown, but then, through her state, she found the letter and placed it into the free hand that awaited.

"Thank you, my dear," the lady whispered again close as she pulled the letter apart. Being unable to read the contents within the dark place they nestled, she gently opened the curtain slightly, and from the torch that flickered within the passageway she managed to tilt the page so the light would catch the words. But at the same time she left no more space between herself and Marie, who managed to find the strength to look up into the face of the one who was spinning her into some thoughts of desire. The flames from the torch flickered into the eyes of Marcela as she gazed at the words. Marie was tumbling like a stone from the clifftop of virtue and into the sinful waters below, there being nothing it seemed to stop her fall into that illicit way.

"Your lady wishes the prince to come to her bedchamber at nine of the clock this eve." Marcela read out the words that were writ upon the letter. She then let the drapes fall back to their secrecy, and to bring darkness once more to the alcove. Folding the note, she placed it within her own keep. "Marie, you must not deliver this letter to the prince, but you must tell your mistress you have done so, and that the prince will, in all eagerness, come to her chamber at the desired time. Say also that 'twas inconvenient at the time for him to return a letter, but spake to you of his desire and wished for you to state his wishes. Do you understand?"

"Yes, my lady, I will do as you bid."

"I wish also that you say that the prince wishes that only one candle may burn in the chamber of his desire, for he wishes to come in some ogre's dress and bedevil her in the blackness."

"I will do as you say, my lady."

Marcela pulled gently her warmth away from the Lady Marie, as the time was almost come to depart the affair; but she held each arm as one would if scolding a child, but 'twas not an act of scolding she brought, but some dire words to the lady who seemed somewhat naive. "And when you have done this bidding, gather discreetly all the chattels you hold dear to you, and keep them secreted, for this night your lady will not long remain about this place, and sometime upon the morrow, we will call upon you so you may bring your goods to your new chamber, and you can settle to serve my mistress, who looks forward with every desire to show her affection for you."

"I will do as you bid, my lady. Will I see you again before the morrow?"

"No, my dear, you will not, but time will soon come when we may spend many hours with my lady, the duchess."

Marie donned her cape then tied up the front; she was about to leave when those soft lips kissed her cheek, and then played upon her ear with such gentle guile did they come to bring desired shivers back to her body. She pulled her hood forward to cover herself from prying eyes, and, with a quick glance through the open drape, tripped her way to her mistress's chamber to deliver the spoken message from the prince imagined.

"And so, Marcela, what news does your little pigeon bring to us?" The duchess sat close to the warming fire that crackled and spat within her closet, as she beckoned her lady closer.

"The Lady Marie brought this note to us, my lady. Sent from her mistress Catherine to the prince. As yet he has not seen the message so writ."

Margaret took the folded note from Marcela and read it silently to herself, then appeared to read it once again as if the first time was of some ramblings. Her face was not pleasing as she looked up at her lady.

"I took the liberty, my lady, of telling the Lady Marie to inform Catherine that she had delivered the note to the prince, and that he had returned his answer verbally to her, and that he would be at her bedchamber as was requested at nine of the clock this eve. And further I added to the Lady Marie to tell her mistress that the prince wished only one candle to burn within her chamber, for he wished to come in some guise and bring some fright to her in the black of night. As the prince is expected in our chamber upon this same eve, my lady, it will leave the Lady Catherine vulnerable to any doings you may choose. If you think I may have gone too far with my suggestion, we can still deliver the note to the prince as so devised."

"No, my lady, you have not overstepped your mark. All is as I would wish it to be. This night all will be done with that whore. No more will I warn her; it will surely be ended, my dearest Marcela."

"What have you planned for her, my lady? Are you thinking that murder may end it?"

"Murder? … No, murder would be too quick; suffering for the rest of her life is what will come upon her. 'Tis the iron for her, my dear, the whore's iron."

Marcela flinched for one moment, for she would be the one to bring about the said punishment. But then she knew how fitting the crime would be, and that which would be suffered upon the soft maiden who did brag of her special virtues. Came now the hint of some smile so wicked upon those lips that but a little while ago were filled with joyous giving, soft and filled illicit with desire.

"Do it, Marcela, at nine of the clock. Do it in the dark as she awaits her lover. She will lay waiting in complete surrender for the desired coming of our prince."

"I will, my lady, do your bidding, and what a pleasure it will be for all of us." She smiled delightfully at her lady, who, with such wicked thoughts in her head, smiled back with little remorse at her desire. For it would be of little good for the prince to become bewitched, and then be unable to honour his pledges. She was doing the only thing she could do to preserve his right to be king … and to spread his wealth about.

The bells chimed its rhythm to strike nine times in the black night. The wind blew and the rain threatened. The ill-fitting windows could stop little, as the torches wafted and spit in their displeasure in the swirl about them. No one walked the passageways, all called they to other duties more pressing than walking the ways of the palace.

They came along, this strange party of ogres and hid faces. A tall figure in a long black gown did lead the way; clopping her shoes upon the stone floor, she stepped with little need for quietness, for were they not expected at nine of the clock? The lady wore upon her face a mask of many colours, bright 'twas, but upon it an evil smile was set with many teeth that did show from the gap that was the mouth. She was followed by the shuffling steps of four. Hid they beneath robes as black as the night, their heads and faces covered with sackcloth with two slits for their eyes and a slit below to suck in air, making ghoulish sounds all about as they did so. To come then two figures, the sleeves of their coats cut at the shoulder to be seen their arms all of muscle. They too wore masks to cover their faces, not painted gaily but black and all full of mischief. Their strong arms glistened as they came along; they held each two rods, passed through a brazier. One upon one side, the other upon the other as they carried it along. The coals, hot and bright, spat and blew about as they trotted the fire behind the others. The length of the rods they hugged in the crook of their arms were long so that the heat from the fire would not burn them, but they still felt the scorch upon their legs and did smell the hairs that singed the skin. There from the coals stuck out the whore's iron. The part that was not in the fire stood black and rusty; the part that dwelled within the coals was past the colour of red, and was closer to being white was it so heated.

To the chamber door of the Lady Catherine they came, that strange party of desire that she awaited. Marcela opened the door with little deftness but bustled in upon a mission. The waiting ladies were gathered about the closet as the party entered, chattering and sewing and relating such tales of intrigues whispered. They at first only looked with some lighthearted faces at those who passed through, deeming 'twas some game that the prince was bringing to their lady's bedchamber. They watched the tall lady in the black dress and the bright mask pass by as she made through the closet and stepped to the doorway of the outer chamber. They giggled as the four hooded men came by with their arms folded before them, and the shuffling of their short steps as if their ankles were tied together. They did not at first grasp what came next, as the two who carried the brazier came through the door one before the other. The brightness then glowed about the closet as the heat from the fire warmed the air, and they saw the iron that stood straight from the coals, and they knew what was afoot. With cries of anguish they left their seats and their chat, to scamper into the corner of the room. All whimpering and crying were they, for they could do nothing to help their lady, only to cower away from those who came upon this mission. And all did lay huddled in the corner, except one … the Lady Marie, who had silently slipped from the scene during the upheaval, and was now upon her way to her closet to gather her things, which lay ready for some quick departure.

The Lady Marcela opened the door to the outer chamber and entered the brightly-lit room, which showed the door to the bedchamber, slightly open and a most inviting gesture for the coming prince. One person sat within this room. He stood and gave a polite bow to the lady who led the party, and then he seated himself again and began to play upon his lute, those tunes of love so requested by the lady abed, and to bring with it his lilting voice that rang about. He cared not for the toings and the froings; all he was bid to do was play his songs and such was all he did. The lady pushed further open the doors to the chamber, where lay in the dark the whore of the night. As was asked, only one candle did burn and flicker in the far reach of the chamber. The wind rattled at the shutters, the bedcovers of silk shone in the little light, the breathing of the lady in some excitement sounded about the chamber.

"My prince, is that you who comes with your wicked ways upon this night? Or are you some stranger in disguise who wishes to take advantage of my frail self?" The Lady Catherine called out at the dark figure that stood in silence before her. But no answer was offered, and still was the room. The four figures, black and hooded, came to the bed. Two stepped to the head and eased the arms of the willing lady, to stretch them out like a bird in flight and hold them at the wrist in tight fashion. The other two took her ankles, which were already spread wide, and held them most firmly. She had carefully placed a cushion beneath herself, to raise herself up for her intruder. She squirmed a little under the thoughts of what advantage may be taken of her, and was in some amorous throes. "Please, please, do not harm me," she bleated in her childlike voice. "I am but an innocent maiden that has never been taken ... I am about to be married, sir, and must still be a virgin for my beloved ... Please do not take such away from me."

The chamber then filled with light; a bright red light that flickered and danced about, showing two giant shadows that danced the same dance upon the walls. She knew not what had entered her chamber and thought 'twas part of the night's game, a new game she knew naught about, but was ready to play. The cauldron was placed upon the floor. The Lady Marcela pulled upon her hands the leather gauntlets. The fire warmed one leg and one side of Catherine's body as she lay prostrate. It seemed to get warmer as she lay upon her soft mattress, and then started to come heat that was becoming uncomfortable. She lifted her head that she may see what delight was coming to her. She saw the cauldron, and the rod that showed from it, and 'twas then she became stricken with fear; her eyes welled and a fearful state came over her body, for now she knew what had come upon her. She had been led down the path, blind to the outrage that was to come this night.

"Do not do this to me, I—"

"Gag her," the voice came with cruel tone. And before she could speak or cry out any more about her misfortune, one of the hooded men stuffed deep into her mouth a cloth that dulled her cries; only her eyes and her arms and her legs struggling showed her state. She could hear little of what was about her, except from the open door the luted song of the minstrel giving forth his songs of love. He did not falter in his tune, for such is what he was beckoned.

The iron's rod that showed from the coals was thinner than the rest, which lay heated deep in the spitting red fire. The lady who would wield it came forward with her black shadow dancing upon the walls. She grasped its rod, and even with the gloves she wore, the heat she felt through the leather, and raised red upon her showed skin. She pulled the iron slowly from the fire. The end that had been hid within the coals was almost white with the heat as 'twas drawn out, and showed then that 'twas fashioned in the shape of manhood. As it threw sparks and glowed bright within the darkened room, Marcela brought the iron toward the lady whose face showed to burst in her anguish.

"You would not listen to the duchess, would you, my fair one?" spake she, and with a slow plunge entered into Catherine the whore's iron.

The eyes that were fearful were closed and the struggle had ceased. With the smell of burnt hair and flesh, the spitting iron was pulled from the lady. The steam rising from that shape of cruel reprise, it now showed but a dull red within the bedchamber, as the lady who wielded it placed it back into the fire. She removed her gloves and, with the others who were so engaged, did all leave the chamber that was but a short while ago a haven of love's gifts, now did lay a place of smoke and burnt flesh. They came to the outer chamber where still strummed the minstrel. "I think, sir, that your jingle will no longer be required, and pray you pack yourself away from this place." The Lady Marcela urged away the strummer who did indeed ready himself to leave the chamber, but then decided to play one last tune for the stricken Catherine. They came to the closet where the tearful ladies waited, still unable to understand the terror that had come upon them. Though they had managed to stand, they stayed in the corner of the room, for there it seemed was the safest place they could be. They cringed back as the brazier, still sparking and glowing bright, came by them, followed by the four hooded ogres who seemed no longer to offer to them any comedy … And as they left the lady in the bright mask spake to them.

"Go to your lady; she will need you now. Be gentle with her, for she has suffered greatly because of her folly. Her great loss will not show to the eye, but she will always have to bear it. I suggest you take her from this place to somewhere that she is not known, for the mark of the whore is upon her."

They gathered up their skirts and hastened to the bedchamber of their mistress. The masked lady left, her mission was done; she heard not the lute's tune as she went along the passageway, only heard were the wails of anguish from the waiting ladies who stayed …

"So, my dear lady, how did you fare upon your task?" the duchess broached the Lady Marcela as she came to report upon the doings of the night.

"All was done as you so desired, my lady."

"And how did she bear under the ordeal?"

"She did not bear it bravely, but quickly she went into some faint, and would feel no more until she awakened."

"So, at last we are rid of her."

"Yes, my lady, her soft tulip so desired is no more. In its stead lays the bark of the elm tree."

The duchess smiled and continued to be readied for the prince who would soon come.

Chapter Twenty-three.

When Black is White.

The time in the dark night had come at last for the prince to make his way to the tantalizing bedchamber of his cousin. Walked he the empty passageways to the duchess, whom he knew was at wait for him. He was dressed in more regal cloth and smelling more sweet than he could ever recall. Looked upon at last was he as a princely person and attired so. The only life he saw upon his way were some green-eyed cats that scurried away from his coming. His boots sounded loud upon the stone floor, but then became silenced as he trod upon the carpet that led to that door, behind which awaited his night's dream with her devouring charms. Few candles lit the chamber showing only dark shapes laid upon black. Richard needed no flame to show him to the bed of his seductress. Were he blind he would find her. He slipped off the garb of a prince, and slid silently into the silken covers where the soft breathing of Margaret he could hear close to his own.

"Where have you been, my prince? It seems long that I have awaited you," the duchess whispered gently into the ear that rested close.

"Chasing cats, my dearest," the prince quipped.

"Come closer to me and chase away your jest with amour."

Soon her softness was close to him as all was divine in his mind. Then in the tremor of his desire two hands with cool touch placed themselves upon his warm skin. Strong hands they seemed and not the softness and warmth he knew from his lover.

"What is this that plays upon me?" the prince quietly pleaded to who would listen.

"Do not be of concern, my dearest, 'tis but my companion, Marcela De Boer who lays her magical ways upon you. Do not stay in your throes but let her add to your pleasure, for she is well enamoured to such ways."

"If it is your desire, mistress, then so be it." And so 'twas in that night, that as they loved, the Lady Marcela plied his receiving flesh and indeed he was most pleasured.

The morn came within the chamber of the duchess, and all were stirred by the coming of the waiting ladies, and of Antonio, who brought warmed water and cloths of soft weave. And all were cleansed of their sinful fare.

Helped in the task by the caring hands of the Lady Marcela, who seemed to relish the task. Soon 'twas that the prince and the duchess sat alone upon the edge of the ruffled bed.

"You have witchy ways, my dear cousin," spake the prince to the duchess.

"Do you not like them such, cousin?" she asked her companion.

"I was indeed entranced by all that transpired in this past night, but something was not as it seemed, but yet I know not of what that tickles my brain."

"Pray, have no bother, my dear boy. Play upon the lute given you." The duchess placed before the prince words that were of good stead, but he still had worms that squirmed beneath his skin that would not let him rest.

Many days had passed at the palace, and 'twas told that the Lady Catherine had been seen leaving her chambers upon a litter, with her ladies about her. All had entered into some kind of carriage and 'twas ridden away in the dark hours of night. Some believed she had been stricken by some malady, others heard that she had gone to a nunnery to spend her days in remorse and prayer. Others knew she was scourged.

The ships for the journey to Scotland were being readied but 'twas taking long hours, for Richard had to have his fleet without any flaws or knotted rope. All had to be perfect. Captains for the vessels were counselled, crews were vetted, supplies ordered, soldiers billeted, and on forever it seemed the tasks did pile.

The kitchen maid was entered with her tray of victuals, to carefully place the unwieldy assemblage upon the table within the chamber of the prince. "Your victuals, sire," she squeaked as she placed them down.

"Thank you, my dear." Her eyes seen fluttering back in some embarrassment to the prince's reply, she curtsied, and skipped the room as quickly as she could, to close behind her the door with quivering hand. The would-be king sat at his desk writing in his ledger of the day's doings. While he was engaged in such his eye caught a movement from the far side of the chamber. He looked up and spied the cat that had slinked in with the maid. Sat 'twas upon his tray chewing at the tempting fare that no one seemed to need. "Be gone you tamed rat!" shouted the prince, who quickly slid off his boot and threw it at the animal. The cat though managed to avoid it by leaping from the table, and ran behind the long seat that pressed against the wall, hiding there in fear from the thing that hurled missiles its way.

Richard carried on his scratching for almost an hour and then upon the coming of Alphonse from the dockside he stretched his arms above his head and spake to his ally. "How was the day? Well, I pray."

"Yes, my lord, we made good our progress this day."

"Come, my friend, let us sup, for I am well in need of some victuals." As up from the desk came the one-booted prince. "Where is that damned boot?" he spake aloud to himself as he limped about. "I threw it at the cat … It must be about somewhere."

"'Tis here, sire," Alphonse spake as he bent to the floor to retrieve the stray missile. "Well thrown, my lord, you must have killed it with one shot."

"What is it you say, Alph?"

"The cat, sire, you must have hit it deftly for here it lies dead."

"Dead? … I did not hit the creature. Ran away it did from my antics to hide out of sight, but I did not fare so well as to strike it." The prince came close with lighted candle to where Alphonse still gazed upon the floor. The candle showed the still body that lay against the wall. The light was brought closer so they may see more of the dark place. "Do you see, Alph, the foaming of the mouth?"

"Yes, sir, I do … Poison!"

"Poison, indeed; poison indeed. We have been subject to some villainy here. 'Twas the tray of food, Alph, meant to bring us down before we could even raise a sword upon English soil. This supposed safe place that is of our repose must be well ordained with spies, and all to Henry's call I fear. Let us relay this happening to the duchess to see if this villain can be found."

In great haste they made to the chamber of the duchess and quickly gained council with her. They stated the event that had fallen upon them. Shocked and dismayed was she as the words chilled her blood. That someone in her care and protection would steal such honour from her, and tread into the mud like some wild horse the trust she had given to all under her roof.

"I have been dishonoured, my dear cousin, that such an outrage has befallen you, and I give you my word we will seek out this vile person. Henceforward we will bring to you a taster with every meal that you partake, so it will not happen again. What a shameful day for my country this is."

"Do not reproach yourself, cousin, 'tis no fault of yours that the King Henry is a man without honour as to ply such a deed upon your house. This act brings him to the level of the slimy toad. But let us not dwell any further on that which is done; we must see if we can find this person before he or she flies the coop. Let us first speak to the kitchen maid who brought to us these sour victuals. I have the utmost belief she knows nothing of the act attempted, but she may have entertained something other in her duties." The prince made the suggestion to the duchess, who in short time had the page away with breeches afire.

Soon he was back with timid Lucy, who came with skirts hitched as she trotted behind him. She came a child in servant's cloth, her face flushed with her trek from the kitchen. Her stomach was twisted, for she knew not the reason she had been summoned.

"The maid, Lucy," spake the page as he bowed in the maid and then returned to his wait at the door's entrance.

"You wished to speak to me, my lady?" The squeaky voice had not improved, the only difference being that it came with gasps of air. The Lady Margaret broached the maid to see what she could relate to them.

"Yes, Lucy, someone this day has tampered with the victuals that you fetched to the chamber of the Prince Richard."

The maid was taken aback by the revelation. Her face turned from the red flush to the palest white. Tears began to well her eyes, dammed up and not, as yet, trickling down their streams of fear upon the young skin so tender. The lips began to tremble, as 'twas beyond herself to stop them, so fearful was she of the reprisal that seemed to be coming upon her innocent self. The prince took it upon himself to step closer to the waif. Though he was still troubled by the attempt upon him, he felt much empathy for the shaking servant girl.

"Be not feared, Lucy; you are in no way suspected of anything foul." His hand rested upon the tiny arm in some compassion to her hurt. "Do not fear so, we wish only to find the culprit, and wish only to speak with you to see if you can recall anything in your duties that was untoward."

"I am not to be dismissed then, sire?"

"No, Lucy, you are not," the duchess interrupted. "We seek from you only information." The wells of water dried as if taken away by an angel, and relief filled her body. She stood silent as if at thought but nothing was spoken. "Well, Lucy, did you see aught?"

"I think not, my lady … I know not what I am to see; it seems nothing was amiss."

"Let us help you, Lucy." The prince tried to bring out from the young girl things she could not recall. "Who readied the tray of victuals?"

"Cook, sir." She brightened with an answer come. "Cook always readies the tray."

"Who was in the kitchen besides you and Cook?"

Silence was about again as she thought with twisted face and itched spot … "The prince's butler was there. He had not eaten since early morn and was at sup." … Time again waned as she tried to picture in her mind the state of the kitchen upon the morn. "Two more kitchen maids were there. Joan and Elizabeth. But, as madam knows, they have been in the kitchen for ages and they would not—"

"There is no reason to defend them, Lucy, for they are under no suspicion. We seek only someone who should not be in the kitchen."

"There was no one, sire; all in the kitchen I have named."

"Then when you left the kitchen with the tray, did anyone distract your way?" Lucy looked at the prince and then at the duchess, for she did not understand the words that were spoken to her. "Tell us of your steps, from when you left the kitchen with the tray."

"I went up the servants' stairway … and saw no one as I climbed the steps … Came I from the stairs and went into the passageway that leads to the chamber of the prince, then walked I—" Her speech tailed to naught as her mind tumbled and the tears that had gone came flooding back once again. Her hand she placed upon her mouth, which stifled some sound as she remembered her journey.

"You remember something, Lucy?" the prince urged her.

"Yes, sir—" She fell silent once again as she fretted.

"Do not be concerned, just say what happened upon your way." The prince again spake softly to her.

"I came along … the tray was so heavy … the cats were about my feet … I am so sorry."

"Lucy, calm yourself, just tell your story; you are in no trouble," the duchess gently spake to her, which helped Lucy, for she had been told of the kindness that she gave.

"I nearly stumbled … He took the tray from me and placed it upon the table."

"*Who took the tray from you?*" Lucy was asked by both Margaret and Richard.

"The gentleman, he took the tray," she answered, and then she began talking faster as her mind recalled the event. "He then sat me upon the bench that was close to the window so I may breathe in the cool air, though I did not feel faint I sat anyway, for he was so kind to one such as I. He told me to close my eyes whilst he counted ten numbers. I did as he asked, for he was a gentleman and I did not want to go against his wishes. Then, as the count finished, I opened my eyes and he told me I was well now. He gave me back the tray and patted my bottom to usher me upon my way. I then went to the prince's chamber and left there the tray of victuals."

"Who was the gentleman? Who helped you?"

"I know not, madam, just a gentleman I have seen about."

"What looks did he have? How was he dressed?—think hard, Lucy."

"Well, he was not tall ... and heavy was his set ... He was dressed handsomely ... He had a beard and long hair down his back ... Oh yes, he had a strange face, like this—" Lucy showed a face that twitched, and eyes that blinked at every twitch.

"What say you, Lucy, he had a face that twitched?" The eyes of the duchess brightened as the words were spake.

"Yes, my lady, like a hooked fish tugged by some line upon his cheek." Lucy began again the act of a caught fish.

"Yes, Lucy, we gather what his twitch was liken to. I know this person," the duchess spake as she turned her words to the prince. "The Lady Lamone's friend ... He was called to her side this last month for her enjoyment, and seen upon sight a poncey rogue, indeed."

"Call the guards and have the lady's toy brought before us now!" The duchess shouted her orders to the guards who stood by the door, and quickly did they rush away to fulfill the order so given. Both excitement and fear spread about the ways and the chambers therein, as the doer of the act was sought. He though could not be found and seemingly was no longer about the palace. The Lady Lamone though was about and asked for a council with the duchess, for it seemed it 'twas her gigolo who had done the mischief, and she was responsible for his presence within these walls ...

"So, my lady, what do you have to say about this matter?" The duchess sat in her chamber, where stood all about those who had an interest in the affair and waited to hear the words of the Lady Lamone. She stood before the duchess. The lady, no longer sprightly but with a pretty face, now plump in her being but still a fetching lady in her finery. A seeker of life's joys, an owner of many properties and land, her coffers were full. A woman most sought by fortune seekers and rogues. She spake with nervous tongue to the duchess.

"I believe my companion, the one you seek, has fled."

"Where to has he taken himself, my lady?" the prince posed to her the first question.

She dabbed at her cheek with her kerchief as it seemed she perspired enough to topple. Her face was flushed and she seemed in some dilemma. A seat was brought for her and she sat heavily in some kind of hysteria. The lady knew all was placed upon her, and that a ladylike faint was in order.

"Come, madam, pull yourself together, a fit of faint will bring no respite to the questions," the duchess spake sternly to the lady. And after seeing her act was not going to bring forth any sympathy, she placed her kerchief back in its folds and continued in the council.

"He has returned to England where I first gained his encounter. He took a great interest in me and showed me much respect, but I know fobs such as he seek only one thing from their encounters, and that is my fortune—Pardon me but I stray from your questions." She pulled again her kerchief from the folds of her dress and dabbed her teary eye that only she knew of. "He, it seems, ordered my manservant to carry his baggage to the harbour, this but two hours past, and to board it upon the ship that was at the ready to leave. My manservant had to throw the chattels aboard, for the vessel was untied and away from the dockside, all ready they to pull sail. The rogue then did run mightily, and with much haste did leap, flapping his arms and his legs liken to some clumsy bird, then landing with much force upon the departing ship. And last seen of him was with his baggage at hand drifting from Flanders' coast. All this I gathered from my manservant who had little choice but to obey the order he was given, for the man spake most harshly to him and he was afeared. And up to that time I myself knew naught of such happenings."

"You are a foolish woman, and it is time you did put such folly aback of you." Margaret spake angrily at the lady who sniffled before her. "You must take care of whom you enter into this palace. These rogues and philanderers who pander you are a blight upon us all. I say to you, any more such activities and you will no longer be welcome within these walls. You will be banished from this court, and the word will be spread to many other courts as well. Do you understand that which I speak?"

"Yes, duchess. I do regret my folly and I will mend my ways." The Lady Lamone spake as best as she was able as she blubbed into her 'chief.

"Do so, lady," were the words of parting plied to her, as she in hasty step left the ordeal afore more retribution fell upon her head. Already though her thoughts were planning as to what next her tryst may be.

"I wager all I own, that bastard who has shipped away is in the pocket of Henry and will soon be telling his tale of our activities here and of our plans to enter his waters." The prince was not pleased with what had transpired. The spy had gone and was not locked away as he had wished.

"He can do naught about it, Richard," the duchess replied to the observation by her cousin. "He has no way to muster his ships and engage you before you land in Scotland, so do not disturb your plans. You can alter naught and indeed you do not have to."

"Again you are right, my dear Margaret. The bridge is crossed; 'tis too late now to check the rope."

The prince and Alph were at chat within their chamber. Low were their voices as close they sat sipping upon the goblets of red wine. Their chairs were pulled close to the table near the window with its fading light.

"My mind is in some jumbled state, Alph."

"What is it that is concerning you, Richard?" His friend wishing to help if he could.

"'Tis the Lady Marcela De Boer, and that Antonio Bercholi, there is some strange happenings with those two, at this time I know not what. But I will soon find that which brings such a puzzle to me, and must so do before we sail."

"They are truly a strange pair, my lord, and, as you say, something is not right in their being. Does not the duchess speak of anything?"

"No, she does not. I have broached her but she always avoids some straight answer. I must, it seems, inquire more into this problem by myself." The prince gulped his wine until the goblet was emptied, the vessel then he brimmed once more from the jug that sat upon the table and continued on to talk to Alph. "Methinks I will venture out this night when the hour is late and seek about the passage near where they reside, and to see if I may spy some happening for I must bottom this matter soon." He laid his head upon the pillow and rested until the hour he wished struck.

Henry was in a mood most foul. Sat he in his closet where no fire was lit, cold and dark the room chilled within the Tower palace. He listening to the rambling excuses of his twitching spy, who once again had failed in his attempt to rid the king of this scourge, "the Perkin Warbeck."

"Enough!" he shouted with raged tone. "You are as much use to me as a bow without twine, a foot without shoe ... a .... a ... spy without his head! Begone from my sight and do not show your twitching self afore me again, for as God looks upon me I will do you harm." The spy scurried away as a ship's rat to shore whilst he was still of one piece. "Is this, sir, the best you can accomplish?" he raised his voice once again to, this time, berate his close adviser the Lord Chancellor. "Time upon time you have tried to end this façade, and time upon time the same result gotten — which, as you are well aware of — is naught!"

"But, sire, if I may —" the chancellor interrupted but only for a breath of time.

"No, sir, you may not. This time I will lay the plot, for that imposter gets closer and closer to me and must be stayed. I have lost the chance to stop him before he lands upon these shores, by buffoons who know not what their game is. Do you not know how serious the situation is becoming? If he gets his toe into England he may gather more to his cause than we can control. We will send letters to the Duchess of Burgundy, to the fact that no further help or sanctuary be given to the said Perkin Warbeck. No monies shall be passed and all correspondence shall be ended. If this is not abided by, we will, without fail, take reprise upon the lands and the life of the duchess and of her subjects and state. She must have no doubt about this action, for it will be so. Make ready these letters and send them in haste to the stated ruler. And upon delivery of these letters, I wish to be informed most quickly of the answer so given to this correspondence. For their word I must have writ, that they will abide by my facts so written. If the Warbeck has no place to flee then soon we will have him and be done with this foolish charade, for it has lingered long enough. And be sure, my Lord Chancellor, this king will end it and it will be bloody."

"Yes sire, I will do your bidding with all haste."

"And send in my army commander. I wish to have some conference with him."

"Yes, my lord," answered the chancellor, bowing and grovelling as he left the closet, which still bounced the raged words from wall to wall, flaying the ears of the lord as he escaped the raging sovereign, pleased enough though to still be keeping his head shouldered for the present time. But the load of the task to be rid of the Warbeck had been taken from him, and he could not be blamed for any other's misfortune, and relief filled his step.

"You desired my presence, your Majesty?" 'Twas the army commander who spake to his sovereign. Light armour he wore, a tall, seasoned campaigner from many a battle, a fighter of the old school stood he.

The king seeming in some urgency spake. "Commander, tell me of your thoughts of this Perkin Warbeck. Tell me of the way you would stop his insurgence into my Realm. Stand easily and speak to me with freedom, be not afraid to tell me of that which I wish not to hear. I am filled enough with smarmy words and words that I wish to hear," the king spake to the one that he had much respect for. "You must know by this time the state of his armies, do you not?"

"Yes, sire, I know he commands in the region of five thousand men."

"Speak out then, tell me of the situation that is about me."

"He has a strong army with many who are well seasoned in war. He hopes that in Scotland to gain more to his following, which would be mainly wild and undisciplined Scots, but even such, would add to his force and we know numbers are all. When he does show his colours south of the Scottish lands, he would need the people of England most dearly, lords and commoners alike, to come to his side and to fight with him. For, my lord, without such loyalties he would fail, and it seems doubtful that such nobles would side with him. For peace and tranquility have been upon this Isle since your good self attained the throne.

"But, if I may say, to further bring your subjects to the fold of their king, I would cut the taxes to these commoners, at least until the problem is done. For then they would have little reason to change their allegiance. If you will offer them this, and the Perkin could only offer to them bloodshed and lost wages at best, then it is writ clear that which they will choose. For they know a lean rabbit in the bag is worth two plump ones running in the meadow. And may I suggest further, my lord, that we do not attack at first show of these rebels, but await at discreet locations to see what falls from the bedcovers as they shake their army southward. I believe they will be repelled by our northern barons and noblemen. And that the king's subjects will turn them back from whence they came."

"If that did happen, commander, then no large army would have to be summoned to repel them, and our coffers would remain filled and not drained for some needless reason." Once again the king would look to his monies in a crisis, for he loved to give such, as a man with no hands. "But the taxes that we would forgo, even for a short time, would bear heavily upon us." A mere drop in the ocean of money was his concern, but a miser he was with little doubt, and most frugal in his ways, except for his own pocket.

"Sire, the country is most devoted to you, except, as you know, the Cornishmen, who continually rise up against the crown, led by that carpenter and that stonemason, who seem to have them beguiled, so I am told. Still, sire, not to be taken without some concern. For with Perkin's forces they could become a threat. But 'tis better to fight such a threat close to London than to march three hundred miles for naught." The officer ended his words.

"Yes, commander, an army marched such a distance with victuals and shelter would deem most costly. But to lose naught by lowering the taxes of the northern peasants, I will increase the taxes upon the Cornishmen, to pay for the army that must be maintained to fight them. And once they concede to us I will forego the taxes imposed and be a most temperate king."

""Tis a good strategy, my lord, and manifests your royal knowledge of tact." The commander, though asked to speak freely, still laid upon his king some humbleness and flattery.

"You have been most informative to me, commander," the king spake as the conference neared its end. "Myself and the queen, and indeed our England, are in your debt, and if all proceeds to your suggestion you will be amply rewarded. Once this Perkin and the Cornishmen are done, we can continue to bringing this England to the might it should be. It has been many years that civil strife has encumbered us, and methinks the people know they can prosper when such unrest is not about them. The Queen Elizabeth has given me a son, the Prince Henry, and she is once again in the quiver of motherhood. Stable is the line of succession, which also brings peace to our land. Our armies have the fastest and strongest horses in all of Europe. Those glorious animals bred by the caring hands of Moran & Smith. Times will be well when the pretender is done."

"My lord speaks with such truths, I am taken aback by your wisdom." Once more the officer spake words that the king wished to hear, and indeed he did seem charmed by them. "May I ask, sir, of the agents that are at the court of the King James? Are they placed and active to this cause?"

"Yes, commander, all seems well in that respect, for I receive regular dispatches, which make good reading. And when Warbeck is ensconced within the Scottish court we will have in our pocket every move that he makes … even before he steps it."

"'Tis well such is our fortune. Would my king give any mind to the murder of the Perkin Warbeck?" asked the officer.

"We will play the game as the die rolls, but, if need be, we will end him. Most preferred is the way of interrogation, whereupon he will be shown to be a liar and a usurper of crowns, and there his story will be ended by the axe. We do not need a martyr to drag along with us for all time." The king gave forth his opinion upon the way he would wish for this scheme to end.

"You speak such true words, your Majesty, for indeed a martyr would not wash well. I wish to thank you, sire, for the honour you have bestowed upon me this day, and pledge my utmost devotion to your House." The commander flourished a bow to his king, and then he was away about his duties into the dusky eve. Leaving his Majesty to ponder the move next to make, but deemed the thing to do was to bring out his patience and wait.

Silently the door closed upon the candlelit chamber. Richard moved to the dim passage, to creep and slink about in the shadowed crevices of the way he trod, quietly in stealth from dark to black he went, to make his queried way to the chambers where lodged the Lady Marcela De Boer. He came to sight the door of her chamber, and close hid himself in the alcove there to wait for a moment, with thumping chest and sucked air. With a sly look to see that naught was about, he moved on, as black as the wall he slithered to the chamber door, lit but dim from the dying flame of the torch that hung from the dank stone, but shone there enough light to show the place of intrigue he sought. He came close to the door and, reaching up, pulled over the cover to the lamp and snuffed out the only light. The lamp with no air to burn gave out its last puffs of black smoke and died into cold tar.

The entrance was darkened as he opened the door in the night's silence, and within the blackness, stepped he in, as some ghostly shape, unseen and unheard, to stand within the chamber of his aim. He stood against the wall as of one with it; the heartbeat loudly but unheard, breathing came in quited gasps. He stilled and listened with unclothed ears to bring to his state the sounds that drifted about. He heard some sighs in constant beat with a creaking cot, as that webbing and oak stretched and slacked to the bodies upon it. He came, still cloaked to the wall as he slinked, to the door that lay ajar. The door that was to the bedchamber where sounds of rapture played the room. He then, with most discretion, peeked with stopped breath into the candlelit chamber. The goblets of wine half-drunk flickered in the candle's flame. The fire just a glow to what it had been. He saw then the bodies dark upon the cot, naked and shiny with passion upon them. All became still as they lay in some rapture flat about upon the crumpled bedclothes, all about in some disarray, sweated and crumbled to no shape of covers but of a raggedy pile. Hard was it for Richard not to exclaim loudly with gasped words at the picture that was played before him, but with much resolve did contain his sound that remained chested within his body bursting. His legs though were not steady, and had became shaky and nerved, as he made his covered way to leave the chamber that was Marcela De Boer's dark intrigue. He came out from the bedchamber, and, in gentle guile, pulled to the door with muffed creak. Along he went, again clinging to the wall to be at the chamber's entrance. Unseen and unheard, he drifted along the passageway to his friendly place, and 'twas with much relief to click his own latch behind him, and to breathe, for it seemed that for much time he had not. He gulped as wine the fresh air, as he stood before the window of his chamber, until he became more composed from his clandestine journey and shook most heartily the stirring body of his ally.

"Alph ... Alph," in a loud whisper he croaked.

"What is it, Richard? ... Oh, my lord, you found out that which you sought?"

"Yes, Alph, I did so and was awed by the sight of it all."

"Come, Richard, tell me all."

"Alph, along the passageway I did slink in such darkness like some evil rat." From the lips came the tale with every pokey detail, of every bug he trod, of every web he broke, of every mouse that scurried away. In such precise words 'twas told to bring all to the shocked end of the intrigue.

"I cannot believe that which you speak, my prince." Alph sat back in some state as the prince finished his drift, finding it difficult to drink in the story so told. "If you were not my prince I would not believe your unlikely tale, for you always speak to me truthfully, though such as you speak seems contrived, yet I know it is not. You will, I suppose, relate to the duchess of your findings?"

"Yes, Alphonse, yes, I will, for she has to know what trickery is afoot beneath her roof. Upon the morrow I will speak with her and tell my tale. 'Tis hourly late now and I must rest, though sleep may come uneasily, like the child before the morrow's birthday."

The day was of rained clouds and darkened skies, bringing gloom over the palace's dark hidings. The candles were lit in the afternoon's murk as if eve had come too soon. Richard had been filled with the duties of his ships, but such of his day was ended and he was dressed in cloth more refined, as he took then his urged steps to his meet with Margaret. In eager state was he to tell his tale of the intrigue he had seen. He was entered into the chamber with little ado and soon embraced his cousin in tender caress, and to kiss the warmed cheeks that glowed from the fire bright, where she had sat until aroused by her prince's coming. She took his hand, and they sat by the fire that brightened the dark chamber, warming their hearts with its crackling desire.

"'Tis but a few days, my dear cousin, until I take up my army and sail to Scotland, where soon I will take my place, and will march to the glory to come upon that land so lost to me. And when I am king, you will reap all the rewards due to you in your unfailing trust in me." The prince led with talk that was not of his mission, but felt he needed to ease himself a little slowly before he brought out the subject of his council.

"Thank you—O kingly one," she playfully spake as she crouched herself closer to the prince.

"I do wish to speak to you though upon another matter." He started to bring out his troubling secret, as the duchess lifted her head and brighter became her eyes, as she moved a little straighter to hear what was upon the tongue of this prince. Though she did not speak, her face showed she was awaiting the tale. "I found, my lady, upon my musings about the palace, something that troubles me greatly, and I feel I must relate it to you, though it may prove most disturbing to your good self. Also, it may bring some disillusionment upon those that are close to you, but indeed I have to speak of it, and for your own well-being you must be told."

"Please, do not hold me in such a fearful state; please, relate to me that which concerns you." The lady was most anxious for Richard to continue and felt it would be morn before it came out.

"'Tis, my lady, regarding the Lady Marcela De Boer, and of your companion, Antonio Bercholi—"

"Please, continue, my prince," spake the duchess as a little smile, so small as almost to be unseen at her mouth's corner, hinted that all was not unknown from the coming words.

"I happened at the Lady Marcela's chamber at the late eve of yesterday, and with much quietness I entered in, for strange noises and movements were about."

"You went, sire, into the lady's chamber unannounced in the darkened night? That is most shameful. I thought that you were true to me, but I see I may have been wrong to think such." The duchess played with words upon the prince.

"No, no, my dearest, 'twas not in my thoughts for such activity, just curiosity took me there and naught else. But, my duchess, what I spied there turned me into some muddled state. Madam, I saw that the gentleman there, Antonio Bercholi, is no eunuch, has never been a eunuch, and has not even seen manhood, for, my lady, he is a woman, with all female parts most pronounced, and what I saw bears no mistake." … The prince waited for some awed reaction from the duchess and paused to allow for it, but no such reaction did she show.

Only spake she in calmed tone. "Please, continue, prince."

The prince was not sure of the state of the duchess, and thought that may she was in some kind of shock and faintness, which made her unable to speak more than she did. "Well, madam, even more appalled was I at the sight that next did meet my eyes, for was not only Bercholi shown in *her* true light, but also shown in that chamber was the Lady Marcela, who was involved with all her wares in this chamber of deceit, to show, madam, that the lady is no lady, for *he* has all the manly trappings of a male, and indeed my lady is a man in all parts." The prince had finished his tale and ended upon the highest note. Proudly he awaited the reaction from the duchess, but none did come, so he deemed her dumbed by the whole tale as if 'twas beyond belief. His wait for some tirade, some jumped anger to leap up again and again against this deception did not come about so.

"Richard," in a calm, amused tone now she spake, "I know of all this you have spake. You think of me that I am so naive of it?"

The prince slumped to lay his back upon the seat where they rested. For after all his trials and shocked state, all his selecting of the right words to bring down such contempt upon the intrigue, he lay shot down as a bird in flight. For, after all of this, the duchess was aware of the situation and seemed little concerned of it.

"You see, my dear," she began talking about the matter as a mother would to her child, "the *Lady* Bercholi, so educated, so clever in her teachings, her languages, her music, and—to face all with blunt words—not the most striking dove in the cote, was unable to pass along her many gifts, for, my prince, she was, as a woman, chained to such prejudice as hangs about women in this age. And so she did decide one day that she would break free from the prison that bound her, and so she dressed as a man and sought positions as a man. In short spate in doing so she gained the reputation of being able to pass on her knowledge with great ease to her students, and all were blessed with her most caring manner and she was filled with accomplishment, the thing she most wanted but thought she would never attain.

"Soon though her charade was stumbled upon, by some spying nobodies who reported the matter to the Church. For her actions she was stripped and whipped before the Church council. And, after this came about, she was banned from all teachings, for so stated was it that corruption and deceit were her guides. She could find no employment in her native land, she was not even allowed to wash dishes. So she fled, with only a bag in hand and a ragged dress upon her back, to this place of Flanders. Soon her outer wounds healed, and then her inner wounds healed. She came to my palace one day in her manly mode, and placed upon the table before me all her cards with none sleeved. And with respect for the hardships she had suffered and for the education she showed to posses, she came to stay and has always been a faithful and sincere person to me. She has given to me much knowledge and true advice, and she is my most cherished friend. To me she relates all within these walls, for she, in her mind, is much debted to me, though she gives more than I. All her activities she truthfully tells and, in doing so, I am surprised at naught for I know.

"Then, my prince, to the *Lady* Marcela De Boer. A most striking figure, do you not think?—possessing the most delicate of manners, more of a woman than of a man she is and all of such sympathy and understanding. A person I need by my side, not fickle, not flitting from one lover to another, not stirring intrigue and deception as others are wont to do."

"But, dear cousin, what of the fact that this is a man that lays beside you almost nightly? Contact so severe must play out," posed such the prince as he listened to the lady's version of the reasons.

"It does not, my prince. When he comes, he comes only to hold me and to caress me and that is all he does. Bound to his leg is his manhood to remain inactive, and so it remains until he is with his companion, the Lady Bercholi. That, my dear, is the story. Not as bizarre as first sighted. And, dear cousin, do not forget the night whence the three of us did revel in such rapture, and the hands of Marcela did lay such delight upon you with her magical ways."

"Do not remind me of the act that we were so engaged in upon that night. Thought I bedded with two ladies, not as such as you have described." Sullied and deceived and most annoyed was he.

The duchess laughed. "Do not feel such, my dearest. In all good faith you joined and naught to soil did happen to you. Are you not still whole?"

"Yes, dear cousin, but I think I cannot look the Marcela De Boer in the eye, for she indeed does hold something over me. 'Tis well I will soon sail from this land of masked players. I know not who is what, nor whether black is white, or that white is black."

He then in some state of melancholy did leave his cousin, his boots more to his gaze than the moon. In dismay he went to his chambers to relate to Alphonse that the story told was no story. No enlightenment, but old stockings full of holes and donned many times. He with tired step sought his cot and fell to sleep, where no one could say that black is white, and where he was his own master. The morn did come and he found himself renewed, the yesterday now more of humour than of sadness. He paid his respects to the duchess, in front of whom he had been in some sad state. He sorriedly excused himself to her for such immature behaviour, and all was a rose garden. But still the prince could not strike his gaze with the Lady De Boer, unable to remove from himself as yet the deception he still did feel.

The duchess gazed out from the window of the watch tower upon that calm morn of September in the year of our Lord fourteen hundred and ninety-three. The harbour of Calais busy far below, the ocean splaying its washy light upon the vessels whose ropes lay slacked. The misty sea stirred with its ghostly drift, as all that could be spied of the boats that awaited in the harbour were their mastheads, with all such banners and flags sagged in the still air. Soon though, in hours come, the breeze would rise and unfold the bright standards and fill the sails to billow. Then the creaking boats like a flock of crows would take its song away.

The duchess looked out upon the scene with many moods about her person, one crossing the other. The courier had arrived from England with the letter from Henry. She knew on parchment to what end her state was. But she also knew that if she ever saw the Prince Richard again he would be standing as the King of England, for no more could she give shelter, care, or finance to his efforts. For surely she would be done as a pig at the butcher's shop. Or, if by some pardon she was not murdered, she would in all sureness lose all she held in property and finance. And 'twas without doubt she could not bear such upon her. The life she lived and the treasures she possessed would not end upon the whim of a prince. A king, surely; a man of no place, never.

The breeze upped the mist to clear, but still was the fog about as the ships moved away from the harbour of Calais. The masts showed their banners and flags with lilting sway in the dragging air. They swayed from one side to the other, seemingly hundreds of them upon the morn of their journey. The fog lifted its cover, but only soon enough to see the black hulls and fading sails drift away on sight's eye, then to be gone. A prince to bring his army against the King Henry, to gain at last the throne or lose all chance to do so. The duchess and her companions watched till naught was sighted. Antonio Bercholi looked across with some evil flashing in his eyes, as the Lady Marcela held the hand of the lady-in-waiting, Marie. It seemed all would not be well upon their return within the walls of Margaret's castle.

Chapter Twenty-four.

This Ship of Peril.

The sails aloft filled; the banners fluttered. All farewells bade to one land, with greetings to come to another. Creaking and splashing they cut through and made good haste upon the calm sea. The prince could see, from the bow of his lead ship, the other boats in his armada, all in good order and following their leader to the Scottish shores. Geese in flight were they, all splayed out at their leader's back. A mighty force did come to bring the usurper Henry to task.

"'Tis good victuals you serve, Captain." Both the prince and Alph were at sup with the captain of the vessel, upon this first eve from port and many miles from any landfall. The prince spake directly to start some conversation, for the tongues did lull. Some mumbled jargon came back from the captain, but most difficult were the words to place as if his mouth were stuffed with chicken feathers.

"Please bear with my captain, sirs," the first mate spake, for he could see there was some difficulty to understand of what was being said. "He is usually of good speak, but due to one of his teeth he is in somewhat of distress. Feared are we that it is abscessed, and pray we make port before the pain worsens. Neither a tooth-puller nor a surgeon do we have here, for the captain himself being the only surgeon of this vessel." The captain nodded in agreement to his mate, as he took no victuals and drank only brandy. His head to one side as he poured the liquid into his mouth, and washed it about the troubled tooth before he swallowed. His cheek glowed as red as the ripened apple and shiny as such. Now and again he would stand and march about the small cabin, with moan and groan and stomped boot, with his clutched hand held at his raged cheek. Then the pain would ease and he would sit once again with his guests.

"We pray upon the morrow that you will find some relief from your angst," the prince spake, hoping his words may bring some relief to the pained old sailor.

"Mmm … Mmm-mmm, mmm—" was all he could answer in his state.

"The captain bids you a good eve gentlemen, for he does wish to rest from his affliction," the mate spake again for his mumbling captain. "And

I must take to the rudder this night to guide us to the morn."

The prince and Alphonse had supped and ate of the seafarer's cake and wine, and made to rest within the rocking hull, creaking as it cut still its way through the cold sea. The planks of the hull leaked the sea into the bottom boards, and seen upon their way the seamen constant with their leather and wooden pumps sucking the slurping water from the hull's keel line. Two hours they would work, all of muscle and blistered hand before relief would come, and the next lowly tars would carry on the ceaseless task for all of the hours the ship was a-sail.

The dark night closed upon them blacker than any night yet seen. The ship rocked evermore, and voices about awakened the half-sleeping pair as they were lurched about in their cots. The prince upped and made his way through the dripping hull to the deck. The shouting was being hurled about the vessel as his head came up from the hold. To spy all about him the activity of a ship entering waters of storm. He looked up to see the sky as black as a rabbit's burrow. But slashed was it by the lightning strike seen all of ten miles ahead, which brought much light to the scene upon the deck. The sailors with their wetted faces glistened in the flash, whiskery and gapped-tooth ruffians were they, but 'twas that no fancy fop would survive such labour as they took upon themselves. Seen most clearly in another flash were they climbing the swaying masts aloft to tie up the billowing sails, still yet in waters not yet stirred by the stick of storm, and time to prepare for that which headed toward them. A flash again came, with thunder rolling from afar, to light up the armada aback and to see the dark figures there toing and froing, engaged all in the same tasks to ready for the storm that would soon come in dreaded fashion.

The strikes were coming quicker now. The sea was riled and did become stirred by hell's wand. The ship began to lurch about and to sway in the turbulent stir. Richard's foot slipped with the rise and fall of the ship, and so he was landed quickly at the stairs' bottom to lay stilled but unhurt, though to stand steady, he was not able, for the rolling and dipping of the vessel made it too severe to put feet upon the dripping boards. He lay still and prayed that soon the night would end and the storm would be gone. The roll of the vessel steadied somewhat, and Richard found he could half stand by clutching upon the wooden steps that led to the deck. He saw the sky through the hatch above him. Dark clouds still chased overhead by the wind that the devil howled about. The sky was streaked with lightning, showing still the rain coming heavy down upon them. The ship it seemed was floundering and no true course did it seem to hold. Not set straight into the wind as was needed, but to sideways and whichway. 'Twas, as Richard saw to be, in danger of sinking, with its hull at odds with the waves. He continued to pull himself from the hatch, fighting the lash that wanted him not upon the upper of the staggered vessel; at last he struggled up and was able to stand upon the deck, clinging tightly to one of the fastened ropes. Through the rain that cut his face and dripped about his eyes, he saw all about in many pieces, the broken mast that had toppled to the deck, bringing ropes and canvas tangled all about. Sailors were there, struggling to bring the flapping sails to some calm, lying then across the once proud canvas that had billowed above them, as others tied them still. Many he saw about the deck holding tight to aught they could grip, their bodies all of sop, their hands cold and numb.

Richard turned then to the stern to see, in the flash of the heaven's glow, one man at struggle with the rudder, the sea all too strong for him to steer the ship into the wind alone, but he knew 'twas the only way the ship could be saved, so he fought on in his lone battle.

"Sire, things look not good. What shall we do?" 'Twas Alph, who it seemed for a long while was not aware of the dire situation, but had at last come to the deck, and had seen such of the disaster that was unfolding.

"To the stern, Alph. We have to make to the rudder before the ship is overcome."

Alph followed the dark shape that struggled against the storm as they both made way to the stern, sometimes standing with lean at strange state, sometimes crawling with fingernails clawing at the wet planking, then to find some rope that draped there to pull themselves further along. Oft the deck would tilt and they would slide in fear to the rail's edge, groping for any object that would stop their fall, only to be thrown to the other side to hang with all their strength once again. With legs and arms flailing they ended sliding into the bulkhead, and to the sailor who fought with the heavy tiller as the unruly rudder washed forth and back again in the wild waters that pushed hard against it. So strong was the pull upon it, the sailor's legs were oft times lifted from the deck, to leave him swinging about with his arms clutching that heavy wooden arm, the only friend he had. The one thing that had stopped him from being swept o'er the side into the churning devil's brew. Richard and Alphonse were able to reach out and grasp the unruly shaft. The three pulled upon it, but seemed it would take ten men to hold it steady. So they struggled as ten men and were able to bring her to right. Two more sailors came the sliding way, and all with great effort brought her straight to point the ship into the storm's rage. Lurching still from bow to stern, as it climbed and then dropped from the sea's mountains and into its valleys. But now 'twas steady and would not sideways flounder.

They, all with salted eyes and cold hands, pushed and pulled the rudder deep into the night, keeping the ship straight into the swell. Their strength was waning as time took all away.

"Where is the mate?" Richard shouted above the wind and waves that crashed.

"'E's gone sire, washed o'er the side, gone to see is brother in the calm below." The sailor who had taken the rudder gave his reply.

"And the captain, where is he?"

"Drunk 'e be, supped rum like water 'e did, trying 'ard to stop 'is pain. Now 'e feels no pain."

"He's not dead, is he?" Richard once more spake to the sailor, finding a place between the crashing of the waves.

"Nay, sire, he ain't be dead, he be just drunk. But 'e ain't no 'elp to us."

They said little more but hung onto the heavy tiller until the dawn was close, and with such did the black clouds break and show the last of the night's stars twinkle. The sun gradually came and chased away that most terrible of nights, and soon calmness came to bring all placid to the churning that was as if all was some mistake and the storm was but a dream. All looked as rats saved from the river, wet and ragged and shivered with cold.

Richard took it upon himself to become captain until the right one was able to bring about his duties. He pointed to the sailor who had first fought the rudder. "You stay at the helm. Do you know where to steer the thing?"

"I do, sir, but only in rough gauge, for I cannot point it proper … I cannot point it exact to the port we seek."

"Do as best you can; as long as we do not return to Calais."

"Yes, sire, I will do my best; as long as I can see the sun, I can find my way."

"We will relieve you as soon as we are able." They left the grinning-toothed sailor at his toy with all his fatigue gone. For 'twas only yesterday he was emptying swill, yet today … captain of the vessel. Richard then gathered four more sailors who were busy gathering up some ropes and throwing the broken mast over the side of the ship. "Take yourselves below and get the pumps working. We have been through a storm. We do not now wish to sink in a calm sea. We will relieve you when we are able."

"Yes, sir," they answered as they made toward the hold.

"And do not bend to any fighting," Richard called after them. "Our lives depend upon your duty this day." They waved some sloppy salute and disappeared below the deck. Then more sailors he gathered and spake to them as a captain would. "Clean up the decks and make ready as best you can the sails. Who is lead amongst you?"

"That be me, sire," an older sailor answered as he stepped forward to show himself.

"You then are in state to oversee these fellows; 'tis your responsibility to keep them to their task and to make this ship worthy again."

"Aye, sire," he acknowledged Richard as they made to their labours. Alph, who had been securing the tiller, stood close to Richard as he started to peer about the ocean.

"What of the other vessels, Alph? Can you see them?" Without any word, Alph climbed a short distance up the scaling rope and looked about the grey waters. Far and near he gathered all he saw.

"I do see some, my lord, all appearing much in the same shape we find ourselves. But they are far and scattered, and not in any formation as an armada should be."

"Well, 'twill be each vessel on its own now. We will assess our state when we reach the Firth of Forth. The captains will bring their ships there as best as they are able … As for captains, 'tis time to seek ours and to what state he harbours."

They walked the slipped deck with its tangled lay all about to come to the cabin of their captain. A rap at the sogged door brought no answer to ear. Richard turned the handle as he tried for entry; the door though was swollen and jammed tight. A strong bump with the shoulder soon threw it open as they stumbled inside with the giving gateway. A stinking cabin met them; awash with the sea's water, mixed with urine and vomit, it came rushing out from the door ajar onto the slimy deck, and to tipple itself into the nearly calmed sea. Soon all the water had left to leave all manner of slime and dirt blaged* to the planked floor. Then, heard from the corner of the cabin where the captain was bunked, moans and foul words searching the air. They came closer and saw where the captain lay. His place of rest was above the line of water, but still his cot filled of stench foul. They came toward the captain—his glowing cheek seemed to guide them as some beacon upon the hill. Nearer they came, trying to contain their breath so as not to suck in the foulness that was about. All was still in the cabin, but then as if by some flag waved, the captain jumped up with sickening cries, raging like someone from the madhouse. Foam came from his bleeding mouth, his hair was matted and full of knots. Dripping wet was he, his clothes covered in vomit and blood. He shouted about loudly in a tongue unknown, and began to throw at the intruders anything he could grasp, hurling with all his might at the visiting ogres that taunted his every minute. The raging tooth had turned him into a madman. Richard

---

* *blaged* [coined] thickly layered or spread

and Alphonse rushed to the door before any hurt befell them, both fighting for the small opening that was the way to their safety. Fresh air blew about their faces as they stumbled out, as sweet as morning flowers, it seemed to be so, compared to the foul hole they had just left. Turning, they slammed the door to close and held upon the latch to keep the brain-poisoned captain within. But still from those wooden walls could be heard frantic cries to rattle and to push at the door from time to time and becoming even madder, for he knew he was within his own prison.

Help was called and in short spate the leader of the crew came to the fracas. Two more sailors, who upon seeing the plight of the others struggling to keep closed the door, came and wrested it from them to hold the captain at bay. Richard and Alphonse leaned themselves against the cuddy wherein ranted their raged captain. Wet and worn they rested for a short while to see what next would be done.

"My dear God, Alph, he is so crazed he should, it seems, be in an asylum. But then 'tis only his tooth that makes him so. It has to be pulled." Richard looked about for some guidance in the matter and so addressed the lead sailor. "What say you of the dilemma?—and what is your name, pray?"

"Jack Thompson, sire."

"Then, Jack, what say you?"

"Well, sire, the captain and the mate are the only ones who know how to navigate the ship. We can manage to keep it afloat and to steer it close to the shore, but as to bring it to the port we seek, no, sir, we cannot. The captain is the only one who can do such."

"I have been told, Jack, that the captain is the only surgeon upon the vessel, is that correct?"

"Yes, sire, that is so."

"Then, gentlemen, as I see it, the only course open to us is to remove the offending tooth so that he may return to sanity."

"Remove the tooth!" The questionable words spilled from the mouth of Alph as if in some disbelief of any attempt to do so. "Who could do such surgery?" he queried.

"I had in mind that you may do such, Alph," Richard spake in some jest, his face though did not relate such.

"No, sir ... No, I cannot. I will do all you may ask of me but I am unable to undertake such a task. No, no, I cannot." Alph was most a-feared that upon him may be placed such a task.

"I only jest with you, Alph; I would not burden you such, for I know your tread would not step upon the beetle. It seems I must attempt the doings myself."

"Thank you, sire," spake Alph, most relieved that he was only being toyed with.

"It will take more than the two of us my friend, for he behaves as a wild boar in a pen." Richard turned again his question toward the seaman, Jack. "Are the surgical tools within his cabin?"

"Yes, sire, they are locked away within his oak chest."

"Then all of us here must assist in this endeavour. He is wild and strong and will fight like a mad dog, so all of us must be ready and wary throughout, for he could rise crazed from some placid state. We will rush in and, without any ceremony, we will subdue him; with one each at an arm and the others to take his legs. The cot must be pulled to the middle of the room and we must lift him upon it. We should then, with all hands, be able to subdue him, long enough to pour as much rum down his gullet as we are able, and pray that he will become docile in some short spate. When such occurs, we can tie him down most securely and proceed with the pulling of the tooth. Does anyone have anything to add about this action?" No replies came, but worried glances abounded from one to the other as the disagreeable task was about to unfold upon them. "Jack." Once again the lead man was called. "Change the crew upon the pumps, and make ready two more to relieve them, for we know not how long this endeavour may be. We will take some victuals and soon be at our task." To the galley they ventured, and there began to fill themselves with foods that they prayed would increase their strength.

The time had come to enter the cage. With flasks of rum, strong ropes, and much apprehension, they gathered outside the door beyond which their captain did lay. Richard, Alphonse, Jack, and the two tars. All stood for a moment, for they understood what depended upon this motley crew. If they would fail in this task they would not in safety be able to put to land at the port of their destination, and 'twoud be more than likely that to an English harbour they would limp. Such a fate would not be greeted with any joy, for they would quickly become prisoners of Henry and few morrows would they see. The other such offering to them would be that they could wreck upon the ill-lit rocks of the craggy coast, and lay washed upon the bottom, sucked by the hungry shrimp.

Richard, with his ear upon the wet door of the cubby, listened for any sound that came from within. All seemed as calm as the sea they floated upon, tranquil and quiet. "Time is nigh," he whispered to his band. "May God help us upon this task."

Quietly the bar was removed that had been placed to secure the entrance. Then, with the tailing words still about, Richard flung open the door and they all tumbled into the slimy cabin. Smashed and broken debris lay about as they staggered in and saw they, standing before them, the raged captain, his face swollen to twice its normal size. To throw himself upon them as soon as he saw the leers of the coming ogres; with their horns and slobbering mouths, they were moving closer to him, they all cruel that sought his blood. Spitting and swearing he came with club in hand; he would take as many with him to the grave as he could. Blood still slurped from his mouth as he brought down the first sailor with the crack of his weapon, ringing about the cabin with its chime, as the tar slid along in the cabin's slime to crumple against the wall, and then to lay still with his bloodied head. Another swing came that was almost laid upon Richard, but he dodged the coming club and, though he slipped to the floor, he managed to clutch onto the legs of the captain to bring him down; slipping and sliding upon the slop, he could stand no more and fell with anguished cries to the hard floor. The others were atop of him now; Jack managed to secure in his grasp one of the flailing legs, as the other sailor held tight upon the other. Stirring in the corner was the tar that had been felled; though still with head spinning, he struggled to his feet; with birds' fluttering within his bloodied top, he managed to bring himself over to the melee and fell atop of the captain, and held the free arm with Richard, gripped tight upon the other. His head still shook about, snapping with snarled teeth, like a mad dog trying to bite these villains who tried for his bone.

"Calm, sire, calm; we try only to give you help," Richard pleaded for some tranquility within the muddled head. The captain's actions did slow from the words spoken, but 'twas known to all that he just was at rest to gain more strength before more anger showed. "Alph, pull closer the rum flasks," Richard gasped to his friend who had been trying to contain the shaking head. He stretched over and was able to grasp one of the flasks and handed it over to Richard, who, with his teeth, pulled the stopper and began pouring the brew into the ranting mouth of the captain. He gulped, he coughed, he spat, but he had to swallow. With Alph holding the captain's head by the ears, Richard was able to keep the steady pour close to the twisting lips. He was taking it down in gurgling slurps. "Methinks he is most thirsty. Come, my captain, drink away," Richard spake with a little more cheer to his voice as the state of the quarry seemed to calm. But then, squirted from the thick blackened lips of the captain, a stream of rum and spit was directed at the voice that chattered above him, to be seen running all over the face of his tormentor. Richard wiped off the mess with one hand but did not stay in his pouring the rum into the hole that showed. The captain gurgled and spat again but was forced to keep swallowing. Then he spat no more, and gurgled no more as the rum overflowed from his mouth, as he seemed filled to the top of his head. To slump and lie in some still state.

"Do you think he is drunk now?" Alphonse asked to Richard.

"He may be, but for sure I know not ... See if you can find the surgical box," Richard spake to Jack, who slowly released a leg, and, as it did not move, he went about to search in the dimmed room. As he did so the others lifted the captain onto the cot, which had been dragged over, and it appeared that he was well drunk. Jack came to find the cupboard that held the instruments, but 'twas secured by a strong hasp and a heavy lock. He searched as best he could for the key but found it not.

"Sire, it is securely locked and there is no key to find. Does he, pray, have it upon his person?" Jack spake hoping that there may be some help coming from Richard. Crack! The fist came up from the captain sending the sailor, who had loosed his grip, sprawling into the slop. The captain was all riled again and was making some effort to break free, but Jack, who saw the happening, came slopping over and fell upon the flailing arm to stop the madness. The stunned sailor was upon his feet again, appearing little hurt from the blow, and came covered in the mire to hold onto the prey once again.

"Is everyone in good state?" Richard asked about.

"Yes, sire, we are so," Jack did answer for all gathered about their captain.

"Then let us see if the key is about him," Richard spake as he searched about the stirring captain, whose glossed eyes followed every move made against him, liken to some puppet did he glare. "Here—I think I may have found it," Richard grubbed about in the mud at the captain's belt. He gave a strong pull from the dark there and free it came to jingle in the air its melody. They were held up so Jack could take them to the cupboard's lock. The rum was then poured once again into the twisted mouth of the captain. He drank and drank as if he himself was an empty barrel, for those about knew not that such an amount could be supped. "More rum," was called for, as another flask was emptied and a new one began its journey down the rasping throat. But then, in little time, the captain lay still, done to a burnt crust, numbed by the golden liquid that had been poured into him. "Give him more!" came the call, so Richard attempted to ply more to the open mouth, but full 'twas and could take no more, as it ran more upon the floor and not down the throat. One by one they eased their hold upon their honourable captain and stood dripping as they looked down upon the sleeping shape; no pain did he feel as he drifted upon those golden waters.

"When he is well, I pray that he will forgive us for that which we are bringing upon this proud being." One of the sailors spake his thoughts, so that all could hear his fear of some reprisal that may come upon them.

"Fear not, my good fellow," Richard gave some speak to the matter raised. "For if this is not done he will not survive; the poison from his affliction will soon bring dire comings upon him. If it is not bled, his brain will be of no use, with no hope of recovery and to the asylum he would go to be fed slop and chastised. So, be not feared; you do only the thing that must be done. If perchance your captain has no heart, which I do not believe, and that indeed he does bring some punishment upon you, in God's eyes you will be a blessed soul."

"Thank you, sire; my heart is deemed much lighter by your council." The sailor it seemed for the moment had forgotten his worries. Clink! The box of instruments was sat upon the small table that had been placed close to the cot of the captain, where he lay seemingly in a helpless state. The tools jingled one upon the other as 'twas placed down, and again each looked at the other pondering the cruel things that sang such a sweet song within that box, a song though of some dire things to come. For all dreaded the tools of the surgeon and the tooth-puller. Sooner they to die in battle than upon some bench.

Jack opened the box with the others grouped about him, they who could not help but to peer reluctantly into the dim opening to see there those shiny, devilish things that glinted in the half-light, winking their sparkle for someone to take them away from their dark home and to play the game they were made for. Leather straps with large buckles they saw and all kinds of metal pieces twisted together. Richard pushed his hand inside the box and delved about pulling out the tool that he sought. Shiny and strong it showed as they all stepped back a little, for they did not wish to be too close to the thing that glimmered. A tooth-puller … Thick teeth they saw with filed grooves to grip the tooth, made liken to the blacksmith's tongs, though of thicker iron for the pulling and twisting 'twas apt to do. A head clamp next was shown. A band for clamping about the head with a bar protruding each side, made for the helpers of the task, so the head could be held still whilst the surgeon did his work. More objects that glittered in candlelight came from the box, as the mouth-stretchers, so needed for this act, were lifted out by Richard. Two clasps were they, one for the upper teeth, and one for the lower teeth, with a screw that was between them, which upon turning would open the clamps as far as one desired. This would keep the mouth open wide for the pulling of the tooth. They all looked at the display that was laid out upon the table, as if in some kind of a trance from the brightness of those evil devices, and they all knew they would never visit such a place as the tooth-puller's chamber, not while their legs could run them away into the bushes.

A stirring moan broke them from their thoughts; 'twas the derelict captain who tried for some movement from his stilled self. But he was not yet able to move his body, for 'twas still weighted down it seemed with a ton of lead.

"Come then, lads, let's to it," Richard began directing his helpers. "Firstly, let us place upon him the head clamp, for then at least we will be able to hold him still if he stirs." The instrument was picked from the table and clamped tight about the goggled-eyed head that flopped about. The band was placed just above the eyebrows and showed like some evil torture upon a criminal. "You boys hold onto the bars tightly; if he awakens, which he may, you will have a good chance to hold him still." Richard ordered the two sailors who then gripped the bars tightly. They stood with their own scars of the battle, and readied themselves with legs braced and hands secure upon the handles, at the ready. The hands and the arms of the captain they tied down with the leather straps, and buckled them tight. The same was also done for the twitching legs and slime-covered feet, which were without boots, being thrown about in one of the captain's frenzies, and lost somewhere in the tumble of the cabin.

"Stand at the ready, Jack, and quickly help where your strength is needed." Richard continued with his charge of the action.

"Aye, sire," Jack answered.

"Alph, give me help here to pry open his mouth so we may secure the clamps." The jaw was locked and stiff, making it hard to open. Richard and Alphonse were both at the head as the others watched the happening whilst they held onto their subdued captain. A wooden pry they took to lever open the tight, stubborn mouth. It opened enough to force in the thin end of the mouth wedge, and with the mallet they tapped it between the grimy teeth to slowly open the gurgling gape. A thicker wedge they tapped in next, and then another that was even thicker, showing then wide enough to place in the mouth-stretcher. Richard gazed into the evil-smelling mouth to see wherein the tooth they sought did lie.

"I see it!" he called out. The gum was red and bloody, and seeping some yellow bile from around the back where lay the tooth. The stretcher was placed as close as they were able to the tooth they were to pull. Richard clipped it in and wound the screw as far as he could with his fingers, then, with the tool that fitted the screw holes, began to turn it. Slowly the mouth opened wider until it had widened enough so they could get the puller in. "Methinks that should be enough, for there is a need not to break his jaw. We look not for a confession. Well, my friends, are we all ready?" Richard asked as the nods were given, and took he firmly into his grasp the tool that would do the task. With sleeves turned high he brought the tooth-puller all shiny and cold to the captain. Placing one knee upon his chest he went in with the tool, rattling upon the other teeth as he found his way to the demon that lurked in silence. There, seen hiding with the others in the dark back, in the gloom of the captain's mouth, looking every bit as good as the ones it stood beside, but its seeping roots told a different tale. Richard peered as best he could into the dark cave to seek out the one that was the giver of such anguish. Then he clamped on, good and strong. "Pray, I have the right one within the tool's grasp, for 'tis like a graveyard in here as black as a moonless night, the stones standing all much the same … 'Tis time, lads." He gripped the puller even tighter and started twisting and pulling at the tooth, not yet knowing if 'twas moving. The captain's eyes opened wide with terror glaring out from them. He tried to shout out in his fear and his pain, but strange noises were all that he could manage as he tried to shake his head free, but 'twas too firmly held and he could not. Pulled he upon his arms and his legs with much strength, but to naught came the effort, held he by the many thick straps. Jack held down firmly the captain's shoulders so Richard could pull even harder in his task. He pulled and twisted the tool even more, so much so he could feel that his strength was ebbing. A loud crack sounded as out the devil came, to make Richard fall back with the tooth grasped in the bright of the metal puller, and seen at dangle from its root, the abscess showed still in its sack, like a white grape swinging back and forth. Richard placed the tool upon the table with the tooth and the abscess still throbbing there, then, taking the rum flask, gulped himself a good mouthful.

"Unfasten his arms and lift up his head, lads." They did such as Richard poured the cleaning liquid into the mouth of evil smell. The captain had recovered enough to wash it about where the pain did lay, and then to spit it out with the vile. He appeared to be in some relief already as more rum was poured in, some he swallowed and some he spat out. Then he laid back upon the sodden cot with eyes closed, as in some repose. They unfastened the others of his bindings and left him to lie there. To pray that he would soon recover to guide this ship of peril, and sail it to the harbour that was in safety's arms. All gathered together and drank from the rum flask, worn as the beggar's coat were they as they barred the captain's door.

The deck was sounding the tread, for Richard as up to the rudder went he, to see how the tar stood, who had took it upon himself the task to sail the vessel. Looking up, Richard saw only two sails left to push along the ship, though it seemed to be making some good pace in the calm weather.

"How are you faring, sailor?" Richard shouted up to the helmsman from the lower deck.

"Well, sire," he called down. "I be following yonder ship." He pointed ahead to the battered vessel that was cutting a good speed but one mile away. "But come nightfall, sir, I will be lost to where we are."

"Continue to follow the ship for as long as you are able, and then we will anchor until dawn and pray our captain will be enough recovered then to guide us."

"Aye, sire," came the answer to Richard, who was troubled, for upon the morn's light he wished not to be the duck spied by Henry's ships that, with little doubt, were searching these very waters for their prize.

They slept most well that placid night, for worn and much fatigued were they. Till soon the morn had come with just a blink of sleep it seemed, as Richard and Alphonse made their way to the cabin of the captain. Knowing not of what would greet them, but still eager to know, their future plans depended upon what would face them in that place where stayed the captain. They removed the bar from the door and rapped upon it. They waited not for any acknowledgement to their call, but were reluctant to step into the slop and the stink of the cabin. They opened the door and looked about, seeing then the captain's shape laid still and unmoved, as if in the state they had left him. Slowly they came until they were close, wary and ready to flee if any sign of trouble showed.

"Captain?" Richard whispered quietly with gentle hand upon the unmoving shoulder. The eyes opened slowly as if from some dream and to gaze to where the voice was heard. "Captain, how fare you?" The pair who watched were still unsure of what state the captain was in. Closer came Richard and looked into the eyes of the once raging boar, and saw he in there only calm and relief from madness.

"'Ow be my ship?" was first to his sane mind.

"'Tis steady, sir; we suffered some damage in the storm that came upon us, but we did manage to ride it out."

"So where are we now?" the captain asked as he began to stir a little.

"We know not for certain. We are anchored somewhere off the northern coast of England; that is as much as we know of our position. We regret your mate was lost in the storm of the night past, which left us without any guidance in our journey. And all prayed that you would be recovered this day so you would be able to right us … Do you feel that you will be able to return to your duties?—for we are dire, sir, and do not know the lay of the coast."

"Methinks I feel well. My mouth is of some pain, but different from the pain before that wracked my mind. I hurt as if I have been chained like some wild animal … And what is this stench in which I lie, this filth, this evil smell?" The captain saw to what state he did lay and looked about at all the chaos.

"'Tis all from the storm, sire, and from the affliction you did bear." Richard answered the captain, who had started to feel about his mouth with his tongue and did find the hole where his tooth was missing.

"My rotted tooth has gone. Who did this thing?" The captain was a little roused.

"'Twas I, sir, with help from Alphonse and Jack Thompson, and two more of the crew chosen by Jack."

"Why so many?" asked the captain.

"It took such to subdue you, sire, for you were liken to a greased boar and with the strength of ten men, it took all our strength to contain you."

A smile of pride came to the mouth of the captain, for proud was he to hear that it did take so many able bodies and strong hearts to contain him, and to know he had fought so bravely for his dignity. "Come then, lads, I must be up, for there is much work to be done to right this vessel."

They helped the captain up, for he was still in some state of weakness. The only victuals he had taken for many hours was an overabundance of rum, which was not standing him in good stead. He stood, disturbing the stench of his affliction and dripping the grime of his cabin. He saw in a better light the grunge of his state and showed much angst at such a circumstance.

"First, gentlemen, call Jack Thompson." Jack was fetched and came in much haste to his captain. "Get the dunking cage ready, for this day there is dunking to be done."

"Yes, Captain, at once," the words still being spoken by Jack, as he went to his duty with some worried look about him. For it seemed the captain was about to reap some justice for the humiliation he had borne in his saddened state. Jack gathered some sailors upon his way and they fetched from its stored place the dunking cage. An open box made with iron strips, all rusty and worn from its journeys into the ocean's salt. A hinged gate was upon one side to enter, with a secure latch upon the outside that could not be reached from within. The cage was large enough to hold one man standing. The party hooked the cage onto the derrick and waited for the captain to show himself, readying for him to bear upon them the rule of ships' captains.

Time 'twas for all to reflect upon the ordeal that was the cage. Placed such for crimes, mild or severe. The guilty were locked inside its rusty bars, white fingers gripping upon the iron and bracing for the ordeal, as the seamen pulled upon the ropes to creak it high and to swing it out above the cold, churning sea. And then upon order to release it into the wicked ocean. The victim to breathe in as much air as he was able, and then when he felt the cold water upon his feet would hold tightly his mouth closed, with the cold washing to his waist, and then to his chest, and then to his head. Then gone was he as all would watch from the ship's side to where their comrade had dipped. Alone was he, not to know when the cage would lift from the biting waters, but for need of air 'twas an eternity, with lungs almost breaking, ready to breathe the air that was not. Then light would show above, and the cage would break the waves to let the victim breathe as much as he could, but no sooner gasped than dunked again; and so it went until all metered punishment had been carried out. And the last time surfaced was to swear by God never to wrong aught, nor to displease another being, for to bear such again could not be.

In such state they awaited their captain. To beg forgiveness would be futile, for a show of weakness would be your undoing, and deemed not worthy to sail the same ship with other brave souls. The stirring of the seamen aside the rail showed the captain was upon his journey. Then showed Richard and Alphonse with the captain but a step behind them. The captain though was naked, walking though as if dressed in his most fine clothes. Straight and sturdy of back, proud of chin, feeling no cold, he marched on unabashed by his unseen cloth. The crew stood in some awe at the sight. He strode on toward the cage, and upon reaching it stopped and turned his head toward his seamen, these sailors who had fought through storms, these sailors he had brought away from the robbers of the sea, whose vessels would seek to plunder them. A hard captain was he, with strict rules applied upon his vessel. Feared be the sailor to break them. But he was revered by his crew, for if you did your duty you would be treated fairly. And, not liken to other captains, if a man was overboard he would turn his ship about and would not leave them to die in the cold waters, as other captains were wont to do just for the sake of a penny.

"Fear not, I have no reprise for you; I owe favour, not pain." And with those words he climbed into the cage and the door was closed upon him. "I am here to be cleansed and not for any punishment, so dip me such and, pray, do not take vengeance out of this act." The crew shouted and cheered as he was swung out. A captain by name. A captain that could stir their hearts. They dipped him many times, though of little duration, until he beckoned to be pulled aboard. Now washed and clean he was swung back upon the deck as the cold began to bite into him. Shivers not of his control painted his body. He climbed out with a wave high to his proud crew, his face smiling broad; for many days there had been little joy, but this day was a good day for the captain. Quickly a blanket was thrown about him, and rubbed roughly upon his skin until relief showed from the effort. Wrapped, he was taken back to his cabin, which had been swilled clean and mopped dry. The cot had been changed and laid with dry covers. All other chattels that belonged in the cabin dried as best could be done. His clean vesture was placed upon the cot, ready for flesh to press upon it. He dressed, he ate, he drank. The captain had returned.

"Come then, sirs, let us see where your helmsman has taken us." At last he was on to his duty, thought Richard and Alphonse, as they scampered behind the captain. His sailor legs carrying him as if he walked the flat road to London Town, feeling no sway or roll from the unsteady plank that he trod. "How fare ye, sailor?" the captain called as he came to the deck where stood the helmsman.

"All is well, Captain," he answered. "We dropped anchor last night, sir, and respectfully await your orders."

"Let us see where you have taken us, lad." The sun was high overhead as the captain took his bearings. "How many hours have we been at sea?" he asked of any who may be able to answer his query, for no one knew for certain, but Richard estimated that 'twas close to ten hours. "Then let us set our course to the northwest, which should bring to sight some landfall that we can follow until some mark becomes familiar. Do you need a change of duties, sailor?"

"No, sir. I am not weary," answered the helmsman. "Some drink and some victuals would be all I need, sir."

"Then we will have some brought to you. We will up anchor now, and when we start to move I wish you to keep the sun to our port side and to the stern of the ship. Within two hours we should sight land and then I will give you a new heading. Do you understand, my lad?"

"Yes, Captain. I hear it loud."

"Land ho!" came the call less than one hour after they were underway. All came upon the deck to see what they all wished for: land. They were not alone in the world, for there in the mist was a place where others dwelt, and lifted now were their spirits.

"Keep 'er steady, lad. Go no closer to the land than we are." The captain's orders went to the helmsman.

"Aye, sir," came the strong reply.

The captain gazed over the side of the vessel with many others also peering the dark line, though they knew not what they looked for, the sight of the land drew them as one to gaze the faint line. The captain shaded his eyes with his hand from the brightness of this day. He stood such in that state peering out for some sign along the rugged coast. For half of an hour was it such, until at last he pointed without yet any word; his thick poke was at arm's length into the air before him, as he looked along the outstretched arm to the ragged rocks that outed from the land crop. A stone tower stood, shadowy and grey, seen little, but lit with a bright flame that blustered about at its top, there belching its curled, black smoke as it spake its silent warning: *Do not close to me, dear seafarer, for my toes unseen will render your ships, to rip open your fragile hulls, and hurry you to the bottom of my cold grave.* The warning beacon for the headland showed its flames. The tower placed but ten miles to the south of the port of Newcastle, which lay in the Realm of Henry.

"Tyneside, lads." The captain pleased to show the prowess of his seafaring skills. "That torch shows us to be but nine hours from our port in the firth, and to the Scotland we seek. We need stay no more, for later when darkness comes the beacons lit all along the coast will guide our way. Upon the morrow, with God's good grace, we will be at harbour." They all who dwelled upon that ship of peril went to their knees to offer their thanks to the Lord that their journey was so blessed, and safe to port would come far from that storm of the devil's doing.

The two sails they had readied pulled them gently into the harbour of Leith, held they in the safety of the Firth of Forth. They saw as they entered the docks many vessels of their armada all in some sorry state, many with heavy damage, but safely at anchor they seemed to be at some rest from their ordeal. Richard's vessel sailed slowly by them, as then heard all about cheers and cries of "God save the prince!" as they saw that their leader was safe, and was still able to command them.

Soon the ship was tied up and the cracked boat gave up its cargo to the earthbound. Richard and Alphonse bade farewell to the captain of their ship, and made way to the chamber of the harbourmaster, wherein awaited the captains of the vessels docked, and the commanders of the troops. The hands were shook and the greetings were spake, then to sit they and listen to the harbourmaster's tally. He stood upon a low table so he may be seen by all so gathered. Spake he of the ships and cargo of the armada, those that were safe and those that were not seen again. He read all from his crumpled document.

"Two ships lost with cargo and all hands. Three ships are still missing. All other ships are safe within this harbour. Those ships in harbour have a total loss of thirty sailors and forty soldiers of the Austrian army. The other boats that did not arrive here, three in all, struck the port of Newcastle. Whether blown there or the port mistook, we know not. The said crews and soldiers and their armoury are being held captive, believed to be detained in the castle at Newcastle. They are awaiting what charges will be brought against them by the King Henry."

"How many are captive there?" the prince asked.

"Sire, we believe from our information that there are sixty seafarers and four hundred soldiers."

"Four hundred soldiers! Well worth the rescue of," Richard spake out with some vigour. "If it were fifty, or even one hundred, then that would be the fortune of our activity, but four hundred good Austrian soldiers is another page in the book. Pray, have your agents obtain more information upon their whereabouts, and let it be known to the captives we aim to spring their heels from the confinement where they are held. And be of haste in this matter, before Henry does them all." Richard had taken the matter quickly into his own hands, for not only did he value the soldiers, but a rescue of them would bring to him much prestige, and would bring favour within the courts of those who had pledged themselves to the side of this prince, and would bring much displeasure in the court of Henry.

Chapter Twenty-five.

Beware, Henry.

A day had passed, and any fatigue had left the prince as all to mind was the plot to rescue those imprisoned, who in Henry's keep did dwell. Though the court at Edinburgh awaited his coming at this time, it mattered not to him, seeking more to impress his followers than to bow in royal presence. Richard and his officers were dwelled within the house of the harbourmaster, in one of the unused chambers there; sparse were the chattels within the cold room, but a table was placed large enough to lay out the maps they had asked for, able they to look them over to see which move would be best for their plan. The commanders were present there, and though their eyes were in a weary state, they were sparked by the prince's endeavour. Alphonse stood by, and the harbourmaster awaited any orders for his agents.

"If we take this route and travel only at night, it should take us but two days to reach the gates. A small band should suffice. One goose is harder to spy than a flock ... Harbourmaster, have your agents meet us upon the road that crosses here, which should be in one day." Richard pointed to the road upon the map, as the harbourmaster came closer to see the place shown. "And be sure, sir, they have the whereabouts of the prisoners."

"Yes, sire, my agent will be informed, and it shall be done with much haste to your request."

"Commander, fifty of your most loyal Austrian soldiers we will need. We will ride at nightfall upon this eve, with ample supplies and four empty carts, for we must also try and retrieve the armoury that has been taken from us … Questions?" None were aired, for there was little to be said, much was still vague, and time would unfold what other may be done. "Then to your duties; be ready at dusk with all prepared."

They parted to their set places to prepare all their tasks. As they drifted away the harbourmaster came to the prince.

"Pardon me, sire, the King of Scotland has sent his envoys to meet with you; they await in the guest chamber to greet you, and to guide your way to the court of Edinburgh."

"Well, sire, they will have to hold close their patience, for I am bound to retrieve my soldiers from the grasp of Henry, and any delay in my action could be fatal to those souls ... Tell them, sir, to stay for my return, whence we will confer our admiration for the King James. Give them a plentiful amount of ale and wine, so their wait may be more pleasurable, and they may lose some of the hours in sodden repose." Richard was eager to be upon his task and spent little time mulling the visitors' desires.

"I will do your bidding, sire," the harbourmaster spake with all due reverence, as the prince departed the office of their council.

The night came cold with blowing wind that rattled leaves and branches, for this night would keep the owl at bay till calm settled the ground. No animals did scurry, no birds did fly, the night as black as pitch draped all. 'Twas the best of nights for warm fires and mulled ale, and the best of nights for to slink unseen upon the soft winding lanes that would take those who wished to be in secret fold. Only of black was their cloth, as black as the night that stirred about them. They all were hooded so no skin did show, and naught seen of shine, for all metals were dulled to glint not. Their weapons with blades and handles that shone were hid beneath their flowed capes. Gently they trod their mounts away from the port. The carts were wrapped with cloth where any rattle may have sounded their coming. They moved along the narrow, winding trail with one ahead of the other. Like the eel were they, black and slithering across the sloping land to make to the water. On they went through the night; the wind blew still with no respite, throwing branches and debris upon the trotting crew.

Dawn did show its coming and all moved from the track to settle in the wooded hide that would keep them from all who may spy upon them. A lookout was posted at the road to keep secure the comrades, and to watch for the informant who would tread the same path. The camp within the wood was kept most quiet as they ate and then slept until the night would come, and their journey would once again begin with foot soon upon English soil.

This night was far changed from the night passed, for calmed was the wind. The stars to be seen floating upon their black drop. The moon lit all that was about, to bounce off the waterways like floating lanterns. An owl's night this night, but not a goodly night for those who wished to slink about. But move on they must, for Henry would not delay his coming whether night was dark or bright with the moon. They moved away from their wooded shield to the ribboned road that showed the way clear. To ride at good pace, the way taken with ease, they were the lone boat upon the river and naught was seen upon these ways. The path, not frequented after dark, brought down its curtain, and they were able to speed as quickly as the carts could pace their way. On they rode beneath the stars, until once again the time of the dawn was coming to end the night's ride, and to wheel off the worn way and into the dark wooded 'scape, bringing guise to their abouts. Guards were posted, they numbered more than before, for deep in the English land were they with more danger to threaten. And also more eyes to see the agent that was hopefully to come. In the bush aside the track they did crouch and waited. Their comrades, with bellies filled, wrapped themselves in their canvas sacks, to sleep as babes in their mother's cradle. The snoring and the whinnies of the horses were far from the way and could be heard not.

In the early afternoon came to sight a lone rider coming at fast pace from the south, his dark blue surcoat at billow in its own wind, as haste drove it to some meet along this way. A likely informant it seemed to the guards, as one of them stepped out into the path of the coming rider. The others were still hidden but watched closely the scene before them, their swords drawn at the ready. Though only one horseman was spied none knew of what his game may be. The guard was in the middle of the narrow road and stepped before the coming rider. Still guised in his hooded cape he raised up his hand to give the comer time for to slow his gait. The other hand held back the bagged cape to show the military sword that was carried. Done such that the comer may see what manner of man stood his way. The rider skidded to a stop in dust and grunt, not at the ready for someone to leap before him. His horse with much discontent to snort and whinny its stay, and the steam soon to rise from the snorting nag. A full ten paces away did he stop, for closer he would not be as yet.

"Hold, sire. From whence have you come this day?" the soldier who stood the road queried. The rider still struggled with his unruly horse, pulling hard upon the reins, and straight did not answer until 'twas calmed.

"I come from the port of Newcastle, sir."

"What business do you have this way?" Once again the soldier tried for more information.

"I take a message from my master at the port, to the harbourmaster at Leith. To whom do I have the pleasure of this meet? Who is thy master, pray?" The rider probed for more than he was shown and treaded he most carefully about his purpose.

"He is one, sir, that awaits a messenger upon such a journey as yours. Are you the said person who brings the news he seeks?" At last some words were spoken by the guard to speak more of the situation but to commit little.

"I know not, sir, until I speak with him." The game played once again by the rider, but 'twas time for the tree to show some fruit and so the guard showed the apple.

"Then dismount, sir, and we will be away to him."

The rider did dismount his horse, but he was still in some distrust and stood his ground beside his steed. He knew that others of the same ilk as the guard before him must be about the bushes, but he had seen the sword and knew 'twas not the style of the English, and deemed 'twas fair to think that he would meet his appointed at this time of the day.

"Come," the caped soldier beckoned him into the wooded shade. He followed to where he was pointed and with horse in hand, went into the cool shelter. Before ten paces were taken the duty guards were upon him, his horse startled at the miffage* but was quickly calmed. The messenger was not thrown to the ground nor abused, but held one at each side steady. The hands of the lead guard roughed all over the body of the man who had come to the meet. A dagger was pulled from his belt and a small knife from his boot. "Is this all the weapons you carry?"

"Yes, that is all I carry," he replied. His tone though showed that he was a little troubled at his treatment. "Why do you treat me such?"

"We take you, sir, to our master not to some cockfight. We find no message upon you. Do you not think that you may be in some distrust—a messenger without a message?"

"I do carry the words given me but writ upon some parchment they are not, for would not I be a fool to carry them such? Once in your pocket, my life would be worth no more than a fatted pig. The message I bring is for only the harbourmaster to hear and to no other."

"Come then, sir, let us see if our harbourmaster is to your liking." They moved on into the woods with two of the guards returning to their place upon the track. The other led the disarmed man with horse in hand deeper into the wooded place. "Guard of the day with rider in hand!" called the soldier to the guards that were dutied close to the camp. He shouted loudly his coming for he wished not to be mistaken for some enemy spy. Closer he came and the guards were able to sight him. "Guard of the day with rider!" he called once again. They stepped back a little so he may pass, to gaze with some curiosity at the fellow who trod the steps of the soldier.

To the clearing they came, and made to the tent that was discreetly set at the edge of the bushes, half hidden by the scratching branches and dripping leaves, the wet canvas steamed its clouds as if afire. Many cloaked soldiers were about—some standing, some asleep, some supping—they with just a glance and no more at the guard and the rider with him.

"Sire, we have stopped a rider who clams to have a message for the harbourmaster at Leith," the guard called into the closed flap of the tent.

---

* *miffage* [coined] disturbance

"He is disarmed, sire." They awaited a coming reply. "Enter!" at last came the shout. The guard took the horse from the rider and ushered him inside. He then stood with the animal outside the meeting place awaiting the outcome of the council within.

The messenger entered the small tent with little room about to make one's way. Commanders and officers about in dark bunches. He was then pointed by one of the cloaked shadows to the table that was almost unseen. He came face to face with whom he believed to be the leader of this band, for he was sat with advisers about him, and though sat he in rough cloth, he seemed to have some air about him.

"You carry information?" the voice in learned tongue asked.

"I do, sir, have such to relay to the harbourmaster of Leith, to the concern of shipping activities and related cargoes that are coming to his port in the coming days." A lot was spoken but nothing was said.

"I represent the harbourmaster, and in his name have come to receive that which was writ to him. I come, sir, as the Prince Richard of York, to retrieve the prisoners from the castle from whence you came. Please, sir, no more dithering, so we may enter in the release of these soldiers, four hundred in all. The agent knew then he was at face with the one he did seek, for no other upon this road would have such information as was spake.

"Please forgive me, my prince," did speak the messenger with due respect to the prince shown. "I am, sire, most mistrustful in my dealings, for my head is worth more than a bleating mouth."

"We well understand your state, sir, and the suspicions you must carry. But to it now, where is the message that you carry?"

"'Tis here, sire," the agent pointed to his head. No letter to be lost, no parchment to be stolen, nothing to find.

"Speak out then, my man," the prince urged.

"Four hundred soldiers are at prison in the walls of the castle at Newcastle. They are kept within the horse barns, for 'twas the only place able to hold that strength. The buildings are lightly guarded but the walls of the castle are guarded well."

"Are the armaments still there?" the prince queried the agent.

"Yes, sir, both the prisoners and the arms are all close, for they await the arrival of Henry's soldiers."

"Do you know how far away they fare?"

"At the last report, sire, they were well north of York and under good pace, but as yet they still ride their old nags and do not ride the faster horse. They should reach Newcastle by the late eve of the morrow."

"Good then, we will still have time to act in some careful manner."

The prince was well pleased with the information he had received, and in such could lay some plan upon the table. "We will have to make our time in the hours of daylight, to able us to make our move before the soldiers of Henry show their force. But naught he can do now, for time he cannot steal. You, my good man," the prince spake toward the agent, "will ride at my side and relate to me all knowledge you have of our destination, and the inners of the castle walls."

"I deem it a pleasure, sire," agreed the agent to the prince.

"Commander, break camp, we move in one half of the hour."

"Yes, sire," answered the officer, as all hustled from the tent and emptied to all places of the camp. The quiet that had hung about was turned to bustle and shout as all was made ready, and true to the half of the hour, the band were ready to leave the welcomed camp.

The prince mounted and started to move the small army away with the agent riding aside him, followed then by the rest of the military. They all still with cloak and hood covered, softly trod to leave the shelter of the wooded shield, the cool and dappled light upon them as they moved along. Blinking in the bright with heads low, their eyes soon likened to the changed place where no shade covered them, and, more familiar with the day, their pace quickened to make good upon the dusty track that was their way. The two afront could be seen in some council, talking as best they could with the jolting rides they were upon. Sly were the eyes upon them, unseen as they passed, in the growth did they lurk.

The night came, but to stop they did not, only to ride on with slowed pace upon the winding stretches of the dark track. Then, before the break of day, may at one hour afore such, they came before the town of Newcastle. From atop their wooded hill, they spied the torches burning in the still town stretched below them as the agent took upon himself the lead. The pigeon may fly to many places but always knows where his home doth lie. He guided them down the track that would bring them close to the castle. The way so narrow that the carts were ripping and breaking the bushes that tried to bar their way, grabbing at the wheels and snagging the drivers as they pushed through their domain. Angered they seemed, the bush and the tree at the intrusion that had come upon them, and so they fought against it with whipping branch and heavy limb.

They came through the tight track to come to a wider way, and there lay at the end, not three chains' distance, stood the walls of the castle. Grey at the top as if newly built, but as lower the eyes came the grey turned to a dull green, and as it neared the ground it showed black and all evil-looking. The light was playing about as the dawn came and the dew soaked their cloth. They moved off the track and into the trees at its edge, continuing onto the side of the road but not upon it, and took upon them a slow gait sheltered by the trees. The prince was seen to dismount and so all others followed his card. Came they to a small clearing that was unseen from about. The horses and carts were stayed and the guards were posted about. The band of soldiers gathered and afoot trod their way. All in line one to follow the other, as the agent led them to a place that was afar from the main gates of the fortress, where more activity dwelt. Here though all was still and without life. The walls of the castle stood before them. But shown just above the grey stone, the sloping roofs of the stables that were within that thick defence. To a small entrance they were guided. The guard paid off to be elsewhere at this hour. A few coins to jingle in his pouch would send him far to buy ale and to sup his cares to far places.

They creaked the door open, the sound like a hundred cats in the dark of night, but, in fact, 'twas just a normal door that creaked. The spy nosed inside and, seeing naught to deter them, beckoned all to follow. Close to the wall they skulked along to come quickly to the corner of the stable and then to the showed entrance. Richard beckoned to three of his most tried officers; they were to enter first and make safe the way for the others to follow. In went they like black cats, as quiet and slinky were they. The smell of horse was all about, so sweet in that strange way; neither man nor any other animal could be smelled with as much pleasure as the horse. Foot trod upon the hay that was spread the floor, made for moves of silence. Seen then, at the far reach of the stable, the guards playing dice, with no thought that danger lurked about. They moved further into the barn and came to the barred door that held their comrades within. The stout piece of wood was lifted from its hooks, and discreetly the door was opened enough for them to peer inside. Then, upon seeing no guards within, they quickly sidled inside. More than eight hundred eyes were upon them, with four hundred mouths below that uttered not one sound at the coming. Well versed were they to the part they were required to play in their escape, and that main part was silence. Some sat, others were standing in their wait. A single chain ran through their clamped wrists; the chain was attached to the hitching posts within the stable, and locked with a keyed clasp—large and rusty, it hung from its black ring. Four hundred sat with not one jingle coming from the metals' hold.

"Guard!" one of the prince's officers called from within the prisoners' keep. "Guard!" he called once more.

"God deliver me, what do they cry about now?" One of the guards, disgruntled and annoyed that he had to leave the dice game, came at last to see what was afoot, and hoped 'twas something worthy of his valuable time. In he came; his keys rattled at his belt, his dagger sheathed, his sword slapped against his leg as he stepped his way. "What pleasure may I bring to—" His sarcasm was cut short by the arm that embraced him from the back, and from the dagger that was pressed against his throat. The one with the dagger he could not see, but before him did see the eyes of many prisoners, and two hooded menaces bearing close to his face.

"Call in another guard," one of the hooded faces, in gruff but whispered tones, sprayed the words into the guard's face. "Do it now with haste." The blade seemed ready to burst through his skin as it pressed with menace against his gulping throat. "Say naught else." He trembled and knew not if the words would come to his mouth.

"Matthew!" he croaked. The knife pressed harder, for 'twas not the best of calls given. "Matthew, come hither, come see this!" he called again, and this time the blade did not press harder.

Another guard trundled to the shout, in as much angst as the other he came. "What say you?—" 'twas all he uttered as he was also taken and dragged into one of the empty stalls. With one stroke his throat was slit with gurgling spurt, to slump down and to lay in his own bloody mess. The eyes of the first guard saw most of the happening as he was held tight, full of fear and tear-filled was he, almost throwing out his stomach's fill.

"Call again," he was urged. "Call the other two."

The voice croaked with much hardship to call out. But the prod of the blade once more urged out the cry. "Come!" he called. "Come quickly and see this!" shouting across the stable as best he could.

The last two could play no game until the return of the others, so they came to the call with curious mind. The slits in the boards of the door showed of their coming, and a nod to the one who held the knife at the throat was all needed as it cut its way into the neck, where the knife had dwelled in patient wait to fulfill its duty, with the warm blood that flowed over it, and to bring death to the one who had played games but a few minutes ago. Now he was just another choking heap slumped upon the bloody hay. The last two guards came in without any fear to see for what troubles they had been called, as then with quick ado they were sent with the others to another place.

The prisoners watched silently at the grisly acts, but with no faze upon them as they awaited the outcome. One of the officers fished about in the mess to search out the key that would fit the locked clasp. Dripping thick 'twas pulled out and then wiped upon the dead man's coat where the blood had not yet soaked it, then taken hurriedly to click open the hasp. The prince and the others of the troop entered the stables, where the prisoners stirred with their cramped legs and growling stomachs. The officer at the far end pulled quickly upon the released chain to free his fellow soldiers.

They cared not that they still did wear the clamps about their wrists, for freedom was theirs.

The agent took the prince to the back of the stables where two large doors showed, and behind which lay another stable. The stable gates were opened wide to show to all, the place where their armoury was kept. Swords and daggers were piled about not in any order, but seemed to have just been thrown in there and the door closed. Clubs and maces, lances and armour all were stacked about. Another pile with horse trappings all at tangle lay. The prince beckoned the freed soldiers to the armoury.

"Take each enough tack for a horse and as much armament as you are able to carry; we have carts at the ready for such as you bring." They delved into the piles that were about, picking saddles and bridles for their needs. Some donned armour to their waist so the carrying would be easier. They gathered up all of the weapons and left naught but some old uniforms and some broken parts that were of little use. Further back they went with their prizes to the part of the stable where row upon row of sturdy horse stuck out their ends, as if to seek out one of the coming riders. And their riders did come, and they quickly saddled the frisky animals that had not been run for some time. And as the soldiers fussed about them, they knew that soon they would feel the wind blowing in their manes, to race again the wild country that was their itch. Saddled now, one by one they came out, led by a rider, with arms filled with weapons of all kinds; following the prince's soldiers along the way, they had come to the carts at wait.

"Do we burn it, my prince?" one of his officers asked.

"Do so," the prince answered. "'Twill at least find them some business about, for guarding seems not to be their ideal." Two officers left to fire the buildings as the others loaded the carts with all they had taken from the stables. They stood and waited, all looking at the roofs of the buildings that showed above the wall. The two officers were once more at the stables. All the horses within had been taken, some to ride and others to be tied to the back of the carts. They took from the wall the unlit torch and sparked it to life, soon 'twas flickering and smoking in the bright morn, then, with little ado, 'twas thrown inside, and watched as it rolled and spilled out its oil upon the dry hay that lay all the floor. It started quickly to break out into a flaming mass. They closed the door upon it and left to see the smoke puffing through the gaps of the boards as they hastened toward the carts. Underway and more than four hundred strong, well armed with little need to hide their jaunt; at a quick pace they went with cloaks flying behind and their hoods down. Their soldiery showed of armour, swords, and studded harness, emblems once hidden beneath black cloaks, seen clear upon the vests that covered their metal. A banner high was unfurled at the lead.

The White Rose shown upon the soil of England once again. Too long hid away in fear, but with pride held high so all would know a regal prince was returned and would take no guff from Henry's lot. They turned from the castle's walls, with the flame and smoke at show, and voices raised from within. The alarm had been given, with no questions to ask, with no one to blame, with no time for aught but to quell the licking flame.

The dust clouded behind them as through hamlet and village they raced, bent they for the border, where the heather would lay its carpet for them in soft tread to bring them welcomed home. A stop overnight, though, afore they felt such beneath them. The inn at the village of Rothbury was their stop. Need was not to be discreet, for too strong a force were they gathered. The local military could not mount enough soldiers to bring any fear to those who drank and ate and caroused under the banner high that stood in the marketplace there. Henry's soldiers were about but could only watch and could bring no threat to the stay. They spied through their slitted eyes once more from some safe distance; the activity in the village was too strong for any confrontation. As they watched the only thing that irked them was that the ale being supped was not tickling their own throats; for many miles 'twas the only tavern to sup and be drunk.

The morn did come and away with much fervour went they o'er the hills, those hills that two hours ago looked too far, but in little time were being raced over with hoofed animal and rattling cart. Soon that day they trod the heather, and their gait slowed to a steady trot as all reprise was left behind.

A most successful enterprise, thought the prince, and easy would be the pickings when he would come with his force. "Beware, Henry, for I have come for my crown."

Chapter Twenty-six.

A Fool to Dally.

The army had all returned to the port at Leith, with the envoys of the King James still at wait. Impatience dwelled upon them, but underlings they were and naught to say of such matters. Greeted was the Prince Richard with much adoration, such as they were expected to do. Gifts were placed upon him and taken with much gratitude by the charmer. The invitation to the palace at Edinburgh was accepted, being but a formality to be asked.

The rested night had passed to show the next morn the army gathered, all arrayed in finery and shined steel, adorned all in the colours of the House of York. The banners waved high, the pipes and drums struck their tune, and the whole assembly moved away to the beat that was played upon them. An army strong to do battle for their leader. Soon they saw the way that would lead them to the place of their invitation. First the black castle would show high upon the rock, seeing o'er the town that dwelled below with the palace huddled close by. The grounds would be the camp for the soldiers; the palace would be the place where plans would be drawn to smite the mighty Henry …

"I am boggled by such as you speak to me." Henry was not pleased and ranted such for all to know his state. "Sever me in half if I am not mistaken. You tell me this pretender—almost shipwrecked—came across the Scottish border with only a gaggle of men, did travel for three days unseen, did ablocate* my prisoners, all armament and horse, set afire the castle's stables, abscond from the place, then did sup ale with much revelry and festivity, and layer their evil lot upon a loyal part of my kingdom? Then, as if in some May parade with pipes and drums wailing, took back his troops to the sanctuary he holds to the King James and does now, as I speak, revel in Scotland?" The king ranted at his army commander. Many heads were at the council so ordered by their monarch. The walls of the Tower of London dripped with the stones' sweat; shining, it ran down the black stone and showed no joy upon all so gathered.

"Sire, we had but little time to reach the castle to belay such activity," the commander bleated out some useless excuse, for mattered not what he

---

* *ablocate* release

had to say he knew too well all was done for him.

"Enough! Sir, you have not the competence to be a commander of troops … A circus you should be in, a tented act, a clown, sir; you would make, sir, a good clown." With head low the commander stood to reap what next may come his way. "Bring in the garrison commander with his guards!" the king shouted, echoing to the far reach of the chamber where ranks were assembled, many praying that they would not be brought into this web of no release. Hustle and bustle ensued, to find and to bring with haste those who the king did call for. Soon, with Henry showing his impatient drummings, the commander called for was ushered in with his trotting troop behind. Flustered and with some fear they came, not yet knowing the reason for their call.

"Your Majesty," the breathless leader bowed before his monarch, and did not lift yet his head toward his king but kept it in some lowly state.

"Take away this buffoon and hang him before the noon hour. I wish not for him to use the air that gives from this Isle; it is but wasted upon such." The king gave forth his orders to the commander, who still did not gaze upon his king for fear of some slight he may give.

"Aye, sire," the guard spake as the commander was taken away, with his trembling legs hardly able to walk as he was helped from the chamber.

"We will find ourselves a new commander!" the king rang his words about the ears of all as the guards left the hostile place. Henry seated himself, and began to speak in a more calmed tone now that he had righted the wrong he believed was done to him. "Our activity will remain the same, and we will stay our place and await the outcome of this pretender's warring into our land. We will then see to what state the commoners give themselves to his cause and upon such information will be based our reprisal." The king next turned his words toward his close adviser. "My lord, seek out another who is able to be our new commander of the army, and brief him upon the activities we will deploy against this warmonger. And, my good man, find someone with a brain and not one who is daft. We will skin this rogue Warbeck before much longer, be sure of that."

The Prince Richard's entourage, with banner and pipe and all pomp at show, came their way along the road that led to the palace known to all with pride as Holyroodhouse. The streets filled with cheered voice as much joy flowed from the throng toward the come prince. He who with humble face waved in acknowledgement for the love shown to him. The army parted from the prince and his companions and made to the open grounds that had been given for their need, to make ready for the soon day when they would be called to horse and would their duty do to bring the prince his crown.

The great doors of the palace opened and beckoned the prince to step through the arched entrance, to echo his steps into the great hall where all the nobility stood await for his coming. They bowed and curtsied as he slowly passed by them and nodded he to their respect, waving his hand in some discreet manner as was the etiquette this day. Reverence was now, council would be later.

Toward the raised throne came he; perfume drifted about as all finery was at display at the court of the King James IV. He looked toward the prince. This prince who would bring glory to his land, and would join his kin to the Plantagenets and so to end all strife with the English. And in this short time as the prince came closer to him, thoughts deep and black skulked about his mind: It may be that, if some tragedy was to befall the prince and his princess, would then not this James be the ruler in his stead?—Begone, such evil thoughts, out of my head, I say, until you are needed; hide away in the goodness I show.

"My dear prince, how fare you?" The king stood in respect to this bringer of a crown.

"I am most well, your Majesty," replied the prince.

"My day was joyed by the news of your foray to retrieve your soldiers; all shows well for us, my prince, for the Henry must be well feared now at your brave and fearless rescue. We pray soon you will march upon him, and bring peace and prosperity to our lands."

"We will, your Majesty, in much haste bring such glory to us all, and to rid ourselves of this Henry."

This day went its joyful way and all were at sup within the great banquet hall. The fine dishes were all finished, and the jugs of brandy had been brought to the table, to bring to the tongue more pleasant things than the course of wars. As the king deemed 'twas the time to broach the prince upon such matters that were close to his heart. He came near to the prince's ear and spake to confide in his ally.

"I wish to speak to you, Richard, upon the subject that was touched upon by my envoys in Flanders. The subject being the offer of my dearest kin into the state of matrimony to your most loved self, the Lady Katherine Gordon being the one so pledged."

"Honoured most deeply am I, your Majesty, but, pray, forgive me my blunt tongue, for as before I am still of the same mind and will only marry for love and will not for convenience tie my bonds." The prince had seen many times afore the hags that had become queens with sight unseen, and swore he would not bear that upon himself. The silken gown may hide the toad.

"I have no fear, sir, for you to state such, for I am rich with maidens of royal blood, and if the dear Katherine does not suit, we have a good choosing for your eyes of all other shapes and demeanours. But, pray, sir, first look upon the one of whom I speak. Set your eyes upon her and you will be enchanted."

"Your bidding will be my command, sire," the prince spake as he condescended to the king's request. They both then straightened from their close conference as the king called for the Lady Gordon. They sat at wait, the king in his chair of honour, and the prince by his side, sat in the most sought place in the court. Honoured indeed was he who sat such.

Those of the court who stood at the rear of the hall began they to part a way for the Lady Katherine. Flanked about her were her fussing waiting ladies, who eased their charge through the curious waves that ogled the one chosen by the king. And knew they, as well as Katherine, that the prince would succumb to her beauty and to her charm, and that such a union leaned to would indeed be so. She came with gentle step and proud bearing, prodded as cattle to the buyer. To the sight of the prince came our lady. The king stood and took the hand of the Lady Gordon and made then the introduction to the prince.

"May I present, sire, the Lady Katherine Gordon, my most treasured kin. My lady, this is the Prince Richard of York to be one day King Richard the Fourth, King of England."

The prince, who now stood, bowed as he took the lady's hand, and kissed gently the silk glove that covered the dainty offering. "It is indeed, my lady, a distinct pleasure to meet with you." As the prince spake the words so polite he looked up to gaze for the first time into the face of the offered maiden. Her green eyes flashed as she upped from her curtsy, a tantalizingly beautiful woman who could charm the mind of any man. Her hair was of black pitch, her shape hidden in her close gown, hidden except to those who wished to see further of the risings and hollows so discreetly offered. Struck was the prince by such tranquil charm and demure nature that seemed to mask her seductive presence.

"I am most delighted to meet you, sir." Her voice was soft and not of the Scottish ilk. She did sound of some good teaching, but mayhap she chatted only of pigs and bread.

"You are taken by her, are you not my prince?" the king whispered from behind the prince to probe his thoughts upon the matter.

"She is, sire, all that you did speak and I am beguiled by her presence … If I may, I would wish to visit with her to see the mind that hides behind such beauty."

"You may do so, sir. Please go with Katherine and her ladies and spend time with her, and you will see she is not only a tempting virgin, but she also has the mind of a scholar and the wit of the jester. And, to whomever she doth marry, she will bring forth many children, for her bearing days are many." The king spake once again of Katherine's virtues as he placed the lady's slender hand upon that of the prince and ushered them away to acquaint themselves. The king knew that the prince was enchanted, and that enchantment was only one of the attributes of this lady. Her manner, her kindness, her demeanour, and her knowledge would all bring the prince close to her and to the union of kingdoms.

The prince and the lady sat aside each other within the closet that was Katherine's. Small was its space, and so was always warmed easily by the fire that burnt and crackled from the hearth. 'Twas not lit by any candle; the only light came from the fire and the small window placed high upon the wall. Rushes were upon the stone floor, and wood panelled the walls dark in the shadows. The ladies were grouped at the far of the fire. Some sewed upon a gown, others stitched at their embroidery. But all listened.

"My lady, I have many things I wish to converse with you; may I beg such permission from you?"

"Of course, my lord, all you wish to know I will in all truth answer."

"By your speech, I gather that you were not schooled in your homeland."

"That is so, my lord. For a number of years I was educated in Paris and taught such as language and politics and of courtly manners. I am converse in many subjects, and I can cook." With twinkled eyes she spake the last words as if she knew what the prince had been thinking, that she was to his mind but a girl from the Highlands who sat beside a peat fire and cooked porridge. The prince was about to offer some reason for the wrongful thoughts he had gained but the lady carried on her council. She came along then with a completely different subject. "And, sire, I know that I can bed you with such antics that you will think you have downed a full crock of wine—your mind befuddled."

"You toy with me, madam, with such words, for yourself is enough to enchant me without such talk."

"Thank you, sire," she half giggled. Her white teeth showed against her smiling lips of rouge of much invite. To kiss the lips of this lady came over him, but to hold her hand as he did brought such bliss to him 'twould be another time for such or he may be overcome by the act.

"Do you wish to know aught of myself?" the prince asked, for he had learned so much from this lady that she must wish as much for herself.

"No, sire, for I know about you, of your escapades, your education, and your bravery. This day I have looked into your eyes and all I need is shown, and no more do I need. I pray that I am all you desire, for, if I am not, I shall be of a broken heart and will not mend."

"Do not fret yourself, Katherine, for I am overcome with you, and I will make my feelings known to the king, that I may take your hand and care for you in constant love."

"I also am overcome, my prince, for such I never thought would happen to me in such a lightning state." Katherine spake with loving words to her prince, and the ladies were in no mood for sew or for stitch; all of giggle and watered eye were they, for the words that had been spoken of their lady. Soon to depart was the prince, and he came to kiss farewell the hand of the Lady Katherine, and, with a blown kiss to the bubbling waiting ladies, he left the closet of his dearest. He had found the one that he had dreamed would come into his life and it did with sudden strike. He floated back to his chamber, smit, to meet his love again upon the morrow, that morrow that would take forever to come. He would not sleep this night, for he was feared that if he did so he may find all was but some dream; so he would stay awake until he saw the lady again.

For the prince, time went quickly. Not so for the soldiers. They had been ready for many weeks, awaiting the call that would take them into glory and legend. The horses were rearing to run and ready to chase from morn until night. They were lively and full of zeal and becoming difficult to control, kicking and prancing in their stalls with impatience. The swords were honed sharp; to sever a blade of grass were they so. Bows and shafts, clubs and maces, all manner of warring things awaited the call. But on went the days, the weeks, the months, and still no call came, bringing upon the army much lethargy that to fight was losing its shine. The prince's interest in war was taken over by his interest in amour, to let his army wash away their desire like a hand in the stream. The days spent with his love were more appealing than the bloody reek he would face.

The King James was restless. The betrothal of the Lady Katherine was most joyful to him, but things were moving slowly and the marriage to the prince was lingering to come. 'Twould soon be one more stitch in the tapestry that he wished to hang, but neither the prince nor the lady could be forced, and time had to name the day. Then the war with Henry hung about him. The war must quickly come, for such a devious one as that King of England could end it all without one head being split.

'Twas a year later when the wedding at last took place. A small, quiet ceremony with no royalty from afar; no lords did come of England, or France, or of Germany. Only Scottish dignitaries walked the way to the small chapel that lay in the grounds of the castle walls. The chapel of Saint Margaret held but fifteen people in all. And in this place did the prince wed his Katherine, to vow to her of his love and fortunes. And the King James was most pleased with another stitch sewn; he prayed this time to a warring cloth. The revelry continued for many days and nights; 'twas all joy within the nation of the match made, that all hoped would bring an end to all days of hostility. Just one more surge of warfare and all life would be of tranquil.

The King of Scotland came striding the passageways of the palace with much menace in his step, for the time had come for some act against Henry. The guards pushed open the door wide to let the king enter into the chamber of the prince. Richard looked up from his book as the door was flung.

"My prince, we have just been informed that the armies of our allies may soon have to depart our land." The king waved about a document that he grasped as he spake with much concern. "The King Henry has brought such threats against our comrades that he, with little doubt, will bring war upon them, unless they recall all their aid so pledged to you. They have been told to end all other activities that threaten England. And, my prince, they will comply, for to war with England they would not relish. To fight the might of Henry is not upon their card. Though we know the army of the English is not what it showed some years past, for they are more devoted to commerce and the peaceful life than those warriors once so feared. But no wish have they to test the fact. So, my prince, it is with haste you must to war afore the act of withdrawing their forces is carried out to Henry's bidding. And, sir, when our allies see how successful you are, they will, in all haste, bring more warriors to our cause, for even Henry does not have the forces to fight both in Europe and in England, and be sure, 'tis in England he will war."

"I agree with you, sire," the prince spake after hearing the change in Henry's stand. "We must hasten our ways and pray that the English people are with us, for without them our day will be short-lived. I oft wonder, do they wish to ride with me? — one who is little known to them. I am young, daring, and warring, but to start can offer them little. Or do they wish to repose in tranquil light holding the hand of Henry? That is the question, sire. If they join us, our might will overcome the king who rules them, and all that would be left of him is that he would be writ about to play no more games upon this board. If they do not come to us in their flock and in a warlike manner, then the story will be told with a different ending, and we will end up as a game played by children."

"Richard, you place obstacles in your way that are only ifs and buts. Go forth, my prince, for we all have faith in you to bring to us the crown so sought." The king showed some concern of the prince's words but knew that once upon the road and not within the bedchamber he would be successful in his enterprise.

Alphonse and the officers were await within the dining room, the food already laid upon the table as Richard alone came to join them. But no sooner had they sat than from afar of the chamber, where the kitchen door did jar, loud voices began to cry out. At first a little muffled, but soon loud and clear as the duty officer came with much bluster from his place within the hot walls.

"Hold, sirs! Hold! Do not take the victuals!" The officer was soon at the table shouting with much anguish. All had stilled there and not a single morsel had yet been taken.

"What is it?" the prince asked as he stood.

"Sire, forgive me, it seems your taster is succumbing to some poison."

"Poison! This cannot be. Was he not in health after his tasting?"

"Yes, sire, he was, but now one half hour later he is in a most sickly state, with twitching and convulsions and foaming mouth. He has, sir, taken some poison from the victuals."

"God's Death, not again; after all our care, we are still in danger. Fetch the surgeon and let him see what this wretch has been bitten with." The prince waited whilst the surgeon was brought, and thought of only one man who would slither so low as to do this deed.

The surgeon came, and the taster examined, still at twitch and groan, curled was he as an unborn, and spitting blood amongst his bile. The table, still piled, beckoned with its tempting victuals; it lay untouched by those who sat and looked upon it, and mulled they what the outcome may have been if the prince had not been delayed. The surgeon came from the kitchen where did lay the tortured body of the food taster, his days of tasting painfully over. Clumping along in his heavy boots he came, his bag of instruments swinging from his hand. A serious frown played upon his face as he came to the prince to state the cause of the happening.

"Sire. Indeed, the taster was poisoned, the poison brewed from the berries of the belladonna and made with much cunning so that its effect would not be immediate, and would make it seem that the victuals were of good state until some time had passed, and then there is no doubt that after eating the food death would certainly follow." The surgeon left them all in silence, as off went he to remove the stiff body that lay twisted in the kitchen. Those gathered could speak no words, for death had brushed them with its nearness.

Much sickened was the prince. "The bastard Henry—will he never stop such evil acts? His spies must number enough to mount a troop. I will have my day with him, that Henry, with his deeds of treachery and wretch. We will not be subject to such acts again, mark me."

The portrait upon the wall within that chamber still looked down upon those assembled there as it always had done. For that knight upon his white charger with painted face was never to change, except for the eyes that moved to spy within its grey face. The stool was placed so that the head could reach and peer through the slots. The black leather shoes squeaked together, the stockings of silk stretched, the royal coat itched as it gathered the dust from within the narrow passage hid. The King James eyed at the happenings below, and his lips smiled at the rage from Richard; angry was the prince and swearing some reprise against the Henry. Stirred was he at last, and well worth the life of one taster, thought he, but one life to stir a prince into battle. Now it will be done, and quickly that fortune of Henry will be paid out to this king. All will soon come our way. He pulled the painted eyes back to their place, stepped down from his stool, and skipped his step back along the narrow way to the hall where the evil victuals lingered, to offer his sadness at the taster's demise.

"The children of all who prepare and supply our victuals, who bring our wines and our ales and any such as we require, all will be kept here at the palace in hostage of any happenings that may bring to us injury. And if we are so injured the innocent will be murdered. Let it be known that this will be so." The prince called out his orders to let all known the rage that he had entered. He was ready to bring down his wroth upon the innocent child, an act that would not stand him in good light if twas learned of his callous ways. "Come, gentlemen, mount your horses and with me ride to the tavern in the near village." They all left the room where the tables spilled with the victuals upon it, for poison tainted its lot, and was not fitted even for pigs. They rode, may twenty of them, to the place that was close by. They tied up their horses and blustered into the jovial den. Quickly they cleared all within the room with threats and shoves and rattling sword, until all the peasants were out, and they could sup within their own company and eat their fill to contentment. When next the time would come to eat at the palace, they would do so with no fear, for the children held would be their foil.

The King James was still not content. After all his intrigue to rile the prince and with all the promises he had been given, the army still wasted away upon the common. Too much thought he had of his wife Katherine, and such raptures engaged to think of aught else. The prince was finally called to the chamber of the king, where he waited in dishumour with his ministers and advisers upon the coming of Richard. For this time there would be given a firm date that the prince would move to his destiny. The waited one arrived, and saw he the gathered party as he entered the chamber, knowing the meaning of the council that showed to him no cheery side.

"My prince, tell me when you plan to enter the kingdom of England?" The words came quickly and blunt even before Richard had sat himself. The king was in no mood for honeyed chat. "I am getting most fretted that time lingers too long and our chance will be gone."

"Do not fear such, sire, I will quickly do your bidding. We will, my lord, bring many rewards and treasures to Scotland. The English will join us in our quest to the throne, and when it is done, joy will dwell in the land." The prince talked on with hands gesturing and arms wafting about, as once more he displayed his promises.

But the king bared not a look toward the antics and spake in such tone. "Enough, prince! All told before, and before that. I need now an answer; I need now a stated day. Tell me no more of deeds to do, tell me only of deeds done. Go to the words, sir, and tell me of deeds done."

"Deeds have not yet been done, sire," sadly spake the prince.

"Then tell me of the day when you can come to me and say, here, sire, here are the deeds I have done, and then I will listen with delight. You are a fool to dally, sir, and I tell you I have had my fill of this faddle. You, my prince, will be gone upon this quest the day after the morrow, so make plan to do so, for we cannot tarry the longer." The king had finished the words bottled within him, and so laid down a royal command to duty bound.

"I will, sire, do your bid." The answer came from the cornered prince, who it seemed had come to the end of his words to do.

"'Tis good you do so, for I have much admiration for you and wish to see you successful." The king calmed somewhat and had spake his last words upon the matter. He could only wait for some result from the prince's foray.

Chapter Twenty-seven.

Henry's War.

The day came, the day to move south to do battle. For the King James the wait was long, for he looked soon to count his fortune reaped from the English. But 'twas no wait at all for the prince, who wished not too soon to leave his Katherine but to dwell and to lay in the comfort of her arms. But the cock crows the need awake, and to fly with the birds at dawn. The heather was unseen as the mist clung to ground upon that morn. The prince moved his army to the south way, to probe his way into Northumberland and to try the waters, to be placid or stormy, soon to be seen. The pipes and the drums blew and rattled as the strong, seasoned army marched its way from Edinburgh. Early still the morn with few to see them away. A few peasants gathered at a corner, waving and shouting with little fervour; stood they shivery and clutching their raggedy cloth, peering grubby through their scarved heads at the soldiery that by them marched.

Further on the army trod, though some aback still within the town's walls marched, watched by another group that had gathered to see the coming. Never before so many soldiers had they seen as the great army passed by. Some tradesmen with tools in hand stood. Their sackcloth bags stitched with hemp, and leather-bound wooden grips that held the jingle of their tools. Treasured lots blessed by the guild. Few in number were they and kept that way, for many they did not wish to hold such skills. Few were better of good wage than many of little wage. Mattered to them not which king or queen ruled the land, for all needed their mansions and palaces. A dead tradesman will build you naught. High upon money's ladder were they, and any strife brought upon them would stop all work over all the land. The guild would not send workers to such places as did not treat their fellows with respect. There they stood watching the hundreds of soldiers that were at march. No cheers from them as they stood with smirky faces, looking at the time at waste they put upon the sight. A poor trade for any man was the soldier. Poorly fed, poorly paid, and poorly honoured. And then to battle and to most death with five hundred more, all thrown into a hole in the ground and covered over. *We have no urge to serve any king. We will build our buildings and our bridges, and when day ends, we will homeward go to sup and lay with our wives.* They sniggered, drank some ale from their crock, and went their way as the tramping army byed them.

Two miles away from the palace at Edinburgh, the banners from the leading horses waved in the still air, moving slowly so the infantry could keep pace. Two miles ahead were they, as the last of the straggling soldiers left the town gates. The king stood at gaze through the high window of his chamber. He had watched the first to leave, and still had stayed his place until the last went into the still mist of the morn. At first seen legless like ducks upon a pond, then soon all were covered in the ghostly hide.

All day they marched with the jingle and jangle of the rocking carts. The soldiers' chatter and laughter about as the miles awayed. The horses' snort and clod upon soft marsh, and then to clop upon hard track. The officers of high horse conversed of military doings. Hangers-on were all about, selling trinkets and ale; they skipped along with the army's beat. Others with lesser morals stealing from the carts and taunting the soldiers to leave their ranks, to draw them away to some dark alley to rob and murder in that dingy place. Street women walked along the way, with bawdy talk and promises when eve would come. And the soldiery with a penny to spend, would then pay for sup or for surrender when cool night came to their weary legs. The night drew as the owl's hoot broke the dark, and the torches' flicker came about to show the guards at watch. Laid upon the grass were the fine soldiery, bundled into small heaps at lie, wet and steaming in the heavy dew, strewn they all around in the guarded clearing. The tents were placed close together where stayed the prince, Alphonse, and the officers. The horses could be heard from afar; restless in the night they stood tethered to the trees, awaiting the dawn's coming to charge again along the murgaling* ways. And come it did the dawn with the twittering and the pots at boil. The smell of fired bread, raw onion, and cheese, all washed away from the ugly mouth with a quaff of ale. Upon these notes the music of the day began. This day was of hope, for all were eager to meet the face of Henry upon the field. They had been cooped for many months and were at the bit to show their guile and manly arts, where they would be as sailors upon the sea, and not as seafarers upon the land. There would be no shaked legs here.

They marched far upon that day but saw naught of any army of the English. Through the hamlet of Belford they went, with few folk about, and no one yet came at the run to join this prince. But soon, Richard believed, the ranks would swell, as the fresh dough by the fire. In the afternoon they came to the fields outside of Ainwick, a town ripe to occupy and there to throw down the gauntlet to Henry. A good place to let all know that the

---

* *murgaling* [coined] fumed; dense air

Prince Richard has come and treads with ease upon the soil of England. They moved closer to the town that looked most tranquil as it laid in the calm at the hills' fold. Around the tree-lined track came the prince, the banners high waved about him as he rode. Many voices then were heard from along the track, but as yet no one was seen. Soon though to view came the makers of the noise. May five hundred people of all kinds barred their coming; with staffs in hand and with clubs and sticks they stood the way. Peasants, farmers, shopkeepers, all manner of them ranged as silent the people of England now did stand. Strong was their belief in the royal right, and were pledged to their king without sway. These were the English the prince sought to his side. Not to be stood afore him with barred way and waving sticks. Their short silence was over as they began again shouting and jeering at the army stopped before them. The prince could not break the throng, for he wished them as allies and not as the enemy. They were dearly of need to ease his regal ambitions, and to bring others to the cause.

"We need you not, sire!" The cries were clearly heard. "Begone back to your wild Scottish laddies." ... "Take away your army! Leave us in peace!" They started to make some threatening moves toward the prince, and he quickly had to refrain his guard from taking some reprisal against them.

"I wish not to bring you any strife." The prince tried to bring some reasoning to the crowd, which had begun to get unruly. "Only to bring to you your true king, and to bring more tranquil to your hard and weary life." They quieted again to hear of what the prince would say, but could he say aught this day that would be of any appeal to them? For riled and angry were they to greet any trouble that may come.

"Begone! We want none of it!" ... "Yes, begone! Leave us in peace!" The cries continued as the prince tried his best to appease them.

"Please, do not rebuff me, but hear my words. For now we will bide our time, but I ask you all to come to the hamlet of Belford upon the morrow at the noon hour, and there to let me speak to you. I have come from afar to bring my message to you the people of this Isle. My army comes to fight only Henry. We offer no harm to you." The prince this day had done all he could to bring some respect to himself, but as the crowd slowly dispersed there were rumblings of discontent amongst them, and the prince knew his task upon the morrow would not be blessed with ease ...

"My dear friends," the prince started his appeal to the large gathering. Stood he upon the hanging stage within the square of the marketplace at Belford. The gallows shadowed its black cross o'er him. A sign not of good intent. An omen seen by many who stood before this pretender, for they were not convinced that he should be called prince. He was dressed not in any regal garb but of plain cloth, though well cut. Seen his hatted top bobbing to the far of the square where many at the tavern swayed about its door, to breathe clean air rather than the smelly crod that filled the tap. They jollied about as they awaited to hear what this prince-pretender would offer. Carts were stopped at the wayside filled with many peasant folk. The doorways of the shops crowded out from within. Children ran about freely as if they had no master. Upper windows spilled out its heads, all these to listen as best they could to this giver of promises … all heard before.

The guard to the prince stood tight to shoulder around the stage. All armed and trouble-ready if it would come, with thoughts to quickly strike the rabble, though 'twas not such to the prince's mind. Five deep stood the regular soldiers facing the crowd that were all about them. Like chickens in a barn were they, all clucking and nodding, moving hither and thither, then stilled to stone as continued the prince to speak.

"I am the true heir to the throne of this most pleasant of lands. I wish not to bring troubles your way, though with but a little strife, and with you by my side, we can regain from that most treacherous Henry that which he has claimed to be his, such claimed with no right of blood and no accession to the crown." The prince stopped there as from the throng a voice seeking some answers called out.

"And so, sir, if such be the way and we pledge our allegiance to you, to what benefit will it bring to such poor souls as we?" From the midst of the crowd came the question, and soon seen was the crier who stood tall, with about him all looking at the man, with a step back to see more of his state. A peasant by dress, but not by words. Then it seemed that all as one turned to look toward the stage, to list to the reply that would come from this Prince Richard with his raptured words.

"I will bring to you a country where war amongst ourselves will never be, and we will all live in some prosperity."

"But, sire, we already have that peace; that peace has laid upon our land since the death of the King Richard, and no uprising have we seen except for the Cornishmen, who are wild and have no leader, and can be quelled by the King Henry in one day when he chooses. What more do you offer besides our blood spilt?" The peasant queried once again to the prince as the crowd gave their "Aye!" to their new speak.

"We will lower your taxes, and will increase your wages to bring more comfort to those dire."

"Sire, we still await such promises from the King Edward, the King Richard, the King Henry, and now, sire, from you. The words of such things never come to pass … And of the Scots—When you are king and the two lands are joined as one and no border remains, this scourge of the English race, who have been our enemies for centuries, will have free rein to come into our lands with their barbaric ways, and to plunder and pillage without any recourse for such as we. And, at best, they will take from us our work, for they will work for little wage, for most have never had any wage, and little is better than naught. So, what say you of this, sire?"

The prince upon his stage looked at Alphonse, who stood his side and relayed to him that seemingly this peasant was no peasant but some rabble-rouser. An agent planted from the King Henry to splash about the stew. The crowd had become riled, for no answer did come straight, and so they started to bring some grief to the soldiers with shout and jostle, and make to them insulting words. Then, like rocks from a catapult, came eggs, no longer fresh, at fly through the air, landing upon the common soldiers, for they sought to stir the weakest part of the army. The stench rose from the rotten missiles with green slime dripping from face and cloth. The uniforms were defiled, which raged the ranks, and so they charged forward at the mob that chided them.

"Hold your line!" the prince shouted to his unruly troops. "Hold! … Hold!" They heard naught of his cries and, in rage, chased the throng about the square. "Do not follow them—their mind is to entrap you!" Use, 'twas not. The peasant-soldiers were a mob who chased a mob. The prince and his officers tried in vain to bring the unruly back to some order, but 'twas to no avail.

Then 'twas Alphonse who called out. "I will try to bring them back to order, sire!" he called out to the prince, as he leapt from the stage and ran into the melee that was all about.

"Stay, Alph! Do not venture into their den." But the call, whether heeded or not, was too late and he was to his duty. Alphonse pushed his way toward the place where the soldiery had broken rank, but afore he could reach them he was pulled to the ground by a hundred hands. His weapons were quickly gone and he feared that death would surely be soon upon him. Upon the cobble he lay among the spit and phlegm that squirted at him. He felt not though the cold steel upon his skin, but, in its stead, rough hands that pulled him to his feet to stand him in his slime and drip. He lifted his head and saw standing before him the rabble-rouser, who came close to his face. The ranting crowd about calling for a bloody end to this ally of the prince.

"This one is not for slicing … Bring him to the cart," spake such the leader of the riot. He was taken by two ruffians who gripped his arms with little care, and pushed him through the human passage. The way was bitter with hate, as blows came upon Alph with such words of abuse never before showered upon him. He was thrown into a cart and tightly shackled, with all ignorant people still about him; they with spit and foul words did curse him and his prince. He lay upon the wooden planks as the wheels began to move. He saw one of the ruffians crouched aside his prostrate body, he who had dragged him to the cart. The driver was the other peasant, a big burly fellow of foul smell, bellowing his shout as he pushed the horse on from the fading melee. And to that well-trod road that was south they did turn, south toward the town of London, to some destination they were not about to share.

"Where, sir, do you take me?" Alphonse with some brave face asked.

"Be silent!" came the gruff voice. "You will know soon enough."

Trouble was upon the stove, trouble was to boil, as the soldiers continued to chase those who continued to jibe at them with insults and spit. Swords were raised as they chased them into the shaded alleys and wynds that were about the square. On they ran, keeping just ahead of the chasers far into the long narrow reaches. Room for only one as each followed the other, till sudden came the stop. The lead soldier—the one with the most anger, who had chosen this place—saw that the alley had opened into a wider space, and he was at face with armed peasants, their knives and swords at the ready. But with little time to respond he was quickly cut down. The next came who could well see the danger ahead but was pushed onward by those at the rear of him, and so came to stumble over his bloody comrade, then hacked across the neck he himself did fall. Four more were done so, before they grasped the fact that a trap laid had come upon them. The remainder thought 'twas best they flee the grisly scene. But as they passed the alcoves that lay upon the way, the last to flee was jumped from the black space and his throat slit, to gurgle and fall upon the blood spilt, as then the next one was done, having little chance to fight back. As the end of the alley came shown to the square, no soldier came out, only bloodied peasants wielding their dripping weapons. All of the alleys that led to the square showed the same gruesome picture: only peasants stood there to warm in the sun's light, for all others lay bloody. They stood shouting out their victory over the intruder, taunting still the soldiers who stood by the prince, but none would come to the peasants' call.

The prince was in much dismay, for he wished not to fight the countrymen he needed; 'twas not the way he wished to tread. With heart at ache he left the stage where the shadow of the gallows bade its farewell, that shadow of witchcraft too left the scene, with the dark clouds that came and stole all such meanings of omens and dark doings. Away went the prince with his army, away from the village that damned his game, and went he along the road that would take them in safety back to Scotland. Lost were fifty soldiers to no avail, all good men gone. Their lives lost with no victory, no soldiers of Henry's army reprised; all were lost for naught.

And then what of Alphonse? The prince questioned all who may have seen him. One of the officers, asked such, believed he saw him overwhelmed by the crowd then thrown into a cart, driven away, and quickly to all sight he was gone.

"Thank God he still lives," spake the prince with eyes that looked to the heavens. "If able, I know he will escape from this act upon him, so I beg all to be wary that he may come, and to be most vigilant and not to mistake him for the enemy."

The embarrassment to the prince's army though was not yet done with, as the peasants used their old ways of demoralizing the enemy. The lines of soldiers that were northward bound were at too much a stretch for a secure march. And so 'twas those who straggled behind were picked away by the true arrow and by the quick leap from the close bushes of the laneways, to slit quickly a throat and begone. No one could tend to the fallen, for all knew that such a move would end in more shed. So they did cling each to the other in file as close as they could, like one snake and not like a thousand worms. Each knew that some would die but prayed it would not be he. Others though did break their rank and ran screaming and waving their weapons, as they chased, into the forests about, the peasants running in fear of them. The soldiers who did such knew of the risk they did take, but better to take some of the peasant mob with them than to wait so in cowering line to be picked away by the lurking, with their shouts and cries along the way, with their insults and their missiles. "I slept with your wife while you were away!" ... "We stole your daughter from your cottage! ... We have her with us! ... Father, Father!" cried out from the trees. "We cut the throat of your mother!" All this was too hard to bear in silence and was too much for their proudness. So they did run into the cool of the forest, all to be cut down by the circle of peasants with their short swords and daggers. The soldiers with their heavy swords were soon turned useless by the bush that hugged so close that they could not be swung. All struggled with the tangling vine that wrapped about them, and were soon felled to the pine floor. The peasants covered them like the ant upon the fly and they were soon done. Death was upon them, but 'twas sweeter to be the fray than to be fodder upon the road to Scotland.

The prince's army moved onward with great distress; the constant warring against them as they went the narrow tracks took its toll of soldiers and the horses they rode. The night came, and in its drape the peasants went upon the roadway not yet trod, and threw upon it all manner of vile. Horse manure, dead rats by the shovel, pig and cow excrement— all dumped to welcome the soldiers of the prince. They had no choice but to tread this way, for the forest was close to the track and they wished not to venture into the thick trees. All with hands over their mouths, they clopped and marched through the ooze that had been laid before them, slipping and sliding about as they went, with some falling over in the slop; a stinking miserable lot were they as they made their way, humiliated in defeat without a battle being fought.

They came two days later across the border to Scotland, no more to suffer both day and night that which was placed upon them ever since they left Belford. They stopped by the river that lay beside their way, and washed away as much of the dirt as they were able. Washed away from the outside all mire, but stayed within more vile and blackness that was not so much of ease to rid.

"What say you, my princely one?" The King James was in council with the prince and asked the question of which he knew the answer, but wished to hear the Prince Richard tell him of the degrading tale. And so he related to the king all the details of the happenings, leaving the pretender with a most dejected air. "Fate, sir, has not raised its happy gaze upon you but has dealt you the evil cut. So, all promises to this kingdom of mine are not to be. I am done by an Englishman again, am I not? for I am sorely in debt with fortunes lost to finance your aim." The king sang his song of sorrowful lyric, though the music was not as sad as the words that were spoken. "But then misfortune strikes us all, does it not? for this war was not your war, but Henry's war, for he has laid down all the rules, and won without a sword raised. Further, sire, ships arrived from Europe to relieve us of our military, so eagerly given and now so eagerly taken. My prince, that which you seek is over; there is no land left that will give you safety, and if one does, be wary of the offer, for Henry has clamped his iron hand over all with threat and bribe."

"I know all of this, my lord, but I am far from the end," the prince spake his words, for he had stood in silence whilst the king brought to him little compassion and even less understanding. "I will leave this Scotland, for I wish you not to be in any compromise because of my presence, and, with all faith, when I do succeed your kindness will be repaid."

The king accepted what had been spoken and bade the prince a farewell in the hope that he still may reach his rightful end. And so the prince did leave with muddled head to move his lot to other places.

Chapter Twenty-eight.

A Cruel Trial.

The cart swayed from one side to the other, the horse at steady trot as
Alphonse feared his meet. He was given water and bread as shackled he
lay with cramped leg and bruised back. They stopped their way at Harrow
but twenty miles from the town of London. As Alphonse tried to look
about the place they had reached, he was just able to see over the side
boards of the cart as four riders came near. Soon they were in council
with one of the peasants. Backs were showed and Alphonse was not able
to see who they were. Heard he, though, the jingle of coin as a moneybag
was passed over from one to the other. Pray, my prince has paid ransom
for my return, thought he in blessed hope. The peasant and the driver
at stink both left the cart a-jingle toward the village that was close to
sight. The four horsemen turned to him and he was able to lift his head
higher, and readied himself to have his chains undone, to be set free from
this undesired state he had been placed in. But then with sunken heart
he saw that soldiers were they, and not soldiers friendly to his cause, but
soldiers in the uniform of the King Henry. No doubt had he now that he
was indeed in a most terrible position, and fear wrapped about him as a
cape. The wrong camp was he in and he was woeful of his fate. One of
the military upped upon the board and took the reins to take the prize
away, the others as if guarding a treasure rode close. They glanced down
with some disdain at their prisoner who lay shivering and wetted with fear
in the stench of the cart. But said they naught as they trotted their catch
toward the smoky cloud that nestled below them. That cloud that dwelled
its time over London and the Tower.

His shackles were loosed and Alphonse was pushed and jostled into
the Tower that had loomed afar. The bright warm day was, within a blink,
changed into dark, cold stone that arched about his head and scraped close
to his sides as they went the narrow passage full of some menace. He
was pushed on until they came to a barred door where he was stopped.
Through the small opening within the black wood came a grisly face, seen
all hairy and unwashed. The breath through twisted teeth was spat o'er the
face of Alph as he stood with numbed mind.

"This 'im then?" was spake from the gape.

"Yes, this is the prisoner; we will leave him in your most pleasant care." The crackled laughter from without and within did not lighten the plight of Alphonse. The rattle of many keys heard he as the guard of the dungeon clicked open the rusty lock, and he was pulled into the grimy chamber that led to the dungeons.

Alphonse looked about at the vile place of dirt and slime, with an evil smell about of blood, of urine and excrement, of rot, and of death. The chamber of truth, the place of torture, placed such that prisoners would have to pass through it, to reach the dungeons that were at the far. As he was urged along he tried not to look into that torched light that sparkled the drip upon the chamber's walls, but black shadows greeted him like demons as he passed, and drew his eyes to places where he wished not to peer. The rack, half seen, the thick rope wrapped about the drum, the levers sticking out like the devil's arms. The body cage with its door swung open showing its black spikes protruding from within. The wall torch close cast a fleeting shadow of the device upon himself as he passed. A bench upon which a brank did lay, a head bridle with a hoop and hinges to enclose the head, with tightening screws showing from it. All manner of things did lay: nail-pullers, teeth-tongs, thumb-screws, finger-cutters, tongue-clamps. But then brightness shone its way and covered the black; a brazier of flickering flames flashed and billowed upon the smoked walls, as it pushed toward the ceiling's opening and out into the air, to send the drift upwards to blend into the dark cloud that o'er London lay. Hot irons of different shapes glowed their red, devilled eyes from the coals that lay beneath the flames. What they wish to know, I will tell them, pledged Alphonse; I am sick and cannot endure that which I have seen.

The keys once again fought each other as the one chosen came forth and opened the door to the dungeon. Alphonse was pushed inside the dark hole. The door clacked behind him as he stood and peered about the dim place. Rats scurried about, but they had no fear of the new visitor. Standing up upon hind legs were they, to screech and peer at the new mate brought to them in their place of rotted smell and dripping walls. Alphonse lay upon some sackcloth all of wet and evildoings. He slept, for 'twas the only relief he could seek as amorphousness took him away from his tragedy.

"C'mon!" the voice at the far side of the kick that was dealt to his side shouted as if angered.

God, 'twas no dream, for I am awakened but still linger in a nightmare; he stood from the dingy rag beneath him that seeped some blood about. Alphonse looked to see from where it had come, and showed his legs had been bitten by the rats, with red spots and bleeding marks upon him as fleas and lice took their sup upon the fresh meat and joyed over his warm stew.

"Get out of here!" came the next cry from the vexed guard. "You flea-ridden wretch, go stand at the table there!" The guard beckoned toward the place he was to be. Alphonse trembled as he made to his place; there he stood and waited to look neither left nor to right. A movement he heard, but he still did not look. A seat raked its legs upon the chamber floor. Books and papers were laid upon the old table; splintered and worn were the boards. The face came to view. The head was hatted, hair to the ears and then cropped, face shaven clean and of grim features.

"I am the interrogator for the King Henry, and upon his orders, I am here to seek out all information I am able with all full rights bestowed to you. Do you understand?"

"Yes, sire, I understand," answered Alphonse with worms that churned his stomach.

"You are the Alphonse Marquette, traitor in league with the Perkin Warbeck?" the interrogator spake his searching line.

"I am, sir, his companion and his friend," Alphonse answered as best he could.

"That is not the answer I seek. Do you wish to give it out once more?" The sounds heard from about showed that others were present, for the rattle of metal, the poking of the brazier, and the smell of the drifting hot spark gave forth meanings other than pleasure. The interrogator, with wafting quill and eyes that only gazed at the script before him, awaited some further answer to his question.

"I am, sir, the traitor in league with the Perkin Warbeck." True or false, Alph had no choice to the words of his answer.

"Now you speak my tongue, sire. Were you in all faith at the ready to do the bidding of the Perkin Warbeck in the murderous acts threatened against the King Henry?" Once more came a question from the king's agent that showed little room for any falsehoods or bent answers.

Alphonse wanted to speak other but he dared not, for those shadowy figures about him rated no heroics. "I was, sir, prepared to do whatever was asked of me."

"Good." The agent was pleased with the answers and liked that this day would be one of little troubles. "And where, sir, did you first meet this said Warbeck?"

"I met him in Portugal, sir." A true answer was easily come to Alph.

"Under what name did you know him when you first did speak?"

"His name, sire, was Piers Osbeck, and then later altered to Perkin Warbeck."

The agent was scratching his quill upon the king's parchment as the questions came and the answers given with all writ as some confession.

"And do you tell me all truth in this matter upon pain of death?"

"Yes, sir, I do." Once more came the answer to the agent's question.

"And do you, sir, give this information to me without duress or torture?"

"Yes, sir."

"You do very well, sir. There is just one more question to be asked." At last the agent looked up from his writings to ask the final question, and was the first time he had looked into the eyes of Alphonse. "Is this Perkin Warbeck indeed the Prince Richard who was incarcerated within this Tower, or is he, sir, an imposter?"

"He is, sir, an imposter," came the answer from Alphonse; it mattered not which he did speak, for the agent looked for only the answers he wished to hear to the questions asked. The eyes did not move their gaze as the parchment was turned and pushed across the table under the gaze of Alphonse.

"Sign at the bottom." The offered quill was taken and the confession was signed. The interrogator took it back, shook upon it some sand from the shaker, and waved it off onto the floor. "And you know, sir, for these heinous crimes that you have atoned to there will be punishment metered?"

"No, sir! Please do not bring death upon me, for I have been foolish and repent all I have done," Alphonse pleaded to the agent in feared tones.

"Do not fret yourself; your life will not be taken; you will be let to live so that others, every day, will see what the outcome of treachery will bring to them. No, sir, we will not be taking your life." He stood and walked away from Alphonse, to leave him holding onto the table and gazing down with blank mind. A lost soul abandoned was he. Voices he heard from the far side of the chamber of words he could not grasp. The agent of the king returned from his council with the guard to sit down once more upon the bench and began to fold the parchment of confession.

Two strong, hairy arms grasped Alphonse and dragged the helpless fish toward a bench with straps and chains that dangled to the floor.

"Come, sir, we will soon fix your nasty problem," one of the guards croaked at him with stinking vile and odour. He was soon strapped down and lay upon his back within the dank chamber. He gazed straight up toward the ceiling, dripping its crusted drips all of slime and grime. The brazier sparked and flashed its glow to make the walls to sparkle in its light. Numbed and wretched did he lay all helpless in his fear-shocked skin. The guards came to him and, lifting up his head, clamped upon it one of the head bridles, securing it tight with the thick screws until 'twas biting into the softness of the forehead. This bridle though was different to the others that were used, for this one was sent from the madhouse where 'twas used to make the inmates docile; it had been brought to the Tower to see if the procedure would be of any help, in that it may clear the head of any who had thoughts of traitorous acts and crimes against the Realm. The brank was fitted with a tube that protruded out from the forehead, with the part that lay upon the skin may two inches above the eyes.

The interrogator upped his books and manuscript and came past the table where lay Alphonse; he gazed at the wretch as he came by and almost stopped at his side, but he did not, and only spake whispery about. "Oh, how sweet death would be for he who wished it not." And then did wend upon his way. The call then shouted above Alphonse. The call that sickened his stomach even more and brought all despair upon him.

"We are ready, sire." The clump of boot came from the creaking door and stopped as a dark shadow spilled over Alphonse, who, in fear's grip, closed his eyes hoping it may remove all that was about him. There were no words spoken as the surgeon from the asylum rattled into his bag and withdrew an iron spike that was one-foot long and as thick as a thumb. One end was pointed and 'twas this end that was slid within the bridle's tube to end upon the skin of Alph, who could feel the warm breath upon his face as the surgeon moved the device about so 'twas placed at the correct place upon the forehead. The breath left and was replaced by another rattle of metal, as pulled from the bag and bathed in the light from the brazier came the heavy mallet. He held upon the rod that showed from the tube, and with a heavy swing did bang the rod into the head of Alphonse. A full three inches it cracked through the skull and cut into the softness beneath. A wrenching cry came from the lips that suffered, but were quickly to silence as he lost all sense. The surgeon came close again to peer upon the mark that had been cut upon the rod, and saw that it still had further to go into the skull. He stood at the side now, and looking as best he could to where the blood was running, gently tapped it until he could see that the mark was level with the skin. Then, with one quick pull, he removed it from the head, wiped it upon his cloth, and placed it back within his carry. His mallet then he placed in and, with that, clicked his bag shut.

"Remove the brank and let the wound continue to bleed. In a few hours it will stop. In two or three days he may awaken and will be cured of all harmful thoughts and be placid of nature and of no mind. If he does not awaken within one week, then you may as well bury him, but I wish to know the outcome, for if he does not awaken I will have to alter my mark upon the rod. Good day to you." He picked up his carry and made his way through the dark chambers to the bright day, climbed upon his steed, and went his way to his asylum-home.

Alphonse knew naught of the happening that had been placed upon him, as the cage was removed from his head and the guards carried him away to another dungeon. This prison had in the middle a high stone where upon the limp body was placed; 'twas built high enough and so smooth that vermin could not climb its tower and reach the body that laid atop—though all twisted and bent without form, it must not be eaten. For 'twas in the orders of the confession that the prisoner best be alive so that all may see the harm that would befall them for any acts of offence against the king. The door was then locked upon the lone body that still breathed within the cold chamber.

"If he lives he will be a wretched sight; if he dies he will be most fortunate." The two guards spake their thoughts as they readied from their day's labour. "Come George, let us finish the rest upon the morrow, for I wish to home and to see my Rose. This day I have had my fill of such misery." They made their way to the outer door and securely did lock the way. Up the steps they came, to the bright sky and the cool air that drifted the smell of the fresh-cut grass about. The sun was bright to their faces as they came to the roadway squinting their eyes with the glare; and soon they had no more discomfort as they breathed in the freshness that was about them; from hell to heaven in quick time. "Good day, George." ... "Good day, William. I will see you upon the morrow." With a wave they parted into the crowd to mingle with others, then gone and lost within the throng that drifted.

The inquisitor was before his king, to retell all he knew from the confession of Alphonse.

"So, sir," spake his king, "do we deal with an imposter?"

"We do, your Majesty; he did confess to such without the use of any torture. He freely spake of the Perkin Warbeck as to be no prince, but a liar and a philanderer just as your Majesty supposed." The words spoken from the agent were those which the king wished to hear above all other matters.

"I know not what game they play upon us—first that usurper Lambert Simnel, and now this Perkin. They must think we are weak and will crumble before them as soon as they spake the words, 'rightful heir.' No, sir, I understand not their ways. Warbeck will soon fall into our open hands, for he is no longer welcome to any land, and he will run himself ragged into our circle of entrapment—mark you my words." The king talked on to his agent as if he were a long-lost friend returned, and spake of the other who had tried to take the English throne, he who had lost his head in the trying, and was deemed such straits would come upon the Warbeck.

"Your prayers will soon bring to bear its fruit, your Majesty, and the usurper will come to that which awaits his deserving." The agent placed butter upon the bread as he spake to his king, seeking to keep him in some goodly humour.

"I must, sir, be informed of all the information you may gather, matters not how trivial." With those words the king waved the servant away, who with reverence bowed to his royal person, and left with such words as to do as he was so bid. The agent closed the door to the king's chamber and turned to move past many who stood in untidy state, they all at wait to have meet with his Majesty upon this day. Many looked at the agent who was to leave, some to wonder of his dealings, others wishing it were their time to be so honoured. All manner stood without that gilded doorway. Cloaked figures of intrigue wishing not to show their faces. Maidens looking of some dubious character chattered and giggled in whispered tones. Ladies and lords and unknowns. Two dwarfs dressed in the garb of the jester practised their rolling and tumbling before the passing waiters. Hoping, no doubt, to become part of the court's entertainers. All at wait to bring their different requests, some with information, some to obtain some reward, some for favours. All waited. Most to no avail.

A long month had passed and 'twas becoming cold now in the November of the year of our Lord fourteen hundred and ninety-eight. And 'twas the day of birth for Alphonse, for was he remembered nothing of any time before, except upon rare occasions where came to his mind vivid pictures and strange words that he would blurt out for no reason, but he knew not what they were, as if a black cloak did shroud him in lonely misery. He had tried to cry out in his anguish but only strange gurgles came from his mouth. His wound still ran with grume[*] and showed to all the act he had been done by. He was now it seemed an imbecile and naught would stay in his head. His mind raced with things to do and to say. His legs were ready to walk him away, but the black cloak lay and he could only stumble and bumble and grope about his prison walls. His eyes looked through some fog, and lightning flashed about in his gaze. Noises ten times loud he heard, talk was all about him, doors forever opening and closing with deafening locks clicking shut. Rats scurried about, like the sound of horses, with screech and scratch. No numbers could he add, no words clear to speak, only of jumbled jargon. His head would loll upon one side at times, and his mouth oft would not close, only to drip his spit. He would soon be subject to squirming fits with no help coming.

The slide of the food door he heard as it broke the rust and opened. The

---

[*] *grume* a clot of blood, a fluid of viscid consistency

tin platter was rattled inside, and the door was slammed shut once again. Alphonse grovelled along the floor upon knuckles and knees to the sound of the food bowl with the stinking victuals slopped into it; he picked it up with shaking hands and then sat back against the dripping wall, tipping some of the gruel into his mouth and managing soon to clean the bowl. He had heard his platter rattle against the tin cup, and so moved his hand about the floor in its blackness until his tingling fingers grasped it, to then bring the cool water to his cracked lips and to pour it down his burning throat.

"C'mon lad," the voice of the guard rang about in the empty head of Alphonse. He was then dragged to his feet, and his child's mind cared not to any happening, as he was led to his groping existence. "Time to show yourself to the pleasures that are away from this chamber and await you without." Alphonse felt something placed about his neck as he swayed without support. The guard had hung there a plaque, and straightened it as if it were a portrait, then he read aloud the words writ upon it, so that the prisoner may hear such that was writ within the law of confession about this cruel trial: "Traitor to the King Henry the Seventh. Wary be all who devise such plots. Not to be removed until death strikes its knell. Signed by the lord privy, constable of the Tower."

The door creaked, the tread slip and wet as Alphonse was led away from the dungeon, pulled along by his bloodied shirt, now ripped and dirt-laden. He felt the cool air upon his face as he came to the outside of the damned Tower. Still dragged along with arms stretched before him, for he could see naught. Then the grip was loosed and the footsteps went. He gripped the stone wall that was his only bearing, and, not knowing of this place or of any other, he slid to the ground to await what fate may be thrust upon him. Footsteps passed him by, others stopped for a moment and then moved on. Others did stop and spit upon him thick gobs to trickle his traitor's face. Then lighter steps did he hear and not the heavy boots as before.

"Come, my dearie," the old, croaky voice laid his ears. His nose smelled the unwashed body that helped him to his feet. Then the hag tied a rope around the waist of Alphonse and pulled him along; he followed behind the clacking shoes. "Steps here," he heard her croak, but did not yet know the meaning of the sounds. He tried to mime them but could only speak babble. Then he felt a wizened hand upon his that placed it upon a stair rail; he then did step and stumble up the wooden way. The cool air that was about him told his mind he was still outside; he sniffed the smells of the street as up and up they went, then to hear the door open, for he knew that sound. He was taken to a loft as the boards' creaking sounded beneath his feet. The door closed; he turned to see but only a foggy shape that meant to him little. Smells came to him who was lost; some meaty stew from a place that gave blessed warmth. He heard others rustling about within the place. The bony hands sat him, and then a warm, hairy thing came close, with a strange breath upon his face and a warm slop, long and wet. "Get thee away, Toby!" the croak called and the dog left to cower away. As he sat, he felt a table before him, and he rested his arms upon the rough wood. It seemed some things had begun to return to his memory. Was this some help before him or was this some evil plot that would squirm and gut him once again? But naught could he do but let fate bring to him whatever it may, for God's plan is not writ, though some compassion did he feel in those bony hands that touched his. Others he felt aside him as he sat with the smelly and raggedy cloth against his own. Naught was spoken by any who came to the table, except the old woman who croaked about, muttering and swearing with every other word. "I be Emma," the voice spake close by. "I fetch in 'ere those 'oo 'ave been butchered, not for the pleasure of your company but to use as beggars." Alphonse sat quiet, but puzzled was his mind, for he half knew from somewhere the meaning of those words, and so he mumbled some of his own, and, as if knowing what he had spoken, the old lady continued with her vile breath of rotting teeth close to his face. "Well, lad, what do you think you are going to do? Dress the royalty? Paint ladies portraits? Or, may, carve wooden birds?" Then came loud all about her croaky laugh, that seemed would never stop until a fit of coughing ended her joyful outburst, with others around the table who laughed just as heartily but with strange voices. Laughter without a tongue; mirth without sight. "You will soon get used to it, my dear, but if you 'aver better way to earn your keep then begone to seek your fortune." Alphonse shook his head, for he could not leave. "See, my cherub, all will be rosy. There be four of you now: Josh, Peter, Mark, and you. Here—" A piece of board was slid over to him and a piece of chalk was pushed into his hand, and it came to him that he was to write his name upon the board, and much to his own surprise he was able to do so, though it took long to mark the letters as his mind juggled with his fingers, and the sight from his eyes watered the board like waves upon the sea. The old lady looked at the writ closely.

"Alph, lads, his name is Alph." Then strange sounds of greetings floated about the table, and came an arm about him that pulled him close in some friendship. Comrades, soldiers of the maimed. "All 'ere have suffered the 'and of Henry," the hag continued; "all with some affliction. Peter though can talk a little for they did not get all of his tongue. Mark can see a little out of one eye, though he walks in a fog. Dear Josh is 'ard done by, for 'e 'as neither sight nor a tongue. And all of them 'ave some fingers missing. You, my dear, are most fortunate, for in time some of your mind will return, whether for good or bad, and you, with God's grace, will learn once again to speak a little.

"I take you out in the mornings to your place of begging and leave you there with your cup. You will 'ear the abbey sound the 'ours so you will know of the day, and when the bell rings five times I will be on my way to fetch you, and before the clock strikes six times you will be taken back to our 'ome to feed you and let you sleep. Alph, listen to me." The shape came closer so he could hear the important words she wished to say. "Be wary as you sit, for upon the streets are many robbers and thieves all out to do mischief upon 'elpless souls. They will with little care steal from such as you. After you 'ear a coin drop into your tin, and the giver 'as gone, put the coin in your mouth for safe keep, for it will matter not that the coin lurk in that 'ole, for you are of all babble anyway." Alph heard some garbled utterings that he could not understand. 'Twas Peter of the half tongue asking Emma some question it seemed. "Peter 'as asked me where you will beg. There is a small alcove outside the walls of the cemetery, which gives good shelter in the winter's cold; that is where you will stake. 'Tis a goodly place, for those about are apt to be generous in their grief, and thieves are little seen about such places."

The cold upon the hand of Alphonse turned to wet, as Toby came to sit close and to nose the new flesh. "'E likes you," Emma spake upon seeing her dog take to the stranger. "'E does not liken to all you know, but 'e likes you. When you have been with us a while and know more of our ways, 'e may take you for a walk, 'e be a good dog." Alph patted the friend to find warmth, gentle soft ears, and dripped tongue. Toby lay with head rested upon the cold feet. Food was brought to the table, and each who sat was given a weak broth, with a little meat, bread, some cheese, and a vessel of water. Alph ate all that was before him and downed quickly the water, and then he heard the cup being filled again. He brought it to his mouth and tasted the cool ale about his lips. Sweeter than nectar was it, and he was more content with the plain offering than anything he might have imagined at some past time. A morsel of meat he saved from his meagre lot, and slipped it upon the eager, lapping tongue of his new-found prince. After the victuals had finished, Emma took the hand of Alph and led him about the room so he would know of where such things did lay. "This be the cooking fire with the irons 'ung 'ere upon these 'ooks." Alph reached his hand forward and heard the irons rattle together, and felt there the warmth of the flames. She moved him further. "'Ere is where I sleep." She bent him over so that he could feel the cot and the wall where 'twas huddled, then she moved on again. "'Ere is the wall with a window and below it a small table with a water jug placed upon it. And 'ere is our cupboard, where is kept all our pans and pots, and our cups and jugs, and our victuals 'ere at the bottom upon the shelves. This corner is where Josh and Peter sleep. 'Ere be the door." Emma kept placing his hands upon the different places she talked of so that Alph would soon know the lay of the chamber, for as yet he could see little but shadows. "This is the corner where Mark and you will lay, and when you are used to the place, you will 'ave to 'elp in any way you can; there is no idle days 'ere." He was seated then back at the table and reached for the board and chalk, for he wished to make some words known. He scratched and slid the board so it could be more easily seen: "Emma tank." She picked up the board and read aloud that which had been writ upon it, so that all would know of the words passed. "No need to thank me, for you will be beholden to me for all things. And I expect you to bring a goodly amount in your cup, or you will end in the gutter where you belong."

Alph was able to understand more of what was being said, and his mind was able to bring to itself questions and answers to the words spoken. Words would not come to his mouth, and his eyes would see only in fogged shapes, but he mouthed, in his strange tones, his reply to the hag's last words. "Emma, you bring to our faces the raging bull, but behind the front is only the gentle lamb." She looked into the face of Alphonse as he spake, and 'twas as before that she seemed to know of what words were spoken from that gawgling* voice.

"We shall see," said she with some little smirk that came to her demeanour, and was quickly hid. "And any rats or mice that you see a-scurrying about this place, kill them and throw them out. I detest such vermin and will not abide them in this 'ome of ours."

They, all tired and weary, lay down upon the rushes and old bedding that did stench of some vile things that were unseen. Other things that slinked about did not delay their sleep. The lice and fleas that chafed mattered little to such tortured beings as they. A princely person came to mind but meant naught to Alphonse as the night's cool took away all aches.

"Time to go, lads ... C'mon, let us away and earn some money." Gentle pulls and tugs did urge them all to rise and to make ready. Emma placed in Alph's hands a small sack wherein was a jug of water, a little bread, and some old cheese. His begging cup then was slipped over his head and hung about his neck upon the top of his traitor's plaque. "Rattle the cup

* *gawgling* [coined] disturbed and severed

good," Emma urged. Each one of the beggars was then begot the same way, each with a bag and a cup about the neck. Soon they were all tied together and moved in a groping line down the wooden stair and on to the laneway with its sewage and swill about their foot. Toby was running far ahead of the slow troop, with stops now and again to be sure they still followed the way he showed. Emma, with rope shouldered, came, with ragged cloth and rotted shoe, clumping and tripping along the lane. With feet wet and muddied, the four broken bodies were dragged along behind to hold upon the rope as best they may.

The strange group made their way through the thick smoky fog that was London. All about them dripped the dewy matte of grime to be covered themselves in the mist deep, looking more a motley lot as they trudged along their path.

"'Ere will be your place, Alph." The line came to a stop as Emma's words were heard. The rope was untied from him as the others leant against the wetted wall. Toby sat at watch, with ears dripping from the morn's dew that clung to his fur, and seemed he was the only one with happy heart as Emma went about her duties. "'Ere's the place; come feel about it." Emma took the hands of Alph and let him feel the lay of the alcove that would be his shelter. "Now, sit you down, and remember all I 'ave told you. We will be back at the end of the day." He heard them ready, and then to stumble and splash away fainter and fainter. "Come, Toby!" he heard as the wet and drip of the dog sprayed upon him as he rushed by to catch up to the others. "How happy would I be if I were you, Toby. Soon will come a prince. He searches." Words tumbled his head once more, but then were lost as if there had been no thought at all.

Nine of the clock he heard struck from the wet tower of the abbey, as its roof searched through the bridal gown of mist. Soon the fog had drifted away, and warmth and light were about the dull streets once hidden. Voices coming closer did Alphonse hear; wheeled carts rattled along the cobbled roadway. Steps heard to come and then to go. Sometimes a kick upon his leg he felt as someone stumbled over him with cursed words. Shuffling steps, heavy of heart, that came from the graveyard. A clink in his cup startled him as the shuffled steps wayed. He tipped it into his mouth and rolled it about amongst the spit there. A bitter taste of copper and grime throgged* his mouth. Chimes came and went in his blackness as came another chink and then another, to slop into his mouth once again the bitter pill that was not to swallow. Then came some steps that seemed to be of stealth. He felt his cup lifted as if someone wished to steal from a blind man. Then blasphemous words were spewed upon him as the steps

---

* *throgged* [coined] a combination of clogged and throat

plodded away. Five of the clock had struck as Alph waited for some sign of Emma's coming. Soon he heard the knowing bark of Toby from afar, then the warm lick with two paws pressing upon his leg, and the wind from the wagging tail wafted about. He knew that at last his day was done, but his mind wondered if he could each day do this task. Then came the voice of Emma, all of rush and hurry to end all such thought.

"Spit them out." Alph did so to hear the jangle as he let the coins drop into his cup. "Good lad, Alph, good lad." The voice above him sounded most pleased as he was helped to his feet. Then he was tied at the waist and dragged along with the others. Garbled gibberish lilted his ears as they tried to talk of their day; they tried, but little came of such, as they were led to their refuge and soon to come the morrow's morn.

Chapter Twenty-nine.

Goodbye, Sweet Prince.

"My dear, we must away from this place. I know it is your home but our time here is done and naught will come to our stay." Richard spake in much earnest to his wife as they stood in their chamber within the castle; its window showed the ocean at Edinburgh, which had brought the prince much promise, but 'twas not fulfilled in any triumph. "Our soldiery here is finished and I must take my way to Cork and arouse the army that awaits there, their favour heartily pledged to me from that green land."

"I will follow you, sire, for by your side is my only need and matters not to any outcome. I will always be so." Katherine spake once more those vows she had pledged, it seemed so long ago.

"Success will come, have no doubt, though bleak times are upon us; fear not, for soon the sun will rise upon our state." Katherine knew well that this could be the last time she would see that sun set upon her Scotland. For had not fate played them a different song? Promise had been much, but then came played that other, that other of deceit, of lost causes and promises gone awry.

They saw the night come with its twinkled blanket, and bedded that night in the blue chamber, where they had dreamed of their ambitions and plans of lovers made.

The morn came with a sharp cold that bit them upon toe and finger as they readied within the yard to leave the place that had been a dear home to them. Frost draped all in white and nothing other showed as far as the eye saw. The grass cracked and crunched as trod 'twas underfoot. The horses' breath steamed like a hundred cauldrons at boil, as they pawed the frosted lay. Only three hundred soldiers from many countries stood at Richard's command. All that remained of the thousands who had stood by his side but a short while ago. Others of the entourage climbed into the carts and upon their horses, those cooks and butlers who still had their children held in surety. Waiting ladies, blacksmiths, stable boys. All to add another one hundred and fifty more to Richard's house, that such as they could not manage without. Away they rode from that once welcoming castle with all its favours once bestowed upon them, to trickle onto the frosty ways, with rattle and clap, of chat and plod.

They, in long order, rode steady pace to Glasgow where ships awaited them to journey the coast to Ireland, and to once more the harbour of Cork, where would await them the loyal cheers and those brave souls who would join them to battle the Henry Tudor.

All were loaded upon the lift and low of the moored ships. Old with many leaks they lay in the harbour, and would take as many men upon the pumps as it would to sail them. But ships they were and 'twere all their monies could bring. Soon the ripped sails were lofted and were taking the breeze in their tattered folds. Masts creaked and groaned in some hidden pain as they made good time to the harbour of Cork. They thanked God for the calm sea and stormless sky, for a battering this fleet could not take. Through the night the blessed ships creaked and heaved upon their set way, to see in the dawn the mist-shrouded Ireland. By noon the mist had gone, and they sailed into the harbour with the hills about seen in their bright green meadows and wooded valleys; the black bogs of peat scarred the tranquil scene. The White Rose was bannered above, as slowly with sails furled they floated with calm to tie up at the dockside. And even before the plank had steadied, the leaders of the army came down with Richard to stand in firm order upon that land that had befriended him so. They stood all of pomp with the armada at their backs billowing the royal banners. The decks filled with the sailors and the soldiers, stood they in some semblance of order upon the lilting planks.

But no crowd did show, though they waited long. No striking band of players luted them to shore. No ribbons seen to wave or soldiers stood straight to greet. But still they did wait, with the ships behind them lifting and falling in the light swell. Those who had stood straight upon the decks were now at the rail watching the lack of happenings before them. Many hung from the rigging above, all awaiting that which was to come. As then through the narrow laneway afront them came a bluster the lord mayor of Cork. Dressed he all fine with red coat stitched with gold, a black hat with white feather flicking in the breeze, his staff of office clutched in his thick hand. Behind him trod his councillors, may twenty in number. At last the coming of the greeting party, and would be soon the lords and the gentry to follow with that grand army at this very moment preparing their parade. They came, the lord mayor and his party, and seen at follow a small group of townsfolk, though not to be seen striking any joyful pose toward the comers. Close came the mayor, his buckled shoes clattering upon the cobblestones, to be within the grasp of Richard. He bowed low.

"Good day to you, my dear prince. We pray you are in good health?"

"I am indeed well, sire; thank you for your concern." The politeness of the meeting was over, though 'twas deemed by both parties to be short, and to cut quickly to the business before them, for seemed need was to be over with it. "There seems to be little shown of any joyful greetings, Mister Mayor. Where, pray, are all the people and the soldiery that did greet me when I last visited your shores?"

"Alas, sire, all soldiery has been disbanded by the King Henry, for 'tis upon death to organize such again. The old lords are no more, all hung and quartered they, and now scattered." The mayor's answer was not pleasing to Richard.

"And of the support pledged to me?" he asked next the most vital question of which he had some inkling of the answer.

"'Tis no more, sire," came the answer he wished not to hear, nor the mayor to speak. "We now have nothing to offer in such warring as you enter. No ships, no soldiery, no monies, sir; we are destitute, for the king stripped us bare for our contrivances."

"I am deeply cut by the words with which you speak. I expected much from this Isle." The prince spake his words of disappointment.

"We know what was expected, sire, but we have nothing to give." The mayor spake of the poor state of his community as he looked forlorn, only to gaze upon his new shoes of expensive leather and silver buckles as he pleaded poverty. Came over the prince in some rage, for he believed little of what he was being told, and could well see the prosperity that was about him, and he needed not to look into any castle to see the same abundance.

"My dear mayor, I take it that you speak for all people here, of all the new lords and owners of land, they who grow rich no matter who holds an iron glove over them. I think, sir, you are all well able to fortune me. But in your state of cowardice, in your fear of Henry, you choose not to join me to destroy him so all will be free of such oppression, is this not so?" The mayor answered not and stood with little feeling upon his face. "You say you are feared now, but the fear you feel will be naught to the fear you will feel when I become king, for believe me of the truth with which I speak. All who gave forth assistance to me, no matter how small, will be treated with uncommon goodness; property and assets will be heaped upon them. For those who refused me will believe the plague to be an easy death, for they will be struck down with such fury. I will raze all your towns and villages, I will kill your women and children, and you will be in a most wretched state. Trust in what I say. Begone and crawl away into your slimed holes; show me no more the face of treachery. The dawn will see us gone, for I will be rid of this place."

The broad plank was upped as the prince boarded his vessel. The soldiers from the ships all about cheered his wicked way, as down below went he to make council in the captain's cabin. His officers stood about him, none to say what was next to come but all at wonder. He turned in the shelter to face them.

"We go to Cornwall where the Cornish are in uprising against Henry. And there, with all endeavour, we will make our say."

"All abide by such, sire; 'tis the honest treat to join with the Cornish, for they will flock like the wandering sheep to your side, for they have all except a leader. The White Rose stands tall amongst the Cornishmen so hateful are they of the Henry Tudor." The prince's commander spake in high tone for all his officers gathered, and all made with high hearts, for 'twas the best plan yet tabled.

The dockside was empty of all life except for the brave seagulls who strutted about with their puffed chests. Would be that others were so proud. The ships set away upon a new tack, no more to be gained to delay their journey. Rocking away they went in the still calm; the breeze was right as they bobbed away like seabirds upon the wave. They looked back upon the land to see many people returning to their town from all directions. Back to their business they, to their fishing and farming and to the bartering in the town's square; all places returning to their new-found tranquil life under the fist of Henry. No reprisals anymore to come to them, no loved ones to sail away, no children to cry for their fathers. *Goodbye, sweet prince, reap all you deserve; we will watch you from afar.*

Chapter Thirty.

Cornishmen.

The shoreline came to sight, another land but one of many seen before. To what fate may our day be? Richard's head once more raced with what could be. If naught was to come from this place then his day would be done; with no place left for him to show his banner, no place he could rest as home in some tranquil; but 'twas the thorny path he had chose, with no arm twisted upon his back. God will guide our way … What of Alph? he pondered; will he not come soon? Sails were furled as the landfall came, and he looked up to see his White Rose fluttering once more as some guardian angel against the blue sky.

Whitesand Bay was before them, the town scattered about the limestone hills that circled the shallow harbour. Came they as close to the shore as they were able before their boats struck the sandbar below that inviting water, and there did lower their anchors. The folk at the town's shore started to gather. Seen from the docks and the cottages close to the shore, they grew quickly in numbers, all peering at the assembly of vessels that had come to their bay, as then arms stretched and began to wave. Scarves were twirled in the air and faintly heard from the far were shouts and cheers. They had seen the angel aflutter above the restless ships. Tenders were lowered from the vessels to take a small party to the land, and to see of the greeting there, and to see if there would be some fearless souls who would relish a war. The oars creaked and splashed as closer came they to the shore. The people there stood in many numbers and their cheering grew louder. Seen then many arms waving clearly, and many banners being swung back and forth as closer they came. Out from the lofts and the cellars, all hid with dust and chaff upon them, came those banners of the White Rose, lofted high in the glory they had long waited for. This day when they would be able to greet their prince, he who at last had come as some lost saviour, from some magical ship from some far time, all happening as the reader of the stones had foretold. Seen tall in the bow of the first boat, his fists upon his hips, his legs braced against the rock of the vessel. Proud stood he, as soon the oars were lifted and the keel cut into the sandy bottom and the waves were just a ripple. They came from the shallow of the sea to the sparkling beach of sand. As they footed once again upon the land of England, most quickly the crowd gathered about them, as they, in wet sloshing boots, walked to the town but fifty paces ahead. All about them now the cheering as they stepped upon the cobbled way. They called out not the name of the prince but of the King Richard the Fourth.

The dignitaries of Whitesand were quickly roused to come to the sea road that dawdled its twisting path along the shoreline. They came in hasty dress, some still being attired, as the carts rolled along. Though a sturdy breed and most warlike in their beliefs, they had no mighty leader and were led only by commoners. A stook without twine. Now though, and known to all about, had come the one they had wished long for. Their might in numbers could at last be led by a royal leader, who had been greeted most reverently as a king though as yet no crown sat his top. They smarmed all over him and guided him upon wings to the mayoral chambers of the town, and there did feast him and all his entourage. And soon 'twas they devised and made their plans for this royal war. Runners were sent out to the reaches of Cornwall, and to Devon, to Somerset, and to Dorset that their king had come, and to join in arms all soldiery and warlike people, and to bring themselves as haste may bear to Morton Hampstead, the place of their meet. To be at the such place upon the sixteenth day of September, the year of our Lord, fourteen hundred and ninety-eight, and to come in all warlike manner. Then to move in great force against the walled town of Exeter, which would be the first blow against the King Henry. That town so dear to the king's heart would be laid to ruin or surrendered.

They moved upon their act the following day. The prince placed ahead of this great force, proud at last to be in his rightful place. Though he had to leave his beloved Katherine behind at the town of Whitesand Bay, for these coming times would be hard and he would not place such misfortune upon her. She was left in secure keep at the burgher's mansion there, which left him in much melancholy though he was regally sat. The prince led his troops to the road that twisted and turned its track to Exeter's way ...

"Your Majesty, Perkin Warbeck has footed this Isle and is now in Cornwall. Followers are flocking to his banner in many numbers and his object is Exeter. He plans to take the town and in doing so bring more followers to his cause. With him are all his commanders and all his army mustered. His wife awaits in secure fashion at Whitesand, and a meet is planned with her husband in more peaceful surrounds." The agent bowed to end his council with the king. He stood, still dusty and parched from his hurried ride, then stepped back humbly to await his next command.

"Do we march against him, sire?" the most senior commander posed the question to his king. But to all seemed that the answer "Yes" was writ and did not warrant the asking. But the king had other things written in his book.

"We do not march ... Not as yet. We lay back without strike, but not without sight. First I wish to know how my commoners will treat this fellow when he raps upon the door of their town. I believe his welcome will be of short time. I believe my people do not want such turmoil upon their step, and, if I am correct, this army of troglodytes he commands will soon tire and disperse from his side. I know of these Cornishmen; they are able to fight but orders they will not abide. They are as a lady's fan, all waving and causing much disturbance at first, then to fold and be naught but two sticks in the wind. I believe our army need not draw a single blade to this scoundrel. I wish not to war with him; I wish to take him with justice; not as a king against another king upon the field, and he to be a martyr, but before legal council as a king against a liar and a usurper; and, until I have him placed such before me, I wish him not harmed in any battle, and for the people to see him as the traitor he truly is. That will mean more to this England than his head upon a platter. As to his Katherine who resides in secure pleasure, we will bring her away from there, and to the palace at Westminster, where the Queen Elizabeth will, in all her compassion, care for her until this play drops its curtain. I will give in writ my honourable pledge that the said lady will not be harmed, or be subject to any discomfort whilst under this given protection. See to it that these things are done and that the lady knows of her rights. Then we will await the outcome.

The prince came to the place of their design and awaited that day for his followers to come in their desire to follow him. And they did come from all places, from the hills far away, from the rich valleys, through the fields of wheat almost ready for the harvest. Cracking underfoot the fallen branches and the cones they came, through the woods and forests to come where their leader stood. Hundreds came with rattling drums and pipes at play. Led by their lords came great hoards of wild Cornishmen, each of a different clan, but all with one endeavour: to finish the Henry Tudor. By day's end stood in the prince's camp six thousand warriors. The warring upon Exeter looked of easy pickings, for each of those souls that huddled within those walls would be outnumbered sixfold. And seemed that when the commoners of the town saw the might before them they would lose all heart and open the gates to welcome this prince and would come in league with him. And high were their spirits, for at last the prince who comes could show his metal.

Upon the morn of the seventeenth day of September they moved away from their encampment, heartened by the pipes and drums that led the army forward, the army that was pledged to bring all glory to the prince. They marched thirty miles, and then came to the crest of a small hill that was close to the north gate of the town of Exeter. This gate, though high, had been chosen for there, upon this side of the town, the wall was lower than the others, and the people within could gather, able to see out from their fortress to the place where Richard's army did gather in great tumult, and could clearly hear the steady beat of the drums as they still came in great numbers, to gather and to fill their ranks. Then began the low chant of those savage Cornishmen, all riled up now, to add to the sight that gathered before those peering eyes atop the wall, who in silence watched. The army, with a signal from the prince, stopped all chant and drum and quiet did they become; to hold their lines steady was the order. The prince wished to take this town without bloodshed if he could.

The commoners' heads were clearly seen as they looked in some awe at those who were gathered before them. No army of Henry dwelled within their stone walls, only a few officers placed to guide the inhabitants in the defence of the town.

The prince rode forward so all could see that indeed 'twas Richard who led this army. He halted his steed and called loudly to the peering lot. "People of Exeter, we, in our right as the heir to this England's throne, have come to take your town within our fold. We wish not to bring strife upon you, but for you to join us freely in our quest, and to bring to your town good fortune." The prince's words were being received with much favour, for they did not want to war, and would concede their position to the prince if all were favourable. His speech made to them turned many minds to his cause and they awaited more of the prince's desires to them. "Be not of fear; my word to you is that you will suffer naught, but you will gain much if you join with us." All was turning to a peaceful settlement, and the bobbing heads seemed to be making some movement amongst themselves, and to open their gate to this prince who spake words of honour and promise. The restless Cornishmen though had taken all they could of the jabber and were itch to fight. Stung by the wasp they started once again their chant of war, and to beating their shields with their broadswords. More joined their cantor, quickening the chant and the beat. "Hold them back!" the prince swinging about called to his commanders. "The orders are to stay! Hold them! We are within a whisper of their submission." But hold they would not and did gather in one force, and charged by the prince toward the gate that stood their way. Shouting and cursing in their Cornish tongue they came in belied fervour, bowling down their commanders who tried to turn this mad lot. They tried with words and then with force to stem the wild men, but they could not be quelled and did race in unruly throng toward the walled city. The prince could only watch with saddened gaze as his campaign melted like the winter's snow in the springtime. "They do all that is wrong; they will succumb with this tact!" he shouted loudly, trying to be heard above the cries and chants. "Do not rush the gates, for they will destroy you!" But the deaf heard naught as they had reached the north gate and began to beat their swords against the thick oak in some useless fashion. The heads that bobbed at the low wall had all gone now, and had taken themselves to the walled top high over the gate. Smoke showed rising to those who were far aback—the prince, his commanders, and those who still stood loyal to his orders. Those close to the city walls saw not, as the pitch was being boiled to tar and was being made ready in the black cauldrons. Then, strangely, one side of the gate opened to the beating swords, and in rushed the warriors with victorious air and shouts of rampage. Some two hundred came through the half gate before the tar came pouring out of the battlements, and was spilled upon all those trying to make the narrow entrance. Down it came, washing all below in its black hand. Crushing and squirming, they rolled and screamed as the boiling black covered them. Burning out their eyes and turning their naked skin into torches. Running away from the gate came those who could. The rest were piled in a miserable heap in straits of searing pain and death, as skin blistered and burst with steaming pop. Came then from within, and clothed in canvas-hooded cloaks and gloves, the commoners, who began to drag away from the open gate the twitching bodies. Smelling most like roasted pie, with many ablaze and crackling loudly. When the gateway was cleared they closed it to those without, and then set about those who were within. Rocks were thrown upon them from the high walls and arrows were leashed from the narrow slots in the battlements. Hacked by the sword in the dark alleys, tripped and stabbed as they scurried about with no escape from the people of Exeter. Welcomed they into their town with open gate and merry greeting. Then a steady slaughter till all were done and none left to suckle the sweet air. The bodies of the Cornishmen were piled high within the market square for all to see and gloat. Weapons were stripped from their bloodied bodies and held high in the hands of Henry's commoners. Not one of those wild men was left to wield against them within their walls.

The rest of Richard's forces, still a mighty band, came and completely surrounded the city to place it under tight siege. But stretched they were thinly about the long wall, and they could not muster enough strength in one place to break through the face that was shown to them. Slowly, as the day dwindled away, the ranks were thinned even more. Rocks were thrown from the high towers that were placed along their stone shield, taking many lives of any who ventured near, and arrows flew to take even more. At the north gate, soldiers were under great duress from the citizens above them, as they began to drag the smouldering bodies of their comrades that lay in great numbers about the gate, that place where such terror had been brought upon them. They stacked high the bodies against the thick oak gate. Some they piled still squirmed and moaned, but there was no hope for them, so they were clubbed to the state where no more anguish would they feel. Mercy given in their sacrifice to come, and then added to the pile. Torches were thrown upon them to set the mess to smoke and flame. Soon high the flames played against the oak mass that blocked their way. High the sparks flew from the human fire as they all stood with weapons in hand and rage in their hearts, ready to charge through the opening soon to show. But the wood was so strong and old it stood like iron and would not burn. The soldiers watched as the fire gave up its raging burn and softened into but a glimmer, with naught done but bodies burnt. Still they watched as if some miracle would swing wide the gates. But no miracle came and the flame died with all hope. Soon many moved away, no longer in any military fashion, but dejected with much misery about them. Others saw the game had ended and moved away from the walls, as word spread about of misfortune and death. Then rumours came of fleeing lords with a prince disguised within their fold. And so they moved into the fields away from those dark walls, and they did not look back, for they had lost too many comrades in grisly fashion against that black drop and wished not to eye it again.

The prince looked upon the sight that unfolded before him; his time was done and 'twas to naught this day of endeavour. The bedraggled army moved away from Exeter and retired to Cullompton, there to regroup and to plan their next move. But many of the prince's followers were leaving him and, with the others who came from the West Country, the rest of the Cornishmen drifted away. Harvest time was now to mind where plunder was before. Many of the commanders and soldiers did not return to the new camp, and to those who did return the prince relayed his position.

"This day, sirs, we are in the most disturbed of minds. We had almost gained a peaceful entry into the town of Exeter and, but for those men of the West Country, we would be in good state. However, they knew nothing of taking orders and were, as I had been told, but dunghill ruffians. They are of painters of manors and palaces who have no references. They come with all their goodly stuff. Barrels of paint and dye, buckets and brushes, tins and rags. By the hundreds they work showing much speed and skill, all of lines straight and with no drips upon the floor. They come and paint with much care, but, when all is finished and 'tis time to view, it is seen most impressive, except it is not the colour that was asked. Worthless bodies who take no direction and have brought my enterprise to an end. My fill is of Cornishmen … I must seek other ways to claim my kingdom, and I must bid you all upon your way to find a better place to occupy; you who are still loyal to my cause, I thank you, but now I must be a lone seeker."

The prince turned and walked slowly away from the gathering with no more words, for he had spake all he could; yet still the crown did not adorn his head, and naught would change even if he were to speak for a fortnight. He mounted his steed and rode away in the dimming of the eve, watched from the camp by the last of his followers, watched until he was gone from sight upon that sad eve of September.

PART FIVE: PERKIN WARBECK

September 1497 …

Chapter Thirty-one.

Confession.

Late was the hour when the prince came to the edge of the New Forest, and did rest over at a small inn there. The night was not pleasant for him, for he turned with such dreams that tormented his mind, and in fear that he may be found by the King Henry's agents before he could find sanctuary. But the morn came upon him with no reprise and he made his way into the forest alone, except with thoughts of his wife and of Alphonse, and the eyes of the king's army. And 'twas midday when he came to the monastery Beaulieu, which lay secluded within the thick of trees. And there upon the twenty-first of September did rap upon the door to gain sanctuary, and 'twas given to him by the abbot there, and, since many days, 'twas the first time he had felt safe in his surrounds. He would be able to find the time without interruption to determine his next scheme. Placed was he within frugal walls, simple food, and goodly guidance. He settled, but his time was short-lived, for after only two days of tranquil state, came to him the abbot in some concerned state.

"Sire, I am ached to bring such tidings to you, but the monastery is surrounded by the king's men, who deem to have knowledge of your presence here. They demand, sir, that you give of yourself to them."

"I am unable to do such, my dear abbot, for am I not in sanctuary here and untouchable under our Lord's keep?" the prince's position was put forth.

"Yes, that is so, my lord, but seemingly they will take you no matter which words you may choose to waylay them," the abbot answered the prince as best as he was able.

"I will speak to the commander. Please, abbot, fetch him to me."

The abbot did as he was bid by the words of the prince, and soon was brought the commander of the king's troop. The officer was tall and of slender build, showing a seasoned appearance. With little doubt a loyal servant of his king to act as he had been ordered, but, Richard thought, that within the request some compromise must have been writ, for 'twould be the king's last resort to break the sanctuary of a prince.

"Good day to you, sire," the officer spake as he acknowledged the prince.

"Good day, sir. You know well that I am in the Lord's house, and under such is deemed that no violence may come upon me."

"I do so, sire, know of your state, but regret my orders offer no such leniency, and I must follow my orders as you are well aware," the officer replied to the prince's statement in a sympathetic but firm tone.

"Are your orders writ, sir?" next inquired our prince.

"Yes, I hold them in my pouch, sire." A hand placed showed the object's concealment.

"Is it reasonable for me to ask to view such as you carry?"

"You may view them, sire, and you will see they are writ in the king's hand and his seal is placed to say such." The officer began to remove the strap upon the pouch.

"I have no doubt of the reality of the orders, and have no cause to think otherwise that they are indeed from the king; doubt, sir, is not my motive. I wish only to read what he has put upon the scroll."

The commander finished retrieving the documents and passed them over to the prince, who took them and placed them flat upon the table before him, then pulled over the candle closer to light the words. All silence was about in the dim place as the prince gazed upon the writ; slowly he read every line that was placed there, for the king was apt to write with mirrors and smoke, for his words writ could be bent so that black was white, and his father a three-legged toad.

"I read, sire, that he wishes me brought to his presence unharmed, and that the deliverer of this message, which, sir, is yourself, must inform me of this fact, and also is writ that my life will be spared and no retribution taken against me. It seems that you have neglected to tell me of these pledges."

"That is so, sire. I wished not to speak of such at this time, for such knowledge was kept aback for use as a bargaining tool in the case 'twas of need. If, sire, you had decided to come with me without reading the document, then it would not be shown and the king would not be obliged to any pledges." The prince listened to the officer who it appeared only followed the orders given to him by his king.

"I wish the abbot and the friars to peruse this document and to remember the writ words contained so they may witness to what circumstance I may leave this sanctuary, and to what laws apply against me in doing so," the prince spake once more to gain for himself some abidance of the writ placed before him.

"You may do as you wish, sire. The king's writ is his word and you will not be harmed in any way. I pledge you that, sir, upon my honour as a soldier of the king's army."

The abbot, upon those words, took the parchment to the far of the monastery where waited the friars in gentle stay, and began there to study the contents of the document. Await of the outcome without a word spake, stood the commander and sat the prince. Came soon from the dim light at the far was seen the abbot upon his way, as quiet whispers came from the brown-hooded robes that were darkly seen behind him. He returned the scroll to the hands of the officer and nodded in meaningful fashion to the prince that all writ was in true meaning and was now recorded within the books of the church.

"Then, sir, I am ready." The prince stood and did gather his few belongings together, placed upon him his cloak and hat, and came out from the dark chamber into the bright of the day. The horsed guard were but black shapes before him as the sun was upon his face; tall, black, and menacing in their duty were they half seen. Soon he was mounted and moved away from the sanctuary of the monastery with his close guard about him. The abbot stood at the iron gate and watched until the last soldier was not sighted. Turned he then to make religious thanks for the bounty received. The coins of the king heavy in the bag he held under his robe. Sold was the prince for one hundred shillings.

Leaving the New Forest they moved southward upon the road that would take them to the town of London. The ride into the town was not the ride he wished. He wished the White Rose to flutter over his head, his queen serene by his side, his guard all about him, and ten thousand soldiers at his command. Alph there upon a white horse as proud as his king. The crowd would be most frantic, and in awe of such a sight, as the king came at last to his rightful place within this Realm.

But this day the guard was not his and numbered they but one hundred. There at ride was no queen, and there was no Alph. The crowd waved not its white banners, they shouted not of their allegiance. Only a few he saw that gathered about who watched in silence as he passed them by; no allegiance did he hear cried but stillness and uncaring gaze. The rain then came, painting the scene with its dark and with its cold, all within the misery that was taking place.

They came to the Tower and clopped onto the wet stone of the yard, as the rain drenched all about them. The prince though was treated with care and respect as would befit someone of royal blood, far from the fact that they did not believe he was such. He was escorted into that darkest of towers, that bloody tower that did hold the young princes in that time long passed. He was taken to a secure chamber where he was blessed with good accommodation—fine victuals and good wines were upon his table. Then he was left alone, knowing that he would be before the king upon the morrow, there to answer such charges as would be laid against him. He fell asleep that night gazing at his new abode, and thinking he wished not to reside there.

The morn came, and soon 'twas time he visit the king at the palace at Westminster. He was given good clothes and fine boots; well was his hat proudly sat. Fresh of shave and with hair trimmed he looked more of a prince this day. Now to be escorted with close guard to the king's carriage that stood at wait. He had but sat when it trundled away; in some hurry were they, but not so the prince who would leisurely ride. The swaying cargo rattled along the cobbled streets and narrow roads. Citizens stood about in many numbers with curious gaze to see the would-be prince as he was sped by, and for the first time to see this man who had dared. The party entered the enclosure at the palace and the prince was taken to the Great Hall there. He shed his cape and his hat and then was paced along the candlelit way. Guards stepped before him and guards stepped behind him as he was led to the court there. Outside the great door he was sat upon a simple bench, and was stayed at the chamber's entrance. The prince waited there for some time, and could hear from within the murmurs of solicitors and judges, and all manner of whispered word bandied. Of tables scraping upon the stone floor, of benches being moved from one place to another, and then, as if in one whisper, all was quiet. "Come!" was heard from within the chamber. The guard who stood, opened one side of the door to enter four guards and the prince. He saw then the high black beams that held the roof, and the ancestral paintings hung the walls. Dark drapes swayed about. 'Twas chilling cold in this place; even the bleak furniture seemed to shiver with all so entered. Tables he saw about with water pitchers and goblets upon them. At the high table, wearing their black coats with white collars, judges and solicitors sat seeing all of miserly face and demeanour. Pages stood a-ready, all with some bug in their breeches. A thousand eyes were upon him as he was guided to the bench that crouched before the tables of the court. Chatter was abound when first that door creaked his whereabouts, but slowly silence had come from the din, to a whisper, then to naught, as all looked at the one who would be king, and to what tale he would bring this day. Would truth out or would lies lay? He looked at the judges as he was sat upon the bench, and to gaze at each one in turn, they who did pretend to be of fair mind and of justice. But the empty seat there that awaited the king was the only place that would call the justice this day. All the pomp and procedure of the assembled lot were of naught. 'Twas the king who would ring the bell of fate. They who sat were but a frame around the picture. Puppets in a farce where all knew of the outcome.

"The King!" was cried from the bearer of the rod. All stood in the chamber, and all did bow in reverence as entered the King Henry in perfumed state, with frivolous attire of lace and of silk, and a large flopped hat upon his head. White cotton stockings stopped at his knees with a red garter shown upon his right leg. His shoes, black and shined with buckles of silver, tightly strapped. The royal staff was held daintily, sparkling with its precious stones in the candles' light. All this displayed as he drifted in some divine fashion to his chair. His flunkies ran about him with sickening swank, to aid him to his seat like bees about their queen. He was at last seated to his pleasure, his coat at last placed most perfectly, his clopped feet at rest upon the velvet stool. He then waved all present to be seated. The prince, though, was told to remain standing; he stood as a weed in a cabbage patch and waited for the next words to come. 'Twould be the king who would lead this trial, and little shown of the other legals about, all looked upon as mere pettifoggers. Henry, though, had some thoughts within his own head, for he knew that he could brand this prince an imposter, but the punishment metered must be well thought, for though not running and shouting in the streets, this prince still had many followers, with many in the upper classes that only waited for the right moment to strike against their king. If Henry put the prince to death then that could be the strike that would light the flame and put out their king, for they would believe that Richard was of royal blood, and above all, such acts against him by another of royal blood would be seen as a murderous act. He would have to tread with care. The noose that hangs this imposter will not be made from the hemp of this king. But Richard will spin it himself and will place his own head within its loop.

"So, sir, you state yourself as being the Prince Richard, heir to this throne that I sit."

"I do so, in all respect, state such, your Majesty," the prince spake his truthful answer to the king's query. The Henry then continued from his regal seat.

"Before you bring to this court your legality in the matter, I have some things you must know of so that you may come to a truthful confession, for I tell you straight, one confession is all you have. If it be truthful, then you will have naught to fear. If you do not speak with truth, you will be subject to interrogation until you do speak the truth. So, as you see, my would-be prince, the truth will out sooner or later." The king began to sort through some documents, playing some game in trying to find that for which he searched, only to give Richard time to mull the words that had already been spoken. He came then with the elusive document and read from its writ words. "Firstly, we have a confession from one ... Alphonse Marquette.

Given without duress, stating, sir, that you are the commoner now known as Perkin Warbeck. And that in fact you have no right of accession to the throne of England. And further to your position, we have in confinement at the palace of Westminster your wife, the Lady Katherine Huntly nee Gordon. She is under the care and protection of the Queen Elizabeth, who, in all kindness and consideration, does dote most kindly."

The prince was riled, and gone from him was his calm demeanour, as the king cut into his heart by the dangle of Katherine before this court. He was placed in the sad position of having no position; whether to speak the truth or to lie, he could give only one confession to this king's court. Though Katherine was unharmed, the threat of some reprise hung heavily upon him.

"So, good sir, speak your plea." Irritated by the delay in the coming answer, the king's words came in some terse manner.

"May I ask your Majesty of my fate in this matter? For I offered no personal harm to your good self and would not will such." The prince spake words that were most suitable for his position, and to not rile the king with harmful intentions.

"If you state that you are the scoundrel Warbeck, you will not be executed for your deeds against this crown. You will be kept in pleasant confinement and with pleasurable excursions available to your request. You will be given an allowance of fair means. You will neither see nor have any contact with your wife whilst you remain in this state. Do you understand such as I have stated?"

"Yes, your Majesty, I understand."

"We wish then to hear the confession from your own lips," the king ordered the sagging prince.

"I plead that I am, indeed, the Perkin Warbeck, and further state that I have no legal accession to the throne of this land, and that I am not the Prince Richard that dwelled in the Tower. I will not contact the Lady Katherine until time gives me the right to do so. All this I state truly before your Majesty and before this court."

As the proceedings came to its promised outcome, the leading judge was at last able to speak the final words. "Your confession will be writ and given to you so you may sign it. Then it will be displayed upon the gates of the Tower so all may know of your shameful act against this land."

With his head bowed and the final words ringing his ears, the once prince was taken away to be confined within the Tower, with all proper amenities stated by the king honoured to him. Much rumblings were about the court chamber, though with quiet were the words, for all knew the acts proffered by this Warbeck were of high treason, and only one act of punishment could be given, and that was of death, and they were at some dilemma at the king's leniency to the matter. The king's adviser was required to broach the question by all that stayed within the court chamber.

"Sire, we are all at wonder of your leniency, for it does not mirror the act of this usurper; we trust you have more in mind than that which you have spoken this day."

The king sat with his adviser and others of the court as they shadowed in closed group to hear of his reasons. He had thought through his situation, but had spake naught of it, nor did writ to any person; but he had to appease those about him, they who looked for justice of this heinous act against their king, for if punishment was a walk in the garden then others may tread the grass.

"Truly, my dear sirs, I cannot in the eyes of our citizens take his head, for there are many who still think of him as Richard, and this contrived confession will be seen for what it is. Does he not look and talk as some royalty? And is not his proud bearing such? We will wait, for will come the day when the people will ask for his head, and I, with great reluctance, will abide to their wishes with great sorrow within my heart."

"Yes, sire, as always you are of astute mind, and we are in regret to have asked such to your most royal Majesty." They all bowed their heads in shame of the question they had proffered.

Chapter Thirty-two.

Lost to Tyburn.

"Perkin" was resided within the Tower, and for many months did abide by all the laws applied to him. He rode horses and hunted whenever he wished; he enjoyed good food and good company. He had monies to spare and dressed most finely; courtesans visited him as often as he wished. He led a life with no troubles or aggravation; an ideal existence was his. All well except for the lion that roared within his chest, and ready to leap out at the smallest chance; the throne of England still aforemost within the royal head.

Upon such a day he came from the king's palace at Westminster, a visit he was obliged to make most frequently to be reminded of his obligations, and to be humiliated with probing questions and rhetoric. Returning he to his Tower chambers, the carriage did rattle along, and was guarded lightly, for alone he posed of little threat. The driver and two guards were all that was his keep. Their voices he heard at chatter, all sat upon the high board. Inside against the plush red velvet did Perkin sit gazing at the young courtesan who sat opposite. She, staring out of the carriage window, little interested in the fellow who opposite did sit. Taking her glass, she pulled her wig straighter, stroked her brows with her finger, and viewed her beauty spot, like a black sheep upon a snowed hill. Dreaming she of the court where all about was gaiety, of rich dresses, of wine and intrigue, of gold and jewels, of royal courtiers, of lords and barons … Of husbands. She wished not to be the companion of some liar and a prisoner of the king. A liaison that would lead to naught. She would never be a lady to this commoner; her payments were meagre from the miserly purse, and, if rumour was any guide, he would not last another year before his head would be taken, he then laid cold, leaving her with thin strings upon a slender purse.

Perkin slumped in some passive state as he looked out from the carriage as it wended the London streets, rattling along this day that was soon to show about the Christmas season. The prince was filled with stately homes and lordly places, and directed the driver to take him upon another route through the tumbling houses and roadways of peasant-town. The peasants about he saw shoeless and with raggedy clothes, dragging small peasants with them, they equally as ragged and desolate. The sun did not shine upon this lot. The carriage took way upon all manner of back streets. They circled about and came back upon the main street where lay the church with the steeple bringing in the hour. Perkin looked about with casual gaze and with little interest upon the way they had travelled. Few people were about except for a beggarly fellow hobbling along. Up straight now eased the prince. "Stop!" he called to the driver. "Stop!" The carriage came to a halt. "Stay for a moment," he called. The coach had stopped its rumbling and was standing still as the prince with his stomach in some sickening state peered through the window, his hand holding steady to the bottom of the sill. Keeping back some in the dimmed light so as not to be seen, he looked at the beggar. The beggar peered back with dimmed eyes to where the noise of the carriage had stopped. He knew through his new sense that he was being spied upon. Stood he in cloth of no more than rags; he was shoeless; his hands showed dirty and bent with winter's cold. A mangy dog was tied to his waist, sitting upon the walk awaiting to guide his master along. "Alph—" the prince gasped in most quiet breath, which was sensed by the shape that watched. The head did lean from one side to the other to gather more sounds into his ears.

The prince? thought he, but no movement came to answer his thought, no prince called him and held him tight. He turned away, tapping his stick upon the cobbles, a sign and a cup swinging about his neck, as the dog pulled upon the rope to take Alph home to Emma. Stumbling some and clacking his stick, the ragged man went his way, watched from the still coach as he turned the corner.

God's Death, what have I done? the prince half cried aloud as his mind spake of the sight. The only sign of his pain was from the inquisitive gaze of the whore, who said naught, for 'twas not her place to offer more than she was paid for. I have brought such ill upon him and he such a loyal friend. I have betrayed him, for he has given all he can and can give no more. I have delivered naught for such sacrifice. No army, no throne, nothing to show for such as Alph has given.

In his hands he sobbed with broken heart, but beckoned the coach to drive onward, and to take him back to his chamber where he would be stayed in royal privilege and fine surroundings, whilst his friend was all at rot.

The prince awakened in the early morning from his disturbed slumber, though the sun had not yet risen. The consort was gone long ago, to ply her trade within the palace where she was more suited. He sat upon his cotside and ran again the thoughts he had played during that sleepless time. He would make another attempt to steal back his throne, he would go about and gather to him another army, and this time with moves more subtle. I will do this with all my heart until death would stay me, for the sake of Alph's sacrifice, who gave all so I may succeed.

He upped in that dim-morned light and dressed himself quickly, then donned his dark cape and hat, pulled on his boots, and, with dagger belted, he slithered out of his unguarded chamber. Along the black passageway he went, his feet treading lightly, as he made his way to the door that opened onto the stable yard. He looked through the peeling bars there, as the cool air washed about his face. All was still within his gaze, for no one thought the pretender would give up his blessed state to flee into the unknown. But 'twas such that he was away to. Fleeted he across the slippery way to the stalls where the horses, restless, pawed about. The prince soon found his steed as black as the night he was to ride into. Saddled quickly, he led the animal as silent as he was able to the laneway that passed by the Tower, across to the far side he went and made down the narrow alley there. He mounted within the narrow way, as on then he went through the town of London. Down a lane here, an alley next, through an entry, and across a field, then soon all was field as he moved his horse to greater speed.

He left the lightening sky that showed the roofs and smoking chimneys behind him, as the dewed wet laid upon himself and steamed his horse. When the full light came he was many miles from the Tower's clutches and closer to that which he did seek …

"And where is the place he seeks?" the king's adviser questioned the guard commander.

"He seems to be heading to Tunbridge Wells, as far as we can ascertain."

"So south he goes?"

"Yes, sire."

"And he saw no one at watch when he made from London?" the adviser continued his council of the guard.

"He saw naught, sire; we were most discreet."

"Then let him run for a while; we will gather him when the hole he is digging covers him o'er."

The prince rode onwards, and in villages and in towns did proclaim himself, and did try to bring those of his ilk to his banner; but 'twas not to be, for none wished to bring themselves to him and were not urged to any revolution. The prince turned from his fruitless tree and made toward the southern coast to seek a vessel away from this lost place and begone from the eyes that would pain him, for did he not run from the king's safe hand and into his own dark making? He rode with speed and without rest, but saw from some distance that each roadway that would relieve his plight was blockaded with the king's soldiery. The way to the sea was stayed and he could not pass. His horse he turned away from such, and made back to the forests and hidden ways to come to the priory of Sheen, and did there take sanctuary with the prior and to dally a while — until the soldiers tired of their search, was to his mind. But, within short spate, the priory was sieged and the prior asked to give up his charge. He would not bend to their wishes, but then saw that the king's guard would not abide by such laws, and, for the sake of his own life, the prince was given up to the guard. The prior, though, was assured that no harm would befall the prince, and so he, under this solemn pledge given, did show the king's men where the prince crouched.

They rode their catch back to London Town, where many people gathered upon the journey, for they had heard of the pretender's movements to rally against the king, and those that watched him pass were not amused by his efforts, for they jeered and ridiculed him as he was driven by. The masses were for the king and not for this want-to-be prince. But the king was not yet ready for his retribution and still bided his time, for he wanted more evidence against this haughty one, to bring him down once and for all.

The prince was placed, with cursing and foul language, within the Tower. His place now but a small barred cell with nothing private. The stone floor was covered with rush and straw running with lice and vermin. A cot he saw placed in the corner made him think he was not yet cast as a peasant. The cold grey walls encased him. No window showed to say was either day or night. 'Twas the mole and not the owl he would be. With only the luxury of a stool and a small table at one side. The ceiling's thick planks lay o'er the beams that hung blackened by the years of dark and mire; seen by many afore as they laid upon the cot and mused their state. That time when they were young and innocent from all turmoil, to now await the hand of justice for their wayward crimes. When did this happen? Why am I here whence I could be in warm climes, of sea and sand, of forests and hills? ... I am but a fool.

The prince, though, was of a different ilk, for never in his life had he been aught but a seeker of a throne. Never had he any other thought to mind than to usurp the crown of England from whoever lurked beneath it. No trial had come upon him for his escape, nor for his attempt to gather followers to his cause; but, with little doubt, one day it would come.

And come it did, for upon the morrow he was awakened by the king's guard who took him as he lay and brought him through the Tower's passages to the outside yard where a cart awaited him. He was bundled upon it, still without his boots and breeches. He sat upon the wet boards and held tightly upon the sides of the narrow wagon as it rattled along the cobbled way. Soon into sight came the palace at Westminster with, outside its gate, a crowd he saw gathered that seemed to be in some merry mood, as shout and laughter sounded and music played. Chestnuts cracking and popping he heard, as closer he came and seemed the carnival was for him. The crowd parted as the soldiers, with little care, broke through the throng beating them as if they were unruly sheep. Jeers and remarks were shouted at Perkin as the crowd came surging close to the cart; they pulled his hair and tugged at his clothes as he slowed by. They came to the door of Westminster, and, as closer they came, the prince saw the grimy stocks that awaited him. He was to be displayed to the citizens and to feel their wroth whilst clamped in a pair of stocks … He was then dragged from the cart.

"Leave me!" he shouted as he pulled from the bearing arms. "I can walk. You have not yet made me a cripple." He struggled free from their grasp and walked without guidance to the seat that was set there before the stocks. He pushed his feet through the lower fetters as he was ordered to. The guard then brought down the top beam and pinned it in place. They pushed forward his head into the upper stock; the prince then placed his hands into the place set for them, as the top was brought down to hold him still. He could not see but did hear the iron locking pin slipped into its catch. He was secured, unable to move any limb and his head locked with little movement into the beam. A statement was read as it would be upon every hour, spake for those who could not read, that they would know of the crime this person had committed.

"Let it be known," the heavy voice rang out from behind the prince, "that this day, and upon the morrow, the said Perkin Warbeck is hereby fettered to all humiliation that may come about. For with malice he did leave the protection of our Majesty, the King Henry, and did attempt to rally forces against this Realm of England and to seek its downfall." The speaker retired as the cart and the guard clopped and rattled away.

Alone now was the prince, helpless before a mob of ignorant peasants. Then joyful music started to play, its lilting sound drifted all about, as they in mischievous mood supped their ale and became more boisterous. The jesters came with their tumbles and falls and their taunting games. The crowd grew even louder.

The prince was in much distress; his wrists ached, his neck stiffened from the angle he had to sit, his back ached, cramping came to his legs. Short was the time that he had been fettered and he felt he could not last the day that was before him, ne'er yet even dream of the morrow. They came then with the abuse …

A big gruff man, smelling like a pig and with ragged cloth, came close and played his stinking breath upon the head that was held tight. Through his mousy teeth came the spit, spraying upon the face of the imprisoned body, to speak at last his mind to the helpless nobility before him. "'Ow does that abide you, *my prince?* Do you enjoy your throne?" He scraped his throat and spit a wet glob of phlegm, all black and green upon the pale that cringed before him. "You are more the jester than those who tumble." He spake once more to the pretender before he spat upon him again. "Am I not more of a prince than you? For who is the one that is fettered, and who is the one that is free? And, as you see, sir, 'tis I, the peasant, who is free and spits upon the one who is not." The crowd about were joining in the taunting egged on by the big fellow who showed no loyalties. They shouted to his words with yeas and nays, and foul cries.

"We are your lords and ladies now," they jibed. "This is your court." Anger came quickly over the prince for he had become sickened of their taunts.

"Begone, you evil lot! If I were free, I would take you to your devil who awaits you."

"Ha! He speaks with a tongue of anger … We should snip it out from that foul mouth," the ruffian spake out loudly to be heard above the rest who jeered. Perkin thought to hold his anger and to stay his mouth, for it may bring upon him more trouble than he was able to deal with. Slop came splash upon his face, pig dung, all ripe and dripping, running from his hair and over his eyes, as then more came, pushed into his face with bony hands to be forced into his nostrils and sucked into his mouth. His eyes stung, and breath was hard to find among the caking mass. They stepped back to see their work, and with laughter saw he looked as a gargoyle upon a castle wall. Locked and still with eyes closed, he could hear the chanting and the taunting, and felt still the vile upon him. His shirt was ripped open at the back, and then felt he the searing hot pain; he writhed, trying not to cry out as he tried to shake it away. Hot chestnuts they had laid upon him from the fired pan, upon him like nails driven into his tender flesh. Though still in some pain, he managed to tumble them off, and only remained were the red welts where they had sizzled. Flies were gathering upon his face, buzzing and sucking at their meal, and bringing great itch and discomfort to him. The day wore on and he was in some senseless trauma, for he could do naught but sink into some half state.

The sounds about had dulled, the crowd was thinned … A small voice spake all of innocence and kindness. "Would you like us to wash your face, sire?" it spake with boyish charm.

"Yes, please," spake Perkin, his mind still numbed from his ordeal. "Get it away this dung and this fly." The three boys stood a few paces away from the stocks as Perkin felt the warm liquid awash upon his face, but it tasted most vile as it trickled into his mouth. They did urinate upon his dunged face, they each seeing who could reach the target from afar back. 'Twas a game of pride in the outcome, and another humiliation for the prince. He heard then their voices laughing, with sounds of friendly fights between them as they left their acid drains upon him. Came the street women who, with skirts raised, showed their all before him, and pressed upon his face the filthy pants they wore, all sticky and smelly, that made him retch and pray for some relief, for seemed more he could not bear. Then the rattle of a cart he heard, and soon came the chatter of soldiers. This day was done. They unpinned his bloody ankles and wrists, lifting out his sagging head to drag the defiled wretch to the waiting cart, where they tossed him in like a sack of grain. Perkin was rocked and bumped as he lay upon the floor of the cart, too much in pain to even move from his coddled lay, for fear more ache may come upon him. Soon was it that he was thrown back into his cell, and did lay there in a heap all bruised and tormented, to wish he had not another day to face such turmoil, but he knew, with sinking heart, he had to tread the path one more time, and felt for certain he could not.

He heard the rattle of keys at the door and the steady creak as it opened. His stomach turned, his eyes looked—another pain to come? The guard entered; he was alone. Perkin had seen him about and gathered that he was assigned to the cells along this passageway, and gave he the impression of bearing some compassion when others had none.

"Some water, sire, so you may wash yourself," he spake softly as he put down upon the table a bowl of warmed water and some drying cloths. He turned then and left Perkin to cleanse the ill from his body. He seemed uncommonly civil to him when all others had not been so.

Perkin struggled with his ached bones and his burned back, as he washed away the dirt and excretion that was caked upon him, to bring back his flesh to some clean air, able to breathe more easily now, as the water washed away all but the humiliation that had been put upon him. He lay with his back against the cold wall as he dried himself, rubbing his face and body until his skin showed with no trace of grime. The cold upon his back eased the burning that he could not reach. Turning, he heard the door creak open once again, there to see the guard bringing some victuals. A bowl of stew and a tankard of ale were placed upon the rickety table. Not usually the fare for such as he in such desperate of times. The guard said naught but took away the washbowl and cloths, and left Perkin alone to eat at the divine table.

He had fallen asleep, but stirred in the middle of the night as voices washed about his ears.

"Richard … Richard," it called in whispered tone. "Richard, look thee up to the ceiling above." Perkin did so, but no angel did he see, only blackness shrouded there. "I am Edward, Earl of Warwick, imprisoned here this many a year; I am confined to the cell above you." Perkin stared into the black space straining both eyes and ears to glean more from the voice. "Be of good cheer and comfort, my prince, for help will soon come." The voice continued in its whispered tones above the prince's head. "I will speak further with you upon the morrow." Then all about the chamber was quiet as if naught had been spoken, as if it were but a dream in the mind of a wishful prince. Sleep covered over him again, but only long enough for Perkin to close his eyes was all it seemed.

He was pulled from his rest once more and taken along the same ways as was trod on the yesterday. *Was that a dream that played upon me or some intent to freedom?*—Perkin tried to place the night's doings as he was being pushed along to the waiting cart. Then on he rattled, to be taken this time to the stocks before the Standard in Cheapside. And he was subject all that day to the same vile attention he had suffered upon the previous day. Though with more resolve was he, for the words of comfort and cheer that he believed he did hear kept him with some hope, and to survive the day was most in his mind so that he may hear more of the promised word.

The long day dragged forever its wearied legs till once more came the cart that would deliver him to his vile abode, but still a sanctuary from that unbearable day. The rain came with heavy drip. Thunder rented the hustling clouds above as he lay in the cart; the wooden sides seemed as a coffin to him as the rain poured to swill about. The great fall of water washed away the thick grime that covered him. Perkin began to rub his hair and washed all he could from his matted locks. He rubbed his face and then thrust it up to the water that tumbled upon him. His clothes clung like skin to his body. He turned cold with the incessant downpour upon him and could not control his shiver or the rattle of his teeth. Better though, thought he, than washed with vile and ridicule.

The sogged mass was thrown shaking upon the stone floor of the cell, and felt he to be most sickly. He heard the boots of the king's guard march their step further and further away, until all was still and he could hear only his breath. The keys rattled their tune upon the cell door and in creaked, once more, the guard.

"Here, sire, some cloths to dry yourself with, and some clothes that will fit. Make thee hastily or you will become sick with the fever. I will bring you hot stew shortly. Be hasty, sire."

Perkin found the strength to stand upon his legs that did shake like the eggs of the tadpole. He struggled to remove the wet clothes that clung to him, but quickly did so, for he feared, as all others, the sweating sickness, that malady that surely would end your days.

In short time he had dried himself and was dressed in the dry clothes offered. He felt then more content as he lay at rest upon the cot. Warmth had come upon him and he felt no illness in his bones. Though the sun did not shine within this hole, he felt 'twas so, for the days passed were of blackness, this place shone with its warmth.

The bowl clanked upon the tankard as the guard placed the victuals aside of Perkin, who now queried his treatment. "How is it, guard, that I am treated in such good fashion by you? For one in my state, it should not be."

"You have friends, sire … More than you know of," came the whispered words of the guard. Spoken as if someone stood by his side to write down all the words that he would relate. He gathered up the wet cloths and the rotting clothes, and said no more to add to those shaded words. To leave with his bundle tied in silence.

The prince was left alone, and in the dark surround knew not the time nor whether 'twas day or night.

"Richard." The floating voice awakened him from his shallow sleep.

"I hear you," Perkin replied to the blackness that was about him.

"'Tis Edward, sire. Many friends who are of your colours are ready to join with you to usurp the crown from Henry. We have faith, sir, that with you at our head we can bring this to fact. What say you to this endeavour, sire?"

"All depends, sir, upon what is in mind. To what plan do you think will succeed when all I have attempted has ended in failure?"

"I beg your forgiveness, sire, but we believe a force of arms such as you aspired to will not bring about that which we seek. We believe the only way to success is to seize the royal treasure, that which lays in some security within this Tower, and to defend ourselves there until our followers relieve us from the said place. To make off then with the treasures, and to declare you, Richard, as the true seat of this land. For without the treasury Henry's place will not be as king." The scheme was unfolded to the prince by the Earl of Warwick who seemed most assured the plan would work, and the cost would be little to accomplish.

"I will have to mull it over, sir," the prince replied. "Though I know my roads are few, 'tis a plot that seems fraught with ifs and maybes."

"Think on it then, sire. I will further make contact with my friends, to set a time and a day, and for them to ready a place if your answer be yea. Good night to you, my lord, and sleep thee well." And quiet came once again as the earl finished his plea, leaving Perkin alone in his chamber of imprisonment.

He thought long of the council as he lay upon his cot, and to which way he would make his move, until deep repose came upon him and he fell soundly to sleep with new games playing within his head.

"Richard ... Richard, are you about?"

"Yes, I hear you," he replied, for with patience he had awaited two days since last their voices had crossed.

"How fare ye, sire?"

"Well enough ... As well as I may in this hole."

"Have you given thought to our plan?"

"Yes, I have, and have done so for many an hour, and it seems that I have but little choice, for you well know my fate is upon the wing of a bird, to fly high or fall to the ground as such may call. I am with you; I will be your king, your leader. This will be my last cause, for to fail I will lose my head without doubt." Perkin, with some reluctance, had to throw in his lot with the earl unseen.

"We are most grateful, sire, and it will indeed be your last turbulent act, for you will, without doubt, be our king, and no more have such turmoil cast upon you. I will relay your words to my friends and we will proceed with the intrigue."

Converse came again a few days later as their plan was discussed, with Edward broaching a request of Richard.

"And what is it you wish of me, sire?" came the words from Perkin, as those incriminating words from Edward were to be spoken from that faceless voice that dropped upon him, from somewhere in the darkness above.

"The followers who come to our side require that you, my lord, do place your name upon the list of friends. We believe all names involved should be writ, for when we take the crown, each will know of the other and to what title he would hold, and to what rewards would come. And to this end, sire, upon the document would be stated that you will be our king, and all writ that you would be titled Richard the Fourth, and would hold all privileges that are constant with such a title."

Perkin understood the dangers of such a document. If they were caught and sent to trial, could be most dangerous to his plea, for it would be marked in his own hand of his intention to take the throne by reason of the king's treasure and turn him into the commoner Henry Tudor, with, no doubt, a most heinous death to come upon him. But naught was left for him, and so the he would take it upon himself. "Bring to me the said document and I will sign it such."

At last 'twas to be writ, that damning script that was so easy to sign.

"'Tis well, sire, for we have made plans that upon the morrow's eve at nine of the clock we will release you from your captivity and go to our future's way."

Perkin writ upon the parchment that the guard had placed before him, glancing at the names that were signed there, but knowing not one that showed. With quill and ink *Richard, Duke of York* scratched he upon the place showed. The guard sprinkled straw chaff and dust that he scooped from the floor upon the wet ink, to blow off until he saw the dryness upon it, and to fold and place it secure within his pouch. He left then with a polite bow as Richard settled and awaited the hour of nine. In some short time after the hour struck, he would either be close to his crown or close to the axe.

The door opened and the light from the passageway broke into the cell of Richard, who stood still within the darkened lot that was his prison. A cold disturbing feeling came over him, for he feared who may enter from that brightness before him. The guard's shadow came firstly, which did not yet relieve his worm. Then came another, tall as such he had to lower his head to enter the cell; then the shape came closer.

"Edward, at your service, sire," spake he as he did shake the hand of Richard with much vigour, and with lowed head did show of reverence to him. "Come, sire, the others await us."

Richard was showed out from the black hole and, followed by Edward, went into the lit passageway. Guards there were stood about with only glances at the comings. Allied to the cause and brought in to replace Henry's toadies, doing naught to hamper their pass. Along they went upon the narrow ways, flat stones beneath their feet, then worn steps to climb, first in light then into dark went they, to come soon to a great door that stood royally before them. The door of the treasury, tall and with great menace, looked down upon the robbers of its pride. Edward brought out a key as large as a dagger, and all of black and rusted iron; he clanged it into the hole and turned the creaking lock. A loud clack gave sound as the lock opened, and hearts beat faster. Their necks craned as the door was pushed open and they tumbled inside. Silent they stood at gaze at the chamber's display, as more seers pushed from the back to stumble those in front further inside into the dim light, and to echo their steps and their voices loud, for naught was about the chamber, and hollow did it lay except for some old boards that stood at lean against the far wall. Even of dust there was none, even of one dead fly there was none. Edward looked at Richard as they stood in the light of the torches that flickered about the emptiness.

"My lord, I am taken aback by this sight. I know not why the treasury is empty, for all our spies told of large amounts of riches being stored here. I will bottom this." Edward was sorely disgruntled at the outcome and was about to hear Richard's wroth also.

"Never mind which and why, what now is our move that we have come upon this? Speak, man. Are you not the great planner?" Edward had no reply, for lost and boggled was he by the situation. A man not of soldiery bearing and seen now as just a parvenu. "Come, we will make to the carts that await us and to quickly haste away from this disaster," Richard urged, as they ran one behind the other as fast as they were able through those dark and dank places.

Who are these people I choose to flee with?—Richard's head spun with thoughts of what swamp he was being sucked into as he fled from the Tower once more—I know them as only voices in the night. I know of no allegiance to them, or of them to I. Does not this prince dangle upon some slim thread of his own choosing? When the time is able, I will depart from these bunglers, for they will soon fall back into Henry's black hole. Yes, I will make away alone, for all is lost when the treasury is not within our keep. To Portugal I will make and lose myself in mist and fog.

"This way," a voice called loud, as through a doorway they went into the cold cover that played their skin. Into the dark outside they ran, close to walls and tight alleys until the neigh of horses met their coming. They bundled into the waiting carts and were away at clatter and creak through the black night of London Town. Twenty in all were piled into the wagons. Twenty would-be nobles of this land, all bathed in riches and properties they dreamed to be. Now though they swayed along in wet carts cringing in the night's cover. The old horses with bones showed dragged the miseried lot to another hole.

Late were the hours and many miles had gone by as they stayed their ride, to stop then at the inn that lay within the town of Walton-on-Thames upon the road to Southampton. The horses were done and could not carry one more mile, given to the stables care, worn and breathless from the heaving ride. The party of schemers left their rotting carts and went to rest and sup at the inn whilst fresh horses were being made ready for them.

"Which way will we take now, my lord?" the earl broached Richard who carried his face of scowl.

"Do not, sir, talk to me of *we*. For now it is *I* and no more we. I will be gone alone as soon as I have supped, and pray I can alone travel unseen. Without the treasure there is no road for us that could be trod. We carry the mark of traitors, and naught we do, nor which way we travel will alter such. I go such, for I wish not to be painted black with the same brush that paints you. For I am more than to be partners with such unlikely lords." Richard, after his tirade, moved to the back of the gathering and made ready to depart from this baggage.

The door was thrown open wide as the king's guard blustered in from the dark outside. Into the lit chamber, grunting and raging, they came with swords raised and cries loud. Rushed quickly to the band who stood in shocked manner, unable to draw upon their weapons before they were overcome and were pushed back against the wall. Richard though, upon first sight of the intruders, had slipped quietly through the small door that was aback, which led him through the empty kitchen where only the fire was of life. The open door with the cool breeze was at the far, and he quickly made for the black opening to be free from this place. He felt the cool air upon his face and the stillness that was about, far from the turmoil within. The club he saw that swung toward him, but too late to move away from. Now, into blackness, was he, as the guard who waited outside had swung with heavy hand to end the escape of the prince with a crack sounded upon his forehead, and to send him slumping to the ground no more pleasantly cool.

The bumping of the cart brought Richard back to his senses, and saw he the others of this party of friends, who sat about with hands bound and dismayed look, the little they did possess of gold and of properties was now naught. Our prince lay full stretched upon the boards to see his allies in pitiful state, then to lapse once more into his faint with head to pound and dreams to scurry.

"Sire ... Sire." The rough hand shook his shoulder, as the prince opened his eyes and felt he the hammer within his head; he slowly eased himself up to sit upon the cot in the cold and dark of the cell. "Come, sir, the trial starts shortly." Yes, the trial, 'tis time I face the inquisitor—the prince tumbled his words about his head, as he stood shakily with his head beating of a thousand drums. A bulge, all blue and black, stood out over his brows like some sickening growth. He was helped by the guard across the cell to the open doorway, where he shook away the helpful hand, to walk the passage under no help from another man, for he had trusted others before, to lean upon and to rely upon, and had always been tripped at the sun's rise.

Two guards stepped before him, two behind him as they guided their catch along the narrow ways of the royal Tower. Always dark 'twas with ne'er few shafts of light to pierce the blackness. The windows were placed high within the walls so no one could look down upon those souls that trod this way. The clump of the boot, the jingle of the weapons, a rasped cough were all that broke the echoed silence, as seemed in a tunnel they did march. Voices from the distance were heard, voices that whispered and broke with muffled laughter, ringing softly about as if wishing not to be heard. The party came close to the whispering group that waited outside the doorway to the court chamber. Solicitors they with their pages, struggling to hold onto thick books and reams of parchment, with heads whacked for fidgeting about whilst elders did talk. Guards stood, and ponced gentlemen, with mouths covered with laced kerchiefs, flounced about.

The prince was brought to the closed door, as he saw all the legals upon one side and, upon the other side, those engaged in the doings of yesterday. They stood in a state of dire melancholy, miserable and forlorn, except for Warwick, who stood with uncharacteristic calm and an air of immortality that Richard did not find to his liking. A guard rapped loudly upon the bright-crested door; three times did he knock. The prince waited as time drew close to enter the chamber. "Come!" The shout from within gave the call for the guard to swing open the heavy door, who, with the creak of the hinge and the grunt from his mouth, managed to push open the gateway to enter all those who awaited without the chamber of court.

Within the sun was shining, striking through the many high windows and eyeing down upon the chamber below. The rising dust from the bustle shone in its whiteness, solid enough to climb out of this place did it seem. The guards guided the prince to the place of his due and stood him there upon the raised dock. He held upon the iron rail, which was upon all sides, except where the entry gate did swing. The others of his band were brought and placed with him, and the small gate was latched as the last one entered, with the guards stood close to the prisoners' keep. All were rambling into their places now. The solicitors and clerks all took their seats; the pages still struggled about under their loads and were still to be abused. Other noises were heard, but the shafts of dusted light made it impossible to know from what or from whom they came. The prince gazed up and saw before him the public gallery, clearly seen high above the shafted blind. Commoners were filling up the benches, but, unlike the scene below, which was of placid calm and duty called, the gallery was full of noise and rasping shout. Pushing and shoving they came in unruly fashion with voices ringing about, of who came first to such a seat and to why the womenfolk should be at the front. They were like children at play. Ragged and shawled women with tattered bonnets sat. Men, unshaven and unwashed, still wearing the dung and dirt from the fields. All pushed together closer and closer as more bodies were forced in, and all those who had waited long were now locked together. Chatter and argument still tarried, and small fights would break out but quickly they melted. Coughing and spitting echoed as the smell rose. The lice crawled from one to the other.

"Silence in this court!"—the cry rang from some unseen person. All was of quiet from the legal shout. A cough, a sneeze, a shuffle, a lowly whispered word from one clerk to another were all that was about.

"The King!"—did come loud the awaited cry. His Majesty entered through a door that was bathed in the misty light, and did so unseen to most. He took his seat upon the stage with the solicitors and the inquisitor before him, naught at his back but the royal guard who all bowed to acknowledge their Henry. The chamber was filled with din as all stood and showed their allegiance to the king. All except the gallery, who were not reverent to the one who kept sway against them, and did keep them in poor state. Though they were prodded by the guards to stand, only those who were close to their swords did so. All then did sit, to rattle and scrape the benches and tables as they settled.

"Silence now for the king's inquisitor!" came the call, as the public gallery hissed and booed, playing a game of their own to each move that was made upon the floor below. "Quiet!" came the call to restore some order. The gallery quieted to await the next chance to disrupt the nobles and legals.

The inquisitor stood. Tall was he, his long cloak all of black and high collared; his face and hands were all that showed of any other hue. No smile he had, no frown he showed, no way was there to know his mind. He spake his words to all of those that huddled close in the dock. Not for comfort did they such, but for the little room that was within that pen that was built to hold but ten prisoners.

"You are here this day to answer to your acts of treachery. Your act of attempting to steal the royal treasure and to usurp the throne from our beloved Henry. And be there no doubt that you will be proven guilty in these heinous acts."

"Wooooo …" The gallery, in feared sound, mocked the opening words of the council.

"Silence!" came the riled cry from the inquisitor. The words heard by all, but just a misty shape in the light and not fully seen. But then, as if upon some set music and at the first sound of his next word, the sun became covered with cloud and the bright shafts of dust were cut and all about was seen clear. The royal court became coloured with shape. Shown was the king sitting nobly, with his royal staff to hand, aloof and haughty from this rabble. The uniformed guard stood at his back like wooden posts. The tables and benches full, with staring eyes liken to frogs in a pond seeking the fly. The inquisitor stood clearly before them. No smile showed; grim indeed was the face now seen. He stared; his steely eyes sought like arrows, piercing the weak minds that stood before him. "So, sir, what name to call you?" spake he directly to the prince and to no other that were confined. "Prince? ... Perkin Warbeck? ... Richard of York? ... Piers Osbeck? Or would you prefer Richard Plantagenet? What name do you deem the most likely, my elusive one?"

"I am, sir, Richard of York, true heir to the throne now sat by the King Henry." The reply with angered words came quickly from the prince.

"Well said, Richard, but why is it that we have a signed confession by one Alphonse Marquette—given freely, I may say—that you are indeed the one known as Perkin Warbeck and as such you are not of royal blood?" The confession was waved about by the inquisitor so that all may see that there was such a document.

"I know not why he would say such, for it is not true."

"So, Richard, say you that your closest of friends, who has suffered greatly for your cause and given up all for you, you call this friend a liar?" Once more the king's speaker niggled at the thoughts of the prince.

"He is no liar, sir, and those words he would not speak, but for such a reason I cannot give."

"That, sir, is no answer. You have no answer, for the truth seems so disenchanted as not to slip from your tongue. You were imprisoned, sir, under great compassion by the King Henry, and showed many amenities, yet you chose to escape from the Tower with your gang of ruffians, then to break into the royal treasury, all in aim to steal from the king his treasures to be used to finance your own schemes, of which we all know of—" The inquisitor was interrupted by the prince, who felt, it seemed, he was not getting enough space to rebuff the words that could lead to his guilt.

"The treasury was entered, sir, but I was not there for to seek any fortune but only to escape from the Tower's confines, and 'twas I, just a bystander in much angst at what was happening, stayed only that they would show to me the way to freedom, for I knew not the passage. There was no act of thievery, for the chamber showed to be empty of treasure, and all left with empty hands."

"Your intention, sir, was to steal, and if you had searched further, you would have found the door that did lead into the inner treasury that was filled with the Realm's fortune. 'Twas fortunate for the king that some building work was being done, and that the tradesmen had left their boards to lean upon the wall where under did sit that fateful door." Richard boiled inside realizing that once more he was but a hair's width of taking the crown. "It is not the court's fault that your gang was incompetent at the task you were bent upon … You then, sir, deny that you intended to steal the king's treasure, escape from the Tower with your ill-gotten loot, and, with your stolen monies, finance a campaign to take the throne from a penniless king?" 'Twas then that the court repeated the charge, so the prince would state, without proof, that he had no intention of such an action, and so he was obliged to answer such to the inquisitor. Spoken as the king, in silence, watched the doings, showing most clearly that he had no sway upon the court or upon its findings.

"I do wholeheartedly deny that accusation; my intent was only to escape from the prison and then to flee the country, and to no more attempt the usurp of the throne. 'Twas only the unruly lot that I became tangled with that, without my knowledge, did attempt to steal from the king. Little choice did I have, I being an innocent man dragged along like a weed in the rush of the tide."

"With words true you state this then, my lord?" A last admission was sought by the inquisitor.

"'Tis the truth I speak, under God."

"Well said, sir, from he who is in such dire straits … for, my lord, I have in my hand a document, given to me by one of your loyal friends who stands with you in the box." The inquisitor flourished the writ high above his head so all may see the intent. His sleeve falling from his raised arm as he did so showed bony and white. The sun came once more from the clouds' curtain to beam its dust-filled light into the chamber, as one window at a time did it move. To the guards who stood at the king's back. To the king dimly gone in that royal light. To the benches full that splayed afore him. The inquisitor, proudly stood, was but a dusty shadow. The dock smoked white. The arm raised with the document still showed clear above the light that had painted all about. "A document, sir, signed by your hand in the name of the Prince Richard, stating that you, in all manner, would be in party to the stealing of the king's treasures, to the financing with such treasures of an army to usurp the throne of our most beloved Henry, and to make him poor in all things. And that you, Richard, would be placed upon the throne of England in his stead … Sir, you did stir in your pot the making of vile schemes and murder."

A clattering noise broke about and more dust did rise from the commotion as tables and benches creaked and all about stood and raised anger. "Shame!" was shouted about. The gallery raged with damning cries. "Cut him now! ... Take his head! ... Murder the liar!" All manner of shouts rang about from the raggedy lot high in the chamber.

"Silence! We must have silence!" a voice called from the sparkling mist, and silence did slowly creep, for all wished to know to what would be next. The silence, though, did not yet reach the gallery that kept its jibes coming; they up there in the shadow cawed. Then were lit brightly as the guarded door was opened upon them. The soldiers shouting loud words upon them to quell the unruly commoners. Then, with rough banter and shouts, they cursed the soldiers for their coming, and only sat after the military began to draw their clubs and to threaten the riled leaders. Quickly calm came upon them as they waited for what may be next spake that would stir them once again. And such did come from the denounced prince.

"No matter the words I so speak, this court has only one verdict to bring upon me. It seems no more will this bird flutter its white wings. I did sign such a document, but only did I do so for I could see no other freedom before me. I had to escape the degrading acts placed upon me, those acts that should not be committed against a rat ne'er a person of royal stature. I had to escape, but in doing so I would not bring forth any danger to our Henry."

"I think not, sir. Your action in writ, and in act, was with every intention to usurp the throne." The last words were spake by the inquisitor and no other words came about, for 'twas declared that all intention was to usurp the throne. That alone being the seed of the fruit, for whether prince or pauper, it did not matter; all that mattered was that this man did try to steal the king's fortune, and such was to be used to raise an army against the monarch. Treason was the word.

The clouds came over the sun once more at this apt time and brought to sight all within the chamber, and seen standing was the king resting easily upon his staff, who was given the floor to bring his thoughts to the trial.

"Gentlemen, the King!" was called loudly about as he started his speech.

"I have listened to all that has been spoken and have concluded that I alone cannot bring judgment to this trial. *Richard* did connive to bring down my house, this after he was treated with royal respect as if he indeed was a prince. But being a prince, that is what a prince would be obliged to do. Even as he stands, he still has many who follow him, and they believe he is Richard. So, I look back and know I cannot fall into the same well as did that Henry, who did kill Becket at Canterbury, or indeed Richard who did spread his murder at the Tower. I wish to be remembered as a goodly king, who ruled with kindness and cared muchly for his people. If I am seen as this man's jury, will I not be bagged as the others and remembered as a villainous king?" Henry pushed forward his face as if showing it to all about. "See this skin—is it not soft and smooth?" Then he removed his hat and showed all the top of his head. "See—is there naught under my hat? No, there is not, but I tell you if I judge this man, it will be writ that my skin was pitted and covered with warts, and that I was of grimaced limp and foul of mouth. And would be storied with shivering fright that when I removed my hat, hid there would be told of two horns showing from the bewitched head. All this would be falsely writ upon my page. One king who did murder an archbishop, and another who did murder princes is enough for all time. I shall not be his brother. I cannot see him free. I cannot see him guilty, for my hands must be unsoiled and fettered with naught. Therefore, I must leave this chamber and place such judgments into the hands of those who do not gain from the outcome." As then with a last glance at Richard, as if he was still muddled by his being, the king, with showed reverence from those of his following, did leave the court to those who would judge this usurper.

"Guilty!" came a lone shout from high in the rafters. "Silence!" rang out in reply.

Free of all encumbrance, now that the king had departed, all the legals sat and appeared to ponder about the decision. Full well the verdict known, though not yet counted.

The inquisitor stood again in full sight of the prisoners' box. "Have you aught to say before a vote is taken?" spake he to all who stood before him.

"Yes, sir." 'Twas Edward, the Earl of Warwick, who stood but five people away from the legal. And whose deed 'twas that did start this whole charade.

"And, pray, what is it you wish to say?" the tiresome voice was spake by the inquisitor.

"Sir, as you are aware, 'twas I who passed on the incriminating document." Though most knew 'twas the earl who had played the game of traitor, much anger seethed within the box from his words, where united they stood in their peril. For if this man did walk away, more than one would risk himself for retribution. But calm prevailed and to await the outcome was embraced. "'Twas given to the office of the prosecutor, who assured me that I would be freed from the Tower for my allegiance to his Majesty."

"It seems, sire, that the said document did not reach our office until after you found that the king's treasury was empty. If the treasury had been full, I daresay we would not have heard of any such writ. You did, in all eyes, carry such a document for your own insurance and this day it does not wash. You, sir, will stay in the box with the others, for we see little difference from one to the other. But, as yet there has been no vote taken upon anyone's guilt, and, if you are innocent, you will be free to leave the Tower. If you are guilty, you will be free to leave the Tower, though your paths will lead to a different place." The earl knew he was done, and stood he with shaked legs and was tarred with the others in that dulled light. "There is no one else who wishes to speak?" the king's man asked once again.

"Yes, sir, I wish to ask of my wife, Katherine, and to know what of her." The lost prince, with sorrow tightening his throat, asked about the only one who seemed to have any care for him.

"She is well and resides with the Queen Elizabeth, and will stay so whether the cloth of innocence or the cloth of guilt is laid upon you. If you are found of guilt, she will be free to marry once again … and, let us pray, this time her head guides her heart."

Richard spake naught to the bladed jibe of the inquisitor. "Sir, when I did come to this place of confinement a royal promise was made before the prior of Sheen, and such was spake upon sacred ground, and writ such in witness that I would be released from the sanctuary into the keep of Henry, and stated that no harm would be seen done to my person, or to place any abuse upon me, and to this the Church has covered me with their blessing. I remain in a state of sanctuary wherever I may reside, and no act of reprise may come upon me." The prince had read from his last card and awaited the answer to come from that man of the king.

"That, my prince, is truly so, but alas our goodly prior, who upon a mission of mercy and whilst making way over common ground, was viciously waylaid by some ruffians and, God rest his soul, did die in such miserable state, left he bloodied in the mire. We shall avenge such a heinous act as this. And we are now seeking the ruffians as I speak. Though of some heartache because of his demise, it does mean, sire, that he will never see you harmed as was writ." The twisted truth was spoken by the inquisitor, as came the only smile to crack his gloomy face, occurred in hand with a fleeting second.

"I am doomed from all sides," lamented the prince. "I rest within the arms of justice, if ever such would come to me."

The judge of the court stood and spake to bring forth the verdict. "I call now upon a hand-raised vote from all who are hereby assembled, from lord to commoner. I will be obliged that such as I ask be done in silence.

For that which we this day have witnessed is a most serious attempt at revolution." He paused in his summary within that cold chamber, for it seemed his words even needed to be understood by the grey walls. Many times had this place seen such, but still it stood through all the turmoil and misery played upon it. "Those who say *guilty* to the charges against this motley lot, raise one hand and be counted." All in that sombre place were seen to raise their hands in the call of guilt. No count was taken, for a glance about did show the call. To those freemen, 'twas seen; to those who prisoners be, 'twas seen. "All who say *not guilty* on the charges, raise one hand." All hands were still and stayed by their side; only heads looked about to see the fool who would raise his hand.

"By the verdict given of nobles and commoners you are hereby found *guilty* of the act of treason, and the punishment you receive will be that which is writ in the laws of this land." Clearly were the words spoken by the inquisitor, who had taken his place to offer forth the punishment owed.

Slumped heads and much anguish did befall the prisoners, for they had brought down the devil's sword upon themselves, and had even helped him to slip it from its scabbard.

"You will be taken from this place and kept overnight, and upon the morrow, at nine of the clock in the morning hour, you will be taken to the cross at Tyburn, where you will be executed by the axe. And, by the grace of our most lenient king, your bodies will not be quartered as is writ in the law, but to be severed at the head only. The heads will be piked and displayed upon the London Bridge. This all to be done upon the same day as the execution, so all may see the quick outcome of any treachery against our king, and against our England. Be wary, all wrongdoers, for this will be your fate. Guards, remove the prisoners to their cells."

The cheering and gleeful shouts from the gallery filled the sombre chamber as the prisoners were taken away, their day was done and all would be lost to the swinging axe at Tyburn. The door to the gallery was opened and they, all cooped, bundled out full of glee and well-being, for they had in their own land helped in the downfall of nobility, and they were most pleased of it.

The court dispersed to their chambers to legalize all the documents appertaining to the trial. The king was not painted black, for all the land would know a jury did find Richard guilty, and 'twas the king who showed much mercy. No, he would not be painted black, but would be shown in tranquil and giving light.

The night had come but alas 'twas not of high adventure; there was no racing upon horseback through forest and field, there was no deer to hunt, no robbers to fight. Only black was about, locked in a prison full of stink and evil. Perkin did sleep; for 'twas the only way he could rid his mind of the feared thoughts of the morrow. Dreamed happenings though came to his head. Tormented and deceived by that word whose space was small. To be king. To triumph. To rule with soft glove. All would be so slept with that little word that came almost at every line: *If.* If treasures I had … soldiers I had … the citizens were with me. If … If … To wash away the mind from such turmoil and lay thee at peace, for my minute in time has passed by and naught will be writ of me now.

He had laid long enough staring at that black ceiling. The fleas that hopped the filthy cot, jumped and itched his limp body. Given up to brush them away, let them feed, thought he, for they will take little and soon all my blood will be plenty spilt. He upped and paced about the small chamber, impatient to be gone now that the dawn had come.

Rattle came to the door as the key unlocked the latch, and 'twas swung open to the low light that came from without. Perkin was on his knees in prayer as entered two of the king's guards.

"Time, sire. Time to go." Perkin did not yet come, for this was the last time he would be able to pray alone and he had much to pledge. "Come, sire, we must go. The cock will crow no matter how much you pray." Perkin still did not move, but kept his head bowed and muttered as if he were alone. "Come, we go now!" Perkin was pulled from his meditation in a most rough manner; the guards tugged and ripped his clothes as he was dragged up. He struggled with the roughness that came upon him and was further abused by the unruly soldiers. They pulled him along like some stubborn mule, causing something to tinkle and rattle upon the floor as it flew from his person, where it rolled and then did stop against the wall; sightless, under the cot, it lay in the thick dust and the dirt there.

Perkin was pulled out from his cell, and pushed and beaten as they made along the passageway. Soon the morn's sun, warm and caressing, bathed his chilled body. He saw ahead the cart that waited with the others of his band crouched in feared state. He tried to step gently between the tangle of arms and legs, but he was quickly pushed in upon the others and forced into a small space. Once more his company was this motley lot.

They rattled away from the Tower, swaying and lurching upon their fateful way. Soldiers afore and soldiers aback marched them along, rocking to the sound of a lone drummer, who struck the slow beat of the dead march. Citizens lined the roadways as the drummer brought them along, and saw many for the first time this man who would be king, but sat he huddled in some old cart that passed their way. They saw no king there, but only a cargo of sinners in some dire straits. On they went upon their cobbled way to their nine of the clock meet.

The square came to sight, this place of Tyburn, this place that would show a bloody day. The houses, all close, hung over the square. The windows above were filled with eager faces, each plying to view the happenings that stirred in the old marketplace. The rickety old buildings looked as if they would fall upon the gathering below so much at lean and bent were they. The square was filled with much tumult as the cargo came closer. The raised stage clearly seen with its dignitaries stood close. The mayor with his insignia shone above all, plump and bursting from his attire was he. Nobles stood about, they all in regal garb there to see that justice would be done. Then the crowds of common folk filled all about, supping their ale, eating their pies, pushing and fighting, laughing and shouting, all gathered about the stage. It stood in the middle of the square, made from old rough-hewn wood; worm-riddled it stood upon its shaky legs. Steps led to its platform, with a wooden board all around to stop any severed parts from rolling off the stage. A rail all around the platform at four paces to stay any turmoil that may come about from the raucous lot.

Axes were lined upon one side of the platform, they all wickedly sharp. Swords also stood, for each crime could be of a different tool. Some were to lose their heads by the axe, some quartered, some to lose their head by the sword; all writ and carried out as the court did levy. Three executioners stood upon the high stage; two were at the back where rested the tools. All were dressed in black, both trouser and shirt, with bagged sleeve to free the arm of cumbrousness. A hood placed over of sackcloth, with eyeholes cut out and a slit for the mouth, ogres three they did stand. The one afront was taking his stance at the wretch whose head hung o'er the block. This day had been dubbed a holiday, for there were so many heads to be taken, the landowners had made it a festival so all may enjoy a pleasing time. The crowd chanted as he readied himself, they all in the mood for celebration. The words rang of derision; wagering was bantered about. The wage? How many blows would be taken before the head did fall? Many of the others before this fellow, who now wept upon his hugged block, had suffered through five tries, for it at first seemed that one of the axemen was with little experience in his trade. But he had then been replaced and carted to the prison at Highgate with his brother, for 'twas found that one brother was wagering for the other, and they did rattle a good many coins in their bag before they had been caught, and a good many ripe necks had been butchered.

"One! ... Two!" came the shout from the crowd, as the executioner had braced himself and was sure that he had delivered a good blow; but his blade did not cut all the way through and had twisted sideways upon the bone. He swung again quickly in the same rhythm and did cut it this time clean. As they counted, they relished each chop, and monies changed hands as they all readied for the next wager. Many this day were to lose their life, for fifty were set for execution; there was much work to done by the hooded men.

"One! ... Two! ... Three!" The head rolled after the third hack and with sickly thud clumped and tumbled upon the stage. Blood gushed from the lifeless shell that was left as the head was picked up with the matted hair and displayed all about to much black-toothed guffaws, thrown then with the others into the basket where they lay with glazed eye and smirked mouth. 'Twas five now in the basket, as then 'twas lifted and placed upon one of the waiting carts; with pikes stacked to one side, they were readied for their last rolling ride to the London Bridge where lay the Thames to sparkle their way. With the body still spewing its blood about and dripping through the boards, 'twas dragged to the body cart, there to be thrown upon the others who huddled in twisted fashion like dead spiders all heaped in a bloody mass. Soon to be taken afar and burnt in a tall pile upon unsacred ground and lost forever. One after the other went the poor souls with their cries of anguish, their sobs, with all control lost, did rent the air with sound and with smell. Some vomiting from the fear that shook them; others unable to contain their functions released themselves where they did stand. Many collapsed in a faint of terror, and had to be lifted upon the block, and were beheaded whilst in their stricken state, knowing naught of what had come upon them. Others stood proudly and did not flinch or show any fear. They took that which was given to them as honourable gentlemen, as knights in past times would in honour stand, so did they ...

The rooftops gave up their cold night to drink in the sun's warmth, as the mist left the tiled tops and drifted away. Smoke reached its fingers upward into the bright sky, as Katherine, named now "the White Rose" for her beauty, showed her as such. She looked afar, past all that should cloud her sight, to bring herself as close as she was able to the prince, whose wife she was. Tearful she did gaze, with the steeple soon to sound that hour of despair. That hour that was so fast to come, that hour of Death. There was no sickness that could say you may die upon the morrow, or may the day after. This was not sickness, for 'twas writ that you will die at nine of the clock.

"Come, my dear, sit with us." Elizabeth tried to console her charge, as she placed about Katherine her caring arm, and eased her away from that window that was all of despair. She brought her slowly over to the waiting ladies who pained for her in her trial. "Be strong, dearest Katherine, we have all seen the pain you endure, but all one day will bring such memories of sweet times, and happiness will dwell with you." Elizabeth held her near as she sobbed in abandon. But then all came close around her to bring to her much comfort in her anguish. They awaited the coming hour together and would suffer together, so caressed all with comforting arms and chanted prayers, huddled within that chamber, as the sun brought its warmth all about those rooftops that did lay before Tyburn …

The cart that held Perkin and the other prisoners was now being emptied, as their names were called and they were hustled into the waiting area; they all would be different in the way they would go to their death. "One! … Two! … Three! … Four!" The shouts still rang about, the heads still rolled, still picked up and tossed into the basket. The bodies still dragged, dripping their life as they were heaved into the body cart. A lull came whilst the stage was washed down with water; the blood, thick and of slime, gave little footing to the swinging executioners. The eager boys only too happy to be upon the stage, soon mopped it dry and blessed it with their miming antics.

"Perkin Warbeck!"… The knees melted as snow near the fire, as rang the name to the prince's ears. The Earl of Warwick sat shaking upon the cold stones. He with no more fortune in his pocket for his betrayal than the others who had not. With the screeching words of a madman he shouted about, doing nothing for his cause, except to bring the roaming dogs to his side, causing them to bark and to snap at the wild thing that ranted in the pen. The others of his lot, who waited in great despair, watched him with saddened eyes and with thoughts of what so nearly came about.

Perkin needed to move but he could not, only to be taken with strong arms and marched to the place at which he would spend little time. As the steps were reached he was able to move alone; his face was numbed with one eye that twitched without control.

"Perkin Warbeck!"

The clerk marked off the name upon his list. "Number forty-one!" he called.

One of the executioners stood forward and began to take some trial swings whilst he waited; time after time he whistled the axe through the warm air like a silver arrow.

The clerk whispered through the sack and into the ear of the king's man, "Number forty-one, the Perkin Warbeck fellow … Behead with axe only." He read direct the orders from his most royal writ.

"Yes, sire," the executioner answered, acknowledging to the act he had to perform.

Standing upon the slipped stage that was still bespattered by bloody gore, the executioner waited. Perkin was shaking as he clung to the rail about, but then he found he could let it go and so was able to stand by himself.

"Anything to say, Warbeck? A last prayer or such?" spake the guard who stood.

Perkin pulled his voice up from his sickening stomach and spake as best as he was able. "I die this day in your eyes as the traitor Warbeck, but, as God looks upon me now, I tell you, in all damnation if I do not speak the truth, that I am, indeed, the Prince Richard, heir to this crown worn by Henry. I am, in right, King Richard, the fourth Plantagenet, and matter not what is spoken, I, in all truth to myself, it is so, for I am no deceiver and did seek nothing that is not by right to be mine. God rest my soul in his Heaven."

"That is enough of this jargon," the clerk spake, most impatient was he to end his long day, and wished to linger no longer about this place than he had to. "You have had your say. Time is now for you to step forward."

Richard then was walked over to the block by the king's guard, and in sad state did reach into his pouch and picked out the only coin there hid, and offered it into the mitted hand of the executioner.

The bloodied hand closed around it and placed it with a clink into his bag. "Thankee, sire," spake he, "I will bring a true stroke to you, and send you gone with no sufferance."

Richard knelt before the block, and, with one last look at the clear sky above him, and of the birds free that fluttered about, he closed his eyes for the last time and laid down his head. Fingers he felt upon his neck, as his locks were pulled away to reveal the soft white neck that was to be struck. He heard peasant voices from afar, their words twisted and foggy, as they still belittled those upon the stage. As fast as the sky would shoot its flash in a storm, so came down the axe with a glint of the sun upon it, to come its wicked way. "One!"

Chapter Thirty-three.

A Trinket.

"I see her not."

"Do not fret, William, she will be here in short time." The two guards peered from the high window, looking out from the Tower of London o'er the narrow streets below. "Look, William, by the baker's shop there … Is that not she?" They both craned their necks at the small opening to spy the scurrying hag that came their way. "Yes, it is her, always late, never here when she is most wanted." Soon her clopping feet they did hear, echoing upon the stone steps that led their way to the cells, dank and dark, and trod many times by others of dubious ilk. "C'mon, Emma, let us get these cells cleaned; they will soon have some new visitors and they like a nice clean place to dwell."

"Shut your ugly mouth. They will all soon be done."

The guards smiled at each other, as their game of taunting the foul-mouthed hag had once more drawn puss from the open wound. She pushed past them with broom and bucket in hand, and into the dirty holes she went. A quick sweep about, a wipe with her wet cloth upon the table, and all was a-sparkle as a new coin. To her eyes 'twas such. From one cell to the other went she with her usual care, to come lastly to the place where that Perkin Warbeck was kept. Emma wiped once more with her deft hand the grimed table, and then moved about the floor with her straw broom. Under the cot she poked and brought out dust and mouldy bits, a dead mouse, and other crummy parts. She scraped them up with her pan and dropped them into her rubbish sack. One more scratch about in the corner with her broom brought out something that rolled from the dust and tinkled its metal along the stone floor. She bent with trying grunt and picked it from the dust and grime. A bloody button, she thought, as she glanced at it and then placed it in her moneybag. She looked around and saw naught else to keep her, as then she made her way from the dungeons, and moved to the doorway of the passage where sat the two guards.

"All bright and sparkling now, Emma?" one of them sniggered.

"Pox on you, toad. Just 'ave my money ready upon the morrow." Emma sprayed out her words through her missing teeth, then she brought her sour-smelling body close to those who mocked, and with her foul mouth whispered close to them. "Do not be amiss or I will kiss you, and if I am in some mind I will jump my fleas and spit my smelly crod upon you."

"Ah, gee!" cried out one of the guards, as the other sat still in numbed fashion, and thought better than to come with any remark, for he wished not Emma to come with some foul anger. "Have no fear, Emma, your wage will be awaiting your coming," he spake as he clutched his throat and grimaced in pain, fearful was he of the threat laid upon them both by the enchanting Emma.

She went her way, Beggar Emma, clip-clop once more along the narrow ways. This path she had many times trod, for all her life she had lived in these alleyways that smelled vile, and in the lanes that were piled with filth. This was her London Town, far from those castles and palaces that towered in the distance. Carts passed her by, they upon the road to London Bridge. Those same carts she had seen earlier in the day, empty then as they waited at Tyburn's Cross. But now they were grisly filled, and rolling about upon the cobbled road, there gruesome cargo covered with canvas. Such placed there to keep eyes from seeing, and to stay the cawing crows that followed them. Many lowly swooped overhead, but some brave to stand upon the canvas trying to rip at the food that lay beneath. But once those heads are upon their poles and swaying about, they will be good victuals for those black devils that looped the sky. A strange hum mingled with the rumble of the carts, and it did seem that there was more beneath the canvas than bloody pieces. For there, under that hot cover and winging their song, droned a million flies, enough beneath it that it seemed they would be able to lift the carts to the skies, and take them away to their maggoty realm.

"Emma! My sweet rose, 'ow be you this day? Are you wanting a ride upon our royal coach?" The cry came from one of the drivers, for all knew of Beggar Emma, and all knew she was always ready to banter words.

"They that roll about in the back be far better 'andsome than you; even though they lie with no neck, and 'ave eyes that flop upon their cheeks, they be far more comely than the one who sits atop."

Laughter rang from the driver as he clopped his way to the bridge, and still he was heard faintly as the cart went from sight.

The light drizzle was come now in the afternoon that grew late of hour. The wet and gloom and the smoke that drifted down from the chimneys dulled the little light even more. Dogs barked at every sound as unseen passers went their way; they seemingly never quiet for little time, always one or t'other would yap.

She came to the rickety stairway that led to her lofty abode and, with slow tread, made her way up; with one hand upon the rail and the other upon her knee, she grunted out each step, like the creak of a water mill, she went in regular beat. Her beggars would be returned and await from their miserable lot. Alphonse, with Toby tied to his waist, would seek out the others, and, with a one-eyed seer and a half-tongued talker, they would grope and trip their way home, pulled along by the homing dog, a party bizarre who did struggle this path every day. No notice was heeded to any who passed, for more beggars than givers did roam these streets.

Toby barked his warning, as the stairs creaked and the door rattled open, and Emma at last came home.

"'Tis me stupid dog," she rasped. The bark turned to spins of joy and a furry welcome. "Git!" A swift swat by her hand sent the greeter scurrying to his corner. Ears no longer perked, but to show flopped down in some sad state, his eyes almost flowed with tears as he rested his heavy head upon his paws, looking only by moving his eyes, as some words were spoken he hoped for him, but still sad, for no kindness came towards him from those who sat about the table. But he knew that soon his guile would bring him to place his head upon the lap of his mistress, and in short spate would feel her hands fussing his ears and his head, and soon would come some table scraps for her most loyal Toby.

"So, my lads, 'ow much 'ave you brung this day?" Emma asked as she sat down at the table with her beggars. The place was not brightly lit, with one lonely torch all that flickered, and low now for want of more oil. They emptied out their tins upon the table. Few clinks did the hearing hear. Few coins did the seers see. "Are they all cheap and miserly that tread their way about? Are there none left that 'ave some charity to us who are in unfortunate of clime?" Emma was not taken by the result of the day's trade, but she was oft to rant at times and it meant not that she had no care for her beggars. "'Tis well I 'ave work at the Tower or we would all starve." She continued with her long-running story, as she scooped up the few pennies and rattled them into her money tin. They supped upon the grimy table their feast of stewed rabbit and turnip, and a jug of ale shared amongst them. Spitting and coughing and with much wind, they ate slovenly with wooden spoons and stumpy fingers, licking and sucking the running drip that ran from them. Toby had slinked over to his friends, and was fussed over by one and then by another as he made his way about the table, and to take gently such morsels as he was offered.

"'Ere."… Alphonse felt the cold metal pushed into his hand. "'Tis wot I found in that cell that 'eld your friend … The one you told me of … That Perkin … Maybe 'twas 'is. 'Tain't no good to 'im now, is it? Looked like it 'ad bin frowed out so I bringed it for you … There be a flower upon it."

Alphonse held the trinket in his twisted hand as carefully as he was able, and seemed to gaze upon it as some cherished object, though he could see very little of its shape or its colour. He mumbled to Emma, who seemed to know of the words he spake. "What colour is the flower, Emma?"

She looked closer at it with her squinting eyes, as Alphonse held it for her. "'Tis white … Shaped like a rose."

He held it tightly, and lowered his head upon the table in some despair, for in his hand he held the button that many years ago a young prince pulled from his doublet and placed it secure upon his person.

"My prince … My prince," he lamented, as he cried his dry tears and sobbed with shaking grief … 'Twas the year of our Lord, fourteen hundred and ninety-nine.

Ne plus ultra

(Nothing more beyond)

About the Author

Eric Owen Burke was born in Nottingham, England, and has lived in southern Ontario, Canada, since 1968, working mainly in the automotive industry. Retired since the late '90s, Mr. Burke enjoys an active life, with his wife and two children.

A natural and gifted writer with an immense vocabulary and a passion for Medieval and Renaissance language and history, the author was truly inspired to write this book.

CPSIA information can be obtained at www.ICGtesting.com
Printed in the USA
LVOW082011091112

306692LV00002B/1/A

9 781425 167264